Pamela Cantrell

Appointment in Samarra

BUtterfield 8

Hope of Heaven

Appointment in Samarra

❖

BUtterfield 8

❖

Hope of Heaven

by

JOHN O'HARA

Random House   New York

CONTENTS

Appointment in Samarra

To F. P. A.

DEATH SPEAKS: There was a merchant in Bagdad who sent his servant to market to buy provisions and in a little while the servant came back, white and trembling, and said, Master, just now when I was in the market-place I was jostled by a woman in the crowd and when I turned I saw it was Death that jostled me. She looked at me and made a threatening gesture; now, lend me your horse, and I will ride away from this city and avoid my fate. I will go to Samarra and there Death will not find me. The merchant lent him his horse, and the servant mounted it, and he dug his spurs in its flanks and as fast as the horse could gallop he went. Then the merchant went down to the market-place and he saw me standing in the crowd and he came to me and said, Why did you make a threatening gesture to my servant when you saw him this morning? That was not a threatening gesture, I said, it was only a start of surprise. I was astonished to see him in Bagdad, for I had an appointment with him tonight in Samarra.

—W. Somerset Maugham

1

OUR STORY opens in the mind of Luther L. (L for LeRoy) Fliegler, who is lying in his bed, not thinking of anything, but just aware of sounds, conscious of his own breathing, and sensitive to his own heartbeats. Lying beside him is his wife, lying on her right side and enjoying her sleep. She has earned her sleep, for it is Christmas morning, strictly speaking, and all the day before she has worked like a dog, cleaning the turkey and baking things, and, until a few hours ago, trimming the tree. The awful proximity of his heartbeats makes Luther Fliegler begin to want his wife a little, but Irma can say no when she is tired. It is too much trouble, she says when she is tired, and she won't take any chances. Three children is enough; three children in ten years. So Luther Fliegler does not reach out for her. It is Christmas morning, and he will do her the favor of letting her enjoy her sleep; a favor which she will never know he did for her. And it is a favor, all right, because Irma likes Christmas too, and on this one morning she might not mind the trouble, might be willing to take a chance. Luther Fliegler more actively stifled the little temptation and thought the hell with it, and then turned and put his hands around his wife's waist and caressed the little rubber tire of flesh across her diaphragm. She began to stir and then she opened her eyes and said: "My God, Lute, what are you doing?"

"Merry Christmas," he said.

"Don't, will you please?" she said, but she smiled happily and put her arms around his big back. "God, you're crazy," she said. "Oh, but I love you." And for a little while Gibbsville knew no happier people than Luther Fliegler and his wife, Irma. Then Luther went to sleep, and Irma got up and then came back to the bedroom, stopping to look out the window before she got into bed again.

Lantenengo Street had a sort of cottony silence to it. The snow was piled high in the gutters, and the street was open only to the width of two cars. It was too dark for the street to look cottony, and there was an illusion even about the silence. Irma thought she could yell her loudest and not be heard, so puffily silent did it look, but she also knew that if she wanted to (which she didn't) she could carry on a conversation with Mrs. Bromberg across the way, without either of them raising her voice. Irma chided herself for thinking this way about Mrs. Bromberg on Christmas morning, but immediately she defended herself: Jews do not observe Christmas, except to make more money out of Christians, so you do not have to treat Jews any different on Christmas than on any other day of the year. Besides, having the Brombergs on Lantenengo Street hurt real estate values. Everybody said so. The Brombergs, Lute had it on good authority, had paid thirty thousand for the Price property, which was twelve thousand five hundred more than Will Price had been asking; but if the Brombergs wanted to live on Lantenengo Street, they could pay for it. Irma wondered if it was true that Sylvia Bromberg's sister and brother-in-law were dickering for the McAdams property next door. She wouldn't be surprised. Pretty soon there would be a whole colony of Jews in the neighborhood, and the Fliegler children and all the other nice children in the neighborhood would grow up with Jewish accents.

Irma Fliegler had hated Sylvia Bromberg since the summer before, when Sylvia was having a baby and screamed all through a summer evening. She could have gone to the Catholic hospital; she knew she was having a baby, and it was awful to have those screams and have to make up stories to tell the nice children why Mrs. Bromberg was screaming. It was disgusting.

Irma turned away from the window and went back to bed, praying that she would not get caught, and hating the Brombergs for moving into the neighborhood. Lute was sleeping peacefully and Irma was glad of the warmth of his big body and the heavy smell of him. She reached over and rubbed her fingers across his shoulder, where there were four navel-like scars, shrapnel scars. Lute belonged on Lantenengo Street, and she as his wife belonged on Lantenengo Street. And not only as his wife. Her family had been in Gibbsville a lot longer than the great majority of the people who lived on Lantenengo Street. She was a Doane, and Grandfather Doane had been a drummer boy in the Mexican War and had a Congressional Medal of Honor from the Civil War. Grandfather Doane had been a member of the School Board for close to thirty years, before he died, and he was the only man in this part of the State who had the Congressional Medal of Honor. Lute had the French Croix de Guerre with palm for something he said he did when he was drunk, and there were a couple of men who got Distinguished Service Crosses and Distinguished Service Medals during the War, but Grandfather Doane had the only Congressional Medal of Honor. Irma still thought she was entitled to the medal, because she had been Grandfather Doane's favorite; everyone knew that. But her brother Willard and his wife, they got it because Willard was carrying on the name. Well, they could have it. It was Christmas, and Irma did not begrudge it to them as long as they took care of it and appreciated it.

Irma lay there, fully awake, and heard a sound: cack, thock, cack, thock, cack, thock. A car with a loose crosschain banging against the fender, coming slowly up or down Lantenengo Street, she could not make out which. Then it came a little faster and the sound changed to cack, cack, cack, cack-cack-cack-cack. It passed her house and she could tell it was an open car, because she heard the flapping of the side curtains. It probably was a company car, a Dodge. Probably an accident at one of the mines and one of the bosses was being called out in the middle of the night, the night before Christmas, to take charge of the accident. Awful. She was glad Lute did not work for the Coal & Iron Company. You had to be a college graduate, Penn State or Lehigh, which Lute was not, to get any kind of a decent job with the Coal & Iron, and when you did get a job you had to wait for someone to die before you got a decent promotion. And called out at all hours of the day and night, like a doctor, when the pumps didn't work or something else happened. And even your ordinary work on the engineering corps, you came home dirty, looking like an ordinary miner in short rubber boots and cap and lunch can. A college graduate, and you had to undress in the cellar when you came home. Lute was right: he figured if you sell two Cadillacs a month, you make expenses, and anything over that is so much gravy, and meanwhile you look like a decent human being and you're not taking chances of being crushed to death under a fall of top rock, or blown to hell in an explosion of black damp. Inside the mines was no place for a married man, Lute always said; not if he gave a damn about his wife and children.

And Lute was a real family man. Irma shifted in bed until her back was against Lute's back. She held her hand in back of her, gently clasping Lute's forearm. Next year, according to Hoover, things would be much better all around, and they would be able to do a lot of things they had planned to do, but had had to postpone because of this slump. Irma heard the sound of another loose crosschain, fast when she first heard it, and then slow and finally stopping. The car was getting a new start, in low gear. Irma recognized it: Dr. Newton's Buick coach. Newton, the dentist, and his wife Lillian who had the house two doors below. They would be getting home from the dance at the country club. Ted Newton was probably a little plastered, and Lillian was probably having her hands full with him, because she had to get home early on account of being pregnant. Three months gone, or a little over. Irma wondered what time it was. She reached out and found Lute's watch. Only twenty after three. Good Lord, she thought it was much later than that.

Twenty after three. The country club dance would just be getting good, Irma supposed. The kids home from boarding school and college, and the younger marrieds, most of whom she knew by their first names, and then the older crowd. Next year she and Lute would be going to those dances and having fun. She could have gone to the one tonight, but she and Lute agreed that even though you knew the people by their first names, it wasn't right to go down to the club unless you were a member. Every time you went, whoever you were the guest of had to pay a dollar, and even at that you were not supposed to go under any circumstances more than twice in any quarter of the year. That was the rule. Next year she and Lute would be members, and it would be a good thing, because Lute would be able to make better contacts and sell more Cadillacs to club members. But as Lute said: "We'll join when we can afford it. I don't believe in that idea of mixing your social life with your business life too much. You get signing checks for prospects down at the country club, and you wind up behind the eight-ball. We'll join when we can afford it." Lute was all right. Dependable and honest as the day is long, and never looked at another woman, even in fun. That was one reason why she was content to wait until they could really afford to join the club. If she had married, say, Julian English, she would be a member of the club, but she wouldn't trade her life for Caroline English's, not if you paid her. She wondered if Julian and Caroline were having another one of their battle royals.

II

The smoking room of the Latenengo Country Club was so crowded it did not seem as though another person could get in, but people moved in and out somehow. The smoking room had become co-educational; originally, when the club was built in 1920, it had been for men only, but during many wedding receptions women had broken the rule against their entering; wedding receptions were private parties, and club rules could be broken when the whole club was taken over by one party. So the feminine members had muscled in on the smoking room, and now there were as many females as males in the room. It was only a little after three o'clock, but the party had been going on forever, and hardly anyone wondered when it would end. Anyone who wanted it to end could go home. He would not be missed. The people who stayed were the people who belonged on the party in the first place. Any member of the club could come to the dance, but not everyone who came to the dance was really welcome in the smoking room. The smoking room crowd always started out with a small number, always the same people. The Whit Hofmans, the Julian Englishes, the Froggy Ogdens and so on. They were the spenders and drinkers and socially secure, who could thumb their noses and not have to answer to anyone except their own families. There were about twenty persons in this group, and your standing in the younger set of Gibbsville could be judged by the assurance with which you joined the nucleus of the smoking room crowd. By three o'clock everyone who wanted to had been in the smoking room; the figurative bars were let down at about one-thirty, which time coincided with the time at which the Hofmans and Englishes and so on had got drunk enough to welcome anyone, the less eligible the better.

So far nothing terrible had occurred. Young Johnny Dibble had been caught stealing liquor from someone's locker and was kicked in the behind. Elinor Holloway's shoulder strap had slipped or been pulled down, momentarily revealing her left breast, which most of the young men present had seen and touched at one time or another. Frank Gorman, Georgetown, and Dwight Ross, Yale, had fought, cried, and kissed after an argument about what the team Gorman had not made would have done to the team Ross was substitute halfback on. During one of those inexplicable silences, Ted Newton was heard to say to his wife: "I'll drink as much as I God damn please." Elizabeth Gorman, the fat niece of Harry Reilly, whose social-climbing was a sight to behold, had embarrassed her uncle by belching loud and unashamed. Lorimer Gould III, of New York, who was visiting someone or other, had been told nine times that Gibbsville was dull as dishwater the year 'round, but everyone from out of town thought it was the peppiest place in the country at Christmas. Bobby Herrmann, who was posted for non-payment of dues and restaurant charges, was present in a business suit, gloriously drunk and persona grata at the inner sanctum (he was famous for having said, on seeing the golf course without a person playing on it: "The course is rather delinquent today"), and explaining to the wives and fiancées of his friends, that he would like to dance with them, but could not because he was posted. Everyone was drinking, or had just finished a drink, or was just about to take one. The drinks were rye and ginger ale, practically unanimously, except for a few highballs of applejack and White Rock or apple and ginger ale, or gin and ginger ale. Only a few of the inner sanctum members were drinking Scotch. The liquor, that is, the rye, was all about the same: most people bought drug store rye on prescriptions (the physicians who were club members saved "scrips" for their patients), and cut it with alcohol and colored water. It was not poisonous, and it got you tight, which was all that was required of it and all that could be said for it.

The vibrations of the orchestra (Tommy Lake's Royal Collegians, a Gibbsville band) reached the smoking room, and the youngest people in the room began to hum Something To Remember You By. The young men addressed the girls: "Dance?" and the girls said: "Love to," or "Sawell," or "Uh-huh." Slowly the room became less crowded. A few remained around one fairly large table in a corner, which by common consent or eminent domain or something was conceded to be the Whit Hofman-crowd's table. Harry Reilly was telling a dirty story in an Irish brogue, which was made slightly more realistic or funny by the fact that his bridgework, done before the Reillys came into the big money, did not fit too well, and Harry as a result always whistled faintly when he spoke. Reilly had a big, jovial white face, gray hair and a big mouth with thin lips. His eyes were shrewd and small, and he was beginning to get fat. He was in tails, and his white tie was daintily soiled from his habit of touching it between gestures of the story. His clothes were good, but he had been born in a tiny coal-mining village, or "patch," as these villages are called; and Reilly himself was the first to say: "You can take the boy out of the patch, but you can't take the patch out of the boy."

Reilly told stories in paragraphs. While he was speaking he would lean forward with an arm on his knee, like a picture you have seen of a cowboy. When he came to the end of the paragraph he would look quickly over his shoulder, as though he expected to be arrested before finishing the story; he would finger his tie and close his mouth tight, and then he would turn back to his audience and go into the next paragraph: ". . . So Pat said . . ." It was funny to watch people listening to Harry telling a story. If they took a sip of a drink in the middle of a paragraph, they did it slowly, as though concealing it. And they always knew when to laugh, even when it was a Catholic joke, because Reilly signaled the payoff line by slapping his leg just before it was delivered. When everyone had laughed (Reilly would look at each person to see that he or she was getting it), he would follow with a short history of the story, where he had heard it and under what circumstances; and the history would lead to another story. Everyone else usually said: "Harry, I don't see how you remember them. I hear a lot of stories, but I never can think of them." Harry had a great reputation as a wit—a witty Irishman.

Julian English sat there watching him, through eyes that he permitted to appear sleepier than they felt. Why, he wondered, did he hate Harry Reilly? Why couldn't he stand him? What was there about Reilly that caused him to say to himself: "If he starts one more of those moth-eaten stories I'll throw this drink in his face." But he knew he would not throw this drink or any other drink in Harry Reilly's face. Still, it was fun to think about it. (That was the payoff line of the story: Old maid goes to confession, tells priest she has committed a sin of immorality. Priest wants to know how many times. Old maid says once, thirty years ago—"but Faa-thurr, I like to think aboat it." Yes, it would be fun to watch. The whole drink, including the three round-cornered lumps of ice. At least one lump would hit Reilly in the eye, and the liquid would splash all over his shirt, slowly wilting it as the Scotch and soda trickled down the bosom to the crevice at the waist-coat. The other people would stand up in amazed confusion. "Why, Ju!" they would say. Caroline would say, "Julian!" Froggy Ogden would be alarmed, but he would burst out laughing. So would Elizabeth Gorman, laughing her loud haw-haw-haw, not because she enjoyed seeing her uncle being insulted, nor because she wanted to be on Julian's side; but because it would mean a situation, something to have been in on.

"Didn't you ever hear that one?" Reilly was saying. "Mother of God, that's one of the oldest Catholic stories there is. I heard a priest tell me that one, oh, it must of been fifteen twenty years ago. Old Father Burke, used to be pastor out at Saint Mary Star of the Sea, out in Collieryville. Yess, I heard that one a long while ago. He was a good-natured old codger. I remember . . ."

The liquid, Julian reflected, would trickle down inside the waistcoat and down, down into Reilly's trousers, so that even if the ice did not hurt his eye, the spots on his fly would be so embarrassing he would leave. And there was one thing Reilly could not stand; he could not stand being embarrassed. That was why it would be so good. He could just see Reilly, not knowing what to do the second after the drink hit him. Reilly had gone pretty far in his social climbing, by being a "good fellow" and "being himself," and by sheer force of the money which everyone knew the Reillys had. Reilly was on the greens committee and the entertainment committee, because as a golfer he got things done; he paid for entire new greens out of his own pocket, and he could keep a dance going till six o'clock by giving the orchestra a big tip. But he was not yet an officer in the Gibbsville Assembly. He was a member of the Assembly, but not a member of the governors and not eligible to hold office or serve on the important committees. So he was not unreservedly sure of his social standing, and damn well Julian knew it. So when the drink hit him he most likely would control himself sufficiently to remember who threw it, and he therefore would not say the things he would like to say. The yellow son of a bitch probably would pull out his handkerchief and try to laugh it off, or if he saw that no one else thought there was anything funny about it, he would give an imitation of a coldly indignant gentleman, and say: "That was a hell of a thing to do. What was the idea that?"

"And I would like to say," Julian said to himself, "that I thought it was about time someone shut him up."

But he knew he would not throw this drink, now almost gone, or the fresh drink which he was about to mix. Not at Harry Reilly. It was not through physical fear of Reilly; Reilly was more than forty, and though a good golfer he was short-winded and fat, and unquestionably would do anything in the world to avoid a fist fight. For one thing, Harry Reilly now practically owned the Gibbsville-Cadillac Motor Car Company, of which Julian was president. For another thing, if he should throw a drink at Harry Reilly, people would say he was sore because Reilly always danced a lot with and was elaborately attentive to Caroline English.

His thoughts were interrupted by Ted Newton, the dentist, who stopped at the table for a quick straight drink. Ted was wearing a raccoon coat, the first season for it if not actually the very first time he had had it on. "Going?" said Julian. That was all he felt like giving to Newton, and more than he would have given him if Newton had not been a Cadillac prospect. Had a Buick now.

"Yeah. Lillian's tired and her folks are coming tomorrow from Harrisburg. They're driving over and they'll be here around one, one-fifteen."

Never mind their schedule, thought Julian. "Really?" he said aloud. "Well, Merry Christmas."

"Thanks, Ju," said Newton. "Merry Christmas to you. See you at the Bachelors'?"

"Right," said Julian, and added in an undertone, while the others said good-night to Newton: "And don't call me Ju."

The orchestra was playing Body and Soul, working very hard at the middle passage of the chorus. The musicians were very serious and frowning, except the drummer, who was showing his teeth to all the dancers and slapping the wire brushes on the snare drum. Wilhelmina Hall, six years out of Westover, was still the best dancer in the club, and was getting the best rush. She would get twice around the dance floor with the same partner, then someone would step out of the stag line and cut in. Everyone cut in on her, because she was such a good dancer, and because everyone said she was not in love, unless it was with Jimmy Malloy, and she certainly wasn't in love with him. At least that's what everybody said. The males who cut in on her were of all ages, whereas Kay Verner, now at Westover, and much the prettiest girl, got her rush almost exclusively from the prep school-college crowd. And she was in love with Henry Lewis. At least that's what everyone said. Constance Walker, the little fool, was not wearing her glasses again, as if everyone in the club didn't know she couldn't see across the table without them. She was known on the stag line as a girl who would *give you a dance*; she was at Smith, and was a good student. She had a lovely figure, especially her breasts, and she was a passionate little thing who wasn't homely but was plain and, if she only knew it, didn't look well without her glasses. She was so eager to please that when a young man would cut in on her, he got the full benefit of her breasts and the rest of her body. The young men were fond of saying, before leaving to cut in on Constance: "Guess I'll go get a work-out."

The curious thing about her was that four of the young men had had work-outs with her off the dance floor, and as a result Constance was not a virgin; yet the young men felt so ashamed of themselves for yielding to a lure that they could not understand, in a girl who was accepted as not attractive, that they never exchanged information as to Constance Walker's sex life, and she was reputed to be chaste. The worst thing that was said about her was: "Yeah, you may think she isn't attractive, and I agree with you. But did you ever see her in a bathing suit? Hot-cha!"

The band was playing Something To Remember You By.

The stag line was scattered over the floor by the time the band was working on the second chorus of the tune, and when Johnny Dibble suddenly appeared, breathless, at the place where his cronies customarily stood, there were only two young men for him to address. "Jeez," he said. "Jeezozz H. Kee-rist. You hear about what just happened?"

"No. No," they said.

"You didn't? About Julian English?"

"No. No. What was it?"

"Julian English. He just threw a highball in Harry Reilly's face. Jeest!"

III

Al Grecco knew the road from Philadelphia to Gibbsville pretty much as an engineman knows the right-of-way. On a regularly scheduled run, an experienced engineman can look at his watch and tell you that in four-and-one-half minutes his train will be passing a schoolhouse to the right of the tracks. Or, he can look out at a haystack or a barn or other landmark, and tell you to the half-minute what time it is. Al Grecco could do almost the same thing. He knew the 94½ miles from Philadelphia to Gibbsville—he knew it cold. And it certainly was cold tonight. The gasps of wind told him that. It was warm in the car, with the heater on. He was driving a V-61 Cadillac coach, and he had lowered the window in the door at his right about three inches from the top. He was an expert driver. He had made the trip to Philadelphia several times under two hours, leaving Gibbsville in the early morning; and tonight he automatically checked his time as he was passing the gate posts which marked the entrance to the Lantenengo Country Club: two hours and a little over forty-five minutes from his hotel in Philadelphia. Not bad, considering the snowdrifts and the condition of the roads down on the lower entrance to Reading, where cars were scattered all along both sides of the road. He was going as fast as he could with safety. It was a business trip.

Although he never had seen anything but the roof of it, Al knew that the country club was built on a plateau. The clubhouse was scarcely visible from the state highway. Cars leaving the club did not come into view from the highway until they were a third of the way down the long drive, which opened upon the highway at the gate posts. Al Grecco noticed as he was passing that another Cadillac, a big sedan job, was just coming into sight on the drive. The moment he saw the car he recognized it. He more or less made it his business to be able to recognize important cars, and this sedan looked important. It was a demonstrator, and would be driven by Julian English, the Cadillac distributor.

"The louse," said Al. But he was not angry with Julian. It was because of an order from Julian that he had had to go to Philadelphia. It looked like Julian was going to have a good party some time between Christmas and New Year's, because he had asked Ed Charney, the big shot, if he could get him a case of champagne, good champagne, and deliver it the day after Christmas. Ed, of course, said he'd be only too glad to get some good champagne, and he had attended to the matter himself. Ed had phoned Philadelphia and made sure that it was good champagne. Ed liked Julian English. Julian English belonged to the Lantenengo Street crowd and he was the kind of a guy that was a high class guy and would be a high class guy in any crowd. You could tell by looking at him he was a high class guy. And he always spoke to the boys on the street. He wasn't like some of them (mostly the older guys), who would do business with Ed, say business at the bank or insurance or something on that order, but they wouldn't even see Ed when they met him on the street. Or even guys who didn't know Ed, they would call up and say this was So-and-so, president of such and such a company, and could Ed do them a favor and get a case of genuine Scotch at a good price. In the early days Ed would try to put himself out for the respectable people, the ones that thought they were high class. But Ed saw it didn't pay; they didn't appreciate it when he did them a favor, and they didn't even say hello to him the next time he saw one of them on the street. So there were only a few of the Lantenengo Street crowd who could get a favor out of Ed without paying cash on the line for it. But Julian English certainly was one of them. And it wasn't only because he spoke to you; it was the way he did it. He spoke to you like a human being, and now and then he even sat down for a cup of coffee with Ed. "That English, he's my boy,"

Ed once said, and that was enough. "For my money," Ed said, "I will take that English. He's a right guy." That was plenty. In Ed's position you had to be a good judge of what a man was like, and the English was copacetic. And Al agreed with Ed. Not that it would have made any difference if he didn't agree with Ed. You either agreed with Ed, between Reading and Wilkes-Barre, or you got a job in the mines. That was the *least* that could happen to you if you didn't agree with Ed: you just weren't in the mob any more. The worst could happen to you was you would get held by a couple of the boys while a couple others kicked you till they got tired kicking you, and then they would put a couple of slugs in you and that was that. But Ed very seldom had occasion to do that kind of thing. In the beginning, yes. There were several cases that the state police were still bothering about that Al knew more about than he wished he knew. That was when Ed was beginning to organize booze and the girls and the numbers racket. He had to put the screws on a few people here and there, or they would have become pests. You had to be tough in this business, or you weren't anything. You didn't get anywhere. Just the same, you had to be regular, you had to be on the up-and-up with those that treated you right. Al Grecco turned up his coat collar. He had felt a chill, and even though there was no one else in the car he felt a little ashamed, because he recognized that the chill was kid stuff; the way you feel when you have done something very good for somebody, or the way you feel about your mother. That was the way he felt about Ed Charney. He felt loyal.

Recognizing this he wanted to do something to show how loyal he could be, and the nearest thing at hand that gave him any chance to do something for Ed was the champagne. He turned to see that the champagne was still covered with blankets and secure against bumps. Ed would want that goods delivered in the best possible shape. Then he remembered the sedan, with English in it. He reduced his speed to thirty miles an hour and allowed the sedan to overtake him.

In a short time the sedan did overtake him, and Al Grecco could see by the way English was driving that he was sore about something. As a rule English was an artistic driver, as good to a car as men used to be to horses. And this particular job that English was driving was a demonstrator, which he kept tuned up all the time. But now English shot the car up over a rut and pushed through a six-foot drift in passing Grecco. Not that there wasn't plenty of room, and not that Al Grecco wouldn't have moved over or stopped if English had blown his horn. English didn't blow his horn, though. He just tramped on the gas and gave the sedan hell. The sedan hit the drift with a hard wallop, swaying from side to side, and almost as soon as he hit the drift and punched a hole in it, English swung the steering wheel and got back on the cleared part of the road. If you could call it cleared.

Stew stuff, Al Grecco decided.

In the few seconds that it took English to pass him Al Grecco noticed that English had his hat on the back of his head, which wasn't like English. English wasn't what you would call a snappy dresser, but he was always neat. Al also noticed that there was a woman in the car, slumped low in the front seat, low and as far away from English as she could get. That would be Mrs. English. It never occurred to Al Grecco that it could be anyone else, because Al never had heard anything about English and other women—and if English had been a chaser Al would have heard about it. Around Gibbsville if you were a chaser it meant you had to go to the roadhouses, and Al made it his business to know who went to the roadhouses. A lot of wise guys in Gibbsville thought they were getting away with murder by taking their girl friends to the country hotels in the Pennsylvania Dutch part of the county. The wise guys thought they were pretty smart, going to those places instead of showing at the Stage Coach, which was the big roadhouse, where the drinks were six bits apiece and there was dancing and a hat-check girl and waiters in uniform and all that front. But if the chasers only knew how wrong they were! Al made it his business to know about the chasers, because you never could tell when it would come in handy to know that So-and-so was cheating, especially if So-and-so happened to be some local big shot that could be useful to Ed up at the courthouse or in politics or even at a bank. Al remembered one time such information had come in handy. There was a councilman who was not on the take. Ed for some reason hadn't been able to get to him with a dime, not a dime. One night Ed got the tip that this councilman was going to shoot off his mouth about a couple of speakeasies which Ed was interested in. This councilman was making a big play to get the Republican nomination for mayor. So Al happened to be there when Ed got the tip, and Al said: "Who did you say's going to do that?"

"Hagemann," said Ed.

"Oh, no he isn't," Al said, and told Ed why Hagemann wasn't going to shoot off his mouth. And was Ed pleased! He went to Hagemann's office and he said to him something like this: Mr. Hagemann, you're a great Church man and you represent the good element in this town and all that, so if it gets around that you've been going places with a

certain lady about thirty years old that wears glasses. . . . And Ed
didn't have to say any more. Hagemann just got up and shut the door
and when Ed left they were the best of friends and still were. Ed even
arranged it that Hagemann could get away with cheating on the one
with glasses. Oh, in this business you had to look for all the angles.

Al Grecco stepped on it to keep up with English, who now had the
accelerator down to the floor, and was keeping it there. You could tell
that that was what he was doing, because when the wheels of the sedan
got out of the tracks the car would leap up to the side of the road,
slapping the long pile of snow. Al noticed that Mrs. English, who had
her fur collar turned up higher than her ears, did not turn on English.
That meant she was mad. Any woman ordinarily would be sitting up
on the seat and bawling her husband out. But if he was any judge, Al
was sure she was not saying a word. He began to wonder about this
English dame.

He just had a feeling, that was all, but he went back in his memory
and tried to recollect something, anything at all, that fitted in with the
idea he was beginning to get about her. The idea he was beginning to
get about her was that she might be a cheater herself. But he could
not remember anything. He knew she never had been to any of the
country hotels. She got loud once in a while at the Stage Coach, but
no worse than a lot of others, and English was always there when
she was. No, it was just one of those things. You got an idea about
some person and you didn't have any reason for it; but Al Grecco in
his twenty-six years had learned one thing, namely, that if you had
a hunch about a person, a real hunch that kept bothering you, something usually happened to prove that your hunch was either dead
wrong or dead right.

It was seven miles and just a little over from the country club to
the Gibbsville Bank & Trust Building, and practically all of the last
three miles was a new and nearly straight stretch of road, which had
been easier to clear; it was protected from winds by a railroad embank-
ment on one side. Al Grecco had to step on it some more when English
hit the stretch, because English was letting it out for all the sedan
would take. Al kept his mind on the driving now. He did not want to
get too close to English, and make English sore; but he did not want
to lose him; he wanted to be close by if English got into trouble. But
English was all right. One of those guys that can drive when they're
drunk or sober, the only difference being that when they're drunk
they have no consideration for what they might be doing to the car.

When the two cars reached Gibbsville Al Grecco made up his mind that he would best please Ed Charney by following English all the way home, so he turned up Lantenengo Street after the sedan. He followed about a block behind the sedan, all the way out Lantenengo Street to Twentieth Street. The Englishes had their house on Twin Oaks Road, but you could see all of Twin Oaks Road from Twentieth and Lantenengo. Al stopped. English had shifted into second for the uphill grade and the snow of Twentieth Street. He made the turn all right, and in a few seconds he stopped in front of the house. The lights of the car went out, and then the porch light went on, and Al could see Mrs. English on the porch, opening the door, the light on in one of the rooms of the downstairs floor. Then English himself on the porch, the downstairs light snapped out just as a light was turned on in a bedroom upstairs. English was leaving the car out all night. He must be cockeyed. Well, that was his business.

Al Grecco put his car in reverse and backed into Twentieth Street and then turned the car and drove down Lantenengo Street. He would go right to the Apollo, the all-night restaurant where you usually looked for Ed Charney. But suddenly he realized he wouldn't find Ed there. This was the one night of the year you wouldn't find Ed there. "Jesus Christ," said Al Grecco. "Me forgetting it was Christmas." He lowered the window of the car and addressed the darkened Lantenengo Street homes that he was passing: "Merry Christmas, you stuck-up bastards! Merry Christmas from Al Grecco!"

2

JULIAN ENGLISH snapped awake, and knew that he had beaten the arrival of Mary, the maid, by one step. He was correct: Mary appeared in the doorway and said: "Mrs. English says it's eleven o'clock, Mr. English." In a lower key she said: "Merry Christmas, Mr. English."

"Merry Christmas, Mary. Did you get your envelope?"

"Yes, sir. Mrs. English give it to me. Thank you very kindly, and my mother says to tell you she made a novena for you and Mrs. English. Shill I close the windows?"

"Yes, will you please?" He lay back until Mary left the room. Such a pretty day. Bright; and there were icicles, actually icicles, hanging in the middle of the windows. With the holly wreath and the curtains they made you think of a Christmas card. It was quiet outside. Gibbsville, the whole world, was resting after the snow. He heard a sound that could mean only one thing; one of the Harley kids next door had a new Flexible Flyer for Christmas, and was trying it out belly-bumpers down the Harley driveway, which was separated from the English driveway only by a two-foot hedge. It would not take long for the room to get warm, so he decided to lie in bed for a few minutes.

There ought to be more days like this, he thought. Slowly, without turning his head, he pulled himself up to a half sitting position and reached out for the package of Lucky Strikes on the table between his bed and Caroline's bed. Then he remembered to know better than to look in the direction of Caroline's bed—and looked. He was right again: Caroline had not slept in her bed. Everything returned to him then, as though in a terrible, vibrating sound; like standing too near a big bell and having it suddenly struck without warning. His fingers and his mouth lit a cigarette; they knew how. He was not thinking of a cigarette, for with the ringing of that bell came the hangover feeling and the remorse. It took him a little while, but eventually he remembered the worst thing he had done, and it was plenty bad. He remembered throwing a drink at Harry Reilly, throwing it in his fat, cheap, gross Irish face. So now it was Christmas and peace on earth.

He got out of bed, not caring to wait for warmth and luxury. His feet hit the cold hardwood floor and he stuck his toes in bedroom slippers and made for the bathroom. He had felt physically worse many times, but this was a pretty good hangover. It is a pretty good hangover when you look at yourself in the mirror and can see nothing above the bridge of your nose. You do not see your eyes, nor the condition of your hair. You see your beard, almost hair by hair; and the hair on your chest and the bones that stick up at the base of your neck. You see your pajamas and the lines in your neck, and the stuff on your lower lip that looks as though it might be blood but never is. You first brush your teeth, which is an improvement but leaves something to be desired. Then you try Lavoris and then an Eno's. By the time you get out of the bathroom you are ready for another cigarette and in urgent need of coffee or a drink, and you wish to God you could afford to have a valet to tie your shoes. You have a hard time getting your feet into your trousers, but you finally make it, having taken just any pair of trousers, the first your hands touched in the closet. But you consider a long, long time before selecting a tie. You stare at the ties; stare and stare at them, and you look down at your thighs to see what color suit you are going to be wearing. Dark gray. Practically any tie will go with a dark gray suit.

Julian finally chose a Spitalsfield, tiny black and white figure, because he was going to wear a starched collar. He was going to wear a starched collar because it was Christmas and he was going to have Christmas dinner with his father and mother at their house. He finally finished dressing and when he saw himself in a full length glass he still could not quite look himself in the eye, but he knew he looked well otherwise. His black waxed-calf shoes gleamed like patent leather. He put the right things in the right pockets: wallet, watch and chain and gold miniature basketball and Kappa Beta Phi key, two dollars in silver coins, fountain pen, handkerchiefs, cigarette case, leather key purse. He looked at himself again, and wished to God he could go back to bed, but if he should go back to bed he would only think, and he refused to think until after he had had some coffee. He went downstairs, holding onto the banister on the way down.

As he passed the living-room he saw a piled row of packages, obviously gifts, on the table in the middle of the room. But Caroline was not in the room, so he did not stop. He went back to the dining-room and pushed open the swinging-door to the butler's pantry. "Just some orange juice and coffee, Mary, please," he said.

"The orange juice is on the table, Mr. English," she said.

He drank it. It had ice, glorious ice, in it. Mary brought in the coffee and when she had gone he inhaled the steam of it. It was as good as drinking it. He drank some of it black, without sugar, first. He put one lump of sugar in it and drank some more. He put some cream in it and lit a cigarette. "I'd be all right if I could stay here," he thought. "If I could just stay here for the rest of my life and never see another soul. Except Caroline. I'd have to have Caroline."

He finished his coffee, took a sip of ice water, and left the dining-room. He was standing in front of the table, with its pile of gifts, when he heard someone stamping on the porch, and almost immediately the door opened and it was Caroline.

"Hello," she said.

"Hello," he said. "Merry Christmas."

"Yeah," she said.

"I'm sorry," he said. "Where've you been?"

"Took some things to the Harley kids," she said. She hung up her camel's hair coat in the closet under the stairs. "Bubbie said to wish you a Merry Christmas and he told me to ask you if you wanted to ride on his new Flexie. I told him I didn't think you would, this morning." She sat down and began to unbuckle her arctics. She had beautiful legs that not even the heavy woolen plaid stockings could distort. "Look," she said.

"I'm looking," he said.

"Don't be funny," she said, and pulled her skirt down. "I want you to listen. This is what I want to say: I think you'd better take that bracelet back to Caldwell's."

"Why? Don't you like it?"

"I like it all right. It's one of the most beautiful things I've ever seen, but you can't afford it. I know how much it cost."

"So what?" he said.

"Well, just this. I think we'll probably need every cent we can save from now on."

"Why?"

She lit a cigarette. "Well, you fixed it last night. No point in going into *why* you threw that drink at Harry, but I just want to tell you this much, you've made an enemy for life."

"Oh, no. Naturally he's sore, but I'll be able to fix it. I can handle that."

"That's what you think. I'll tell you something. Have you any idea how news travels in this town? Maybe you think you have, but listen to me. I just came from the Harleys', the only people I've seen except Mary since last night, and almost the first thing Herbert Harley said when I got in the house was, 'Well, I'm glad somebody put Harry Reilly in his place at last.' Of course I tried to laugh it off as if it were just a joke between you and Harry, but do you realize what that means, Herbert Harley's knowing about it so soon? It means the story's got all over town already. Somebody must have told the Harleys over the phone, because I know Herbert hasn't had his car out. There aren't any tracks in their driveway."

"Well, what of it?"

"What *of* it? You stand there and ask me what of it? Don't you realize what that means, or are you still drunk? It just means that the whole town knows what you did, and when Harry realizes that, he'll do anything short of murder to get even with you. And I don't have to tell you that he won't have to commit murder to get even with you." She stood up and smoothed her skirt. "So—I think you'd better take the bracelet back to Caldwell's."

"But I want you to have it. I paid for it."

"They'll take it back. They know you."

"I can afford it," he said.

"No, you can't," she said. "Besides, I don't want it."

"You mean you don't want to take it from me?"

She hesitated a moment, and bit her lip and nodded. "Yes. I guess that's what I mean."

He went to her and put his hands on her arms. She did not move except to turn her head away from him. "What's the matter?" he said. "Reilly doesn't mean anything to you, for God's sake, does he?"

"No. Not a thing. But you'd never believe that."

"Oh, ridiculous," he said. "I never thought you were having an affair with him."

"Didn't you? Are you sure you didn't?" she freed herself. "Maybe you didn't actually think I was having an affair with him, but part of the time you wondered whether I was. That's just as bad. And that's the real reason why you threw the drink in his face."

"I might have thought you kissed him, but I never thought you were having an affair with him. And the only real reason why I threw a drink in his face was I just happen to dislike him. I can't stand his stupid Irish face, that's all. And those stories."

"His face looked pretty good last summer when you needed money, and by the way, here's something you'd better not overlook. Perhaps you think people are going to be on your side if it comes to the point where people take sides in this. Perhaps you think all your friends will stick by you, and maybe you think that's going to frighten him because he wants to run the Assembly. Well, just don't count too much on that, because practically every single one of your best friends, with one or two exceptions, all owe Harry Reilly money."

"How do you know?"

"He told me," she said. "Maybe Jack and Carter and Bob and the rest would like to be on your side, and maybe in any other year they would stick by you, but I don't have to tell you there's a depression in this country, and Harry Reilly's practically the only man around here with any money."

"I'll bet he comes to our party," said Julian.

"If he does you can thank me. I'll do my best, but my heart won't be in the work." She looked at him. "Oh God, Ju, why did you do it? Why do you do things like that?" She began to cry, but when he went to her she held him away. "It's all so awful and I used to love you so."

"I love you. You know that."

"It's too easy. The things you called me on the way home—whore and bitch and a lot worse—they weren't anything compared with the public humiliation." She accepted his handkerchief. "I've got to change," she said.

"Do you think Mother and Dad know about it?"

"No, I doubt it. Your father'd be over here if he knew. Oh, how should I know?" She walked out and then came back. "My present is at the bottom of the pile," she said.

That made him feel worse. Under all the other packages was something she had bought days, maybe weeks, before, when things were not so bad as they now appeared to be. When she bought that she was concentrating on him and what he would like; rejecting this idea and that idea, and deciding on one thing because it was something *he* wanted or something *he* would want. Caroline was one person who really did put a lot of thought into a gift; she knew when to choose the obvious thing. One time she had given him handkerchiefs for Christmas; no one else had given him handkerchiefs, and they were what he wanted. And whatever was in that package, she had bought with him alone in mind. He could not guess from the size of the box what was inside it. He opened it. It was two gifts: a pigskin stud box, big enough to hold two sets of studs, with plenty of room inside for assorted collar buttons, collar pins, tie clasps—and Caroline had put in a dozen or so front and back collar buttons. The other gift was of pigskin, too; a handkerchief case that collapsed like an accordion. Both things had J. McH. E. stamped in small gilt letters on the top cover, and that in itself showed thought. She knew, and no one else in the world knew, that he liked things stamped J. McH. E., and not just J. E., or J. M. E. Maybe she even knew why he liked it that way; he wasn't sure himself.

He stood at the table, looking down at the handkerchief case and stud box, and was afraid. Upstairs was a girl who was a person. That he loved her seemed unimportant compared to what she was. He only loved her, which really made him a lot less than a friend or an acquaintance. Other people saw her and talked to her when she was herself, her great, important self. It was wrong, this idea that you know someone better because you have shared a bed and a bathroom with her. He knew, and not another human being knew, that she cried "I" or "high" in moments of great ecstasy. He knew, he alone knew her when she let herself go, when she herself was not sure whether she was wildly gay or wildly sad, but one and the other. But that did not mean that he knew her. Far from it. It only meant that he was closer to her when he was close, but (and this was the first time the thought had come to him) maybe farther away than anyone else when he was not close. It certainly looked that way now. "Oh, I'm a son of a bitch," he said.

II

In the middle of the front page of the *Gibbsville Sun*, the morning paper, there was a two-column box, decorated with Santa Claus and holly doo-dads, and in the center of the box was a long poem. "Well, Mervyn Schwartz finally got it."

"What?" said Irma.

"Shot in a whorehouse last night," said her husband.

"What!" exclaimed Irma. "What are you talking about?"

"Here it is," said her husband. "Right here on the front page. Mervyn Schwartz, thirty-five, of Gibbsville, was shot and killed at the Dew Drop—"

"Let me see," said Irma. She took the paper out of her husband's hands. "Where? . . . Oh, *you*," she said, and threw the paper back at him. He was laughing at her with a high, soft giggle.

"Think you're funny," she said. "You oughtn't to say things like that where the children might hear you."

He continued to laugh and picked up the paper and began to read Mervyn Schwartz's Christmas poem. Mervyn Schwartz formerly had contributed his holiday poems (Christmas, Washington's Birthday, Easter, Memorial Day, July 4, Armistice Day) to the *Standard*, the afternoon paper; but the *Standard* had not run his Armistice Day poem on the front page, so now he was in the *Sun*. Lute Fliegler read the first verse aloud, very sing-song and effeminate.

"What time do you want dinner?" said Irma.

"Whenever it's ready," said Lute.

"Well, you only had breakfast an hour ago. You don't want dinner too early. I thought around two o'clock."

"Okay by me," he said. "I'm not very hungry."

"You oughtn't to be," she said. "The breakfast you ate. I was thinking I'd make the beds now and Mrs. Lynch could put the turkey on so we could eat around two or ha' past."

"Okay by me."

"The kids won't be very hungry. Even Curly was stuffing himself with candy a while ago till I hid the box."

"Let him eat it," said her husband. "Christmas comes but once a year."

"Thank heaven. All right. I'll give them the candy, on one condition. That is, if you take care of them when they have stomach ache in the middle of the night."

"I'll be only too glad. Go ahead, give them all the candy they want, and give Teddy and Betty a couple highballs." He frowned and rubbed his chin in mock thoughtfulness. "I don't know about Curly, though. He's a little young, but I guess it'd be all right. Or else maybe he'll take a cigar."

"Oh, you," she said.

"Yes-s-s, I think we better just give Curly a cigar. By the way, I'm going to take Teddy out and get him laid tonight. I—"

"Lute! Stop talking like that. How do you know one of them didn't come downstairs without you hearing them? They'll be finding things out soon enough. Remember what Betty said last summer."

"That's nothing. How old is Teddy? Six—"

"Six and a half," she said.

"Well, when I was Teddy's age I had four girls knocked up."

"Now stop, Lute. You stop talking that way. You don't have any idea how they pick things up, a word here and there. And children are smarter than you give them credit for. You don't have to go anywhere today, do you?"

"Nope. Why?" He lit a Camel, taking it out of the package in the lower right pocket of his vest.

"Well, no reason. Last Christmas remember you had to drive to Reading."

"That was *last* Christmas. Damn few Caddies being given for Christmas presents this year. I remember that trip. That was a sport job. A LaSalle, it was, not a Caddy. That Polish undertaker up the mountain, Paul Davinis. He wanted it delivered Christmas and he didn't want his kid to see it so we asked to keep it in Reading. And then when we did deliver it the kid knew he was going to get it all along. His mother told him beforehand. He smashed it up New Year's Eve."

"You never told me that," said Irma.

"You never asked me, as the snake charmer said to her husband. By the way, did Mrs. Lynch say she'd mind the kids tonight?"

"Uh-huh."

"Well, then I better phone Willard and tell him we'll go along. I'll get that Studebaker sedan. We can get six in it comfortably. It's a seven-passenger job, but we can sit three in the front and three in the back and we won't have to use the extra seats. How many are going?"

"I think twelve. Ten or twelve. It depends. If Emily's father and mother come down from Shamokin she and Harvey won't be able to come along, but it won't make any difference. They were going in Walter's car, so if they don't go, that makes two less in that car."

"I better call the garage and make sure about the Studebaker." He went to the telephone. "Hello, this is Lute Fliegler. Merry Christmas. Listen, that Studebaker sedan, the black one. The one we took on a trade-in from Doc Lurie. Yeah. Doc Lurie's old car. Well, listen. Don't let anybody take it out, see? I asked the boss if I could use it tonight and he said okay, see? So I just wanted to make sure none of you thieves took it out. If you want to go any place you can use my Rolls. Seriously, Joe, you want to do me a favor, you can put the chains on the Studie. Okay? Swell." He hung up, and addressed Irma. "Well, that's settled."

"You can call Willard later," she said. "I told him we'd call if we couldn't go, so he'll take it for granted we're going."

"What about liquor?" said Lute.

"Well, it's Willard's party. I should think he'd supply the liquor."

"Oh, yeah? Do you know how much liquor costs at the Stage Coach? Seventy-five cents a drink, baby, and they won't sell it to everybody. I don't think Willard intends to supply the liquor, not at six bits a shot. I think I better make some gin and take a quart along, just in case. It wouldn't be right to expect Willard to buy all the liquor and everything else for a party of twelve people."

"Maybe there'll only be ten."

"All right. What if there *is* only ten? They have a cover charge of a dollar and a half or two dollars, and there goes twenty bucks already, not including ginger ale and White Rock, and sandwiches! You know what they charge for a plain ordinary chicken sandwich at the Stage Coach? A *buck*. If Willard gets away under forty bucks he's lucky, without buying a single drink. No, I better make some gin. Or on second thought, there's that quart of rye the boss gave me. I was going to save it, but we might as well use it tonight."

"Oh, the gin's good enough. You make good gin. Everybody says so."

"I know I do, but gin's gin. I think I'll turn square for once in my life and take the rye. Maybe the others will bring their own, so we won't have to get rid of the whole quart."

"I don't want you to drink much if you're going to drive," said Irma.

"Don't worry. Not over those roads. I know. I'll put the quart into pint bottles and keep one pint in my overcoat pocket when we get to the Stage Coach. Then the others will think I only have a pint and they'll go easy. But I imagine everybody will bring their own, if they have any sense."

"I imagine," she said. "I'm going upstairs now and make the beds. I'll see if the pants of your Tux need pressing."

"Oh, God. That's right. Do I have to wear that?"

"Now, now, don't try and bluff me. You look nice in it and you know it. You like to wear it and don't pretend you don't."

"Oh, I don't mind wearing it," he said. "I was just thinking about you. You'll be so jealous when all the other girls see me in my Tux and start trying to take me outside. I just didn't want to spoil your evening, that's all."

"Applesauce," said Irma.

"Why don't you say what you mean? You don't mean applesauce."

"Never mind, now, Mister Dirty Mouth." She left.

What a girl, he thought, and resumed reading his paper; Hoover was receiving the newsboys for Christmas. . . .

III

It was about two o'clock, U. S. Naval Observatory Hourly By Western Union time, when Al Grecco appeared in the doorway of the Apollo Restaurant. The Apollo was a hotel and restaurant. There had been a hotel on the site of the Apollo for close to a century, but the Pennsylvania Dutch family who had the restaurant before George Poppas took it over had not kept the hotel part open. Then when George Poppas, who actually was wearing those white Greek kilts when he arrived in Gibbsville, began to make money on the restaurant, someone mentioned that the building had been a hotel for nearly a hundred years, and George spent a lot of money on making the place a hotel again. The rooms were small and had a fireproof look about them, with steel beds and other furniture. The hotel was clean, the rooms were small and cheap, and the Apollo got a big play from salesmen who had their swindle sheets to think of. The John Gibb Hotel. Gibbsville's big inn, was expensive.

Al Grecco was one of the few permanent guests of the Apollo. He had a room there, for which he paid nothing. Ed Charney had some kind of arrangement with George Poppas, in which no money changed hands. Ed wanted Al to be at the Apollo to receive messages and so on. Whenever there were strangers from other mobs in town on business, or friends who just happened to be passing through Gibbsville, they always looked up Ed Charney at the Apollo. And if Ed was not there, he wanted someone to be on hand, and that someone usually was Al Grecco.

Al had his hat on but was carrying his dark blue overcoat. There was not a customer in the place. Smitty, who was a taxi driver and two-bit pimp, was sitting at the marble counter, drinking a cup of coffee, but Smitty was always at the counter drinking coffee. George Poppas was standing behind the cigar counter. He looked as though he were sitting down, but Al knew better. George leaned with his fat hands folded, supporting himself on the cigar counter, and appearing to be in great pain. George always appeared to be in great pain, as though he had eaten, an hour ago, all the things that can give you indigestion. Al once had seen him in a crap game make fifteen straight passes and win over twelve thousand dollars, but he still appeared to be in great pain.

Loving Cup was behind the counter, and seemed to be the only waiter in the place. Loving Cup was about twenty, perhaps less; slight, with a bad complexion and a terrible breath. The boys were always kidding Loving Cup about his ears, from which he got his name. They were at least a third as long as his whole head, and stuck out. Also, the boys often had kidded Loving Cup about his lonely sex life, until one night for a gag they took him to the Dew Drop and paid for his entertainment. But when he came downstairs Mimi said to them: "Well, you wise guys, this kid got more than any of you. Howdia like that? He's the only man in the crowd." And Loving Cup listened delightedly, his eyes bright and gleaming and wicked and small. From that night on the boys make no cracks about Loving Cup and his lonely sex life. They still referred to him as Loving Cup, and called him Bertha, but they had some respect for him.

Al did not speak to George Poppas. They had a mutual contempt for each other; George for Al, because Al was a minor member of the mob; and Al for George because George did not belong to the mob at all. They never spoke, except in crap games, when they confined their remarks to "You're faded" and the other language of the game. Al placed his coat on a hanger and removed his hat, using both hands in taking off the hat so as not to disturb his hair.

He took the *Philadelphia Public Ledger*, which was lying on the counter in front of George. He sat down at the mob's table, which was in the very front of the restaurant, in a corner just back of the front window, where various crustaceans were squirming about in a pool. Al looked at the front page and saw that Hoover was going to entertain some newsboys for Christmas. He turned over to the sport pages.

"Hyuh," said a voice. It was Loving Cup.

"Oh, hyuh, Loving Cup," said Al.

"Two over? Bacon well done? Coffee?" said Loving Cup.

"No," said Al. "Gimme the bill of fare."

"What for?" said Loving Cup. "You can read the paper."

"God damn it! Get me the bill of fare before I cut your heart out."

"All right, all right," said Loving Cup, running away. He came back with a menu and laid it beside Al's right arm. "There."

"What are you, a Jew or something? Didn't they tell you it's Christmas, or don't they have Christmas where you come from? Say, where *did* you come from, anyway, sweetheart?"

"That's my business," said Loving Cup. "The turkey is all right. You want some of that? I thought you was having breakfast."

"It's Christmas, you lug," said Al.

"Yeah, I know," said Loving Cup. "What are you gonna have, or do I have to wait here all day while you spell out the words?"

"Crack wise, Bertha," said Al. "I'll have that a dollar and a half dinner."

"What kind of soup you want?"

"I don't want any soup," said Al.

"It goes with the dinner, so you don't have to pay extra. I'll bring you the cream of tomato. I just seen the chef spit in it." He jumped away as Al reached out for him. He went laughing to the kitchen.

Al read his paper. There was always some stumble bum from Fargo fighting in Indianapolis. Every time you picked up the paper and looked under Fight Results there was somebody from Fargo doing a waltz somewhere. Either they were all would-be fighters in that town, or else they just used the name of the town and didn't come from there at all, like the Gibbsville Miners, the pro football team. Practically every man on the team was an All American, but they never heard of Gibbsville before they came there to play football. They all talked like Snake Eyes O'Neill, who came from Jersey City and was one of the mob. Snake Eyes never said r. Dollah. Fawd. Hoit. Boint. Thoid. Likka. Never said r. Al wondered where Fargo was. It was past Chicago. He knew that. They had one good boy from that town. Petrolle. Billy Petrolle, the Fargo Express. But the rest of them! God, what a gang of tankers they were. He wondered just what was the angle on there being so many fighters from Fargo. Maybe Ed would know. Ed could usually tell him when something puzzled him.

Ed had said he wouldn't be down till around four o'clock. He had to spend Christmas with the wife and kid, God knows why. Al did not like to think of Annie Charney. The kid was swell; six years old and fat and healthy-looking. He wasn't like Ed, but for the present more like Annie. She was fat and healthy-looking and blonde, like most Polacks. Ed didn't care for her any more. Al knew that. Ed cared for Helene Holman, who was a torch singer like Libby Holman and sang at the Stage Coach. Ed really cared for Helene. He played around a little, but Al knew Helene was the only one he really cared for, and Helene really cared for him. With her it was slightly different, because nobody else would even look cockeyed at Helene as long as Ed cared for her, but even taking that into consideration Al knew Helene really cared for Ed. And she was good for him. You could tell when Ed and Helene were getting along. Ed was easier to get along with then. Tonight, or this after', when Ed showed up at the Apollo, he probably would be in a bad humor. That was the way Annie affected him. Whereas if he had spent the day with Helene he would have been in a good humor. But Al knew that Ed wouldn't think of spending Christmas with Helene. Ed was a family man, first and last, and that was the one day in the year he would spend with the kid, at home.

"Here," said Loving Cup.

Al looked at the blue plate. "For a buck fifty I don't call that much turkey," he said.

"What's the matter, Mr. Grecco? Is it too small?" said Loving Cup.

"Small? For Christ's sakes. And wuddia say, how about giving me some white meat? If I'm gonna pay a buck fifty for turkey I wanna get some white meat, not this God damn dark meat."

"Shall I take it back?"

"Sure, take it back," said Al. "No, wait a minute. The hell with it, and the hell with you. You'll take a couple hours."

"That's right, Mr. Grecco. It's Christmas. You said so yourself just a minute ago."

"Screw, bum," said Al. Loving Cup pretended to pay no attention to him and dusted off the table cloth, but out of the corner of his eye he was watching Al, and when Al made a grab for his wrist Loving Cup leapt away. Then he snickered and went back to the counter.

Al usually had breakfast at this time, if he was up. He ate eggs and bacon for breakfast, had a small steak or something like that at seven in the evening, and then after midnight he usually ate what he called his big meal: a thick steak with boiled potatoes, piece of pie, and many cups of coffee. He was about five feet six with his high heels, and weighed about 130 pounds with his suit on. He had been with Ed Charney and eating regularly for four years, but he still did not gain much weight. Stayed about the same. His bones were small, and he was a thin little man in every part of him. He was born in Gibbsville, the son of Italian parents. His father worked on a navvy gang and supported six children, of whom Al was the third. Al's name was not Al, and it was not Grecco. His real name was Anthony Joseph Murascho, or Tony Murascho, until he was eighteen. He had been kicked out of the parochial school for striking a nun when he was fourteen; carried newspapers, stole, was house-man in a poolroom, served a year in prison for burgling the poorbox in one of the Irish Catholic churches, and was arrested several other times: once when a false alarm was turned in (he had an honest alibi); once for attempted rape (the girl could not positively identify more than two of the six suspects); once for breaking the seals on a freight car (the railroad detectives listened to his father's plea, and they had a good case against four other boys, so out of kindness to the old man they did not prosecute Tony); once for stabbing a colleague in a poolroom argument (no one, not even the victim, could swear Tony had done it; and anyway it was only a slight wound).

It was when he was eighteen, the same year of his life that he went to the county jail, that he got the name of Al Grecco. At that time he decided to be a prizefighter, and though he had a lingering touch of gonorrhea, he went into training and studied the sweet science under Packy McGovern, Gibbsville's leading and only fight promoter. Packy told him he was a born fighter, had the real fighting heart, and that the clap was no worse than a bad cold. He made Tony lay off women, alcohol, and cigarettes, and do a lot of bag-punching. He showed Tony how to hold his elbows and how to keep his right foot in position so he could move his body backward without taking a backward step; that was footwork. He taught Tony how to scrape an opponent's eyes with the palm of the glove, and also how to use his thumb, and also how to butt. He of course instructed Tony never to enter a ring without first knocking a few dents into the aluminum-cup supporter which is supposed to be a protection against foul blows. You never know when you can claim foul and get away with it, and if the cup is not dented no club physician would dare allow the claim. Tony Murascho, who up to that time had been known only as a tough little guinny, was matched to fight a preliminary bout at McGovern's Hall.

As it happened, Lydia Faunce Browne was assigned to write a feature story about that fight card. Lydia Faunce Browne was not a Gibbsville

girl originally. She came from Columbus, Ohio, and had been in Gibbsville five years when her husband deserted her. He was younger
than Mrs. Browne, who at the time of the desertion was forty-nine,
and he left behind, besides Lydia, a large bill at the Lantenengo Country Club, another big bill at the Gibbsville Club, and several other
bills. For a time Mrs. Browne eked out a living and paid a little on the
bills by teaching auction bridge to the wives of the Jewish storekeepers,
but she finally flattered Bob Hooker, editor of the *Standard* into giving her a job on the staff of the *Standard*. She told him he was a real
man for his editorial on his dead dog. She became the pest of the
Standard office on her own hook, and was being built up big by Bob
Hooker, who regarded himself as the William Allen White-Ed Howe-
Joseph Pulitzer of Gibbsville. He began to regard Lydia as the local
Sophie Irene Loeb, and paid her $35 a week, with three exceptions
the highest journalistic salary in the town.

Lydia was always being sent down in the mines, much against the
wishes of the miners, who think it is unlucky for a woman to enter a
mine; or riding in locomotive cabs, or spending a night in prison, or in-
terviewing visiting celebrities, such as George Luks (who later wanted
to know where in the name of God they dug her up) and Rabbi Stephen S. Wise and Gifford Pinchot (five times). Lydia's secret favorite
adjective for herself was keen; and she went around looking keen during all her waking hours. She felt sorry for prostitutes on all occasions;
she thought milk for babies ought to be pure; she thought Germany
was not altogether responsible for the World War; she did not believe
in Prohibition ("It does not prohibit," she often said). She smoked
cigarettes one right after the other, and did not care who knew it; and
she never was more than five minutes out of the office before she was
talking in newspaper argot, not all of it quite accurate. She had a hell
of a time with the spelling of names.

She went out to cover the prizefights with Doug Campbell, sports
editor of the *Standard*. No nice women ever went to prizefights in
Gibbsville, no matter what they did in New York, and Lydia's story
the next day began:

I went to the boxing match last night.

I went to the boxing match, and to be completely frank and honest,
I enjoyed myself. What is this taboo that man-made convention has
placed upon women going to boxing matches? Can it be that men
are just a little selfish, depriving women of the fun and beauty of the
boxing match? And I use the word beauty advisedly, after long and

careful consideration. For there was beauty in McGovern's Hall last night. Let me tell you about it.

To you women who cannot attend boxing matches because of the aforementioned masculine taboo that has been placed on attendance at the "fights" by women, permit me a few words of explanation. The principal contest of the evening, like all good things, is called the "wind-up" and it comes last. It follows the introductory "bouts" which are known as "preliminaries" or "prelims" I believe they were called by my friend Mr. Doug Campbell, popular sports editor of the *Standard*, who escorted me to McGovern's Hall and showed me the "ropes." In the "prelims" one sees the lesser known lights of the boxing fraternity, and it is considered a kind of obscurity to be relegated to the "prelims." But it was in a "prelim" that I saw real beauty.

A mere strip of a lad, hardly more than a boy he was, and his name is Tony Morascho. Doug Campbell informed me that it was the début of Tony Morascho but I sincerely trust it will not be Tony's last, for there was beauty personified, grace in every ripple of his lithe young frame, symmetry and rhythm and the speed of a cobra as it strikes the helpless rabbit. Beauty! Do you know El Grecco, the celebrated Spanish artist? Surely you do. Well, there was El Grecco, to the life. . . .

That was how Al Grecco got his name.

He could not live the name down. The gang at the poolroom and at the gym called him El Grecco, and for a gag Packy McGovern billed him as Al Grecco on the next card. The name followed him into prison —was, in fact, waiting for him there; Lantenengo County Prison was ruled by a warden who, though no deep student of penology, believed in permitting his wards to have newspapers, cigarettes, whiskey, assignations, cards—anything, so long as they paid for it. And so when Al Grecco was sent up on the poorbox burglary matter he was not altogether unknown at the Stoney Lonesome, as the prison was called.

When Al had served his time he came out with some idea of turning square. He wanted to turn square, because he had seen so many ex-convicts in the movies who came out with one of two plans: either you turned square, or you got even with the person who got you sent up. He could not get even with Father Burns, the curate who had caught him burgling the poorbox, because it was a sacrilege to hit a priest, and anyhow Father Burns had been transferred to another parish. And so Al decided to turn square. First, though, there were two things he wanted to do. There was no one to give him money while he was in prison, and he felt he had been deprived of the two most important things you can have. He had about ten dollars, his earnings in prison, but that was not enough for a big night. He wanted twenty. So he got in a game of pool, to get his eye and his stroke back, and surprised himself by being pretty good. That gave him confidence, and he asked if he could take a cue in a money game. He lost all his money in the game and Joe Steinmetz, the crippled man who owned the place, would not stake him. Steinmetz would give him a job, he said, but no money to shoot pool with. So Al walked out of the place, wishing he had insulted Joe. Outside the poolroom, which was the next building to the Apollo hotel and restaurant, Al saw Ed Charney, sitting in his Cadillac sedan. Ed was smoking a cigar, and seemed to be waiting for someone. Al waved his hand and said, "Hyuh, Ed." All the poolroom gang spoke to Ed, although Ed did not always answer. Now he beckoned to Al. Al made the distance to the car in three jumps.

"Hello, Ed," he said.

"When'd you get out? Somebody spring you?" said Ed. He took his cigar out of his mouth and smiled benevolently at Al. Al was surprised and pleased that Ed Charney should know so much about him.

"No, I did my time," he said. "I got out today." He leaned with one arm on the rear door of the sedan. "I didn't know you knew me."

"I make it my business to know a *lot* of people," said Ed. "How'd you like to make a sawbuck?"

"Who do you want knocked off?" said Al.

Ed glared and put the cigar back in his teeth, but then took it out again. "Don't talk tough, kid. That don't get you any place. That don't get you any place except up in that jail house or else—" he snapped his fingers. "Nobody has to knock anybody off, and the sooner you get them ideas out of your head the better off you are."

"You're right, Ed," said Al.

"I know I'm right. I make it my business to be right. Now if you want to make that sawbuck, all I want you to do—can you drive a car?"

"Yeah. What kind? This one?"

"This one," said Ed. "Take it out to the Gibbsville Motors or whatever you call it. English's garage. Tell them I sent you out to have it washed and wait till they're done with it and then bring it back here." He reached in his pocket and took a ten-dollar bill from a roll. "Here."

"A sawbuck for that? Do you want me to pay for washin' it?"

"No. Charge it. I give you the sawbuck because you just got outa the can. Keep your nose clean." Ed Charney got out of the car. "Keys in the car," he said. He walked toward the Apollo, but turned after a few steps. "Say," he said. "Who the hell ever told you you was a prize-fighter?"

Al laughed. There was a guy for you: Ed Charney, the big shot from here to Reading and here to Wilkes-Barre. Maybe the whole State. What a guy! Democratic. Gave a guy ten bucks for doing nothing at all, nothing at all. Knew all about you. Made it his business to know all about you. That night Al Grecco did not get quite so drunk as he had planned; he waited until the next night, when he had thirty dollars from a crap game. *That* night he got good and drunk, and was thrown out of a house for beating up one of the girls. The day after that he took a job with Joe Steinmetz.

For three years he worked for Joe Steinmetz, more or less regularly. No one could beat him shooting straight pool, and he had great skill and luck in Nine Ball, Ouch, Harrigan, One Ball in the Side and other gambling pool games. He saw Ed Charney a couple of times a week, and Ed called him Al. Ed seldom played pool, because there were only six tables in the place, and though he could have had any table by asking for it or even hinting that he wanted to play, he did not take advantage of his power. When he played he played with Snake Eyes O'Neill, the wisecracking, happy-go-lucky guy from Jersey City, who was always with Ed and, everybody said, was Ed's body-guard. Snake Eyes, or Snake, as Ed called him, carried a revolver unlike any Al ever had seen. It was like any ordinary revolver except that it had hardly any barrel to it. Snake was always singing or humming. He never knew the words of a song until after it was old, and he used to make sounds "Neeyaa, ta ta ta tata, tee ta tee, laddie deetle," instead of singing the words. He was not called Snake Eyes because he had eyes like a snake. Far from it. The name was a crap-shooting term. He had big brown eyes that were always smiling. O'Neill was tall and skinny and in Al's opinion was the snappiest dresser he ever had seen. Al counted up one time and he figured O'Neill had at least four-teen suits of clothes, all the latest cut from Broadway, New York City. Ed Charney was not a very snappy dresser. Ed had quite a few suits, but he did not change them much. His pants often needed pressing, and he often put his hat on so that the bow on the band was on the wrong side of his head. There were always cigar ashes on the lapels of his coat. But Al knew one thing: Ed wore silk underwear. He'd seen it.

In the last year before he got a job with Ed, Al frequently sat at Ed's table in the Apollo. By that time Al was shooting such good pool that Joe cut him in on the weekly take of the poolroom, and Al had permission to use house money when he wanted to play pool for money. He was only twenty-one and thinking of buying a half interest in the place. He spent plenty, but he made plenty; anywhere from fifty to two hundred bucks a week. He had a car—a Chevvy coupé. He bought a Tuxedo. He went to Philadelphia when there was a musical comedy and he knew a girl there that worked in night clubs and shows, who would sleep with him if he let her know he was coming to town. He liked the name Al Grecco, and never thought of himself as Tony Murascho. The boys who sat at Ed Charney's table would not have known who was meant if the name Tony Murascho had been mentioned. But they knew Al Grecco for a good kid that Ed liked well enough to ask him to eat with him once in a while. Al Grecco was no pest, and did not sit at the table unless he was asked. He never asked any favors. He was the only one who ever sat at the table who had nothing to do with the stock market, and that was a big relief. All the others, from Ed Charney down, were in the market or only temporarily out of it.

Al lived then at Gorney's Hotel, which was not quite the worst hotel in Gibbsville. He never went near his home and did not go out of his way to speak to any of his brothers or sisters if he saw them on the street. They did not try to persuade him to come home, either. When they needed money badly they would send one of the younger kids to the poolroom, and Al would give the kid a five or a ten, but Al did not like this. It put him off his game. After giving away a five or ten he would get overanxious in trying to make it up, and the result would be he would lose. He wished the old man would support his family himself. And what about Angelo and Joe and Tom; they were all older than Tony—Al. And Marie, she was old enough to get married and the other kids didn't have to go to school all their life. *He* didn't. The old man ought to be glad he didn't have to work in the mines. Al knew that the old man would have worked in the mines, and glad to get the bigger wages, but all he could do was navvy gang work. Even so, the old man ought to be glad he had outdoor work instead of mucking in a drift or robbing pillars or being on a rock gang in tunnel work. That kind of work was hard work. Or at least Al thought so. He never had been in the mines himself—and never would, if he could help it.

One afternoon Joe Steinmetz didn't come to work and he didn't come to work. Joe did not like the telephone, because it interfered with a man's privacy, and the next day when he again did not show up, Al took the Chevvy up to Point Mountain, where Joe lived with his wife. There was a crêpe on the door. Al hated to go in, but he thought he ought to . . . It was Joe, all right. Mrs. Steinmetz was alone and hadn't been able to leave the house except to have a neighbor get a doctor. Joe had died of heart disease and was good and dead by the time the doctor had sent the undertaker.

Joe left everything to his wife. She wanted Al to work for her, keep the poolroom going, and at first he thought it would be a good idea. But a few days of taking the day's receipts all the way out to her house showed him he didn't want to work for her. She offered to sell the good will and fixtures for five thousand dollars, but Al never had had that much money all at once in his life and there were only two ways he could borrow it; from the banks or from Ed Charney. He didn't like banks or the people who worked in them, and he didn't want to ask Ed. He didn't think he knew Ed well enough to ask him for money. Anyhow, not that kind of money; five grand. So the poolroom went to Mike Minas, a Greek friend of George Poppas's, and Al went to work for Ed Charney. He just went up to Ed and said: "Viz have any kind of a job for me, Ed?" and Ed said yes, come to think of it, he had been thinking of offering him a job for a long time. They agreed on a fifty-dollar-a-week salary, and Al went to work. At first he merely drove Ed around on business and pleasure trips; then he was given a job of some importance, that of convoy to the booze trucks. He would follow two or three Reo Speedwagons, in which the stuff was transported. If a state policeman or a Federal dick stopped the trucks, it was Al's business to stop too. It was an important job, because he took a chance of being sent to prison. When he stopped, it was his job to try to bribe the cops. It was an important job, because he carried up to ten thousand dollars cash of Ed's money in the Nash roadster which he used on these trips. It was up to him to use his head about bribing the cops; one or two of them wouldn't be bribed, but most of them would listen to reason unless they had been sent out to pinch a truck or two to make a showing. He had to be smooth in his bribery offers to some of them. Some of them would take anything from a gold tooth to ten thousand dollars, but hated to be approached in the wrong way. On the few occasions when the cops refused to be bribed, it was Al's job to get to the nearest telephone, tell Ed, and get Jerome M. Montgomery, Ed's lawyer, working on the case. Al never was arrested for attempted bribery. In fact he was so successful generally that Ed took him off the convoy job and made him a collector. Ed trusted him and liked him, and made a lot of money for him, or gave him a lot of money. Sitting there at breakfast on this Christmas morning Al Grecco could write a check for more than four thousand dollars, and he had thirty-two one-thousand-dollar bills in his safety deposit box. For a kid of twenty-six he was doing all right.

Now Loving Cup suddenly was standing at his table. "On the phone, you," said Loving Cup.

"Who is it? Some dame?" said Al.

"Don't try and bluff me," said Loving Cup. "I know you're queer. No, it's a party I think they said the name was Jarney or Charney. That was it. Charney."

"Wise guy," said Al, getting up. "I'll cut your ears off. Is it Ed?"

"Yeah," said Loving Cup, "and he don't sound like Christmas to me."

"Sore, eh?" Al hurried to the telephone. "Merry Christmas, boss," he said.

"Yeah. Same to you," said Ed, in a dull voice. "Listen Al, my kid got his arm broke—"

"Jesus, tough! How'd he do that?"

"Oh, he fell off some God damn wagon I bought him. So anyhow I'm staying here till he gets the arm set and all, and I won't be down till I don't know when. Annie is all hysterical and yelling her head off —shut up, for Christ's sake, can't you see I'm phoning. So I'm staying here. Now listen, Al. Do you have a date for tonight?"

"Nothing I can't break," said Al, who had no date. "I had a sort of a date, but it can wait if you want me to do anything."

"Well, I hate to ask you, but this is what I want you should do. Drive up to the Stage Coach and stay there till they close up and keep an eye on things, see what I mean? And tell Helene I'll be there if I can make it, but you stay there anyhow, will you kid? There's fifty bucks in it for you on account of lousing up your date. Okay?"

"Kay," said Al. "Only too glad, Ed."

"Okay," said Ed. "Just stick around and keep an eye on everything." He hung up.

Al knew what he meant. Helene was not a teetotaler by any means. In fact Ed encouraged her to drink. She was more fun when she drank. But she was liable to get drunk tonight, because it was Christmas, and Ed didn't want her to become reckless with the spirit of giving.

3

ANYONE IN Gibbsville who had any important money made it in coal; anthracite. Gibbsville people, when they went away, always had trouble explaining where they lived. They would say: "I live in the coal regions," and people would say, "Oh, yes, near Pittsburgh." Then Gibbsvillians would have to go into detail. People outside of Pennsylvania do not know that there is all the difference in the world between the two kinds of coal, and in the conditions under which anthracite and bituminous are mined. The anthracite region lies roughly between Scranton on the north and Gibbsville on the south. In fact Point Mountain, upon which Gibbsville's earliest settlement was made, is the delight of geologists, who come from as far away as Germany to examine Gibbsville Conglomerate, a stone formation found nowhere else in the world. When that geological squeeze, or whatever it was that produced veins of coal, occurred, it did not go south of Point Mountain, and coal is found on the north slope of Point Mountain, but not on the south side, and at the eastern face of Point Mountain is found Gibbsville Conglomerate. The richest veins of anthracite in the world are within a thirty-mile sector from Gibbsville, and when those veins are being worked, Gibbsville prospers. When the mines are idle, Gibbsville puts on a long face and begins to think in terms of soup kitchens.

The anthracite region, unlike the bituminous, is a stronghold of union labor. The United Mine Workers of America is the strongest single force in the anthracite region, and under it the anthracite miner lives a civilized life compared with that of the miner in the soft coal regions about Pittsburgh, West Virginia, and the western states. The "coal and iron" police in the anthracite region have been so unimportant since the unionization of the mines that they seldom are mentioned. A candidate for governor of Pennsylvania cannot be elected without the support of the U.M.W.A., and the Pennsylvania State Police never are called "black cossacks" in the anthracite region. A candidate for any political office in the anthracite counties would not think of having anything printed without getting the typesetters' union label on his cards and billboards. The union is responsible for the Pennsylvania mining laws, which are the best in the world (although not yet the best there could be), and labor conditions, so far as labor strife was concerned, were all right in 1930, and had been all right since the disastrous strike of 1925. At that time the union called a strike which lasted 110 days, the longest strike in anthracite history. There was no violence beyond the small squabble, and there was no starvation among the miners. But anthracite markets disappeared. Domestic sales were hurt permanently; the oil burner was installed in thousands of homes. Anthracite is practically smokeless, and was satisfactory to home owners, but they could not get anthracite during the strike, and when the oil burner was installed there was no point in going back to coal. And so, as a result of the 1925 strike, the anthracite industry went back to work without nearly the demand for the product that there had been when the strike was called 110 days before. There had been another long strike in 1922, and the two strikes taught consumers that the industry was not dependable. The feeling was that any time the union felt like it, it would call a strike, shutting off the supply of anthracite.

Thus what were boom times for the rest of the country were something less for Gibbsville. The year of Our Lord 1929 saw many of the mines near Gibbsville working on a three-day a week basis. The blasts of the giant whistles at the collieries, more powerful than those of any steamship, were not heard rolling down the valleys as they had been before the 1925 strike, every morning at five and six o'clock. The anthracite industry was just about licked.

Still there were a great many people in Gibbsville who had money in 1930. The very rich, who always had money, still had a lot of money. And the merchants and bankers, doctors and lawyers and dentists who had money to play the market continued to spend their principal. Mr. Hoover was an engineer, and in a mining country engineers are respected. Gibbsville men and women who were in the market trusted that cold fat pinched face as they had trusted the cold thin pinched face of Mr. Coolidge, and in 1930 the good days work of October 29, 1929, continued to be known as a strong technical reaction.

II

William Dilworth English (B.S., Lafayette College; M.D., University of Pennsylvania), father of Julian McHenry English, had a salary of $12,000 a year as chief of staff of the Gibbsville Hospital. He lived within that salary, almost to the dollar. His income from private practice was about $10,000, and this totaled up to more than he could spend in a year, without being foolish. In addition to that his wife, Elizabeth McHenry English, had an income which in 1930 was about $6,000. In other years it had been more than that, but Dr. English, in investing his wife's money, had been no wiser than a lot of other men whose wives had money to invest.

Dr. English came from one of the oldest families in Gibbsville. He was of Revolutionary stock. He wore a ring with an indistinguishable crest (he took it off when he operated). Adam English, one of his ancestors, had come to Gibbsville in 1804, two years after Gibbsville was re-founded (Gibbsville was founded by Swedes in 1750, as nearly any-one could make out; the Swedes had been massacred by the Leni Lenape Indians, and the Swedish name of the original settlement has been lost). Old Adam English, as Dr. English called him, who cer-tainly would have been old if he had lived till 1930, was a Phila-delphian. It was not old Adam's father, but *his* father who had fought in the Revolution.

The Englishes were not exactly coal people. They were more in the railroad, the Philadelphia & Reading. But of course the railroad and the coal and iron once had been all one company. It was much better in those days, Dr. English said, because you could get passes on the railroad if someone in your family happened to be connected with either the railroad or the coal company. But Dr. English did not desire a return to those days, the days when he was in college and at The University (whenever a Gibbsvillian speaks of The University he means Pennsylvania and nowhere else). He rarely spoke of those days, for, as he said, a dark and bitter cloud had been drawn over what should have been remembered as the happiest days of his life. He re-ferred, of course, to the fact that the summer after he got his M.D., his father, George English, stuck a shotgun in his mouth and blew his head all over the hayloft of the English stable. Dr. English thought of his father as a coward. Two or three times in their married life the doc-tor had said to his wife: "If George English had been anything but a coward he would have gone to the directors like a man and said, 'Gen-tlemen, I have been using the bank's funds for my own uses. I am willing to work hard and make it up.' And I know the directors would have admired that stand, and they would have given him a chance to make good. But. . . ." And his wife would sympathize with him and try to comfort him, although she knew that her father, for one, would have tried to send George English to jail. As it was, he opposed her marriage to Billy English. Her father had said: "He may be all right. I don't know. But his education was paid for out of stolen money. That's enough for me." But how was Billy to know that? she argued. "He knows it now," said her father. Yes, he knew it, she went on, and he was anxious to start private practice so he could make good every penny. And he had. Within ten years of his graduation Billy English had paid off the money his father had taken from the bank. It had been a struggle, in a way; what with young Julian's arrival in the world. Still, Julian had not been deprived of anything, thanks to her own income. Despite the dark, bitter cloud that hung over Dr. English's college days, Julian, who wanted to go to Yale, was sent to

Lafayette. And, probably out of spite, Julian did not accept the invitation to join Phi Delta Theta, his father's fraternity, but had joined Delta Kappa Epsilon. By that time his father had given up hope that Julian would study medicine. He had pointed out to Julian that "when I die, you'll have this practice that I've been years building up. I don't understand it. Plenty of boys in this town would give their right arm for just this chance." Poor Dr. English, people would say; starting out that way, with that handicap, and then his only son not taking advantage of that wonderful opportunity. No wonder the doctor was such a stern-looking man. He'd had his troubles.

He represented the best things in the community. He was a member of the County Medical Society, the Medical Club of Philadelphia, the Gibbsville Chamber of Commerce, the Gibbsville Community Chest (director), the Children's Home Association (life subscriber), the Y.M.C.A. (director), Lantenengo County Historical Society, the Gibbsville Club (board of governors), the Lantenengo Country Club (board of governors), the Gibbsville Assembly (membership committee), the Union League of Philadelphia, the Ancient and Arabic Order-Nobles of the Mystic Shrine, the Scottish Rite Masons (32°), and the Liberty (formerly Germania) Hook & Ladder Company Number 1 (honorary). He also was a director of the Gibbsville National Bank & Trust Company, the Gibbsville Building & Loan Company, the Gibbsville-Cadillac Motor Car Company, the Lantenengo Lumber Company, and the Gibbsville Tap & Reamer Company. Episcopalian. Republican. Hobbies: golf, trapshooting. All that in addition to his work at the hospital and his private practice. Of course he didn't do nearly the private practice he used to. He was more or less giving that up and specializing on surgery. He left the little stuff to the younger men that were just starting out—childbirth and tonsils and ordinary sickness.

If there was one thing he loved, outside of his wife and son, it was surgery. He had been doing surgery for years, in the days when the ambulances from the mines were high black wagons, open at the rear, drawn by two black mules. It was almost a day's drive from some of the mines to the hospital, in the mule-drawn-ambulance days. Sometimes the patient or patients would bleed to death on the way, in spite of the best of care on the part of the first-aid crews. Sometimes a simple fracture would be joggled into a gangrenous condition by the time the ambulance got off the terrible roads. But when that occurred Dr. English would amputate. Even when it didn't look like gangrene Dr. English would amputate. He wanted to be sure. If the case was a skull fracture and Dr. English knew about it in time, he would say to the one man in the world he hated most: "Say, Doctor Malloy, I've ordered the operating room for five o'clock. Man brought in from Collieryville with a compound fracture of the skull. I think it's going to be very interesting, and I'd like you to come up and see it if you have time." And Mike Malloy, in the old mule-ambulance days, would be polite and tell Dr. English he would be very glad to. Dr. Malloy would get into his gown and follow Dr. English to the operating room, and by saying "I think this, Doctor English" and "I think that, Doctor English," Dr. Malloy would direct Dr. English in trephining the man on the table. But that was in the old days, before Dr. English overheard one of the surgical nurses saying: "Trephine this afternoon. I hope to God Malloy's around if English is going to try it." The nurse later was dismissed for being caught undressed in an interne's room, a crime of which she had been guilty many times, but which had been overlooked because she knew at least as much medicine as half of the men on the staff, and more surgery than several of the surgeons. But even without her assistance Dr. English continued to do surgery, year after year, and several of the men he trephined lived. The dismissal of that nurse had one effect: Dr. Malloy never again spoke to Dr. English. "Need I say more?" Dr. English said, in telling his wife of Malloy's strange behavior.

III

One look at his father told Julian that the old man had not heard anything about the scene in the smoking-room of the country club. The old man greeted him about as usual, with Merry Christmas thrown in, but Julian expected that. He knew there was nothing wrong when he saw the old man's mustache flatten back and the crow's feet behind his shell-rim spectacles wrinkle up in the smile that he saved for Caroline. "Well, Caroline," said the doctor. He took Caroline's right hand in his own and put his left hand on her shoulder. "Help you with your coat?"

"Thanks, Father English," she said. She put her packages down on the hall table and was helped out of her mink coat. The old man took it to the closet under the stairs and put it on a hanger. "Haven't seen you in I guess it must be two weeks," he said.

"No. Christmas preparations—"

"Yes, I know. Well, we didn't do very much in the way of shopping.

I thought it over and I told Mrs. English, I said I think checks would be more acceptable this year, wherever we can—"

"Doc-tor!" came a voice.

"Oh, there she is now," said the doctor.

"Merry Christmas!" Caroline called out.

"Merry Christmas, Mother," shouted Julian.

"Oh, you're here," she replied, and appeared at the top of the steps. "I was just about to say we ought to call you up. It must have been a good party at the club." Julian saw his father's expression change. Mrs. English came downstairs and kissed Caroline, and then Julian.

"Now let's all have a nice cocktail," said Mrs. English, "and then we can tell Ursula to start serving while everything's still hot. You two are so late. What kept you? Did you really get in so late last night? How was the dance?"

"I couldn't get the car started," said Julian. "Cold."

"What?" said the old man. "Couldn't get it started? I thought that apparatus you put in your garage, I thought—"

"It wasn't in the garage. I left it out all night," said Julian.

"Our driveway was blocked," said Caroline. *"We're* out in real *country.* It was drifted as high as the roof."

"Was it?" said the doctor. "I never knew it to drift that high out where you are. Remarkable. Well, I s'pose a Martini. Martini, Caroline?"

"Fine for me," said Caroline. "What about you, Julian?"

"Now, Caroline," said the doctor. "He'll drink anything, and you know it."

"See our tree?" said Julian's mother. "Such a skimpy little thing, but they're so much trouble. I like a spruce, but they're so much trouble I don't think it's worth it when there aren't any children in the house."

"We have a small tree, too," said Caroline.

"When Julian was a boy, do you remember those trees? You must have been here during the holidays when we had a tree, weren't you, Caroline?"

"No, I don't think I ever was. Julian used to hate me then, remember?"

"Funny, isn't it?" said Julian's mother. "Tsih, when I look back. You're right. He didn't like to play with you, but my gracious, I don't think he disliked you. He was in awe of you. But we all were. Still are." Caroline gave her mother-in-law a hug.

"Oh, now, Mother," she said. "Julian did hate me. Probably because I was older."

"Well, you wouldn't think it now," said the older woman. "I mean that both ways. You wouldn't think he ever hated you, and you certainly wouldn't think you were older. Julian, why don't you go to the 'Y' or something? Let me look. Turn your face over that way. . . . You are. You're getting a double chin. Julian, really."

"Very busy man," said Julian.

"Here we are," said the doctor. "Drink this one, Caroline, and you and I can have another before we sit down."

"We can all have another one," said his wife, "but we'll have to take it in to the table with us. I don't want to keep the girls any later than necessary. But that doesn't mean you're to bolt your food. Bad for the digestion."

"It is if you don't masticate—" said the doctor.

"Doctor, please don't say that," said his wife. "Chew your food is just as good a word. Well, shall we have a toast?"

"Yes, I think so," said the doctor. He raised the glass. " 'God bless us, everyone,' " he said; and all momentarily serious and self-conscious, they drank their drinks.

IV

Caroline and Julian, in the car, waved to Dr. and Mrs. English, and then Julian slowly took his foot off the clutch and the car pulled away. The clock on the dashboard said 4.35.

Julian reached in his pocket and took out the Christmas envelope, which had been on his plate, exactly like the envelope that had been on Caroline's plate. He laid it in Caroline's lap. "See how much it's for," he said.

She opened the envelope and looked at the check. "Two hundred and fifty," she said.

"How much was yours?" he said.

She opened her envelope. "Same thing," she said. "Two hundred and fifty. Really, that's too much. They're sweet." She stopped herself and he looked at her without turning.

"What is it?" he inquired.

"Oh," she said. "It's just that they're so swell. Your mother is such a darling. I don't see how you—if she finds out about last night, your performance, do you realize how ashamed she'll be?"

"She's my mother," he said.

"Yes, she is. It's pretty hard to believe sometimes."

"Am I going to be bawled out the rest of the way home?" he said.

"No," she said. "What's the use? What are you planning to do about Harry?"

"Harry? I don't know. I could call him up," he said.

"No, that's not enough. I think the best thing is for you to take me home and then go to his house and apologize in person."

"Fat chance," said Julian.

"All right. But if you don't, I go to no more parties with you. That means I'll stay home from everything that we've accepted, and another thing, *our* party is *off*. If you think I'm going to make a spectacle of myself for people to talk about, going around to parties and having people feel sorry for me because of your behavior—I just won't do it, Ju, I won't do it, and that's that."

"If there's anything I hate, it's that's that," he said. "All right. I'll go to his house. He's probably forgotten about it, and my going there will bugger things up proper."

"Please promise me you *won't* bugger things up. You can handle him, Ju, if you're just careful. I didn't mean it when I said you couldn't. You can. Turn on some of that English charm and he'll fall for it. But please make it right so there won't be a situation for the rest of the holidays. Will you, darling?" Her tone had changed completely, and her earnestness thrilled him. She was not quite so handsome when she was being earnest, but she so seldom wanted anything enough to be earnest about it that she became a new and rare Caroline.

"One condition," he said.

"What?"

"Will you do it?" he said.

"I won't promise till I know what it is. What's the condition?"

"That you be in bed when I get home," he said.

"Now? In the afternoon?"

"You always used to love to in the daylight." He reached over and put his hand high on the inside of her leg.

She nodded slowly.

"Ah, you're my sweet girl," he said, already grateful. "I love you more than tongue can tell."

She spoke no more the rest of the way home, not even good-bye when she got out of the car, but he knew. It was always that way when they were away from their home, and made a date to go to bed when they got home. When they made a date like that she thought of nothing else until they got home. She wanted nothing else, and no one else could take anything of her, not even the energy that goes into gregarious gayety. Always she seemed then to crouch a little, although she didn't actually crouch. But whenever they did that, from the moment she agreed, to the ultimate thing, she began to submit. And driving away he knew again, as he had known again and again, that with Caroline that was the only part of their love that was submission. She was as passionate and as curious, as experimental and joyful as ever he was. After four years she was still the only woman he wanted to wake up with, to lie glowing with—yes, and even to have intercourse with. The things that she said, the words he had taught her, and the divining queries that they put to each other—they were his and hers. They were the things that made her fidelity so important, he believed; and when he thought of how important those things were, the words and the rest, he sometimes could understand that the physical act in unfaithfulness can be unimportant. But he doubted that infidelity is ever unimportant.

He stopped the car at Harry Reilly's house, where Reilly lived with his widowed sister and her two sons and daughter. It was a low stone and brick house, with a vast porch around three sides. He pushed the bellbutton, and Mrs. Gorman, Reilly's sister, came to the door. She was a stout woman with black hair, with a dignity that had nothing to do with her sloppy clothes. She was nearsighted, wore glasses, but she recognized Julian. "Oh, Julian English. Come on in," she said, and left the door open for him to close. She did not bother to be polite. "I guess you want to see Harry," she said.

"Yes, is he here?" he said.

"He's here," she said. "Go on in the living-room and I'll go up and tell him. He's in bed."

"Oh, don't disturb him," said Julian, "if he's still asleep."

She made no answer. She went upstairs. She was gone less than five minutes.

"He can't see you," she said.

He stood and looked at her, and she returned his look without a word and her expression said, "It's up to you."

"Mrs. Gorman, you mean he won't see me?" said Julian.

"Well, he said to tell you he can't see you. It's the same difference."

"I came here to apologize for last night," said Julian. . . .

"I know you did," she said. "I told him he was a fool to raise a stink about it, but you can't change him. He has a right to stay sore if he wants to."

"Yes, I know."

"I told him what he should of done was give you a puck in the mouth when you threw the drink at him, but he said there were other ways of fixing you." She was completely ruthless and honest, but Julian had a suspicion that she was a little on his side.

"You don't think it would do any good if I went upstairs?"

"Only make matters worse, if you want my opinion. He has a black eye."

"Black eye?"

"Yes. It isn't much of a one, but it's there. The ice from the drink. You must of slung it pretty hard. No, I guess the best thing you can do is go. You won't get anywhere hanging around here now, and he's upstairs waiting till you go so he can curse you out once you get outside."

Julian smiled. "Do you think if I leave and he curses me out, I'd be all right if I came back then?"

Her face became a little angry. "Listen, Mr. English, I don't want to stick my two cents in this one way or the other. It's none of my affair. But I want to tell you this much. Harry Reilly is a sore pup, and there isn't anything funny about it when he gets sore."

"Okay. Well, thank you."

"All right," she said. She did not go to the door with him.

He did not look back, but he knew as well as he could know anything that Harry Reilly was watching him from the upstairs window, and probably Mrs. Gorman was watching with him.

He drove home, parking the car in front of his house, and went inside. He took as long as he could with his hat and coat, scarf and arctics. He walked slowly up the stairs, letting each step have its own full value in sound. It was the only way he knew of preparing Caroline for the news of Reilly's refusal to see him, and he felt he owed her that. It would not be fair to her to come dashing in the house, to tell her by his footsteps that everything was all right and Reilly was not sore, only to let her down.

He sensed that she had understood the slow steps. She was in bed, the dazzling light coming in the windows from the west, and she was reading a magazine. It was *The New Yorker*, and not the newest one. He recognized the cover. It was a Ralph Barton drawing; a lot of shoppers, all with horribly angry or stern faces, hating each other and themselves and their packages, and above the figures of the shoppers was a wreath and the legend: Merry Xmas. Caroline had her knees up under the bedclothes, with the magazine propped against her legs, but she was holding the cover and half of the magazine with her right hand.

She slowly closed the magazine and laid it on the floor. "Did you have a fight with him?" she said.

"He wouldn't see me." Julian lit a cigarette and walked over to the window. They were together and he knew it, but he felt like hell. She was wearing a black lace negligée that he and she called her whoring gown. Suddenly she was standing beside him, and as always he thought how much smaller she was in her bare feet. She put her arm inside his arm, and her hand gripped the muscle of the arm.

"It's all right," she said.

"No," he said, gently. "No, it isn't."

"No, it isn't," she said. "But let's not think of it now." She moved her arm so that it went around his back under the shoulder blades, and her hand moved slowly down his back, along his ribs, his hips and buttocks. He looked at her, doing all the things he wanted her to do. Her reddish brown hair was still fixed for the day. She was not by any means a small girl; her nose rubbed under his chin, and he was six feet tall. She let her eyes get tender in a way she had, starting a smile and then seeming to postpone it. She stood in front of him and kissed him. Without taking her mouth away she pulled his tie out of his vest and unbuttoned his vest, and then she let him go. "Come on!" she said, and lay with her face down in the pillow, shutting out everything else until he was with her. It was the greatest single act of their married life. He knew it, and she knew it. It was the time she did not fail him.

v

It was dark when Al Grecco bundled up, preparatory to starting his lonely drive to the Stage Coach. He bought cigarettes and chewing gum. He regretted that there was no one to see him getting into Ed Charney's "coop." He liked doing that, driving away alone, in that car, before the muggs who hung around the Apollo. It showed them how he stood with Ed, compared to them.

It was an eighteen-mile drive, with a dozen tiny coal-mining patches to break up the stretches of lighted highway. The road was pretty good, but Al told himself that if he was any judge, it would be drifted again before he got home. In the patches the snow was piled high on each side of the streets. He counted only six persons in all the patches between Gibbsville and Taqua, the next fairly big town, fourteen miles from Gibbsville. That showed how cold it was. In all the houses in the patches the curtains were down, and the hunkeys, the schwackies, the roundheaders, the broleys—regional names for non-Latin foreigners—probably were inside getting drunk on boilo. Boilo is hot moonshine, and Ed did not approve of it, because if the schwackies once stopped drinking boilo, they would drink his stuff. Still, there was nothing to do about it. But it was cheating, in a way, for the schwackies to be celebrating Christmas; they celebrated Christmas all over again on January 6, Little Christmas. In each patch there was one exception to the curtained windows of the houses; that was in the doctor's house. There was a doctor in each town, living in a well-built house, with a Buick or a Franklin in front of the house. More than once Al had found it a good thing to know, that the doctors usually kept one car in front of the house—either the Buick or Franklin, or the Ford or Chevvy. More than once Al had drained gasoline from the doctors' cars, and never once had been caught.

He tore along the highway, clipping off the fourteen miles to Taqua in twenty-one minutes. His best time was twelve minutes, but that was in the summer, with a load of "white"—alcohol. Twenty-one minutes tonight wasn't bad. But he gave up trying to make time from Taqua to the Stage Coach. Too many turns in that road, and all uphill. You come to a fairly steep hill on that stretch, you climb the hill and think you're set, but then you find it's only the beginning of the real hill. Once you get on top of the hill it is only a few hundred yards to the crossroads, which is where the Stage Coach is built. If you want to you can go on and climb some more hills, because the Stage Coach is built on a plateau, one of the coldest places in Pennsylvania. There has been an inn on the site of the Stage Coach as long as there has been a road. It was one of those things that had to be. Anyone who climbed that hill in the old days had to rest his horses—and get a toddy for himself. And motorists liked to pause there for the same reason. It was a natural place to stop traveling.

A wrought-iron coach-and-four, six feet long over all, hung from a post in front of the inn. The Stage Coach was only two years old, still new as Gibbsville things went, and Ed was making improvements all the time. A business acquaintance of Ed's in New York had sent Ed a fat, rosy-cheeked young man to do the decorating. The young man had been driven once back to New York by the practical jokes of the boys, but Ed gave out the word to leave him alone, so the pansy came back and did a very good job of the Stage Coach. People from the cities often commented on the Stage Coach, how surprising it was to see such a really nice place in all that coal-region squalor.

Ed, of course, owned the place, but it was run by Foxie Lebrix, who had been headwaiter in one of the big New York hotels—which one he never would say. Foxie was a strong, bulky Frenchman, about fifty-five years old, with white hair and a black mustache. He could tear a deck of cards in half, or break a man's jaw with a single punch. He also could cook stuff that only a few of the Lantenengo Street crowd ever had heard of, and just as few could pronounce. He was thought to be a killer, but nobody knew that for sure. Al Grecco treated him with respect.

"Hello, Fox," said Al, in Lebrix's office.

"Hello," said Lebrix.

"The big boy tell you I was coming?" said Al.

"He dit," said Lebrix. He was dipping a cigar in brandy, using his left hand, and giving the impression of not letting his right hand know what the left hand was doing. He saved the right hand for his little gestures. "Thee lady is resting," he tossed his head back to indicate upstairs. "She was a little onder the wather wan Ed phoned."

"She know I'm coming?"

"She will. If you want the truth, she was cockeye dronk."

"Oh, yeah? She's liable to—"

"She wawnt leave the room. I have Marie to watch her." Marie was Lebrix's common law wife. Anyhow, that's what she said. "You want to see her? She started to drink when she got op, without eating break-fast. She can't do dat. She can't drink at all. But no. 'It's Christmas. I have to drink. I have to get dronk. It's Christmas.' God damn son of a bitch a bastard. I wish Ed would take her some other place. She is more trobble than she is worth."

"Oh, well," said Al.

"Aw, well. Sure. Aw, well. If I had a woman do like that you bet she would not do it twice."

"Oh, well, you know how it is, Fox," said Al.

Lebrix nodded. "Oh, pardon," he said. "You have your dinner? Have a drink?"

"No, just a cuppa coffee."

"Café Royale?"

"No, thanks, Fox. Just coffee. No drinks for me tonight."

"Too bad. I'll order coffee." He pushed a button under the top of the desk and told a waiter to serve Al's coffee. "Lots of reservations tonight. Several parties from Gibbsville, and a big dinner from Taqua. Jews. And that politician, Donovan, he has the nerve to reserve a table for ten for tonight. Cheap bastard son of a bitch."

"He'll pay," said Al.

"Sure he'll pay. He'll hand me a century, like a big heavy spender, and I'm soppose to thank him politely, but then I give him his change and it's ten sawbucks. The waiters are lucky if they get a tip. That's the way he is, the cheap bastard son of a bitch. I'd like to give him a Mickey Finn. I never gave one of those in my life, but if I do, he will be the first."

"You can't do that."

"I know. You want to sit with Helene tonight?"

"I guess that's the best way."

"Yes, I think so. Some of our guests, they get some of this so-called champagne in their bellies, and Miss Hilman will begin to think she is Mistinguette."

"What?"

"French entertainer. Yes, if your job is to keep an eye on her, you better be where she can see you so she will not forget herself. It's Christmas, my friend. She may give something away."

"Huh. That's exactly what I was thinking."

"So?" said Lebrix.

4

THEY WERE driving south on the way to the club, down South Main Street. Caroline was smoking a cigarette and holding Julian's hand. He took the hand away to do *shave-and-a-haircut* on the horn button, signaling to the Cadillac just ahead of them.

"Who's that?" said Caroline.

"A good prospect," said Julian. "Young Al Grecco."

"Who's he? I know him by name. Who is he?"

"He's a sort of a yes man for Ed Charney," said Julian. The coupé in front turned off to the left, to the Lincoln Street bridge, and apparently Al Grecco did not hear the signal. He did not turn his head or answer with *bay-rum* on the horn of the coupé.

"Oh, he's the one that went to Philadelphia for the champagne. Did he get it?" said Caroline.

"If Mr. Charney wants champagne, whoever is told to get it, gets it."

"Oh, I don't believe it. Why are people so afraid of him?"

"I'm afraid of him," said Julian.

"You are not. You're not afraid of anyone. My big strong man. My mate."

"Nuts to you, sister," he said.

"Don't call me sister, and don't say nuts."

"Say masticate," said Julian. "God, did you ever hear anyone like Mother? Did you hear her telling the old gent not to say masticate? You know she hasn't the remotest idea why she doesn't like the word."

"I'll bet she has. Women aren't that dumb."

"I say she hasn't the remotest idea why she doesn't like the word. Somewhere in the back of her mind the sound of the word has a dirty connotation, but what it is she isn't sure. So she thinks she prefers simple language. Did you ever masticate?"

"None of your business."

"Did you?"

"I'm getting a little tired of this," said Caroline.

"So am I," said Julian. They rode for a while, and then he said: "When are we going to have a kid?"

"I don't know. When *are* we?" she said.

"No, seriously, *when* are we?"

"You know. The five years will be up soon."

"The Five Year Plan," he said slowly. "Well, maybe you're right."

"I know I'm right. Look at these kids, Jeanie and Chuck. Married less than two years, hardly more than a year, and Jeanie may have to have false teeth. Mind you, false teeth, and do you remember her teeth? She had the loveliest strong white teeth I ever saw—"

"Except yours."

"Well, except mine. But hers were beautiful and just right. Smallish and nice and really sparkling. Mine are bigger, and they don't sparkle."

"They dazzle me," he said. He snapped off the headlights. "We'll use your sparkling teeth for headlights."

"Put the lights on, you fool," she said. "No kidding, it's awful. She's only twenty-one. Just twenty-one, and she's absolutely a married woman. A married woman with a child. And—"

"And a husband. And what a husband."

"Exactly!" said Caroline. "Chuck. That little twirp. Jeanie. Why, he isn't good enough to . . ."

"To what. Finish it."

"No, I'm not fooling. Chuck running around with that girl from Kresge's and the other day at bridge club Barbara Schultz spoke up and said, 'Well, I think someone ought to defend poor Chuck.' Poor Chuck! She said, 'If Jeanie had taken the trouble to keep herself attractive, Chuck wouldn't chase after other girls.' Golly it made me mad. She must have read that somewhere. I didn't say anything, and neither did anyone else, but you could see what everybody was thinking. Barbara's such a fool for letting herself in for that. Why, she did everything but handcuff Chuck to make him marry her."

"She did? I didn't know that. I knew they had dates, but I never thought—"

"No? Well, here's something else you didn't know. Mrs. Schultz was so sure Barbara was going to get Chuck that she made reservations for two for a trip around the world—"

"Well, she and old Stinker went around the world."

"Yes, but Mother told me that she was in Mr. Schultz's office when—"

"God damn it to hell!" said Julian. He stopped the car. "Cross-link broke. I might as well fix it now while I'm sober." He got out of the car and fixed the link. They did not speak to each other during the five-minute wait. Cars drove by and one or two stopped, recognizing Julian and the car, asking if they could help, but he sent them on.

He started the car again. "Hyuh, baby," he said. "What were we talking about? Had we finished with Chuck?"

"Mm."

"What's the mattah, honey sugah lamb pie, what's the mattah you all?"

"Listen, Ju. Listen to me, will you?"

"Listen to you? Why, Mrs. English, one of the most attractive features of the Cadillac is the minimum of noise in the motor. Just let me show—"

"No. Don't be funny."

"What's the matter? Did I do something wrong? Did I say something? Christ, I thought we were getting along fine."

"We were, but something you said worried me. See, you don't even remember saying it."

"Well, come on. Out with it, dearie. What did I say?"

"When you stopped the car. When you got out to fix the chain, you said something about you were going to fix it now, while you were sober."

"Oh," he said.

"As if—"

"I get it. You don't have to draw a map."

"Now you're annoyed. Aren't you?"

"No. Yes, slightly. I don't know. What the hell. I don't blame you."

"I'm sorry, darling. I don't want to be a wet towel or anything, but

I couldn't go through another half hour like that last night—I'd rather die."

"I know. I'm terribly sorry, Callie. I won't get drunk."

"Please don't," she said. "Please. And I'll do anything. Let's get through these holidays without any more mess or jam or anything. I don't want to give you a pep talk—"

"I know you don't. I don't blame you."

"You're my sweet Ju and I love you. I don't mean don't drink. You know."

"Uh-huh. I promise."

"No, don't promise. Just don't. You don't have to. Lots of times you go to parties and don't get crazy. So be like that tonight. I'll do anything, any of the things you like. Anything. Do you know what I'll do?"

"What?"

"I'll come out in the car with you at intermission and stay with you, the way we used to."

"I know, but—that's what I'd love. It *would* be fun."

"We haven't done that since we've been married."

"Yes we did. At Lake Placid."

"Yes, but we haven't here, at home, and I want to, don't you?"

"Yes, but what about, you know, business?" he said. She hated to name the contraceptive devices.

"I won't bother. We can start having a baby."

"Do you mean it?" he said.

"I never meant anything so much in my life," she said. "And there's one way to prove it."

"Yes, that's true. Just by being here. Just by coming out here." They had arrived at the club parking grounds.

"Uh-huh."

"Oh, my sweet lovely Caroline," he said.

"Not now," she said. "I said intermission."

They got out of the car. Ordinarily Julian would have stopped the car at the steps near the vestibule, where the women got out of chauffeur-driven and husband-driven and beau-driven cars, but tonight they had not thought of it. Julian drove the car in and out of lanes, twisting and maneuvering until he had got as close to the verandah as he could, to make as short as possible the walk through the snow. Arm in arm he and Caroline, their arctics flopping, went up to the verandah and around to the vestibule. Caroline said she would be right down, and Julian went out again to the verandah and all the way around the clubhouse to the men's locker room.

It was a grand night for a party. It was cold, and the snow-covered golf course seemed not to be separate from the farmlands that bounded the course on the second, fourth, and seventh holes. In the summer the golf course was so neatly shaved that it made him think of a farmer in his Sunday suit surrounded by other farmers in overalls and straw hats. But now in the night there was no way of telling, if you did not know, where club property ended and real farmland began. As far as you could see the world was white and blue and purple and cold. You learn by living with your mother and father and people that it is bad to lie in the snow for a long time, but when all the world is covered with snow and moonlight it doesn't look as if it would do you any harm. But it was just a picture now, so it doesn't do you any harm. Julian took in a deep breath and felt very much like a healthy, clean-living person for so doing. "I ought to get more of that," he said, and went in to the locker room.

Many men said hello and hyuh to him, and he said hyuh and hello back at them six or seven times. He didn't have an enemy in the place. Then he heard someone say, "Hello, Socker." He looked to see who it was, although he knew who it was. It was Bobby Herrmann.

"Hello, Rum Dumb," he said.

"Yeah, Rum Dumb," said Bobby in his slow difficult way of speaking. "Jesus Christ. You have a nerve calling me Rum Dumb, I'll say."

"Nuts," said Julian. He was taking off his coat and hat and putting them in his locker.

Everyone seemed to think that the job of kidding Julian was being taken over by Bobby. "Jesus Christ," said Bobby. "I've done a whole lot of things in my life, but by Jesus if I ever sunk so low that I had to throw ice in a man's face and give him a black eye. My God."

Julian sat down at the table. "Cocktail. Straight liquor. Highball. What'll you have, Ju?" said Whit Hofman.

"Cocktail, I guess."

"Martinis in this shaker," said Hofman.

"Fine," said Ju.

"Trying to ignore me," said Bobby. "Trying to give me the old high hat. The old absent treatment. Well, all right. Go ahead. Ignore me. Give me the old high hat. I don't care. But the least you can do, English, the least you can do is go in there and pay for an extra subscription to the dance."

"Huh?" said Julian.

"You heard me. You're responsible for there being one less man here tonight and the club needs the money, so don't forget, you sock out an extra five bucks when you pay your subscription."

"Who is this man?" said Julian to Whit. Whit smiled. "Did he come here with a member?"

"That's all right," said Bobby. "Don't worry about me."

"Depression or no depression, I think the membership committee ought to draw the line somewhere," said Julian. "I don't mind Jews or Negroes, or even a few people with leprosy. They have souls, the same as you or I. But when a man goes to his club he likes to think he's going to associate with human beings, and not some form of reptile life. Or is it insect? Turn around, Herrmann, till I decide just what you are. Have you got wings?"

"Don't worry about me. I'll get by."

"That's just the trouble," said Julian. "We ought to have state cops stationed at the club entrance, just to keep people like you away."

"It's a good thing we didn't have state cops here last night. As it was it's a wonder somebody didn't send for them. Or the God damn marines or something."

"There you go, talking about the war again," said Julian. "You never got over that God damn war. That's your trouble. You don't hear Whit, or Froggy—"

"That's all right," said Bobby. "When there was a war, I was in it. I wore a uniform. I wasn't one of these God damn slackers playing sojer boy at some college. Lafayette or Lehigh or wherever it was. S.A.T.C. Saturday Afternoon Tea Club. Yes, sir. When old Uncle Sam needed me, I heeded the call and made the world safe for democracy, and when the war was over I stopped fighting. I didn't do like some people that put on a uniform back in 1917 and then did their fighting by throwing drinks around in the presence of respectable people at a country club, thirteen or fourteen years after the war was over. Nineteen-thirty. That's what some people are. Veterans of 1930. The Battle of the Lantenengo Country Club Smoking Room. Surprise attack."

The others were laughing, and Julian knew he was coming off a very bad second best. He finished his drink and rose to go.

"Not driving you away, are we?" said Bobby.

Julian looked at Whit, deliberately turning his back on Bobby. "Something wrong with the can, Whit? Or don't you smell it?"

Whit gave a neutral smile. "Going in?" he said.

"Let him go, Whit," said Bobby. "You know how he is when he has a drink in his hand. Of course you're safer when it's a cocktail. There aren't any lumps of ice in a cocktail to give you a black—"

"Well, bye bye," said Julian. He walked out of the locker room, but as he left he heard Bobby say in a very loud voice, loud enough not to be missed by Julian: "Say, Whit, I hear Harry Reilly's thinking of buying a new Lincoln. He doesn't like that Cadillac he bought last summer." The locker-room loved it.

Julian walked on, through the smoking-room, through the dining alcoves, out to the dance floor, through to the foyer at the foot of the stairs. That was where you waited for your lady. Julian said hello and good evening to a great many people, and waved especially gayly to Mildred Ammermann, who was giving tonight's dinner. She was a tall, toothy girl, captain of the women's golf team. Her father was a drunken roué, quite rich in real estate, and nominally a cigar manufacturer. He never came to the club except on nights like this, when Mr. and Mrs. Ammermann would entertain a few of their—her—friends at a smaller table. Mildred, towering above Losch, the club steward, and pointing, daintily for her, with one finger as she held a small stack of place-cards in her left hand, apparently was one woman who had not heard about the business of the night before. It was axiomatic in Gibbsville that you could tell Mill Ammermann anything and be sure it wouldn't be repeated; because Mill probably was thinking of the mashie-niblick approach over the trees to the second green. Julian derived some courage from her smile. He always had liked Mill anyway. He was fragmentarily glad over again that Mill did not live in New York, for in New York she would have been marked Lesbian on sight. But in Gibbsville she was just a healthy girl. Good old Mill.

"What are you thinking?" said Caroline, suddenly standing beside him.

"I like Mill," he said.

"I do too," said Caroline. "Why, did she do something or say something?"

"No. I just like her," he said. "I've been learning how to take it."

"How?"

"Mr. Robert Herrmann is in his best form, ribbing me about last night—"

"Oh, Lord, where? In the locker room? Were there a lot of people there?"

"Yes, Whit and Froggy and the usual crowd. He told me I ought to sock out five bucks to cover Harry's subscription to the dance. And then he started kidding me about the war being over or something.

How I waited till 1930 before I did my fighting, and a lot of stuff about calling out the state police."

"Mm. I suppose we can expect an evening of that."

"Why? Has anyone said anything to you?"

"No, not exactly. Kitty Hofman came in the johnny while I—"

"God, you women, going to the can together! Why do you always—"

"Do you want to hear what she had to say? Or are you going to go into all that again?"

"I'm sorry."

"Well, Kitty, you know how she is. Comes right out with it. She said she heard Harry had a black eye, and I said yes, I knew he had. And she said Whit is worried. Did he say anything to you?"

"No. He didn't get much chance, with Bobby holding forth. I didn't wait to talk to Whit."

"Well, apparently Whit knows Harry has money in the garage."

"Sure he knows. It's no secret. As a matter of fact I think I told Whit myself. Yes, I did. I had to tell him, because when Whit heard about it last summer he wanted to know why I hadn't come to him, and I told him everybody came to him. Didn't I tell you that?"

"No, you didn't. But anyhow, Kitty said Whit's worried, because Harry is a bad man to have as an enemy. I told you that."

"I know you did. Well, we can't go on standing here like this. There's Jean and Froggy. Let's go over there."

They went over there. Jean was Caroline's best friend, and Froggy was one of the group whom Julian regarded as his best friends. He had no single best friend, had had none since college. His best friend in college was with the Standard Oil in China, and he never heard from him except about once a year. With these people Julian felt safe and at ease. Froggy, thirty-four, was not quite five years older than Julian. Froggy had lost an arm in the war, and probably because of that Julian felt less close to him than to the other men of the same age who had been in France. Julian's war record had been made in college, as a member of the S.A.T.C., and he still had the feeling that he should have enlisted to fight and not to go to college. Year by year the feeling grew less strong, and he believed he did not care any more, but he still did. He always did when he saw Froggy for the first time on any day; Froggy, who had been a beautiful swimmer and tennis player. With Jean, Julian had complete ease. Everything that they ever could have been to each other, Jean and Julian had been. They had been passionately in love all one summer long ago; a demi-vierge affair that left them, when it did leave them finally, with a feeling toward each other which was far more innocent than that of two children, and made them ready really to love someone else. Julian knew, because Jean had told him, that she had "gone the limit" with Froggy the very first night she had a date alone with him, and Julian honestly believed he was glad for her.

Now they talked about people who were visiting the So-and-sos; whether the Reading crowd was coming up for the dance; how swell or how perfectly terrible some of the girls looked; whether Julian had had a flat tire, as they had seen his car stopped on the road to the club; wasn't it wonderful, or wasn't it? the way the highway department got the roads clear so quickly; such a lovely corsage; oh, smoke a Camel, you can't tell the difference; Mill's father looks worse than ever; there was one thing about the Ammermanns, and that was when they gave a party they didn't spare the pennies. Then Mill and her mother and father were seen to take their places, standing just inside the ballroom (living-room when the furniture was not cleared away), and forming a little reception line. In less than three minutes there was a milling crowd in the foyer, all waiting to say good evening a bit stiffly to Mr. and Mrs. Ammermann, and very friendly hello to Mill. The orchestra, Ben Riskin and his Royal Canadians from Harrisburg, took their places and with two thumps of the bass drum burst forth into (boom boom) Oh, Give Me Something To Remember You By. "Now please don't drink too much," said Caroline, and went to find her place at the festive board.

II

The festive board now groaned under the Baked Alaska. The Ammermann dinner party was just about over. Until one o'clock the men, young and old, would see to it that Mill was not left standing without a partner; after that whatever dances she got she would have got without giving the dinner. Tomorrow's papers would carry the list of guests, and then the dinner would be history. Next Christmas the big dinner at the club Christmas dance would be given by someone else. Whatever she did, Mill Ammermann must not give another large dress-up party for at least a year.

Tonight's dinner, as almost every guest was able to tell at a glance, was the club's two-fifty dinner. This was a club dinner dance, and all members were invited. At a dinner such as the Ammermanns', the hostess could arrange with the steward for the dollar-fifty (roast chicken), the two-dollar (roast turkey), or the two-fifty (filet mignon), and this had been the filet mignon dinner. The Ammermanns had just that much money, and their position in Gibbsville was just that certain and insecure, that they had to give the best of everything. Conforming to custom, the Ammermanns did not supply drinks, nor did they pay the dance subscriptions. A man on accepting an invitation to the dinner was paired off with a woman or girl. The custom for unmarried, unengaged men was to accept the dinner invitation with his card, and then to telephone the hostess and ask if she wanted him to escort someone to the dinner. All this was arranged beforehand, much more subtly than might be supposed. There were certain sad birds among the girls who had to be invited to many dinners, and it was understood by the hostess that certain men would make themselves available to take these sad birds to the dinner. But it was also understood by every hostess that a popular, attractive young man should not be designated the escort of any but popular attractive girls. Then there was another group of girls, to which Mill Ammermann herself belonged, who got to the dance somehow, usually with a married couple who were friends of hers, or as extra girl on a party of four or six. Mill, and girls like her, could tell almost to the foot how far they would dance, and if they danced more than that distance they could inquire of themselves what was wrong. Usually the answer, to girls like Mill, was that some young husband was sore at his wife and wanted to tell Mill all about it because Mill was such a pal. So understanding. And didn't misunderstand when you gave her what amounted to a rush. Sometimes, of course, Mill and the girls like her would get a real rush—by a man who had drunk more than usual. Whatever was cruel about the system, there were some things to be said for it; for one thing, by the time a girl was twenty-five she usually was prepared, knew precisely what to expect, of every dance that she went to. Only a very few girls of Mill's type went to a dance with sadly foolish hopes that this dance would be different from any other. And there was one other unwritten, unspoken agreement among the dancing men: if a Gibbsville girl of doubtful popularity inveigled an out-of-town man to come to a club dance, the Gibbsville men did go a little bit out of their way to see that she made a good showing. They danced with her twice instead of once in a night; with the result that all but the saddest of the sad birds married themselves off to out-of-town men. Of course when they once married their ugly duckling days were forgiven and forgotten; such girls took their places with the most popular girls. But it had to be marriage, not merely an engagement, but the man could be the worst heel, stupid, badly dressed—anything, so long as he was not a Jew. Not that any Gibbsville girl of the country club-Lantenengo Street set ever married a Jew. She wouldn't have dared.

By the time a man reached junior year in college he knew how he was situated in the country club social life. Julian, for instance, had known for years that what had happened tonight would always happen: that he would sit at table between one attractive girl and one sad bird. Always the attractive men, or those who were accepted as attractive in Gibbsville, were given a sad bird as a duty and an attractive girl as a reward. The attractive girls far outnumbered the sad birds. On Julian's right sat Jean Ogden; on his left was Constance Walker, who danced as though her sex life depended on it. Constance was a distant cousin of Caroline's.

All during dinner Julian's thoughts kept returning to Caroline. Constance, prolonging what had long since ceased to be a slightly amusing tradition, always called Julian, Cousin Julian, or plain Cousin. He danced once with Constance between courses, and he found himself incredulous all over again at her physical resemblance to Caroline. The two girls were almost exactly the same height and weight, and there was no denying that Constance had a lovely figure. Yes, she had it a little on Caroline, or at least he thought she had; she was fresher than Caroline—to him. He knew that under a bright light the small of Caroline's back showed an unmistakable patch of down. He knew where the cicatrix of Caroline's vaccination stood out on her left thigh; but though he had seen Constance many times in a bathing suit, he wasn't sure that she had been vaccinated at all. He was thinking of this as he danced with Constance, and he was on the verge of asking her whether she was vaccinated when he became aware that he was holding her tight and she was holding him just as tight, and for good reason. He felt ashamed of himself and sorry for Constance. It was a dirty trick to get this kid excited. It was a low trick to be excited himself. He slowly relaxed his hold.

But the process of comparing the girl he was dancing with, eating with, with the girl he had married, who was her cousin, gave him something to enjoy in secret. Whenever he was on a party and did not drink too much he needed a secret game to play or a mental task to perform the while he apparently was observing the amenities. Caroline was thirty-one and Constance was still in college and probably about ten years younger than Caroline. The cousins were pretty good types of their respective colleges: Caroline had gone to Bryn Mawr, Constance was at Smith—the plain girl who goes to Smith and competes with the smart Jewesses for Phi Beta Kappa, as distinguished from the pretty girls who go to Smith and write to Yale. Caroline was the perfect small-town girl at Bryn Mawr; from private school in her home town, to a good prep school, to Bryn Mawr and the Bryn Mawr manner, which means quick maturity and an everlasting tendency to enthusiasms. Constance knew everything, but Caroline still was finding things out—the capital of South Dakota, the identity of Mike Pingatore, the location of Dalhousie, the handicap system in polo, the ingredients of a Side Car. He wondered why he put so much stress on the education of the two girls, and then he stumbled upon a truth: that Caroline was an educated girl whose education was behind her and for all time would be part of her background, whereas with Constance and girls like her—oh, what difference did it make? Constance was an unimportant little girl. But he was glad he discovered that about Caroline and her education. It was worth remembering, and as happened so often when he made a discovery about her, he wanted to tell Caroline about it, to try it out on her and see if she agreed with it. He knew what she would say. She would say—and it would be the truth—that she had been telling him practically that for years.

The dinner guests stood up and he looked for Caroline. He saw she was too far away to have it worth making a point of going to her. That turned out to be an error in judgment.

When the Ammermann dinner party rose, that did not mean all the people eating in the dining room rose too. The Ammermann party was the largest and therefore the most important, but there were many smaller parties of varying size and degrees of importance. One of these was a squat little dinner given by Mrs. Gorman, Harry Reilly's sister. There were eight at her table: two Irish Catholic doctors and their wives; Monsignor Creedon, pastor of the Church of SS. Peter & Paul; and Mr. and Mrs. J. Frank Kirkpatrick, the Philadelphia criminal lawyer and his wife. They were having the two-fifty dinner, and champagne from a bucket under the table, in more or less open defiance of Sec. 7, Rule XI, House Rules & Regulations, Lantenengo Country Club. Mrs. Gorman always went to the big dances at the club, and always she was the hostess at a small dinner, like tonight's. Her guests all took each other for granted after the first awkward politeness. They ate in silence and at the coffee, which was served at the table, the men would sit back and burn their cigars, and the men and women would watch, completely un-selfconsciously, the gay folk at the largest dinner party. They would watch without staring—except Monsignor Creedon, who would sit with his hands folded somewhat ecclesiastically on the table in front of him, sometimes folding the tin-foil of his cigar, sometimes telling a story in a softly musical voice and a beautifully modulated brogue. He knew everyone in Gibbsville, and he was a member of the club; but he belonged to the club for the golf, and in the dining-room he never spoke to anyone unless he was first spoken to. It was a spurious display of dignity, but it had the right effect on his non-Catholic acquaintances, as well as on his parishioners. He had been made old and philosophical before his time, because Church politics had deprived him, his parish, and Gibbsville of the bishopric they all had been trying for years to get. The Cardinal hated his guts, everyone said, and fought against making SS. Peter & Paul's a cathedral and Father Creedon a bishop. Instead he was elevated to the monsignori, made rural dean and irremovable rector of SS. Peter & Paul's—and thereby tacitly informed that he was to discontinue all activity tending to make a cathedral out of SS. Peter & Paul's. It was a sad blow for him as well as for the rich laymen of his parish, who loved Creedon, and for the more powerful Masons in the Coal & Iron Company, who respected this man whom they never could understand. "I'm a strong Presbyterian," they would say, "but let me tell you, nobody says anything against Father Creedon in my hearing and gets away with it, Catholic or no Catholic."

There were those among his parishioners who secretly resented Monsignor Creedon's serving on non-sectarian committees in community activities, but this sort of criticism could be traced to disgruntled Knights of Columbus. The Coal & Iron was ruled by the Masons, who admired Monsignor Creedon, and who tolerated the Knights of Columbus. The latter felt that their pastor ought to use his influence more frequently in advancing "Knights." He never did. He used his influence in coaxing better company houses for the miners' families out of the directorate; or in wangling contributions for poorer parishes than his own. The U.M.W.A. organizers and field workers hated Monsignor Creedon because he was so close to the bigwigs of the company.

On the other hand, he did sometimes use his influence to help a Protestant. He got them bail, helped them get jobs. He had bought a Cadillac from Julian, instead of a Lincoln from the Ford dealer, who was a Catholic. He bought three Fords for his curates to atone for patronizing Julian's business. Three years ago he had driven his car, a Buick, to Julian's garage and went in Julian's office and said: "Good morning, son. Do you have any nice black Cadillac sedans today?" He bought a car right off the floor and paid cash for it. His curates' cars went to the Ford dealer for repairs and service, but he always bought his tires and other needs at Julian's garage.

Julian wanted to go to the bathroom after the dinner party stood up, and on his way to the men's locker-room he had to pass Mrs. Gorman's table. He looked at Mrs. Gorman and she did not speak to him, but that was not unusual. But he felt the chill that passed between him and the men at the table. Kirkpatrick nodded politically and showed his teeth, but the doctors frankly snubbed him, and Monsignor Creedon, whose round, bluish face usually smiled sadly above that purple thing he wore under his Roman collar, nodded just once and did not smile. It took Julian a few seconds to figure it out, because in his dealings with Catholics he so often forgot to consider the Catholic point of view. But by the time he was alone in the men's room he had it figured out: they all regarded his insulting Harry Reilly as an insult to themselves. There was no other reason why he should throw a drink at Reilly, so it must be because he was an unattractive Irish Catholic whom he could insult freely. He did not believe they were quite right. But one thing he knew; if the Catholics had declared war on him, he was in a tough spot. In the Smith-Hoover campaign two men, one a jeweler and the other a lime and cement dealer, had let it be known that they were members of the Ku Klux Klan and were outspokenly against Smith because he was a Catholic. Those two were the only Gibbsville business men who had come out in the open. And now both of them were bankrupt.

Drying his hands Julian thought it might be a good idea to sound out Monsignor Creedon, and he sat down to wait for the priest to come back to the locker-room. He pushed the button and told William, the locker-room waiter, to get a bottle of Scotch out of his locker and put it with two glasses and ice and club soda on a small table near the locker. He poured himself a mild drink and lit a cigarette.

Men and boys wandered in, making cracks about his being exclusive. Bobby Herrmann came in and before he could say anything Julian told him to keep his trap shut. One or two of the younger kids showed by the expression of their faces when they saw the extra empty glass and the bottle of Scotch that they thought Julian was being ignored. It was pretty funny. They wanted to be nice, he could see, and they wanted to have a drink, but their wanting to be nice and their wanting a drink were not enough to make them associate with an outcast. What the hell had he done? he wondered. He had thrown a drink in a man's face. An especially terrible guy who should have had a drink thrown in his face a long while ago. It wasn't as if Harry Reilly were a popularity contest winner or something. If most people told the truth they would agree that Reilly was a terrible person, a climber, a nouveau riche even in Gibbsville where fifty thousand dollars was a sizable fortune. Julian thought back over some other terrible things, really terrible things, that people had done in the club without being made to feel they had committed sacrilege. There was the time Bobby Herrmann or Whit Hofman or Froggy Ogden—no one knew which—wanted to test a carboy of alcohol which Whit had bought. One of the three (they all were very drunk at the time) touched a match to the alcohol to see if it was genuine, and a table, chairs, a bench, and part of a row of lockers were ruined or destroyed before the fire was extinguished. There was the time a member of a visiting golf team was swinging a mashie in the locker-room and Joe Schermerhorn walked into the swing and got a broken jaw, lost his beautiful teeth and went a little bit nuts so that two years later, when his car went off the Lincoln Street bridge, people said it was suicide. Did they hold that against the visiting golfer? Hardly. He still visited the club and got drunk with the boys. There was the time Ed Klitsch wandered stark naked upstairs to the steward's living quarters and presented himself, ready for action, to the steward's wife. That was remembered as a good joke. There were innumerable vomitings, more or less disastrous. There was the hair-pulling, face-scratching episode between Kitty Hofman and Mary Lou Diefenderfer, after Kitty heard that Mary Lou had said Kitty ought to be suppressed by the vice squad. There was the time Elinor Holloway—heroine of many an interesting event in club history —shinnied half way up the flagpole while five young gentlemen, standing at the foot of the pole, verified the suspicion that Elinor, who had not always lived in Gibbsville, was not naturally, or at least not entirely, a blonde. There was the time, the morning after a small, informal party for a visiting women's golf team, when a Mrs. Goldorf and a Mrs. Smith, and Tom Wilk, the Reverend Mr. Wilk's son, and Sam Campbell, the caddy-master, all had to have the stomach pump. That was complicated by the fact that they were all together, in bed or on the floor, in Sam's room upstairs in the caddy-house. There was the time Whit Hofman and Carter Davis got so sore at a New York orchestra that wanted too much money to play overtime, that they broke all the instruments and pushed the bass drum all the way down the club hill to the state highway. The result of that was a nice suit, some Philadelphia publicity, and a temporary blacklisting of the club by the musicians' union. There were numerous physical combats between husbands and wives, and not always the husbands that matched the wives. Kitty Hofman, for instance, had been given a black eye by Carter Davis when she kicked him in the groin for dunking her head in a punch bowl for calling him a son of a bitch for telling her she looked like something the cat dragged in. And so on. Julian had another drink and a fresh cigarette.

And then there were people. Terrible people, who didn't have to do anything to make them terrible, but were just terrible people. Of course they usually did do something, but they didn't have to. There was (Mrs.) Emily Shawse, widow of the late Marc A. Shawse, former mayor of Gibbsville, and one-time real estate agent, who had developed the West Park section of Gibbsville. Mrs. Shawse did not participate in club activities, but she was a member. She came down to the club summer afternoons and sat alone on the porch, at one end of the porch, watching the golfers and tennis players and the people in the pool. She would have a fruit lemonade on the porch, and have one sent out to Walter, her Negro chauffeur. She would stay an hour and leave, and go for a drive in the country, presumably. But if she wasn't having an affair with Walter, Gibbsville missed its guess. No one ever had seen her speak with Walter, not even good-morning-Walter, good-morning-Mrs. Shawse; but it certainly looked fishy. Walter had the car, a Studebaker sedan, at all hours of the day and night. He always had money to bet on the races, and he was a good customer at the Dew Drop Inn, where the Polish and Lithuanian girls had not been brought up to draw the color line. Julian prided himself on the fact that he had blocked the sale of a Cadillac to Mrs. Shawse. She had wanted one, or at least was ready to buy one in exchange for a little attention, in a nice way, from Julian. She had put him in a tough spot for a while. He couldn't just say he didn't want to sell her a car. He eventually solved the problem by telling her he would give her only a hundred and fifty in a trade involving the Studebaker, which then was worth, trade-in value, about six times that much, and when she still was not rebuffed he sent Louis, the pimply, bowlegged carwasher, with the demonstrator, instead of going himself. Mrs. Shawse kept the Studebaker. There was Harry Reilly's own nephew, Frank Gorman, a squirt if ever there was one. Frank got drunk at every last party the minute his mother went home. It was because of him that she came to the club dances. He was at Georgetown, having been kicked out of Fordham and Villanova, not to mention Lawrenceville, New York Military Academy, Allentown Prep and Gibbsville High School. Frank was a spindle-shanked young man who wore the most collegiate clothes, the kind that almost justify the newspaper editorials. He had a Chrysler roadster, a raccoon coat, adenoids, and some ability as a basketball player. He was a loud-mouth and a good one-punch fighter, who accepted invitations of the younger set as though they were his due. He was the kind of young man who knows his rights. His uncle secretly hated him, but always referred to him, with what was mistaken for bashful pride, as that crazy kid. There was the Reverend Mr. Wilk, who had had the club raided under the Volstead Act. There was Dave Hartmann, who wiped his shoes on clean towels and in seven years had not been known to violate the club rule against tipping servants and caddies, and who belonged to the club himself but would not let his wife and two daughters become members. Dave manufactured shoes, and he needed the club in his business, he said. Besides, what would Ivy and the girls get out of the club, when the Hartmann home was in Taqua? It'd be different, he said, if he had his home in Gibbsville. Julian had another Scotch and soda.

He wanted to go on thinking about the terrible people, all members of this club, and the people who were not terrible people but who had done terrible things, awful things. But now he got nothing out of it; it made him feel no better, no surer of himself. It had in the beginning, for there were many things he had thought of that were worse things than he had done. What Ed Klitsch had done, for instance. A thing that could have a terrible effect on a decent woman like Mrs. Losch; or it might have made Losch think that his wife invited Klitsch's little attention. And so on. But the trouble with making yourself feel better by thinking of bad things that other people have done is that you are the only one who is rounding up the stray bad things. No one but yourself bothers to make a collection of disasters. For the time being you are the hero or the villain of the thing that is uppermost in the minds of your friends and acquaintances. You can't even say, "But look at Ed Klitsch. What about Carter and Kitty? What about Kitty and Mary Lou? Aren't I better than Mrs. Shawse?" The trouble with that is that Ed Klitsch and Carter and Kitty and Mary Lou and Mrs. Shawse have nothing to do with the case. Two more kids looked at Julian and said hyuh, but they did not hover thirstily and wait for him to offer them a drink. He wondered about that again, and as it had many times in the last year and a half, Age Thirty stood before him. Age Thirty. And those kids were nineteen, twenty-one, eighteen, twenty. And he was thirty. "To them," he said to himself, "I am thirty. I am too old to be going to their house parties, and if I dance with their girls they do not cut in right away, the way they would on someone their own age. They think I am old." He had to say this to himself, not believing it for a moment. What he did believe was that he was precisely as young as they, but more of a person because he was equipped with experience and a permanent face. When he was twenty, who was thirty? Well, when he was twenty the men he would have looked up to were now forty. No, that wasn't quite right. He had another drink, telling himself that this would be his last. Let's see; where was he? Oh, yes. When I was forty. Oh, nuts. He wished Monsignor Creedon would heed the call of nature. He got up and went out to the verandah.

It was a fine night. (Fine had been a romantic word in his vocabulary ever since he read *A Farewell to Arms,* but this was one time when he felt justified in using it.) The fine snow was still there, covering almost everything as far as the eye could see. The fine snow had been there all the time he had been inside, having dinner, dancing with Constance and Jean, and sitting by himself, drinking highballs too fast. He took a deep breath, but not too deep as experience had warned him against that. This was real, this weather. The snow and what it did to the landscape. The farmlands that once, only a little more than a century ago, and less than that in some cases, had been wild country, infested with honest-to-God Indians and panther and wildcat. It still was not too effete. Down under that snow rattlesnakes were sleeping, rattlers and copperheads. A high-powered rifle shot away, or maybe a little more, there were deer, and there were Pennsylvania Dutch families that never spoke English. He remembered during the war, during the draft, when someone had told him about families near the Berks County line but still in this county. They not only couldn't understand about the war; many of them never had been to Gibbsville. That alone was enough to make a story when he first heard it. Now he wished he had heard more. He resolved to go into it further, find out more about the peculiarities of his native heath. Who did Kentucky think it was that it could claim exclusive rights on hillbillys? "I guess I love this place," he said.

"Good evening, son," said a voice.

He turned. It was Father Creedon. "Oh, Father. Good evening. Cigarette?"

"No, thank you. Cigar for me." The priest took a cigar from a worn, black leather case. He amputated the end of the cigar with a silver cutter. "How are things with you?"

"Fine," said Julian. "Huh. As a matter of fact, anything but fine. I suppose you heard about my performance last night with a friend of yours."

"Yes. I did. You mean Harry Reilly?"

"Uh-huh."

"Well, it's none of my affair," said Monsignor Creedon. "But I wouldn't let it worry you if I were you. I don't imagine Harry Reilly likes to be missing the dancing and all that, but he's a reasonable kind of a fellow. Go to him and tell him you're sorry, and make him think you mean it. He'll listen to reason."

"I did go. Didn't Mrs. Gorman tell you? I went to see him this afternoon and he wouldn't see me."

"Oh, he wouldn't, eh? Well, the next time you see him tell him to go to hell." He chuckled. "No. Don't. I wouldn't want to have that on my conscience. A priest of God stirring up animosities and so forth and so on. I don't know. You didn't ask me for my advice anyways. But if you can forget for a minute that I'm a priest, and just between you and me, I think Harry Reilly is a horse's ass."

The old man and the young man laughed. "You do?" said Julian.

"I do. If you ever tell that I'll fix your feet, young man. But that's what I think."

"So do I," said Julian.

"We're both right, son," said Monsignor Creedon. "Harry is ambitious. Well, Cæsar was ambitious. A lot of people are ambitious. I was ambitious myself, once, and I got a nice kick in the teeth for it. Ambition's all right, if you know when to stop. As F. P. A. would say, I can take my ambition or leave it alone. Oh, yes, ambition is all right, just as long as you don't get too ambitious."

"Do you read F. P. A.?"

"My God, yes. I get the *World* every day. Of course I'm a Republican, but I have the *World* delivered with the *Ledger*. I miss Broun, though, since he isn't with the *World* any more. Do you read the *World*? I didn't know Cadillac dealers could read. I thought all they had to do was make an X mark on the back of a check."

"I never was meant to be a Cadillac dealer or any other kind of dealer, Father," said Julian.

"That sounded to me as though—you're not a frustrated literary man, by any chance, are you? God forbid."

"Oh, no," said Julian. "I'm not anything. I guess I should have been a doctor."

"Well—" the priest stopped himself, but his tone made Julian curious. "What, Father?"

"You won't think this sounds awful? No, of course you won't. You're a Protestant. Well, I'll tell you. I've had my moments of wishing I'd taken some other life work. That doesn't sound bad to you, because you weren't brought up to believe in the true vocation. Well, I guess I better go inside. I keep forgetting I'm an old man."

"How about a drink?" said Julian.

"I will if it isn't too late. I'm fasting." He looked at his big silver watch. "All right. I've time. I'll have one with you."

Surprisingly, no one had taken the bottle of Scotch off the table in Julian's absence. The thieves, which was to say everyone, probably thought the owner of the bottle was in the toilet and was apt to surprise them in the act of stealing the liquor, a heinous offense.

"Oh, Scotch. Fine," said the priest. "Do you like Irish whiskey?"

"I certainly do," said Julian.

"I'll send you a bottle of Bushmill's. It isn't the best Irish whiskey, but it's good. And this stuff is real. Ed Charney sent me a case of it for a Christmas present, heaven only knows why. I'll never do anything for that one. Well, your very good health and a happy New Year. Let's see. Tomorrow's St. Stephen's Day. He was the first martyr. No, I guess we better stick to happy New Year."

"Cheerio," said Julian.

The old priest—Julian wondered exactly how old he was—drank his highball almost bottoms up. "Good whiskey," he said.

"That came from Ed Charney, too," said Julian.

"He has his uses," said the priest. "Thank you, and good-by. I'll send you that Bushmill's tomorrow or next day. 'Bye." He left, a little stoop-shouldered but strong-looking and well-tailored. The talk had given Julian a lift, and the air had sobered him up. The tails hanging over his buttocks, the sleeves of his coat, the legs of his trousers were still cold, covered with cold, from his stand on the verandah, but he felt fine. He hurried out to dance with Caroline and others.

The orchestra was playing Three Little Words. He spotted Caroline, dancing with—it would be—Frank Gorman. Julian cut in, being no more polite about it than he had to.

"Have we met?" said Caroline.

"Ouimet. The name of a golfer. Francis Ouimet," said Julian. "How did you ever remember the name?"

"Where have you been? I looked around for you after I came down from the johnny, but were you anywhere to be seen? Did you greet me at the foot of the stairs? Did you come dashing forth to claim the first dance? Did you? No. You did not. Then an hour passes. And so on."

"I was having a very nice chat with Father Creedon."

"Father Creedon? You were not. Not for long. He's been sitting with

Mrs. Gorman and her party most of the evening. You were getting drunk and you just happened to give him one drink so you could truthfully say you'd been with him. I know you, English."

"You're wrong as hell. He was with me for a long time. And I learned something."

"What?"

"He thinks Harry Reilly is a horse's ass," said Julian.

She did not reply.

"What's the matter with that? I think so too. I see eye to eye with Rome on that."

"How did he happen to say that? What did you say that made him say that?"

"I didn't say anything to make him say that. All I said was . . . I don't remember how it started. Oh, yes. He asked me how I felt and I said fine, and then I said no, anything but fine. I was standing outside on the verandah, and he came out for a breath of air, and so we got to talking and I said I supposed he'd heard about my altercation with Harry and I told him I'd been around to apologize, and I said Harry had refused to see me, and then Creedon said he thought Harry was a horse's ass."

"That doesn't sound much like him."

"That's what I thought, but he explained it beforehand. He said he wasn't talking as a priest, but just as man to man. After all, darling, there's no law that says he has to dearly love all the people who go to his church, is there?"

"No. Well, I'm just sorry you talked to him about it. Even if he doesn't go right back and tell—"

"Oh, for God's sake. You were never so wrong in your whole life. Father Creedon's a swell guy."

"Yes, but he's a Catholic, and they stick together."

"Oh, nuts. You're trying to build this up into a world catastrophe."

"Oh, yeah? And what are you doing? You're trying to pass it off as though it were the least important thing in the world, just a little exchange of pleasantries. Well, you're wrong, Julian."

"Aw-haw. Now we're getting to the Julian stage. I get it."

"Will you listen? This thing isn't going to blow over and be forgotten, and I wish you'd stop thinking it is. I've tried to tell you what you should have known yourself, that Harry Reilly is a bad enemy."

"How do *you* know? How do you know so much about Harry Reilly's characteristics or avenging moods or what-have-you? If you don't mind my saying so, you give me a pain in the ass."

"Okay," said Caroline.

"Oh, I'm sorry. Believe me? I'm sorry. Please forgive me." He held her closer. "Have we still got a date for midnight?"

"I don't know."

"You don't know? Just because I said that?"

"Oh, I think you're unfair. I think it's a dirty trick, and you always do it. You make me very angry about something and then you refuse to go on with the discussion, but instead you blithely talk about love and going to bed. It's a dirty trick, because if I refuse to talk about loving you, you become the injured party and so on. It's a lousy trick and you do it all the time."

The music stopped but almost immediately resumed with Can This Be Love? The orchestra was not doing so well with the back-time, and that disturbed Julian, whose ear for jazz was superb.

"See?" said Caroline.

"What?"

"I was right. You're sulking."

"For God's sweet sake, I'm not sulking. Do you want to know what I was thinking?"

"Go ahead."

"Well, this'll make you mad, I have no doubt, but I was thinking what a lousy band this is. Does that make you sore?"

"In a way, yes," said Caroline.

"I was thinking what a foolish economy it is to save money on an orchestra. After all, the most important thing at a dance is the music, isn't it?"

"Must I talk about that?"

"Without the music there would be no dance. It's like playing golf with cheap clubs, or playing tennis with a dollar racket, or bad food. It's like anything cheap." He drew his head back, away from her so he could observe the effect of his words. "Now you take a Cadillac—"

"Oh, cut it out, Ju. Please."

"Why?"

"Because I want you to. Because you ought to."

"What's the matter? My God, you're sourball tonight. You ask me not to drink, and I don't drink. You—"

"Oh, yeah?"

"Well, you asked me not to get tight, and I'm not a bit tight. You said I could drink. Let's go outside. I want to talk to you."

"No. I don't want to go out."

"Why not?"

"It's too cold, for one thing. And I don't feel like it."

"Well, that's the best reason. Does that mean you're not going to keep our date at intermission?"

"I don't know. I'm not sure." She spoke slowly.

He said nothing. Then presently she spoke. "All right," she said. "I'll go out with you."

They danced to the foyer, broke, and ran to the anonymous sedan nearest the verandah. They got in and she sat with her arms drawn close to her ribs. He lit a cigarette for her.

"What is the matter, darling?" he said.

"God, I'm cold."

"Do you want to talk, or are you going to just say how cold you are?"

"What do you want to talk about?" she said.

"About you. Your attitude. I want to try to find out what's eating you. There isn't a single thing I've done tonight that you can find fault with."

"Except calling me a horse's ass."

"You're crazy! I didn't call you that. That was what old What's Iss called Harry Reilly. I said you gave me a pain in the ass, which isn't quite the same."

"All right."

"And I said I was sorry, and I am sorry. But that's not the point. We're just quibbling—"

"You mean I am."

"Yes, frankly. I do mean that. Oh, Christ! What the hell is it? Please say something. Tell me what's the matter. Bawl me out or do anything you like, but don't sit there freezing like a martyr. Like some kind of a St. Stephen."

"What?"

"St. Stephen was the first martyr. Father Creedon told me that."

"My, you kept the talk on a high plane, didn't you?"

"Will you for the last time, will you tell me why you have a fig— what's the matter?"

"I'm freezing, Julian. I've got to go in. I shouldn't have come out without a coat."

"I'll look around in the other cars and borrow a robe, if you'll stay."

"No, I don't think we'd better," she said. "I'm going in. This was a mistake, coming out here."

"You had no intention of talking when you came out."

"No. I don't suppose I did, but I didn't want to have a scene on the dance floor."

"Have a scene on the dance floor! All right. You can go. I won't keep you. Just one question. *Is* there something I've done? Any one thing that you're sore about?"

"No. Not exactly. No. There isn't."

"One more question. Maybe I'd better not ask it."

"Go ahead," she said, with her hand on the door of the sedan.

"All right: Is there something you've done? Have you done anything? Have you fallen in love with someone else?"

"Or necked someone else?" she said. "Or laid someone else while you were sneaking your drinks in the locker room? No. My attitude, as you call it, comes from something much more subtle than that, Julian, but we won't go into it now."

He took her in his arms. "Oh, I love you so much. I always will. I always have and I always will. Don't do this." She held up her chin while he kissed her neck and rubbed his mouth and nose against her breast, but when he cupped his left hand over her right breast she said, "No. No. I don't want you to do that. Let me go, please."

"Have you got the curse?"

"Please don't talk that way, say things like that. You know perfectly well I haven't."

"That's right. I do. I thought you might have got it suddenly."

"You think that's the only possible explanation for the way I feel?"

"At least there is some explanation, or there ought to be. You won't tell me what it is?"

"It'd take too long. And now I *am* going. It isn't like you to keep me waiting out here with the temperature near zero."

"Mm. Giving me a break. Okay. Let's go." He got out of the car and made one last effort to take her in his arms by carrying her to the verandah, but she was on the steps without even seeming to spurn his gesture. She went inside and immediately went up the stairs to the ladies' quarters. He knew she did not expect him to be waiting when she came down, so he went out and joined the stag line. He saw Mill Ammermann and he was waiting for her to dance or be danced close enough to the stag line and he was going to cut in on her, when suddenly something happened that was like migraine: he did not see anyone in the room nor anything, yet the people and the lights and the things hurt his eyes. And the reason for it was that in one and the same instant he remembered that he had not asked Caroline to say yes or no about the date at intermission—and he realized that he did not need to ask her.

He recovered a sense which may not have been sight, but whatever it was it enabled him to find his way back to the locker-room, where there was enough liquor for anyone in the world to get drunk.

5

WHEN CAROLINE WALKER fell in love with Julian English she was a little tired of him. That was in the summer of 1926, one of the most unimportant years in the history of the United States, and the year in which Caroline Walker was sure her life had reached a pinnacle of uselessness. She was four years out of college then, and she was twenty-seven years old, which is as old as anyone ever gets, or at least she thought so at the time. She found herself thinking more and more and less and less of men. That is the way she put it, and she knew it to be sure and right, but she did not bother to expand the -ism. "I think of them oftener, and I think of them less often." She had attained varying degrees of love, requited and unrequited—but seldom the latter. Men, and damn good men, fell in love with her with comforting regularity, and she had enough trouble with them, in one way or another, to make it impossible for her to tell herself honestly that she was unattractive. She was sorry she was not beautiful—until a nice old gentleman, a Philadelphian who painted society women's portraits, told her that he never had seen a beautiful woman.

That summer she thought of her life after college in three ways: she thought of it as unicellular, but a life that reversed the amoeba's performance. The days got together and formed one life, losing their separate identities. Again, she thought of those four years as calendar years, broken formally by the Assembly (New Year's Eve), the July 3 Assembly, Easter, Hallowe'en, Labor Day. Put together they made four years, the length of time she had passed at Bryn Mawr, and like the years of college in that they seemed so long a time and so short a time, but also not at all like the college years, because she felt she had got something out of college. These four years had not had the compactness of college, and they seemed wasted.

They were wasted. She took her turn teaching the Italian and Negro children at the Gibbsville Mission, which is what passes for the Junior League in Gibbsville. But she didn't like it. She had no poise or assurance with those children, or any group of children, and she knew she was not a teacher. She almost loved two or three of the children, but somewhere in the back of her mind she recognized the reason: the Mission children that she liked best were the ones who were least like the other Mission children and more like Lantenengo Street children, the children of her friends. There was one exception: a red-headed Irish brat who she was certain had let the air out of her tires and hid her hat. He never called her Miss Walker or Miss Car'line, as the other little sycophants did. He was about eleven years old— the limit of Mission children was twelve years of age—and he had a face that it would take him at least twenty more years to grow up to. She liked him but she hated him; she was afraid of him and the way he sometimes would stare at her when he wasn't making trouble. At home when she thought of him she would tell herself that he was a child whose great energy could and ought to be directed into useful channels. He was just a mischievous kid, and he could be "saved." . . . Thus practically her entire sociological knowledge at the time. She was to learn a little more.

The Gibbsville Mission was an old, three-story brick house in the very dingiest part of Gibbsville, and was supported by Lantenengo Street contributions. Babies were brought there to be cared for through the day by girls like Caroline, and a professional nurse. Then in the afternoon, after the parochial and public schools closed for the day, the children up to twelve came to play and be read to until six o'clock, when they were sent home, their supper appetites spoiled by a pint of milk.

One afternoon in the spring of 1926 Caroline had said good-by to the children and had gone around, tried doors, getting ready to close the Mission for the day. She was putting on her hat, standing in front of the mirror in the office, when she heard a footstep. Before she could see who it was—she saw it was a child—two arms went around her legs and two hands slid up under her skirt, and a red little head was burrowing into her stomach. She slapped down at him and tried to push him away, and finally succeeded, but he had touched her where he wanted to with his vile little fingers, and she went insane and struck him many times, knocking him to the floor and kicking him until he crawled and ran away, out of the office, crying.

Her great fear for days after that was that his grimy hands had given her a venereal disease. He never came back to the Mission, and she resigned the next week, but for weeks she was sure she had syphilis or *something*. The incident finally sent her, dying of mortification, to Doctor Malloy, to whom she told all. He very seriously examined her— he was not the family physician—and told her to come back the day after the next for the laboratory report; and then soberly informed her that she was free to marry and have babies, that there was nothing wrong with her. When she insisted on paying him he charged her fifteen dollars. This money he gave, without Caroline's knowledge, to be sure, to the mother of the redhead, on the theory that the mother of such a child would appreciate anything in the way of a gift, without inquiring into the reason for the gift.

That was Caroline's first completely unpleasant encounter with the male sex. She thought of it constantly in the days that followed. When she asked herself, "Why did he do it?" she always came to the same answer: that that was what you could expect of men, what she had been brought up to expect of men. She had had many men run over her with their hands, and there were some with whom she permitted it. She was still a virgin at that time, but until the child made his mysterious attack she thought she had sex pretty well under control. After the attack she reorganized, or entirely disorganized, her ideas about men and the whole of sex; and the one permanent effect of "that afternoon at the Mission," as she referred to it in her frequent introspection, was that her ignorance of sex was pointed up. She knew herself for a completely inexperienced girl, and for the first time she began to remember the case histories in Havelock Ellis and Krafft-Ebing and the lesser psychologists as more than merely pornography.

Up to that summer Caroline had been deeply in love twice in her life, although from the time she put her hair up she was always in love with someone. One of the men, the first, was a distant cousin of hers, Jerome Walker. He was an Englishman by birth and education, and he came to Gibbsville in 1918. He was about twenty-five and a captain in the British Army. He was through, so far as the war was concerned; they were taking more and more bone out of his left leg, and putting in more and more silver. His presence in the United States, which he never before had visited, was to teach modern warfare to the draft army. Gibbsville girls threw themselves at him when he turned up at Caroline's house on a month's leave, and he was invited everywhere, a catch. He wore slacks, which were slightly unmilitary, and the stick he carried had a leather thong which he wrapped around his wrist. His tunic was beautifully tailored, and the little blue and white ribbon of the Military Cross, which no one identified, gave a nice little touch of color to his uniform. His lack of height fitted in with the fact that he was an invalid, a "casuality," as most of the Gibbsville women—and men—called him. He took one careful look at Caroline and then and there decided for himself that this girl in the three-cornered hat and long gray spats and nicely cut suit was going to be something worth trying for. He was quite confident he could swing it in a month's time.

He very nearly did. Caroline's father was dead, and her mother was deaf, the kind of deaf person who, not wishing to yield to her deafness, refuses to learn to read lips or to wear earphones. In the Walker mansion on South Main Street were Caroline, her mother, the cook and the maid. And Jerry.

The first time he kissed her he all but gave up his ideas of having an affair with her. It was awfully far from the war, this warm room in Gibbsville in Pennsylvania in America, and there was nothing particularly warlike about "Oui, oui, Marie, will you do ziss for me?" which was going round and round on the phonograph. Caroline, except for her horrible accent, might have been an English girl, a sister of a friend, at home. But when she got up to change the needle and the record he reached out and took her hand and drew her to him, sat her on his right knee, and kissed her. She went to him without resistance but only the thought: "Well, we can kiss, can't we?" But the kiss was not very successful, because they bumped noses in trying to get their heads at the right angles, and he let her go. She stopped the Victrola and came back and sat beside him. He took her hand and she looked at it and then looked up presently at him. They did not speak, and when she looked at him he was smiling very gently. A nervous smile came and went on her face and then she moved closer to him and really kissed him. But the moment of unscrupulousness had passed for him. She was all body and sensation and he had the terrible consciousness that while she felt this way, anything he chose to do to her, anything, would not be resisted.

This lasted a minute, two minutes, maybe five, before she squeezed back into herself and put her head on his shoulder. She was ashamed and grateful, because she never before had let herself go that way. "Let's have a cigarette," she said.

"Do you smoke?"

"I'm not allowed to, but I do. You hold it and I'll take a puff."

He got his silver case out of his trousers pocket and she smoked, not holding the cigarette very expertly, but taking appalling inhales. Cute was the word for her as she sat there, blowing smoke out of her mouth and nostrils, smoking the cigarette too fast. He took it from her to cool it off, and then they heard the quick catch of her mother's car, a Baker electric, in the driveway on the way back to the stable. Caroline got up and put Poor Butterfly on the Vic. "That's one of our old records," she said, "but I like it because it's so syncopated." Anything that had the sound of the trap-drummer's wood blocks in it was syncopated.

They often kissed after that, in the halls, the butler's pantry, and in her Scripps-Booth roadster, which had a peculiar seating arrangement; the driver sat a foot or so forward of the other seat, which made kissing an awkward act.

He went away without telling her that he loved her, and without changing her status as woman or girl. He was dead of gangrene within six months of his visit to Gibbsville, and it was another two months before his family remembered to write to them. That had something to do with lessening Caroline's grief: that he could have been lying dead in a grave while she went on thinking of him as the love of her life, while she was having a lovely time with the boys who were back from France and Pensacola and Boston Tech and the Great Lakes Naval Training Station. She was in demand, and she kissed a good many men with as much abandon as she had kissed Jerome Walker, except that now she knew how and when to stop. She was getting to be a prom trotter, too, as much as Bryn Mawr would permit, and having a perfectly wonderful time with the college boys. They were gay again now that the war was over and their universal embarrassment at not being in the fighting army was at an end, now that it was all right to be gay publicly. She was leaving for a weekend at Easton, where Ju English was in college, when her mother read the letter from England, which was mostly about how grateful the Cecil Walkers were for the hospitality their boy had received in Gibbville, as they called it. There was one reference to Caroline. It was: ". . . and if you and your dear little girl should come to England, we shall . . ." Oh, well. But not oh, well. She knew, or hoped she knew, that the reason he did not tell his mother more about her was that he didn't want his mother to think things. Still, on the ride to Easton she was depressed. When our minds run that way we date periods in our lives, and Caroline in later days and years fixed the train ride to Easton as the end of her girlhood. All her life, until she fell in love with Julian English, she was to feel that if things had been different, she would have married her cousin and lived in England, and she always thought very kindly of England. She did not, however, visit Jerome's family when she went abroad in 1925. She was only going to be gone two months altogether, and by that time she was in love with a living man.

Joe Montgomery could be classified under many headings. Drunk. Snake. Rich boy. Well-dressed man. Debbies' delight. Roué. Bond salesman. War veteran. Extra man. And so on. They all added up to the same thing. His chief claim to distinction was that he had known Scott Fitzgerald at Princeton, and that made him in Caroline's eyes an ambassador from an interesting country, full of interesting people whom she wanted to meet and to see in action. She did not know, of course, that she was a member of good standing of the community which she thought Joe Montgomery represented, which Fitzgerald wrote about. She only knew that Gibbsville was her home town, but it or the people who lived in it certainly were not worth writing about.

Joe Montgomery's home was in Reading, which is across two state lines from New York, but actually in the same radius as Hartford or New London—a fact which apparently is not known to any New Yorkers or to most Reading people, but was taken for granted by Joe Montgomery. His father was so rich that he had gone down in the *Titanic*, and it was told of Henry Montgomery, as it has been told of almost every other male on that vessel's passenger list, that he had been (a) a hero, and (b) that the captain had had to shoot him dead to keep him out of the women's and children's lifeboats. Things in Joe's background included vague recollections in Caroline's mind of a Stutz Bearcat, a raccoon coat, Brooksy clothes, and some local reputation as a golfer. He knew a few people in Gibbsville, and he was a friend of Whitney Hofman's, but he seldom came to Gibbsville.

He was hardly more than a name to Caroline in 1925, when she was thrown with him for a festive week in East Orange, just before her trip abroad. She was being a bridesmaid and he an usher at a wedding there, and she was elated when he said: "Lord, God, don't introduce me to *Caroline Walker*. She and I are old pals. Or are we, Caroline?" He was about the best there was at the wedding, and she probably kissed him more frequently and more ardently than she did the other ushers. He must have thought so, because he stayed over in New York for her last week before sailing. The wedding fuss ended Sunday, the last day of May, and she was sailing in the *Paris* the next Saturday. He tried to monopolize her time, and all but did. He took her to see shows—"Lady Be Good," with the Astaires and Walter Catlett, which she had seen in Philadelphia; "What Price Glory?"; "Rose Marie"; Richard Bennett and Pauline Lord in "They Knew What They Wanted"; the Garrick Gaieties. It was a stifling week, although only the first week of June. The whole country seemed to want to die, and, led by a former vice president who once made a remark about what this country needed, die many of them did. Joe kept saying *"Jee-zuzz,"* unable to forget the heat, and after the first act of "What Price Glory?" he had no trouble persuading her to not go back. He had his car, a red

Jordan roadster, in town, and he suggested driving out to Long Island, Westchester, anywhere. "I'll swear for you and tell you some war stories," he said. "And you'll think you're still at the play."

He had enough sense or intuition not to try to talk much until they got out of the city. The heat was awful; it got up her nose, and everyone whose eyes met hers had a silly smile on his face that seemed to apologize for the weather. And she guessed she looked that way herself.

They finally came to a place on Long Island which Joe told her was called Jones's Beach. "How are you fixed for underwear?" he said.

"Oh. So that's it?"

"Yes, I guess it is. I won't go in unless you do."

Her heart was thumping and there was a shaking in her legs, but "All right," she said. She never had seen a grown man with all his clothes off at one time, and when he walked away from his side of the car and stepped toward the water she was relieved to see that he was wearing shorts, part of his underwear. "You go on in," she said. She wanted him to be in the water when she moved from the shelter of the car in her brassiere and step-ins. He got the idea and did not look until she was swimming a few yards away from him.

"What this is going to do to my hair," she said.

"Too late to worry about it now," he said. "You cold?"

"Not now," she said.

"I should have built a fire. I didn't think of it."

"God, no! And have people see it and come running down? Gosh, I'm glad you didn't."

He came out first. "Better not stay in too long," he said. "You can use my undershirt for a towel." He went back to the car and started the motor and held his undershirt, which was damp from perspiration, near the engine. "Better come out now," he said.

She came out, pulling her soaking step-ins about so as to get a maximum of modesty. Her brassiere was no good at all, and she was so angry at her swinging breasts that she wanted to cry; no matter how nice he was he couldn't fail to notice her "chest."

"Don't be embarrassed," he said. "I've seen a naked woman."

"Oh—" she mumbled. "You haven't seen me. Or hadn't."

"Please don't. You'll take the enjoyment out of the swim. Go on back and swim a little more and then come out without being self-conscious. Or anyhow, embarrassed. Go on."

She did as he said and felt better. She felt fourteen years old. Less. She had not overcome her embarrassment, but she no longer was afraid.

She dried herself with his warm undershirt. "I don't know what I'm going to do about my hair."

"Here." He threw her a clean handkerchief. "That'll help a little." It didn't.

He gave her the coat of his dinner suit and made her put it on over her evening dress, and they had cigarettes and were only vaguely aware of the discomfort. "I guess we could have saved all this trouble by going somewhere to a regular beach, or pool."

"I'm glad now we didn't," she said.

"Are you? That's what I wanted you to say."

"Did you? I'm glad I said it then."

He put his arm around her and tried to kiss her.

"No," she said.

"All right," he said.

"Don't spoil it," she added.

"It wouldn't spoil it. Not now. At least I don't think so. I waited till you were dressed."

"Yes, and I'm glad you did. I like you for that, Joe. But even now. *You* know."

"No, frankly. I don't know what you mean."

"Yes, you do. You—oh, hell."

"Oh, you mean because I saw you without any clothes on."

"Mm-hmm," she said, although up to then she had been thinking that technically he had not seen her without *any* clothes on. Now she wished she had been completely nude. It was something you had to get over, and with Joe it had been a grand chance.

"All right," he said, and took his arm away.

They talked about her trip abroad. It was her first. He said he wished he were going with her, or could go in time to take her around Paris and so on, but he couldn't make it; he had to be a good boy at the National City, because it was time he was getting somewhere and making some money. A crooked lawyer and his mother's stupidity had reduced his father's estate. So he was working for the National City, with an office in Reading and a salary that just proved to him how worthless he was. She couldn't muster much pity for him; she had seen the Montgomery home, Mrs. Montgomery's Rolls.

"Well, this is all very nice," she said, "but I think maybe we'd better start back to town. How far is it?"

"Oh, plenty of time. It isn't far. I don't really know how far it is exactly. Let's not go back right away. You're going away so soon, and for such a long time."

"But I have so many things to do," she said. "You've no idea."

"Oh, yes, I have. Turkish towels, six. Heavy woolen underwear, six. Handkerchiefs, twelve. Two sweaters. The school will supply sheets and bed linen, but we recommend, and so on. All marked with indelible ink or Cash's woven labels."

"But I have. I have to—"

"Parents are specially urged to exercise restraint in providing boys with pocket money. A dollar and a half a week will be sufficient for most needs."

"Oh, Joe."

"The use of motorcycles is absolutely prohibited."

"What about cigarettes?"

"Members of the Upper Middle and higher forms are permitted to use tobacco on written permission of one or both parents."

"I could tell you some you don't know," she said.

"Such as?"

"Oh—girls' schools."

"Oh, that's easy. In cases where a girl is likely to be absent from class and other activities at frequent intervals during the school year, a letter from the family physician, addressed to the school nurse—"

"That's enough," she said. She was embarrassed and angry with herself. Here she was, talking about the most intimate part of a woman's life, with a man whom she did—not—really—know. It was the second time tonight that she had done a "first" thing with him: he was the first to see her with nothing on (she had well-founded misgivings about the protection the step-ins had given her), and he was the first to talk to her about That. She hated all the euphemisms for it, and when she thought of it she thought of it in the Bryn Mawr term: "Off the sports list."

His arm was around her again and his head was close to hers. He thought she was angry with him, and for the moment she did not care; but then she rested her face on his shoulder, and she put up her mouth for the kiss and then she let herself coast with him. He took down her dress and kissed her breasts and she patted and rubbed his head. She waited without tension for what he would do next. She thought she knew what that would be, and she did not prepare to fight against it. But she was wrong. He suddenly slipped her shoulder straps up her arms and back where they belonged. Her breath was coming as though she had stopped running a few minutes ago, slowly and deeply.

"You virgin?" he said.

"Yes," she said.

"Are you sure? Please tell me the truth."

"Mm-hmm. I am."

"Do you love me?" he said.

"Yes, I think I do, Joe."

"How old are you?" he said.

"Twenty-five. Twenty-six soon. No. I *am* twenty-six."

"Oh. Then you want to be a virgin when you get married. That's why you are now."

"I guess so," she said. "I don't know." She ran her teeth over her lower lip. "It's never been like this before." She put her arm around his neck. He kissed her.

"Will you be engaged to me?" he said. "Is there anyone else?"

"No, there's no one else important right now."

"Well?"

"Yes," she said. "You don't want to announce it now, or anything like that, do you?"

"No. I suppose we'd better be sensible and let you have your trip and two months away from me and see if you still love me."

"Do you love me?" she said. "You haven't actually said so."

"I love you," he said. "And you're the first girl I've told that to in—nineteen twenty-five—eight years. Do you believe me?"

"It's possible," she said. "Eight years. You mean since 1917. The war?"

"Yes."

"What happened?" she said.

"She was married," he said.

"Do you still see her?"

"Not for two years. She's in the Philippines. Her husband's in the Army and now they have three children. It's all over."

"Would you marry me if I weren't a virgin?"

"I don't know. I honestly don't know. That wasn't the reason I asked you if you were. I wanted to know because—do you want me to tell you the truth?"

"Of course."

"Well, I was going to ask you to spend the night with me if you weren't."

"In which case you probably wouldn't have asked me to marry you."

"Maybe. I don't know. But I do want you to marry me. You will, won't you? Don't get a yen for some Frenchman."

"I won't. I almost wish I weren't going, but I guess it's a good thing I am." Her voice was low and dramatic.

"What makes you say it like that?"

"The obvious reason. I have a theory, Joe. I've always told myself that when I loved a man enough to want to marry him, I'd have an affair with him before we announced the engagement, and then have a short engagement and get married practically right away."

"Oh. That means you haven't really been in love all your life."

"No. It doesn't mean that. Not quite. But I haven't been in love since I made that decision. Since I've found out more about sex. God! Is that clock right?"

"A few minutes fast."

"How many minutes fast?"

"Oh. I don't know."

"No, honestly. Even if it's a half hour fast look what time that means. We've got to go back. I hate to, but please, darling?"

"All right," he said.

Half way back to town she remembered something that made her want to let out a cry, to melt away, to die. The worst of it was she would have to tell him now.

"Joe, darling," she said.

"Yes, ma'am."

"I just remembered something, the worst thing I can think of. Oh, damn it all. I wish people . . ."

"What is it?"

"I'm not going to be able to see you tomorrow night."

"Why not? Can't you break it?"

"No. I should have told you before, but I didn't know we were— I was going to. All this tonight, about us. Some people are coming over from Gibbsville to see me off."

"Who? Who is the guy?"

"Well, it's not just one person. There is a man—"

"Who? Do I know him?"

"I don't know. Julian English. He's coming, and some people named Ogden. I think you know them."

"Froggy? Sure. I've met English a couple of times, too. He's a college boy, isn't he?"

"No. He's out."

"Are you in love with him? I hope not. He isn't so hot. He cheats at cards. He takes dope."

"He does not!" she exclaimed. "He doesn't do any such thing. He *drinks* too much, maybe."

"Oh, darling, don't you know when I'm fooling? I don't know anything about him. I'm not even sure I'd know him if I saw him. Yes, I would. But you're not in love with him, are you?"

"I'm in love with you. Oh, I do love you. And that's what makes it worse. I wish you could come along tomorrow night, my last night before I sail. But I don't think that'd be so good."

"Oh, no. Mr. English wouldn't like it."

"It isn't that. I'm not only thinking of him. But Jean and Froggy are coming all the way from Gibbsville just to see me off and we planned a big bender in New York tomorrow night. I'm not a bit pleased about it now, but there's nothing I can do at this late date."

"No, I guess you're right, damn it. You certainly are the will o' the wisp if I ever saw it."

"Are you going to write to me, a lot?"

"Fourteen Place Vendôme, every day."

"How did you know?"

"Oh, you're a Morgan, Harjes girl, as distinguished from an American Express girl. I'll write every day and cable every week-end. And what will I get for it? A postcard that I'd be ashamed to show to my own mother and a scarf from Liberty's and maybe a Dunhill lighter."

They stopped and bought a comb at a drug store before she would go in the Commodore, where she and Lib McCreery and Is Stannard, Bryn Mawr classmates who were going abroad with her, were stopping. The breeze ended when they stopped the car, and the heat came back and everything began to get a little unsatisfactory and she wanted to go to her room and lie in the water. Their farewell was hurried and she was too conscious of looking like the wrath of God to enjoy any minute of it.

That was one of the things he commented on in his first letters. He had to stay in New York, in the heat, while she was cooling off and feeling like a human being on shipboard. Her letters were ardent and pleasant and pleased, full of new and sudden love. Nicholas Murray Butler and Anne Morgan and Eddie Cantor and Genevieve Tobin and Joseph E. Widener were on board. "I wonder if I love him" became a song the way she said it, and she would sing over and over to herself: "I wonder, I won-der."

"Who? Joe Widener?" said Lib.

"The Joe part is right."

"Joe English, the boy that came down to the boat?"

"His name is Ju, j u for Julian."

"Well, who is it, then?"

"You wouldn't know," said Caroline.

"Oh, I know. The man who brought you back to the hotel in that awful condition."

"That's the one."

But when his letters came they did not match her mood. Discontent and some petulance, and though she snatched at the love passages, she had to be honest with herself and admit that they read more like postscript material. She blamed the heat of New York and Reading and felt sorry for him and said so in her replies. He was the man all during her first trip to Europe whom she missed, with whom she wanted to share the fun of her discovery of foreign lands. And she missed him very much. Then she got a letter from him that soured her trip, or at least divided it into two phases. He wrote and wrote, for pages, but it all boiled down to one thing, which in subsequent days she recognized to be true: ". . . The truth is, darling, some kind of fate threw us together, but the same fate kept us apart the night before you sailed. Those people were fated to come and take you away from me that night. I have a feeling that if they hadn't, you would have put into practice that theory that you spoke of the night we went swimming. But they did come, didn't they? That being the case, you went away without putting your theory into practice and since then I have spoiled it as far as we're concerned with another girl. So I suppose this ought to be quits. I feel like the devil . . ."

She didn't believe the words, and then she wanted to cable him that another girl couldn't make a difference. She loved him, and she regretted as much as he did that she had not spent her last night in New York with him. If only she could have talked to him. But that was impossible, and letters or cables were no good. Late in the afternoon of the day she got the letter she groped through to an explanation for the shock of his letter (which, however, did not make her any less unhappy): he had jolted her by being, so far as she knew, the first man who had tried to be honest with her. Reason did that for her, and then for the first time in her life she made up her mind to get drunk. And that night she did get drunk, with a handsome young Harvard Jew, who turned out to be something fancy in her sex life; he took her by easy stages down the scale of Paris entertainment, ending with a "circus." She didn't remember about that until the next afternoon, when the memory, which she knew she could not have dreamt, came through her hangover. Then and there she wanted to pack and go home, but Is Stannard saved her sanity. When Lib McCreery had gone out to do some shopping Is came in and sat on Caroline's bed. "Where did Henry take you last night?"

"Oh, God. If I only knew."

"Were you that blotto?"

"Oh, Lord," said Caroline.

"Don't you remember anything?"

"Very little."

"Did he—do you remember going to a place where a man and a woman—you know?"

"I think so. I'm afraid so."

"That's where he took me, too. I thought I'd die when I went with him. I don't understand him. I wasn't nearly so drunk as you were. *I remember*. Every detail. But I can't understand Henry. He never touched me. All he did was to keep watching me. He didn't watch *them*, just me. I think he must have got pleasure out of the effect it had on me, those people. I don't think we'd better see that crowd again, that he goes around with. He wants me to go again and he wants you to come."

"God, I feel so terrible. Do you think he did anything to me?" said Caroline.

"Oh, no. I'm sure he didn't. He gets some kind of pleasure out of watching us. There are people like that. You never went the limit, did you, Callie?"

"No."

"Neither did I, and I think someone like Henry can tell that just by looking at you. I really do."

"Then why does he—oh, I wish I were home."

"Don't worry. You notice he didn't ask Lib. I've thought for years that Lib had an affair, probably more than one. So you and I are together on this. Just don't say anything about it to Lib, and if Henry becomes too insistent we can leave Paris. Can I get you some aspirin or something?"

Caroline had had her scare, and she got drunk no more. For the rest of her trip she traded nothing but her dancing ability for the attentions of the English-speaking young men who were attracted to her; and for a year after that the frightening experience with Henry What's His Name, and the disillusioning and humiliating experience with Joe Montgomery dictated her preference in men: they had to be clean, preferably blond, and not in the least glamorous or unusually attractive.

Back home, she had nothing to do in Gibbsville except to play bridge with the girls in the afternoon bridge clubs, and the mixed clubs in the evening; to take a course in shorthand and typewriting at the Gibbsville

Business College, with vague notions of a winter in New York in the front of her mind; to turn out for the Tuesday women's golf tournament-and-luncheon; to wheedle contributions on the various tag days; to act as chauffeuse for her mother, who could not learn to drive a combustion-engine car; to give her share of parties. She kept her weight under 115 pounds. She bobbed her hair. She drank a little more than the sociable amount, and she grew mildly profane. She came to know herself to be the most attractive of the Lantenengo Street girls. Without getting the rush that the girls still in school would get at dances, she still was more universally popular; the boys in the school crowd danced with her and so did the males of all ages up to forty, and a few did who were more than forty. She never had to pretend that she was having a better time sitting with a highball than she did on the dance floor. The girls she knew liked her without calling her a good sport or trusting her too far with their husbands or fiancés. They really did trust her, but they did not trust their men.

At the beginning of the summer of 1926 she recapitulated, and acknowledged that she was getting a little hard. She saw most frequently Julian English, Harry Reilly, Carter Davis, and a man from Scranton named Ross Campbell. Julian English was a habit, and she suspected that he went on seeing her because she never said anything about his Polish girl, who was reputed to be beautiful, but whom no one had seen. Harry Reilly was lavish and considerate; in his way, so crazy about her that he was almost self-effacing. Carter Davis was too predictable; she was certain she could tell how many years it would be before the day came when Carter stopped drinking and trying to pick up Irish girls after church Sunday night, and settled down and married a Lantenengo Street girl. "But it won't be me," she said. "Imagine life with a man whose deepest passion was bridge. And the Philadelphia Athletics. And the Cornell football team. God!" Ross Campbell was the most likely prospect for marriage. He was older than the others except Reilly, and he was something that did not exist in Gibbsville; one of those Harvard men, tall and slim and swell, who seem to have put on a clean shirt just a minute ago—soft white shirt with button-down collar—and not to have had a new suit in at least two years. He was not rich; he "had money." He had big strong teeth and his charm had something to do with a deceptive awkwardness, a result of his height, and his St. Paul's-Harvard voice and accent. He became a non-resident member of the Lantenengo Country Club as a matter of course when he began to see Caroline, and that was when Caroline first noticed that he was, besides everything else, a snob. He told her he was going to join. "I'll ask Whitney Hofman to put me up. I think it'd be best to ask him to get someone to second me. I don't really know anyone else." He knew some others as well as he knew Whit Hofman, but Caroline saw that what he meant was that Whit Hofman, being the richest and the impeccable young man of Gibbsville, was the only man of whom he would ask a favor. And so Ross was put up by Mr. Whitney Stokes Hofman, seconded by Mrs. Whitney Stokes Hofman; initiation fee $50, annual dues $25. Then she noticed that he was a bit on the stingy side. He always added restaurant charges before signing the checks. He rolled his own cigarettes, which may have been an honest preference in tobacco, but looked like an economy; and once after winning a few dollars in a bridge game at the club he pocketed his winnings with the remark: "That covers my gas and oil expenses this trip. Not bad." This somehow did not fit in with what you would expect of a man whose life work was "keeping the estate's affairs in shape. I have to. Mother doesn't know the multiplication table higher than the six-times table." Caroline began to see that she was right about his not being a coal-region rich man. Some of the things that made him himself were things that she liked—his manners, his manner, his way of walking into any party with a smile that was pleasant enough but at the same time said, "What have you got to offer me?" She liked the simple fact of his not ever trying to kiss her; she liked it and kept postponing her inquiry as to the reason for it. But by postponing that, for any and all inquiry, she did something else; she lost interest in him. The day came when she did not have to postpone the analysis of his diffidence, and she became merely satisfied with his diffidence. There was no showdown, because she let him see what had happened: she did not care if he never came to Gibbsville. She did not condone her behavior. She knew that her friends—and not only those of her own sex—were for the first time a little in awe of her, practically rediscovering her, because Ross Campbell so obviously was interested in her. She was sorry for her friends, who already were thinking of the New York and Boston ushers; and in a not quite sincere way, she was sorry for herself. After all, there had been six or seven times when she had liked him so enormously at particular moments that she wanted to get closer to him, to put her arms around him. But she never had, and the whole thing spilled away. It wasn't long before it became very, very easy to think of him as a stick, a stuffed shirt.

At the same time she was worried and angry with herself. There was something wrong and incomplete in her relations with all the men she had liked best and loved. They were wrong, and circumstances were wrong; Jerome Walker had been too decent because she was too young; Joe Montgomery was the man she had loved most in her life, but because of an engagement with other people, she had not seen him on the night before she sailed; Ross Campbell, who was not a great love but certainly was the right man for her to marry, had turned into nothing, right before her eyes. And there weren't any other men; led by Julian English there were a lot of men whom she had kissed or necked with, whom she disliked in retrospect with what approached a passion. Altogether she was contemptuous of the men she had known, no matter how tenderly she remembered minutes in automobiles, motorboats, trains, steamships; on divans or a few times on beds at house parties; on the porches of country clubs, in her own home. But she thought with anger that there was nothing of her that the race of men had not known—except that no one man ever had known her completely. Up to now the passion she had generated would have been enough to —she never finished that. She made up her mind to one thing: if she wasn't married by the time she was thirty, she was going to pick out some man and say, "Look here, I want to have a child," and go to France or some place and have the child. She knew she never *would* do that, but one part of her threatened another part of her with it.

Then, in the spring of 1926, she fell in love with Julian English, and she knew she never had loved anyone else. It was funny. Why, it was the funniest thing in the world. Here he was, taking her out, kissing her good night, ignoring her, seeing a lot of her and then not seeing her at all, going together to dancing school, kindergarten, Miss Holton's School—she'd known him all her life, had hidden his bicycle up a tree, wet her pants at one of his birthday parties, been bathed in the same tub with him by two older girls who now had children of their own. He had taken her to her first Assembly, he had put clay on her leg when a yellowjacket stung her, he had given her a bloody nose —and so on. For her there never had been anyone else. No one else counted. She was a little afraid that he still loved the Polish girl a little, but she was sure he loved Caroline the most.

They dodged being in love at first, and because they always had been friends, his seeing her increasingly more frequently did not become perceptible until he asked her to go with him to the July 3 Assembly. You asked a girl at least a month in advance for the Assemblies, and you asked the girl you liked best. It was the only one he ever freely had asked her to; she knew his mother told him to ask her to the very first one. The Assembly was not just another dance, and in the time between her accepting and the night of the dance they both were conscious of it. A girl gave preference in dates to the man who was taking her to the Assembly. "You're my girl now," he would say. "Or at least till after the Assembly." Or she would call him up and say: "Do you want to drive to Philadelphia with Mother and me? You're my beau now, so I thought I'd ask you first, but don't say yes unless you really want to." When he would kiss her she could tell he was trying to find out how much she knew. The long kisses in the beginning were like that; no overwhelming passion, but lazy and full of curiosity. They would halt in a long kiss and she would draw back her head and smile at him and he at her, and then without speaking he would put his mouth to hers again. He left it at kissing until one night when he brought her home from the movies and she went upstairs for a minute and saw that her mother was sound asleep. He was in the lavatory on the first floor and he heard her come down the back steps and try the kitchen door. They went to the library. "Do you want a glass of milk?" she said.

"No. Is that why you went to the kitchen?"

"I wanted to see if the maids were in."

"Are they?"

"Yes. The back door's locked." She put up her arms and he came in to them. He lay with his head on her shoulder for a few minutes and then she reached up and pulled the cord of the floor lamp, and moved in on the davenport so that he could lie beside her. He rolled up her sweater, up to her armpits, and unhooked her brassiere, and she unbuttoned his vest and he dropped it and his coat on the floor.

"Don't—don't go the limit, will you, sweetheart?" she said.

"Don't you want to?" he said.

"More than anything in the world, my darling love. But I can't. I never have. I will for you, but not here. Not—you know. I want to in bed, when everything is right for it."

"You never have?"

"Not all the way. Don't let's talk about it. I love you and I want you all the way, but I'm afraid to here."

"All right."

"Do that. Ah, Ju. Why are you so nice to me? No one else could be so darling to me. Why are you?"

"Because I love you. I always loved you."

"Oh, love! Sweetheart?"

"What, darling?"

"I can't help it. Have you got a thing? You know?"

"Yes."

"Do you think it'd be all right? I'm so afraid, but it's just as wrong to stop, isn't it? Isn't it just as wrong to stop?"

"Yes, darling."

"I'm so crazy about. . . ."

6

THERE WERE Lute and Irma Fliegler, Willard and Bertha Doane, Walter and Helen Schaeffer, Harvey and Emily Ziegenfuss, Dutch (Ralph) and Frannie Snyder, Vic and Monica Smith, and Dewey and Lois Hartenstein. From where he sat, at the side and to the rear of the orchestra, practically in the drummer's lap, Al Grecco could see them all. He knew all the men by sight, and Lute Fliegler and Dutch Snyder he knew by their first names, and the others he knew to say hello to without his using any name on them and without their calling him Al or Grecco or anything but Hyuh. He knew Irma Fliegler to speak to; he called her Mrs. Fliegler. He knew Frannie Snyder to speak to; he could have called her Frannie or Baby or practically anything that came into his mind, but he never said more than hello, with a distant nod, to her. What the hell; she was married, even if that was no bargain she was married to that Dutch, and for all Al knew she had been straight as a dye (Al sometimes wondered how straight as a dye was; a dye wasn't straight) for close on to two years. So there was no sense speaking to her. That loud-mouthed punk she was married to, if he saw her speaking to Al Grecco there was no telling what he would think. And do. And anyhow, you couldn't judge a baby by just one night two years ago. Maybe that had been the only time she ever cheated on that loudmouth, and you couldn't hold that against her. She had been the easiest job of work Al ever had, or one of the easiest. He had known her in sisters' school and then as they grew up he hadn't seen much of her around town; just see her on the street now and then, and she'd say "Hello, Tony Murascho," and he'd say "Hello, Frances." And he read in the paper where she got married to Dutch Snyder and he felt sorry for her, because he knew what Dutch was: a loud-mouthed Kluxer, who was always getting his face pushed in for making cracks about the Catholic church, but was always trying to get dates with Catholic girls—and getting them. When Al read about the marriage he figured Frances had got herself knocked up, but he was wrong: what had happened was that Frances's father, Big Ed Curry, the cop, had caught his daughter and Snyder in an awkward position and had given Snyder the choice of marriage or death. Al did not know this. He did know that it wasn't long after the marriage before Dutch, who was known as Ralphie to some of the girls at the Dew Drop Inn, was around the Dew Drop again, a sucker for cigarette money and one of the most unpopular customers of the institution. So one afternoon, two years before the night at the Stage Coach, Al was driving through Collieryville and he saw Frances waiting for a bus and he stopped his car. "You want a ride?" he said.

"No—oh, it's you, Tony," she said. "Are you going back to town?"

"Nothing else but," said Al. "Get in."

"Well, I don't know—"

"Okay. No skin off my ass," he said, and reached for the door to close it.

"Oh, I don't mean—I'll go with you. Only, will you leave me off somewhere—"

"Get in and do the talking on the way," he said.

She got in and he gave her a cigarette. She had been to her grandmother's in Collieryville and she wanted a cigarette and accepted a drink and was easily persuaded to go for a short ride. The short ride was short enough: half a mile off the main road between Gibbsville and Collieryville to a boathouse on the Colliery Dam. There was something queer about the whole thing, like going with your cousin or somebody. He had known Frances as a little girl in school, and then all of a sudden one day you discover that she is a woman that has had her experience and all that—it was queer. It was like finding money on the street; you didn't have to earn it, work for it, go on the make for it. And she must have felt the same way, because if there was ever an easy lay she was it—that day. But she said on the way home: "If you ever tell anybody this I'll kill you. I mean it." And you could see she did. And she refused to see him again and told him never to call her up or try to see her. She was a little sorry, what she had done, but he could not be sure that even that was not putting on an act. He often thought of it. He thought of it now, watching her watching Dutch dancing with Emily Ziegenfuss, with his leg rammed in between the Ziegenfuss woman's legs and trying to make out as if he was just dancing like anyone else. The son of a bitch. Frannie was all right. Al liked Frannie. But that Dutch—he'd like to paste him one. That was the trouble: women (he did not call them women, or girls, but another name which he used for all female persons except nuns) nearly always got the dirty end of the stick. Only once in a while they got a right guy, like Fliegler, for instance.

Then he began to feel a little angry at Irma Fliegler. He wondered whether she appreciated what a right guy she was married to. Probably not. She probably just took him for granted. That was the other side of it: a woman married a louse that beat her and cheated on her, and she got so she took that for granted; and another woman married a real guy, a square shooter from the word go, and she didn't see anything unusual about that. Al almost but not quite reached the opinion that all women are so used to getting the dirty end of the stick that they took it for granted when they did get it, and took it for granted they were going to get it when they didn't. The hell with them. He wanted to forget about them.

But that was not possible here, at the Stage Coach. It was a woman's place. All dance places, night clubs, road houses, stores, churches, and even whorehouses—all were women's places. And probably the worst kind of woman's place was a place like this, where men put on monkey suits and cut their necks with stiff collars and got drunk without the simple fun of getting drunk but with the presence of women to louse things up. Wherever there was an orchestra there were women, you could always be sure of that. Women singing the first words of songs: I got rhythm, Three little words, You're driving me crazy, Thinking of you dear, My heart is sad and lonely for you I pine for you dear only I'd gladly surrender. "Surrender my ass!" said Al Grecco, and looked across his table at Helene Holman, whom he hated now a thousand times worse than he ever hated anyone in his whole life. All evening long he had been hating. In the early part of the evening he had hated the job Ed Charney had given him, the job of keeping tabs on Helene. She knew what he was there for all right, and she took it out on him, she took it out on him that Ed was staying home with his kid. And wife. She was the only person he could think of who had open contempt for him, and tonight it was worse than ever. "This is a swell way for you to be spending Christmas," she said. And went on from there; why didn't he get himself fixed up? What kind of a life did he lead? Was he nothing but a yes-man? Was he a unique? Did he know what a unique was? A unique, she told him, was a morphadite. . . . And he had had to take it for a couple of hours, getting no rest from her except when she would get up to sing a song. But then along about ten or eleven she began to lose her spunk. She got a little tired of panning him and she took a different attitude.

She was wearing a dress that was cut in front so he could all but see her belly-button, but the material, the satin or whatever it was, it held close to her body so that when she stood up she only showed about a third of each breast. But when she was sitting down across the table from him she leaned forward with her elbows on the table and her chin in her hands, and that loosened the dress so that whenever she made a move he could see the nipples of her breasts. She saw him looking—he couldn't help looking. And she smiled.

"You wouldn't want to get your teeth knocked down your throat, would you?" he said.

"And by who, may I ask?" she said.

"You wouldn't want them nice molars all smashed, would you?"

"Aw-haw. Big talk. Little Allie is sore because—"

"Never mind about little Allie, baby. I'm telling you something for your own good. A word to the wise is sufficient."

"I'm shaking all over," she said.

He suddenly did not desire her, but he weakened in another way. "Cut it out, will you? I'm not here because I want the job. You ought to know that by now."

Her eyes stabbed at him. "All right, then, scram. Get outa here and leave me have some fun. My God."

"Sure. Scram. Are you off your nut? Where would I go? I'd have to go plenty far if I went outa here before I get my orders. Plenty. I wouldn't even get outa here. Wuddia think that French bastard would be doing when I left? Dya think he'd leave me go? He *would* not."

"Oh, no?" said Helene.

That was interesting. It sounded as though the Fox had been making passes at Helene, which Al had suspected for a long time. But he didn't care about that now. All he cared about now was for Helene to behave herself so he wouldn't get in a jam with Ed. "I got my orders," he said, "and I'm staying here whether I like it or not or whether you like it or not."

"So I see," she said.

"And my orders is to see that you keep your knees together, baby."

"Horse feathers," she said. "Well, is it all right if I have a drink?"

"No, it ain't all right if you have a drink. You got cockeyed once today."

"Well, then do you want to dance with me? I gotta do something besides get up there and give these butter and egg men hot pants, don't I?"

"No, I don't want to dance with you," he said. "That ain't my orders."

"Oh, you're afraid."

"All right," he said. "I'm afraid. If you want to leave it that way, I'm afraid."

She recognized the introduction to Body and Soul, which was one of the songs she sang. She walked slowly to the center of the orchestra platform.

"What does she call herself?" said Emily Ziegenfuss.

"Helene Holman," said Dewey Hartenstein.

"Holman? She has a nerve," said Emily.

"Why so?" said Vic Smith.

"Why, that's the name of a real singer. Libby Holman. Isn't that it? Libby? Or Liddy. No, Libby's right. Yes. Libby Holman. She makes records," said Emily.

"Well, she has as much right to the name as Libby Holman has," said Irma Fliegler.

"She has not," said Emily.

"She has so," said Irma. "Libby Holman isn't Libby *Holman's* real name."

"Oh," said Emily. "Well—how do you know, Irma?"

"Because I have these friends out in Cincinnati, Ohio, or at least they're friends of Lute's. Lute?"

"What?" said Lute.

"What was it those friends of yours in Cincinnati, Ohio, remember, they had that meningitis that took away their two children—"

"Spinal meningitis," said Lute, who had been talking with Willard Doane.

"I know that," said Irma. "What was their name?"

"Oh, Schultz. Harry Schultz. Why? Shall we call him up and tell him to join the party or what?"

"No, wisecracker. I wanted to know what Libby Holman's real name was. The singer."

"Oh, well, why didn't you ask me that in the first place?" said Lute.

"Well, come on, tell us what it was."

"Fred. Her right name was Fred," said Lute.

"Oh, bushwah on you," said Irma. "He never talks like anyone else. Anyhow these friends, these people named Schultz in Cleveland—"

"You just got through telling us it was Cincinnati," said Emily. "I don't think—"

"Cincinnati, then. All right, Cincinnati. Whatever city it is this Holman comes from. Anyhow, they came from the same town as her, and they told us her real name."

"Fred, I guess," said Emily. "Oh, I don't believe it. I don't think you know anything about it, if you asked me." Emily had had her fourth highball.

"She's good. I like her singing," said Frannie Snyder.

"You *like* it?" said Emily. "You mean you actually can sit there and say you like that kind of a voice? You must be crazy, Frannie."

"I like it all right," said Harvey Ziegenfuss.

"Oh, who asked you?" said Emily Ziegenfuss.

"Nobody asked me. Can't I express my opinions?"

"No. Who asked you for your opinions? Look at her. If she's going to sing why don't she sing, and if she's going to do a hootchy-kootchy dance then why don't she do it? But at least she ought to make up her mind. She's like a burlesque show dancer."

"How do you know what a burlesque show dancer is like?" said Harvey Ziegenfuss.

"How do I know?" said his wife. "You ask me that? You, Harvey Ziegenfuss, ask me that? All right, I'll tell you. I know because you showed me. When we were first married you used to get me to get undressed one by one, one thing after another. That's how I know."

Everyone, except Harvey Ziegenfuss, laughed. "Aw, you're nuts," he said. But that only made them laugh a little more.

"Drinks!" shouted Lute Fliegler. "Emily, how 'bout you? Dutch, you're ready for another. Frannie, you could stand it. Vic, what's the matter with you? Not drinking?"

"I'm going easy," said Vic Smith.

"You better, too, Lute Fliegler," said Irma Fliegler.

"No worse than a bad cold, Vic," said Lute. "What was that strange noise I heard?" He held his ear in the direction of Irma.

"You heard what I said. You better go easy yourself. Vic's right."

"No worse than a bad cold," said Lute. "You're not a man till you had it once. Dewey, how about you? You know what the governor of North Carolina said to the governor of *West* Virginia."

"You mean the governor of *South* Carolina," said Emily.

"You meant North Dakota," said Lute. "Come on, let's get drunk, people."

"I'm cockeyed already," said Dewey Hartenstein.

"I'm getting an edge on myself," said Harvey Ziegenfuss.

"Oh, you. Who asked you?" said Emily Ziegenfuss.

"Hey, there, Ziegenfusses, quit necking right out in public," said Lute. "Wait till you get home."

"Here's to good old Yale," said Dutch Snyder, who had been All-

Scholastic guard on the Gibbsville High championship team back in 1914, the year Gibbsville beat both Reading *and* Allentown.

"Embrace me, my sweet embraceable you. Embrace me, my irreplaceable you, *la* la, *la* la, *la* la, *la* la, *la* dada, da, um, ha, um ha, um ha, um ha, *lum* dada da." Monica Smith was singing.

"Low-zee," said Emily. "Our cat sings better than that."

"Embrace me, my sweet embraceable you," Monica sang. "Embrace me la la replaceable you. Don't be a naughty baby. Come to papa, come to papa do. My sweet embraceable you."

"Everybody got their drink? Emily," said Lute, "what you need is a drink."

"Yeah," said Harvey Ziegenfuss. "What she needs is a drink. Yeah."

"Sure she does," said Lute. "I didn't say of what, did I?"

"Carbolic acid, I suggest," said Monica Smith.

"Oh, cut fighting, you two," said Helen Schaeffer, who up to this time had taken no part in the conversation.

"Another country heard from!" said Emily.

"Who wants to dance? I got rhythm, I got rhythm!" sang Dutch Snyder.

"Yeah. You got rhythm. You said it you got rhythm," said Emily.

"Well, come on, what's holding you?" said Dutch.

"Frannie," said Emily.

"I am not," said Frannie. "Go ahead and dance with him if you want to." In a slightly lower tone she added: "You like it."

"What you say?" said Emily.

"I said you like it. Go ahead and dance with him," said Frannie.

"All right," said Emily. "I *will* dance with him. Come on, Dutch."

"Let's go," said Dutch. "I got sweet dreams in green pas-tures."

The others, except Lute and Frannie, chose or were somehow maneuvered into taking partners. Lute got up and moved to a chair beside Frannie.

"That Emily Ziegenfuss," she said. "What does she think she is? I know what *I* think she is."

"Uh-huh. Don't say it," said Lute, "don't say it. If there's one thing I don't like, I don't like to hear one woman call another a bitch."

"Well, that's what she is, all right," said Frannie. "It's partly your fault, too, Lute. You know she can't drink. Why do you keep on giving her drinks?"

"She'd be just as bad on two as she is on four or five," he said. He dropped the levity for a moment. "The only thing to do now is make her pass out. She will."

"Well, she can't pass out any too soon for me," said Frannie. "And that husband of hers, that Harvey. Trying to give me a feel under the table. Honestly! Can you imagine that? Just because she makes a fool out of him he thinks because Dutch is a sap, I guess he thinks that gives him the right to try to paw over me."

"I don't blame him," said Lute. "I'd like a little of that myself."

"Oh, you," said Frannie, but pleased. "Gee, if they were all like you, married men I mean, it wouldn't be so bad. Anyhow I burnt Mr. Ziegenfuss with a cigarette. He thought he was getting along fine and then I reached down and pushed the lighted end of the cigarette on the back of his hand."

"Oh, swell. I saw him kind of jump there for a minute."

"He jumped all right," said Frannie. She sipped her drink and she was looking round the room, over the rim of the glass. "Say, look," she said. "Isn't that your boss there, just coming in?"

"My God! Yes," said Lute. "Oh, and has he a nice package?"

"I'll say. That's his wife with him, isn't it?"

"That's her, all right," said Lute. "That's funny. They were supposed to go to the dance at the country club tonight. I know that for sure."

"Oh, that's nothing," said Frannie. "They often come here when they get tired of the club dances. I often heard them talking when I go to have my hair waved. They often leave the country club dances."

"He's nice and drunk, all right," said Lute.

"He doesn't look so drunk," said Frannie. "I've seen a lot worse."

"Yes, but that boy can drink. When he's that way you can tell he had plenty. He can drink all night without showing it. When he shows it, boy, you can be pretty sure he has damn near a quart under his belt."

"That's Carter Davis with him," said Frannie.

"I know. Carter Davis, and I can't see who the girl is."

"I can't either, but wait a minute. Oh, it's Kitty Hofman. Yeah. Kitty Hofman, and there comes Whitney Hofman. I guess he was parking the car."

"Yeah. I guess he was parking the car. I wonder if English drove," said Lute.

"Oh, I don't imagine so," said Frannie. "Not if Whitney Hofman had to park the car."

"You can't be so sure about that. English gets that way sometimes. He can always drive when he's stinko, but a big thing like parking the car—no, sir. That's asking too much."

"Well, they got a good table," said Frannie. "Look at that old Frenchman, What's His Name, moving that Taqua crowd around to make room for English."

"To make room for Hofman, you mean," said Lute.

"Oh, of course. I didn't think of that. I like that Whitney Hofman. He's so democratic."

"Well, I guess if I had fourteen million bucks I imagine I'd be democratic, too. He can afford it," said Lute.

"What are you talking about, Lute?" said Frannie. "They're the ones that you never see democratic, those with the money."

"No, you're wrong there. The ones with the dough, the big dough, they're always democratic," said Lute.

"Oh, you have everything upside down," said Frannie. "The ones that have a lot of money, they're the ones you always think of as being the high-hat ones."

"Not me, Frannie. I always think of the ones that really have more money than I'd know what to do with, I think of them as the democratic ones. If you don't have money you're not democratic. You don't have to be democratic. You just act natural and nobody ever thinks of it as democratic or anything else. It's like a story I heard about Jim Corbett."

"Jim Corbett? Is he the one that's staying at Y.M.C.A.? The electric engineer?"

"Hell, no. His name is Corbin. No, Jim Corbett was the fighter, heavyweight champion. They used to call him Gentleman Jim."

"Oh, Gentleman *Jim*. Oh, I heard of him. I always thought he was some kind of a crook. I heard of him all right. What's the story?"

"Well, when he was here two years ago—"

"Was he here? In Gibbsville? I never knew that," said Frannie.

"Yes, he was here for a banquet. Anyhow, one of the reporters got to talking to him about his title of Gentleman Jim, and he told the story about how he was in the subway in New York or something and somebody started pushing him around—no, that's the one about Benny Leonard. Wait a minute. Oh, yes. This is it. Somebody was asking him why he was always so polite to everybody. He is the politest man in the world, I guess, and he said, 'Well, when you've been heavyweight champion of the world, gentlemen, you can afford to be polite.'"

"What did he mean by that?" said Frannie.

"*What!*" said Lute. "Let it go, Frannie. It isn't that important."

"Well, I just don't see what that has to do with Whitney Hofman being democratic. I think he's very democratic."

"I think you better have a shot," said Lute.

"Am I dumb or something?" she said. "You act as though I said something dumb or nay-eeve."

"Not at all. You want ginger ale with yours, or straight?" said Lute.

"I'll have a straight one I guess, then you can give me another in a highball."

"That's talking," said Lute. "Oh. Don't look right away, but I think we're going to have a little company. You can look now."

"You mean English? He's coming over. Introduce me to him, will you?"

"Sure. If he ever makes it," said Lute.

Julian English had stood up and looked around the room and had recognized Lute Fliegler. Immediately he told Caroline and Kitty and Whit and Carter that he had to talk to Lute. Matter of business that couldn't wait. He excused himself and began to make his way, assisting himself by taking hold of the backs of chairs and people's shoulders, to the table where Lute and Frannie were seated.

He extended his hand to Lute. "Luther, I came all the way over here to wish you a happy birthday. All the way over here. Happy birthday, Luther."

"Thanks, boss. Will you sit down and have a drink with us? This is Mrs. Snyder. Mrs. Snyder, this is Mr. English."

"I'm pleased to meet you," said Frannie, and began to get up.

"Not leaving?" said Julian.

"Oh, no," said Frannie. "I'll stay."

"Very good. Very, very good. Very good. Luther, I came over here to talk to you on a matter of business—no, sit down, Mrs. Snyder. Please sit down. You can hear what I have to say. Luther, have you any Scotch?"

"No, I only have rye, I'm sorry to say."

"What of it?" said Julian. "Who is that man over there, Luther?"

"Where?"

"The one that's staring at us. I think he's dead. Did you ever hear the story about the dead man in the subway, Luther?"

"No, I don't think I did."

"Lucky boy. Lucky boy, Luther. I always said you were a fine fellow. Are you having a good time?"

"Pretty good."

"How about you, Mrs. Snyder? Have I the name right?"

"Yes, that's right, Mr. English. I'm having a pretty good time."

"Well, I'm not. Or at least not till I came to this table. Are you married, Mrs. Snyder?"

"Yes, I'm married."

"She's Dutch Snyder's wife," said Lute.

"Oh. Oh, of *course*. Of course. Dutch Snyder. Well, I'll be God damned. What ever became of old Dutch? I haven't seen old Dutch in years."

"He's dancing," said Frannie.

"Dancing, is he? He was always a great one for dancing, was our Dutch. So you married Dutch. How nice. How jolly. Do you think Dutch has any Scotch, Luther?"

"No, he only has rye, too," said Lute.

"What of it? Is that any my business who has rye or who has Scotch? Wellp. I think I have to leave you now, my friends. It's been a great little visit and I want to tell you I enjoyed every minute of it. You be nice to Mrs. Snyder, Luther. She is my ideal woman. But now I have to go. I see little Al Grecco over there and I think if I play my cards right I could get a drink of Scotch out of him. I understand he knows a fellow that can get it for you."

"So I hear," said Lute.

Julian stood up. "Mrs. Snyder—a pleasure. A pleasure indeed. Luther —I'll see you some other time. Luther and I work together, Mrs. Snyder. We're buddies. He's my buddy, and I'm his buddy. He's my buddy, I'm her Joe. Ju. If a buddy, meet a buddy, looking for the Scutch. If a buddy, meet a buddy, how's my old friend Dutch? Auf wiedersehen."

"Auf wiedersehen," said Lute.

Julian moved away, and they saw him sitting down at Al Grecco's table, in Helene Holman's chair. Helene was singing Love for Sale: "Let the poets pipe of love in their childish way; we know every type of love better far than they. . . ."

"Don't get up, Al, don't get up," said Julian.

"Oh, that's all right," said Al Grecco.

"I wanted to see you on a business proposition," said Julian.

"Well," said Al, rising, "I guess we can—"

"Oh—" Julian put a hand on Al's shoulder. "Sit down, sit down. We can talk here. I wanted to know if you knew anybody that could let me have some Scotch."

"Why, sure," said Al. "What's the matter? Don't Lebrix know you? He ought to. I'll fix it right away. Waiter! Eddie!"

"No, no," said Julian. "I can get it here all right. They'll sell it to me. But I don't want to buy it. I simply don't want to buy drinks, Al. If there's anything I don't want to do it's buy a drink. I'll buy *you* a drink.

I'll buy—oh, that man over there, I'll buy him a drink. But I don't want to buy a drink. See what I mean?"

"No. I don't exactly see what you mean, Mr. English."

"Just call me Mr. English, Al. You call me Mr. English and I'll call you Al. The hell with this formality. We've known each other all our lives. You know, we Gibbsville people, we have to stick together in a place like this. If we don't you know what happens? Those Hazleton people gang us. What was I talking about just before you said that?"

"What?"

"Oh, yeah. About drinks. Uh, if I don't want to do anything it's buy a drink. You know why? You want to know why I feel that way?"

"Sure."

"Well, it's like love, Al," said Julian. "You know what I mean? Or don't you see what I mean? You buy a drink, and that's all it is, just a bought drink. Whereas, on the other hand, au contraire, au contraire, Al, uh, you uh, uh, somebody gives you a drink and that's like love. Why, say, who is this?"

"You got my chair, Mister," said Helene Holman, who had finished her song.

"Not at all," said Julian. "Sit right down. Don't apologize. Just sit down. If this is your chair you needn't apologize. Just sit right down and Al will get another chair for us, won't you, Al?"

Al pulled a chair from another table.

"Shake hands with Mr. English," said Al. "He's a friend of Ed's."

"Are you a friend of Ed's?" said Julian to Helene.

"Yes, I guess you'd call it that," said Helene.

"Fine," said Julian. "Ed who?"

"Ed Charney," said Al.

"Oh-h-h. Ed *Char*ney," said Julian. "Well, my God, why didn't you say so? My God. Jesus Christ Almighty, why didn't you say so? I didn't think you were a friend of Ed *Char*ney's. My God."

"What Ed did you think he meant?" said Helene.

"Oh, I don't know. Do we have to go into that?" said Julian. "What's your name?"

"Helene Holman," she said.

"Oh, yes, yes," said Julian. "What? Will you say that again, please?"

"Helene, Hol-man," she repeated.

"Oh. Helene *Hol*man. You're the one that married Dutch Snyder. How is old Dutch? Does he still dance as much as ever?"

"I never heard of him," said Helene.

"Neither—did—I," said Julian. "You're my pal. Neither did I. And

I don't want to again. My goodness that's a nice gown you have on."

"I like it," she said, smiling at Al.

"Miss Holman is a very, very good friend of Ed Charney's," said Al.

"That's fine. I like that," said Julian. "And I'll tell you something else. *I'm* a very *very* good friend of Ed Charney's."

"Oh, I know," said Al. "I was just telling you, Miss Holman is, too. A very good friend. You know what I mean?"

"You don't have to draw a map, do you?" said Helene.

"You mean—Miss Holman is Ed's mistress? Is that what you mean?" said Julian.

"Yes, that's what he means," said Helene.

"Well, I don't know what to say," said Julian, and then: "Except—I do like that dress. I like that dress."

"I like it," said Helene.

"So do I," said Julian. "How about you, Al? What's your opinion on Miss Holman's dress? Come on, speak up."

"It's all right," said Al. "It's all right."

"I should say it is," said Julian. "How about dancing, Miss Holman?"

"She's tired," said Al.

"Well, in that case, she better go to bed," said Julian.

"Hey," said Al.

"What do you want?" said Julian.

"Nothing. Only remember what I told you about Miss Holman and Ed," said Al.

"My friend, I've already forgotten that little bit of gossip," said Julian. "I'm not a bit interested in Miss Holman's affairs, am I, Miss Holman?"

"Not a bit."

"Right," said Julian. "So let's dance."

"Check and double check," said Helene, and got up and went to the dance floor with Julian.

Everyone in the big room watched them. She was a gool dancer, and so was Julian. And they *danced*, which was a kind of disappointment to several persons, who expected another kind of exhibition. It also was a kind of surprise to Helene, and a kind of surprise to Al Grecco. When they sat down again Al relaxed and was able to laugh at the things Julian said. Presently they were joined by Carter Davis. After he was introduced he said: "Caroline wants you."

"I happen to know she doesn't," said Julian.

"Well, she does," said Carter.

"Carter, sit down before there's an ugly scene," said Julian.

Carter hesitated, and then sat down. "All right," he said, "but only for a minute. Ju, you've got to—"

"Did you all meet my friend Mr. Davis?" said Julian.

"Yes."

"Yes."

"Yes, they met me," said Carter.

"So they did," said Julian. "Well, let's talk about something else. Books. Uh, Miss Holman, have you read *The Water Gipsies?*"

"No. I don't believe I have," said Helene. "What is it about?"

"I haven't the faintest idea," said Julian. "I got it for Christmas, or rather a member of my family did."

"A member of your family," said Carter.

"Yes, a member of my family," said Julian. "My wife, Miss Holman. Mr. Davis, this is Mr. Davis right here, he gave my wife *The Water Gipsies* for Christmas. What did you give me, pal?"

"You know what I gave you," said Carter.

"Of course I do, and I'm a bastard for not remembering it." Julian leaned forward to explain to Helene and Al: "Mr. Davis gave me a tie, from Finchley's. All the way from Finchley's. Do you remember which tie you gave me, Carter?"

"Sure I do," said Carter.

"I'll bet you five dollars you don't," said Julian. "Al, you hold stakes. Here's my five. Is it a bet, Carter?"

"I don't want to take your money," said Carter.

"Oh, yes you do. Oh, yes you do. Put up your five bucks. There, Al. Now."

"How can we prove it?" said Julian. "Oh, I have an idea. You tell me what kind of tie it was, and then go over to Caroline and repeat the description of the tie, see? And if you're right she'll shake her head yes, and if you're wrong she'll—"

"She'll shake her head no," said Carter. "O.K." He got up and went over to the table.

"Do you want to dance some more?" said Julian.

"Don't you want to wait till your friend proves who won the bet?"

"The hell with him. I just did that to get rid of him," said Julian.

"But you lose five bucks," said Helene.

"Yeah, you lose five bucks," said Al.

"It's worth it," said Julian. "I got rid of him, didn't I? Come on, let's dance."

"Check and double check," said Helene. They ignored Al completely and went to the dance floor. "Is that your wife?" said Helene.

"Which one do you mean?" said Julian.

"Oh, I know Kitty Hofman," said Helene.

"Well, my wife is the other girl, yes," said Julian. "You're a swell dancer, or have I said that before?"

"No, you didn't say it before. You're not so bad yourself, Mr. English."

"Oh, call me Malcolm."

"Is that your name? Malcolm? I thought he—oh, you're giving me the razz. Okay."

"No, I'm sorry. My name is Julian. Call me Julian."

They said no more until the music stopped, and as they stood there, Julian applauding and Helene standing with her hands folded in front of her, he suddenly said: "Are you in love with any person?"

"Isn't that a personal question?" she said.

"Of *course* it is. *Are* you?"

"What makes you ask that all of a sudden?" she said.

"I wanted to know. I—" the music continued. "I wanted to ask you to go out with me. Will you?"

"When do you mean? Now?"

"Yes."

"It's awful cold out," she said.

"But you will?" he said.

"I don't know," she said. "I have a room here."

"No, I want to go outside. Out in the car."

"Well, maybe that'd be better. We can't stay long. I have to sing again in about a half an hour. Oh, I better not go. Your wife will see us, and so will Al."

"Will you go?" he said.

"Yes," she said.

They glided to the edge of the floor and broke into a walk and disappeared. Three persons, over and above all the others in the big room, saw them go. Three persons: Caroline, Al Grecco, Foxie Lebrix.

In a little while Julian fell asleep in the car, and Helene went back to the house by herself. It was long after three when Julian felt himself being shaken and came slowly half awake. "Wha'?" he said.

"Don't wake him up," someone said.

"We have to wake him up to put his coat on. Come on, Ju. Snap to." It was Whit Hofman. "Come on."

"Here, let me," said Kitty Hofman. She started to get in the car.

"Get away," said her husband. "Come on, Ju. Carter, get in the other side. Here, take his coat. I'll hold him up and you put his coat around him and the two of us can put his arms in the sleeves."

"I know," said Kitty. "Let's put snow on his face."

"Oh, drop dead," said Whit.

"The snow might be a good idea," said Caroline.

"Who sai' pu' snow my face?" said Julian.

"Are you awake, Ju?" said Whit.

"Sure I'm 'wake," said Julian.

"Well, then, put your coat on," said Whit. "Here. Hold the other arm, Carter."

"I dowanna put my coat on. Why do I have pu' my coa' on? Hu? Who do I?"

"Because we're going home," said Whit.

"Go on, darling, put your coat on," said Kitty.

"Oh, hello, Kitty," said Julian. "How about a dance, Kitty?"

"No, we're leaving," said Kitty.

"Oh, get out of the way, Kitty, for Christ sake," said Whit.

"I think I'll go to sleep," said Julian.

"Come on, Julian. Snap out of it," said Caroline. "Everybody wants to go home and it's freezing out here. Put your coat on."

Without another word Julian put his coat on, scorning all assistance. "Where's my hat?" he said.

"We can't find it," said Whit. "The hat check girl said she must have given it to someone else by mistake. Lebrix said he'd buy you a new one."

"Turn your collar up," said Caroline.

Julian turned up the deep collar of the coat, which was a husky garment of raccoon skins. He slumped back in a corner of the car and pretended to go to sleep. Carter sat in the other corner and Kitty Hofman sat in the middle of the back seat. Caroline sat up front with Whit, who was driving Julian's car. The whooping of the wind and the biting crunch of the tire chains in the snow and the music of the motor were the only sounds that reached the five persons in the car. The married four understood that; that there was nothing to be said now.

Julian, lost in the coonskins, felt the tremendous excitement, the great thrilling lump in the chest and abdomen that comes before the administering of an unknown, well-deserved punishment. He knew he was in for it.

WHEN HE was a boy, Julian English once ran away from home. In a town the size of Gibbsville—24,032, estimated 1930 census—the children of the rich live within two or three squares of the children of parents who are not rich, not even by Gibbsville standards. This makes for a spurious democracy, especially among boys, which may or may not be better than no democracy at all. In any case, in order to get a ball game going the sons of the Gibbsville rich had to play with the sons of the non-rich. There were not even nine, let alone eighteen, boys of Julian's age among the rich, and so the rich boys could not even have their own team. Consequently, from the time he was out of kindergarten until he was ready to go away to prep school, Julian's friends were not all from Lantenengo Street. Carter Davis would stop for him, or he would stop for Carter, when they were going to play baseball or football. They would go down the hill to Christiana Street, the next street, and join the gang. The gang's members had for fathers a butcher, a motorman, a "practical" surveyor (that is, a surveyor who had not gone to college), a freight clerk, two bookkeepers for the coal company, a Baptist minister, a neighborhood saloonkeeper, a mechanic in a garage (which he called a garridge), and a perennial convict (who was up this time for stealing 100,000 cigarettes from the Gibbsville Tobacco Company).

These boys had enough to eat. They did not have to sell papers, although the minister's son sold subscriptions to *The Saturday Evening Post* and was always talking about blue vouchers or green vouchers and the Ranger bike he was going to get when he had enough vouchers. He was not available on certain days of the week, when he had to go to meetings of the other *Post* salesmen. He was an industrious boy, and his nasal Indiana twang and the fact that he was a stranger (he had come to Gibbsville when he was five) and was bright in school all helped to make him unpopular in the gang. You could always tell his voice from the others: it was high, and his enunciation was not sing-songy like the other boys', which showed strong Pennsylvania Dutch influence. Julian liked him least of all. Best of all he liked Walt Davis, the son of the cigarette thief. Walt was no relation to Carter. Walt was cross-eyed, which somehow made him handsome, or Julian thought so. In the nights preceding Hallowe'en it was Walt who remembered the various Nights: one night was Gate Night, when you took people's gates off the fences; another night was Tick-Tack Night, when you held a button through which string had been run and wound up, against window panes, making a very effective sound until the string ran down; another night was Paint Night, when you painted sidewalks and people's houses. On Hallowe'en you dressed up as ghosts and cowboys and Indians and women and men, and rang doorbells, and said: "Anything for Hallowe'en?" If the people gave you pennies or cakes, all right. If they didn't, you stuck a pin in the doorbell and threw the doormat out in the street and carried away the porch furniture and poured buckets of water on the porch so it would freeze in the night. Walt knew which Night was which; he got the information from his father.

The leader of the gang was Butch Doerflinger. He was fat and strong and brave. He had killed more copperheads than anyone else and was a better swimmer than anyone else and knew all about older people because he had watched his father and mother. They didn't mind, either. They thought it was funny. Julian was afraid of Butch, because Julian's mother had threatened to "report" Butch's father for beating his horse. Nothing ever came of it, and every year or two Butch's father would get a new horse.

There were things not to talk about in the gang: you did not talk about jail, because of Walt's father; nor about drunken men, because there was a saloonkeeper's son; nor about the Catholics, because the motorman's son and one bookkeeper's son were Catholic. Julian also was not allowed to mention the name of any doctor. These things did come up and were discussed pretty thoroughly, but usually in the absence of the boy whom the talk would embarrass. There was enough to talk about: girls; changes in boys which occurred at fourteen; parades, which would you rather have; if you had a million dollars what would you do; what were you going to be when you got big; is a horse better than a dog; what was the longest you'd ever been on a train; what was the best car; who had the biggest house; who was the dirtiest kid in school; could a policeman be arrested; were you going to college when you got big; what girl were you going to marry and how many children were you going to have; what was the most important instrument in the band; what position was most important on a baseball team; were all the Confederates dead; was the Reading better than the Pennsylvania railroad; could a blacksnake kill you. . . .

There were all sorts of things to be done. There was marbles, and there was a game of marbles called Dobbers, played with marbles the size of lemons. You played it in the gutter on the way home from school, throwing your Dobber at the other fellow's and he would throw his at yours. It wasn't much of a game except it made the way home from school seem short. Some days the gang would hop a wagon—preferably a packing-house wagon or a wholesale grocery wagon; coal wagons were too slow—and ride out to the state police barracks and watch the staties drill and shoot. The gang would go out on the mountain and play "Tarzan of the Apes," jumping around from tree to tree and skinning their behinds on the bark. You had to be careful on the mountains, careful of air-holes, which were treacherous, or supposed to be treacherous, places where the ground was undermined and liable to cave in. In the memory of the oldest citizen no life had been lost in Gibbsville as a result of a mine cave-in, but the danger was there. There was a game called Run, Sheepie, Run, and sometimes the gang would play Ku Klux Klan, after having seen "The Birth of a Nation." Games that had their source in a movie would be played and played for days and then dropped and forgotten, to be revived months later, unsuccessfully. The gang had a Fisk Bicycle Club for a while. You were supposed to have Fisk tires on your bike, and that made you eligible to send away to the Fisk people and get pennants and caps and all the other stuff; buttons, books of instructions on wig-wag and so on. Julian's father made him buy two Fisk tires, and Carter Davis had one Fisk tire, but these were the only Fisk tires in the gang. The other members of the gang were saving up to buy Pennsylvania Vacuum Cups, and meanwhile when they had a puncture they filled the tire with Neverleak. There were cigarettes to be smoked: Ziras, Sweet Caps, Piedmonts, Hassans. Julian sometimes bought Condax cigarettes, which were more expensive. Butch and Julian were the heavy smokers of the gang, but Julian liked the smell of someone else's cigarette better than he liked smoking, and he discovered that smoking did not get him in better with Butch. He stopped after a year, using the excuse that his father had detected the nicotine stains on his fingers. Sometimes the gang would sit on the rocks on the mountain and watch the coal trains coming down the valley from the east, and they would count the cars: seventy-eight battleship cars was the highest number they ever saw and agreed upon. Sometimes they would go down in the valley and when the train slowed up or stopped at Gibbsville Junction they would get on and ride four miles to Alton or the five miles to Swedish Haven. It was a cold and dangerous ride, and about once a year some boy would fall off and lose a leg or be killed under the wheels, but the practice of hopping coalies went on. It was not wise to go beyond Swedish Haven, because after that the railroad veered off too far from the highway. There was a coalie that slowed down at Gibbsville Junction every day at about three-fifteen, and it reached Swedish Haven at four o'clock, which usually gave the gang time enough to get home, either by bumming rides on the grocery wagons or stealing rides on the trolley cars, or walking. You could get home only moderately late for supper.

There was one other game that Julian did not like, because he was afraid of the consequences. That was known simply as Five-Finger Grab. There were two five-and-ten stores, Woolworth's and Kresge's, in Gibbsville, and about once a month after school the gang would wander through the stores. Sometimes they would not take a thing, usually because they were watched carefully by the clerks and the manager, whose office was placed so that he could look down on every counter. But sometimes after a tour of the store the gang would meet, and two or three of the boys would say: "Look what I got," and show what they had got in the Five-Finger Grab: pencils, magnifying glasses, screw drivers, pliers, spools of wire, nickel Rocket baseballs, hard candy, school tablets, toys, cotton gloves, friction tape—these were some of the things that would be produced by the proud-five-finger grabbers. The other boys would be ashamed, and the next time they went to the store everyone would try to get something.

Julian at first would refuse to participate in the Five-Finger Grab, but when Carter Davis abandoned his side and went over to the grabbers, Julian had to do something. Once he tried to buy something—a jar of hard candy—to be able to show something after a grab, but he could not do this often; he was not given much money. A quarter a week was his allowance, and he had to have a nickel on Friday and a nickel on Saturday for two movie serials he was following, and that meant he could not buy much at the five-and-ten if he wanted to have a cinnamon bun and pickle, two cents, at recess. And so he became a five-finger grabber.

He was very successful, and when he saw how successful he was he wanted to do it all the time. Most of the other fellows in the gang stole only for the sake of stealing; that explained why some of them, emptying their pockets after a grab, would pull out white feet for women's stockings, baby rattles, cards of safety pins, wash cloths, soap, and other useless articles. But Julian became so proficient that he could tell beforehand what he was going to get, and usually he would get it. The gang would separate on entering the store, and there would be so many boys wandering around that it was hard to keep track of them.

Julian did not know that he was being watched. He had been watched for a long time, and the manager saw that Julian was not taking things and stopped watching him. But when he began to have success as a grabber the salesgirls learned to keep on the lookout for him. They knew who he was; a Lantenengo Street kid, who did not have to steal. Several of them reported him to the manager, who thereafter forgot all about the other kids in order to keep an eye on Julian.

One day after school the gang decided to have a Five-Finger Grab, and they all trooped down to Kresge's. When they entered the store a bell rang, but they paid no attention to it; bells were always ringing in the store—signals to cash girls, signals to the assistant managers and floorwalkers and stock boys. Bells were always ringing. Julian had announced beforehand that he would get a flashlight for Butch, in return for which Butch was going to steal a large hunk of summer sausage from the Doerflinger meat market. Not just an ordinary *slice*, that he could get for the asking, but a hunk at least a foot long.

The flashlight came as a case, battery, and lamp: ten cents for each part, thirty cents altogether. The electrical supplies counter was very near the front door, and Julian went right to it. The girl standing in front of the counter—the clerks stood in front of counters that were against the walls—asked him what he wanted, and he said he was only waiting for a friend who had gone to another part of the store. She looked at him without saying anything and kept looking at him. Well, he was not going to let her scare him, and he could outsmart her. He took out a package of Ziras, put one in his mouth, and pretended to reach in his pocket for a match, but all the cigarettes dropped to the floor, as Julian planned. The girl automatically leaned over, which was more than Julian had counted on—he merely wanted to distract her. He too leaned over, and as he did his right hand reached over the counter and he had the flashlight in his pocket before he began to pick up the cigarettes. "No smoking in here," the girl said.

"Who said so?" said Julian, and at that moment his arm was grabbed tight.

"I saw you, you little thief!" It was the manager. "I saw you take that flashlight. Miss Loftus, go get the policeman."

"Yes, sir," said the girl.

"I'll show you. I'll fix your feet for you," said the manager. Julian tried to reach in his pocket to get rid of the flashlight. "Oh, no you don't," said Mr. Jewett. "That flashlight stays right in your pocket till the policeman comes. I'll put a stop to this. Little highbrow, eh? Doctor English's son. Lantenengo Street boy. Well."

Quickly there was a crowd around, and some of the fellows were in the crowd. They were frightened, and a couple of them left, which gave Julian a sinking feeling but he did not blame them, and he was glad to see that Butch and Carter stayed.

"Go on away, you people," said Mr. Jewett. "I'll settle this." The group slowly moved away, and that was the chance Butch had been waiting for. He moved closer to Jewett and said:

"What did he do, Mister?"

"Never you mind what he did. You know damn well what he did," said Jewett.

Butch kicked Jewett square in the shin and ran, and so did Julian. They got out of the store and ran to the left, knowing that Leffler, the policeman, would be coming from the 'squire's office, at the right. They ran down one street, up another, down another, until they came to the railroad freight yards. "Jesus, I never ran so much in all my life yet," said Butch.

"Me either," said Julian.

"It's good I gave him a kick," said Butch.

"You bet. If you didn't I'd be there yet. What would they do?"

"I do' know. Send you to reformatory, I guess. I guess me too now maybe," said Butch.

"Gee," said Julian.

"What'll we do now?" said Butch.

"Gee. I do' know. What should we?"

"Well, if you go home—they know who you are at the store—so if you go home they'll have the cop, Leffler, he'll wait there for you."

"Do you think they will?" said Julian.

"Sure. He'll arrest you and the 'squire'll send you to reformatory till you're eighteen years old yet."

"Honest?" said Julian.

"That's right," said Butch.

"I won't go to any reformatory. I'll run away before I do that."

"Me too," said Butch. "I'm instigated."

"Oh," said Julian.

"I'm instigated because I kicked Jewett in the shins and that makes me instigated the same as you are."

"Well, I won't go to any reformatory. They won't catch me and send me to any reformatory. I'll run away before I get put away," said Julian.

"Well, what will we do?" said Butch.

Julian thought a minute. He watched them making up a train; the shifting engine collecting cars from all over the yard and backing them into a track near where they were sitting. "Let's hop the freight and run away?" said Julian.

"Gee," said Butch. "I don't know where they go. A coalie you know where it goes and you can get off down at the Haven, but a freight."

"We gotta do something. We don't want to get sent away to reformatory, do we?" said Julian.

"Yes, but who wants to hop a freight that they don't know where it's going. Philly, maybe, without stopping," said Butch.

"Philly without stopping! You're crazy. You know more about trains than that. It'll stop all right. They have to put water in the engine tender, don't they? They have to put on more cars and take them off, don't they? Don't they? Anyhow, what do we care where it's going? It's better than the reformatory, isn't it? Do you know what they do there?"

"No."

"Sure you do. They have priests there, Catholics, and they beat you and make you go to church every morning at five o'clock. That's what I hear."

"From who did you hear that? Who from?" said Butch.

"From—oh, lots of fellows told me that. I know it for a fact. That came from somebody that knows all about it and I'm not allowed to tell you his name. So will you go? We can sell papers in Philly. I was there often and they have fellows the same age as us selling papers there, so so can we. Younger than us. I've seen little kids I bet they weren't more than about nine and a half years old, they were selling papers right in the Bellevue-Stratford."

"Aw," said Butch.

"They were so," said Julian. "I bet you don't even know what the Bellevue-Stratford is. Where is it?"

"In Philly. Anybody knows that."

"But *what* is it?"

"Oh, I don't know. You don't know everything."

"See? You don't know. Well, it's the hotel where we always stay—" Julian was brought up then to the fact that if he was going to Philadelphia, this time he was not going to stay at the Bellevue-Stratford. "Well, are you going with me?"

"I guess so."

They waited until the train was beginning to move, and then they got on the front platform of the caboose. They had to get off a couple of times at way stations, and finally they were caught. They were turned over to the railroad police in Reading, and were brought back to Gibbsville on the "late train." Butch Doerflinger the elder, and Dr. English were standing on the platform of the Gibbsville station when the train pulled in. The elder Doerflinger had made many, too many, remarks about his son being a chip off the old block, and he was amused and a little proud of his son. "Only twelve years old yet and hopping freights already. By Jesus, you don't know what kids are today, say, Doc?" His plans were made: a good beating for young Butch and make him work on the delivery wagon every day.

But William Dilworth English, M.D., was not thinking of the immediate punishment of his son; that was something which could be decided upon. He was not thinking of the glory of having a son who hopped freight trains. The thing that put him in the deep mood and gave him the heavy look that Julian saw on his face was that "chip off the old block" refrain of Butch Doerflinger's. William Dilworth English was thinking of his own life, the scrupulous, notebook honesty; the penny-watching, bill-paying, self-sacrificing honesty that had been his religion after his own father's suicide. And that was his reward: a son who turned out to be like his grandfather, a thief.

Julian never stole anything else, but in his father's eyes he was always a thief. In college Julian about once a year would be overdrawn at the bank, invariably because of checks he wrote while he was drunk. His father never spoke to him about it, but Julian knew from his mother what his father thought of his money habits: ". . . do try to be more careful (his mother wrote). Your father has so many worries and he is specially worried about you where money matters are concerned because he thinks it's in the blood, because of Grandfather English."

It was nine-thirty, the morning after the night at the Stage Coach. It couldn't have been more on the dot of nine-thirty by the modern little clock on Caroline's dressing-table. The little clock had no numerals but only squares of metal where the numerals were supposed to be. He lay there thinking about the pictures evoked by the sound of "nine-thirty": people still hurrying to work, coming in to Gibbsville from Swedish Haven and Collieryville and all the other little towns nearby; people with worried faces, worried because they were late to work. And the early shoppers. But there would be no early shoppers today, Friday, the day after Christmas. It was too early to start to exchange Christmas gifts. Monday would be time enough for that. But the stores had to be open, and the banks, and the coal company offices, and the business men who made a business of being conscientious about getting to work, got to work. "Me, for instance," he thought, and got out of bed.

He was wearing his underwear. His tailcoat and trousers were folded and hanging on a chair, and other things told him that Caroline had taken the studs out of his shirt, the garters from his socks, his tie, his waistcoat, and put the things in the laundry that belonged in the laundry. That meant she was up, because in the mood she must have been in when they came home last night she wouldn't have bothered to take care of his things. He shaved, bathed, dressed, and went downstairs and poured himself a drink.

"Oh, you're up," said Mrs. Grady, the cook.

"Good morning, Mrs. Grady," said Julian.

"Mrs. English come down for breakfast but she went back to bed," said Mrs. Grady.

"Any mail?"

"I don't think anything important. Christmas cards, by the look of them," she said. "Do you want eggs for breakfast or what?"

"Sure."

"Well, I didn't know," she said. "I seen you was taking a drink of liquor so I didn't know if you wanted the eggs. I'll have them ready for you. The coffee's ready. I was just having a little cup myself when I heard you in here."

"Oh, one of those little cups," said Julian.

"Humm?"

"Nothing. Nothing at all. Three and a half minutes for the eggs, remember?"

"I ought to after four years, I ought to remember how long you want your eggs done."

"Yes, you ought to, but you don't always," said Julian. He was annoyed with her contemptuous manner.

"Now listen here, Mister English—"

"Oh, go boil the eggs, will you, and for Christ's sake shut up." There it was again: servants, cops, waiters in restaurants, ushers in theaters— he could hate them more than persons who threatened him with real harm. He hated himself for his outbursts against them, but why in the name of God, when they had so little to do, couldn't they do it right and move on out of his life?

There was no newspaper on the table, but he did not want to speak to Mrs. Grady, so he sat there without it, not knowing whether the damn paper had come, with nothing to read, no one to talk to, nothing to do but smoke a cigarette. Five minutes of ten, for God's sake; there ought to be a paper here by this time, and that old cow probably had it out in the kitchen and was just keeping it out there to annoy him. By God, she ought to be—oh, nuts. She got along all right with Caroline. That was it; the old cow, she probably knew from Caroline's manner that there was something wrong about last night, and her sympathies were, of course, all with Caroline. Well, she wasn't being paid to take sides in family quarrels, and she certainly wasn't being paid to—he got up and walked noisily to the kitchen.

"Where's the paper?" he said.

"Huh?"

"I said, where's the *paper!* Don't you understand English?"

"I understand one English," she said.

"Oh, for Christ's sake, Mrs. Grady, even you ought to know that's old stuff. Where's the paper?"

"Your wife took it upstairs with her. She wanted to read it."

"How do you know? Maybe she wanted to build a fire with it," he said, on his way out.

"There ain't no fireplace upstairs, smartie."

He had to laugh. He had to laugh, and pour himself a drink, and he was putting the top back on the bottle, which had a little chain holding a plate marked Scotch around the neck, when she brought in the large breakfast tray. He wanted to help her with it, but he would be damned if he would.

"Maybe she's asleep now and I can get the paper," said Mrs. Grady.

"No, thanks, don't bother," said Julian. He had a suspicion that Caroline not only was not asleep, but had heard every move he made from the time he got up. She was sleeping in the guest room again.

"Will you be coming home for lunch?"

"No," said Julian, although he had not given it any thought.

"Well, then, about the stuff for the party tonight."

"Oh, God. I forgot about it," said Julian.

"Well, Mrs. English says to tell you to leave a check for the liquor and champagne wine. It's to be delivered this afternoon."

"How much, did she say?"

"She said to make it out to cash and she'd fill in the amount when Grecco brings it."

Grecco. She would bring that up. And it was strange that Caroline wanted him to make out the check. She had her own money; right now she had more than he had. She had her own money, and always when they gave parties she would pay for the liquor when it was delivered, if she happened to be home, and they would settle it up later. On a party like this, which was as much hers as his, he would buy the liquor and she would pay for everything else. He wished there was going to be no party.

He finished his breakfast and drove downtown to the John Gibb

Hotel, where every morning he stopped to have his shoes shined. John, the Negro who had the shine concession, was not there. "He ain't been in this morning yet," said one of the barbers. "I guess he had too much Christmas cheer, like a lot of us." Julian watched the man carefully, but he did not seem to mean anything by the remark; and Julian reflected that his conduct the night before was not something that would be talked about in barber shops. Friends meant something, and they did not talk about that sort of thing in barber shops. Still, on his way out to the car he remembered that last night was only the second of two big nights for him, and it was extremely likely that barbers and everyone else had heard about his performance with Harry Reilly. "Good God," he said, remembering. This morning he had forgot all about Harry Reilly.

He changed his mind about driving out to the garage right away. Harry Reilly had an office in the bank building and he decided to call on Harry there. It was two blocks from the hotel, and he might get a ticket for parking, but if he couldn't get the ticket fixed, it was worth the two-dollar fine to have things straightened out with Harry.

Some places the sidewalk was all clean, some places there was only a narrow path cleared away, and the snow got down in his shoes when he stepped out of the way for women. Another minor annoyance. In front of J. J. Gray's jewelry store he met Irma Fliegler. "Hello, Julian," she said.

"Hello, Irma," he said, and stopped.

She was wearing a raccoon coat and she had some packages under her arm. It was still so cold that from a short distance away women did not seem to have any distinctive features, but close up she became Irma Doane, or at least Irma Fliegler, again; still pretty, a bit on the stout side, but stout in a way that did not make her unattractive. You knew that she was not going to get stouter, or definitely fat. She had very pretty legs and hands. You remember how pretty her hands were when you saw them with gloves on.

"Well, you certainly were a fine example of the young mother last night," said Julian. He knew it was the wrong thing to say, but some mention had to be made of last night. Better to make some mention of it than to be self-conscious about not bringing it up.

"Me? What did I do? Julian, you're nuts."

"Now, now, Irma, you don't think I don't remember. Didn't you know you stole the trombone player's hat?"

"Oh, you're kidding. You're a fine one to talk, you are. What a load you had. Did you get home all right?"

"I guess so," he said. Then he thought quickly. "I felt a little sick, haven't felt that way in years, and I was dancing, too, so I had to go out."

"Oh," she said. Maybe she believed him.

"I pulled a complete pass-out in the car. I think it was some girl from your party that I was dancing with," he said. Maybe she might believe him.

"Oh, no it wasn't. Not that they didn't want to, but you went out with the singer."

"What singer?"

"Helene Holman her name is, she sings at the Stage Coach."

"Oh, it's worse than I thought. I guess I have to send her flowers. I had some vague idea it was Frannie. I remember talking to her."

"She was there, but you didn't dance with her," said Irma. "She was having her own troubles. Well."

"See you soon," said Julian.

" 'By," she said.

He walked on, a little afraid that he had made a fool of himself, that Irma had not believed a word of his too-ready story that he had gone out with Helene because he was sick. But he knew that whatever he did, Irma would stick up for him. He always had liked Irma; she was the prettiest girl in high school, and a big girl, when he was a kid running around with Butch Doerflinger and Walt Davis and the rest of his kid friends. She had taught him in Sunday School, and did not report him on Sunday afternoons when he "bagged it" to go to a ball game. He wished he could tell her all his troubles, and he knew that if there was one person to whom he would tell them, it would be Irma. But she was Mrs. Lute Fliegler, the wife of one of his employees. He told himself that he must not forget that.

He went up in the elevator to Harry Reilly's office. "Hello, Betty. Your boss in?" Betty Fenstermacher was a stenographer who also ran the switchboard in Harry's office. Betty also had given her all to Julian and at least a dozen of his friends when they were all about nineteen or twenty.

"Hello, Ju," she said. "Yes, he's in all right. Can't you hear him? He's going away, and you'd think he was never away before in his life. Do I have to announce you?"

"I think you'd better. Where's he going?"

"Oh, New York," she said, and spoke into the telephone. "Mr. English is here to see Mr. Reilly. Shall I send him in?"

Just then Harry appeared, bag in hand, hat and coat on. "I'll be back by Tuesday at the latest," he was saying. "Phone Mrs. Gorman and tell her I made the train all right." He turned his face, and for the first time Julian was able to see that Harry's eye was decorated with a shiner, there was no other word for it. The ice apparently had smacked his cheek bone, and the pouch of flesh under the eye was blue and black and red and swollen. "Oh, it's you," said Harry.

"Yes, I thought I might as well come—"

"Listen, I can't wait another minute. I'm catching the ten-twenty-five and I have about four minutes. I'll be back next week." He ran through the office. Julian thought of going along with him to the station, but rejected that plan. He couldn't get anything said to a man who had four minutes to catch the train. On her own hook Betty Fenstermacher was calling the station and telling them to hold the train; Julian became conscious of this, and when she finished he said:

"What's it all about?"

"I don't know. I heard him shoot off his mouth about a lot of railroads going together. You'd think he was the one that was getting them together, the fuss and fury we been having around this office this morning. I hear you gave him the shiner, Ju. What was he, making passes at your wife or something?"

"No. Good-by, darling," he said. Ordinarily he would have stopped to kid Betty, to whom you could say anything without insulting her, but now he was still blank from Harry's breezy walk-out. It wasn't like Harry.

On the way back to the car Julian recalled that he had heard some talk about a merger of the New York Central, the Chesapeake & Ohio, Nickel Plate, Baltimore & Ohio and the Pennsylvania, and such a merger certainly might have an effect on Harry Reilly's fortune. Harry had large holdings in Virginia and West Virginia, in the soft coal fields. But Harry was a teller of elaborate lies, too; and he might be using the merger as an excuse to leave Gibbsville until the black eye was less black. Julian wished he knew whether the merger really was going through. Not that he would do anything about it now, but he still had the curiosity about such things that anyone who has traded in the stock market never quite loses: inside dope is fun to have, and he might risk a hundred or so on it. No, he guessed he wouldn't. If he knew anything, there was not going to be any merger; Harry Reilly was still a four-flusher; couldn't even leave town without making it appear that he was leaving on an errand of big business.

Driving out to the garage he could think of only one thing that occurred so far this morning that wasn't especially designed to annoy him; and that was that the fact of Harry Reilly's going away, the fact that Harry was going to be away with a legitimate reason would keep people from talking when he did not show up at the party tonight. Considering the way things were going today, that was a good break. . . . Yes, there was one other good break this morning; he had not been given a ticket for parking. At that moment a cross-link on the tire chains broke, and he rode the rest of the way to the garage with the link banging, cack-thock, cack-thock, cack-thock, against the left rear fender.

He blew the horn at the garage door, and it was fully two minutes before Willie, who washed cars and was an apprentice mechanic, opened the door. Julian had left orders at least fifty times that no one was to be kept waiting at the door, and he was going to bawl Willie out, but Willie called out: "Merry Christmas, boss. How'd Santa Claus treat you?"

"Yah," said Julian.

"Well, thanks for the Christmas present," said Willie, who had received a week's pay. "That fifteen bucks come in handy." Willie was closing the door and talking above the sound of the idling motor and the sounds of the mechanics working upstairs. "I said to my girl, I said—"

"Cross-link busted on the left rear chain," said Julian. "Fix it."

"Huh? When'd it break?"

"Right now, at Twelfth Street."

"Well, say, it held up pretty good. Better'n I thought. Remember, I told you Wensdee already, I said you better leave me fix them cross-links."

"Uh-huh." Julian had to admit that Willie *had* told him. He went to the office, which was in the rear of the big show room on the street floor. "Good morning, Mary," he said.

"Good morning," said Mary Klein, his secretary.

"What's doing?"

"Pretty quiet," she said, adjusting her spectacles.

"Have a nice Christmas?"

"Oh, it was all right I guess. My mother came downstairs in the afternoon, but I guess the excitement was too much for her. She had another spell around a quarter after five and we had to have Doctor Malloy out."

"Nothing serious, I hope," said Julian.

"Oh, I don't think so. Doctor Malloy said not, but those doctors, they don't always tell you the truth. I want her to go to Philadelphia to see a specialist, but we're afraid to tell Doctor Malloy. You know how he is. If we told him that he'd say all right, get another doctor, and we owe him so much already. We do the best we can, but there doesn't seem to be any sign of my brother getting a job yet, although it isn't for the lack of trying. Dear knows he isn't much of an expense and my mother, she has *some* money, but I have to keep up the building and loan and the insurance and food is so high again, my goodness."

One nice thing about Mary's morning recital of her woes was that usually you could stop her at any point and she would not be offended. "I guess we all have our troubles," he said. He had said this at least three mornings a week since Mary had come to work for him, and always Mary responded as though it were a shining new idea.

"Yes, I guess so," she said. "I was reading in the paper on the way to work about the man that used to write those comical articles in the *Inquirer*, Abe Martin, he died out west somewhere. I thought he was from Philadelphia but it said Indiana. Indianapolis, I think. Now *there* was a man—"

"Hello, Julian." It was Lute Fliegler. Mary immediately ended her talk. She disliked Lute, because he had once called her the biggest little windbag this side of Akron, Ohio, and to her face, at that.

"Hello, Lute," said Julian, who was reading a letter from a dealer in another part of the state, planning a gay party for the week of the Auto Show. "Want to go to this?" he said, throwing the letter to Lute.

Lute read it quickly. "Not me," he said. He sat down and put his feet up on Julian's desk. "Listen, we gotta make a squawk again about Mr. O'Buick."

"Is he at it again?" said Julian. O'Buick was their name for Larry O'Dowd, one of the salesmen for the Gibbsville-Buick Company.

"*Is* he?" said Lute. "I tell you what happened this morning. I went out to see Pat Quilty the undertaker this morning. I had him out a couple times in the last month and he's ready to go, or he was. He wants a seven-passenger sedan that he can use for funerals and for his family use. Or he *did*. Anyhow, I honestly figured, I said to myself, this is the one day the old man won't be expecting me to come around, so maybe I'll surprise him into signing today. And he'll pay cash on the line, too, Julian. So I took a ride out to see him and I went in his office and started kidding around—he likes that. Makes him feel young. So I noticed I wasn't getting a tumble from him, so finally I broke down and asked him, I said what was the matter, and he said to me in that brogue, he said: 'Will now Oi'll till you, Meesturr Fliegler, the way to hear it the coompany you do be working for, I hear they don't like people of my faith.'

"'What?' I said. 'Why the Cadillac car is *named* after a Catholic,' I said. I said 'Old Duke Cadillac, he was a Catholic.'

"'I don't mean Ginrul Mawtors, Mr. Fliegler,' he said. 'I mean Julian English, that's who I mean.'

"'Why, Mister Quilty,' I said, 'you're all wrong about that,' I said. I told him about Reverend Creedon, what a good friend of yours he is, and how you did this and that and the other for the sisters and so on, but he wouldn't hear any of it. He said he didn't always see eye to eye with Reverend Creedon, as far as that goes, but that wasn't the point. The point was, he said, he'd been hearing some stuff about you and Harry Reilly having a fight. What the hell's he talking about?"

"I threw a highball in his face the other night," said Julian.

"Oh, that," said Lute. "I heard about that. But you weren't having a fight over religion, were you?"

"No. Certainly not. I was cockeyed and I just let go with the drink. What else? What about O'Buick?"

"Well, that's the trouble. I can't get anything on him," said Lute. "Old Quilty, he wouldn't tell me any more than what I told you, except to say he was going to take a little time to think it over before he bought anything off us. I'm afraid we're not going to move that car unless you go out and talk to him yourself, Julian."

"Do you think that would do any good?"

"To tell you the God's honest truth, I don't know. I'm up a tree. When one of these Irish bastards gets the idea you're against their church, you have your hands full bucking it. The only explanation for it in a case like this is young O'Dowd, the son of a bitch, he heard about you and Reilly having this fight or whatever it was, and he went right out and gave old Quilty this story. That's my guess. I'd like to punch him one in the nose."

"So would I."

"Well, don't *you* do it or we won't be able to *give* the product away in 1931. I might as well tell you all the bad news while I'm at it."

"You mean more bad news?" said Julian.

"That's what I mean nothing else but," said Lute. "Julian I don't want —wait a minute. *Miss* Klein, would you mind going out on the floor a minute while I talk with Mr. English?"

"Not at all. The language you use." Mary Klein left the office.

"Listen, Julian," said Lute. "Your private affairs are your own business, and you're boss here and all that. But I'm ten years older than you and you and I always hit it off pretty damn good, so do you mind if I give it to you straight from the shoulder?"

"No. Go ahead."

"Well, I don't want you to take offense at this, and you can fire me if you get sore, but you been making a fool of yourself, and last night up at the Stage Coach—Jesus, I don't know what to say. But you oughtn't to done that, taking that dame out, that torch singer. You know whose girl she is? Ed Charney's. One of the best friends we have, in a business way. There's a guy, a lot of people don't want to have anything to do with him, and I guess a lot of your friends think you contaminate yourself by selling him an automobile. But meanwhile Ludendorf is selling plenty of Packards to the same friends, so what they think don't matter. Ed Charney is a right guy, a square shooter. He pays his bills regular, and they're pretty big bills. He likes you personally. He told me that many's the time. He says you're the only one in the whole high-hat crowd that he considers on the up and up. Well, what's the result? The result is, any time one of his bootlegger friends is on the market for a high-priced automobile, Ed sees to it that we make the sale. You don't see Ludendorf selling Packards to any of Ed Charney's pals.

"So then what? So then you turn around and pay him back by giving his girl a lay and making a monkey out of him right in his own spot, not to mention making a fool of yourself with your own wife and friends right there. You know what'd happen to any of Ed's own crowd that tried to pull a fast one like that, don't you? Why it'd be suicide, and just because your father happens to be a big shot here, Julian, don't think you're in such a good spot yourself. I don't mean Ed's going to have his guerrillas turn a Tommy gun on you or anything like that. But why can't you be more careful? I happen to know Ed is plenty burned up, and, my God, I don't blame him. He's been keeping that dame for over two years now, and everybody says he's nuts about her, and then you get cockeyed and take her out for a quick jump and ruin the whole works. My God, Julian."

"You're wrong about one thing," said Julian.

"What's that?"

"I didn't lay that girl."

Lute hesitated before answering. "Well, maybe you didn't but everybody thought you did and that amounts to the same thing. She was out in the car with you long enough, and when she came back she didn't look as if you'd been sitting there listening to Father Coughlin on the radio. What surprised me was that you'd have anything to do with her at all. Not that it's for me to say, but you always struck me as the ideal married couple, you and Caroline, Mrs. English. That's what Irma said too. I know it's the first time I ever knew of you going on the make for some dame. Honest, Julian, I don't want to talk out of turn, but if you and your wife are having family troubles, you ought to do your best to fix it up. You have the nicest, the swellest girl in the whole God damn Lantenengo Street crowd, and everybody in town thinks so, and if you take it from me—and mind, I'm ten years older'n you—you do the wise thing and patch it up. Irma and I, we have our troubles, but she knows how it is between she and I, and I think you feel the same way about Mrs. English.

"There. I've shot off my face more than I intended to, but I'm glad I got it off my chest. If you want to give me the air, that's your business, but everything I told you is the truth and down in your heart you know it, pal. I can get another job, or if I can't, I'll get by somehow. If you're the kind of a guy that'd fire me for what I been telling you, then you're not the kind of a guy I always took you for, and I don't want to work for you. So that's that." Lute stood up slowly.

"Sit down, Lute." Julian was unable to say more than that. The two men sat opposite each other for a few minutes. Lute offered Julian a cigarette and Julian took it, and Julian gave Lute a light. Presently Julian said: "What do you think I ought to do, Lute?"

"Gee, I wish I knew. I guess let it ride for the time being. You were cockeyed, and that's one consolation. Maybe Charney will take that into consideration. Aw, what the hell. We'll get by. Don't take it to heart too much. I'll see you this afternoon around quitting time. I have to go to Collieryville now, but it'll work out one way or another. Shake?"

"Shake," said Julian. They shook hands and smiled, and Lute left, and Julian heard him telling Mary Klein that everything had been decided; they weren't going to handle automobiles any more; just airplanes.

"It isn't true, is it, Mr. English? What Luther Fliegler just told me?"

"What did he tell you?"

"That we were going to stop selling cars and sell airplanes instead. I don't think there's any market for airplanes around here."

"Don't let it worry you for a couple of years, Mary," said Julian. "You know Lute."

"And how!" said Mary Klein.

It was one of those mornings when he could tell himself that he was up to his ears in work or that he had nothing to do, and either with equal honesty. His hangover did not bother him inordinately; he knew he could work in spite of whatever effect the night before still maintained. He wanted to work; the difficulty was in getting started. He wanted to work to put things out of his mind, and he tried to the extent of getting out some scratch paper and pencils with the idea of working out some sort of summary or recapitulation of the year's business of the Gibbsville-Cadillac Motor Car Company. This was a good time to do that; when no salesmen would disturb him, and when there was nothing much else he could do. But the words, summary, recapitulation—they made him think of Lute and how he had recapitulated and summarized his performance of the night before, including the consequences. The Quilty business—well, he thought he knew what to expect there: O'Dowd probably hadn't said a word to old Quilty, but when O'Dowd did hear about Julian's throwing the highball at Harry Reilly, he would hotfoot out to Quilty and make the sale. O'Dowd was a good salesman, and he knew how to handle a situation like this. Julian hated to lose that sale, too, because no matter how people joke about it, when you place a car with an undertaker, you have a pretty good advertisement. Undertakers keep their cars in the best of shape, black and gleaming and polished and clean. Julian knew this from his own reaction; he often had thought that if you had to die, it wouldn't be so bad to ride to the cemetery in Quilty's luxurious hearse, followed by Quilty's well-kept Studebaker sedans. Whenever he heard the tune, Saint James' Infirmary, he always thought of old Quilty. And the sale would be for cash. That wouldn't be hard to take. It certainly made it hard to lose. He wondered if Harry Reilly had gone to work already. Harry was a very rich man and handling his investments and holdings was a full-time job, but he also managed to know what was going on in other people's businesses, and it would be just like him to know that old Quilty was thinking of buying a Cadillac. It was just the kind of thing he would know. After all, why shouldn't he know it? He had lent Julian twenty thousand dollars last summer, and that was a nice piece of change no matter how much Harry might be worth. It was enough to excuse any extraordinary interest Harry might be taking in Julian's business.

Twenty thousand dollars! Why in God's name had he ever asked for that much? He knew perfectly well why he had asked for that much: at the time he needed ten thousand, but he figured he might as well get a good hunk while he was at it. Ten thousand had gone in no time: it cost, even with the cheap labor and construction costs of last summer, about eight thousand to build the inclined driveway inside the building, which he had calculated would mean eventually a great saving in electric power bills through decreased use of the elevator. So far it hadn't made much difference, if any. In fact, Julian would not have argued very long if someone suggested that the driveway was an ill-advised project. Then what else was there? Well, there were those two three-wheel motorcycles. The idea of them was a mechanic could ride the motorcycle to, say, the Davis' garage, hook some kind of gadget on the Davis' Cadillac, and drive the car, with the motorcycle trailing along behind, back to the Gibbsville-Cadillac Motor Car Company for servicing or repairs. That was another idea that was going to make a saving, but the saving, Julian was sure, had failed to make a showing on the books. And why *two* motorcycles. One was enough. More than enough. Then there were the trees, those beautiful, slender trees. Julian had conditioned himself against ever seeing them when he passed them, but now he made himself think of them. There they were out there in the little strip of grass along the curb. Seven-hundred and sixty-six dollars and forty-five cents' worth of them, including freight and planting. Julian knew to the penny what they cost, but he still was not sure of the name of them. They had been purchased while he was in a fine, naturalistic mood as an aftermath of a City Beautiful luncheon. There had been trees a long time ago where the Gibbsville-Cadillac Motor Car Company now stood, and there had been trees along the curb, but they had been chopped down. Then one day Julian went to a City Beautiful luncheon and everybody got up and said a few words about trees and what they did for a residential section—Julian's garage was in a residential section—and by the oddest coincidence there chanced to be a man from a nursery at the luncheon, and Julian signed. And that about took care of the extra ten thousand dollars.

The other ten thousand had gone for expenses, real ones, like payments on notes, payroll, and so on.

Lute was right on another score: Ed Charney was a good customer. "I'm a good customer of Ed's," Julian reminded himself, "but he's a better one of mine." Something ought to be done about Ed, but he supposed the best thing to do for the present was to lay off trying to fix it up. Yes, he certainly had loused things up last night: Ed Charney sore at him, Caroline—well, he wouldn't think of that now; he was at work, and he would try to think of things only in so far as they affected his business. If Ed Charney got really sore—but he wouldn't do that; he wouldn't throw a pineapple at the garage. This was Gibbsville, not Chicago. And after all, the English name meant something around here. "No thanks to me, however," Julian said under his breath.

"Darn his buttons anyhow," said Mary Klein.

"What is it, Mary," said Julian.

"Luther Fliegler," she said. "He makes out these slips when he gets gas, but you can never tell whether he means ten gallons or seventy gallons, the way he makes figures."

"Well, I don't think he'd be making out a slip for seventy gallons. A car doesn't hold that much gas," said Julian. "Besides, that's not your headache. Let Bruce worry about it."

Mary turned to look at him. "Sure, but you forget. You told Bruce he could go to Lebanon over the week-end." She spoke as a woman who was carrying on in spite of all injustice. Bruce Reichelderfer was the bookkeeper, and Julian had given him the week-end.

"That's right, I did. Well, let me see it."

She handed him the slip. She was right as usual; you could not tell from the figures whether Lute had meant 10 or 70. "We ought to use the French seven," he said. "Then we'd always know. However, I guess we can take a chance that he meant ten gallons. He wouldn't be signing for seventy gallons all at once."

"Well, I just wanted to be right on it. Sixty gallons of gas, that costs money, and we can't just—"

"I know, Mary. You're right." Somehow her tone filled him with terror, the kind that he felt when he knew he was doing something bad. It was an old experience; he still thought of it in the terms of boyhood: "—when I'm doing something bad." And it wasn't her tone alone; it was her manner, and it was not a new manner. For weeks, and probably months, she had behaved like someone, a school teacher, who was meaning to speak to him about his lessons or conduct. She was Right, and he was Wrong. She could make him feel like a thief, a lecher (although God knows he never had made a pass at her), a drunkard, a no-good bum. She represented precisely what she came from: solid, respectable, Pennsylvania Dutch, Lutheran middle class; and when he thought about her, when she made her existence felt, when she actively represented what she stood for, he could feel the little office suddenly becoming overcrowded with a delegation of all the honest clerks and mechanics and housewives and Sunday school teachers and widows and orphans—all the Christiana Street kind of people who he knew secretly hated him and all Lantenengo Street people. They could have their illegitimate babies, their incest, their paresis, their marital bestiality, their cruelty to animals, their horrible treatment of their children and all the other things which you could find in individual families; but collectively they presented a solid front of sound Pennsylvania Dutch and all that that implied, or was supposed to imply. They went to church on Sunday, they saved their money, they were kind to their old people, they were physically clean, they loved music, they were peace-loving, they were good workers. And there they sat, with their back curved in at the small part, their oilcloth cuffs covering their sleeves, their fresh blouse as neat after five hours' wear as Julian's shirt after two. And they were thinking what a pity it was that this wonderful business wasn't in the hands of one of their own men, instead of being driven into the ground by a Lantenengo Street—wastrel. And yet, Julian made himself admit, Lute Fliegler is a Pennsylvania Dutchman and one of the swellest guys that ever lived. Thinking that over Julian returned to his old theory: it was possible, wasn't it? that Lute's mother had had a quick one with an Irishman or a Scotsman. A hell of a thing to think about that old Mrs. Fliegler, who still baked the best pie crust Julian had ever tasted.

Every few minutes Julian would jot down some figures as they came into his head. All the time he looked very busy, and he hoped he was making a good impression on Mary Klein. The sheets of paper that lay before him were filling up with neat, engineering style lettering and numerals. Addition, subtraction, multiplication, and division. . . .

He did. What's the use of trying to fool myself? I know he did. I know he did and no matter what excuses I make or how much I try to tell myself that he didn't, I'll only come back to the same thing: He did. I know he did. And what for? For a dirty little thrill with a woman who—oh, I thought he'd got all that out of his system. Didn't he have enough of that before he married me? Did he still think he was a college boy? Did he think I couldn't have done the same thing to him, dozens of times! Did he know—oh, of course he didn't know that of all his friends, Whit Hofman was the only one that I can truthfully say never made a pass at me. The only one. Ah, Julian, you stupid, hateful, mean, low contemptible little son of a bitch that I hate! You did this to me, and *know* that you do this to me! *Know* it! Did it on purpose! Why? It wasn't only to get even with me. It wasn't only because I wouldn't go out in the car with you. Are you so dumb blind after four and a half years that you don't know that there are times when I just plain don't feel like having you? Does there have to be a reason for it? An excuse? Must I be ready to want you at all times except when I'm not well? If you knew anything you'd know I want you probably more then than any other time. But you get a few drinks in you and you want to be irresistible. But you're not. I hope you found that out. But you didn't. And you never will. I love you? Yes, I love you. Like saying I have cancer. I have cancer. If I did have cancer. You big charmer, you. You irresistible great big boy, turning on the charm like the water in the tub; turning on the charm like the water in the tub; turning on the charm, turning on the charr-arm, turning on the charm like the water in the tub. I hope you die.

I hope you die because you have killed something fine in me, suh. Ah hope you die. Yes-suh, Ah hope you die. You have killed something mighty fine in me, English, old boy, old kid, old boy. What Ah mean is, did you kill something fine in me or did you kill something fine. I feel sick, sick as a dog. I feel sick and I would like to shoot my lunch and I would like indeed to shoot my lunch but I will be damned if I want to move out of this bed, and if you don't stop being nasty to servants—I said r. I said a word with r in it, and that makes me stop this silly business. I wonder why. I wonder why r?

Oh, I guess I better get up. There's nothing to be gained by lying here in bed and feeling sorry for myself. It's nothing new or interesting or novel or rare or anything. I'm just a girl who just feels like dying because the man I love has done me wrong. I'm not even suffering any more. I'm not even feeling anything. At least I don't think I am. No, I'm not. I'm not feeling anything. I'm just a girl named Caroline Walker, Caroline Walker English, Caroline W. English, Mrs. Walker English. That's all I am. Thirty-one years old. White. Born. Height. Weight. Born? Yes. I always think that's funny and I always will. I'm sorry, Julian, but I just happen to think it's funny and you used to think so too, back in the old days when I knew you in an Eton collar and a Windsor tie, and I loved you then, I loved you then, I love you now, I love you now, I'll always love you to the day I die and I guess this is what they call going to pieces. I guess I've gone to pieces, because there's nothing left of me. There's nothing left of me of days that used to be I live in mem-o-ree among my souvenirs. And so what you did, what you did was take a knife and cut me open from my throat down to here, and then you opened the door and let in a blast of freezing cold air, right where you had cut me open, and till the day you die I hope you never, never know what it feels like to have someone cut you open all the way down the front of you and let the freezing blast of air inside you. I hope you never know what that means and I know you won't, my darling that I love, because nothing bad will happen to you. Oh, lovely Callie, your coat is so warm, the sheep's in the meadow, the cow's in the corn. *"No, I don't think I'll get up for a while, Mrs. Grady."*

It was inevitable that every time Al Grecco went to the garage in which Ed Charney kept his private cars, he should think of a photograph one of the boys from the west had shown around. Probably a great many men—and the women of those men—in Al Grecco's line of work had the same thought, inspired by the same photograph (there were thousands of copies of the photograph), whenever they looked inside an especially dismal garage. The photograph showed a group of men, all dead, but with that somehow live appearance which pictures of the disfigured dead give. The men were the victims of the St. Valentine's Day massacre in Chicago, when seven men were given the Mexican stand-off against the inside wall of a gang garage.

"It'd be a nice wall for it," Al said, as he opened the garage door.

He went upstairs and lugged a case of champagne down the steps. Then he went up again and lugged a case of Scotch down, and then he lifted them into a dull black Hudson coach, which was used for deliveries. He backed the car out into the street, Railroad Avenue, and then got out and slid the garage doors shut. He took one more look at that blank wall before he finally closed the door. "Yes. It sure would be a nice wall for it," he said.

No man could call him what Ed Charney had called him and get away with it. Not even Ed Charney. He thought of his mother, with the little gold earrings. Why, he could remember when she didn't own a hat. She would even go to Mass on Sunday with that scarf over her head. Often in the far past he had told her she was too damn lazy to learn English, but now, thinking of her, he thought of her as a good little woman who had had too much work to learn much English. She was a wonderful woman, and she was his mother, and if Ed Charney called him a son of a bitch, all right; if he called him a bastard, all right. Those were just names that you called a guy when you wanted to make him mad, or when you were mad at him. Those names didn't mean anything anyhow, because, Al figured, if your mother was a bitch, if you were a bastard, what was the use of fighting about it? And if she wasn't, you could easily prove it. What was the use fighting about it? But this was different, what Ed Charney had said: "Listen you God damn dirty little guinny bastard, I sent you up there last night to keep an eye on Helene. You didn't have to go if you didn't want to. But what do you do? You double-cross me, you son of a bitch. I bet English gave you a sawbuck so he could take her out and give her a jump, and you sit back there collecting fifty bucks from me becuss I'm sap enough to think you're on the up-and-up with me. But no. Not you. Not you. Why, you small-time chiseling bastard, you. You dirty lousy mother —— bastard." And more like that. Automatically Al had tried to explain: all she did was dance with him; she wasn't outside long enough to do anything with English ("You're a dirty liar. Foxie told me she was out a half an hour."); English was stewed and not on the make ("Don't tell me about English. I'm not blaming him. I'm blaming you. You knew she was my girl. English didn't."), and so on. In his heart Al wanted to tell Ed the real truth; that he could have made Helene himself if he hadn't been on the up-and-up. But that wouldn't do any good now. Or it wouldn't do enough harm. Ed was crazy mad. He was so crazy mad that he said all these things to Al over the telephone from his own house, most likely in front of his wife. Oh, positively in front of his wife. If she was in the same house she couldn't help hearing him, the way he was yelling into the telephone. So Al just stood there at the phone and took it without making any real comeback. At first he had been stunned by the accusation of being a double-crosser. But in Al's and Ed's line of work it is never wise to call an associate a double-crosser; if the associate is guilty, the thing to do is punish him; if he isn't guilty, it puts the idea into his head. And then when he remembered the bad thing that Ed had called him, that began to put the idea into Al's head. He hadn't made any plans about what he was going to do. Not yet. But something would have to be done. "I guess it'll be me or him," he said, thinking of that wall.

But meanwhile he had his work to do. Little jobs here and there. Odds and ends, daily routine work. Ed had been in such a rage, so burnt up, that he had forgot to fire Al, and despite everything he had said, he had not indicated that he intended to fire Al. In their line of work it was one thing to have a scrap, a mouth fight, or to be angry for a day or two at an associate. But to fire a man was something else again. You didn't just fire a guy like *that* (finger-snap). Not even in Gibbsville, which was not Chicago.

That was the trouble, in a way. In a way maybe it was a break that it wasn't Chicago, because out there they knocked each other off with less excuse than a fight over a dame. But in another way Al was sorry it wasn't Chi. In Gibbsville they never had a gang war, because Ed Charney simply didn't have any competition. Whereas on the other hand, in Chi they did. They had gang wars all the time. They were used to it. In Chi you could get away with it. In Gibbsville it would be just a murder, and they would have to make a pinch and have a court trial and all that, and the juries around here were so screwy, they might even send you to the chair. "That Rock View, I don't want any part of that," said Al.

So now he had a nice little job to do. A little odds and ends. He had to take this champagne and this Scotch out to where English lived. English, the mugg that caused all the trouble in the first place. Although as he drove along he could not stir up any very strong hatred of English, because the truth of the matter was, if you wanted to know who was responsible, it wasn't English or it wasn't even Helene with her hot pants. It was Ed Charney himself. A married man with a kid, and absolutely haywire on the subject of another woman not his wife. That was where the trouble was. He wanted everything, Ed did. Well, that remains to be seen, as the elephant said.

"I'm above this kind of work," Al said, as he lifted first one case, then the other, out of the Hudson and laid them down on the kitchen porch of the English house. He rang the bell.

"How much is it?" said the old woman.

"You don't have to pay me," said Al, who knew that English had credit with Ed.

"I said how much is it?" said the old woman, the cook, he guessed she was.

"A hundred and seventy-five. A hundred for the champagne, seventy-five for the Scotch."

The woman closed the door in his face and in a few minutes she came back and handed him a check and a five-dollar bill. "The cash is for you. A tip," said the woman.

"Stick it—" Al began.

"Don't you say that to me, you dago wop," said the old woman. "I got two boys would teach you how to talk. If you don't want the money, give it here."

"The hell I will," said Al.

"Aw, my goodness. Where you going, beautiful lady? You going somewhere?" said Foxie Lebrix.

"Can that stuff," said Helene Holman. "Will you phone down to Taqua and get me a taxi? I'll pay you for the call."

"Aw, but I hate to see you leave. I t'ought you and I—"

"I know you thought, but we ain't, see? If you don't want to get me a taxi, say so and I'll walk it," said Helene.

"Wit' all dose bags?"

"You're damn right. The quicker I get out of this place the better I like it. Well, what about the taxi?"

"Wall, I would not see you walking in the snow. Maybe we see each other in New York some day, and you get me a taxi when I leave your place, eh? Sure I get you a taxi."

8

MARY KLEIN had gone home to lunch and Julian was alone in the office, with a small array of sheets of paper on which were rows of figures, names, technical words: Number of cars sold in 1930; our cut on new cars sold; gas and oil profit 1930; tires and accessories profit 1930; profit on resale of cars taken in trade; other profit; insurance on building; ins. on equipment; ins. on rolling stock; interest on bldg.; taxes; advertising; graft, expenses, light, other elec. outlay; heat; tool replacement; licenses; office stuff, incl. stationery; workmen's compensation; protective association; telephones; bad debts; stamps; trade-in losses; lawyer & accountant fees; building repairs; losses not covered by ins.; plumber; depreciation on bldg.; deprec. on equipment; depr. on trade-in jobs; depr. on new cars not moved; contributions to charity; cash advance to self; notes due at bank; cash needed for payroll. . . . As a result of his figuring Julian announced to the empty room: "I have to have five thousand dollars."

He stood up. "I said, I have to have five thousand dollars, and I don't know where I can get it. . . . Yes, I do. Nowhere." He knew he was lying to himself; that he did not need five thousand dollars. He needed money, and he needed it soon, but not five thousand dollars. Two thousand would be enough, and with any break in the beginning of the year, after the auto shows in New York and Philadelphia (which are attended by a surprising number of Gibbsville automobile enthusiasts), he would be able to get back on his feet. But he reasoned that it was just as hard to get two thousand as five, five thousand as two. It was easier to get five, he told himself; and as he had argued less than a year ago, when he had gone to Harry Reilly for a loan, he might as well go for a neat, convenient-sounding sum. The question seemed to be: Where to get it.

Tempers are better in summer than in winter, in Gibbsville; Julian's summer life had included a good deal of Harry Reilly last summer, and it was easy enough to get away from him. If you didn't want to play golf with Harry, you said you had promised Caroline to play a match for blood with her, which did away with the necessity of asking Harry to play along. On the other hand, it was not bad to drink with Harry in a party of undershirted convivials in the locker-room, and Harry was a fair tenor and even knew songs about the roll of Delta Kappa Epsilon, Lafayette was Lafayette when Lehigh was a pup, the Lord Jeff of Amherst, and a lot of other college songs. Of course Harry got the words wrong sometimes, but Julian was no purist who would discourage the progress of a fair tenor. No, a good tenor, as locker-room tenors go.

He thought of these things. Harry must have changed since then, become obnoxious or something. Julian reasoned that he could not have asked the Harry he now knew to invest so much money in the business. Well, maybe the winter had something to do with it. You went to the Gibbsville Club for lunch; Harry was there. You went to the country club to play squash on Whit Hofman's private court, and Harry was around. You went to the Saturday night drinking parties, and there was Harry; inescapable, everywhere. Carter Davis was there, too, and so was Whit; so was Froggy Ogden. But they were different. The bad new never had worn off Harry Reilly. And the late fall and winter seemed now to have been spoiled by room after room with Harry Reilly. You could walk outside in the summer, but even though you can walk outside in winter, winter isn't that way. You have to go back to the room soon, and there is no life in the winter outside of rooms. Not in Gibbsville, which was a pretty small room itself.

Well, what was the use of trying to build up Harry now as having been a swell guy last summer. Last summer Julian had needed money, and Harry Reilly had money, so he had asked Harry. And Harry had said: "Jesus, I ain't got that much cash at this present minute. Do you need it right away?" Julian had said he needed it pretty soon. "Well, I don't see how I can get it for you before tomorrow. . . . Oh, hell, sure I can." Julian had almost laughed in his face: in one minute the little worry that Harry wanted to have a month to think it over and raise the cash had come and gone. Julian had had a lot more trouble in college, trying to borrow forty-four cents to go to the movies. . . . Harry had been no different then from the Harry he knew today. Might as well face that. As for the Caroline angle, Julian believed in a thought process that if you think against a thing in advance, if you anticipate it—whether it's the fear that you're going to cut yourself when you shave, or lose your wife to another man—you've licked it. It can't happen, because things like that are known only by God. Any future thing is know only to God; and if you have a super-premonition about a thing, it'll be wrong, because God is God, and is not giving away one of His major powers to Julian McHenry English. So Julian thought and thought about Caroline and Harry, and thought against them, against their being drawn to each other sexually, which was the big thing that mattered. "By God, no one else will have her in bed," he said, to the empty office. And immediately began the worst fear he had ever known that this day, this week, this minute, next year, sometime she would open herself to another man and close herself around him. Oh, if she did that it would be forever.

Julian reached in the second drawer of the desk and took out a Colt .25 automatic and got up and went to the washroom. He was breathless with excitement and he felt his eyes get the way they got when he was being thrilled, big but sharp. He sat down on the toilet, and he knew he was not going to do it that way. But he wanted to sit down and look at the pistol. He looked at it for he knew not how long, and then snapped himself to without changing his position in the slightest degree. He put the barrel in his mouth and some oil touched the inside of his lower lip. He made a "Guck" sound, and took a long breath, and then he put the pistol in his pocket and got up and washed his mouth with cold water and then he took off his upper garments, except his undershirt, and washed himself all over the head and face and arms to the elbow. He used four towels, drying himself. Then he put on his clothes again, wiped stray drops of water off his shoes, and went back to the office and lit a cigarette. He remembered a bottle of whiskey he had in the desk, and he had a longlasting drink of one whiskey glass of it. "Oh, I couldn't," he said, and he put his arms on the desk and his head on his arms, and he wept. "You poor guy," he said. "I feel so sorry for you."

He heard the first of the mechanics' post-luncheon sounds: the thump of a baseball in a catcher's mitt. That meant the mechanics were through lunch, because one of the men pitched on a semi-pro team, and he kept himself in shape all winter. Julian held his head up and the phone rang. "Hello," he said.

"I just tried to get you at the club. Where'd you have lunch?" It was Caroline.

"I didn't," he said.

"Well, I don't suppose you felt much like it. Now listen, Julian, the reason I called is, if you talk the way you did to Mrs. Grady again, we're through. Do you hear?"

"Yes."

"I mean it this time. I'm not going to have you take your hangovers out on any servants. Mrs. Grady should have slapped your face."

"Say!"

"It's about time someone slapped your face. Now I want you to understand this, old boy. If you come home drunk this afternoon and start raising hell, I'll simply call up every person we've invited and call off the party."

"You'll simply, huh?"

"Oh, shut up," she said, and ended the call.

"She'll simply," he said to the telephone, and gently replaced the handpiece in the cradle. "She'll simply." He got up and put on his hat. He stopped and debated, a very short debate, whether to leave a note for Mary Klein. "Naa, who's Mary Klein?" He struggled into his coat and drove to the Gibbsville Club.

The usual crowd was not in the club this day. "Hello, Straight," said Julian to the steward.

"Good afternoon, Mr. English. I hope you had a merry Christmas. Uh, we all want to thank you for your, uh, generous, uh, subscription to the club employes' Christmas fund. Uh." Old Straight always spoke as though he had just been sniffing ammonia.

"Well, you're very welcome, I'm sure," said Julian. "Have a nice Christmas?"

"Quite nice. Of course, uh, well, of course I have no family that you'd, uh, really call a family, uh. My nevview in South Africa, he—"

"Mr. Davis in the club? Who's here? Never mind. I'll go look."

"Not many members here today. The day, uh, day after—"

"I know," said Julian. He went into the dining-room and at first glance it appeared that it was occupied solely by Jess, the Negro waiter. But there was a small table in one corner, by common consent or eminent domain, the lawyers' table, at which sat a few lawyers, all older men and not all of them Gibbsville men, but residents of the smaller towns who came to the county seat when they had to. You did not have to speak to the men at the lawyers' table. In fact, some of the men who sat there did not speak to each other. Julian had hoped Carter Davis might still be in the club, but there was no sign of him. He sat down at a table for two, and he no sooner had given his order than he was joined by Froggy Ogden.

"Sit down and eat. I just ordered. Jess'll take your order and serve it with mine if you want to."

"I don't want to," said Froggy.

"Well, then, sit down and take the load off."

"You're feeling pretty snotty today," said Froggy, sitting down.

"Snotty isn't the word for it. Cigarette?"

"No, thanks. Listen, Julian, I didn't come here for a friendly chat."

"Oh, no?"

"No," said Froggy. You could see he was getting angry.

"Well, then, come on. I've been hearing the anvil chorus all day, so you might as well join it. What kind of a fig have you got—"

"Now listen, I'm older than you—"

"Oh, it's going to be one of those. And you have my best interests at heart? That one? Jesus Christ, you're not going to give me that."

"No. I'm not. I'm older than you in more ways than one."

"What you're trying to say is you lost your arm in the war. Do you mind if I help you? You lost your arm in the war, and you've suffered, and that makes you older than me, and if you had both arms I guess you'd thrash me within an inch of my life."

Froggy stared at him until they heard the wall clock ticking. "Yes. I have a notion to bust you one right now. You God damn son of a bitch, Caroline is my cousin, and even if she wasn't my cousin she's one of the finest girls there is, Caroline is. You want to know something? When she told me she was going to marry you, I tried to stop it. I always hated you. I always hated your guts when you were a kid, and I hate you now. You never were any damn good. You were a slacker in the war—oh, I know how old you were. You could of got in if you'd tried. You were yellow when you were a kid and you grew up yellow. You chased around after that Polish girl till she had to go away or her father would have killed her. Then you put on some kind of an act with Caroline, and God help her, she fell for it. I tried to stop it, but no. She said you had changed. I—"

"You're a dirty God damn one-armed bastard, and I wish you had that other arm."

"You—don't—have to wish it," said Froggy, and he picked up the glass of water and threw the water in Julian's face. "Come on outside. I'll fight you with one arm." Trembling with rage, Julian stood up, and then he felt weak. He knew he was not afraid; he knew he could not fight Froggy. He still liked him, for one thing; and for another, he could not see himself fighting a man who had only one arm.

"Come on. Anywhere you say," said Froggy.

Julian wiped the water off his face with a napkin. "I don't want to fight you." He wondered, but did not turn his head to ascertain it, whether the men at the lawyers' table had seen the incident. He heard some children playing in the street and he thought of horrible Saturday mornings at the dentist's, when he was a kid and horses were being whipped and children were playing in the street and the car to Collieryville will be ringing its bell.

"Come on. Don't stand there because I only have one arm. I'll worry about that. Don't you."

"Go away. Beat it," said Julian. "You're showing off. You know I can't fight you."

"Come outside or by Jesus I'll sock you in here."

"No, you won't. I won't let you sock me in here, hero, and I won't fight you outside. You think I'd give people the chance to say that about me? You're crazy. Go on, beat it, General. The war's over."

"Yeah? That's what you think. You're right. I knew you wouldn't fight. There isn't a spark of manhood in you. I knew you wouldn't fight. There isn't a spark of manhood left in you, if there ever was one."

"Run along, cousin. Go on home and count your medals."

Froggy swung on him and Julian put up his open hand and the punch made a slight smack sound on his wrist, and hurt his wrist.

"Gentlemen!"

"Don't be a God damn fool," said Julian.

"Well, then, come on outside."

"Gentlemen! You know the club rules." It was Straight. He stood in front of Froggy, with his back toward Froggy, facing Julian. He certainly made it look as though he were protecting Froggy from an attack by Julian. By this time there was no doubt about the lawyers being in on the quarrel. They were all watching, and two of them were standing up. Julian heard one of them say something about "see what he *did* . . . one arm." He knew they were doing just what everyone else would do who heard about this: they were taking for granted that he had socked Froggy. One stout man, whom Julian knew only as a lawyer face around the court house and Gibbsville restaurants during court terms, walked over and put his hand on Froggy's shoulder. "Did he hit you, Captain Ogden?"

"Captain Ogden!" Julian laughed.

"We know all about him up the mountain," said the stout man.

"Are you by any chance a member of this club?" said Julian.

"A member, and what's more you never see my name posted," said the man. "Don't you worry about me being a member."

Well, that was all right. It was a slap at Julian, who had been posted two or three times, but it also was a slap at Froggy, Carter, Bobby Herrmann and just about everyone else. It was no distinction to be posted at the Gibbsville Club; it could mean that you had not paid your bill six days after the bill was presented.

"Is this man a member, Straight?" said Julian.

"Oh, yes. Mr. Luck is a member."

"Luck? Lukashinsky, if I know anything."

"What's that got to do with it. This is between me and you," said Froggy.

"Not any more, it isn't. No, Captain, it's between me on the one side, standing here alone, and you and the Polack war veterans and whoremasters on the other side. I'll stay where I am."

"Hey, you!" said the lawyer.

"Aw," said Julian, finally too tired and disgusted with himself and everyone else. He took a step backwards and got into position, and then he let the lawyer have it, full in the mouth. The man fell back and gurgled and reached fingers in his mouth to keep from choking on his bridgework. Another lawyer came over, another Polack whose name Julian never could remember. He had a club soda bottle in his hand.

"Put that down!" said Froggy. "He has a bottle!" He grabbed a bottle himself, and Julian got a water carafe. All through it Straight kept saying Gentlemen, gentlemen, gentlemen, and kept out of the way.

"Come on," said Julian, to the man with the bottle. The man saw the carafe and hesitated. The other lawyers took the bottle away from him without a great struggle. The man could not keep his eyes off Froggy. He could not understand why Froggy had warned Julian.

"Go on out and get a warrant, Stiney," called the lawyer whom Julian had socked. Julian hit him again, hit him in the hands, which were covering the sore mouth. He hit him again in the ear. Froggy grabbed Julian's shoulder to pull him away, and Julian pulled up his shoulder so suddenly that it hit Froggy in the chin. The lawyer went down, not to get up for a while, and then Julian rushed Froggy and punched him in the ribs and in the belly and Froggy lost his balance and fell over a chair. Julian picked up the carafe again and hurled it at the man who had come at him with the bottle, and without waiting to see what it did, he ran out of the room, taking his coat and a hat off the hall rack. He hurried to the car.

"Hi, boy." Someone called to him. Julian had his foot on the starter and he identified the greeter as Whit Hofman. Well, Whit was a son of a bitch, too. Whit probably hated him and had hated him for years, just as Froggy had done. The car jumped out of the snow and Julian drove as fast as he could to the quickest way out of Gibbsville. The worst of that drive was that the sun glare on the snow made you smile before you were ready.

Your home is the center of many zones. The first zone is your home, the second can be the homes around you, which you know only less well than you do your home. In the second zone you know where the rainpipes have stained the shingles on the houses, you know where the doorbell button is, how much of a bedpost can be seen in an upstairs window; the length of slack taken up in the porch-swing chains; the crack in the sidewalk; the oil spots from the drip-pans in the driveway; the lump of coal, which you remember from the time it was not swept away, and its metamorphosis from day to day as it is crushed and crushed into smaller lumps and into dust and then all that is left of it is a black blot, and you are glad one day that it has been crushed and it no longer is there to accuse you of worrying about your neighbor's slovenliness. And so on.

The next zone is the homes and buildings you pass every day on your way to work. The tin signs outside little stores, the trees with the bark gnawed away by horses, the rope on the gates and the ancient weights, the places where the street ought to be repaired, the half-second view of the town clock tower between two houses. And so on.

And more zones, zones that the farther you get from the center, the longer spaces there are in the familiar things. In one zone a hundred yards of highway will be familiar, while in another zone the familiar spaces are a matter of inches. In the familiar zones remembering is effortless. An outside zone is where your brain begins to tell you where to make a turn in the road and where to keep going straight and where to blow your horn and where to slow down for a curve. Julian was in an outside zone, southwest of Gibbsville and in the Pennsylvania Dutch farming country, when he first brought himself up. He was first able to perceive that he had been driving, judging by the distance at least a half hour, when he became aware of not having a hat on. He reached over and picked up the hat beside him, but his fingers rejected the dents in the crown, and he examined the hat. The brim did not snap down in front. It was a Stetson, and Julian wore Herbert Johnson hats from Brooks Brothers. But he did not like to see men driving hatless in closed cars; it was too much like the Jews in New York who ride in their town cars with the dome lights lit. He put the hat on the back of his head, and lowered the window at his side. The first breath of air made him want a cigarette almost immediately, and he slowed down to light one from the torch on the dashboard.

The road was his. He wanted to drive on the left side and zigzag like an army transport and idle along at four miles an hour. But one time when he thought the road was his he had done all these things, finally to be arrested for drunken driving by a highway patrolman who had been following him all the while. "You'd think you owned the road," the patrolman had said; and Julian could not answer that that was exactly what he had been thinking.

So long as the engine did tricks for him he knew he was safe, but when he discovered this about the car, that it was occupying his mind and keeping it off the events of the last hour, two hours, twenty-four hours, forty-eight hours—although it was not forty-eight hours since he had doused Harry Reilly with a highball—the discovery forced his eyes to the clock. And the clock said three-eleven. It was three-eleven back at the garage, and he had to get back to see Lute Fliegler. He slowed down and stopped just beyond a country lane, he backed the car in the lane and then drove out, and the radiator now pointed in the direction of Gibbsville and not away from it. The faster he drove the less he liked the zones he was getting into. He wished he had gone on instead of turning around. To go on until he had spent his money, write a check in Harrisburg, write another in Pittsburgh, until his money was gone; then sell the car, sell it and buy a second-hand Ford, sell his coat, sell his watch, then sell the Ford, then get a job in a lumber camp or something—where he wouldn't last a minute, not a day. There was something awfully good and lucky for him in being guided out of the club and into the car and away, but something else had pulled him back. You did not really get away from whatever it was he was going back to, and whatever it was, he had to face it. His practical sense told him that the idea of going away, writing checks, selling the car and so on, eventually would catch up to him. He probably would break a law. Oh, more than that. The way things were now at the garage, he had no right to sell this car, nor even to run away. He was too tall to run away. He would be spotted.

And so he kept his foot on the accelerator, hurrying back to Gibbsville. The cigarette burned down to his glove—he could not remember putting the gloves on—and made a little stink. He threw the cigarette out and he yawned. Always when he felt sleepy while driving he would light a cigarette and it would revive him, but now he was sleepy and tired and did not want to be revived. Even the little fight in him annoyed him. He did not want to fight and he did not want to be awake.

You would look at Mrs. Waldo Wallace Walker, dressed in a brown sweater with a narrow leather belt, and a tweed skirt from Mann and Dilks, and Scotch grain shoes with fringed tongues, and a three-cornered hat. You would know her for all the things she was: a woman who served on Republican committees because her late husband had been a Republican, although she always spelt it tarriff. She would be a good bridge player and a woman who knew the first two lines of many songs, who read her way in and out of every new book without being singed, pinched, bumped, or tickled by any line or chapter. Between doing the last thing and the next she would beat her hands together in little claps, rubbing her pure, once pretty fingers together for the warmth she generated in the fingertips, and making you expect her to say something good and wise about life. But what she would say would be: "Oh, fish! I *must* have my *rings* cleaned."

A stranger, spending his first hour with her, would look at her clothes and think what trunkfuls of once stylish suits and hats and dresses she must have—and she had them. She was the prettiest woman of her age in Gibbsville, and though she did not know it and would not have accepted it, her hair-dresser would have been glad to do her for nothing, she was such a good ad. She also would have made a good ad for spectacles; but she also would have made a good ad for drinking a cup of hot water in the morning, Don't Worry, take a nap every afternoon, walk a mile every day, the Golden Rule, visit your dentist twice a year, and all the other codes that she had the time and the means to live by.

Judge Walker had not left a great fortune, but there was money there. Mrs. Walker gave $250 to this, $15 to that, and never personally turned a hungry man away from her kitchen door. When Caroline was at Bryn Mawr, Mrs. Walker, according to Caroline, became president ex officio of the college, and in later years it was always with difficulty that Caroline restrained her mother from calling on Dr. Marion every time they motored through Bryn Mawr, the town. Someone once told Mrs. Walker that Caroline had great independence of spirit, and this delighted the mother and caused her to allow Caroline to develop as much as possible unassisted. Whatever independence of spirit Caroline possessed had developed unassisted before Mrs. Walker made a philosophy of it, but at least Mrs. Walker did make it much easier for Caroline, and Caroline made it as easy as possible for her mother to develop unassisted too. There had been nothing but placid love in their relationship from the time Caroline began taking her own baths. It was a comfortable relationship, only slightly disturbed, if at all, by the fact that from the time of that necessary talk when Caroline was thirteen, Caroline always thought of her mother as a person who could say "the mouth of the womb" without leaving the tiniest inference of any excitement to be had there. In the beginning of her love with Julian, Caroline sometimes felt sorry for her mother as she felt sorry for all the females she liked because of what they were missing, but after a year or two she wondered if it could not be possible that her mother simply had forgot the hours of her own passion. Julian said that a lovely lady had to be passionate to get that look—and Mrs. Walker had been a lovely lady. Julian was fond of his wife's mother, a fondness that was incomplete only because he was not sure that she really liked him. But Mrs. Walker gave everyone who knew her well that feeling; and the truth was that at the moment of ordering the groceries, Mrs. Walker was as fond of Joe Machamer, the clerk at Scott's, as she was of anyone except her daughter, and the dignity in the memory of her husband, and Abraham Lincoln. (Mrs. Walker had an uncle whose home had been part of the underground railway for slaves.)

Mrs. Walker was turning the pages of a Christmas book, *Mr. Currier and Mr. Ives,* when she heard the front door open and close. "Who is it?" she sang.

"Me." Caroline took off her gloves and coat and hat, and her mother put up her hand as though to ward off a too-affectionate kiss (it gave that impression), but when her daughter lowered her head to kiss her, Mrs. Walker cupped Caroline's chin in the palm of her hand. "Dear," she said. "Did you have a nice Christmas. Never even telephoned, did you?"

"Yes, I did, but you were out."

"Yes, I was. I did go to Uncle Sam's. You look well, dear."

"I don't feel well. I feel like the devil. Mother, what—"

"Yes, a little tired. A little strained. Why don't you make Julian take you—"

"What would you do if I got a divorce?"

"—to Pinehurst. Divorce? Oh, now, Caroline. Four years, almost five. Divorce."

"I thought so," said Caroline. She relaxed. "I'm sorry. I just came here because I had to speak to somebody and I didn't want to talk to somebody that'd blab it all over."

"Are you serious?"

"Yes, I'm serious."

"But are you? Are you serious, Caroline? That's a very serious thing, when people start talking about a divorce. We've never had a divorce in our family, and I don't think there was ever one in Julian's family either. What is it?"

"I'm just fed up. I'm sick and tired and miserable. I'm so miserable and unhappy. I'm so unhappy, Mother, I don't care if I die."

"Die, dear? Are you pregnant? Are you, dear? You could be wrong, you know. It might just be the strain, Christmas." She got up and sat beside Caroline. "Come here, dear. Tell me about it. Mother wants to hear all about it."

"Caroline wants to cry," said Caroline, and laughed.

"Oh, this *is* serious. Dear, don't. Have you missed the second period, dear?"

"Yes. Someone was in our seats. Oh, Mother, please. I'm not pregnant. That's not it."

"Are you sure, dear?"

"I'm positive. Mother, please don't worry about that. That's not it at all. It isn't that. I guess I don't want to talk about it," said Caroline. "I'll tell you what's the matter. I might as well. I'm through with Julian. I want to go away and get a divorce and never hear his name again for a long time. We can go to France, can't we? Can't we?"

"Well, I suppose so. This year we ought to be a little more careful, Mr. Chadwick says and Carter. Carter isn't very optimistic. But we could if we had to, go to Europe I mean. Seven. Twenty-five. Hundred and. Oh, we could go. You wouldn't want to buy many things, would you, dear?"

"I don't want to buy anything. I want a divorce. I want to stop being with Julian English and this life. All I am is tired. It's nothing more than that. I'm just tired and fed up. I'm all washed up and I want to go away. I want to sleep here tonight and all other nights. I want to forget Julian and I want to talk to somebody and go away. I want to talk to somebody with an English accent or I don't know. I'm sorry."

"This is serious. Tell me all about it if you want to. Of course if you'd rather not."

"I'm not making much sense, am I?"

"Did you have a quarrel? Oh, you must have, of course."

"No. Strangely enough, we didn't. Not what you'd call a quarrel. That is, we didn't have any scene or anything. It isn't as easy as that. That could be fixed, I guess."

"Well, what then? Julian isn't in love with someone else, is he? I can't somehow I can't believe that. I don't profess to know much about Julian, or any men, for that matter, but if Julian's in love with someone else, then I'm no judge at all. If it's just another woman temporarily, dear, don't wreck your life on that account, I beg of you. Don't wreck your whole life. Men are different from us women. An unscrupulous woman can make a man—"

"Period."

"What, dear?"

"Nothing."

"Well, as I was saying, dear, please listen. A woman without any scruples—and it might be someone we know. I don't know a thing about this other woman, but there are unscrupulous women in every strata of life."

"Mother?"

"Yes, dear."

"Mother, what did you do with all the old records?"

"What old records, dear? Do you mean the Victrola records? Those?"

"Yes. What did you do with them?"

"Oh, don't you remember I gave them to the Y.M.C.A. camp three years ago. You said at the time you didn't want them, only a few. You took *some*."

"Oh, so I did."

"If there's any special one you want we could send for it. Mr. Peters would be glad to get it I'm sure. He wants me to buy an autophonic and trade this one in, this Victrola. But I'd never use an autophonic. I never use this one."

"Orthophonic, Mother."

"Orthophonic? It sounded like autophonic. Are you sure? Mr. Peters, I was sure he said autophonic. Or, Caroline, see?"

"What, Maman?"

"See? It's all over, isn't it? Your bad spell. Here we are, having one of our discussions about words. You and Julian. You didn't leave any foolish notes, did you, dear?"

"Oh, God no. I never thought to. Mother, do you really think I came running to you with a silly five-minute quarrel?"

"Well, after all, you're not upset any more, are you?"

"Do you really think I'm not?"

"Yes. I do. I really think the worst of it has passed, gone. Your father and I had our quarrels, too."

"When he died you said you never quarreled."

"I never said that. At least, I never tried to give the impression that we didn't have our differences. That would be untrue. All high-strung people, people in love, they always have their differences. As a matter of fact, Caroline, I've been thinking all along, something told me there wasn't much to this. I'm nothing if not sympathetic and you know there's nothing I wouldn't do to see you happy, but I don't want you to behave like a foolish child and do things and say things you'll be sorry for later. Divorce! Why the very idea is—it's wrong, Caroline, and I don't see how you could say such things. You go on back to Julian, or stay here a while if you want to punish him, but stop this talk about divorce. Understand, I'm not defending Julian, but I should think you'd know how to handle him by this time. Flatter him, use your feminine wiles. You're a pretty girl and he loves you. Believe me, Caroline, when a wife can't hold a husband and there's no other woman, the wife had better stop and see where the lack is in herself. Oh, my. It's all so much like the time your father and I had our first quarrel."

"What was your first quarrel about—not that this is my first, but go on, dear. Tell me. Caroline wants to know."

"It wasn't anything much. It was personal. Just between your father and I, dear."

"Sex?"

"Caroline! Yes, it was, in a way. Is that—is—are you and Julian—does he want you to do something you—something . . ."

If she only knew Julian, Caroline thought; if she only knew me! "No, dear, Julian's always been very good about that," she said.

"Oftentimes men don't understand. Many girls' lives are ruined, completely wrecked, because men don't understand how a nice girl feels. But let's not talk about that. I told you when you were married, I told you to take a firm stand on certain things."

"You never told me what things, though."

"Well, dear, a nice girl. I couldn't very well tell you some things till the matter came up. Apparently it never did, or you'd have come to me, I'm sure. You're still only a girl, though, Caroline, and if you're having trouble that way, that sort of trouble, please come to me instead of going to some friend your own age. I think things of that sort ought to be talked over between mother and daughter, not outsiders. I finally learned how to handle your father and my experience isn't worth a thing, not a snap of the fingers, unless I'm able to help you, hand it on to you. But let's not talk about it unless you want to."

"Tell me more about Father," said Caroline.

"No. No. That's sacred. Your father never worried me about another woman, not even before we were married. Julian, I think probably Julian—not that it's anything against him, because he was quite grown up when he fell in love with you. But I don't think you were the first girl in Julian's life. I've often thought so. That may be a good thing in some cases, but I don't know."

"Mother, don't talk about it if you don't want to. I'm sorry."

"Conversations like this aren't good, Caroline. I'd rather go on, living my poor useless life and loving your father for what he was, a good, decent man, than exhume chapters of our life together. Men are weak, darling. In the hands of a woman the strongest man in the world is weak, so don't think any the less of Julian or your father or any other man if he has a momentary weakness. . . . Oh, here I am, talking away about something I don't know the first thing about. But you do feel better toward Julian, don't you? If you do, that's all that's necessary."

"I'm sorry if I was inconsiderate."

"Oh, you weren't inconsiderate. You couldn't be. You were just curious. That shows you're still a little girl. Want some gum?"

"I'd love some."

"It's really very good for the digestion, and I think the muscles of the jaw need the exercise. How are your teeth, Caroline?"

"I'm going to have a wisdom tooth out, Dr. Patterson says."

"Well, he probably knows his business. I still like Dr. Baldwin."

"Not after lunch, though, Mother."

"What? Why?"

"He bolts his food or eats too much or something. His stomach rumbles."

"I never noticed that when I went to him," said Mrs. Walker. "Are you sure?"

"Oh, yes. I wouldn't make up a thing like that."

"Do you want to stay here tonight? Isn't there a dance tonight?"

"There's one in Reading. No, I guess I better not stay here. As a matter of fact, we're having a party."

"Oh, I didn't know that. A big party? Who are you having?"

"The usual crowd. The young crowd, a few from the school crowd, and our own friends. Which reminds me."

"Is there anything you want?"

"No, but I must go. I was going to call it off when I first came here, but I might as well go through with it, so I must do some shopping, odds and ends. I'll see you tomorrow or next day. Give me a nice Beech-Nut kiss. Good-by."

"Good-by, darling. You're a sweet girl."

"You're the one that's sweet," said Caroline. She put on her things in the hall, knowing that her mother was standing at the window, waiting to wave to her. Well, at least she had made some kind of gesture for tradition; she had run to mother. The visit had been a fiasco, but she was glad in a way that it had been—glad that it had been a fiasco in the way that it had been, but sorry if it were to result in awakening disturbing memories, whatever they were, for her mother.

She ran down the steps and turned and waved to her mother before getting in the car. Her mother waved and then the curtains fell into place and her mother withdrew from the window. Then Caroline heard a long blast of a Cadillac horn, and she saw Julian in his car, half a block down the street, on the other side. He was waiting. She drove her car near his, staying on her side of the street, and stopped. He got out and sauntered over. He looked like hell.

"Well," she said.

"You were in there long enough. What did you have to see her for?"

"Now really, Julian. Is that reasonable?"

"Is it reasonable for you to be down here now? What's it all about? I suppose you had to take down your back hair and have a good cry and so forth."

No answer.

"Oh, that's it. Giving her a song and dance about me, I suppose. Little bride runs to mother because hubby doesn't like her biscuits. For Christ's sake. Good God, I tried to—what did you tell her? Come on, what did you say?"

"This is no place for a scene."

"It's as good a place as any. Better, in fact. It's safer for you, because I probably won't do here what I feel like doing."

"You mean punch me in the face, I suppose."

"How did you ever guess it?"

"If you take your foot off the running-board I'd like to get going."

"I suppose you heard about the club."

"I didn't. What club? What do you mean, the club? Has the club suspended you on account of the other night?"

"Now she's interested. No, the club hasn't suspended me, not as far as I know. This is a different club, this time."

"The Gibbsville Club?"

"The Gibbsville Club no less."

"What happened there? What did you do there?"

"I had a little get-together with Mr. Ogden, Captain Ogden, the war hero, the one-armed wonder and snooper extraordinaire."

"What do you mean?"

"You'll find out. You'll find out soon enough. You said something about going a minute ago. Go ahead."

"I don't want to go now till I find out what you're talking about. More trouble. God, I'm so tired of it." Her voice broke and she began to cry.

"No scenes on the street, dearie. No scenes on the street. No street scenes, if you please. It's your idea. Can't have things like this in public."

"Oh, Julian, what did you do? My God." She was now really crying. Her voice had the far-away sound of hollow pain, despairing women in removed rooms down a hospital hall, wailing women at the mouth of a blown-up mine.

"Listen, will you go away with me? Now? This minute? Will you? Will you go away with me?"

"No, no, no, no, no. What did you do? Tell me what you did? What did you do to Froggy?"

"I can't talk to you like this. Let's go home."

"Oh, no. I don't want to go home. You'll make me stay with you. Oh, go away, Julian. Please let me alone." A horn sounded and a small coupé passed. Caroline waved. Julian waved. It was Wilhelmina Hall and the visiting Gould man from New York. "Are they going to stop?" said Caroline.

"No. They're going on. Me too," he said.

"No. What did you do? Tell me. Come in to Mother's with me. She knows we're having a quarrel. She won't bother us."

"Like a whole lot of hell I will. I'm not going in there. I'm going."

"If you leave I'm going to call off the party and I'm going to stay here. Be reasonable, Julian. Tell me what happened."

"No. Come on home with me and I'll tell you. Otherwise no. This is a pretty good time for you to stick by me."

"I can't stick by you if you don't tell me what for."

"Blind, without knowing, you could stick by me. That's what you'd do if you were a real wife, but, what the hell."

"Where are you going? To get drunk I suppose."

"Very likely. Very likely."

"Julian, if you leave now it's for good. Forever. I won't ever come back to you, no matter what happens. I won't ever sleep with you again or see you, not even see you."

"Oh, yes, you will. You will, all right."

"You're pretty sure of yourself, but this time you're wrong. It's no go."

"I didn't mean that. I didn't mean I was sure of myself. What I meant was, you'd see me. You wouldn't be able to help it."

"Why should I want to?"

"To gloat, probably. Either you'd want to gloat, if you were absolutely out of love with me, or you'd want to see me if you still loved me."

"You're so wrong it isn't even funny."

"It isn't even funny. Lord and Taylor! Wouldn't that jar you? I'll say. You tell 'em casket, I'm coffin. I'll tell the world. Don't take any wooden nickels. . . . I'm going."

"Oh, go ahead. But remember, I'm not going to be home tonight. Not me. I'm going to call off the party, unless you want to have it. Anyway, I won't be there."

"That's all right. It only makes a different kind of a party."

"Oh, there's no need to tell me that. But you'd better be careful with your torch singer. She knows how to handle people like you."

"You're a dear. You're a sweet girl. I knew you'd be a good sport about it. I knew all along you would be."

"Oh, go to hell, you and your cheap sarcasm."

"No wonder the chaps at the club say I'm henpecked," said Julian. He regretted it the moment he said it; club was not a word he wanted to use now. "You'll attend to the details about the party, calling people up and telling them I broke my leg and so on, will you?"

"Of course, unless you want to have it yourself and say I have a broken leg."

"That's better. I don't mean about you having a broken leg. But it's nicer for us to be agreeable and sort of phony about it. You know what I mean?"

"You're the authority on phony, of course, but, yes, I know what you mean. I know."

"All right, dear. Cheerio, I mean cherro. Stout fella."

"Funny boy. You're a scream."

So he left.

9

GIBBSVILLE MOVED UP from the status of borough and became a third class city in 1911, but in 1930 the city still had less than 25,000 inhabitants (estimated 1930 population in the notebooks sent out by the Gibbsville banks to their depositors). In Gibbsville a party becomes an institution the moment the hostess tells her plans to one other person, and nothing short of a death or other act of God must postpone the party, once the invitations are given. To the persons who eventually had been invited and to those who wished they had, the English party got in the institution class a day or two after the Lafayette-Lehigh football week-end. On their way home from Easton, Caroline and Julian decided to have a party "some time during the holidays." They were riding in Whit Hofman's car, with Whit and Kitty, and Kitty immediately said it would be a swell idea, and began to count off the nights when the party could not be given on account of conflicting parties. It couldn't be given the night of any of the Gibbsville dances nor the afternoon of the tea dances. Kitty Hofman finally decided upon the date. "There's the Junior League dance in Reading the night after Christmas Day," she said, "but I'm sick of going to Reading. Let them come up here for a change. We go down there and spend our money on their lousy Junior League parties, but if we ever tried to have a Junior League in Gibbsville you know what support we'd get from Reading."

No argument.

"So let them come to our parties this year," Kitty continued. "The Assembly. That money goes to charity, doesn't it, Whit?"

"In theory it does," said Whit.

"It usually ends up with Whit paying for the Assembly," said Julian.

"Don't forget, you pay your share," said Whit. "We all do. But they do come to the Assembly, sometimes they do."

"All right. Let them come again. Let's not go to their Junior League dance. Let them help our charity. Caroline, you have your party that night. The twenty-sixth."

"How about it, Ju? That's all right, isn't it?"

"You're God damn right. I won a hundred dollars on the game. No, two hundred. But anyway, a hundred that I'll get. Bobby Herrmann will owe me his hundred."

"Well then, that's settled. The twenty-sixth we'll have our party. Our own crowd and some of the school kids, the ones that can drink. Not Johnny Dibble and kids that age, but a little older."

"Oh, dear me," said Julian. "My goodness sakes alive. Oh, my. We have to have Johnny. We must have Johnny Dibble. Why, he's practically a Deke. No matter where he goes to college, he's going to be a Deke."

"Not if he goes to State," said Whit.

"Right. Not if he goes to State. No Dekes at State. How'd you know that, Whit? You know more about D. K. E. than I do. Why can't we have Johnny, Caroline? He's a nice kid. . . . Well, *kind* of nice."

"All right, we'll have him, if you insist. He drinks as well as you do, for that matter. He'll make a good Deke. Who else shall we blackball?" Caroline and Kitty worked on the list, and the next week it was in Gwen Gibbs' column on the society page of the *Standard*. Gwen Gibbs' column was a dumping ground for all society gossip on the *Standard*. There was no Miss Gibbs, of course. There was an Alice Cartwright, graduate of the University of Missouri School of Journalism, and daughter of the current Baptist minister. Miss Cartwright knew very few of the Lantenengo Street crowd and except for the Purim Ball and K. of C. Promenade she was not on any of the invitation lists. She certainly never for a second expected to be on the list of the invited guests for the English party. And she wasn't. Yet the night of the party she was the only one who arrived at the attractive home of that leading young business man and that charming leader of the younger married set; in this case, Mr. and Mrs. Julian M. English.

Julian got afraid of something the moment he walked away from Caroline and climbed in his own car. He never looked her way again after he left her. He treated his car more considerately. He moved along, approaching the business district at a moderate rate of speed, extra-careful of the rights of other motorists and of pedestrians, and resolved that since he was already a quarter of an hour late for his date with Lute Fliegler, he would break the date entirely and without explanation. He did that with a clear conscience because he effected an exchange in himself: in exchange for accepting in advance the hell and the fury of what he was going to have to face with his father and Harry Reilly and the lesser stockholders in the company, who were going to have to save him from bankruptcy—he paid himself off by keeping the rest of this day to himself. If ever there was a man in a jam, he was it, he was sure. It was no more difficult to face a fist or to enter the front-line trenches than it was going to be to meet these people, especially his father. Nobody would have the crust to tell his father about the Stage Coach episode, because his father was a kind of man who would have the Stage Coach raided for less reason than that his son had been a fool there. But someone was sure to tell him about throwing a drink in Harry Reilly's puss. It was the sort of thing Gibbsville men, their identities masked by hot towels, would be hearing often in the hotel barber shop for the next couple of weeks. And yet it was not so bad as the mess at the Gibbsville Club. The Polack lawyers would tell every— "Good Christ! Polacks are Roman Catholics!" Julian thought of that for the first time. And now he remembered seeing the emblem of the Benevolent and Protective Order of Elks in the lapel of the man he had knocked down. "Is there anything I haven't done? Anyone I haven't insulted, at least indirectly?" . . . He tried to be honest and to figure out every possible bad angle to the last few days' work, in order that he could go back and find something comforting. He thought of the bad way he had treated Caroline, the many bad ways; doing something that permitted her to accept disgrace, as with the drink thrown at Harry Reilly; doing something that publicly and unequivocally and personally humiliated her, which was going out with Helene Holman. His manner toward Mrs. Grady this morning—a thing Caroline especially (and, sometimes, a little unreasonably) campaigned against. And then, a little before he was ready for it, he thought of the thing that in its way was more important than anything between himself and Caroline; that thing was the never-to-be-buried discovery that all this time Froggy Ogden had been his enemy. That was worse than anything he could do to Caroline, because it was something that did something to him. It made a change in himself, and we must not change ourselves much. We can stand only so many—so few—changes. To know that there were people who he thought were his friends, his good friends, but who were his enemies—that was going to make a change, he knew. When was the last time there had been a change in himself? He thought and thought, rejecting items that were not change but only removal or adornment. He thought and thought, and the last time there had been a change in himself was when he discovered that he, Julian English, whom he had gone on thinking of as a child with a child's renewable integrity and curiosity and fears and all, suddenly had the power of his own passion; that he could control himself and use this control to give pleasure and a joyous hiatus of weakness to a woman. He could not remember which girl it had been; to forget her had been a simple manifestation of his ego; the important part of the discovery, the change, had been a thing for himself, his own moment. But he saw how deep and permanent the discovery, the change, became. It was almost as important, and no doubt precisely as permanent, as the simplest discovery of physical manhood. And there again it was the change and not the act that had been lasting and great; for he could not recall with accuracy the circumstances of that discovery.

It was easier to bear now, the discovery that it was possible that to him it might happen that there were people who bothered to hate him. Why did they bother, really? Yet they did. People also liked him. Still it was no shock to find out, for example, that a girl had been loving you for a long time before you found it out. Part of you expected people, girls especially, to like you, and there was no jolt but only a corroboratory pat on the back in the experience of hearing a girl say, "Darling, I've loved you so much longer than you have me." Girls fitted easily into their own and your own picture of someone dying of unrequited love. If they slipped out of it before you were ready, that was all right too; their slipping out frequently was the necessary reminder that an affair had run its course. It also was the necessary reminder that the realist in a woman, the good appraiser, makes her want to take a loss and get out before she is—for the purposes of the analogy—ruined.

Often Julian had faced this suspicion: the suspicion that a man who is good with women, as good as he had been, is not wholly trusted and liked by men. In the past he had thought of this many times, but he dodged the conclusion as applying to himself. Men liked to have him on poker parties, in golf foursomes, at luncheons (the Lions Club finally got him after he had squirmed away from Rotary and Kiwanis). But now he wondered if there was the slightest meaning to their including him in their gregariousness. No, there was no meaning more flattering than their habit. And as he drove the car in the garage at the side of his house he began to see things. Froggy Ogden, making a boastful confession of treachery and long hatred of him, had seemed proud of having done the job so well that Julian had not thought of him as anything but a friend. There must be others like him. Froggy had been one of his best friends. What about Carter? Whit? Bob Herrmann (who was a fool, but had a life and was leading it)? What about the wives of the men he liked? Those men, many of whom could have hated him and probably did hate him, must have told their wives. Jean Ogden, for instance. She'd known all along that Froggy hated him, but never gave any sign of warning. Did Kitty Hofman's bad manners come from the assurance she got from knowing that Whit hated him? . . . And if it only was hate! It would be so much better hate than just being disliked and held in contempt. It came back again to women; the fellows, those who knew him best, had kidded him about his Polish friend. But all the time they had kidded him they were being moral, and all the time they were being moral, underneath that they were wishing they had Mary. But Mary had been his girl. He closed the door of the garage. Mary had been his girl and he got again the sensation of looking at her. Just for a second the sensation came back; the embarrassment he had felt so many times, with wanting to look at her beautiful body but with his eyes held by her quiet, shining smile until then she would look at her breasts and then look at him and the smile would be gone. And he was sure now of what he had not quite wanted to be sure of then: that Mary had loved him and never would love anyone else the same way. He put her out of his mind and went in the house and sat down and stretched out on the couch in front of the fireplace. Oh, he went to sleep, wishing he knew more things.

It was dark and one hand of the clock was on ten, but Julian could not be sure that it was the big hand or the little hand and he was too comfortable to move so he could see his watch. Then he knew why he was awake. The doorbell was ringing. He got up and ran his fingers through his hair and pulled his vest and coat around and fixed his tie. It could have been Caroline at the door. The girl was about the same height. But when he got closer he saw she was wearing glasses. He opened the door and the air was good.

"Oh, good evening, Mr. English. I'm Miss Cartwright from the *Standard*. I'm sorry to disturb you. I thought you were having a party."

"It's been postponed. Won't you come in?"

"Well, I don't think I ought to really. But that's news." She was confused by Julian's smile. "I don't mean it's news when I don't come in."

"Well, come on in and have a drink," he said. God knows why he wanted to talk to her, but she was somebody.

"Well, for a minute. I meant to say it's news if you're not going to have the party. Is it postponed? Sickness in the family? Is Mrs. English not feeling well, or what?"

"No. I think you'd better call Mrs. English at Mrs. Walker's. She'll tell you about it."

"Oh, dear," said Miss Cartwright, lighting a Spud. "Now that means I have to get something to fill the column. I don't suppose I could run it and say the following will attend—when is the party postponed to, Mr. English, or is it indefinitely?"

"Indefinitely, I think. Do you like Scotch or rye? Or would you rather have a Benedictine or something like that?"

"Rye and ginger ale, if you have it," she said.

"Is that your car outside?" he said.

"My brother's. That is, it belongs to him and another boy. It's just an old flivver, on its last legs, but it saves me a lot of steps and trolley fares when he comes home. He always lends it to me when he's home, but he takes it to college with him. He goes to Brown."

"Oh, Brown."

"Yes. Providence, Rhode Island."

"Yes, I've been there."

"Oh, did you go to Brown, Mr. English? There aren't many from around here go to Brown."

"No. I went to Lafayette, but I've been to Brown, just to visit."

"Aren't you going to have one?"

"Yes, I think I will."

"I hate to drink by myself. They say that's the sign of an insane person, when they drink alone."

"That's probably one of those things started by the saloon-keepers. You know, like three on a match was started by the match trust in Sweden."

"Oh, that's very interesting. I never heard that. Yes, I did. Come to think of it."

"Won't you take off your coat?"

"I really shouldn't. I can only stay a minute and get the story. Uh. Postponed. Would you care to tell me why you're postponing it, Mr. English?"

"Mrs. English would be able to tell you better. I think you ought to ask her, because it's really her party. I'd rather not talk to the press, because after all it *is* her party."

"Oh, I see," said Miss Cartwright. "Oh, don't hang it up. Just put it on the chair or some place. This is awfully strong. I'm not used to drinking. I don't suppose I average more than a drink a week, all year round."

"I'll give you some more ginger ale."

"This is an awfully attractive house. Did Mrs. English do it herself?"

"Yes."

"She has terribly good taste. Oh! Foujita! I *love* Foujita! Is it a real Foujita or a copy? I mean—"

"It's a print. You look quite different without glasses."

"I have to wear them when I'm driving or walking. I couldn't get a license unless I wore them and if I drive without them I'm liable to be fined or have my license taken away. Why don't you try a Spud?"

"No, thanks. I can't get used to them."

"That's what *I* thought, but I did finally, and now I can't smoke any other kind. I hope I'm not keeping you from anything, Mr. English."

"Far from it. I'm glad you came."

"I shouldn't have come, but I did want to get the list of guests right. People are so touchy. Not that Mrs. English is. She's very considerate, and believe me, that's a lot. But I've made some mistakes lately about who was at whose party and so on, and some of the Gibbsville matrons have raised the devil down at the office. So I only have this list we printed in Gwen Gibbs a month ago and I wanted to be sure if there were any changes. Additions and so on, to the original list."

"It's a tough job, isn't it?"

"Oh, is *it ever tough?* It isn't really, most of the time, but once in a while we have a sort of wave of indignation or something. Women call up and just raise the devil because names were left out or parties weren't given the prominence they thought they ought to have. And of course I always get it in the end, they pass the buck to me. Some people named Bromberg, Jews, they almost got me fired last week. They took out their ad and everything, just because I didn't use a story they sent in about some imported English perambulator they bought for their baby. You should have seen the story! I couldn't possibly use it or the paper would have been a joke, but did they back me up? They did not. I finally had to run a half a stick about it, but I killed the gushy part, and so the Brombergs put their ad in again and I have to lick everybody's boots and kowtow to everybody that appears on the society page. Not Mrs. English, but I can't say as much for some of your friends. Well, thanks very much for the drink and I'm sorry you're not having the party. It's very nice to have met you. I often see you driving those beautiful Cadillacs around town. When we first came to Gibbsville I used to wonder who you were. . . . My goodness, what made me say that?"

"Have another drink before you go. Stay and tell me more."

"Oh, yes. Oh, my yes. Can't you just see me? No, I better go while the going's good. Oh, I don't mean that the way it sounds, Mr. English, but people talk so much in this town." Julian had a quick recollection of a story about the Baptist minister's daughter going without stockings. Unwillingly he looked at her legs, and she apprehended the look. "That's it," she said. "You heard it yourself. I'll never live it down, going without stockings. It's all right in front of Queen Mary, but not in Gibbsville. Well, thanks again. See you again some time."

"Don't go," he said. Unaccountably he liked her. More than that, he didn't want her to put on her glasses. She wasn't bad-looking. She wasn't pretty. But she wasn't bad-looking, and she had an interesting figure; not sensationally good, but you could have fun with it. He hated himself, but he had an enormous desire to discover this girl.

"What time is it?" she said.

"It isn't even ten o'clock. It's still in the nine class. Nine-thirty-five, nine-thirty-seven, something like that. It's very early."

"Well, one more drink, although why you want me to stay I don't know. I look a wreck. Haven't even been home from the office." She gazed around the room, just getting ready to sit down, and then she said: "Mr. English, I'd feel a thousand per cent better if you'd let me wash my hands."

"Oh, I'm terribly sorry. I'll show you."

"Just tell me where it is, I'll find it."

"I better show you. There's no light, I don't think."

"This is terribly embarrassing, or would be if you weren't so nice. I always feel more at ease with a married man. Tell you the truth, my back teeth are floating."

He was shocked and he was glad it was too dark for her to see his face. Either that one drink had had an unusual effect, or little Miss Cartwright—who was not little, but rather reedy—could turn out to be fun. He lit the lights and then came downstairs and made himself a drink. He heard her, and then he saw her coming down the stairs, slowly now; step by step, at ease. Her steps might have meant self-confidence, in which case he did not like it and did not like her. He wanted to seduce this girl, but he wanted to do it because he was able to through experience and superior knowledge. He didn't want her to have anything to do with it except to acquiesce. Still, she was near-sighted or something. That might explain the way she walked.

"Rye and ginger ale," he said.

"Right," she said. She sat down, and now he was sure it was confidence. He almost laughed in her face. She was not a girl who would be included in anyone's list of attractive damsels, but she had as much confidence at this moment as Norma Shearer or Peggy Joyce or somebody. He knew now that she was not a virgin, no matter what he had thought ever before; and while he made a drink for her he imagined the ridiculous scene with probably a veterinary student with two or three scholastic keys and fraternity pins on his vest—the rush of life in the direction of Miss Cartwright, and the quick rush away. He wondered how old she was, and he asked her as he handed her her drink.

"Old enough to know better," and then, "I'm twenty-three. Why do you ask that? Just curiosity or what?"

The Big Ten confidence. "What, probably. I don't know. I just wondered. I couldn't make an accurate guess myself, so I asked you."

"That's refreshing nowadays. Now how old are you?"

"Thirty."

"That's what I thought. I thought about twenty-eight, but you go around with so much older people that I thought in a town like this you —oh, I don't know what I thought. It doesn't make much difference. This drink is *much* stronger. I suppose you know that."

"Yes. I made it exactly as strong as mine. As a matter of fact I had an extra one while you were upstairs. Where'd you go to school?"

"University of Missouri."

"Oh, did you? I was thinking of going to one of the Western Conference schools one time."

"Well, you wouldn't have gone to Missouri, then. Missouri isn't in the Conference."

"Oh, I thought it was."

"No," she said. "I started at Missouri before we came to Gibbsville. I was thinking of transferring to Columbia, to save the expense of train fare and so on, but I decided to stay out there. I studied journalism."

"Oh, I see," he said. Her breasts were small. Practically non-existent while she had her dress on, but they would be neat.

"I'm sorry in a way I didn't transfer, because I'd like to have spent a year or two in New York. Soon as I get enough money I'm going to try to get a job on a New York paper. The *World* is the paper I'd like to work on, but it's awfully hard to get a job there. It's awfully hard to get a job anywhere nowadays, at least on a paper. I have this friend of mine on the St. Louis *Post-Dispatch*, one of the best men they have, getting an awfully good salary. He went to New York on his vacation and he dropped in just to look around at one of the papers, and do you know what they offered him?"

"What?"

"Forty dollars a week! Good Lord, I'm getting twenty, and I don't know a thing compared to him, but forty dollars a week. That was as high as they'd go. You can imagine what *he* told *them*." She shook her head and reminisced with her eyes, not looking at Julian. So she felt more at ease with married men.

"How on earth does a man support a family on forty dollars a week? Oh, I know it's done, but on a paper I should think you'd have to dress pretty well?" Julian asked.

"That's exactly what this friend of mine said. He has a wife and child. He couldn't begin to afford to live in New York. His friends are always saying, why doesn't he go to New York. Well, that's the answer."

It certainly was, Julian reflected. It certainly was the answer. So a man with a wife and child had done it? That meant, most likely, that it had been done with more skill—and regularity—than if it had been done by a college boy. "Drink?" he said.

"Oh, all right," she said.

He made the drinks and went back to her with a drink in each hand. But instead of handing her hers he put both drinks down together on the small table and sat down beside her. He put his hand under her chin and she turned her face and smiled and then she closed her eyes and her mouth was open before it touched his. She brought up her

knees and pushed herself full-length out on the couch, and held his
head with her hands over his ears. "Just kiss me," she said, but she put
her hand under his coat and opened his vest and his shirt. "No," she
said. "Just kiss me." She was terribly strong. Suddenly she jerked away
from him. "Whew! Come up for air," she said. He hated her more than
anyone ever had hated anyone.

"Drink?" he said.

"No, I don't think so, I must go."

"Don't go," he said. He wanted to call her all kinds of bitches.

"Now is the best time," she said, but she did not get up.

"Well, it's up to you," he said.

"Listen, Joo-lian," she apologized by exaggerating the u in his
name, "if I stay here you know what'll happen."

"All right," he said.

"Not all right at all. You're married to a swell girl. I don't know her
at all, but I know she's swell, and you don't give a damn about me.
Oh, I don't want to talk about it. I admit. I have a yen for you, but—
but all the same I'm going. Good-by," she said, and she would not let
him help her with her coat. He heard the wurra-wurra of the starter
in her car, but he was not thinking of her. He was thinking of the
time after time he was going to hear those words in the future. "You're
married to a swell girl. I don't know her at all (or, "Caroline's one of
my best friends"). . . . I have a yen for you, but all the same I'm
going." Miss Cartwright was already deep in the past, the musty part
of the past, but now her words came out of the mouths of all the girls
he wanted to see. Telephone operators, department store clerks, sec-
retaries, wives of friends, girls in the school crowd, nurses—all the
pretty girls in Gibbsville, trying to make him believe they all loved
Caroline. In that moment the break with Caroline ceased to look like
the beginning of a vacation. Now it looked worse than anything, for
he knew that plenty of girls would do anything with a married man
so long as he was married, but in Gibbsville for the rest of his life he
was Caroline's husband. There could be a divorce, Caroline could
marry again for that matter, but no girl in Gibbsville—worth having—
would risk the loss of reputation which would be her punishment for
getting herself identified with him. He recalled a slang axiom that
never had any meaning in college days: "Don't buck the system;
you're liable to gum the works."

He didn't want to go back and make a more definite break
with Caroline. He didn't want to go back to anything, and he went
from that to wondering what he wanted to go to. Thirty years old.

"She's only twenty, and he's thirty. She's only twenty-two, and he's thirty. She's only eighteen, and he's thirty and been married once, you know. You wouldn't call him young. He's at least thirty. No, let's not have him. He's one of the older guys. Wish Julian English would act his age. He's always cutting in. His own crowd won't have him. I should think he'd resign from the club. Listen, if you don't tell him you want him to stop dancing with you, then I will. No thanks, Julian, I'd rather walk. No thanks, Mr. English, I haven't much farther to go. Listen, English, I want you to get this straight. Julian, I've been a friend of your family's for a good many years. Julian, I wish you wouldn't call me so much. My father gets furious. You better leave me out at the corner, becuss if my old man. Listen, you, leave my sister alone. Oh, hello, sweetie, you want to wait for Ann she's busy now be down a little while. No liquor, no meat, no coffee, drink plenty of water, stay off your feet as much as possible, and we'll have you in good shape in a year's time, maybe less." He had a drink. He had another and he got up and took off his coat and vest and tie. He had another and he brought the Scotch over and stood the bottle on the floor, and he got out his favorite records, which were in three albums. He put the albums on the floor. When he got drunk enough he would want to play them, but he wanted to have them near now. He lay down and then got up and brought the seltzer and the ice bucket and stood them beside the Scotch. He examined the Scotch bottle and saw there was not much more than a pint left, so he went to the dining room and got another and opened it, then put the cork back. He drank while walking and this demonstrated the inadequacy of the glass. He had a smart idea. He took the flowers out of a vase and poured the water out, and made himself the biggest highball he ever had seen. It did not last very long. He got up again and got a plate of hors-d'œuvres from the kitchen. They made him thirsty. He lowered his suspenders and felt much better.

"I think, if you don't mind, I think we shall play a little tune," he said aloud. He played Paul Whiteman's record of Stairway to Paradise, and when the record came to the "patter" he was screaming with jazz. The phonograph stopped itself but he was up and changing it to a much later record, Jean Goldkette's band playing Sunny Disposish. He laid a lot of records out on the floor without looking at their titles. He spun a spoon around, and when it stopped he would play the record to which it pointed. He played only three records in this way, because he was pounding his feet, keeping time, and he broke one of his most favorites, Whiteman's Lady of the Evening, valuable because it has the fanciest trick ending ever put on a record. He wanted to cry but he could not. He wanted to pick up the pieces. He reached over to pick them up, and lost his balance and sat down on another record, crushing it unmusically. He did not want to see what it was. All he knew was that it was a Brunswick, which meant it was one of the oldest and best. He had a drink out of the glass. He used the vase for resting-drinking, and the glass for moving-drinking. That way he did not disturb the main drink while moving around, and could fill the glass while getting up and sitting down. Unintentionally he lay back. "I am now," he said, "drunk. Drunk. Dronk. Drongk." He reached like a blind man for the fresh bottle and with eyes that he knew were sober he watched himself pour himself a drink. "No ice I get drunk kicker. Quicker," he said that aloud. To himself he said: "I bet I look like something nice now." He found he had two cigarettes burning, one in the ash tray on the floor, and the other getting stuck in the varnish on the edge of the phonograph. He half planned a lie to explain how the burn got there and then, for the first time, he knew it would not make any difference.

He got to his feet and went to the stairs. "Anybody in this house?" he called.

"Anybody in this house?

"Any, body, in, this, *house!*"

He shook his head. "Nope. Nobody in this house. You could wake the dead with that noise," he said.

He got a package of cigarettes from the table and took the new bottle of Scotch. He wished he had time to look around the room to see if everything was all right, no more cigarettes burning or anything like that, but there wasn't time. There wasn't time to put out the lights or pick up anything or straighten the rugs. Not even time to put on a coat, pull up his suspenders or anything. He went out on the porch and down the steps and opened the garage door and closed it behind him. He shivered a little bit from the cold, and it was cold in the garage, so he hurried. He had to see about the windows. They had to be closed. The ventilator in the roof was closed for the winter.

He climbed in the front seat and started the car. It started with a merry, powerful hum, ready to go. "There, the bastards," said Julian, and smashed the clock with the bottom of the bottle, to give them an approximate time. It was 10:41.

There was nothing to do now but wait. He smoked a little, hummed for a minute or two, and had three quick drinks and was on his fourth when he lay back and slumped down in the seat. At 10:50, by the clock in the rear seat, he tried to get up. He had not the strength to help himself, and at ten minutes past eleven no one could have helped him, no one in the world.

10

OUR STORY never ends.

You pull the pin out of a hand grenade, and in a few seconds it explodes and men in a small area get killed and wounded. That makes bodies to be buried, hurt men to be treated. It makes widows and fatherless children and bereaved parents. It means pension machinery, and it makes for pacifism in some and for lasting hatred in others. Again, a man out of the danger area sees the carnage the grenade creates, and he shoots himself in the foot. Another man had been standing there just two minutes before the thing went off, and thereafter he believes in God or in a rabbit's foot. Another man sees human brains for the first time and locks up the picture until one night years later, when he finally comes out with a description of what he saw, and the horror of his description turns his wife away from him. . . .

Herbert Harley said he thought he heard a car about ten o'clock. It sounded like a Ford, starting in front of the English home, but he could have been mistaken. Or, as Deputy Coroner Moskowitz pointed out, it could have been just any car that happened to stop in front of the English home. Dr. Moskowitz wanted to have the thing all neat and no loose ends, and he wished the driver of the car would come forth and reveal himself; but he guessed he never would; that part of town was pretty secluded, you might say, and necking couples often went there. So the car probably was just some necking couple, Dr. Moskowitz said, and anyway it was an open-and-shut case of suicide by carbon monoxide gas poisoning, the first of its kind in the history of the county (and a damn nice, clean way of knocking yourself off, he added off the record). What happened, as he reconstructed it, was: Mr. English had had difficulties with Mrs. English, so he went home and got drunk and while temporarily deranged through alcohol and grief, he, being well acquainted with the effects of carbon monoxide, being in the automobile business, why he committed suicide. There was no doubt about him being insane, at least temporarily, because from the broken Victrola records in the house, and the clock that was smashed in the car, deceased manifestly had been in a drunken rage and therefore not responsible. His widow, Caroline W. English, was apparently the last one to see him alive, and that was about four o'clock in the afternoon. Mrs. English had telephoned the two servants in the house and informed them that a party scheduled for that night was postponed, and they could go home so they went.

Fortunately deceased had seen fit to vent his rage and smash the clock in the front part of the car, which readily enabled the deputy coroner to fix the time of death at about eleven o'clock P.M., the night of December 26, year of Our Lord one thousand nine hundred thirty. Thus it will be seen that seven hours elapsed between the last time Caroline W. English had seen her late husband and the time of his death. This was verified by Mrs. Judge Walker, mother of Caroline W. English, at whose home Mrs. English had been stopping from the time she last saw deceased up to the time she had been informed of his death.

This had been done by Dr. William D. English, chief of staff, Gibbsville Hospital, and also father of deceased, the first physician called after the body was discovered.

The body had been discovered by Herbert G. Harley, next-door neighbor of deceased. Mr. Harley was an electrical engineer, employed by the Midas Washeries Company, operators of the Midas, Black Run, Horse Cave, and Sadim washeries. Mr. Harley was at home reading, the night of the death of Mr. English. Mrs. Harley had gone to bed early, being exhausted as it was the day after Christmas and with children in the house, the day after Christmas you know how it is. Well, so Mr. Harley was reading a book called *N by E,* by Rockwell Kent. He happened to remember that because he had met Mr. Kent once while on a visit to New York; he had met him at the Princeton Club. And that was how he happened to remember the name of the book. He was reading it, or rather to be exact studying the pictures in it, when he heard the car start in Mr. English's garage. The time, he should judge, as nearly as he could place it, was roughly about ten-thirty. In the evening. Ten-thirty P.M. He thought nothing of it at the time, as he and Mr. English came and went and while they were always very friendly and polite in a neighborly way, they never were what you would call good friends, as Mr. English traveled with, well, a different crowd from the one Mr. Harley traveled with. He had known Mr. English about four years and saw him on the average about once a day usually.

Well, so he went on reading the book and then for some reason that he couldn't explain, he got some sort of a premonition. It wasn't a premonition exactly, but more like the feeling you get when you *know* someone is in the room even before you *see* the person. That was the feeling he got, and Mr. Harley wanted to be sure to make it clear that he did not believe in spiritualism or anything like that, as he had a scientific education and he did not believe in that kind of bunk. It was all right for some people; they could believe what they liked. But Mr. Harley did not hold with that school of thought, and to prove it, he had an explanation, what might be called a scientific explanation, of why he had that feeling. The explanation was this: he had been sitting there perhaps a half an hour, and something inside him told him something was wrong. In a minute he understood what it was; it was the motor running.

All that time the motor had been running in Mr. English's car. You could feel the low vibration of it, hear the distant sound of it. Not loud, the sounds weren't; and the vibrations weren't strong. But out where they had their home you get so you know every little sound, and it was very unusual for a motor to be running that length of time. Mr. Harley debated with himself and finally decided to go take a look and see what was what. He thought perhaps Mr. English was having trouble with his car, and he was going to volunteer his assistance.

Well, the moment he stepped out on his front porch he knew there was *something* amiss. The motor was running, but the garage was dark. He got closer to the garage and he looked in a window—the one in the west wall of the garage—and all he could see was the car. The dash lights were the only lights in the whole garage that were burning. He thought it best to go tell Mr. English that he had left his motor running and to warn him against staying in the garage any length of time. Mr. Harley of course knew the danger of carbon monoxide and had known one or two cases of carbon monoxide poisoning in his engineering experience. He went up and rang the bell of the English home, then he opened the door and called out, but there was no answer from anyone. Then he ran as fast as he could back to the garage. He opened the big door and the windows so as to create a draft, and then he opened the front door of the car, and there was Mr. English.

He was lying sort of slumped down on the seat, half of his body almost off the seat. Mr. Harley had a little trouble, as Mr. English was not a small man, but finally he got him and carried him, fireman-fashion, out of the garage and laid him down on the driveway. He felt Mr. English's heart and there were no beats, and he felt his pulse, and there was no pulse. He tried giving him artificial respiration, because he knew the value of artificial respiration in such cases, and he yelled as loud as he could to his wife, and when Mrs. Harley stuck her head out the bedroom window he told her to call Dr. English.

He continued giving artificial respiration until Dr. English came, but Dr. English examined his son and pronounced him dead. They carried the body inside the house and then Dr. English thanked Mr. Harley and Mr. Harley went back to quiet Mrs. Harley, who by that time was almost out of her wits, with not knowing what it was all about.

As nearly as Mr. Harley recalled, Mr. English was attired in dark gray trousers, white shirt without a tie, black shoes. There was a strong odor of whiskey about his person. His eyes were open and his face was pinkish, or, rather, pallid with a pinkish tinge. Mr. Harley asked permission to add that in his opinion, judging by the position of the body and what he knew about such cases, Mr. English may have wanted to commit suicide when he first got in the car, but that he had changed his mind just before becoming unconscious, but had not had the strength to get out of the car.

Well, that did not alter the main fact, in the opinion of Dr. Moskowitz. All they had to go on proved pretty conclusively that deceased had taken his own life, no matter what else might have been in his mind. The jury returned a verdict to that effect.

Dr. English thought it best not to try to influence the verdict of the jury. In this case let the little kike quack Moskowitz have his revenge, which Dr. English knew Moskowitz was doing. Dr. English knew Moskowitz loved every bit of testimony that pointed toward suicide, for it gave Moskowitz a chance he had wanted ever since the time Dr. English had given a dinner to the County Medical Society and failed to invite Moskowitz. Dr. English thought he had good reason: the dinner was at the country club, and Jews were not admitted to the club, so Dr. English could not see why he should violate the spirit of the club rule by having a Jew there as his guest. Anyway he despised Moskowitz because Moskowitz once had said to him: "But, my dear Doctor, surely you know the oath of Hippocrates is a lot of crap. I'll bet your own wife uses a pessary. Or did. Mine always has, and still does." . . . Let Moskowitz have his revenge; Dr. English would have something to say hereafter about the deputy coronerships. Without that Moskowitz could not live.

Dr. English thought of himself as crushed by Julian's death. He knew people would understand that; crushed. His wife, on the other hand, was a little silly, bewildered. She cried, but he did not think he heard pain in her cry. He thought he might expect a nervous breakdown when the enormity of her grief touched her, and he began immediately to plan something, say a Mediterranean cruise, which they could take together as soon as Julian's affairs were settled. Julian had been dead only twelve hours when the thought first entered the doctor's head, but it was well to have something ahead to look foward to when a sad loss crushed you. He would recommend the same thing to Mrs. Walker, and at least offer to pay Caroline's share of the trip. Not that Mrs. Walker needed it or would accept it, but he would make the offer.

Dr. English was not afraid of what he knew people were saying—people with long memories. He knew they were recalling the death of Julian's grandfather. But inevitably they would see how the suicide strain had skipped one generation to come out in the next. So long as they saw that it was all right. You had to expect things.

It was a lively, jesting grief, sprightly and pricking and laughing, to make you shudder and shiver up to the point of giving way completely. Then it would become a long black tunnel; a tunnel you had to go through, had to go through, had to go through, had to go through, had to go through. No whistle. But had to go through, had to go through, had to go through. Whistle? Had to go through, had to go through, had to go through, had to go through. No whistle? Had to go through, had to go through, had to go through.

"Caroline dear, please take this. Sleep will do you good," her mother said.

"Mother darling, I'm perfectly all right. I don't want anything to make me sleep. I'll sleep tonight."

"But Dr. English gave me this to give to you, and I think you ought to get some sleep. You haven't slept a wink since one o'clock this morning."

"Yes, I did. I slept a little."

"No, you didn't. Not a real sleep."

"But I don't want to sleep now. Specially."

"Oh, dear, what am I going to do with you?" said Mrs. Walker.

"Poor Mother," said Caroline, and she held out her arms to her mother. She was sorry for her mother, who had no great grief in this, but only sadness that was stirred by her own grief. She was just sort of on-call, ready to supply sadness which made her eligible actively to share Caroline's grief.

She tried, that first day, not to think about Julian but what on earth else was there to think about? She would think back to the early morning, when her mother came in her old room and told her Julian's father was downstairs and wanted to see her. Sometimes when she thought about it she would say, "I knew it right away. I got it immediately," but again she would be honest and accuse herself, for she had not got it right away. That there was something wrong she knew, but the truth was she was on the verge of refusing to go downstairs. She knew it concerned Julian, and she did not want to hear more of him, but her intelligence and *not* her instinct pointed out to her lying in her warm, sweet bed that Julian's father was the last man in the world to wake you up at that hour of the night—one o'clock in the morning, almost—without some good reason. He said he had terrible news for her—and it was just like prefacing a story with "this is the funniest thing you ever heard," or "this will kill you." Nothing Dr. English could say could come up to his prefatory words. But he was a considerate man; he told it all at once and did not wait to be asked questions. "Mr. Harley found Julian lying in the car, in the garage, and he was dead then, although Mr. Harley didn't know it at the time. He died of carbon monoxide, a poison gas that comes out of a car. The motor was running." Then, after a pause. "Caroline, it looks like suicide. You didn't get any note or anything like that, did you?"

"God, no! Don't you suppose I'd be up there now if I did?"

"I didn't mean to imply anything," said the doctor. "I just wanted to be sure. The coroner will ask things like that. I don't see how we can avoid a verdict of suicide, but I'll try. I'll see what I can do." He had the sound of a politician who doesn't want to admit that he can't get a new post office.

"Why should you want to? Of course he killed himself," said Caroline.

"Caroline, dear!" said her mother. "You ought not to say that till you're sure. That's a terrible thing to say."

"Why is it? Why the hell is it? Who said so? God damn all of you! If he wanted to kill himself whose business is it but his own?"

"She's hysterical," said her mother. "Darling—"

"Ah, go away. You did it. You, you don't like him. You did, too, you pompous old man."

"Oh, Caroline, how can you say things like that?"

"Where is he? Come on, where is he? Where'd you take him. Do *you* know he's dead? *How* do you know? I don't think you even know when a man is dead."

"He's my son, Caroline. Remember that please. My only son."

"Yaah. Your only son. Well, he never liked you. I guess you know that, don't you? So high and mighty and nasty to him when we went to your house for Christmas. Don't think he didn't notice it. You made him do it, not me."

"I think I'll go, Ella. If you want me you can get me at home."

"All right, Will," said Mrs. Walker.

"Why did you call Mother first? Why didn't you tell me first?"

"Now, dear. Good night, Will. I won't go to the door."

"Aren't you going to take me to him? What's the matter? Is he burnt up or mangled or what?"

"Oh, please, darling," said Mrs. Walker. "Will, do you think—for a minute?"

"Yes, I guess so. I just thought it'd be bad for her while the news is fresh."

"Well, then, if you really want to see him tonight, dear," said Mrs. Walker.

"Oh, God. I just remembered. I can't. I promised him I wouldn't," said Caroline.

"You *promised* him! What is this? What are you talking about? You knew he was going to kill himself!" Now the doctor was angry.

"No, no, no. Don't get excited. Keep your shirt on, you old—" in her mouth was one of Julian's favorite words, but she had shocked her mother enough. She turned to her mother. "We both made a promise when we were married, we promised each other we'd never look if one of us died before the other. If he died first I—oh, you know." She began to weep. "Go away, Doctor. I don't want to see you. Mother."

They stayed there a long time, Caroline and her mother. "It's all right, it's all right," Mrs. Walker kept saying, and she kept herself from weeping by thinking of the sounds that Caroline made. It was strange and almost new to hear Caroline crying—the same shudders and catches of breath, but in a firmer voice. That made it new, the firmer voice, the woman part. The little girl in woman's clothes, who never could put on girl's clothes again. What was it Pope said? Was it Pope? This dear, fine girl. A thing like this to happen to her. It was as though Julian had not existed. Only Caroline existed now, in pain and anguish. Poor girl. Her feet must be cold. They went upstairs together after a while, the mother prepared for a long vigil; but she was not used to vigils any more, and sleep won.

All night Caroline did not sleep, until long after daylight she lay awake, hearing the heartless sounds of people going to work and going on with their lives regardless. The funny thing was, it was a nice day. Quite a nice day. That was what made her tired, and in the morning she did sleep, until near noon. She got awake and had a bath and some tea and toast and a cigarette. She felt a little better before she remembered that there was a day ahead of her—no matter how much of it had been slept through. She wanted to go to Julian, but that was just it. Julian was more in this room, more in the street where he had walked so angrily from her car yesterday, much much more in the room downstairs where once upon a time she had become his girl—than what was lying wherever he was lying was Julian. She looked out the window, down at the street, not one bit expecting to see that he had left footprints in the street. But if the footprints had been there she would not have been surprised. The street sounded as though it would send up the sound of his heels. He always had little metal v's put in his heels, and she never would hear that sound again, that collegiate sound, without—well, she would hear it without crying, but she would always want to cry. For the rest of her life, which seemed a long time no matter if she died in an hour, she would always be ready to cry for Julian. Not for him. He was all right now; but because of him, because he had hit her, and she would not hear the sound of the little metal v's on a hardwood floor again, nor smell him, the smell of clean white shirts and cigarettes and sometimes whiskey. They would say he was drunk, but he wasn't drunk. Yes he was. He was drunk, but he was Julian, drunk or not, and that was more than anyone else was. That was what everyone else was not. He was like someone who had died in the war, some young officer in an overseas cap and a Sam Browne belt and one of those tunics that button up to the neck but you can't see the buttons, and an aviator's wings on the breast where the pocket ought to be, and polished high lace boots with a little mud on the soles, and a cigarette in one hand and his arm around an American in a French uniform. For her Julian had that gallantry that had nothing to do with fighting but was an attitude and manner; a gesture with a cigarette in his hand, his whistling, his humming while he played solitaire or swung a golf club back and forth and back and forth; slapping her behind a little too hard and saying, "Why, Mrs. English, it *is* you," but all the same knowing he had hit too hard and a little afraid she would be angry. Oh, that was it. She never could be angry with him again. That took it out of her, that made him dead. Already she had begun the habit of reasoning with him: "But why did you do it? Why did you leave me? Everything would have been all right if you'd waited. I'd have come back this afternoon." But this time she knew she would not have come back this afternoon, and he had known it, and God help us all but he was right. It was *time* for him to die. There was nothing for him to do today, there was nothing for him to do today. . . . There, that was settled. Now let the whole thing begin again.

"Kitty Hofman's downstairs," said her mother. "Do you want to see her?"

"No, but I will," said Caroline.

It was the news room of the Gibbsville *Standard.* "Don't forget everybody, it's Saturday. We have early closing. First edition goes over at one-ten, so don't go to lunch." Sam Dougherty, the city editor of the *Standard,* had been saying that every Saturday for more than twenty years. It was as much a part of him as his eyeshade and his corncob pipe and his hemorrhoids. As city editor he also had to read copy and write the Page One headlines. "Say, Alice," he said, putting down his pencil and interrupting his reading of a story.

"What?" she said.

"What do you hear on this English suicide? Any of your people have anything to say on it?"

"No," she said.

"Did you *ask* anybody about it?" he said.

"No," she said. Then: "I heard the boss tell you to play down the story."

He shook his head. "See?" he said. "That's your trouble, Alice. A good reporter knows ten times as much as he ever prints. That's the kind of stuff you ought to know. Off the record stuff. The angles, girl. The angles. You oughta always get the angles of every big story, even when you can't print it. You never know when it's going to come in handy, see what I mean?"

Harry Reilly went up to his hotel to wash up a bit before meeting a man for lunch. There was a message for him, and when he got upstairs he put in a call for Mrs. Gorman at Gibbsville one one one eight, Gibbsville, Pennsylvania.

"Hello."

"Hello."

"Hello. Hello, is that you, Harry?"

"Yes. What can I do for you?"

"Listen, Harry. Julian English killed himself last night."

"He what?"

"Killed himself. He took some kind of a poison in his garage. Carbon oxide."

"You don't mean carbon *mon*oxide?"

"That's it. It's a poison."

"I'll say it's a poison, but he didn't take it. It comes out of the motor."

"Is that it? Well, I didn't know that. I just knew it was some kind of a poison and he took it in his garage."

"When? Who told you?"

"Last night. Everybody in town knows it by now. I heard it from four or five different people and I didn't leave the front porch all morning. I went to seven o'clock Mass, but otherwise I haven't been—"

"How do they know it's suicide? Who said so? It could happen to anybody. Was he drunk?"

"Yes."

"Well, then, he might of fell asleep or something."

"Not at all. He went in the garage and closed the door. He had a bottle of liquor with him, I heard. The way I heard, Caroline was going to leave him. She was at her mother's."

"Oh."

"That's why I called you, Harry. You didn't have anything to do with it, did you?"

"Christ, no!"

"Well, you know how people are—"

"I know how *you* are."

"Never mind the insults. I'm trying to do a favor for you. You know what people are apt to say. They'll say you had something to do with it, because English threw that drink in your face the other night. They'll put two and two together and get five."

"What are you talking about?"

"Are you dumb or what? They'll say he was sore at you because you have a crush on Caroline."

"Aw, where's it eatin' you, for God's sake, woman. English was in my office yesterday. He came to see me. He was in my office twenty-four hours ago and I talked to him."

"What did you talk about?"

"I didn't have time to talk much. I was hurrying to catch the train to New York. You're trying to make trouble where none is. Is that all you wanted to talk about?"

"Isn't it enough? You wanted to know about English, didn't you?"

"Only so I could go right out and send some flowers right away, that's all. I liked English and he liked me or otherwise he wouldn't have borrowed money from me. I know that type. He wouldn't borrow a nickel from me if he didn't like me. Calm yourself, honey, don't get excited about nothing. That's your trouble. You have nothing to do any more so you sit home and worry. What will I bring you from New York?"

"I don't want anything, unless you want to go down town to Barclay Street. I noticed this morning Monsignor needs a new biretta and it might make a nice little surprise for him, but remember. Purple. He's a monsignor."

"Don't you think I know that? All right, I'll buy him one and have it sent in your name. Anything else? Because I have a lunch appointment any minute now."

"No, I guess that's all."

"Everything all right otherwise?" he said.

"Yes, everything's all right. So I guess I'll hang up. Good-by Harry."

"Good-by." He hung up slowly. "He was a real gentleman. I wonder what in God's name would make him do a thing like that?" Then he picked up the telephone again. "I want to order some flowers," he said.

The girl stood waiting while the man checked his hat and coat. She was tall and fair and had been told so many times she looked like a Benda mask that she finally found out what it was. The man was tall and stoop-shouldered and expensively comfortable about his clothes. He took her elbow and guided her to a tiny table across the room from the bar. They sat down.

A young man who had something to do with the place stopped and said hello, and the other man said, "Hello, Mac, nice to see you. Mary, this is Mac, Mac, Miss Manners." They smiled, and then Mac went away, and the man turned to Mary and told her Mac was the brother of one of the men that owned the place and what would she like or a Martini?

"A Martini, rather dry," she said.

"Two," said the man, and the waiter left them.

They lit cigarettes. "Well," said the man, "how do you feel?"

"Hmm," she said, with a smile.

"Ah, you're darling," he said. "Where do you come from?"

"Originally I came from Pennsylvania," she said.

"Why, so do I. Where are you from? I'm from Scranton."

"Scranton? I'm not from there," she said. "I live in a little town you never heard of."

"But what part of the State? What's it near?"

"Well, did you ever hear of Gibbsville?"

"Sure I heard of Gibbsville. I've visited there often. Are you from Gibbsville?"

"No, but near there. A place called Ridgeville."

"I've been there. Just driven through, though. Who do you know in Gibbsville? Do you know Caroline Walker? That's right, she's married. She married Julian English. Do you know them?"

"I know him," she said.

"Do you know Caroline at all?"

"No. I never met her. I just knew Julian."

"Well, I didn't know him very well. I haven't seen either of them in years. So you're from Pennsylvania."

"Uh-huh."

"Mary Manners," he said, "you're the prettiest girl I ever saw."

"Thank you, kind sir, she said," she said. "You're all right yourself, Ross Campbell."

"I am now. I will be if you go away with me this afternoon."

"Not this week-end."

"But next week-end I won't have Ed's car."

"You can hire one. No, I have to watch my step. We shouldn't of come here, Ross. Rifkin comes here sometimes and his friends, a lot of movie people, they all come here."

"Come on, while I have the car."

"No, positively not. Not this week."

"Lute, give me five dollars. I want to pay the garbage man."

Lute Fliegler was lying on the davenport, his hands in back of his head, his coat and vest on the chair beside him. He reached in his trousers pocket and took a five dollar bill from a small roll. His eyes met his wife's as the money appeared, and she was grateful to him for not saying what they both were thinking: that maybe they had better be more careful about money till they saw how things were. She went out to the kitchen and paid the garbage man and then came back to the living-room. "Can't I make you a sandwich, Lute? You ought to have something."

"No, that's all right. I don't feel like eating."

"Don't worry. Please don't worry. They'll make you the head of it. You know more about the business than anybody else, and you've always been reliable. Dr. English knows that."

"Yeah, but does he? What I'm afraid of is he'll think we were all a bunch of drunks. I don't mean that against Julian, but you know."

"I know," she said. If only daytime were a time for kissing she would kiss him now. All this, the furniture, the house, the kids, herself—all this was what Lute was worrying about. She was almost crying, so she smiled.

"Come here," he said.

"Oh, Lute," she said. She knelt down beside him and cried a little and then kissed him. "I feel so sorry for Caroline. You, I—"

"Don't worry," he said. "I still get my check from the government, and I can get lots of jobs—" he cleared his throat "—in fact, that's my trouble. I was saying to Alfred P. Sloan the other day. He called me up. I meant to tell you, but it didn't seem important. So I said to Al—"

"Who's Alfred P. Sloan?"

"My God. Here I been selling—he's president of General Motors."

"Oh. So what did you say to him?" said Irma.

BUtterfield 8

Starting on December 16, a distinguishing numeral will be added to, and become part of, each central office name in New York City. For example:

HAnover will become HAnover 2

(From an advertisement of the New York Telephone Company, December 8, 1930.

1

On this Sunday morning in May, this girl who later was to be the cause of a sensation in New York, awoke much too early for her night before. One minute she was asleep, the next she was completely awake and dumped into despair. It was the kind of despair that she had known perhaps two thousand times before, there being 365 mornings in a calendar year. In general the cause of her despair was remorse, two kinds of it: remorse because she knew that whatever she was going to do next would not be any good either. The specific causes of these minutes of terror and loneliness were not always the words or deeds which seemed to be the causes. Now, this year, she had come pretty far. She had come far enough to recognize that what she had done or said last night did not stand alone. Her behavior of a given night before, which she was liable to blame for the despair of any today, frequently was bad, but frequently was not bad enough to account for the extreme depth of her despair. She recognized, if only vaguely and then only after conquering her habit of being dishonest with herself, that she had got into the habit of despair. She had come far away from original despair, because she had hardened herself into the habit of ignoring the original, basic cause of all the despair she could have in her lifetime.

There *was* one cause.

But for years she had hardened herself against thinking of it, in the hope of pushing it away from her and drawing herself away from it. And so mornings would come, sometimes as afternoons, and she would awake in despair and begin to wonder what she had done before going to sleep that made her so full of terror today. She would recollect and for a fraction of a fraction of a second she would think, "Oh, yes, I remember," and build up an explanation on the recollection of the recognizably bad thing she had done. And then would follow a period of inward cursing and screaming, of whispering vile self-accusation. There was nothing she knew of that she would not call herself during these fierce rages of self-accusation. She would whisper and whisper the things men say to other men when they want to incite to kill. In time this would exhaust her physically, and that left her in a state of weak defiance—but not so weak that it would seem weak to anyone else. To anyone else she was defiance; but she knew that it was only going on. You just go on.

For one thing, you get up and get dressed. On this Sunday morning she did something she often did, which gave her a little pleasure. The drawstring of the pajamas she was wearing had come undone in the night, and she opened the pajamas and laughed. She said to herself: "I wonder where he is."

She got out of bed, holding the pajamas to her, and she was unsteady and her body was pretty drunk, but she walked all over the apartment and could not find him. It was a large apartment. It had one large room with a grand piano and a lot of heavy, family furniture and in one corner of that room, where there was a bookshelf, there were a lot of enlarged snapshots of men and women and boys and girls on horseback or standing beside saddle horses. There was one snapshot of a girl in a tandem cart, a hackney hitched to it, but if you looked carefully you could see that there was a tiestrap, probably held by a groom who was not in the picture. There were a few prize ribbons in picture frames, blues from a Connecticut county fair. Some pictures of yachts, which, had she examined them carefully, the girl would have discovered were not many yachts but duplicate snapshots of the same Sound Inter-Club yacht. One picture of an eight-oared shell, manned; and one picture of an oarsman holding a sweep. This picture she inspected closely. His hair was cut short, he was wearing short, heavy woolen socks, a cotton shirt with three buttons at the neck, and a small letter over the heart, and his trunks were bunched in the very center by his jock strap and what was in it. She was surprised that he would have a picture like that hanging in this room, where it must be seen by growing girls. "But they'd never recognize him from that picture unless someone told them who it was."

There was a dining-room almost as large as the first room. The room made her think of meats with thick gravy on them. There were four bedrooms besides the one where she had slept. Two of them were girls' bedrooms, the third a servant's room and the fourth was a woman's bedroom. In this she lingered.

She went through the closets and looked at the clothes. She looked at the bed, neat and cool. She took whiffs of the bottles on the dressing table, and then she opened another closet door. The first thing she saw was a mink coat, and it was the only thing she really saw.

She left the room and went back to his room and picked up her things; her shoes and stockings, her panties, her evening gown. "Well, I can't wear that. I can't go out looking like that. I can't go out in broad daylight wearing an evening gown and coat." The evening coat, more accurately a cape, was lying where it had been carefully laid in a chair. But when she took a second look at the evening gown she remembered more vividly the night before. The evening gown was torn, ripped in half down the front as far as the waist. "The son of a bitch." She threw the gown on the floor of one of his closets and she took off her pajamas—*his* pajamas. She took a shower and dried herself slowly and with many towels, which she threw on the bathroom floor, and then she took his tooth brush and put it under the hot water faucet. The water was too hot to touch, and she guessed it was hot enough to sterilize the brush. This made her laugh: "I go to bed with him and take a chance on getting anything, but I sterilize his tooth brush." She brushed her teeth and used a mouth wash, and she mixed herself a dose of fruit salts and drank it pleasurably. She felt a lot better and would feel still better soon. The despair was going away. Now that she knew what the bad thing was that she was going to do, she faced it and felt all right about it. She could hardly wait to do it.

She put on her panties and shoes and stockings and she brushed her hair and made up her face. She used little make-up. She opened a closet door and put her hand in the pockets of his evening clothes, but did not find what she wanted. She found what she wanted, cigarettes, in a case in the top drawer of a chest of drawers. She lit one and went to the kitchen. On the kitchen table was an envelope she had missed in her earlier round of the apartment. "Gloria," was written in a round, backhand style, in pencil.

She pulled open the flap which was sticky and not tightly held to the envelope, and she took out three twenty-dollar bills and a note. "Gloria—This is for the evening gown. I have to go to the country. Will phone you Tuesday or Wednesday. W." "You're telling me," she said, aloud.

Now she moved a little faster. She found two hats, almost identical black felt, in one of the girls' closets. She put one on. "She'll think she took the other to the country and lost it." She was aware of herself as a comic spectacle in shoes and stockings, panties, black hat. "But we'll soon fix that." She returned to the woman's closet and took out the mink coat and got into it. She then went to his bedroom and put the sixty dollars in her small crystal-covered evening bag. She was all set.

On the way out of the apartment she stopped and looked at herself in a full length mirror in the foyer. She was amused. "If it wasn't Spring this would be just dandy. But—not bad anyway."

She was amused going down in the elevator. The elevator operator wasn't handsome, but he was tall and young, a German, obviously. It amused her to think of what would happen to his face if she opened the mink coat. "Shall I get you a taxi, Miss?" he said, without turning all the way around.

"Yes, please," she said. He would not remember her if anyone asked him to describe her. He would remember her as pretty, as giving the impression of being pretty, but he would be a bad one to ask for a good description. All he would remember would be that she was wearing a mink coat, and anyone who wanted to get a description of her would know already that she had been wearing a mink coat. That would be the only reason anyone would ask him for a description of her. He was not the same man who had been running the elevator when she came in the apartment house the night before; that had been an oldish man who did not take his uniform cap off in the elevator. She remembered the cap. And so this young man naturally did not question her wearing a mink coat now instead of the velvet coat she had worn coming in. Why, of course! He probably didn't even know what apartment she had come from.

She waited for him to precede her to the big iron-and-glass doors of the house, and watched him holding up his finger for a taxi. She decided against tipping him for this little service—that would make him remember her—and she got in the taxi and sat back in the corner where he could not see her.

"Where to, Ma'am?" said the driver.

"Washington Square. I'll tell you where to stop." She would direct him to one of the Washington Square apartment houses and pay him off, and then go in and ask for a fictitious person, and stall long enough for the driver of this taxi to have gone away. Then she would come out and take another taxi to Horatio Street. She would pay a surprise call on Eddie. Eddie would be burned up, because he probably would have a girl there; Sunday morning. She was in good spirits and as soon as she got rid of this cab she would go to Jack's and buy a quart of Scotch to take to Eddie and Eddie's girl. At the corner of Madison the driver almost struck a man and girl, and the man yelled and the driver yelled back. "Go on, spit in their eye," called Gloria.

In the same neighborhood another girl was sitting at one end of a rather long refectory table. She was smoking, reading the paper, and every once in a while she would lay the cigarette in an ash tray and, with her free hand, rub the damp short hair at the back of her neck. The rest of her hair was dry, but there was a line deep in the skin of her head and neck that showed where a bathing cap had been. She would rub her hair, trying to dry it, then she would wipe her fingers on the shoulder part of her dressing gown, and her fingers would slide along the front of her body and halt at her breast. She would hold her hand so that it partly covered her breast and the fingers rested under her arm, in the armpit. Then she would have to turn a page of the paper and she would pick up the cigarette again and for a while she would hold it until the heat of the lighted end warned her that it was time to get a shorter hold on the cigarette or get burned fingers. She would put it in the ash tray and start all over again with the rubbing of the hair at the back of her neck.

Presently she got up and was gone from the room. When she came back she was naked except for a brassière and panties. She did not go back to the table, but stood on one foot and knelt with the other knee on a chair and looked out the windows that ran the length of the room. She was in this position when a bell rang, and she went to the kitchen.

"Hello. . . . Ask him to come up, please."

She walked hurriedly to the bedroom and came out pulling a cashmere sweater over her shoulders and wearing a tweed skirt, light wool stockings and brogue shoes with Scotch tongues that flapped a little. Another bell rang, and she went to the door.

"Greetings. Greetings, greetings, and greetings. How is Miss Stannard? How is Miss Stannard."

"Hello, Jimmy," said the girl. She closed the door, and immediately he took her in his arms and kissed her.

"Mm. No response," he said. He tossed his hat in a chair and sat down before she did. He offered her a cigarette by gesture and she declined it with a shake of her head.

"Coffee?" she said.

"Yes, I'll have some coffee if it's any good."

"Well, I made it and I drank two cups of it. It's fit to drink, at least."

"Ah, but you made it. I doubt if you'd throw away coffee you made yourself."

"Do you want some or don't you?"

"Just a touch. Just one cup of piping hot javver for the gentleman in the blue suit."

"How *about* the blue suit? Didn't you get What's His Name's car? I thought we were going to the country." She looked down at her own clothes and then at his. He had on a blue serge suit and white starched collar and black shoes. "Did you get a job in Wall Street since I last saw you?"

"I did not. That goes for both questions. I did not get the car from Norman Goodman, not What's His Name. You met him the night we went to Michel's and you called him Norman. And as for my getting a job in Wall Street—well, I won't even answer that. Norman phoned me last night and said he had to drive his father to a circumcision or something."

"Is his father a rabbi?"

"Oh—don't be so—no, dear. His father is not a rabbi, and I made that up about the circumcision."

"What are we going to do? You didn't get someone else's car, I take it. Such a grand day to go to the country."

"I am in the chips. I thought we could go to the Plaza for breakfast, but seeing as you've had breakfast. I'm supposed to be covering a sermon, but I should cover a Protestant sermon on a nice day like this. I don't know why they ever send me anyway. They get the sermons at the office, and all I ever do is go to the damn church and then I go back to the office and copy the sermon or paste it up. All I do is write a lead, like 'The depression has awakened the faith of the American people, according to the Reverend Makepeace John Meriwether, don't spell it with an *a* or you're fired, rector of Grace Methodist Episcopal Free Patrick's Cathedral.' And so on. May I have some cream?"

"I'm afraid I've used up all the cream. Will milk do?"

"Damn, you have a nice figure, Isabel. Move around some more. Walk over to the window."

"I will not." She sat down. "What do you really contemplate doing?"

"No Plaza? Not even when I'm in the chips?"

"Why are you rich?"

"I sold something to the *New Yorker*."

"Oh, really? What?"

"Well, about a month ago I was on a story up near Grant's Tomb and I discovered this houseboat colony across the river. People live there in these houseboats all winter long. They have gas and electricity and lights and radios, and all winter the houseboats are mounted on piles, wooden piles. Then in the Spring they get a tug to tow them out to Rockaway or some such place, and they live out there all summer. I thought it would make a good story for the Talk of the Town department, so I found out all about it and sent it in, and yesterday I got a check for thirty-six dollars, which comes in mighty handy. They want me to do some more for them."

"You're going to do it, aren't you?"

"I guess so. Of course I can't do a great deal, because believe it or not I have a job, and the novel."

"How's the novel coming?"

"Like Santa Claus. And you know about Santa Claus."

"I think I'll leave you."

"Permanently?"

"A few more like that last one and yes, permanently. Such a lovely day to go to the country." She got up and stood at the window. "Look at those men. I never get tired of watching them."

"What men? I'm too comfortable to get up and look at men. You tell me about them."

"The men with the pigeons. They stay up on the roof all day, every Sunday, and chase the pigeons off. Our maid said the idea is that a man has a flock of pigeons, say eighteen, and the reason he chases them off is that he hopes that when they come back there'll be nineteen or twenty. A pigeon or two from another flock gets confused and joins them, and increases the man's flock. It isn't *exactly* stealing."

"But you won't have breakfast at the Plaza?"

"I've had breakfast, and I'll bet you have too."

"As much as I ever have. Orange juice, toast and marmalade, coffee. I just thought we'd have kidneys and stuff, omelette, fried potatoes. Like the English. But if you don't want to, we won't. I just thought it'd be fun, or at least different."

"Some other time. But I'll dress and we can spend your money some other way, if you insist."

"I am not unmindful of the fact that I owe you ten dollars."

"We'll spend that first. Now I'll go dress."

He picked up a few sections of the paper. "The *Times!*" he shouted. "You'll never see my stories in the *Times*. What's the idea?" But she had closed the door of the bedroom. In ten minutes she reappeared.

"Mm. Nice. Nice. Mm."

"Like it?"

"It's the best dress I've ever seen. And the hat, too. It's a cute little hat. I think girls' hats are better this year than they've ever been. They're so damn *cute*. I guess it has something to do with the way they do their hair."

"I guess it has a whole lot to do with the way they do their hair. Mine's still damp and looks like the wrath of God, and that's your fault. I wouldn't have taken a shower if I'd known we weren't going to the country. I'd have had a real bath and wouldn't have got my hair wet. Remind me to stop at a drug store—"

"Darling, I'm so glad!"

"—for a decent bathing cap. Jimmy, before we go, I want to tell you again, for the last time you've got to stop saying things like that to me. I'm not your mistress, and I'm not a girl off the streets, and I'm not accustomed to being talked to that way. It isn't funny, and no one else talks that way to me. Do you talk that way to the women on newspapers? Even if you do I'm sure they don't really like it all the time. You can't admire my dress without going into details about my figure, and—"

"Why in the name of Christ should I? Isn't the whole idea of the dress to show off your figure? Why does it look well on you? Because you have nice breasts and everything else. Now God damn it, why shouldn't I say so?"

"I think you'd better go." She took off her hat and sat down.

"All right, I'll go." He picked up his hat and walked heavily down the short hall to the door of the apartment. But he did not open the door. He put his hand on the knob, and then turned around and came back.

"I didn't say anything," she said.

"I know. And you didn't move. I know. You know I could no more walk out that door than I could walk out those windows. Will you please forgive me?"

"It will happen all over again, the same thing, the same way, same reason. And then you'll come back and ask me to forgive you, and I will. And every time I do, Jimmy, I hate myself. Not because I forgive you, but because I hate those words, I hate to be talked to that way, and I know, I *know* the only reason you do talk to me like that is because I *am* the kind of girl you talk to that way, and that's what I hate. Knowing that."

"Darling, that's not true. You're not any kind of girl. You're you, Isabel. And won't you ever believe me when I tell you what I've told you so often? That no matter what we do, whenever I see you like this, in the morning, in the daytime, when there are other people—I can't believe that you're my girl. Or that you ever were. And you're so lovely in that dress, and hat. I'm sorry I'm the way I am."

"You wouldn't talk to Lib that way. Or Caroline."

"I wouldn't talk to them *any* way. I couldn't be annoyed. Let's go before I say something else wrong."

"All right. Kiss me. Not hard." She put out her hand and he pulled her out of the chair until she stood close to him.

"I *have* to kiss you hard. Me not kiss you hard? Impossible." He laughed.

"Not quite impossible," she said. "There are times." She laughed.

"Now I don't want to go," he said.

"We're going. See if I have my key." She rummaged in her bag. "Yep. Lipstick, Jimmy. Here, I'll do it. Me your handkerchief. There."

He held the door open for her and with his free hand he made as if to take a whack at her behind, but he did not touch her. She rang for the elevator and after it groaned and whirred a while the door opened.

"Good morning, Miss Stannard," said the elevator man.

"Good morning," she said. They got in and the car began its descent, but stopped one floor below, and a man and woman got in. The man was precisely the same height as the woman, which made him seem smaller.

"Good morning, Mr. Farley, Mrs. Farley," said the elevator man.

"Good morning," said the Farleys.

None of the passengers looked at one another. They looked at the elevator man's shoulders. No one spoke until the ground floor was reached, then Isabel smiled and allowed Mrs. Farley to leave the car first, then she followed, then Farley nodded to the open door and indicated with his eyes that Jimmy should go first—and was obviously surprised when Jimmy did go first. But the Farleys beat them to the door and the doorman was standing there with the large door of their car open for them. The car, a Packard four-passenger convertible, sounded like some kind of challenge of power, and not unlike the exhaust of a speedboat gurgling into the water.

"And to think we walk while punks like those people ride in a wagon like that. Never mind, all that will be changed, all that will be changed. I guess you know who made the loudest noise in Union Square the day before yesterday."

"I guess I do," said Isabel.

"I don't think I like your tone. Somehow, I don't quite like your tone," but he began to whistle and she began to sing: "Take me back to Man-hattan, that dear-old, dirty, town."

At Madison Avenue they were almost struck by a huge Paramount taxi, and when Jimmy swore at the driver, the driver said, "Go on, I'll spit in your eye." And both Isabel and Jimmy distinctly heard the lone passenger, a girl in a fur coat, call to the driver: "Go on, spit in their eye." The cab beat the light and sped south in Madison.

"Nice girl," said Isabel. "Did you know her?"

"How would I know her? She's someone from this neighborhood obviously. Downtown we don't talk that way, not in the village."

"No, of course not, except I could point out that the taxi is on its way downtown, in a hurry."

"All right, point it out. And then for a disagreeable couple I give you the man and woman in the elevator. Mr. Princeton with the glasses and his wife. I'll bet they're battling right this minute in that beautiful big chariot. I'd rather know a girl that yells out of a taxi, 'Spit in their eye,' than two polite people that can't wait to be alone before they're at each other's throats."

"Well, that's the difference between you and me. I'd rather live in this part of town, where the people at least—"

"I didn't say anything about living with them, or having them for neighbors. All I said was I'd rather know that kind of girl—that girl— than those people. That's all I said."

"Still stick to my statement. I'd rather *know* the man and his wife. As a matter of fact I happen to know who they are. He's an architect."

"And I don't really give a damn who they are, but I do give a damn who the girl is."

"A girl who would wear a mink coat on a day like this. She's cheap."

"Well, with a mink coat she must have come high at some time."

He was silent a few seconds before continuing. "You know what I'm thinking, don't you? No, you don't. But I'd like to say it if you'd promise not to get sore? . . . I was just thinking what a powerful sexual attraction there is between us, otherwise why do we go on seeing each other when we quarrel so much?"

"We only quarrel, if you'll look back on it, we only quarrel for one reason, really, and that's the way you talk to me."

He said nothing, and they walked on in silence for several blocks.

When Sunday morning came Paul Farley never liked to be alone with his wife, nor did Nancy Farley like to be alone with Paul. The Farleys were Roman Catholic, although when they were married, in the fourth summer after the war, you would not have been able to guess from their dossiers in the newspapers, without looking at their names, that the wedding was taking place in the Church of St. Vincent Ferrer. Of Paul it was said: "He attended Lawrenceville School and Princeton and served overseas as second lieutenant in a machine gun company of the 27th Division. He is a member of the Association of Ex-Members of Squadron A, the Princeton Club and the Racquet and Tennis Club." Of Nancy it said: "Miss McBride, who is a member of the Junior League, attended the Brearley School and Westover, and she was introduced to society last season at a dance at the Colony Club and later at the Bachelors' Cotillion in Baltimore, Md."

After their marriage they had children, three of them, rapid-fire; but when the third, a girl, died, Nancy, who had wanted a girl very much, came to a decision. It was a major adjustment in her life. Up to that time Nancy had been a girl who always did what people told her to do. A succession of people: her mother, to a lesser degree her father, a nurse, a governess, her teachers, and the Church. The odor of sanctity was faint but noticeable in the McBride household, as Nancy's paternal uncle had been quite a good friend of the late Cardinal Gibbons; and the McBrides, as they themselves put it, realized their position. It was a religious household, including the servants, and at the time of Nancy's various debuts the big house in the East Seventies still had its quota of holy pictures, and there was hardly a bureau which did not contain one drawer full of broken rosary beads, crucifixes with the corpus missing, Father Lasance's *My Prayer Book, The Ordinary of the Mass,* and other prayer books for special occasions. One of Nancy's losing battles against the domination of her elders (and they were all defeats) was fought for the removal of a small, white china holywater font which hung at the door of her bedroom. She finally capitulated because a Westover friend who was visiting her was curious and delighted by the sacred article.

Nancy was the youngest of four children. The first-born, Thornton, was ten years older than Nancy. He was out of a high-priced Catholic prep school, Yale, and Fordham Law School. He was with his father in the law firm and cared about nothing except the law and golf.

Next in age was Nancy's only sister, Mollie. She was eight years older than Nancy, and when Nancy was married Mollie was in the Philippines, living the life of an army officer's wife.

Two years younger than Mollie was Jay—Joseph, but always known as Jay. He was unable to finish prep school, and had lived almost all his life, from the time he developed a case of T.B., in New Mexico. He was at work on a monumental history of the Church and the Indian in the Southwest.

There would have been a child between Jay and Nancy, but it had been a Fallopian pregnancy from which Nancy's mother almost died. This was kept from Nancy not only all through her girlhood, but even after she was married and had her own two children. Nancy did not know about her mother's disastrous Fallopian pregnancy for the reason that her mother did not quite know how to explain it. It was kept quiet until Nancy's little girl died in early infancy, and then Mrs. McBride told her. It infuriated Nancy to be told so late in life. It might not have made any difference in her attitude toward having children, but it gave her the feeling of having been insulted from a distance, this taciturnity of her mother's. People ought to tell you things like that. Your own mother ought to tell you everything about that—and then she would recall that what ought to be and what actually was were two quite different things so far as her mother and sex were concerned. Mrs. McBride accepted the working theory of the Church that sex education of children was undesirable, unsanctioned; and when Nancy was fourteen her mother told her that "this is something that happens to girls"— and that was all she ever told her until Paul and Nancy were to be married. Then Mrs. McBride provided the second piece of information to her daughter: "Never let Paul touch you when you are unwell." Whatever else Nancy learned was from the exchange of knowledge among school acquaintances, and from her secret reading of the informative little propaganda pamphlets which the government got out during the World War, telling in detail the atrocities which the Germans committed upon Belgian maidens, nuns, priests, old women. These pamphlets did not incite Nancy to turn her allowance into Liberty Bonds, but they made her understand things about her anatomy and the anatomy of the young men with whom she swam summer after summer on the South Shore of Long Island.

Sex had been healthy and normally strong and only a trifle unpleasant for Nancy up to the time of the death of her daughter. Paul was considerate and tender and fun. Child-bearing, the incomparable peace of nursing the boys, the readjustment after the nursing periods—all were accomplished with a minimum of fright and pain, and sometimes with a pleasure that—especially at nursing time—was heavenly joy, because at such times Nancy felt so practically religious. She wanted to have a lot of children, and she was glad that things were that way: that the Church approved and that there was such high pleasure in motherhood. Then the little girl died and for the first time Nancy discovered that you cannot blame your body alone for the hell it sometimes gives you. Nancy broke with Rome the day her baby died. It was a secret break, but no Catholic breaks with Rome casually.

The man carrying the black Gladstone refused the help of the Red Caps. Who wanted a little thing like that carried for him? A little thing like that. What did they think? Did they think he wasn't strong enough to carry it? Didn't he look strong enough to carry a little bag, a little Gladstone like this? Did they think he wasn't young enough to carry a bag like this? Did they think he—they didn't think he was old, did they? Huh. If they thought that they had another think coming, by Jove. Ablative of Jupiter. They were young and looked pretty strong, most of these Red Caps, but the man drew a deep breath as he walked rapidly up the ramp and out into the great station. He would wager he was as strong as most of them. He could break them in half, and they thought he was old and wanted to carry his little Gladstone! He thought of how they would look on a chain gang, with the sweat pouring down on their satiny hides. Satiny hides. That was good. Ugh. He wanted to be sick, he wanted to think away from bodies; he patted his belly and pinched his Phi Beta Kappa key and started to curl the watch-chain around his finger, but this was somehow getting back again to the things of the flesh, and he wanted to think away from things of the flesh. He wanted to think of the ablative, the passive periphrastic, the middle voice, the tangent and cotangent, the School Board meeting next Tuesday. . . . He wished he hadn't thought of the School Board meeting next Tuesday or any Tuesday. He wished he'd always thought of the School Board meeting next Tuesday.

He got into a taxi and gave the address, and the driver was so slow starting the meter that the man repeated the address. The driver nodded, showing half his face. The man looked at the face and at the driver's picture. They didn't look much alike, but they never did. He supposed this was a reputable taxicab company that operated the taxicabs at the station. Oh, well, that wasn't important.

"If only I'd always thought of the School Board meetings I wouldn't be here now, in a filthy New York taxicab, living a lie by being in this city on a cooked-up pretext. Living a worse, worse lie by having any reason to be here. God damn that girl! I am a good man. I am a bad man, a wicked man, but she is worse. She is really bad. She is bad, she is badness. She is Evil. She not only is *evil*, but she *is* Evil. Whatever I am now is her fault, because that girl is bad. Whatever I was before, the bad me, was nothing. I never was bad before I knew her. I sinned, but I was not bad. I was not corrupted. I did not want to come to New York before I knew her. She made me come to New York. She makes me trump up excuses to come to New York, makes me lie to my wife, fool my wife, that good woman, that poor good woman. That girl is bad, and hell's fire is not enough for her. Oh, *more* fresh air! It is good, this fresh air, even in a taxicab. Fresh air taxicab! God! Amos and Andy. Here I'm thinking of Amos and Andy, and all that they mean. Home. Seven o'clock. The smell of dinner in preparation, ready to be served when Amos and Andy go off the air. Am I the man who loves to listen to Amos and Andy?" The door opened and he got out and paid the driver.

2

THE YOUNG MAN got out of bed and went to the kitchenette and pushed the wall button that unlatched the front door. He was in his underwear, one-piece cotton underwear and it had not been fresh the day before. He rumpled his hair and yawned, standing at the door and waiting until whoever it was that rang would ring the apartment bell. It rang, and he opened it half a foot.

"Oh," he said, and opened the door all the way.

"Hel-lo, darling, look what I brought you." Gloria held up the parcel, a wrapped-up bottle.

"Oh," he said, and yawned again. "Thanks." He went back to the bed and lay on it face down. "I don't want any."

"Get up. It's a lovely Spring morning," said Gloria. "I didn't think you'd be alone."

"Uh, I'm alone. I haven't any soda. You'll have to drink that straight, or else with plain water. I don't want any."

"Why?"

"I got drunk."

"What for?"

"Oh, I don't know. Listen, Gloria, I'm dead. Do you mind if I go to sleep a little while?"

"Certainly I do. Where are your pajamas? Did you sleep in your underwear?"

"I haven't any pajamas. I have two pairs and they're both in the laundry. I don't even know what laundry."

"Here. Here's twenty dollars. Buy yourself some pajamas tomorrow, or else find the laundry and pay what you owe them."

"I've some money."

"How much?"

"I don't know."

"Well, take this, you'll need it. I don't believe you have any money, either."

"Why are you suddenly rich? Isn't that a new coat?"

"Yes. Brand-new. You didn't ask me to take it off. Is that hospitable?"

"Good God, you'd take it off if you wanted to. Take it off, if you want to."

"Look," she said, for he was closing his eyes again. She opened the coat.

He suddenly had the expression of a man who has been struck and cannot strike back. "All right," he said. "You stole the coat."

"He tore my dress, my new evening dress. I had to have something to wear in the daytime. All I had was my evening coat, and I couldn't go out wearing that."

"I guess I will have a drink."

"Good."

"Who is the guy?"

"You don't know him."

"How do you know I don't know him? Damn it, why don't you just tell me who it is and save time? You always do that. I ask you something and you say I wouldn't know, or you talk around it or beat about the bush for an hour, and you make me so God damn mad—and then you tell me. If you'd tell me in the first place we'd save all this."

"All right, I'll tell you."

"Well, go ahead and *tell* me!"

"His name is Weston Liggett."

"Liggett? Liggett. Weston Liggett. I do know him."

"You don't. How would you know him?"

"I don't know him, but I know who he is. He's a yacht racer and he used to be a big Yale athlete. Very social. Oh, and married. I've seen his wife's name. What about that? Where did you go?"

"His apartment."

"His apartment? Is his wife—does she like girls?" He was fully awake now. "Did she give you the coat? You're going in for that again, are you?"

"I think you're disgusting."

"You think *I'm* disgusting. That's what it is. That's started again, all over again. That's why you came here, because you thought I had someone here. You know where you ought to be? You ought to be in an insane asylum. They put people in insane asylums that don't do a tenth of what you do. Here, take your lousy money and your damn whiskey and get out of here."

She did not move. She sat there looking like someone tired of waiting for a train. She did not seem to hear him. But this mood was in such contrast to her vitality of a minute ago that there was no doubting that she had heard him, and no doubting that what he was saying had caused her mood to change.

"I'm sorry," he said. "I'm terribly sorry, Gloria. I'd rather cut my throat than say that. Do you believe me? You do believe me, don't you? You do believe I only said it because—"

"Because you believed it," she said. "No. Mrs. Liggett is not a Lesbian, if you're interested. I went to their apartment with her husband and I slept with him. She's away. I stole the coat, because he tore my clothes. He practically raped me. Huh. You think that's funny, but it's true. There are people who don't know as much about me as you do, you know. I'll go now."

He got up and stood in front of the door.

"Please," she said. "Let's not have a struggle."

"Sit down, Gloria. Please sit down."

"It's no use, Eddie, I've made up my mind. I can't have you for a friend if you're going to throw things up at me that I told you in confidence. I've told you more than I've ever told anyone else, even my psychiatrist. But at least he has professional ethics. At least he wouldn't get angry and throw it all up to me. I trusted you as a friend, and—"

"You *can* trust me. Don't go. Besides, you can't go this way. Listen, sit down, darling." He took her hand, and she allowed herself to be guided to a chair. "I'll call up a girl I know, I was out with her last night, and ask her to bring some day clothes over here. She's about your build."

"Who is she?"

"You wouldn't—her name is Norma Day. She goes to N. Y. U. She's very good-looking. I'll call her and she'll come right over. I have a sort of date with her anyway. All right?"

"Uh-huh." Gloria was pleased and bright. "I think I'll take a bath. Shall I? Okay?"

"Sure."

"Okay," she said. "You sleep."

Weston Liggett walked up the platform to where the line of parked cars began, and as he reached the beginning of the line he heard a horn blown six or seven times. A Ford station wagon was just arriving. It was driven by a young girl, and two other girls about the same age were on the front seat with her. Liggett took off his hat and waved.

"Hello, pretty girls," he said. He stood beside the right front door. The girl in the driver's seat spoke to him:

"Daddy, this is Julie Rand; this is my father."

"How do you do," he said to the new girl, and then spoke to the girl in the middle: "Hello, Frances."

"'Lomistliggett," said Frances.

"Where's Bar'?" he said.

"She drove Mother over to the club. We're all going there for lunch. Get in, we're late."

"No, we're not. Mother knew I was coming out on this train."

"Well, we're late anyway," said Ruth Liggett, the driver. "We're always late. Like the late Jimmy Walker."

"Oh, ho, ho." Miss Rand laughing.

"Is that door closed, Daddy?" said Ruth.

"Think so. Yes," he said.

"It rattles so. We ought to turn this in while we can still get something on it."

"Uh-huh. We'll turn this in and sell the house. Would that suit you?" he said.

"Oh. Always talking about how broke we are. And in front of strangers."

"Who's a stranger? Oh, Miss Rand. Well, she's not exactly a stranger, is she? Aren't you Henry Rand's daughter?"

"No. I'm his niece. My father was David Rand. I'm visiting my Uncle Henry and Aunt Bess, though."

"Well, then you're not a stranger. *You* like this car, don't you?"

"Don't call it a car, Daddy," said Ruth.

"I like it very much," said Miss Rand. "It's very nice, I think."

"Ooh, what a prevaricator! She does not. She didn't want to ride in it. You should have seen her. When she came out of the house she took one look and said, 'Is this what we're going in?' Didn't you? Own up."

"Well, I never rode in a truck before."

"A truck!" said Ruth.

"Aren't there station wagons where you come from?"

"No. We just have regular cars."

"She comes from—what's the name of the place, Randy?"

"Wilkes-Barre, P A."

"And a very nice town it is," said Liggett. "I remember it very well. It's near Scranton. I have a lot of very dear friends in Scranton."

"Do you know anybody in Wilkes-Barre?" said Miss Rand.

"I don't believe so—*Ruth!*"

"Well, he ought to stay on his own side of the road."

"You can't count on that. I don't mind taking chances, but when there are other people in the car."

"Oh, he wouldn't have hit me."

"That's what you think. No wonder this car's all shot."

"Now you can't blame that on me, Daddy. I don't drive this car that much."

"Well, I'll admit you're not responsible for this car, but the Chrysler, you are responsible for that. Clutch is slipping because you ride it all the time. Fenders wrinkled."

"Who wrinkled it—not them. It. The left hind fender. That happened when someone else was driving, not me."

"Well, let's not talk about it."

"No, of course not. I'm right. That's why we won't talk about it."

"Is that fair? Do I change the subject when I'm in the wrong, Ruth? Do I?"

"No, darling. That wasn't fair." She reached her hand back to be held. He kissed it.

"Why, Daddy!" The others did not see.

"Shh," he said and then was silent until they came to the club. "Here we are. I'll go around and wash up. I'll meet you in three minutes."

In the locker room he rang for the steward and arranged to cash two checks. The club had a rule against cashing a check for more than twenty-five dollars on any single day, but he made them out as of two dates and the steward, who had done this many times before, gave him fifty dollars. The sixty dollars Liggett had left for Gloria and the other money he had spent on her had left him short, and he knew Emily would think it strange that he had spent so much in one night.

He had a highball, and as he prepared it and drank it he wondered what it was that made him feel so tender toward Emily, when he was sure that what he ought to be feeling was unwillingness to see her. Yet he wanted very much to see her. He wondered what had made him kiss Ruth's hand. He hadn't done that for a long time, and never had he done it quite so warmly and spontaneously. Always before this it had been a part of a game he played with Ruth in which Ruth played a flirtatious girl and he was a hick from the country. He joined the party in the grill.

He went straight to Emily and kissed her cheek.

"Oh-ho, somebody had a highball," she said.

"Somebody needed a highball," he said. "Somebody has a hangover and badly needed a drink. How about the rest of you? Cocktail, dear?"

"Not I, thanks," said Emily, "and I don't think the girls had better have anything if they're going to play tennis. Let's order, shall we?"

"Steak," said Ruth. "How about you, Randy? Steak?"

"Yes, please."

"We all want steak," said Ruth. "You do, don't you, Frannie?"

"I don't," said Barbara, the younger Liggett girl. "Not that it makes any difference to Miss Smarty Pants, but steak is exactly what I don't want. Julie, if you'd rather not have steak just say so. You too, Frannie. Mother, do you want steak?"

"No, dear, I think I'd rather have just a chop. Will that take too long, Harry?"

"'Bout ten minutes, Mizz Liggett. Course you be having soup maybe, first, 'n' by the time yole get finished with your soup chop'll be ready."

"Daddy, steak?" said Ruth.

"Right. Tomato juice cocktail first for me, if that's all right, Ruth?"

"Absolutely. Have we decided? Chops for how many? Mother, chops. Miss Barbara, chops. Randy, chops. Daddy, steak. Frannie, steak, and me, steak. Have you got that, Harry?"

"Yes, Miss Liggett. What about vege'ables?"

"Just bring in a lot of vegetables," said Ruth.

All through the ordering Liggett watched Ruth and thought of Emily. Emily—and he did not remember this at the moment—who retained the mouth, nose, chin, bone structure and, to some extent, the complexion Emily had had and that made her handsome; but she was handsome no longer. What Emily retained only made you ask what had happened that left her a plain woman with good features. The eyes, of course they made the difference. They looked nowadays like the eyes of someone who has many headaches, although this did not happen to be the case. Emily was apparently very healthy.

Now he watched her busying herself with her hands; unfolding her napkin, touching without changing the position of the silverware, folding her hands. She had a way of watching her hands when she was using them. He wondered about that, noticing it for the first time. He could not recall ever having seen her watching her hands when they were resting and still, the way she would have if she were conscious of them in the sense of being vain. What she did was to watch them as though she were checking up on their efficiency, their neatness. It was just another part of the way she lived. Her life was like that.

Often she would sit at home with a book of poems in her hand and she would be looking in the direction of the window, a dreamy look in her eyes. He would look again and again at her, wondering what pretty thoughts had been started by what line in what poem. Then she would say suddenly something like: "Do you think I ought to ask the Hobsons for Thursday night? You like her, don't you?" Liggett supposed a lot of husbands were like him; two or three, at least, of his own generation had confided to him that they didn't know their own wives. They had been married, some of them, as much as twenty years; reasonably if not strictly faithful, good providers, good fathers, hard workers, and temperate. Then after a year or so of the depression, when they saw it was not a little thing that was going to pass, these men began taking stock of what life had given them or they had taken. Usually men of this kind began counting with, "I have a wife and two children . . ." and go on from there to their "investments," cash, job, houses, cars, boats, horses, clothes, furniture, trust fund, pair of binoculars, club bonds, and so on. They were—these men—able to see right away that the tangible assets in the Spring of 1931 were worth on the whole about a quarter of what they had cost originally, and in some cases less than that. And in some cases, nothing. By the time the depression had reached that point such men accepted as fact the fact that nothing that you could buy or sell was worth what it once had been worth. At least it worked out that way. Then a few men, a few million men, asked themselves whether the things they had bought ever had been worth what had been paid for them. Ah! That was worth thinking about, worth buying heavy and expensive books to find out about. Some of the keenest practical jokers on the floor of the Stock Exchange went home nights to see what the hell John Stuart Mill said—to find out who the hell John Stuart Mill was.

But among Liggett's friends there were men who, beginning their inventories with, "I have a wife and two children—" went through the list of their worldly goods and then came back to the first item: wife. Then they discovered that they could not really be sure they had their wives. The mortality rate for marriages in Liggett's class is fairly close to 100%, but until the great depression there was no reason to find this out; most of these men believed that they were working for the happiness of their wives and children as well as for their own advancement, but an idle woman is an idle woman, whether her husband is downtown making millions or downtown trying to hold on to a $40-a-week job. Men like Liggett—in 1930 you would see them on the roads of Long Island and Westchester, in cap and windbreaker and sport shoes, taking walks on Sunday with their wives, trying to get to know their wives, because they wanted to believe that a wife was one thing they could count on. Of course there was nothing deliberately insulting in this attitude, and as often as not the wife was not conscious of insult, so it was all right. She knew that he always had taken her to football games and the theater, he paid her bills, he bought her Christmas presents, he was generous to her poor relations, he did not interfere with the education and rearing of the children. Sometimes she did not even ask why, when he became more curious, tried to become more companionable. She knew there was a depression, and she saw the magazine articles about the brave wives who were standing shoulder-to-shoulder with their husbands; she read the sermons in the Monday papers in which clergymen told their parishioners (and the press; always the press) that the depression was a good thing because it brought husbands and wives closer to each other.

Liggett was not quite one of these men; Emily certainly was not one of these women. For one thing, Liggett was a Pittsburgher and Emily a Bostonian. That was one thing, not two. Liggett was precisely the sort of person who, if he hadn't married Emily, would be just the perfect person for Emily to snub. All her life she seemed to be saving up for one snub, which would have to be delivered to an upper-class American, since no foreigner and no lower-class American could possibly understand what she had that she felt entitled her to deliver a snub. What she had was a Colonial governor; an unbroken string of studious Harvard men; their women. Immediately and her own was, of course, the Winsor-Vincent Club-Sewing Circle background. She had a few family connections in New York, and they were unassailable socially; they never went out. It came as a surprise which he was a long time understanding for Liggett to learn, after he married Emily, that Emily never had stopped at a hotel in New York. She explained that the only possible reason you went to New York was to visit relations, and then you stopped with them, not at a hotel. Yes, that was true, he agreed—and never told her the fun he had had as a kid, stopping at New York hotels; the time he released a roll of toilet paper upon Fifth Avenue, the time he climbed along the ledge from one window to another. He was a little afraid of her.

But she was better off with him than she might have been with a Boston man. He was rich and handsome, a Yale athlete. Those qualifications were enough to explain his attraction for her. But he was more than that. She was handsome, she was healthy, and therefore she was passionate, and she wanted him from the moment she first met him. In the beginning Liggett himself was all mixed up about her; he was awed by her manner and her accent (he never got over the accent, and only got accustomed to the manner). She was less handsome than other girls he had known, but he had not known anyone like her, not so close. They met at a deb party, on one of her infrequent visits to New York—his last before beginning training for crew. He made a date with her for tea the following day, but had to break it, and thus began a correspondence which on his part was regulated by the necessity of staying in college and rowing at the same time, and on her part by a schedule: never answer more than one letter a week, and never until two days after the letter has been received. Because of her he decided to go to Harvard Business School. This pleased his father, who gave him a Fiat phaeton and anything else he asked for. There was one thing he could not ask his father for, and that was Emily's fair white body. Emily gave that without being asked, one winter's night in Boston. After waiting three miserable weeks to see if anything was going to happen, they decided to be engaged.

She was better off married to Liggett than she might have been with a Boston man because he never took her passion for granted. A Boston man might have, and might not be long looking around for more of the same from someone else. Liggett could not take her for granted. There is something about those good, good words of sleeping together, the language of sleeping together, when spoken in the tones of Commonwealth Avenue, that no man who has been brought up west of the Connecticut River can fail to notice. And when a man is listening for the words, when he teaches them to a woman, when he asks her to say them, he does not take everything all at once. He will want more.

There was that, and there was the secrecy. Their intimate moments were their own, so much so that Liggett did not once mention Emily's pregnancy to anyone, not even to his own sister, while she was carrying their first child. It was nothing they agreed upon; Emily herself told Liggett's sister. But it was part of the way he felt about Emily. Anything that had to do with their intimate life was not to be discussed with a third person, so far as he was concerned.

To a degree this was true of everything else in their relationship. Liggett's impulse was always to talk about Emily, but he had gone that important step above vulgarity: he secretly recognized his own temptation to vulgarity. However valuable an asset this may be, it had one bad effect. A man ought to be able, when it becomes necessary, to discuss his wife with a third person, man or woman. Since it was impossible for him to bring himself to discuss Emily with another man he found himself in a spot where he had to talk to some woman. It had to be someone who knew Emily, someone close to her. He looked around and for the first time became aware that Emily in the years she had lived in New York—at that time, seven; it was in 1920—had not made a single close friend. Her best friend was a Boston girl, Martha Harvey. Martha was a divorcee. She had been married to a young millionaire who was practically illiterate, always drunk, was three inches shorter than she, and never had spoken an uncivil or impolite word to anyone in his life. Martha had grown up with Emily and they saw each other frequently, but when it came time to discuss Emily with her, Liggett saw how impossible it would be. Martha in a way was Emily over again.

The occasion, however, was urgent. Emily's family's money was mostly in cotton mills. Emily's father was a doctor, a pleasant, unimaginative man who studied medicine in a day when surgeons still spoke of "laudable pus." (He never quite got over the surprise of learning that Walter Reed was right.) In fact his presence in medicine is explained by a fondness for the dissection of cats. It was the only cerebral activity he ever had been interested in, so his father and mother steered him into medicine. A merit-badge boy scout would have been as useful in an emergency as Emily's father, but a few friends went to him for colds and sore throat, and they constituted his practice. His practice was his excuse for neglecting his financial responsibilities, but every year or two he would have an idea, and at this time his idea was to get rid of all his cotton holdings and turn the cash into a vague something else. This time the vague something else was German marks. He just knew they were going to be worth something, and as he had traveled in Germany as a young man, he thought it would be pleasant, since his fortune would soon be doubled, to have a castle on the Rhine, where even at that moment you could have a castle, they said, fully staffed and equipped for $100 a month.

Liggett did not care a very great deal what the old man did with his own money, but that money, he felt, was not altogether the old man's to fool with. The doctor had not earned it; he had inherited it, and since he had inherited it, it seemed to Liggett to be a kind of trust which the doctor had no right to violate. At least it was not to be squandered. If the doctor could go on year in, year out without assuming a permanent responsibility for the money, then he ought not to be permitted to risk losing all of it when he had a foolish hunch. Cotton was high that year, and while it was debatable whether it was the height of shrewdness to dump so much stock on a favorable market, Liggett at least conceded that there was a chance the market would absorb the doctor's holdings without strong reaction. No, with the old gentleman's decision to sell Liggett could not seriously quarrel (indeed, it would have been more like the old man to sell at the bottom of the market). But German marks, for Christ's sake!

Liggett wished Emily had a brother, or even the kind of sister some people have. But Emily's sister was a total stranger, and brother she had none. Next was friend, and friend was Martha. He rejected the plan of talking to Martha the moment her name conjured up a picture of her. But the more he thought the more he was convinced that he had to talk to somebody about the situation. Emily and the two little girls were in Hyannisport that summer, and he did not want to speak to Emily if he could help it. She was taking the children very seriously at the time and talk about her father would worry her.

Martha was just going out when he telephoned, going out to dine alone, and she was not surprised or curious at his calling her for dinner. She said yes. He asked her if she would like a drink, and she said she would, very much, and he said he would bring a bottle of gin. He stopped at a place in Lexington Avenue, bought a bottle of the six-dollar gin, had a drink on Matt, the proprietor, and took a taxi, one of those small, low Philadelphia-made un-American-looking Yellows of that period.

Martha lived on Murray Hill between Park and Madison, in an automatic-elevator apartment. They had orange blossom cocktails, which Liggett liked. She asked once, and only once, about Emily. She said: "How's Emily? She's at Hyannisport, isn't she?" He said she was fine, and was on the verge of correcting himself to say that whether she knew it or not she was not fine at all. Then later, when he saw Martha did not come back to Emily, he was in more real danger of talking about Emily; a girl who had what Martha had, the assurance and poise that gave her courage to accept his wanting to have dinner because she was herself and not merely a trusted friend of his wife's—you could confide in that girl. But at the same time the thing he wanted to talk about began to recede. He began to enjoy himself because he was enjoying Martha's company.

They had two cocktails, and then she told him to take off his coat. Next he thought she would offer him a cigar, because take his coat off was exactly what he wanted to do. It was so comfortable here. "Are you hungry?" he said.

"Not specially. Let's wait. It'll be cool around nine o'clock, if you're in no hurry."

"Gosh, I'm not in a hurry."

"Have some more cocktails, shall we? You know, I like to drink. I never knew I did—gosh, I never even knew about drinking—till I married Tommy, and he used to try to get me drunk, but that was no good. I don't like to have people try to get me drunk. If I want to get drunk I'll do it."

He took the cocktail shaker to the kitchen and made very strong cocktails, not entirely on purpose, but not entirely accidentally, for what she had just been saying reminded him of a physical, biological, whatever-you-want-to-call-it fact: that Martha had been married and therefore had slept with a man. It meant no more to him for the time being. It was just strange that he had somehow ceased to think of her as a girl with a life of her own. Almost always he had thought of her as someone who, when he knew her better, would become finally a good sport, a sexless friend of Emily's.

"Today is Bastille Day in Paris," he said, when he returned with the cocktails. (It was also the day Sacco and Vanzetti were convicted.)

"So it is. I hope to be there next year on Bastille Day."

"Oh, really?"

"I think so. I couldn't go to the Cape this summer because Tommy finds out where I am and comes calling at all hours."

"Isn't there some way to put a stop to that?" he said.

"Oh, I suppose there is. People are always suggesting things like the police. But why do that? They don't seem to remember that I like Tommy."

"Oh, do you?"

"Very much. I'm not in love with him, but I like him."

"Oh, I didn't know that."

"Well, of course you couldn't be expected to."

"No, that's true. I guess this is the first time you and I've really talked together."

"It is." She had her arm across the back of the sofa. She put down her cigarette and crushed it in the tray and picked up her cocktail. She looked away from him as she raised the glass. "As a matter of fact, I never thought we ever would be like this, the two of us, sitting, talking, having a cocktail together."

"Why?"

"Do you want the truth?" she said.

"Of course."

"Well, all right. The truth is I never liked you."

"You didn't."

"No," she said. "But I do now."

Why? Why? Why? He wanted to ask. Why? Why do you like me now? I like you. How I like you! "But you do now," he repeated.

"Yes. Aren't you interested in knowing why I like you now after not liking you for such a long time?"

"Of course, but if you want to tell me you will and if you don't there's no use my asking."

"Come here," she said. He sat beside her on the sofa and took her hand. "I like the way you smell."

"Is that why you like me now and didn't before?"

"Damn before!" She put her hand on his cheek. "Wait a minute," she said. "Don't get up. I'll do it." She went to one of the two large windows and pulled down the shade. "People across the street."

He had her with her clothes on. And from that moment on he never loved Emily again.

"Do you want to stay here tonight?" she said. "If I'm going to be with child for this we might as well be together all night. If you want to stay?"

"I do, I do."

"Grand. I'll have to phone the maid and tell her not to come in early tomorrow. You'll be out of here before ten, tomorrow I mean, won't you?"

They had a wildly passionate affair that summer. They would have dinner in little French restaurants, drinking bad whiskey out of small coffee cups. She was sailing in September and the night before she sailed she said to him: "I don't care if I die now, do you?"

"No. Except I want to live." All summer he had been doing arithmetic on scratch paper—financial arrangements for getting a divorce from Emily. "Once again, marry me."

"No, darling. We'd be no good married to each other. Me especially. But this I know, that for the rest of our lives, whenever we see each other, if I look into your eyes and you look into mine, and we see the thing that we see now—nothing can stop us, can it?"

"No. Nothing."

The next time he saw her was two years later in Paris. In the meantime he had met and lain with ten other women, and Martha was in the White Russian taxi-driver phase. They didn't even have to give each other up, for there was scarcely recognition, let alone love, when again their eyes met.

It got around that he was on the town, but if some kind friend ever told Emily she never let it make any difference. He was comparatively discreet in that he avoided schemers. Among the women he slept with was an Englishwoman, right out of Burke's Peerage, who gave him gonorrhea, or stomach ulcers as it was then called. To Emily he confided that in addition to the ulcers he had a hernia, and she accepted that, not sure what a hernia was, but knowing that it was not a topic for dinner-table conversation. She was so incurious that he was able to keep at home the paraphernalia for the treatment of his disease.

Dr. Winchester, by the way, did not buy the marks. An honest broker dissuaded him.

Liggett addressed his wife: "Are you coming in town tonight or in the morning?"

"Not till Tuesday morning. The girls have a day off tomorrow."

"Why?"

"One of the kids got diphtheria and they're fumigating the school," said Ruth. "Are you staying out?"

"I'd like to. I'd like to really get going on the boat. But I've got to go back to town tonight, so what about you and Bar and Frannie and Miss Rand all getting paint brushes and going to work tomorrow?"

"Pardon me while I die from laughing," said Ruth.

"I will if the others do," said Barbara.

"You're safe and you know it," said Ruth.

"Girls?" said Emily.

"Let's save the Plaza?" said Isabel Stannard.

"Nope. I'm for blowing it up," said Jimmy.

"What?"

"Let it go, dear. It wasn't worth it."

"What wasn't worth what?" she said.

"Please, will you go back to whatever it was you said first? Let's save the Plaza. All right, let's save it. Save it for what? Do you want to go some place else?"

"I think we ought to go there some time when we're feeling more like it."

"Well, I don't exactly see what you mean. I feel like it. I felt like it before I saw you, I felt like it up at your apartment, and you did too—"

"No, not exactly. Remember I was dressed for the country. I thought we were going for a drive."

"Mm. Well, where to, then?" he said.

"Let's keep walking down Fifth—"

"Till we get to Childs Forty-eighth Street."

"All right," she said. "That's all right with me."

"I thought it would be."

"We could go to Twenty-One."

"It's Sunday."

"Aren't they open Sunday? I'm sure I've been there Sunday some time."

"Oh, I know you have, some time. But not at this hour. It's too early, dear. It's too early. They don't open till around five-thirty."

"Are you sure that isn't something new?"

"When the same people were at 42 West Forty-ninth they had the same rule about Sunday. Now that they're at 21 West Fifty-second Street, damned if they haven't the same rule they had at 42 West Forty-ninth. The same people, the same rule, different places."

"Another one of those hats," she said.

"Another one of what hats?"

"Didn't you see it? I think they're rather cute, but I don't know whether to buy one or not. Those hats. Didn't you notice that girl that went by with the foreign-looking man? She was smoking a cigarette."

"She gets paid for that."

"Paid for it?"

"Yes, paid for it. I read that in Winchell's column—"

"The way you wander about from subject to subject, you're like a mountain goat jumping from crag to crag—"

"From precipice to precipice, and back—"

"I know that one, don't say it. Why does she get paid?"

"Why does who get paid, my lamb, my pet?"

"The woman. The one with the hat. The one I just commented on. You said Walter Winchell said she gets money."

"Oh, yes. She gets paid for smoking a cigarette on Fifth Avenue. Winchell ran that in his column after the Easter parade. They're trying to popularize street smoking for women—"

"It'll never go."

"It'll never take the place of the old Welsbach burner, if—hello. Hello." He spoke to two people, girl and man.

"Who are they? See, she has one of those Eugenie hats. She's rather attractive. Who is she?"

"She's a model at Bergdorf Goodman's."

"She French?"

"She's about as French as you are—"

"That's more French than you think."

"Well, than I am. She's—are you still interested?—a Jewess, and he's a lawyer, a Broadway divorce lawyer. He's the kind you see in the tabloids every Monday morning. He tips off the city editors of the *News* and *Mirror* and gets a free ad on page three. The story's always about his client, of course, but he gets his name printed in the third paragraph, with his address. Winthrop S. Saltonstall, of Fourteen-Something Broadway."

"Huh. Winthrop Saltonstall's hardly a Jewish name."

"That's what *you* think."

"Then I suppose she's getting a divorce—although of course she may just know him anyway."

"That's right. You're catching on."

"I've always wanted to go to a service at St. Patrick's. Will you take me some time?"

"What do you mean, a service? Do you mean Mass?"

"Yes, I guess so."

"All right, I'll take you some time. We'll get married in St. Pat's."

"Is that a threat or a promise?"

He stopped dead. "Listen, Isabel, will you do me a favor? A big favor?"

"Why, I don't know. What is it?"

"Will you just go on being a Bryn Mawr girl, nice, attractive, worried about what Leuba taught you, polite, well-bred—"

"Yes, yes, and what?"

"And leave the vulgarities of the vernacular to me? When you want to be slangy, when you want to make a wisecrack, stifle the impulse."

"But I didn't make any wisecrack."

"Oh-ho-ho, you're telling me."

"But I still don't see what you mean, Jimmy."

"They ought to take those fences down and let the people see what they're doing. I am an old construction-watcher, and I think I will take it up with Ivy Lee."

"What are you talking about?"

"I was just thinking as we passed where they're building Radio City, if they took the fences away I'd be able to check up on the progress and report back to the Rockefellers. Ivy Lee is their public relations counsel."

"Ivy Lee. It sounds like a girl's name."

"You ought to hear the whole name."

"What is it?"

"Ivy Ledbetter Lee. He gets $250,000 a year. Here we are, and we probably won't be able to get a table."

They got a table. They knew exactly what they wanted, including all the coffee you could drink for the price of one cup. On the dinner you could even have all the food you wanted for the prix fixe.

"What are we up to this afternoon?"

"Oh, whatever you like," she said.

"I want to see 'The Public Enemy.'"

"Oh, divine. James Cagney."

"Oh, you like Cagney?"

"Adore him."

"Why?" he said.

"Oh, he's so attractive. So tough. Why—I just thought of something."

"What?"

"He's—I hope you don't mind this—but he's a little like you."

"Uh. Well, I'll phone and see what time the main picture goes on."

"Why?"

"Well, I've seen it and you haven't, and I don't want you to see the ending first."

"Oh, I don't mind."

"I'll remind you of that after you've seen the picture. I'll go downstairs and phone. If King Prajadhipok comes in and tries to pick you up it won't be a compliment, so have him put out."

"Oh, on account of his eyes. See, I got it."

"Will you try that number again, please?" said the old man. He held the telephone in a way that was a protest against the hand-set type of phone, a routine protest against something new. He held it with two hands, the one hand where it should be, the other hand cupped under the part he spoke into. "It's Stuyvesant, operator. Are you dialing S, T, U? . . . Well, I thought perhaps you were dialing S, T, Y."

He waited, but after more than five minutes he gave up again.

Joab Ellery Reddington, A.B. (Wesleyan), M.A. (Harvard), Ph.D. (Wesleyan), had come to New York for a special purpose, but the success of his mission depended upon his first completing the telephone call. Without making that connection the trip was futile. Well enough, too well, he knew the address, and the too many taxicabs, the bus systems, the subway and elevated, the street car lines all helped to annihilate space and time for anyone who wanted to present himself in person at the door of the home of Gloria Wandrous. But one of the last things in the world Dr. Reddington wanted to do was to be found in the neighborhood of the home of Gloria Wandrous. The very last thing he wanted to do was to be seen with her, and it went back from there to the other extreme: the thing he wanted most, eventually, was to be so far removed from the company of Gloria Wandrous, from any association with her, that, as he once heard a Mist' Bones say to a Mist' Interlocutor, it would cost twenty dollars to send her a postcard. No, he definitely did not want to go near her home. But he did want to get in touch with her, just this one more time. He wanted to talk with her, he wanted to reason with her, make a deal with her. Failing in making a deal with her, he—he was not prepared to say, even to himself.

But no one answered the telephone. What was the matter with her mother, her uncle? It was no surprise to Dr. Reddington to learn that Gloria was not at home. She was seldom home. But he often had called at her home and been given a number to call. Full well he knew that whether her mother and uncle knew it or not, the number they gave was a speakeasy or a bachelor's apartment; a Harlem beer flat was one number Dr. Reddington had called on occasion (he hated to think of that now, the way those Negroes were not surprised or shocked by the appearance of his kind of man, Phi Beta Kappa key and severely conservative clothes and all, at a beer flat one Saturday noon, calling for a drunken girl who greeted him on terms that too plainly indicated that he was not a stern parent coming to fetch a recalcitrant daughter, but—just what he was).

Dr. Reddington sat on the edge of the bed and (as he expressed it to himself) cursed himself for a blithering idiot for never having written down the numbers he had called. No, that was being unjust to himself. The reason he had not written down those numbers was a good one; he didn't want to be found dead with those numbers on him.

He sat on the bed and his finger searched the soft, faintly damp, white skin of his jowls for a hair that had escaped his razor that morning. There was none. There never was. Only when the barber shaved him. He sat in an attitude that is classically pensive, but he could not think. God, wasn't there one name that would come to him? One name in the numbers that he had called?

It was useless to try to think of the names of speakeasies. His personal experience with speakeasies was slight, as he never drank; but he knew from going to them with Gloria that a place would be known familiarly as Jack's or Giuseppe's—and then when the proprietor gave you a card to the place (which you threw away the moment you were safe outside), it would be called Club Aristocrat or something of the sort. So it was no use trying to think of the names of the places, and too much trouble, practically a life work, to try to find them from memory. No telling what a taxi driver would think if you told him to drive up and down all the streets from Sheridan Square to Fourteenth Street in the hope of recognizing a basement entrance through which you had passed one night long ago. No, the thing to do was to recall a name, a person's name, the name of someone Gloria knew.

A. Ab, Ab, Ab, ante, con, de—no, this was no time to be thinking of the Latin prepositions. Thinking of things like that would only rattle him now. Think viciously, that was the thing. A for Abbott. A for Abercrombie. A for Abingdon. A for Abrams. Wonder what ever happened to that Abrams girl that was so good on the piano? He could think kindly of her now and remember her as a girl who had a nice touch at the piano. She was a degenerate at heart, though, and when her father came to him and asked him what was the meaning of this what his daughter had told him, Dr. Reddington had almost felt like telling the girl's father what kind of child he was raising. But instead he had said: "Look here, Abrams, this is a terrible thing you are saying to me, a serious charge. Am I to infer that you are taking an impressionable child's word against mine?" And the little man had said he was only asking, only wanted to know the truth so if it was the truth he could go farther. "Oh, indeed? Go farther, eh? And who might I ask would take your word against mine? I was born in this town, you know, and for five generations my ancestors have been prominent in this town. I myself have spent twenty-two years in the teaching profession, and you have been here how long? Two years? Well, six years. What's six years against hundreds? Do you think even your own people would take your word against mine? Dr. Stein, for instance. Do you think he would believe you rather than me? Mr. Pollack at The

Bee. Do you think he would believe you, risk his standing in this community where there are mighty few of your people, to side with you in an attack on me with a story that has no foundation in fact? Mr. Abrams, I could thrash you within an inch of your life for coming to me with this accusation. The only thing that prevents me from doing that is that I am a father myself. I think we've said enough about this. Your daughter is your problem. My job is to see that she is given an education, but my job begins at nine in the morning and ends at three in the afternoon." The Abramses. They probably were in New York, at least they took their daughter out of school and sold out their store shortly after the two fathers had their conversation. Abrams. A lot of Abramses in New York.

B. C. D. E. F. G. H. Think of all the people in this city, the money the telephone company must make. All those people, all with their problems. B. Buckley. Brown. Brown with an e on the end. Barnes. Barnard. Brace. Butterfield. Brunner! Gloria knew someone named Brunner. Dr. Reddington found the number and gave it to the operator.

He heard the signal of the number being rung, and then the practiced voice: "What number did you call, please? . . . I'm sorry, sir, that telephone has been dis-con-nec-ted."

He replaced the transmitter. This was a hunch. He looked up the address and memorized it, and went downstairs and took a taxi to the address. He told the driver to wait at the corner of Hudson Street and the driver gave him a good look and said he would.

Dr. Reddington walked down the street, following a girl with a large package under her arm. Any other time she might have interested him, but not today. She was just the back of a girl with a good figure, from what he could see, carrying a bundle. Then to his dismay she turned in at the number he sought, and he had to walk on without stopping; and he thought of the taxi driver, who would be looking at him and wondering why he had passed the number. All confused he turned around and went back to the taxi and they left the neighborhood and drove back to the hotel in the sunshine.

"This is terribly nice of you," said Gloria.

"Oh, that's all right," said Miss Day.

"Thanks a lot, Norma," said Eddie Brunner.

"Oh, I don't mind a bit. I know how it is," said Miss Day. "You'd roast in that mink coat today."

"Eddie, you look out the window a minute," said Gloria.

"Oh! You really did need these," said Miss Day when Gloria took off her coat. "I'm glad I had them. Usually on Sunday my extra things are at the cleaners'. I didn't think to bring a slip."

"I won't need one with this skirt. This is a marvelous suit. Where did you get it?"

"Russek's. Were you playing strip poker?"

"It looks that way, doesn't it? Yes, I was, in a way. That is, we were shooting crap and I was 'way ahead at one time and then my luck changed, and when I offered to bet my dress the men took me up and of course I didn't think they'd hold me to it and it wasn't the men that held me to it, it was the girls on the party. Fine friends I have. It made me very angry and I left."

"Are you going to school in New York?"

"No, I live here, but I couldn't go home looking like this. My family —they won't even allow me to smoke. All right, Eddie."

"Looks better on you than it does on me," said Norma.

"I wouldn't say that," said Eddie.

"I wouldn't either," said Gloria, "but Eddie never says anything to make me get conceited. We've known each other such a long time."

"Eddie, I thought you went on the wagon after Friday," said Norma. "I did."

"Oh, that. That's mine," said Gloria. "I bought it for Eddie because I wanted to get in his good graces. You see I thought I was going to have to spend the day here and I was going to bribe Eddie to go uptown to one of the Broadway shops, I think there are some open on Sunday night, they always seem to be open. But then he suggested you, and I think you're perfectly darling to do this. I'll hang this up in one of your closets, Eddie, and call for it tomorrow. I've been intending to put it in storage but I keep putting it off and putting it off—"

"I know," said Miss Day.

"—and then last night I was glad I hadn't, because a cousin of mine that goes to Yale, he and a friend arrived in an open car and it was cold. No top. They were frozen, but they insisted on driving out to a house party near Princeton."

"Oh. Weren't your family worried? You didn't go home then?"

"The car broke down on the way back at some ungodly hour this morning. Bob, my cousin's friend, took us to a party when we got back to town and that's where I got in the crap game."

"But what about your cousin? I should think—"

"Passed out cold, and he's not much help anyway. Not that he'd let them make me give up my dress, but he can't drink. None of our family can. I had two drinks of that Scotch and I'm reeling. I suppose you noticed it."

"Oh, no. But I can never tell with other people till they start doing perfectly terrible things," said Miss Day.

"Well, I feel grand. I feel like giving a party. By the way, before I forget it, if you give me your address I'll have these things cleaned and send them to you."

"All right," said Miss Day, and gave her address.

"Let's go to the Brevoort, but my treat."

"I thought you lost all your money," said Miss Day.

"I did, but I cashed a check on the way downtown. A man that works for my uncle cashed it for me. Shall we go?"

The nose of the Packard convertible went now up, now down. The car behaved like an army tank on a road that ordinarily was used only by trucks. Paul Farley, driving, was chewing on his lower lip, and the man beside him, looking quite pleased with himself and the world at large, was holding his chin up and dropping the ashes of his cigar on the floor of Farley's car.

"Let's stop," said the man. "Just take one more look. See how it looks from here."

Farley stopped, none too pleased, and looked around. It did please him to look at the nearly finished house; it was his work. "Looks pretty swell to me," he said.

"I think so," said Percy Kahan. He was just learning to say things like "I think so" when he meant "You're damn right." People like Farley, you never knew when they were going to say something simple, like "You're damn right," or something sophisticated, restrained, like "I think so." But it was better to err on the side of the restrained than the enthusiastic. Besides, he was the buyer; Farley was still working for him as architect, and it didn't do to let Farley think he was doing too well.

"A swell job. I know when I've done a swell job, and I've done one for you, Mr. Kahan. About the game room, my original estimate won't cover that now. I could have done it earlier in the game, but I don't suppose you're going to quibble over at the most twelve hundred dollars now. You understand what I meant about the game room itself. That could be done for a great deal less, and still can, but if you want it to be in keeping with the rest of the house my best advice is, don't try to save on the little things. I was one of the first architects to go in for game rooms, that is to recognize them as an important feature of the modern home. Up to that time a game room—well, I suppose you've seen enough of them to know what most of them were like. Extra space in the cellar, so they put in a portable bar, ping-pong table, a few posters from the French Line—"

"Oh, I want those. Can you get them?"

"I think so. I never like to ask them for anything, because I have my private opinion of the whole French Line crowd, but that's a mere detail. Anyway, what I want to point out is that I was one of the first to see what an important adjunct to the home a game room can be. I'd like to show you some things I've done out in the Manhasset section. The Whitney neighborhood, you know."

"Oh, did you do the Jock Whitney estate too?"

"No, I didn't do that, but in that section I've—two years ago I had eleven thousand dollars to spend on one game room out that way."

"But that was two years ago," said Mr. Kahan. "Whose house was that?"

"Weh-hell, I, uh, it isn't exactly ethical to give names and figures, Mr. Kahan. You understand that. Anyway, you see my point about not trying to chisel a few dollars in such an important feature of the home. For instance, you'll want a large open fireplace, you said. Well, that's going to cost you money now. You see, not to be too technical about it, we've gone ahead without making any provision for fireplaces on that side of the house, the side where it would have to be if you wanted it in the game room. And, you have the right idea about it. There *should be* an open fireplace there.

"You see, Mr. Kahan, I want this house to be right. I'll be frank with you. A lot of us architects just can't take it, and a lot of fellows I know are pretty darn pessimistic about the future. Naturally we've been hit pretty hard, some of us, but I personally can't complain. So far this year I've done well over a half a million dollars' worth of business—"

"Net?"

"Oh, no. Not net. I'm a residence architect, Mr. Kahan. But that stacks up pretty well beside what I've been doing the last three years. I had my best year oddly enough last year, Mr. Kahan."

"No kidding."

"Oh, yes. I had a lot of work in Palm Beach. And so far this year I've had a very good, a very satisfactory year. But next year, I'm a little afraid of next year. Not because people haven't got the money, but because they're afraid to spend it. There's an awful lot of hoarding going on. I know a man who is turning everything he can into gold. Gold notes when he can't get the actual bullion. Well, that isn't so good. The general spirit of alarm and unrest, and next year being a Presidential year, but I've got my overhead, I've got my expenses, Presidential year or no Presidential year. So far I haven't had to lay off a single draftsman and I don't want to have to do it, but great heavens, if people are going to take their money out of industry and let it lie gathering dust in safe deposit vaults, or in secret vaults in their own homes, the general effect is going to be pretty bad.

"Now with a house like this, people will see this house and they can't help being enchanted with it, and it's been my experience that a house like yours, Mr. Kahan, with a page or two of photographs in *Town and Country* and *Country Life* and *Spur*, people who might be tempted to hoard their money—"

"You mean pictures of this house in *Town and Country?*"

"Naturally," said Farley. "You don't suppose I'd let this house go without—unless you'd rather not. Of course if you'd—"

"Oh, no. Not me. I'm in favor of that. Don't tell Mrs. Kahan, though. It'd make a nice surprise for her."

"Certainly. Women like that. And women are mighty important in these things. As I was saying, I'm counting on people seeing this house, and your friends and neighbors coming in—that's one reason why I'd like to see you have a good game room, when you entertain informally, people will see what a really fine house you have, and they'll want to know who did the house. It's good business for me to do a good job for you any time, Mr. Kahan, but especially now."

"*Town and Country,* eh? Do I send in the pictures or do you?"

"Oh, they'll send for them. They call up and find out my plans in advance, you know, and I tell them what houses I'm doing, or at least my secretary does—it's all routine. I suppose I've had more houses chosen for photographing in those magazines than any architect within ten years of my age. Shall we go back to the club? I imagine the ladies are wondering what's happened."

"Okay, but now listen, Mr. Farley, I don't want you paying for dinner again. Remember last time we were out here I said next time would be my treat?"

"Huh, huh, huh," Farley chuckled. "I'm afraid I cheated, then. I have to sign. Some other time in town I'll hook you for a really big dinner, and I might as well warn you in advance, Mrs. Farley knows wines. I don't know a damn thing about them, but she does."

They drove to the club, where the ladies were waiting; Mrs. Farley fingering her wedding ring and engagement ring and guard in a way she had when she was nervous, Mrs. Kahan painlessly pinching the lobe of her left ear, a thing she did when she was nervous.

"Well," said the four, in unison.

Farley asked the others if they would like cocktails, and they all said they would, and he took Kahan to the locker-room to wash his hands and to supervise the mixing of the drinks. As they were coming in the locker-room a man was on his way out, in such a hurry that he bumped Kahan. "Oh, I beg your pardon, sir," said the man.

"Oh, that's all right, Mr. Liggett," said Kahan.

"Oh—oh, how are you," said Liggett. "Glad to see you."

"You don't know who I am," said Kahan, "but we were classmates at New Haven."

"Oh, of course."

"Kahan is my name."

"Yes, I remember. Hello, Farley."

"Hello, Liggett, you join us in a cocktail?"

"No, thanks. I've got a whole family waiting in the car. Well, nice to have seen you, Kann. 'By, Farley." He shook hands and hurried away.

"He didn't know me, but I knew him right away."

"I didn't know you went to Yale," said Farley.

"I know. I never talk about it," said Kahan. "Then once in a while I see somebody like Liggett, one of the big Skull and Bones fellows he was, and one day I met old Doctor Hadley on the street and I introduced myself to him. I can't help it. I think what a waste of time, four years at that place, me a little Heeb from Hartford, but last November I had to be in Hollywood when the Yale-Harvard game was played, and God damn it if I don't have a special wire with the play by play. The radio wasn't good enough for me. I had to have the play by play. Yes, I'm a Yale man."

3

"WELL, I can see why you didn't want me to see the ending first. I never would have stayed in the theater if I'd seen that ending. And you wanted to see that again? God, I hope if you ever write anything it won't be like that."

"I hope if I ever write anything it affects somebody the way this affected you," said Jimmy.

"I suppose you think that's good. I mean good writing," said Isabel. "Where shall we go?"

"Are you hungry?"

"No, but I'd like a drink. One cocktail. Is that understood?"

"Always. Always one cocktail. That's always understood. I know a place I'd like to take you to, but I'm a little afraid to."

"Why, is it tough?"

"It isn't really tough. I mean it doesn't look tough, and the people—well, you don't think you're in the Racquet Club, but unless you know where you are, I mean unless you're tipped off about what the place has, what its distinction is, it's just another speakeasy, and right now if I told you what its distinguishing characteristic is, you wouldn't want to go there."

"Well, then let's not go there," she said. "What is peculiar about the place?"

"It's where the Chicago mob hangs out in New York."

"Oh, well, then by all means let's go there. That is, if it's safe."

"Of course it's safe. Either it's safe or it isn't. They tell me the local boys approve of this place, that is, they sanction it, allow it to exist and do business, because they figure there has to be one place as a sort of hangout for members of the Chicago mobs. There's only one real danger."

"What's that?"

"Well, if the Chicago mobs start shooting among themselves. So far that hasn't happened, and I don't imagine it will. You'll see why."

They walked down Broadway a few blocks and then turned and walked east. When they came to a highly polished brass sign which advertised a wigmaker, Jimmy steered Isabel into the narrow doorway, back a few steps and rang for the elevator. It grinded its way down, and a sick-eyed little Negro with a uniform cap opened the door. They got in and Jimmy said: "Sixth Avenue Club."

"Yessa," said the Negro. The elevator rose two stories and stopped. They got out and were standing then right in front of a steel door, painted red, and with a tiny door cut out in the middle. Jimmy rang the bell and a face appeared in the tiny door.

"Yes, sir," said the face. "What was the name again?"

"You're new or you'd know me," said Jimmy.

"Yes, sir, and what was the name again?"

"Malloy, for Christ's sake."

"And what was the address, Mr. Malloy?"

"Oh, nuts. Tell Luke Mr. Malloy is here."

There was a sound of chains and locks, and the door was opened. The waiter stood behind the door. "Have to be careful who we let in, sir. You know how it is."

It was a room with a high ceiling, a fairly long bar on one side, and in the corner on the other side was a food bar, filled with really good free lunch and with obviously expensive kitchen equipment behind the bar. Jimmy steered Isabel to the bar.

"Hello, Luke," he said.

"Howdy do, sir," said Luke, a huge man with a misleading pleasant face, not unlike Babe Ruth's.

"Have a whiskey sour, darling. Luke mixes the best whiskey sours you've ever had."

"I think I want a Planter's punch—all right, a whiskey sour."

"Yours, sir?"

"Scotch and soda, please."

Isabel looked around. The usual old rascal looking into a schooner of beer and the usual phony club license hung above the bar mirror. Many bottles, including a bottle of Rock and Rye, another specialty of Luke's, stood on the back bar. Except for the number and variety of the bottles, and the cleanliness of the bar, it was just like any number (up to 20,000) of speakeasies near to and far from Times Square. Then Isabel saw one little article that disturbed her: an "illuminated" calendar, with a pocket for letters or bills or something, with a picture of a voluptuous dame with nothing on above the waist. The calendar still had not only all the months intact, but also a top sheet with "1931" on it. And across the front of the pocket was the invitation. "When in Chicago Visit D'Agostino's Italian Cooking Steaks Chops At Your Service Private Dining Rooms," and the address and the telephone numbers, three of them.

By the time she had studied the calendar and understood the significance of it—what with Jimmy's advance description of the speakeasy—their drinks were served, and she began to lose the feeling that the people in the speakeasy were staring at her back. She looked around, and no one was staring at her. The place was less than half full. At one table there was a party of seven, four men and three women. One of the women was outstandingly pretty, was not a whore, was not the kind of blonde that is cast for gangster's moll in the movies, and was not anything but a very good-looking girl, with a very nice shy smile. Isabel could imagine knowing her, and then she suddenly realized why. "Jimmy," she said, "that girl looks like Caroline English."

He turned. "Yes, she does."

"But the other people, I've seen much worse at Coney Island, or even better places than that. You wouldn't invent a story just to make an ordinary little place seem attractive, would you?"

"In the first place, no, and in the second place, no. In the first place I couldn't be bothered. In the second place I wouldn't have to. People like you make me mad, I mean people like you, people whose families have money and send them to good schools and belong to country clubs and have good cars—the upper crust, the swells. You come to a place like this and you expect to see a Warner Brothers movie, one of those gangster pictures full of old worn-out comedians and heavies that haven't had a job since the two-reel Keystone Comedies. You expect to see shooting the minute you go slumming—"

"I beg your pardon, but why are you talking about you people, you people, your kind of people, people like you. *You* belong to a country club, you went to good schools and your family at least *had* money—"

"I want to tell you something about myself that will help to explain a lot of things about me. You might as well hear it now. First of all, I am a Mick. I wear Brooks clothes and I don't eat salad with a spoon and I probably could play five-goal polo in two years, but I am a Mick. Still a Mick. Now it's taken me a little time to find this out, but I have at last discovered that there are not two kinds of Irishmen. There's only one kind. I've studied enough pictures and known enough Irishmen personally to find that out."

"What do you mean, studied enough pictures?"

"I mean this, I've looked at dozens of pictures of the best Irish families at the Dublin Horse Show and places like that, and I've put my finger over their clothes and pretended I was looking at a Knights of Columbus picnic—and by God you can't tell the difference."

"Well, why should you? They're all Irish."

"Ah, that's exactly my point. Or at least we're getting to it. So, a while ago you say I look like James Cagney—"

"Not look like him. Remind me of him."

"Well, there's a faint resemblance, I happen to know, because I have a brother who looks enough like Cagney to be his brother. Well, Cagney is a Mick, without any pretense of being anything else, and he is America's ideal gangster. America, being a non-Irish, anti-Catholic country, has its own idea of what a real gangster looks like, and along comes a young Mick who looks like my brother, and he fills the bill. He is the typical gangster."

"Well, I don't see what you prove by that. I think—"

"I didn't prove anything yet. Here's the big point. You know about the Society of the Cincinnati? You've heard about them?"

"Certainly."

"Well, if I'm not mistaken I could be a member of that Society. Anyway I could be a Son of the Revolution. Which is nice to know sometimes, but for the present purpose I only mention it to show that I'm pretty God damn American, and therefore my brothers and sisters are, and yet we're not American. We're Micks, we're non-assimilable, we Micks. We've been here, at least some of my family, since before the Revolution—and we produce the perfect gangster type! At least it's you American Americans' idea of a perfect gangster type, and I suppose you're right. Yes, I guess you are. The first real gangsters in this country were Irish. The Mollie Maguires. Anyway, do you see what I mean by all this non-assimilable stuff?"

"Yes. I suppose I do."

"All right. Let me go on just a few sticks more. I show a sociological fact, I prove a sociological fact in one respect at least. I suppose I could walk through Grand Central at the same time President Hoover was arriving on a train, and the Secret Service boys wouldn't collar me on sight as a public enemy. That's because I dress the way I do, and I dress the way I do because I happen to prefer these clothes to Broadway clothes or Babbitt clothes. Also, I have nice manners because my mother was a lady and manners were important to her, also to my father in a curious way, but when I was learning manners I was at an age when my mother had greater influence on me than my father, so she gets whatever credit is due me for my manners. Sober.

"Well, I am often taken for a Yale man, by Yale men. That pleases me a little, because I like Yale best of all the colleges. There's another explanation for it, unfortunately. There was a football player at Yale in 1922 and around that time who looks like me and has a name something like mine. That's not important."

"No, except that it takes away from your point about producing public enemies, your family. You can't look like a gangster *and* a typical Yale man."

"That's true. I have an answer for that. Let me see. Oh, yes. The people who think I am a Yale man aren't very observing about people. I'm not making that up as a smart answer. It's true. In fact, I just thought of something funny."

"What?"

"Most men who think I'm a Yale man went to Princeton themselves."

"Oh, come on," she said. "You just said—"

"All right. I know. Well, that's not important and I'm only confusing the issue. What I want to say, what I started out to explain was why I said 'you people, you members of the upper crust,' and so on, implying that I am not a member of it. Well, I'm *not* a member of it, and now I never will be. If there was any chance of it it disappeared—let me see—two years ago."

"Why two years ago? You can't say that. What happened?"

"I starved. Two years ago I went for two days one time without a thing to eat or drink except water, and part of the time without a cigarette. I was living within two blocks of this place, and I didn't have a job, didn't have any prospect of one, I couldn't write to my family, because I'd written a bad check a while before that and I was in very bad at home. I couldn't borrow from anybody, because I owed everybody money. I'd borrowed from practically everybody I knew even slightly. A dollar here, ten dollars there. I stayed in for two days because I couldn't face the people on the street. Then the nigger woman that cleaned up and made the beds in this place where I lived, she knew what was happening, and the third morning she came to work she brought me a chicken sandwich. I'll never forget it. It was on rye bread, and home-cooked chicken, not flat and white, but chunky and more tan than white. It was wrapped in newspaper. She came in and said, 'Good morning, Mr. Malloy. I brought you a chicken sandwich if you like it.' That's all. She didn't say why she brought it, and then she went out and bought me a container of coffee and pinched a couple of cigarettes—Camels, and I smoke Luckies—from one of the other rooms. She was swell. She knew."

"I should think she was swell enough for you to call her a colored woman instead of a nigger."

"Oh, balls!"

"I'm leaving."

"Go ahead."

"Just a Mick."

"See? The first thing you can think of to insult me with. Go on, beat it. Waiter, will you open the door for this lady, please?"

"Aren't you coming with me?"

"Oh, I guess so. How much, Luke?"

"That'll be one-twenty," said Luke, showing, by showing nothing on his face, that he strongly disapproved the whole thing.

Exits like the one Isabel wanted to make are somewhat less difficult to make since the repeal of Prohibition. In those days you had to wait for the waiter to peer through the small door, see that everything was all right, open at least two locks, and hold the door open for you. The most successful flouncing out in indignation is done through swinging doors.

He had to ring for the elevator and wait for it in silence, they had to ride down together in silence, and find a taxi with a driver in it. There were plenty of taxis, but the hackmen were having their usual argument among themselves over the Tacna-Arica award and a fare was apparently the last thing in the world that interested them. However, a cruising taxi appeared and Isabel and Jimmy got in.

"Home?" said Jimmy.

"Yes, please," said Isabel.

Jimmy began to sing: ". . . How's your uncle? I haven't any uncle. I hope he's fine and dandy too."

Silence.

"Four years ago this time do you know what was going on?"

"No."

"The Snyder-Gray trial."

Silence.

"Remember it?"

"Certainly."

"What was Mr. Snyder's first name?"

"Whose?"

"Mister *Sny*-der's."

"It wasn't Mister Snyder. It was Ruth Snyder. Ruth Snyder, and Judd Gray."

"There was a Mr. Snyder, though. Ah, yes, there was a Mr. Snyder. It was he, dear Isabel, it was he who was assassinated. What was his first name?"

"Oh, how should I know? What do I care what his first name was?"

"Why are you sore at me?"

"Because you humiliated me in public, calling the waiter and asking him to take me to the door, barking at me and saying perfectly vile, vile things."

"Humiliated you in public," he said. "Humiliated you in public. And you don't remember Mr. Snyder's first name."

"If you're going to talk, talk sense. Not that I care whether you talk or not."

"I'm talking a lot of sense. You're sore at me because I humiliated you in public. What the hell does that amount to? Humiliated in public. What about the man that Ruth Snyder and Judd Gray knocked off?

I'd say he was humiliated in public, plenty. Every newspaper in the country carried his name for days, column after column of humiliation, all kinds of humiliation. And yet you don't even remember his name. Humiliation my eye."

"It isn't the same thing."

"Yes, it is. It's exactly the same thing. If I got out of the taxi now would that be humiliating you publicly?"

"Oh, don't. It's so unnecessary."

"Please answer my question."

"I'd rather you didn't. Does that answer it?"

"Yes. Driver! Pull over, please, over to the curb, you dope. Here." He gave the driver a dollar and took off his hat. "Good-by, Isabel," he said.

"You're being silly. You know you're being silly, don't you?"

"Not at all. I just remembered I was supposed to be covering a sermon this morning and I haven't put in at the office all day."

"Good heavens, Jimmy! Will you call me?"

"In an hour."

"I'll wait."

Liggett took a late afternoon train back to town. He almost enjoyed the ride. It had been a strain, being with the girls. Not so much with Emily; for the time being she was out of this, and she would only be in it if something slipped. So she was not a strain. Not that he expected anything to slip; but there was always the possibility that that fool girl might still be asleep in the apartment, or that she had left something behind, and he wanted to have plenty of time for a thorough search before Emily and the kids got back. Whatever got over him, he asked himself, that he should take that girl to his apartment? He'd never done that before, not even when Emily and the girls were away for the summer, or in Europe. Well . . .

Europe. This had been a tough winter. The things that were supposed to happen this last winter, hadn't happened. He was beginning to think that the things that were promised to happen were not going to happen, either. Privately, secretly, he did not delude himself as to his own importance in his own economic scheme; he was the New York branch manager for the heavy-tool manufacturing plant his grandfather had founded as a tap and reamer plant. Liggett could read a blueprint; he could, with a certain amount of concentration, pass upon estimates with sufficient intelligence to see the difference between cost and eventual purchase price, which was a not inconsiderable part of his job, since one of his best customers was the City of New York. He also had to deal with large utility corporations and he had to have at least a working knowledge of the accounting and valuation systems of these corporations, which make a practice of carrying, say, a $5,000 pneumatic drill outfit as a $5,000 capital investment ten years after the purchase, allowing nothing for depreciation. He had to know the right man to see among all his prospective customers—which did not by any means always turn out to be the purchasing agent. He did not know how to use a slide rule, but he knew enough to call it a slip-stick. He could not use a transit, but among engineers he could talk about "running the gun." Instead of handwriting he always used the Reinhard style of lettering, the slanting style of printing which is the first thing engineers learn. He would disclaim any real knowledge of engineering, frankly and sometimes a little sadly, but this had a disarming effect upon real engineers: they would think here is a guy who is just like a kid the way he wants to be an engineer and he might have made a good one. The superficial touches which he af-fected—the lettering, the slang, the knowing the local engineering gos-sip like who was the $75-a-week man who did the real work on a certain immense job—all these things made him a good fellow among engineers, who certainly are no less sentimental than any other group of men. They liked him, and they did little things for him which they would not have done for another engineer; he was a non-competing brother.

A crew man, he always had something to talk about to M. I. T. men. He would talk about the spirit of the M. I. T. navy, taking its beatings year after year. His own father had gone to Lehigh, so he al-ways had a word of Lehigh engineers. He would recognize Tau Beta Pi and Sigma Xi keys a mile away. He was even known to remark, in the presence of non-Yale men, that he wished he had at least gone to Sheff and learned something. He never made the mistake of saying of Tau Beta Pi and Sigma Xi men, as he once said to a man he did not like: "I never saw a Phi Beta Kappa wear a wrist watch."

The "personal-use clause" which required Yale men to sign state-ments that they hoped their mothers dropped dead this minute if these football tickets that they were applying for were to be used by someone else—that was a gift from the gods to Liggett. He would apply for his tickets, sign the pledge that went with the tickets—and then when some properly placed Tammany man came to him for a pair for the Harvard game, Liggett would explain about the pledge but he would turn over the tickets. Liggett did not think it entirely necessary to justify this violation of his word of honor, but he had two justifications ready: the first was that he did not approve of the pledge; the second, that he had got boils on his ass year after year for Yale, four years of rowing without missing a race, and he felt that made him a better judge of what to do with one of the few benefits he derived from being an old "Y" man than some clerk in the Athletic Association office. On at least one occasion those tickets made the difference between getting an equipment contract and not getting it. And so, looking at it one way, he was a valuable man to the firm. The plant no longer belonged to the Liggett family, but he was a director, as a teaser for any lingering good will that his father and grandfather might have left. He voted his own and his sister's stock, but he voted the way he was told by the attorney for his father's estate, who was also a director.

It took the whole year 1930 to teach him that he just did not know his way around that stock market. Business was a simple thing, he told himself: it was buying and selling, supply and demand. His grandfather had come over here, a little English mechanic from Birmingham, and supplied a demand. His father had continued the supply and demand part, but had also gone in more extensively for the buying and selling. In 1930 Liggett reasoned with himself: the buying and selling is not up to me the way it was up to my father, and neither is the supplying of the demand up to me the way it was up to Grandfather. I am in the position of participating in the activities of both my grandfather and my father, and yet since I am not right there at the plant, I have something they didn't have. I have a detached point of view. Liggett & Company are supplying—and selling. Now wherever I go I see buildings going up, I see excavations being made. A few common stocks—all right, *all* common stocks—have taken a thumping, but that's because some of them were undoubtedly priced at more than they were worth. All right. Something happens and the whole market goes smacko. Why? Well, who can explain a thing like that; why. But it happened and in the long run it's going to be a good thing, because when those stocks go up there again, this time they're going to be worth it.

On that basis he brought his income down from the $75,000 he earned in 1929 to about $27,000 for 1930. His salary was $25,000 and this was not cut, for his Tammany connections were as good in 1930 as they were in 1929, and he sold. In 1929 his income from Liggett & Company, aside from salary, was $40,000, including commissions. In addition he had an income of about $10,000 from his mother's estate, which was tied up in non-Liggett investments in Pittsburgh. In 1930 his profits from Liggett & Company amounted to $15,000, which went to his brokers, as did the $5,000 he got from his mother's estate. But he and another man did make $2,000 apiece from an unexpected source, and they thought seriously of doing it every year.

Liggett convinced himself he had to go abroad in the Spring of 1930, and a man he had known in college but less well in the after years, came to him with a scheme which took Liggett's breath away. They talked it over in the smoke room, and as part of the scheme they bought out the low field in the ship's pool. The next day shortly after high noon the ship stopped, and was stopped for a good hour. As a result of the delay Liggett and his friend, holding the low field, won the biggest pool of the voyage, and Liggett's end was around $2,000. It was not clear profit, however; $500 of it went to the steward whom they had bribed to fall overboard at noon that day. In Liggett's favor it must be said that he refused at first to go into the scheme, and would not have done so had he not been assured that a financier whom he always had looked up to as a model of righteousness and decorum had once given the bridge an out-and-out bribe, with subtle threats to back it up, to win a pool that didn't even pay his passage. Also, Liggett had to be assured that his fellow-conspirator would choose a steward who could swim. . . .

He hurried from the train to a phone booth and called his home number. No answer. That didn't mean anything, though. It only meant that this Gloria was not answering his telephone. He took the subway to Times Square, but instead of taking the shuttle to Grand Central he went up to the street out of that horrible subway air (it was much better when there were a lot of people in it; you could look at the horrible people and that took your mind off the air) and rode the rest of the way home in a taxi.

He looked for signs of something in the face of the elevator operator, but nothing there, only that six-months-from-Christmas "Good afternoon, sir." He hurriedly inspected the apartment, even opening the kitchen door that opened upon the service hall.

"Well, she's not here," he said aloud, and went back to take a better look at the bathroom. She certainly had made a nice little mess of that. Then he noticed that his toothbrush, which always, always stood in a tumbler, was lying on the lavatory. A tube of toothpaste had been squeezed in the middle and the cap had not been replaced. He held the toothbrush to his nose. Yes, by God, the bitch had brushed her teeth with his brush. He broke it in half and threw it in a trash basket.

In the bedroom he saw her evening gown and evening coat. He picked up the gown and looked at it. He turned it inside out and looked at it at approximately the point where her legs would begin on her body, expecting to find he knew not what, and finding nothing. It was a good job of tearing he had done and he was embarrassed about that. From the way she had behaved when once he got her into bed there was no reason to suspect her of being a teaser, but why had she been so teaser-like when he brought her home? They were both drunk, and he had to admit that she was a little less drunk than he, could drink more was what he was trying not to admit. She had come home with a man she had met only that night, come to his apartment after necking with him in a taxi and allowing him to feel her breasts. She had gone to his bathroom and when she came out and saw him standing there waiting for her with a drink in his hand she accepted the drink but was all for going back to the livingroom. "No, it's much more comfortable here," he remembered saying, and remembered thinking that if he hadn't said anything it would have been better, for as soon as he spoke she said she thought it was more comfortable in the livingroom, and he said all right, it was more comfortable in the livingroom but that they were going to stay here. "Oh, but you're wrong," she said, and looked at him in the face and then slowly down his body, the frankest look anyone ever had given him, the only time he ever was completely sure that he was looking at someone's thoughts. He got up and put his drink on a table and took her in his arms as roughly as possible. He squeezed her body against his until she felt really small to him. She kept her drink in her hand and held it high while she leaned her head back as far as she could, her face away from his face. She stopped speaking, but she did not look angry. Tolerant. She looked tolerant, as though she were dealing with a prep school kid, as though she were suffering but knew this would be over in a little while and she would be there, with her drink in her hand and her dignity unaffected. That finally was what made him release her, but not for the reason she supposed. She thought he was going to give up, but that dignity was too much for him. He had to break that some way, so he let her go, took his arms from around her, and then snatched the top of the front of her dress and ripped it right down the front. It tore right down the middle.

Instantly there were changes. He had frightened her and she was pitiful and sweet. He didn't even notice that her dignity was at least genuine enough to cause her to hold on to the drink and walk two steps with it to a table. For a minute, two minutes, he was ready to love her with all the tenderness and kindness that seemed to be all of a sudden at his command, somewhere inside him. He followed her to the table and waited for her to put down the drink. He was aware now, the day after, but hadn't been last night, that she looked a little posed, in a trite pose, with her chin almost on her shoulder, her eyes looking away from him, her right arm making a protective V over her chest, her left hand cupped under her right elbow. He put his hands on her biceps and pressed a little. "Kiss me," he said.

"As a reward," she said.

She turned her face toward him, sufficient indication that she would kiss him. He put his hands in back of her again and kissed her tenderly on the mouth, and then she slowly lowered her arms from in front of her and put them around him, and she walked up to him without moving her feet.

Thinking of it now he knew that it went beyond love. It was so completely what it was, so new in its thoroughness and proficiency that for the first time in his life he understood how these guys, these bright young subalterns, betray King and Country for a woman. He even understood how they could do it while knowing that the woman was a spy, that she was not faithful to them; for he did not care how many men Gloria had stayed with since she left this apartment; he wanted her now. He hadn't remembered this all afternoon, so long as he was with Emily and the girls, but right now if he could have Gloria here he would not care if Emily and the kids came in and watched. "God damn it!" he shouted. She couldn't possibly know the things he knew. He was forty-two, and she wasn't less than twenty years younger than he, and—aah, what difference did it make. Wherever she was he'd find her, and he would get her an apartment tonight. This, then, was what happened to men that made people speak of the dangerous age and all that. Well, dangerous age, make a fool of yourself, whatever else was coming to him he would take if he could have that girl. But he would have to have her over and over again, a year of having her. And to make sure of that he would get her an apartment. Tonight. Tomorrow she could have the charge accounts.

He telephoned her at home, not expecting to find her there, but there was always the chance. A timid male voice answered; probably her father, Liggett thought. She was not home and was not expected back till later this evening. That did not discourage Liggett. He thought he knew enough about her to know where to find her. He made a bundle of her evening clothes and took it with him and went downstairs and took a taxi to the Grand Central. He checked the bundle there and was going to throw away the check, but thought she might like to have the dress for some reason, maybe sentimental, maybe to patch something. Women often saved old dresses for reasons like that, and he had no right to throw away the check. Besides, the coat was all right. He hadn't thought of that at first, because all he thought of was the torn dress. It was annoying the way he kept thinking of that. He liked to think of tearing the dress and stripping her, all in one thought, with the memory of how she had looked at just that moment, her body and her terror. But the fact of tearing a girl's dress was embarrassing and he did not like to be left alone with that thought. He went to a speakeasy in East Fifty-third Street, the one in which two men inside of two years shot themselves in the men's toilet. They were taking the last few chairs off the tables, getting ready to open up, but the bar was open and a man in a cutaway and a woman friend were having drinks. The man was a gentleman, in his late forties. The woman was in her early thirties, tall and voluptuous. They were a little drunk and having an argument when Liggett entered the bar, and the man took the woman's arm and steered her away from the bar to a table in the same room but away from Liggett. Obviously the woman was the man's mistress and he was helplessly in love with her.

"Ever since I've known you," she said, very loud, "you've asked me nothing but questions."

Liggett got some nickels and went to the phone booth to call an engineer friend. The engineer did not answer. He tried two other engineer friends because he wanted to go on a tour of the speakeasies where he would be likely to find Gloria, and he wanted to be with a man but not one of his real friends. They would be at home with their wives or out to parties with their wives, and he wanted to go out with a man whose wife did not know Emily. He tried these engineers, but no soap. No answer. He tried a third, a man he did not specially like, and the man was very cordial and tried to insist on Liggett's coming right up and joining a cocktail party where there was a swell bunch. Liggett got out of that. In another minute he was sure he could have had the company of the man in the cutaway, judging by the conversation between the man and his woman. The conversation had taken a renunciatory turn and the woman was any minute now going home and sending back everything he had ever given her, and he knew what he could do with it. Not wishing to be left alone with the man, Liggett drank the rest of his highball, paid his bill and went to another speakeasy, next door.

The first person he saw was Gloria, all dressed up in a very smart little suit. She gave him a blank look. She was with a young man and a pretty young girl. He went over and shooks hands and Gloria introduced him to the other people and finally asked him to sit down for a second, that they were just leaving.

"Oh, I thought we were going to have dinner here," said Miss Day. "I'm really getting hungry."

There was a silence for the benefit of Miss Day, who was being tacitly informed by everyone at the table that she should have known better than to say that. "Are you waiting for someone?" said Liggett.

"Not exactly," said Gloria.

"I really feel like an awful stupid and rude and all when you were so kind to invite us for dinner," said Miss Day, "but really, Miss Wandrous, I'd of rather stayed at the Brevoort and ate there because I was hungry then. I—" Then she shut up.

"I think we ought to go," said Mr. Brunner. "Gloria, we'll take a rain check on that dinner." He had not been drinking, and he had a kind of surly-sober manner that men sometimes get who are temporarily on the wagon but usually good drinkers. Liggett quickly stood up before they changed their minds. Miss Day apparently had postponed her appetite because she got up too.

When they had gone Liggett said: "I've been trying to get you. I phoned all over and I was going to look everywhere in New York till I did find you. What are you drinking?"

"Rye and plain water."

"Rye and plain water, and Scotch and soda for me. Do you want to eat here?"

"Am I having dinner with you?"

"Well, aren't you?"

"I don't know. What do you want that you've been calling me all over, as you put it, although I don't know where you'd be apt to call me except home."

"And the Manger."

"That's not funny. I was drunk last night. That won't happen again."

"Yes. It *must* happen again. It's got to. Listen, I don't know how to begin."

"Then don't, if it's a proposition. Because if it's a proposition I'm not interested." She knew she was lying, for she was interested in almost any proposition; interested in hearing it, at least. But so far she could not tell which way he was headed. He had said nothing to indicate that he had discovered her theft of the coat, but his avoiding that topic might be tactical and only that. She resolved not to say anything about it until he did, but to wait for the first crack that would indicate that he wanted the coat back. She was not at this point prepared to take a stand about the coat. Later, maybe, but not now.

He looked down at his hands, which were making "Here's the Church, here's the steeple, open the door and there's all the people."

"Do you know what I want?" he said.

It was on the tip of her tongue to say yes, the mink coat. She said, "Why, I haven't the faintest idea."

He reached in his pocket and brought out the check for the bundle he had left at Grand Central. "You," he said.

"What's this?" she said, taking the check.

"The rye is for Miss Wandrous. Scotch for me," said Liggett to the waiter who had sneaked up with the drinks. When he went away Liggett went on: "That's for your dress and coat. You got the money I left. Was it enough?"

"Yes. What do you mean you want me?"

"Well, I should think that would be plain enough. I want you. I want to—if I get you an apartment will you live in it?"

"Oh," she said. "Well, I live at home with my family."

"You can tell them you have a job and you want to be uptown."

"But I didn't say I wanted to live uptown. What makes you want me for your mistress? I didn't know you had a mistress, I know that gag, so don't you say it."

"I wasn't going to. I want you, that's why."

"Do you want me to tell you?"

"Well—"

"First you want me because I'm good in bed and your wife isn't. Or if she is—don't bridle. I guess she is, judging by the way you took that. But you're tired of her and you want me because I'm young enough to be your daughter."

"Just about," he said. "I'd have had to have you when I was very young."

"Not so very. I saw pictures of your daughters in your living room, and they're not much younger than I am. But I don't want you to feel too old so we'll pass over that. You want me, and you think because you paid the rent for an apartment that I'd be yours and no one else's. Isn't that true?"

"No. As a matter of fact it isn't. I was thinking not an hour ago, before I knew where you were, Gloria, I discovered something and that is, I didn't care who you were with or in what bed, I still wanted you."

"Oh. Desperate. You *are* getting a little, uh, you're getting worried about how near fifty is, aren't you?"

"Maybe. I don't think so. Men don't get menopause. I may have as many years left as you. I've taken good care of myself."

"I hope."

"I hope you have, too."

"Don't you worry about me. The first thing I do tomorrow is go to my friend on Park Avenue."

"Who's your friend on Park Avenue?"

"My friend on Park Avenue? That's my doctor. I'll be able to tell you this week whether there's anything the matter with you, and me."

"Do you always go to him?"

"Always, without fail. Listen, you, I don't want to sit here and talk about venereal disease. You didn't let me finish what I was saying. You think I'd be faithful to you because you gave me an apartment. My handsome friend, I would be faithful to you only as long as I wanted to be, which might be a year or might be till tomorrow afternoon. No. No apartment for me. If you want to take an apartment where we can go when I want to go with you, or where you can take anyone you please, that's entirely up to you. But after looking around at your apartment and making a guess as to how you live? Not interested. You haven't enough money to own me. Last year, last fall, that is, I got a pretty good idea how much I was worth. Could you pay the upkeep on a hundred and eighty-foot yacht? Diesel yacht?"

"No, frankly."

"Well, this man could and does, and I'll bet he doesn't use it half a dozen times a year. He goes to the boat races in it and takes a big party of young people, and has it down in Florida with him when he goes, and before it was his I saw it at Monte Carlo."

"I guess I know who that is."

"Yes, I guess you do. Well, he wanted me, too."

"Why didn't you take him up if you want money?"

"Do you know why? Because do you know those pictures of pygmies in the Sunday papers? Little men with legs like match sticks and fat bellies with big umbilicals and wrinkled skin? That's what he looks like. Also I can't say I enjoy his idea of fun. Ugh."

"What?"

"I honestly wouldn't know how to tell you. I'd be embarrassed. Maybe you've heard, if you know who it is."

"You mean he's peculiar?"

"Huh. Peculiar. Listen, darling, do you know why I like you? I do like you. Do you know why? You're just a plain ordinary everyday man. You think you're something pretty hot and sophisticated because you're unfaithful to your wife. Well, I could tell you things about this rotten God damn dirty town that—ugh. I know a man that was almost elected— Well, I guess I better shut up. I know much too much for my age. But I like you, Liggett, because you want me the way I want to be wanted, and not with fancy variations. Let's get out of here, it's too damn effete."

"Where do you want to go?" Liggett said.

"Down to Fortieth Street to my practically favorite place."

They went to the place in Fortieth Street, up a winding staircase. They were admitted after being peered at, it turned out, by a man with a superb case of acne rosacea. "I was afraid you wouldn't remember me," said Gloria.

"What? Fancy me not remembering you, Miss?" said the man, who was the bartender.

"And what will be your pleasure to partake of this Lord's Day?" said the bartender. "Little Irish, perhaps?"

"Yes, fine."

"And you, sir?"

"Scotch and soda."

"Fine. Fine," said the bartender.

It was the longest bar in New York in those days, and the room was bare except for the absolute essentials. One half of it held tables and chairs and a mechanical piano, but there was one half in front of the bar which was bare concrete floor. Liggett and Gloria were getting used to themselves and smiling at each other in the mirror when a voice rose.

"Laddy doo, Laddy doo, Lie die dee. Tom!"

"Please control your exuberation, Eddie," said Tom, the bartender, and smiled broadly at Gloria and Liggett.

"Gimme a couple nickels, Tom, Laddy doo, Laddy doo."

They looked at the man called Eddie, who was down at the other end of the bar, rubbing his fat hands together and sucking his teeth. He had on a uniform cap and a gray woolen undershirt and blue pants, and then they noticed he had a revolver, chain twister, handcuffs and other patrolman's equipment. His tunic lay on a chair. "I beg your pardon, Miss and Mister," he said. "Serve the lady and gentleman first," said Eddie.

"I was doing that very thing," said Tom, "and when I get done I'll be giving you no nickels and stop askin'."

"Laddy doo. Gimme a beer, my Far Doon friend," said Eddie. "After serving the lady and gentleman, of course."

"When I get good and ready I'll give yiz a beer. It's almost time for you to ring in anyway. What about we taxpayers of this great city? When we go to exercise our franchise at the polls we'll change all this."

"Civil Service. Did you never hear of the Civil Service, my laddy-buck? The members of the Finest are Civil Service and what the likes of you repeaters do at the polls affects us not one single iota. A *beer!*"

"Get outa here. Go on out and ring in. It's twenty-five to, time to box in."

"The clock is fast."

"God can strike me dead if it is. I fixed it meself comin' in this evening. Go on or you'll be wrote up again."

"I'll go, and I'll be back with a hatful of nickels," said Eddie. He pulled his equipment belt around and put on his tunic and straightened his cap and as he was leaving he said, "Will I bring you a paper?"

"Go on, don't be trying to soft-soap me now," said Tom.

A party of four young men came in and began to play very seriously a game with matches, for drinks. A man in an undershirt and black trousers, wearing a cap made out of neatly folded newspaper, came in and waved his hand to the match-game players, but sat alone. A man with his hat on the back of his head came in and spoke to the players and to the man with the newspaper cap. He sat alone and began making faces at himself in the mirror and went into a long story which Tom showed by nods that he was listening to. During the story the man never once took his eyes off his reflection in the mirror. Tom was attentive with the man who looked at himself, chatted about baseball with the man with the newspaper cap, kidded with the match-game players, and was courtly with Liggett and Gloria. The cop came back bearing several newspapers and a large paper bag, from which he took several containers. Out of these he poured stewed clams into dishes which Tom got out of the bottom of the free lunch bar. The cop said: "Let the lady have hers first," and then everyone else was served while the cop looked on, happy; then he took off his tunic and laid it on the back of a chair, and then he went over to the piano.

"Get away from that God damn piano," yelled Tom. "Beggin' your pardon, Miss. Eddie, you lug you, get away from that t'ing, it's out of order."

"You go to hell," said Eddie. "Beg your most humble pardon, Lady, I have some rights here." The nickel he had dropped had set the motor humming, and in a minute the place was filled with the strains of "Dinah, is there anyone finah?"

"Oh, Jesus, Mary and Joseph, the wrong record," said the cop, in real pain. "I wanted 'Mother Machree.'"

A special delivery letter which arrived at the home of Gloria Wandrous the next morning:

Dear Gloria—I see that you have not changed one whit your deplorable habit of breaking appointments, or did you not realize that we had an appointment today? I came, at great inconvenience, to New York today, hoping to see you on the matter which we are both anxious to settle. I brought with me the amount you specified, which is a large sum to be carrying about on one's person, especially in times like these.

Please try to be at home tomorrow (Monday) between 12 noon and one p.m., when I shall attempt to reach you by long distance telephone. If not, I shall try again at the same hour on Tuesday.

If you realized what inconvenience it costs me to come to New York you would be more considerate.

Hastily,
J. E. R.

Gloria read this letter late Monday afternoon, when she went home after spending the night with Liggett. "*Poor* dear," she said, upon reading the letter. "If I realized what inconvenience, meeyah!"

4

EDDIE BRUNNER was one of the plain Californians. He was one of those young men whose height and frame make them look awkward unless they are wearing practical yachting clothes, or a $150 tailcoat. He did not gain much presence from his height, which was six feet two. When he talked standing up he made a gesture, always the same gesture; he put out his hands in the position of holding an imaginary basketball, about to shoot an imaginary foul. He could not talk with animation unless he stood up, but he did not often talk with animation. Like all Californians he made a substantive clause of every statement he made: "It's going to rain today, is what I think . . . Herbert Hoover isn't going to be our next President, is my guess . . . I only have two bucks, is all."

In his two years in New York he had had four good months, or make it five. At Stanford he was what is known as well liked, which tells a different story from popular. Popular men and women in college make a business of being popular. Well-liked people do things without getting disliked for them. Eddie Brunner drew funny pictures. He had a bigger vogue away from Stanford than at it, because the collegiate magazines republished his drawings. He had taken the work of several earlier collegiate comic artists—notably Taylor, of Dartmouth—and fashioned a distinctive comic type. He drew little men with googly eyes whose heads and bodies looked as though they had been pressed squat. He had a rebus signature: a capital B and a line drawing of a runner. It was a tiny signature. It had to be because the men Eddie drew were so small. In college he drew no women if he could help it; with his technique women would have to have fat legs and squat little bodies. Occasionally he did a female head as illustration for He-She gags, most of which he wrote himself.

The *Stanford Chaparral*, as a result of Eddie's drawings, had a high unofficial rating among college humorous monthlies during the three years Eddie contributed to it. He did nothing in freshman year; he was just barely staying in college, what with his honest laziness, his fondness for certain phonograph records, and a girl.

When he got out of college, with the class of '29, he was secretly envied by a good many classmates. Even the wealthy ones envied him. He had something; back East they knew about Eddie. Hadn't his drawings been in *Judge* and *College Humor* time after time? Eddie's father, a lucky sot who had made the fourth of a series of minor fortunes in miniature golf courses, had become bored with the golf courses and in the nick of time had converted them, wherever the zoning laws would permit, into drive-in car-service eateries, which were doing fabulous business in Eddie's last year in college. Brunner the elder was never so happy as when accompanying a party of "sportsmen" and newspaper writers to a big fight back East. Jack Dempsey was a great friend of his. He himself was an alumnus of the University of Kansas, but he gave huge football parties at Stanford and then at the St. Francis after the games. These did not embarrass Eddie, as Eddie had not joined his father's fraternity, and when the old gent came down to Stanford he called at his own fraternity and otherwise busied himself so that Eddie could follow his own plans. Eddie had for his father the distant tolerance that sometimes compensates for a lack of any other feeling, or, better yet, is a substitute for the contempt Eddie sometimes was in danger of feeling.

Eddie accepted his father's generosity with polite thanks, knowing that Brunner père spent every week in tips at least as much as the $50 allowance he gave his son in senior year. Eddie spent his allowance on collectors' items among old Gennett records, and on his girl. Almost regularly every six months Eddie fell in love with a new girl, and he would be in love with her until some extra-amatory crisis, such as a midyear examination, would occur. That would take his mind off the girl, and he would resume his routine existence to find that he had been thoughtless about breaking dates, and he would have to get a new girl. With a good second-hand Packard phaeton and a seeming inability to get too much to drink, his instinctive good manners and what the girls called his dry sense of humor, he could have just about his choice of the second-flight Stanford girls.

The idea was that the allowance was to continue and he would come to New York and stay until he got a job. So with his records and some Bristol board and the rest of his equipment packed in a seaman's chest, and enough hand luggage to carry his clothes, Eddie and two cronies drove to New York.

His father had arranged with his secretary about the allowance, and so it came regularly. With the cronies he took an apartment in a good building in Greenwich Village, and each of the friends furnished a bedroom and divided the cost of furnishing the common living-room. They bought a bar, a quantity of gin, installed a larger electric icebox and began doing the town. One of Eddie's roommates played pretty fair trombone, the other played a good imitative piano, and Eddie himself was fair on a tenor banjo with ukulele stringing. Eddie also purchased a slightly used mellophone, hoping to duplicate the performance of Dudley —— in the Weems record of "Travelin' Blues," which Eddie regarded as about as good a swing number as ever was pressed into a disc. He never learned to play the mellophone, but sometimes on Saturday and Sunday nights the three friends would have a jam session, the three of them playing and drinking gin and ginger ale and playing, complimenting each other on breaks and licks or making pained faces when one or the other would play very corny. One night their doorbell rang and a young man who looked as though he were permanently drunk asked if he could come in and sit down. He brought with him a beautiful little Jewess. Eddie was a little hesitant about letting them in until the drunk said he only wanted to sit and listen.

"WELL!" shouted the roommates. "Sit you down, have a drink. Have two drinks. What would you like to hear?"

" 'Ding Dong Daddy,' " said the stranger. "My name is Malloy. This is Miss Green. Miss Green lives upstairs. She's my girl."

"That's all right," they said. "Sit down, fellow, and we'll render one for you." They played, and when they finished Miss Green and Malloy looked at each other and nodded.

"I have drums," said Malloy.

"Where? Upstairs?" said Eddie.

"Oh, no. Miss Green and I don't live together that much, do we, Sylvia?"

"Not that much. Almost but not quite," said Sylvia.

"Where are they, the percussions?" said Eddie.

"At home in Pennsylvania, where I come from," said Malloy. "But I'll get them next week. Now do you mind if Sylvia plays?"

The boy with the trombone offered her his trombone. Eddie handed up the banjo.

"No," said Malloy. "Piano."

"Oh, piano. That means I mix drinks," said the boy at the piano.

"Yes, I guess it does after you hear Sylvia," said Malloy.

"As good as that?" said the trombone player.

"Go ahead, Sylvia," said Malloy.

"I ought to have another drink first."

"Give her another drink," said Eddie. "Here, have mine."

She gulped his drink and took off her rings and handed them to Malloy. "Don't forget where they came from," she said. "*And* a cigarette." Malloy lit a cigarette for her and she took two long drags.

"She better be good," said one roommate to the other.

Then with her two tiny hands she hit three chords, all in the bass, one, two, three. "Jee-zuzz!" yelled the Californians, and got up and stood behind her.

She played for an hour. While she played one thing the Californians would be making lists for her to play when she got finished. At the end of the hour she wanted to stop and they would not let her. "All right," she said. "I'll do my impressions. My first impression is Vincent Lopez playing 'Nola.' "

"All right, you can quit," said Eddie.

"None too soon," she said. "Where is the little girls' room, quick?"

"What does she do? Who is she? What does she do for a living?" the Californians wanted to know.

"She's a comparison shopper at Macy's," said Malloy.

"What is that?"

"A comparison *shopper*," said Malloy. "She goes around the other stores finding out if they're underselling Macy's, that's all."

"But she ought to— How did *you* ever get to know her?" said the piano player.

"Listen, I don't like your tone, see? She's my girl, and I am a very tough guy."

"Oh, I don't think you're so tough. Big, but not so tough, is my guess."

"No, not so tough, but plenty tough enough for you," said Malloy, and got up and swung at the piano player. The trombone player grabbed Malloy's arms. The piano player had caught the blow on his upraised forearm.

"I'm for letting them fight," said Eddie, but he took hold of Malloy. "Listen, fellow, you're one to three here and we'd just give you a shellacking and throw you downstairs if we had to. But we wouldn't have to. My friend here is a fighter."

"Make them shake hands," said the trombone player.

"What for?" said Eddie. "Why should they shake hands?"

"Let him go," said the piano player.

"All right, let him go," said Eddie to the trombone player. They let him go and Malloy went in after the piano player and stopped suddenly and fell and sat on the floor.

"You shouldn't have done that," said the trombone player.

"Why not?" said the piano player.

"Why not? He asked for it," said Eddie.

"Well, he's plastered," said the trombone player.

"He'll be all right. I'm afraid," said the piano player. He went over and bent down and spoke to Malloy. "How you coming, K.O.?"

"Um all right. You the one that hit me?" said Malloy, gently caressing his jawbone.

"Yes. Here, take my hand. Get up before your girl gets back."

"Who? Oh, Sylvia. Where is she?"

"She's still in the can."

Malloy got up slowly but unassisted. He sat in a deep chair and accepted a drink. "I think I could take you, sober."

"No. No. Get that idea out of your head," said the piano player.

"Don't be patronizing," said Malloy.

"He can afford to be patronizing," said Eddie. "My friend is one of the best amateur lightweights on the Coast. Do you know where the Coast is?"

"Aw, why don't you guys cut it out. Leave him alone," said the trombone player.

Sylvia appeared. "Did you think I got stuck? I couldn't find the bath-room light. Why, Jimmy, what's the matter?"

"I walked into a punch."

"Who? Who hit him? You? You big wall-eyed son of a bitch?"

"No, not me," said the trombone player.

"Then who did? *You!* I can tell, you sorehead, because I showed you how to play piano you had to assert your superiority some way, so you take a sock at a drunk. Come on, Jimmy, let's get out of here. I told you I didn't want to come here in the first place."

"Wait a second, Baby. Don't get the wrong idea. It was my fault."

"Stop being a God damn gentleman. It ill becomes you. Come on, or I'll go alone and I won't let you in, either."

"I'll go, but I was in the wrong and I want to say so. I apologize to you, Whatever Your Name Is—"

"Brunner."

"And you, and you, and thank you for being— Anyway, I apologize."

"All right."

"But I still think I could take you."

"Oh, now wait a minute, listen here," said the piano player. "If you want to settle this right now I'll go outside, or right here—"

"Oh, shut up," said Eddie. "You're as bad as he is. Good night. Good night." When the door closed he turned on the piano player. "He was all right at the end. He apologized, and you can't blame him for want-ing to think he could lick you."

"A wrong guy. If I ever see him again I'll punch his face in for him."

"Maybe. Maybe it wouldn't be so easy if he was sober. He had to walk on a loose rug to take that haymaker at you, remember. I don't want to hear any more about it. The hell with it."

"Ah, you give me a pain in the ass."

"You took the very words right out of my mouth. All you tough guys," said Eddie.

"Gee, but that little Mocky could play that piano," said the trombone player.

That was the first of two meetings between Eddie Brunner and Jimmy Malloy. Eddie's life went on as usual for a while. He did a few drawings and sold none. His stuff was too good for a syndicate manager to take a chance on it; too subtle. But it was not the type of thing that belonged in the *New Yorker*, the only other market he could think of at the time. So the three friends would have their jam sessions, and some nights when they did not play they would sit and talk. The names they would talk: Bix Beiderbeck, Frankie Trumbauer, Miff Mole, Steve

Brown, Bob MacDonough, Henry Busse, Mike Pingatore, Ross Gorman and Benny Goodman, Louis Armstrong and Arthur Shutt, Roy Bargy and Eddie Gilligan, Harry MacDonald and Eddie Lang and Tommy and Jimmy Dorsey and Fletcher Henderson, Rudy Wiedoeft and Isham Jones, Rube Bloom and Hoagy Carmichael, Sonny Greer and Fats Waller, Husk O'Hare and Duilio Sherbo, and other names like Mannie Kline and Louis Prima, Jenney and Morehouse, Venuti, Signorelli and Cress, Peewee Russell and Larry Binion; and some were for this one and some for that one, and all the names meant something as big as Wallenstein and Flonzaley and Ganz do to some people.

Early in October of that year Eddie got a telegram from his mother: PAPA DIED OF A STROKE THIS MORNING FUNERAL SATURDAY PLEASE COME. Eddie counted the words. He knew his mother; she probably thought the indefinite article did not cost anything in a telegram. He overdrew at the bank and cashed a check large enough to take him home, cashed it in an uptown speakeasy where he was known. He went home, and his maternal uncle told him how his father had died; in the middle, or the beginning maybe, of a party in a Hollywood hotel, surrounded by unknown Hollywood characters. They kept that from Eddie's mother, who had been such a sad, stupid little woman for so many years that she could have taken it without shock. All she said, over and over again, as they made plans for the funeral was: "I don't know, Roy always said he wanted to be buried with the Shrine band. He wanted them to play some march, but I can't think of the name of it." They told her not to worry about it; they couldn't have the Shrine band for a funeral, so don't keep worrying about it. After the services she said she noticed that Mr. Farragut was at the funeral. "That just showed, you know," she said. "I think Roy could have got in the Burlingame Club if he'd of tried just once more, or why would Mr. Farragut be here today?" Mr. Farragut was the man Mr. Brunner always had blamed for blackballing him from membership in the only organization he might have joined that he did not join.

Roy Brunner was one jump ahead of the sheriff when he keeled over with his cerebral hemorrhage in his eyes. He had been letting the drive-in car-service eateries get along without him, as he figured to do something new with all those lots he had tied up. He had gained a local reputation for sagaciousness and public-pulse-feeling as a result of getting out of the miniature golf course business ahead of time. His new idea was a nickel movie on every available corner; showing newsreels and short subjects for a nickel. A half-hour show, and turn them out. That did not give them much for their money, as it meant only one short and two newsreels, but on the other hand it was a lot for their money. A nickel? What did they want for a nickel? It was only a time killer anyway. He was in Hollywood ostensibly working on this project at the time the grim reaper called. No papers had been signed, and he hadn't seen the top men, but he was going to let them know he was in town tomorrow or the day after, and this party was just a little informal get-together with a couple of football coaches and golf professionals and what are known in the headlines as Film Actresses—extra girls. He had all the confidence in the world, and not without some reason. A man who is able to show the motion picture producers one example of how he called the turn of the public fancy can sell them practically anything, so long as he calls it Showmanship. But no papers had been signed.

"Your mother's going to stay with Aunt Ella and me for the present," Eddie's uncle told him, and that settled a problem for Eddie. He did not want to stay around his mother. He loved her because she was his mother and sometimes he felt sorry for her, but all his life (he had realized at a time when he was still too young for such a realization) she was so engrossed in her own life work of observing the carryings-on of her husband that she was like some older person whom Eddie knew but who did not always speak to him on the street. She was a member of a Pioneer Family, which in California means what Mayflower Descendant means in the East. The Mayflower Descendants, however, have had time to rest and recover from the exhausting, cruel trip, and many have done so, although inbreeding did not speed recovery. But the Pioneers had a harder trip and not so long ago, and it is reasonable to suppose that many of their number were so weakened when they got as far as the Pacific littoral that they handed down a legacy of tired bodies. Roy Brunner had come out from Kansas on a train, and his wife became his wife—a little to his surprise—the first time he asked her. She'd never been asked before, and was afraid she never would be again. She would willingly have learned, in married life, the one important thing her husband was able to teach her, but he was tolerantly impatient with her, and went elsewhere for his fun. When it came time to acquaint Eddie with the facts of sexual life, and Roy acquainted him with them, his wife said to him: "How did you tell him?" The reason she asked was that she still had hopes at that time of finding out herself. But Roy's answer was: "Oh, I just told him. He knew a lot already."

Eddie knew that in his mother his uncle was figuring on a profitable paying guest. That annoyed him a little, but what was there to do? She wanted to be there, and it took care of everything satisfactorily. Mrs. Brunner gave Eddie five hundred dollars out of her own money, and having signed a power of attorney in favor of his uncle, Eddie returned to New York, believing that his allowance would continue.

It never came again. His father's estate was tangled enough, and the Crash fixed everything fine. Eddie's uncle was hit, though not crippled. He wrote to Eddie, who was a month and a half behind in the rent with a lease to run exactly a year longer. He told Eddie they all were comparatively lucky. "You are young," he said, "and can earn your own living. I hope you will be able to send your mother something from time to time, as we can give her a roof over her head, a place to sleep and eat but nothing else. . . ."

Eddie sold his car for $35, he hocked his beautiful mellophone for $10. He gathered together, early in December, all his money and found he had not quite $200. His roommates had jobs and they were more than willing to have him keep his share of the apartment and owe them his share of the rent, but in January one of them lost his job in the first Wall Street purge, and in March they all were ousted from their apartment.

They went their separate ways. One of the roommates had a married sister living somewhere in suburban New Jersey. He went there. The other, the fighter, died of pneumonia in a room off Avenue A. Eddie did not even hear about it until long after his friend's body had been cremated. Eddie went from rooming-house to rooming-house, in the Village at first, and then in the West Forties, among the Irish of Tenth Avenue. He stayed uptown because it saved a dime carfare every day. He tried every place, everyone he knew to get a job. He was a helper in a restaurant one week, picking dirty plates off tables and carrying trayfuls of them to the kitchen. He dropped a tray and was fired, but he paid something on his rent and he had kept his belly full. He thought of driving a taxi, but he did not know how to go about it. He knew there had to be licenses and other details, and he did not have the money for a license. He tried to be an actor, saying he could play comedy character parts. The only time he was picked he revealed right away that he had had no experience: he did not know what a side was, nor anything else about the stage. One night, very hungry, he allowed himself to be picked up by a fairy, but he wanted his meal first and the fairy did not trust him, so he punched the fairy one for luck and felt better, but wished he had had the guts to take the fairy's bankroll. He sold twenty-five cent ties in fly-by-night shops and was a shill at two auctions but the auctioneer decided he was too tall; people would re-

member him. Then, through his landlady, for whose children he sometimes drew funny pictures, he heard of a marvelous opportunity: night
man in a hotel which was more of a whore-house. It was through her
Tammany connection that she heard about the job. He operated a
switchboard and ran the elevator from six in the evening to eight in
the morning, for ten dollars a week and room, plus tips. Customers
would come in and the password was, "I'm a friend of Mr. Stone's."
Then Eddie would look the customer over and ask him whom he
wanted to see, and the man would give the name of one of the three
women. Eddie then would call the room of the woman named, and
say: "There's a friend of Mr. Stone's here for you," and she would say
all right, and Eddie would say: "She says she's not sure she remembers
you. Will you describe her to me?" And the man would either describe
her or say quite frankly that he'd never been there before, and all this
was stalling. It gave Eddie a chance to look him over carefully and it
gave the woman a chance to prepare to entertain the visitor, or get
dressed and get ready to be raided, if Eddie pulled back the switchboard key which rang her room. He was instructed to turn down men
who were too drunk, as the place was not paying the kind of protection
that had to be paid by clip joints. Eddie never turned anyone down.

On this job he met Gloria. She came in one night, plastered, with a
sunburned man, also plastered, who wore in his lapel the boutonniere
of the Legion of Honor. Eddie was a little afraid of him at first, but he
guessed it would be too early in the season for a cop to have the kind of
tan this man had. And the man said: "Tell Jane it's the major. She'll
know." Jane knew and told Eddie to send him right up. The girl,
Gloria, went with him. Eddie made the wise guess that this was Gloria's first time here, but not her first experience being a spectator. The
major kept smiling to himself in the elevator, humming, and saying to
Gloria: "All right, honey?"

The major gave Eddie a dollar when they reached Jane's floor, gave it
to him as though that were the custom from time immemorial. Eddie
returned to the switchboard. Then in about twenty minutes he heard
footsteps, and standing before him was the girl, Gloria.

"Will you lend me that dollar he gave you?" she said. "Come on, I'll
give it back to you. You don't want any trouble, do you?"

"No. But how'll I know you'll give it back to me? Honestly, I need
that buck."

"You don't have to pimp for your money, I imagine."

"That's where you're wrong, but here, take it."

"I'll bring it back tomorrow. I'll give you two bucks tomorrow," she said. "What are you doing here, anyway?"

"You mean what is a nice girl like me doing in a place like this," said Eddie.

"Good night," she said, "and thanks a million."

He had a feeling she would return the money, and she did, two nights later. She gave him five dollars. She said she didn't have change for it, and he took it. "What happened the other night, anything?" she said.

"Your friend got stinko and Jane had to send out for a bouncer," he said.

"Oh, you're not the bouncer?"

"Do I look like a bouncer?"

"No, but—"

"But I don't look like an elevator boy in a whore-house either, is what you're trying to say."

"Are you from the West?"

"Wisconsin," said Eddie.

"What part of Wisconsin?"

"Duluth," said Eddie.

"Duluth is in Minnesota."

"I know," said Eddie.

"Oh, in other words mind my own business. Okay. Well, I just asked. I'll be seeing you."

"I have something belonging to you, Miss Wandrous."

"What!"

"Your purse, you left it in Jane's room when you left in such a hurry. That's why you had to borrow the buck, remember? I took the liberty of trying to identify the owner, but I couldn't find you in the phone book. I didn't think I would."

"Oh."

"I was going to take a chance that you were still living at the address on your driver's license. You better get a new license, by the way. The 1928 licenses aren't any good any more. This is 1930."

"Did you show this to anybody?"

"No."

"Why not?"

"I just didn't think it was anybody else's business. It wasn't mine, for that matter, but it's better for you to have *me* look at it than turn it over to, well, one of the boys we have around here sometimes."

"You're a good egg. I just happened to think who it is you remind me of."

"I know."

"Do you?"

"I ought to. I've heard it often enough."

"Who?"

"Lindbergh."

"Yes, that's right. I guess you would hear that a lot. When is your night off?"

"The second Tuesday of every week."

"No night off? I thought they had to give you a night off."

"They break a lot of ordinances here, ordinances and laws. Why, what do you want to know about my nights out for?"

"We could have dinner."

"Sure. Do you think I'd be here if I could take girls out to dinner?"

"Who said anything about taking me? I just said we could have dinner. I have no objection to paying for my own dinner under certain circumstances."

"For instance."

"For instance eating with someone I like."

"Now we're getting somewhere," he said, but he could not prolong the flippancy. This was the first time in months that anyone had spoken a kind personal word to him. She understood that.

"Get somebody to work for you, can't you?"

"Why should I? . . . Hell, why shouldn't I? There's a jiggaboom had this job before me is working down the street now. He just runs the elevator at a hotel now, maybe he might work for me if they said it was all right. I don't want to lose this job, though."

The Negro said he would be glad to take over Eddie's job for a night, and Mrs. Smith, Eddie's boss, said it would be all right but not to make a practice of it, as the girls upstairs did not like Negroes for agents.

Thus began the friendship of Gloria and Eddie.

It would be easy enough to say any one of a lot of things about Gloria, and many things were said. It could be said that she was a person who in various ways—some of them peculiar—had the ability to help other people, but lacked the ability to help herself. Someone could write a novel about Gloria without ever going very far from that thesis. It was, of course, the work of a few minutes for the 1931 editorial writers (who apparently are the very last people to read the papers) to find in Gloria a symbol of modern youth. She was no more a symbol of modern youth than Lindbergh was a symbol of modern youth, or Bob Jones the golfer, or Prince George, or Rudy Vallée, or Linky Mitchell, or DeHart Hubbard or anyone else who happened to be less than thirty years old up to 1930. There can be no symbol of modern youth any more than there can be a symbol of modern middle age, and anyway symbol is a misnomer. The John Held Jr. caricature of the "flapper" of the 1920's, or the girls and young men whom Scott Fitzgerald made self-conscious were not symbols of the youth of that time. As a matter of fact there was no tie-up between the Scott Fitzgerald people and the John Held people. The Scott Fitzgerald people were drawn better by two artists named Lawrence Fellows and Williamson than by John Held. Held drew caricatures of the boys and girls who went to East Orange High School and the University of Illinois; the Held drawings were caricatures and popular, and so people associated the Fitzgerald people with the Held drawings. The Fitzgerald people did not go in for decorated yellow slickers, decorated Fords, decorated white duck trousers and stuff like put-and-take tops and fraternity pins and square-toed shoes and Shifter movements and trick dancing and all the things that caught on with the Held people. The Held people *tried* to look like the Held people; the Fitzgerald-Fellows people were copies of the originals.

The average man, Mr. Average Man, Mr. Taxpayer, as drawn by Rollin Kirby *looks* like the average New York man making more than $5,000 a year. He wears Brooks clothes, including a Herbert Johnson hat, which is a pretty foreign-looking article of apparel in Des Moines, Iowa, where J. N. Darling is the cartoonist; but in New York, Kirby's territory, the Kirby taxpayer is typical. He is a man who wears good clothes without ever being a theater-program well-dressed man; it is easy to imagine him going to his dentist, taking his wife to the theater, going back to Amherst for reunion, getting drunk twice a year, having an operation for appendicitis, putting aside the money to send his son to a good prep school, seeing about new spectacles, and looking at, without always being on the side of, the cartoons of Rollin Kirby. But no one would call this man a symbol of middle age or American Taxpayer. If he walked along the streets of Syracuse or Wheeling or Terre Haute he would be known as a stranger. He would be picked out as a stranger from a bigger city, and probably picked as a New Yorker. And a Held flapper would have embarrassed any young snob who took her to a Princeton prom. And a Fellows young man, driving up in his Templar phaeton to the Pi Beta Phi house at a Western Conference University would have been spotted by the sorority girls even before they saw the Connecticut license on his car. There *are* typical men and women, young and old, but only editorial writers would be so sweeping as to pick out a certain girl or a certain boy and call him a symbol of modern youth.

There could be a symbol of modern young womanhood, but the newspapers would not be likely to print her picture. She would have to be naked. The young girl who was about twenty years old in the latter half of the 1920's did conform to a size. She was about five feet five, she weighed about 110. She had a good body. There must be a reason for the fact that so many girls fitted that description, without regard to her social classification. And the reason may well be that between 1905 and 1915 the medical profession used approximately the same system in treating pregnant women and in the feeding and care of infants. Even the children of Sicilian and Ghetto parentage suddenly grew taller, so the system must have been standard; there seems to be no other explanation for this uniformity. It is noticeable in large families: the younger children, born during and after the World War, are almost invariably tall and slender and healthier than their older brothers and sisters.

Gloria missed by ten years being a "flapper"; that is, if she had been born ten years sooner she might have qualified in 1921 as a flapper, being twenty-two years old, and physically attractive. One of the differences between Gloria as she was and as she might have been was that in 1921 she might have been "considered attractive by both sexes," and in 1931 she was considered attractive by both sexes, but with a world of difference in the meaning and inner understanding of it.

It has been hinted before that there was a reason for the recurring mood of despair which afflicted Gloria. When Gloria was eleven years old she was corrupted by a man old enough to be her father. At that time Gloria and her mother and uncle were living in Pittsburgh. Her father, a chemist, had been one of the first people to die of radium poisoning. The word father, spoken with any tenderness or sentimental intent, always evoked a recollection of her father's college class picture. It was the only picture her mother had of her father, as something had happened to their wedding pictures when they were moving from one house to another. The class picture was not much help to a child who wanted to be like other children; she saw her father as a man with a white circle around his head, in the second row of three rows of young men standing on the steps of a stone building. Through her childhood she could not see a haloed saint's picture without thinking of the picture of her father, but she would wonder why the halo did not go around the front and under the chin of the saint, and why the white circle around her father's head did not end at the shoulders the way it did with the saints; and thinking first one thing and then the other she never thought of her father as a saint, and never thought of the saints except as reminders of her father.

Her uncle, a man named William R. Vandamm (R for Robespierre), was the older brother of her mother. He, too, was a chemist and had been a classmate of Gloria's father at Cornell. Vandamm and Gloria's father had gone to Chile after college, and had stayed long enough to hate it jointly and break their contracts together. They came back together and Wandrous married Vandamm's sister. There was a little money on all sides, and both bride and groom brought equal advantages to the union, and it was one of those obscure, respectable marriages that take place every Saturday. When Wandrous died it was Vandamm who went to the radium company and used his Masonic and professional and political connections to see to it that money was provided for the upbringing and education of Gloria. They wanted to give the widow stock in the radium company, but Vandamm was too smart for that and thereby lost close to a million dollars, as it later turned out, but Vandamm was the only one who noticed that, and he did not call his sister's attention to it.

Vandamm was a good enough industrial chemist, and a very good uncle. He lived away most of the time while Gloria was a small child. He would take a job, hold it a year or so, and then take a better job, gaining in money and experience and acquaintance. He would live in men's clubs and Y.M.C.A.'s all over the country, taking half of his annual vacation at Christmas so that he could spend the holidays with his sister and niece. He would bring home beautiful presents, usually picked by one of the succession of nice young women to whom he was attentive. In every town where he worked it was the same. He was clean and respectable and had a good job, and he was unmarried. So he would single out one of the young women he met, and he would be polite to her and take her to nice dances and send her flowers, and tell her all the time what a wonderful thing this friendship was. Each time he quit his job and moved to another town he would leave behind a bewildered young woman, who had had him to her house for Sunday dinner fifty times in a year, but had nothing to show for it, candy and flowers being the perishable things that they are. There were two exceptions: one was a young woman who fell in love with him and did not care how much she showed it. He had to depart from his Platonic policy in her case, because she was making what were then known as goo-goo eyes at him every time she saw him, at parties or alone. At the risk of not being permitted to finish, he told her that she had made him feel as no other girl had made him feel, and for that reason he was quitting his job at the factory. If he stayed on, he said, he would be tempted to ask her something he had no right to ask her. Why had he no right to ask her? she wanted to know. Because of his sister and his niece. They had only what money he could give them, and never would have more. For that reason he hated to quit this job; he had been able to do things for them that he never had been able to do before. "I will never marry," he stated, as though it had national political significance. That fixed her. It also fixed him; instead of making him less attractive it made him look tall and husky, a philanthropist who gave millions in secret. It made her feel something she never had felt before. Before that she and all women like her were a little afraid that all bachelors were comparing all eligible women. But William, he wasn't comparing. He had decided on her, even though he could not, because of his dependents, have her. It turned out to be only a question of time before he did have her. "Take me," she said, one moonlight night, and she threw her arms back. He wasn't quite ready to take her at that moment, but he was in a minute. For the rest of that year he would take her every Sunday night, after paying a visit to a drug store in another part of town every Saturday night. In nice weather they would wander casually in the backyard and dart suddenly into the carriage house. In bad weather they would have to wait until her father and mother had gone to bed, and then they would go down cellar. They would leave a scrub-bucket just inside the cellar door so that if anyone started to come down, whoever it was would knock the bucket down the steps with a warning racket. It was better in the carriage house, as she did not get her petticoat so dusty in a barouche as on the cellar floor.

The second exception was the girl in the next town he came to. He fell in love with her and asked her to marry him. She turned him down with such finality that she was sorry for him and suggested that they could still be friends. He snatched at this eagerly, and there was nothing he would not do for her. Years later he read about her. She and a married man, a doctor in the same "set" died together in a Chicago hotel. The doctor shot her through the heart and then turned the revolver on himself. That, after all those years, made Vandamm understand why she would not have him; there was someone else.

The arrival of the World War was propitious for Vandamm, who was getting a little tired of all but the freedom part of his freedom. He was beginning to hate the visits to the drug stores on Saturday night; he hated not being able to go right to sleep; he hated keeping his mind active so that he would not be led into a proposal of marriage. He detested the little university clubs he lived in. He hated American accents. In no town that he ever lived in had he made an impression on the first three families. He could see, when he met them, how they regarded him: an Easterner who wasn't good enough for the East and thought he would be a king among monkeys rather than a monkey among kings. He decided he had had enough experience, and from now on would make money.

He went to Pittsburgh and had no trouble getting a job. In the war years he made excellent salaries and he and his sister bought a house in the East End. It turned out that he had to move again, this time to Wilmington, Delaware, but his visits home—and he thought of it as home—were more frequent than they had been. One of the results of these frequent visits was his discovering that he adored his niece. He never would have put it that way. Even love was a word he had schooled himself against using. But he began to look forward to seeing her every time she was out of his sight. Here was someone he could love without watching what he said and did. It was such a relief after the long cautious years. What started it was the child's beauty, and he took pride in the relationship. She photographed well and he carried snapshots of her in his wallet. He was glad she was not his daughter, because he could love her more. Fathers *have to* love their daughters and sometimes there is nothing else, but an uncle can love his little niece, and they can be friends, and she will listen to him and he can be as extravagant with her as he pleases. His sister was in favor of this obvious enthusiasm on the part of her brother, although she was not unaware that her brother more and more gave to her the status of a privileged governess.

The war, his work, the money it brought him—they were half his life. Gloria was the other half, that he did not talk much about.

He took his sister's money and doubled it for her, not really for her but for Gloria. Then when he saw what he had done, he had what he thought was a brilliant idea. For the first time in his life he indulged the dangerous thrill of planning someone else's life. He wanted to get his sister married off. That would be all for the present. Get her married off, and then see what happened. But he could not stop thinking what might happen, and did not see why he should not enjoy his plans. His sister was young enough to have children, and if she had a child, a new baby, with a living husband, there was no telling what might happen. He reasoned that his sister ought to be glad to let him have Gloria. She would have a child of her own, and he would have Gloria. He would think later on about marriage for himself. If the right woman came along and Gloria liked her, and he liked her for Gloria, he might marry her. In the course of a few months of thinking along these lines Vandamm planned a whole new life for himself. He thought of it only as rearranging his own life, and never as deliberate, planned rearranging of the lives of anyone else, except little Gloria, who was after all, so young. . . .

In Wilmington he had met a man, a major in the Army Ordnance Department. Major Boam was not like most of the men who, without previous military experience, walked into captaincies and majorities in the Ordnance Department and Quartermaster and Medical Corps; he looked well in uniform. He looked fit, healthy, strong. This man worked out of Washington, and spent most of his time in Wilmington, Eddystone, Bethlehem, and Pittsburgh. Vandamm remained a civilian all through the war. He was nearsighted, underweight, flat-footed, and the Army didn't want him. Not that they were rude about it; they wanted him to remain a civilian.

"Next time you're in Pittsburgh stop in and see my sister," Vandamm told Major Boam. The major said he would be glad to, and did, and when next he saw Vandamm he said he had stopped in and had dinner with Mrs. Wandrous, a very nice dinner. Vandamm wanted to know if he had seen Gloria, but the major said he had been so late that Gloria had been asleep, oh, hours, when he got there. To Vandamm that meant that Boam had arrived late and must have enjoyed himself if he stayed, and he found out that Boam had stayed until almost train-time.

Boam was a widower with a grown daughter. Must have married very young, Vandamm decided, to have had a daughter old enough to be married. The daughter lived in Trenton, but Boam never saw her. "She has her own household to look after now," Boam said. "I don't like to go there as a father-in-law." It sounded a little as though Boam were lonely, and that fitted in with Vandamm's plans. A lonely widower, young-middle-aged, well set up, good job probably if they gave him a major's commission right off the bat. "How'd you like Major Boam?" Vandamm asked his sister. She liked him, she said. She judged men by their size. She liked a tall man better than a short man, and a tall husky man better than a tall thin man.

The Armistice interfered with Vandamm's plans. Major Boam took off his Sam Browne belt, his boots and spurs, his uniform with its two silver chevrons on the left sleeve. He stopped in to see Vandamm in Wilmington on his last trip around his circuit, and for the first time in the friendship he relaxed. Leading up to it in the most roundabout way, he finally said to Vandamm: "Well, it's time I went out looking for a job." It developed that Boam was not going back to some highly paid position. He was not going back to anything. He told Vandamm that when the United States entered the war he wanted to be a dollar-a-year man, but that he couldn't afford it. He had had expenses in connection with his daughter's marriage, and a lot of other things. The only way he could serve his country was to get a commission. Working for a major's pay was a financial loss, he said, and as much as he could do for his country. And now there was no job waiting for him.

This suited Vandamm. He told the major he would see to it that he got a job. The major thanked him and said he would try to use his own connections first, and if nothing came of them Vandamm was not to be surprised if one fine day Boam turned up in Pittsburgh or Wilmington.

He turned up in 1921, not to ask for a job, but just to pay a social call. He had found a vague job with the political end of the chemical game, he said. The vague job was lobbying. Peace with Germany was about to be signed, and it was his job to see to it that when the German dye factories reopened they did not wreck the American dye industry, such as it was. This was difficult, he pointed out, because many of the German factories were American-owned, or had been until war was declared, and Americans had to move carefully. There were some Americans who wanted their plants back nearly intact, and it was going to be a risky business if the Germans saw that the German dye industry was going to be discriminated against. Official Germany would not dare do anything, but the workers in the German dye factories could not be counted on to keep their sabotaging hands off the factories if they heard that their means of livelihood was being cut off in the American Congress. In other words there were two camps in America; one camp, those who had owned factories in Germany, didn't want Congress to take any tariff action until after they saw what was going to happen about the plants. The other camp consisted of the Americans who had more or less entered the dye industry for the first time when the British navy bottled up German maritime activity. These Americans had spent a lot of money building up our dye industry (under the tremendous handicap that the trade secrets of dye manufacture were kept in Germany), and they didn't want to see their money go to waste just because Germany was licked. What was the use of winning the God damn war if we couldn't get something out of it?

And so Major Boam, who retained his military title partly because the hotel and restaurant people in Washington knew him as Major Boam, and partly because he thought it gave him standing with members of Congress—had been staying in Washington ever since the Harding Administration moved in. He spoke fraternally of Congress: "We're getting a lot of work done down there. You wouldn't believe it the amount of work we're getting done—why, who is this?"

"This is Gloria. Say how do you do to Major Boam," said Mrs. Wandrous.

"How do you do," said Gloria.

"Come here till I have a look at you," said the major. He held out his hands, his big brown fat hands. "Say, this is quite a young lady. How old is she? How old are you, Gloria?"

"I'm almost twelve," she said.

"Come up here," he said. "Sit on my lap."

"Oh, now, Major, she'll be a nuisance," said Mrs. Wandrous.

"Well, if the Major wants her," said Vandamm. "Go on, Gloria, be sociable."

"Shooooor she will," said Major Boam. "Ups!" He picked her up and sat her down on his left leg. He held his left hand on her back and went on talking. As he talked his hands moved, now he would pat and squeeze her bare thighs, now he would pat her little behind. She looked up at him as he did these things, and he went on talking so interestedly and in such a strong easy voice that she relaxed and laid her head on his shoulder. She liked the pressure of his hands, which did not hurt her the way some people's did. She liked the rumble of his voice and the smell of his clean white shirt and the feel of his soft flannel suit.

"Look," said Vandamm, interrupting and indicating with a nod how relaxed Gloria was.

Boam nodded and smiled and continued what he was saying. In a little while Gloria fell asleep—it was past her bedtime. Her mother picked her up off Boam's lap, and Boam immediately jumped up.

He tried to stay away from the Wandrous-Vandamm home after that, but the harder he tried, the more excuses he invented. He would plan to go there after he was sure Gloria would be asleep; but then he would be saying: "How's little Gloria?" and Vandamm would immediately say: "Come up and see her when she's asleep." Boam had business in Pittsburgh that was supposed to keep him there three or four days. He stayed a fortnight. All that time he knew what was happening to him. He did not know what he wanted to do with the child. He did know that he wanted to take her away, be alone with her.

Up to that time Gloria had been only another beautiful child, with a head of dark brown curly hair, and eyes that were startlingly beautiful at first glance, and then the longer you looked at them the more uninteresting they became. But each time you saw them anew you would be seeing for the first time how beautiful they were. Their beauty was in the set and the color, and being dark brown and the eyes of a child, they did not change much and that was what made them uninteresting. Gloria was like most female children. She was cruel to animals, especially to dogs. She was not at all afraid of them until after they had made friends with her and then she would hit them with a stick, and after that she would be afraid of them, although for the benefit of her elders she would call nice doggy. A Negro hired girl named Martha would come out from Wiley Avenue every afternoon to take Gloria for her walk. The other child's nurses were white and they did not encourage the colored girl to sit with them. They did like to have pretty little Gloria with them, and pretty little Gloria knew this, knew that her company was preferable to Martha's, so Martha had no control over her. Her mother did not try to exercise any control over her, except to see that she always looked nice before she went out. Barring only an occasional enema and trips to the dentist, Gloria's childhood was lived according to Gloria's rules. School was easy for her; she was bright, and any little brightness she displayed was rewarded out of proportion to its worth. She liked all little boys until they played rough, and she would fight any little boy who was being mean to a little girl, any little girl. There was one continual paradox all through her childhood: for a child who frequently heard herself called a little Princess she was very neglected. She had no one to create or to generate childhood love.

On the way out to Gloria's home Boam did not allow himself to think of what might happen, of what he hoped would happen. He had been out to the house every second day while he was in Pittsburgh, but this one sunny day he knew was to be the day. He knew he was going to do something. It was after lunch, and he had a hunch Mrs. Wandrous would be out. She was. The maid who answered the door knew him, and when he did not seem disposed to leave when she said Mrs. Wandrous was out, she asked him to come in. "You don't know what time she'll be back?" he said.

"No, sir, but I don't imagine for quite a while. She went all the way downtown shopping. You only missed her by about a half an hour. Can I get you a cup of tea or something?"

"No, thanks, you go ahead with whatever you were doing. I'll just sit down a little while and if Mrs. Wandrous doesn't come along. Little Gloria out playing?"

"No, sir, she's in. The nurse-girl didn't come today. I'll send her in."

"I'd like to say good-by to her. I'm leaving tonight."

The maid was only too glad to get rid of Gloria. She had her own work to do and Mrs. Wandrous did not accept excuses when it wasn't done.

Gloria came running in and then stopped short and looked at him. Then she smiled faintly.

"How's my little girl today?" he said.

"Very well, thank you," she said.

"Come here and I'll read you the funny section," he said, and picked up the paper. He nodded to the maid, who left.

Gloria went to him and stood between his legs while he sat and read comic strips. She had an attitude of attention, but no attention in her eyes. The pressure of her elbow on his leg was becoming unbearable, and he looked into her eyes as he would have looked into a woman's. She showed no fear. Was it possible that this child had—was Vandamm the kind of man—did that explain Vandamm's adoration of this child?

He stopped reading the paper. "Let me feel your muscle," he said. She made a muscle for him. "Mm," he said. "That's quite a muscle for a girl." Then a silence.

"All ready for the summer, aren't you?" he said.

"Yes," she said.

"Not much on," he said. Then panic and fright and the need of haste came on him, and his hands went wild. He kissed her so hard on the mouth that he hurt her and she could not be sure what else was going on, but she knew enough to struggle.

He tried to pass it off with acrobatics. He held her high in the air and spoke to her and tried to laugh. He wanted to get out of this house, but he was afraid. He had not done anything but touch her, but he was afraid of the story she might tell. He could not leave until he was sure she would not run frightened to the kitchen and babble something to the maid. Then he said: "Well, I've kissed you good-by now, so I guess I'll go. All right?"

She did not know what was the polite thing to say.

"You going to miss me?" he said. "I'll bring you a nice present next time I come back. What would you like?"

"I don't know," she said.

"Well, I'll bring you something pretty nice all the way from New York, next time I come here. That's our secret, isn't it?"

"Yes," she said.

"Are you going to say by-by to me?"

"Yes," she said.

"Well."

" 'By," she said.

"Tha-a-at's right. Good-by, Gloria. You tell your mother and uncle I said good-by to them, too." He was tempted to give her money but some kind of hog's caution prevailed. He went away and he never came back, but he was remembered.

Gloria wanted to tell someone what he had done. The minute he left she forgot how he had hurt her with his teeth. She remembered his hand. She went to the kitchen and stood watching the maid, who was polishing silverware. She watched the maid and did not answer when the maid said: "Well, what are you looking at?" She could not tell *her*.

It took a year for her to tell the story, which was doubted word by word by her mother and denied by her uncle. But Vandamm knew something was wrong, because Gloria suddenly did not like him or anything he bought her or did for her. He thought it had something to do with her age. She was twelve years old, and she might be having her menstruation earlier than most girls. Lots of reasons. She was moody. A little depressed always. You couldn't expect her to be a child all the time, though. But the story did come out, little by little, until mother and uncle were able to reconstruct the scene. They took Gloria to their doctor, but Gloria would not let him touch her. They had to take her to a woman physician. Vandamm hired a private detective to look up Boam, and instituted his own campaign to have Boam ousted from his job in Washington. This was not necessary. Boam had gone back to Washington after his maltreatment of the child, quit his job, and left no forwarding address. The private detective ascertained that Boam had got into another similar mess a year or two before the war. His daughter's fiancé found out about it and daughter and fiancé eloped and never saw her father. That was the reason he never went to see his daughter in Trenton.

There was no physical aftermath to the Boam incident, except that her mental state affected Gloria's general health. Vandamm thought it would be a good thing to move away from Pittsburgh. A change of scene. New York.

For three years New York turned out to be a good idea. They put Gloria in a High Church day school where the girls wore uniforms. Thus from the first day she was like all the other girls. Her mother took her to school every day and met her after school. Here Gloria was not the prettiest nor the brightest, and was singled out for no special attention. She made a few friends, and in the summer she went with these friends to a camp in Maine, which was run by two members of the school faculty. There were enough girls at the camp from other schools to keep her from getting tired of the same faces. Then back at school there were always new girls. She improved to such an extent that it was she who asked to be sent away to school. She wanted to go to school in California, but when it came down to giving reasons her only reason was that she loved a tune, "Orange Grove in California," which was popular at the time. At that her uncle almost indulged this fancy, and would have had it not been for the—he trusted—momentarily depleted state of their finances. He tried to get a job in California, and found out for the first time that he was a lucky man; good men were working out there for monthly salaries smaller than the rent of his apartment in New York. And whatever chance there was of Gloria's being sent to California or anywhere west of the Hudson disappeared when two crimes of violence occurred within a week of each other, solidifying for all time Vandamm's inherent prejudice against the West. One crime was the Leopold-Loeb affair, which was too close a reminder of what had happened to Gloria; and the other was the suicide-pact of the woman and the doctor Vandamm had known long ago. A good, not spectacularly fashionable New England school was decided upon for Gloria. She was there almost the whole year before another man, who eventually made Boam seem like a guardian angel, was attracted to her.

When you are a year away from a day that (because of some Thing) was not like other days you are as far away from the day and as far away from the thing, good or bad, as you will ever get. If it is bad, it is far enough away. Its effect may last, but there is no use kidding yourself that you live the thing over again. Something is missing. One thing that is missing in living it in retrospect is the reality; you know when you start that what you are about to recall is only, so far as this moment is concerned, a kind of dreaming. If a year ago you saw yourself cut open, your blood coming out of you, and everything outside was pain coming in you—you still cannot live that over again. Not the day, and not the moment. You can and do live back to the moment when the awful thing, whatever it was, began. Or the good thing (but of course life is not made up of many good things; at least we don't make milestones out of the good things as much as we do the bad). The still beautiful word poignant does not apply to ice cream, medals you won in school, a ride on a roller coaster, something handsome to wear, or "The Star-Spangled Banner"; although "The Star-Spangled Banner" comes closest. It is music, and poor old music, whether it's Bach or Carmichael, it knows when it starts that it is making a forlorn effort to create or recapture something that it of itself does not possess. Music is synthetic, so how can poor, lovely old music, which is the highest art, have by itself a fraction of the poignancy of an important day, an important event that day, in the life of a human being? The answer is it can't. You may shut your eyes for a second while the Maestro is conducting, but you will open them again, and to show how completely wrong you are in thinking that you have been listening to the music he brings out, you will catch yourself noticing that he has shifted the baton from his tired rheumatic right arm to his left. It is nothing to apologize for, however. Only a phony would say that he does not really notice the man Toscanini, but a phony would say it. A phony would think he gained by saying he could overlook the genius because he is a man, a human being. Who the hell wrote the music? A disembodied wraith?

We have had long and uncomfortable periods when we built chairs, forgetting that a chair is meant to be sat in. Music, too, is to be enjoyed, and we might as well face it: it must have human associations if it is to be enjoyed. The same way with love. It can happen to be pure when for one reason or more, two people do not go to bed together; and sometimes it is enough, and better, that they do not go to bed together. Love *can* be as far away from the idea of going to bed together as hate is from the idea of killing. But a chair is meant to be sat in, music is good for what it does to you, love is sleeping together, hate is wanting to kill. . . .

Three years can pass, and for two of them Gloria can be safely away from the ability to live again the time with Major Boam. This is not to say that Boam did her a favor. He was bad for her because he made her different, inside herself, and made her have a secret that was too big for her but was not the kind she could share. But she got bigger and stronger, not in the metaphorical sense, and what she knew—that a man as big as Major Boam, a man that you didn't even know what he looked like undressed, wanted to do the same things to you that little boys did—became final knowledge. It became knowledge that made up for your lack of curiosity, or your willingness to learn. Out of fear you did not want to find out too much when you were thirteen and fourteen, but you could always tell yourself that you knew quite a lot, something the other girls did not know.

The other girls respected Gloria for what they thought was genuine innocence. Children do respect that. All it was was that she did not want to hear talk, to ask questions, to contribute information. But it passed for true innocence. It deceived her mother as well as her contemporaries. When Mrs. Wandrous had to tell Gloria what was going on inside her body she felt two ways about it: one was that it was partly an old story to a girl who had been "violated" by a grown man; the other was that it was awful to have to remind the child that she had a sex. But she told her, and Gloria took the information casually (there was little enough information in what her mother told her) and without questions. Mrs. Wandrous breathed with relief and hiked Gloria off to boarding school.

Coming down from school for the Spring vacation Gloria was with five other girls. It was a bad train and the day was not warm, and every time the train stopped a man who was sitting in a seat that was almost surrounded by the six girls would get up and close the door after the passengers who left the door open. After closing the door he would go back to his seat, the third seat away from the door, and begin to doze. All her life the sound of snoring fascinated and amused Gloria, and this man snored. It made her like this man, and at the next station-stop she got up and closed the door, as she was one seat nearer the door than he was. He smiled and nodded several times, and said thank-you. At Grand Central when her mother met her the man, carrying a brief case and handbag, went to Mrs. Wandrous, who greeted Gloria first off the train, and said: "I want to compliment you on your little girl's manners and consideration. A very polite and well-mannered little girl," he smiled and went away. Mrs. Wandrous wanted to know who he was —he was either a clergyman or schoolteacher she knew that, and thought he must be from Gloria's school. Gloria said she guessed she knew why he had said that, and told her mother. Her mother looked at the man, walking up the ramp, but her instinctive alarm did not last. "There are good people in the world," she told herself. It was easy for her to think thus; Gloria's manners were the personal pride and joy of her mother.

On the way back after the holiday Gloria was with one other girl, but they did not get seats together. She was displeased with the prospect of not talking to anyone all the way back, and very pleased when a man's voice said: "We won't have to worry about the door in this nice weather." It was the man who had snored. He asked her where she was going to school, said he knew two or three girls there, told her who they were, asked her what her studies were, asked her how she liked teachers in general, explained he was one himself if you could call a principal a teacher.

Not altogether by accident he was on the train that brought her back to New York at the end of school. She was with a lot of her friends but she saw him and spoke to him like an old friend. This time in Grand Central her mother was late, and he was lagging behind. She told her friend she would wait for her mother, and the man when he saw she was alone went to her and said he would see that she got a taxi. He could even give her a lift.

It was all too easy. Two days later she called at his hotel in the afternoon, and she was sent upstairs with a bellboy because the man had been a steady patron of the hotel, was known as a respectable schoolteacher, and probably was expecting her but forgot to say so. Within a month he had her sniffing ether and loving it. It, and everything that went on in that room.

She did not see him as often as she wanted to; they could be together only in New York. She stayed two more years in that school but did not finish her college preparatory course there. In May of the second year the house mistress found a bottle of gin in Gloria's room, and she was "asked not to come back." Her mother worried a little about this but attributed it to the fact that Gloria was getting to be very popular with boys, and deep down she was glad; she thought it indicated that the Boam business was a thing of the past. Gloria was immensely popular with boys, and in a less strict school she could have been intercollegiate prom-trotting champion. She went to another school, passed her College Boards for Smith, and then thought better of college. She wanted to study Art. In New York. With her own apartment.

Her uncle enjoyed her popularity because it was the easiest thing for him to do. He never had forgiven himself for bringing Boam into their home, but neither had he ever completely blamed himself. Gloria's current popularity made up for that, and Vandamm was liberal and always on her side in disputes between his sister and his niece.

Neither Mrs. Wandrous nor Vandamm was getting any younger. Gloria won out on her refusal to go to college and on studying art in New York. They said they would see about the apartment. For the present they would move to a house in the Village which was theirs by inheritance, and fix up the top floor as a studio. Vandamm was trading luckily in the market at that time and he seriously thought Gloria had a real talent. She did have a kind of facility; she could copy caricatures by Hugo Gellert, William Auerbach-Levy, Covarrubias, Constantin Alajálov, Ralph Barton—any of the better-known caricaturists. That year she talked a great deal about going to the Art Students' League, but each time a new class would form she would forget to sign up, and so she went on copying caricatures when she had nothing else to do, and she also did some posing, always in the nude. But the thing that about that time became and continued for two or three years to be the most important was drinking. She became one of the world's heaviest drinkers between 1927 and 1930, when the world saw some pretty heavy drinking. The Dizzy Club, the Hotsy-Totsy, Tommy Guinan's Chez Florence, the Type & Print Club, the Basque's, Michel's, Tony's East Fifty-third Street, Tony's West Forty-ninth Street, Forty-two West Forty-nine, the Aquarium, Mario's, the Clamhouse, the Bandbox, the West Forty-fourth Street Club, McDermott's, the Sligo Slasher's, the News-writers', Billy Duffy's, Jack Delaney's, Sam Schwartz's, the Richmond, Frank & Jack's, Frankie & Johnny's, Felix's, Louis', Phyllis's, Twenty-one West Fifty-third, Marlborough House—these were places where she was known by name and sight, where she awed the bartenders by the amount she drank. They knew that before closing she would be stewed, but not without a good fight. There was no thought of going on the wagon. There was no reason to go on the wagon. She drank rye and water all day long. When she remembered that she had not eaten for twenty-four hours she would go to a place where the eggs were to be trusted, order a raw egg, break it in an Old Fashioned cocktail tumbler, shoot Angostura bitters into it, and gulp the result. That night she would have dinner: fried filet of sole with tartar sauce. Next day, maybe no food, maybe bouillon with a raw egg. Certain cigarettes gave her a headache. She would smoke Chesterfields or Herbert Tareytons, no others. For days at a time she would have no sex life, tying up with a group of young Yale remittance men who in their early twenties were sufficiently advanced alcoholics to make it desirable to their families that they stay in New York. It was understood and agreed that the big thing in life was liquor, and while she was with these young men she believed and they believed that she was—well, like a sister. You did not bother her. Only one disgusting little fat boy, who came on from the Middle West twice a year, ever did bother her, but he stopped when he saw it was not the thing to do. The other young men were in the stock market from noon to closing, by telephone. By three-thirty they knew how they stood: whether to celebrate at Texas Guinan's or to drown their sorrows every other place. There was considerable riding around in automobiles with non-New York license plates, but the cars seldom got out of the state except during football season. The summers were fun in New York. Planters' Punches. Mint Juleps. Tom Collinses. Rickeys. You had two or three of these to usher in the season, and paid a visit or two to the beer places, and then you went back to whiskey and water. What was the use of kidding yourself? Everything was done at a moment's notice. If you wanted to go to a night club to hear

Helen Morgan or Libby Holman you made the decision at midnight, you scattered to dress, met an hour later, bought a couple of bottles, and so to the night club. The theater was out. The movies, a little. Private parties, no, unless they were something special. Weddings, by all means. The young men were happiest when they could arrive at "42," stewed and in cutaways, "glad to be back with decent people, not these people that think champagne is something to drink."

"Down with Princeton!" Gloria would say.

"Down with Princeton," the young men would say.

"To hell with Harvard!" Gloria would say.

"The hell with Harvard," the young men would say.

"Hurray for our side!"

"Hurray for our side."

"Bing-go, bing-go, bingo, bingo, bingo that's the ling-go," Gloria would sing, and the young men would smile and join in a little weakly, drinking very hard until they could get like her, except that she could do these things while apparently not drunk. She was not invited to the weddings that they were ushering at, and there were times when she was not exactly a pest, but if she would only understand that a telephone call to a broker was important. On wedding days she would be waiting for them when they finally got away from the sailing of the French ships that in those days were well liked, but when they met her she would have a bill for drinks waiting for them that indicated she had been waiting too—since lunch. Not that she was poor. She always had fifteen or twenty dollars for taxis and things, and if you ran short she would hand it right over. It was just that she was unthinking.

She used to see Weston Liggett sometimes. He would come in, sometimes alone, sometimes with a man, sometimes with women. He would stand at the bar, have his drinks and behave himself. The second or third time she saw him she noticed he was looking at her longer than it was wise to do even in the best-regulated speakeasies. "Who is that man you spoke to?" she said to the Yale boy.

"Oh, a fellow called Liggett. He was in college with my brother."

"Yale?"

"Uh-huh. Yeah. He was one of the atha-letic boys. Crew."

It meant that he could never pick her up, and she would never speak to him until they were properly introduced. He could see her every day of the year after that, but because they had connections in common she would not have anything to do with him; and Liggett understood that and soon became a strange familiar face that Gloria saw unrecognizingly even when she was alone and he was alone. She might never have spoken to him had it not been for one accident: she got pregnant.

One night in the winter of 1929–30 she went home with the surviving two Yale boys. The others had gone back to the provinces to wait out the crash, but these two remained. This night they were prematurely drunk; the liquor was beginning to be harder to take. Gloria usually got undressed in the bathroom when she stayed at their apartment, and they would lend her pajamas. Up to that point this night was as always. But when she lay down on the sofa Bill said: "Come on over and sleep with me."

"All right," she said.

She picked up her pillow and dragged her comforter after her and got into bed with him. She turned her back and settled herself, but she knew immediately that Bill was not going to be pal Bill tonight. He was holding her too close for any doubt about that. She let him worry for a few minutes, and then she turned around and put her arms around him and kissed him. After all, they had been friends a long time, and she liked Bill.

She also liked Mike, who was in the other bed, and not missing a thing. "How about me, Gloria?" he said.

"All right," she said.

Then they called up another girl, or rather Gloria did. The girls they called would not come over at that hour, but Gloria knew one who would, so long as there was another girl. It was all a lot more than the Yale boys anticipated, and it put an end to the drinking companionship. After that night, which was not unpleasant, Gloria went into another phase of her life; although it was in a way a return to a former phase. The next day, when she and Jane left the boys' apartment, Gloria went with Jane to a date Jane had, and the man got another man and Gloria never went out with the Yale boys again. She meant to, they meant to, but it was time she was moving on.

It was the summer of that year, 1930, when she met Eddie Brunner. She had gone to the place where he worked with "the major" because she had met the major in a speakeasy and had the sudden fear that he might be Major Boam and she might not be recognizing him. In all her life she had met only one other major, and that was Boam, and it became a terribly important thing to find out if this could be he. What if she had forgotten that man's face? It was the first time she had thought of the possibility of having forgotten Boam's face, and when the thought came she had to admit that she might easily have seen Major Boam on the street without recognizing him. This major turned out not to be Boam, but not immediately. When she asked him his name (it was lost in the mumble of a speakeasy introduction) he told her it didn't make any difference, just call him Major. That was enough to strengthen her fear that it could be Boam without her recognizing him. For the rest of the night she pestered him for his name, and he amiably refused to tell her unless she went to this place and that place with him. His name turned out to be O'Brien or Kelly or some Irish name, but by the time she learned this she had learned too many other things about him.

Many men had the pleasure of sleeping with Gloria in the year 1930, and Eddie was the only one who could have who didn't. He began by being afraid of getting a social disease, and then when Gloria became a friend he thought he saw something in her that he did not want to sleep with. He saw a kid sister. When they were together, going to the movies, having breakfast, having a couple of beers or a highball at his house, he would feel that he was in the presence of the real Gloria. The other part of her life was shut out. They would talk about the things of their childhood (it is always a wonderful thing to discover with someone through memories of childhood how small America is). "When you were a kid did you count out by saying Ibbity-bibbity-sibbity-sab, ibbity-bibbity-ka-nah-ba, or did you just say eenie-meenie?"

"We said ibbity-bibbity."

"When you were a kid did you yell at girls named Marguerite like this: 'Marguerite, go wash your feet, the Board of Health's across the street'?"

"No, we never yelled that."

"Adam and Eve and Pinch-Me went out the river to swin. Adam and Eve were drowned and who was saved?"

"Pinch-Me." Then: "Ouch!"

"Did you go to dancing school?"

"Oh, sure."

"Did your fella used to carry your ballet slippers for you in the fancy bag?"

"I didn't have a fella."

"Brothers and sisters I have none, but this man's—"

"Oh, God, I could never do those."

Or long stories beginning: "Once when I was a kid—" about killing a snake or breaking a finger or almost saving someone's life. They would talk about the stories in *The American Boy*, both of them having been great admirers of Marcus Aurelius Fortunatus Tidd, the stuttering fat boy created by Clarence Budington Kelland; and the Altschuler Indian stories, and the girls of Bradford Hall, and Larry the Bat and Silver Nell—wasn't that her name? In the Jimmie Dale stories? They were for older people, but after reading them Eddie had gone around sticking gray seals all over the neighborhood. What kind of car did Gloria have? No car, until she was twelve or something like that, then her uncle bought a Haines, which he traded in on a National. Oh, but those weren't old cars. Eddie's father had a Lozier, an Abbott-Detroit, a Stutz Bearcat (which he smashed up three weeks after he bought it), a Saxon, an Earl, a King Eight—always buying cars. Of course a lot of Fords, a second-hand Owen Magnetic, and an airplane. He won the airplane as a gambling gain, but he was afraid to learn to fly. Had Gloria played Diabolo? Once, and got knocked on the head. Did you ever sell Easter egg dyes to win a motion picture camera? Did you ever know anyone who won a real Shetland pony by selling subscriptions to some magazine? No, but she had saved bread wrappers and won a pushmobile. What were your words for going to the bathroom? Did you ever really know a boy who robbed birds' nests? No, that was like people making bathtub gin. Neither of them ever had seen gin made in a bathtub.

"I love you, Eddie darling," she would say.

"I love you, Gloria," he would say, but always wanting to say more than that, like: "No matter what they say about you," or "I wish I'd known you five years sooner," or "Why don't you pull yourself together?"

She knew that and it had a sterilizing effect, which was what they wanted, but no good when they had it. "Eddie," she would say, to change the subject, "why don't you go to a dentist. You're going to lose that tooth and it'll spoil your smile. Go to my dentist tomorrow, now will you promise?"

He would take her home, but they knew she would go right out again, and after these happy evenings that always ended with their knowing they had nothing to look forward to, the next man who had her would say to himself: "Well, I thought I knew everything, but after all the places I've been, all the women, a kid, an American kid. . . ."

Because of the Yale boys she had an abortion, and after that many benders. The night she picked up Weston Liggett for the first time she was coasting along from a bender which had begun after seeing Eddie. She had been home twice during this bender to change her clothes (she long since had had it well understood at home that she did not like to be questioned when she told her mother that she was staying with a friend uptown). A bad thing about days like that was to come out of a speakeasy in the afternoon and find it still daylight, and she would hurry downtown to fill in the remaining daylight with a bath and a change of clothes. The place where she encountered Liggett was a converted carriage house, with no character except for that. It was patronized by kept women and people in moderately good circumstances who lived in the vicinity. Gloria went there when some people she knew telephoned her and said they were all meeting there instead of another place. She went there—it was about nine-thirty in the evening—and discovered she was alone except for a couple, a sort of military grandfather and a young woman out to take him for whatever could be got out of him. Gloria said to the husky Italian who let her in: "I'm meeting Mrs. Voorhees and her party. I'll wait for her at the bar." She had a drink and was smoking and in walked Liggett. He sat at the other end of the bar, munching potato chips and drinking Scotch and soda. When he recognized Gloria he picked up his drink and joined her. "We've never met, but I've seen you so often—"

"Yes, with Billy."

"I went to college with his brother."

"Yes, he told me."

"My name is Liggett."

"He told me that, too. I'm Gloria Wandrous." The bartender relaxed then.

"Wandrous. I'll bet people—it's so much like wondrous."

"Yes, they think I made it up, like Gladys Glad and Hazel Dawn and Leatrice Joy, names like that. I didn't though. It's spelt with an a. W, a, n, d, r, o, u, s, and it's pronounced Wan-drous, pale and wan."

"Not pale and won."

"Mm. Not bad. Not *good*, but not bad."

"Well, I don't make any pretense of being a wit. I'm just a hard-working business man."

"Oh, are business men working again? I hadn't heard."

"Well, not as much as we'd like to. What I was leading up to was, I suppose you have a date."

"You didn't think I came in here every night, the mysterious veiled lady that always sits alone sipping her apéritif?"

"That's exactly what I thought, or hoped. I thought you came here to get away from the usual places—"

"Place, as far as you and I are concerned."

"Right. But now look here, Miss Wandrous, don't dodge the issue. Here is a hard-working business man with Saturday night as free as the air—"

"As free as the air. I have a friend a writer, he'd like to use that some time. As free as the air. That's good."

"You won't go places with me, then?"

"Why go places? Isn't this all right?" she said. "No, Mr.—"

"Liggett."

"Mr. Liggett. No, I'm waiting for some people. It'll probably be all right if you join us. You can sit here till they come and I'll introduce you to those I know."

"Oh, you don't know them. Maybe you won't like them."

"That's possible—here they are, or at least it sounds like. Hello there."

"Gloria darling, you've never been so prompt. Why, Weston Lee-gett. I didn't know you knew each other. Weston, why, you dog, you've broken up my party, but it's all right. That means we have an extra man. See now. Gloria, this is Mr. Zoom, and uh, Mr. Zoom, and you know Mary and Esther, and, everybody, this is Weston Liggett, a great friend of Peter Voorhees. Didn't you go to school together or something?"

"Prep school. Look, I don't want to mess up your party. I'll—let me buy you a drink, and—"

"There are four more people coming down from my house," said Mrs. Voorhees. "Elaine and three men, so you really will be an extra man when we all get here. Oh, I wonder what I want to drink. A Stinger, I think. Elaine. If those men knew you were going to be here they wouldn't have waited with Elaine."

"They knew," said Gloria.

"Only by name. Isn't she lovely, Weston? She's young enough to be your daughter, Weston. You know that, don't you? You're not pretending otherwise, I hope."

"I'm going to adopt her," said Liggett. "That's what we're here for, a few papers to sign and she's my daughter."

"What do you want with two more daughters I'd like to know?"

"Is anybody hungry?" said one of the Messrs. "Zoom." "I'm gonna order some food. A nice filet mignon."

"That's not very nice after the dinner we had at my house."

"Squop chicken? I never get enough to eat when I eat squop chicken. I told you that when we sat down. You gotta give me that. I told you when we sat down, I said frankly I said this is not my idea of a meal, squop chicken. I'm a big eater. Were you in the Army, Mr. Liggett?"

"Uh-huh."

"Then you know how it is. One thing I said to myself in France. I promised myself if I ever got back home the one thing I was never gonna do was go hungry. When I want to eat I eat."

"Watch this trick," said Mrs. Voorhees. The other Mr. Zoom was doing a trick. You balance a fifty-cent piece on the rim of a glass with a dollar bill between the coin and the glass. You snatched the dollar bill out from under the coin and—if the trick is successful—the coin remains balanced on the glass. "Fascinating," said Mrs. V.

"I can do a better one than that with friction. You get friction in your fingers—"

"Shhhh. Marvelous! I can't even get it to stay on the glass, let alone make it stay after you pull the bill away. You have a wonderful sense of—I think I do want something to eat, after all. Waiter, have you any uh, that uh, you know, begins with a Z? It's a dessert."

"Zabag—"

"That's it. I'll have some. Nothing for you, Mary?"

"I know one with friction. You get friction in your fingers by rubbing them on the table-cloth. Wait till he puts the table-cloth on the table and I'll show you. And you have to have a fork or a spoon. That's the idea of it. You lift up the spoon with the—"

"Listen, Hoover's all right."

"Will you look at that old fool. Can't he see she's making a fool out of him? I'm glad my father died before he was old enough—"

"I'm sorry, Madame, the chef says—"

"Look at him. Does he get any thrill out of that?"

"It's exactly like the old place. Exactly. The only difference is it's on the uptown side now instead of the downtown side. It used to be on the downtown side but *now* it's on the *up*town. I think they were terribly smart to preserve the same atmosphere. I said to—"

"Did you see that thing they had in *The New Yorker* I think it was the week before last?"

Listening, Gloria and Liggett found themselves holding hands. On her part a tenderness had come over her; at first because she felt responsible for Liggett, and then because she liked him; he was better than these other people. "When the others come we can leave, if you want to," she said.

"Good. Perfect," said Liggett. "Will it be all right with—"

"She won't mind. She just hates to be alone. Two people more or less won't make any difference."

"Good. We'll go some place and dance. I haven't done any volunteer dancing for a long time. That's a compliment, I hope you appreciate it. I haven't done any volunteer dancing since I don't know when. Of course I dance the Turkey Trot. You do the Turkey Trot, of course?"

"Mm-hmm. And the Bunny Hug. And the Maxixe. And the Can-Can. By the way, what was the Can-Can? Was it worth all the excitement they made about it or that I suppose they made about it?"

"Listen, beautiful Miss Wandrous, I am *not* old enough to remember the Can-Can. The Can-Can was popular around the turn of the century, and I wasn't. I wasn't at all popular at the turn of the century."

"I can hardly believe that. At least I can hardly believe my ears now, hearing you admit that you weren't popular any time in your life."

"There have been lots of times when I wasn't popular, and I'm beginning to think this is one of those times."

They went to a lot of speakeasies, especially to the then new kind, as it was the beginning of the elaborate era. From serving furtive drinks of bad liquor disguised as demi-tasse the speakeasy had progressed to whole town houses, with uniformed pages and cigarette girls, a string orchestra and a four- or five-piece Negro band for dancing, free hors d'œuvres, four and five bartenders, silver-plated keys and other souvenir-admittance tokens to regular patrons, expensive entertainment, Cordon Bleu chefs, engraved announcements in pretty good taste, intricate accounting systems and business machinery—all a very good, and because of the competition, necessary front for the picturesque and deadly business of supplying liquor at huge financial profit—powerful radio stations, powerful speedboats and other craft not unlike the British "Q" ships, powerful weapons against highjackers, powerful connections in the right places. And often very good liquor and enough good wine to set in front of the people who knew good wine and still cared about it.

Having got thoroughly drunk, picking up couples and dropping them, joining parties and deserting them, Gloria and Leggett went to his apartment as the last place to go. He had been wondering all night how he was going to suggest a hotel. He thought it over and thought it over, and kept putting it off. At the last place they went to, which they closed up, they took a taxi, Liggett gave his home address, and it was as easy as that. When Gloria heard the address she guessed it was no love nest she was going to, and when she saw the apartment she knew it wasn't.

5

ON MONDAY AFTERNOON an unidentified man jumped in front of a New Lots express in the Fourteenth Street subway station. Mr. Hoover was on time for the usual meeting of his Cabinet. Robert McDermott, a student at Fordham University, was complimented for his talk on the Blessed Virgin at the morning exercises in her honor. A woman named Plotkin, living in the Brownsville section of Brooklyn, decided to leave her husband for good and all. William K. Fenstermacher, the East 149th Street repair man, went all the way to Tremont Avenue to fix a radio for a Mrs. Jones, but there was no Jones at the address given, so he had to go all the way back to the shop, wasting over an hour and a half. Babe Ruth hit a home run into the bleachers near the right field foul line. Grayce Johnson tried to get a job in the chorus of The Band Wagon, a new revue, but was told the show was already in rehearsal. Patrolman John J. Barry, Shield No. 17858, was still on sick call as a result of being kicked in the groin by a young woman Communist in the Union Square demonstration of the preceding Friday. Jerry, a drunk, did not wake up once during the entire afternoon, which he spent in a chair at a West 49th Street speakeasy. Identical twins were delivered to a Mrs. Lachase at the Lying-In Hospital. A Studebaker sedan bumped the spare tire of a Ford coupe at Broadway and Canal Street, and the man driving the Ford punched the Studebaker driver in the mouth. Both men were arrested. Joseph H. Dilwyn, forty-two years old, had all his teeth out by the same dentist he had gone to for twelve years. A woman who shall be nameless took the money her husband had given her to pay the electric light bill and bought one of the new Eugenie hats with it. Harry W. Blossom, visiting New York for the first time since the War, fell asleep in the Strand Theatre and missed half the picture. At 3:16 P.M. Mr. Francis F. Tearney, conductor on a Jackson Heights No. 15 Fifth Avenue bus, tipped his cap at St. Patrick's Cathedral. James J. Walker, mayor of the City of New York, had a late lunch at the Hardware Club. A girl using an old curling iron caused a short circuit in the Pan-Hellenic Club. An unidentified man jumped in front of a Bronx Park express in the Mott Avenue subway station. After trying for three days Miss Helen Tate, a typist employed by the New York Life, was able to recall the name of a young man she had met two summers before at a party in Red Bank, N. J. Mr. and Mrs. Harvey L. Fox celebrated their thirtieth wedding anniversary with a luncheon in the Hotel Bossert, Brooklyn. Al Astor, an actor at liberty, woke up thinking it was Tuesday. John Lee, a colored boy, pulled the wings out of a fly in Public School 108. The Caswell Realty Company sold a row of taxpayers in Lexington Avenue to Jack W. Levine for a sum in the neighborhood of $125,000. Gloria Wandrous, after taking a warm bath at home, went to sleep while worrying over what she should do about Mrs. Liggett's mink coat. Eddie Brunner spent the afternoon at Norma Day's apartment, playing the phonograph, especially "The Wind in the Willows," the Rudy Vallée record.

Monday afternoon Emily Liggett and her daughters came home by train. They got out of their taxi, carrying their coats and leaving the few bags for the doorman to see to. Emily went straight to her room and of all the things that happened to all the people in New York that day, none was more shocking to any individual than Emily's discovery that her mink coat was not in her closet.

It had been such a good week-end; quiet and peaceful. Saturday was warm, Sunday morning was warm and in the afternoon it turned cool and made Emily think of the coat. It was time, really, to put it away, and she made a note of it as the first thing to do Tuesday morning. This year she would insure it for $3,000, half what it cost in 1928. She would insure it and hope something would happen to it so that she could get the money out of it. There were things she could do with $3,000, and she was getting tired of having a mink coat. She never had been happy with the actual possession of it. Something about the New England conscience; when you added up the maximum number of times you wore the coat in a season, multiplied that by three for three seasons, and divided that into $6,000 you got the cost of the coat each time you had worn it. And it was too much. It was a fair calculation, because she knew she could not get $3,000 for the coat now in any other way than insurance. As for getting $6,000 on it—ridiculous. Well, it had been a good week-end.

She opened the closet door, and the closet might as well have been empty. The coat was not there. She called the cook and the maid and questioned them, but her questioning and her own and their search did not result in finding the coat. Her questioning did not bring about any of the disclosures which the maid was pondering—the inference the maid had taken from certain little things she had noticed about Mr. Liggett's bedroom and bath.

Emily telephoned Liggett, but he was not in the office and his secretary did not expect him back. Emily was going to call his two clubs
and a speakeasy or two, because she thought the theft of the coat
ought to be reported immediately; but she decided to wait and talk to
Weston before notifying the police. When Liggett came home she told
him about the coat. He was frightened; he was twice frightened, because he did not know it was gone, but when he learned it had disappeared he knew right away who had it. He told Emily it was best
not to notify the police; that losses like that were immediately reported
to the insurance company and that it was a bad thing to have to report
to the insurance company. "All the insurance companies work together,"
he said, "and they keep a sort of exchange blacklist. If your car is
stolen all the other companies know about it in a week, and it affects
your rating with the companies. It makes you a bad risk to lose a thing
like that, and when you're a bad risk it's sometimes impossible to get
insurance, and the least you get out of it is you have to pay a much
higher preminum, not only on, for instance, the coat, if they get it
back, but also anything else you decide to insure." Liggett did not believe all this—in fact knew some of it to be inaccurate; but it covered
up his confusion. That that girl, that swell kid, could be the same
girl he had slept with last night, for whom he was feeling something
he never had felt before, and all the time she was a common ordinary
little thief—it was beyond him. It was more than beyond him. The
more he thought of it the angrier he got, until he wanted to take her by
the throat. He told Emily he would have a private detective agency
look for the coat before reporting to the insurance company or the
police. This was not the way Emily would have done it, and she said
so. Why go to the expense of a private detective agency when the insurance company assumed that and would be glad to assume it rather
than risk the loss of $3,000 for the coat? No, no, he insisted. Hadn't
she been listening to him? Didn't she pay any attention? Hadn't he just
finished telling her that the insurance company kept blacklists, and
the chances were the disappearance of the coat would have some simple
explanation. The detective agency wouldn't charge much—ten dollars,
probably. And he would save that much in premiums by not reporting
the loss to the insurance company. "Now please let me handle this," he
told Emily. Well, it seemed pretty irregular to her, and she didn't like
it. What if the private detectives didn't find the coat? Wouldn't the insurance company be very annoyed when he did finally report the theft
of the coat? Wouldn't they ask why he hadn't immediately reported to
the police? Wouldn't it be better in the long run to do the regular

thing? She thought it was always best to do the regular thing, the conventional thing. When someone dies, you get an undertaker; when something is stolen, you tell the police. Liggett almost said: "Who are you to talk about the conventional thing? You slept with me before you married me." He was ashamed of that, of thinking it; but he guessed he always had thought it. It was just beginning to dawn on him that he never had loved Emily. He was so flattered by what she felt for him before they were married that he had been blinded to his true feeling about her. His true feeling was passion, and that had gone, and since then there had been nothing but the habit of marriage—he really loved Gloria.

And then he remembered that he did not love Gloria. He could not love a common thief. She *was* a common thief, too. You could see that in her face. There was something in her face, some unconventional thing along with the rest of her beauty, her mouth and eyes and nose —somewhere around the eyes, perhaps, or was it the mouth?—she did not have the conventional look. Emily, yes. Emily had it. He could look at Emily dispassionately, impersonally, as though he did not know her— objectively? wasn't it called? He could look at her and see how much she looked like dozens of girls who had been born and brought up as she had been. You saw them at the theater, at the best cabarets and speakeasies, at the good clubs on Long Island—and then you saw the same girls, the same women, dressed the same, differing only in the accent of their speech, at clubs in other cities, at horse shows and football games and dances, at Junior League conventions. Emily, he decided after eighteen years of marriage, was a type. And he knew why she was a type, or he knew the thing that made the difference in the look of a girl like Emily and the look of a girl like Gloria. Gloria led a certain kind of life, a sordid life; drinking and sleeping with men and God knows what all, and she had seen more of "life" than Emily ever possibly would see. Whereas Emily had been brought up a certain way, always accustomed to money and the good ways of spending it. In other words, all her life Emily had been looking at nice things, nice houses, cars, pictures, grounds, clothes, people. Things that were easy to look at, and people that were easy to look at; with healthy complexions and good teeth, people who had had pasteurized milk to drink and proper food all their lives from the time they were infants; people who lived in houses that were kept clean, and painted when paint was needed, who took care of their cars and their furniture and their bodies, and by so doing their minds were taken care of; and they got the look that Emily and girls—women—like her had. Whereas

Gloria—well, take for instance the people she was with the night he
saw her two nights ago, the first night he went out with her. The man
that liked to eat, for instance. Where did he come from? He might have
come from the Ghetto. Liggett happened to know that there were places
in the slums where eighty families would use the same outside toilet.
A little thing, but imagine what it must look like! Imagine having spent
your formative years living like, well, somewhat the way you lived in
the Army. Imagine what effect that would have on your mind. And of
course a thing like that didn't only affect your mind; it showed in your
face, absolutely. Not that it was so obvious in Gloria's case. She had
good teeth and a good complexion and a healthy body, but there was
something wrong somewhere. She had not gone to the very best schools,
for instance. A little thing perhaps, but important. Her family—he
didn't know anything about them; just that she lived with her mother
and her mother's brother. Maybe she was a bastard. That was possible.
She could be a bastard. That can happen in this country. Maybe her
mother never was married. Sure, that could happen in this country.
He never heard of it except among poor people, and Gloria's family
were not poor. But why couldn't it happen in this country? The first
time he and Emily ever stayed together they took a chance on having
children, and in those days people didn't know as much about not
getting caught as they do today. Gloria was even older than Ruth,
so maybe her mother had done just what Emily had done, with no
luck. Maybe Gloria's father was killed in a railroad accident or something, intending to marry Gloria's mother, but on the night he first
stayed with her, maybe on his way home he was killed by an automobile
or a hold-up man or something. It could happen. There was a fellow
at New Haven that was very mysterious about his family. His mother
was on the stage, and nothing was ever said about his father. Liggett
wished now that he had known the fellow better. Now he couldn't
remember the fellow's name, but some of the fellows in Liggett's crowd
had wondered about this What's-His-Name. He drew for the *Record*.
An artist. Well, bastards were always talented people. Some of the most
famous people in history were bastards. Not bastards in any deroga-
tory sense of the word, but love children. (How awful to be a love
child. It'd be better to be a bastard. "If I were a bastard I'd rather be
called a bastard than a love child.") Now Gloria, she drew or painted.
She was interested in art. And she certainly knew a lot of funny people.
She knew that bunch of kids from New Haven, young Billy and those
kids. But anybody could meet them, and anybody could meet Gloria.
God damn it! That was the worst of it. Anybody could meet Gloria.

He thought that all through dinner, looking at his wife, his two daughters, seeing in their faces the thing he had been thinking about a proper upbringing and looking at nice things and what it does to your face. He saw them, and he thought of Gloria, and that anybody could meet Gloria, and Anybody, somebody she picked up in a speakeasy somewhere, probably was with her now, this minute.

"I don't think I'll wait for dessert," he said.

"Strawberries? You won't wait for strawberries?" said Emily.

"Oh, good. Strawberries," said Ruth. "Daddy, you'll surely wait for strawberries. If you go I'll have to eat yours and I'll get strawberry rash."

"You won't *have* to," said Emily.

"Gotta go. I just thought of a fellow. About the coat."

"Can't you phone him? A detective agency, surely they'd have a phone."

"No. Not this fellow. He isn't a private detective. He's a regular city detective, and if I phoned him he'd have to make a report on it. If I went through the regular channels. I'll get in touch with him through a friend of mine, Casey, down at Tammany Hall."

"Well, where? Can't you phone this Casey and make an appointment?"

"Emily, *must* I explain everything in detail? I just thought of something and I want to do it now. I don't want any strawberries, or if they're that good you can put them in the icebox till I get back."

"Well, all right. I hope this doesn't mean one of your all-night binges with your Tammany Hall friends."

If the girls had not been there he would have given a more blistering answer than: "I should have been a doctor."

A taxi took him to a drug store in the Grand Central zone and he tried to get Gloria on the telephone. He tried her home, several speakeasies, and—he did not quite know why—had her paged at two of the Times Square hotels. A woman he guessed was her mother said Gloria was out for dinner and the evening. It sounded so respectable, the voice and the words, that he wanted to laugh in the mouthpiece. He could not tell (and he tried) whether he was now angry with Gloria for stealing Emily's coat, or because he had her, in his mind, grappling with some young snot-nose from Princeton. He came out of the telephone booth sweating and uncomfortable, with his hat on the back of his head. He had a Coca-Cola standing up at the fountain, and when he set the glass down on the fountain it made the hollow *cloup* sound those glasses make, but this glass must have been imperfect because it cracked and broke and he cut his finger, ever so slightly, but enough to cause an industrial crisis in the store. The pharmacist and the soda jerker were so solicitous and made him so angry with it that he was rude to them, and away went his resolution not to drink. He had been feeling so respectable and superior up to then, but the cut on his finger, which was minutely painful but enormously annoying, and the store people with their attentions got him upset. "Jesus Christ, why don't you send for a God damn ambulance," he said, and went out in search of a drink.

Fifty-second Street between Fifth and Sixth Avenues was packed solid with automobiles and their sound, never changing. The *eep* sound of the taxis and the *aa-oo-aa* of Lincoln town cars predominated in the chorus. It was like an evening wedding in a small town; with the invited, those who had cards, inside, and the big noise going outside independent of the rest.

He went inside and had a Scotch and soda at the bar. It appeared to be full of people trying to be late for the theater, and out-of-town men in light tan suits, drinking Old Fashioneds and laughing too loud for the humor in anything they could possibly say. Liggett did not want to talk to anyone, not even the bartenders. He drank and smoked and drank and smoked, and when his cigarette was done he ate potato chips and when his drink was done he lit another cigarette and then had more to drink. This way he waited out the people who were going to the theater, and was alone at the bar. By that time the men in the tan suits were kissing the handsome women. Those men were getting drunk much too soon, Liggett decided, getting drunk. He realized he was drinking too much and he put it up to himself squarely, whether to go home now or get really stewed. He decided to get stewed, because he would be uncomfortable if he went home, where he never got drunk; and because if he got drunk here he might think of some crazy thing to do that might lead to his finding Gloria. Where could she be? New York's a big place, but the places Gloria went to were not many. The theater was out; she never went to the theater. The only other place she could be was in any apartment in town. Any other, from the houses that hung over the Harlem River branch of the New York Central to the apartments that hung over the East River, or in a one-room apartment in the Village, or an artist's studio in the West Sixties, or some place on Riverside Drive. Any apartment.

He went home late, having gone to nine speakeasies in one block, having been refused admission to two others. He went home without seeing Gloria.

She was spending the evening with Eddie. She went to his apartment and they had dinner at a restaurant, where Eddie ate a lot of spaghetti, winding it expertly around his fork. They had a bottle of red wine. It was a good little restaurant, with sawdust on the floor and a pool table, where some elderly Italians played a game which Eddie never understood; something to do with shooting the cueball between two tiny bowling pins. A small radio was turned on. They did not change the dial, and the program went from music to speech to adventure story to torch-singer, with no editing on the part of the proprietor of the place. It was probably the only station that came in good, because of the "L," which was only half a block away. Gloria and Eddie were the only Americans in the place, and no one paid any attention to them. When they wanted the waiter they had to call him from his card game with three other patrons.

"What did you do last night?" said Eddie.

"Oh, went to a movie."

"Which one?" Eddie asked.

"The Strand."

"What did you see?"

"Uh, Norma Shearer, in 'Strangers May Kiss.'"

"Oh, did you? How'd you like it? Any good?"

"Not very. I like her, though. I think she's terribly attractive."

"She's a Canadian. From Montreal. You know, Montreal, Nova Scotia," said Eddie.

"Montreal isn't in Nova Scotia," said Gloria.

"I know. And 'Strangers May Kiss' isn't at the Strand, in case you're interested. Of course I'm not. I don't give a damn, only I don't know why you think you have to lie to me."

"Well, I could have got the theater wrong."

"No, you couldn't. You could have got the theater wrong, but not the picture, and 'Strangers May Kiss' isn't playing on Broadway. It was, but it isn't now. So don't lie any more than you have to."

"I'll lie to you if I want to. What I do isn't your affair anyway."

"You won't lie to me often, because I won't be around to listen."

"Why? Are you going away?"

"No. Where would I go? No, it's just that I won't see you. I don't want to see you if you lie to me. I know practically everything about you that there is to know, and I don't mind the kind of life you lead, because that's your business. But just don't go to all the trouble of lying to me. Save your lies for someone you have to lie to."

"Oh—"

He laughed. "Unless of course you want to *practice* on me. You ought to do a little more practicing, by the way. If you think Norma believed that story the other night about you and your imaginary cousin and the crap game where you lost your clothes. What do you think people are? Don't you give them credit for any sense at all? You know it's a form of insult, making up a screwy story to explain something that you don't have to explain. You know, Norma's my girl, and she hasn't any wrong ideas about us."

"Did you tell her?"

"Certainly I told her."

"How? What did you say to her?"

"I told her we weren't having an affair."

"Who brought it up? Did you say it first, or did she ask you? How did you happen to tell her?"

"I don't know," said Eddie, and reflected. "It was when I first knew her. She asked me if I was in love with anybody, and I said no, and she said what about the girl named Gloria that someone said I saw all the time. Someone told her I was seeing you, but all she knew was your first name. So I said you were a platonic friend, and that's all."

"Is it?"

"About all. Nothing else worth repeating."

"Didn't she say that if you and I were platonic friends, you were my only platonic friend?"

"No. Not exactly."

"Not exactly, hah? You know she said something like that, though, don't you?"

"A little like that. Oh, what the hell, Gloria, yes. She didn't put it that way. She wanted to know how I could see a good-looking girl like you and keep up a platonic friendship. I mean keep it platonic."

"And you were peeved because you thought she was laughing at you. It didn't make you look so good to be the one man I didn't sleep with."

"There you're wrong. If I started to resent that now it'd be pretty late in the game."

"Did you ever resent it?"

"No."

"Why not?"

"I don't know."

"Because I'm not attractive to you?"

"No. Not that either."

"Well then, *what?*"

"Well, we didn't start off that way, is the only reason I can give right now. Do you want a psychological reason?"

"Yes."

"Well, I haven't got one for you. Do you want some more wine?"

"Yes, I guess I ought to have some wine from sour grapes."

"Oh, for God's sake," said Eddie. "Am I supposed to infer that you're sour grapes because I like Norma better than you?"

"Why not? Isn't that the truth?"

"No, certainly not."

"You don't like me because you feel superior. You know all about me and that's why you never ask me to sleep with you."

"I've asked you to sleep with me."

"Yes. Sleep with you. Good Samaritan. When I'm tight and you think I'll get the devil if I go home drunk. You ask me if I'll sleep in your apartment. Why, that's the most insulting thing you can do, in a way. It *proves* how you feel about me. You're above my sex appeal. You could sleep with me and not feel a thing."

"Good Lord."

"Yes, good Lord. I'm no good. I'm not fit to touch. You'd be contaminated if you touched me. That's the way you feel about me, isn't it?"

"No."

"It is! You hate me, Eddie Brunner. You can't stand the sight of me. You're so damned superior you—"

"Oh, stop."

"Why should I stop? Because I'm talking too loud. I'm embarrassing you by talking too loud. That's it, isn't it?"

"You *are* talking above a whisper."

"God damn it, why not? Here! You!" She called to one of the elderly Italians.

"Me, Miss?"

"Yes. Come here."

The old man came over and tipped his hat. "Yes," he said.

"Am I talking too loud?"

"Oh, no. Not at all, Miss. You have a good time." He smiled at Eddie.

"I didn't ask you if I could have a good time. I asked you if I were talking too loud."

"Oh, no. We don't mind it," said the Italian.

"Doesn't it disturb your card game to have me talking so loud?"

"No. No. Oh, no."

"All right. You may go."

The old man looked at her and then at Eddie, and smiled at Eddie, and then tipped his hat and went back to the game. He explained in Italian the interruption, and each of the players turned and looked at Gloria before resuming the game.

Eddie went on eating.

"There you sit," she said.

"Uh-huh. Just as though nothing happened. Drink your wine, bad girl, and feel sorry for yourself some more. John!" The waiter came. "Another bottle of wine," said Eddie.

They did not speak while the waiter went to fetch the wine. He opened the bottle and poured some in Gloria's glass.

"That's an insult!" said Gloria.

"Miss?" said the waiter.

"That's an insult. Didn't you see what he did? You know you're supposed to pour it in his glass first."

"I'll take your glass," said Eddie.

"That's not the idea. He's supposed to pour some in your glass first and then fill mine and then fill yours. You know that, so why shouldn't he know it?"

"This wine is just bottled, Miss. It is only when the wine has been in the bottle a long time."

"You don't have to tell me about wine. I know more about wine than you do."

"Yes, Miss. This is home-made wine and it is only bottled this evening."

"I didn't ask you the history of it. I won't drink it. I want a highball."

"Give her a highball. Rye and soda," said Eddie.

"Humor her," said Gloria. "Let her have her own way. Well, I don't want a highball. I want another bottle of wine, and you pour it the right way, whether it was bottled in 1926 or five minutes ago. I've never been so insulted in all my life."

"Are you drunk, by any chance?" said Eddie.

"No, and you know I'm not."

"Well, what are you sore about? All right, John, another bottle of wine. What's the matter with you, Gloria? Did someone do something to you? You're never like this with me. In a minute I'll begin to be sorry for myself. Maybe you hate me and you don't want to tell me."

"No."

"Tell me, what is it?"

"I don't want to talk about it."

"You can talk to me. You always have."

"I don't even know what it is myself. It isn't against you. I love you, Eddie. Oh, I'm so awful."

"Are you in love with someone?"

"Not the way I want to be."

"You mean me?"

"No. Yes. But you're not the one I'm thinking of. No, it's this Liggett."

"You're in love with Liggett?"

"Oh, I think so. I don't know."

"Does he know it?"

"No."

"Really in love with him?"

"I am, yes. He isn't. I know what he thinks. He thinks—well, just a pushover. First night I go out with him I go to bed with him. Even worse than that. He picked me up in a speakeasy."

"Well, being picked up in a speakeasy is better than being picked up in the Grand Central station."

"*Why did you say that! Answer me!* Why did you say that?"

"Hell's bells, I don't know. Did I say the wrong thing?"

"What made you say the Grand Central station? What do you know about the Grand Central station?"

"Well—it's—a *station*."

"You said it was better to be picked up in a speakeasy than in Grand Central. Why did you say that? Do you know anything about my being picked up in the Grand Central?"

"No, were you?"

"Oh, God. Oh, Eddie. Take me out of here. Let's go to your apartment."

"Sure. John! Tell John I don't want the wine. Just bring the check."

They went home and she told him about Dr. Reddington. She spent the night there because she was afraid, and Eddie went to sleep in a chair, watching her while pretending to read. He became exhausted by the first experience of the desire to kill a man.

The next morning, Tuesday, Liggett got awake with an average hangover, the kind that reminded him of mornings after football games and boat races, except that after a night's drinking like last night's he could count on partial recovery within a few minutes after answering the call of nature, and after a day of strenuous athletics nature does not always call, at least not before he was at top form. It always seemed to Liggett that too hard rowing stiffened the muscles of the intestines, resulting in constipation, which resulted in boils. Drinking had for him no such effect. A trip to the bathroom and the worst of this kind of hangover was gone. A shot of tomato juice with a generous dash of Worcestershire sauce, and a cup of black coffee and a plate of cream of tomato soup—that was his breakfast on mornings like this.

Emily came in while he was eating his soup. "Did anything happen about the coat?"

"I couldn't find Casey. I'll get in touch with him today."

"There's some on your vest. Here, I'll get it."

"No, it's all right. I'll do it."

"I'll do it. You'll stain it. Let me." She scraped off the splash of soup with a knife. "There."

"Thanks."

"Let's go to the theater tonight. I want to see Bart Marshall. And you like Zita Johann."

"Bart Marshall? Who is he?"

"Herbert Marshall. I was being funny."

"What are they playing in?"

" 'Tomorrow and Tomorrow.' By Philip Barry."

"Oh, yes. Well, all right if you get the tickets. Who shall we ask?"

"I thought we could ask the Farleys. We'll be going to the country soon and I dislike not having seen her since last summer. What made me think of them was they were at the club Sunday, and Mrs. Farley's a nice woman. I like her."

"Yes, I saw him. He was with a fellow that said he knew me at New Haven. A Jew."

"Oh, ho. You?" Emily laughed.

"What are you laughing at? I have nothing against Jews. I have some good friends Jews. Paul and Jimmy. You know I like them."

"Oh, I know, but not while you were in college."

"Listen, don't you go around saying things like that. This is no time for that kind of snobbishness. Have the Farleys by all means. Her brother is a great friend of Al Smith's. You get the tickets, and what about dressing?"

"I think a black tie."

"Yes. Farley's always very well dressed, and if you don't specify black tie he's liable to come in tails, and I'll be damned if I want to put on tails this late in the season. Is this play any good?"

"Josie liked it."

"What the hell does she know about anything?"

"You *like* Josie. I've heard you *say* you liked her."

"Oh, you mean Josie Wells. I thought you meant Josie Demuth." He wiped his mouth with the napkin lengthwise. He looked at his watch, and then had to look again to see what time it was. "I'll be home as early as I can. I'm going to Philadelphia on the ten o'clock, but I'll be back in plenty of time for dinner, I hope. I'm not going to the office at all, unless I stop in after I get back from Philadelphia. Good-by." He kissed her.

"This is Emily Liggett, Mrs. Farley. I tried to wave to you at the club Sunday."

"I saw you, and the *girls.* Was that really Ruth?"

"It was. Isn't she—"

"Oh, she must be such fun. I knew Barbara, but I had to look twice to be sure that was Ruth. She used to be *pretty*, but now she's *handsome.*"

"Oh, thank you. I wish I could tell her that, but I think I'll save it for her. When she needs cheering up. I wondered if you and Mr. Farley could come to dinner tonight on such short notice. I wanted to ask you on Sunday, but it would only be the four of us, you and Mr. Farley and my husband and I. I thought we might go to the theater."

"Tonight? Why, yes, I think so. I'm almost positive."

"Oh, fine. Have you seen 'Tomorrow and Tomorrow'?"

"No, we haven't. Paul said this morning that that was one of the things he wanted to see. I thought it would get the Pulitzer Prize, or at least a lot of people seemed to."

"Oh, have they given the Pulitzer Prize again?"

"Yes, it's in this morning's paper. 'Alison's House,' by Susan Glaspell, won it."

" 'Alison's House.' Oh, yes. That was about Emily Dickinson, but I never did see it. They do so many good things at the Civic Repertory but it's such a nuisance to go all the way down there. Well, I'm so glad you can come. At seven-thirty, and black tie for our husbands."

"Grand, and thank you so much," said Nancy.

She liked Emily Liggett, and she was pleased because she knew Mrs. Liggett had not tried to wave to her on Sunday. That lie was one of the amenities. Nancy Farley knew that what had happened was that Mrs. Liggett had seen her at the club, had thought of her some time, perhaps several times, on Monday, and had decided probably last night to invite her to dinner. Nancy had no hope of being or desire to be an intimate friend of Emily Liggett's. Emily Liggett was one of a few women whom Nancy always spoke to, addressing them as Mrs., seeing them a lot around the club in the summer and over the heads of people at the theater. She knew Emily liked her—which meant little more than liking her looks, but that was quite all right—and that the liking had in it such qualities as mutual respect and approval. They never would be close friends, because they never would have to be. Nancy knew that if she ever happened to be taking a boat trip or a long train ride with Emily Liggett they would find they had friends in common other than the same general group they knew in New York; but Nancy was satisfied to take that for granted, along with probable tastes in common. There was warmth now in her admiration for Mrs. Liggett; it took a kind of courage for Mrs. Liggett to invite the Farleys to dinner, and it was that which Nancy admired. She called Paul's office and left word with his secretary that they were going to the Liggetts' for dinner. Then she went to Paul's room to see that one of his two dinner jackets was pressed and ready to wear, and she made a routine inspection of his shirts and collars and ties.

The Farley boys were long since at school and Nancy had nothing to do until five o'clock. Every day at five, unless Paul had other plans, Nancy would drive down Lexington Avenue to the neighborhood of the Graybar Building, where Paul had his offices. She had been doing this for four years. It began accidentally. She happened one afternoon to be in the neighborhood of his offices, which were then at 247 Park Avenue, and she waited for him and caught him coming out. It was such a good idea, they agreed, that it would be fun to do it every day she could. It did have its points; there were many afternoon parties in those days, and she would stop and pick him up and they would go to the parties together. Although they never happened to say so to each other or to anyone else, both Nancy and Paul hated to enter a room alone. But together they put up a good united front, and they were two people who in the minds of their friends were thought of always as husband and wife. Only to his draftsmen and to the employees of his clubs and a few business acquaintances did Paul have an identity of his own. After working hours everyone thought of him as the one in masculine attire of the inseparable Mr. and Mrs. Paul Farley. It was almost true of Nancy, too; as true as it could be of a woman, who, if she has anything at all—beauty, ugliness, charm, bad taste, good taste, sex appeal—begins with a quicker identity and holds it longer than a man does. And so they would go to parties together, or simply go home together. Every day she would meet him.

After a while it began to be a habit that to Nancy was not an un-mixed blessing. At first occasionally, and then every day, Paul would come up in back of the car and gently pinch the back of Nancy's neck. In the beginning it was cute, she thought. Then she found that she was expecting it. Then she found she was setting herself against it, tightening her nerves and sitting in the very middle of the front seat, hoping he would not be able to take her by surprise. But he always did. It became a game with him, and she could count on the fingers of one hand the number of times when luck was with her and she was quicker than he. They had a phaeton then, a Packard. When they were buying a convertible one thing she had in mind was that she would be able to raise the window on her side and he would not be able to touch her neck. This was no good, though; he would get the same surprise effect by rapping hard with his ring on the raised win-dow. Little by little the custom of meeting Paul every day became a nuisance, then almost a horror. It made her jittery, and all because he was doing something she at first thought was cute, sweet. After they would get in the car it would take her a few minutes to get her mind on what he was saying. A few times, on days when the weather was fine and he had reason to expect her to meet him, she just could not bring herself to face it—although face it was precisely not the word—and she would find excuses not to turn up. At such times he would be so hurt that she would tell herself she was a little beast; Paul was so kind and considerate and sweet in everything else, what on earth was the matter with her that she couldn't pass over such a slight fault? But this self-reproach did not have any lasting effect. It was a form of self-indulgence that certainly did not solve the problem.

As for coming right out and telling Paul she objected to his pinching the back of her neck—that was out of the question. From conversa-tions with her friends, and from her own observations, Nancy knew that in every marriage (which after all boils down to two human beings living together) the wife has to keep her mouth shut about at least one small thing her husband does that disgusts her. She knew of a case where the marriage was ruined because of the husband's habit of al-lowing just a little of the white of egg to hang from the spoon when he ate soft-boiled eggs. In that case the disgusting thing occurred every morning. She knew of another case where the husband walked out on his wife because he said she was unclean; it took one of those psycho-analytical quacks a month to get the man to reveal that the woman never went to the bathroom without leaving toilet paper floating in the bowl of the toilet. Things like these that you kept quiet about, they were worse than the things you could quarrel about; your husband's behavior in bed, or your wife's; his taste in clothes, or hers; cheating at games, flirtatiousness, bad manners, differences of opinion, repetitiousness, bragging and humility and punctuality and the lack of it and all the other things that people can quarrel openly about. Then there was always the hope that please God he might stop. But, no; he probably did it because he thought it was expected of him.

Now this Tuesday Nancy Farley, with nothing to do all day, began thinking of Paul's little trick early in the day. It was going to be a fine day. There wasn't a cloud in the sky and no chance of any legitimate excuse not to meet Paul. This same day, this idleness gave her plenty of chance to think from time to time of John Watterson, the homely actor who everyone said had more charm than—well, everyone said he had more charm than anyone they ever knew. Watterson came of an awfully good Boston family and he had gone to Harvard, and he usually played hardboiled parts, although he looked well in tails. He reminded some people of Lincoln; he was tall and homely like Lincoln, and Lincoln must have had a marvelous voice too. Watterson had. What with one play and another, Watterson had reached that point where he could be identified by his first name: "Are you going to John's opening?" meant Watterson as surely as Kit and Alfred and Lynn and Helen and Oggie and Jane and Zita and Bart and Blanche and Eva and Hopie and Leslie meant the people that those names meant. Watterson certainly had arrived, and having arrived he had quietly settled down to the practice of his profession, on and off the stage.

The first thing Nancy said about him when she first laid eyes on him was that there was an honest man, which she amended to there is a man with honesty. He had hair like an Indian's, straight and black and it fell over his forehead—never with any attempt on his part to keep it from falling. He had big thick lips and out of them came the sounds of this hard strong voice of his in a Chicago accent which he never tried to change, except when he played the captain of an English minesweeper and in his one try at the films, when he played an Indian. He was used to being told he had beautiful hands. They were big, and on the little finger of each hand he wore a signet ring which had had to have more gold put in to fit his fingers. He liked women whose buttocks just fit his spread hands, and although Nancy did not quite qualify, she was still on the small side. He wanted Nancy.

She had seen him probably a dozen times offstage. This was extremely painful to him, as he was every bit as aware of the number of times he had seen her as Nancy was of the number of times she had seen him. But it had always been Mr. Watterson and Mrs. Farley. The last three times she had seen him he had asked her to come in some afternoon, any afternoon, when she was in the neighborhood and had a minute. That was as far as he would go. If she came it would be with the understanding, et cetera. She knew that. And he knew as well as the next one what his reputation was, and all the women he knew also knew his reputation. "I have no etchings," he would say, "but I'll bet I can get you tight." Yes, he had honesty, and he was in the phone book.

It was Spring and Nancy had nothing to do all day until the daily ordeal with Paul, and last week she had seen Watterson and that time he had said: "You haven't come in for a drink, Mrs. Farley. What about that?"

"I haven't been thirsty."

"Thirsty? What has thirsty got to do with it? I'm going away for the week-end, but I'll be back Tuesday and I'm in the phone book, so I think you'll need a drink Tuesday. Or Thursday. Thirsty on Thursday. Or Wednesday. Or any other day. But beginning Tuesday." Then he had laughed to take the curse off it a little and also to let her know that of course he didn't think for one minute she'd come.

Once in her life with Paul, Nancy had let herself go in a kiss with another man, a hard kiss, standing up, with her mouth open and her legs apart. Now that she thought of it, that had been an actor too. A young actor, a practically unknown juvenile. This day, thinking about Watterson, and then about the juvenile, she went back to a truth which she had discovered for herself. It was something she discovered watching the progress of the extra-marital love life of her friends—while pretending not to watch at all. The truth was that there is a certain kind of man, attractive and famous in his way and sought after by women, whom sound women, women like Nancy herself, can conceivably have an affair with, but would not marry if he were the last man on earth. Once Nancy had heard the French wisecrack: that you can walk in the Bois without buying it. (It sounded better than the American: why keep a cow when milk is so cheap?) She would use the Bois remark to justify the behavior of some men whom she liked without liking their behavior. Only in the past three or four years had she even attempted to apply it woman to man. Well, she would not marry a man like Watterson, but since there were men like Watterson, why not find out about them? Why not find out about at least one other man? She knew every hair on Paul's body; they knew everything about each other that they might be likely to learn. A new man would be all strange, and Nancy wondered about herself, too. Maybe she was all strange, to herself as much as to any new man. And this was a good time to find out. As coolly as that she made up her mind to have an affair with John Watterson the actor.

She was sitting down with *The Good Earth* in front of her. She put it aside the moment she made her decision, got up and went to the closet where her hats were perched on things that looked like huge wooden collar-buttons. She took two hats, tried on both of them, and went back to the closet and took out a third, which she kept on. Gloves, purse, cigarette extinguished, and she was ready to go.

The car was parked outside. She got in and drove the few blocks to the block in which Watterson lived. When she came to his house she drove right past without changing her speed. Somehow—not today. She had a hunch. "If my foot had eased its pressure on the accelerator I'd have gone in. But it didn't, so, not today." She went to the movies—dear George Arliss, in "The Millionaire." "I suppose that's passing up an opportunity," she said to herself, thinking of Watterson, and enjoyed it over and over again.

"Do you want some coffee? I made some coffee if you can stand it," said Eddie.

"Huh?" said Gloria. "Oh. Eddie. Hello, Eddie darling."

"Hello, sweet. How about some coffee?"

"I'll make it. Just give me a minute to wake up."

"You don't have to make it. It's made. All you have to do is drink it."

"Oh, thank you." She sat up in bed and reached with both hands for the cup and saucer. She drank some. "Good," she said. "You make this?"

"Yes, ma'am," said Eddie.

He sat down easy on the bed so he would not jounce it and cause her to spill the coffee. "Did you have a good sleep?"

"Mm. But marvelous," she said. Then: "What about you? Where did you sleep? My beamish boy."

"Right here."

"Where 'right here'?" she repeated.

"There. On the chair."

"There, there, under the chair. Run, run, get the gun," she said. "No, where did you sleep, Baby?"

"The chair, I told you."

"You couldn't. With those legs? You couldn't sleep in any chair with those legs. What did you do with your legs?"

"I didn't do anything with them. I just put my fanny deep in the chair, and my legs—I don't know. Extended. They extended in a, uh, southwesterly direction and I went to sleep and my legs went to sleep."

"Ooh, you must feel like the wrath of God. Are you stiff?"

"No, as a matter of fact I feel fine. I was so tired when I went to sleep. I read a while after you dropped off, and I went to sleep with the light on. I woke up I guess around three or four and doused the light and got up and got an overcoat. Reminds me. You know that fur coat you came here in Sunday. It's still in my closet. You better haul off and do something about it. Take it back where you got it, will you?"

She seemed to think about it.

"Will you?" he said. "It's none of my business, Gloria, and what you do is—as I just said, it's none of my business, only I wish you'd return that coat. That's the kind of a fast one that—maybe you had every reason in the world to take it at the time, but you can't keep a coat like that, that cost four or five hundred dollars or more."

"Four or five *thousand*."

"Jesus! All the more reason. My God, Baby, a coat like that, that kind of money, they insure those things. The first thing you know they'll have detectives parked on our doorstep."

"I doubt it. I imagine I could keep that coat as long as I wanted to."

Eddie looked at her but not long. He stood up. "Do you want some more coffee? There is more if you want it."

"You don't like that, do you?"

"What difference does it make whether I like it or not? I told you what I thought. I have no say over you."

"You could have. Come here," she said. She held up her hands. He sat on the bed again. She put her arms around his head and held him to her bosom. "Oh, you don't know what I'd do for you, my precious darling. You're all I have, Eddie. Eddie, you're afraid of me. I'm no good, Eddie. I know I'm no good, but I could be good for you, Eddie, Eddie, my darling. Oh. Here. One second, darling. One second. My baby. My baby that needs a haircut. Ah, my— *What's that!*"

"Phone," he said.

"Answer it. It's bad luck not to answer it."

"I never heard that."

"It is. Go on, darling, answer it."

"Hello," he said into the telephone. "What? Yes. Speaking."

Pause.

"Why, you son of a—," he slammed the phone into its cradle. "The Bush Brothers Hand Laundry. The bastards."

"Is that the laundry you owe the money to?"

"Oh, God. Maybe it is. I forgot the name of that one. I don't think I ever did know it. No, it couldn't be the same one. The Bush Brothers were soliciting new work, so that's not the laundry that has my stuff. *They* don't want any new work. I want you."

"Do you? Here I am. Can anybody see us from those windows over there?"

"They might. I'll get it. I'll do it."

"I ought to get up."

"No, don't."

"I'll have a child."

"Don't you want a child?"

"Yes, very much. But, all right."

He sat up again and looked away. He made his gesture of shooting a foul in basketball, but with his fists clenched. "No," he said.

"It's all right, Eddie," she said. "It's all right, darling."

"No," he said. "No, it isn't. It's anything *but* all right."

"I'm clean. You needn't worry about that, if that's what's worrying you."

"Oh, I know. I wasn't thinking that."

"You used to think it. Didn't you?"

"A long time ago. Before I knew you."

"I'd never do that to you."

"I know. I don't think that any more. That's not what I'm thinking now."

"Don't you love me? Do you love Norma?"

"Nope."

"Have you told her you love her?"

"Once or twice."

"Does she love you?"

"No. I don't think so. Maybe."

"You're not sure."

"Oh, I'm sure. She doesn't love me. No, it hasn't anything to do with Norma. I love you."

She touched his shoulder. "I know. And I love you. The only one I ever did love, and the only one that ever loved me."

"I doubt that. Aw, you're *crazy*."

"No. I know. I know what it is even if you don't. Or maybe you do know and won't say it. It's because I've stayed with so many men that you think—"

"Don't talk. Don't say anything."

"All right," she said, and was silent, as was Eddie. Then she went on: "If you didn't know I'd stayed with so many men would you love me?"

"I do love you."

"But it would be different, wouldn't it? Of course. It's stupid of me to ask you that. But will you answer this truthfully? If you had just met me, without knowing a thing about me, what would you think of me?"

"How do you mean? There isn't a better-looking girl in this town, is my honest opinion. Your face, and you have a beautiful build." He stopped. She was staring ahead, not listening to him.

Despair.

"What are you thinking?" he said.

"Mm?"

"What are you thinking about so seriously?"

"It's all right with you now, isn't it? You'll be all right if I get up now, won't you? I mean and get dressed. Will you be all right?"

"I'll be all right."

"Because I know about men when they get excited and nothing happens. I wouldn't do that, either. If it's just a question of—oh, I don't know. I don't know how to talk to you now, Eddie. If you're going to be uncomfortable the rest of the day because we started something and didn't finish it, then let's finish it."

"Not that way I won't. I don't even feel like it now."

"No, neither do I, but I don't want you to feel as if you'd been pulled through a wringer."

"I won't. Don't worry about me."

"Then I guess I'll get up and take a shower."

"I'll get you a clean towel. I have one."

"All right."

"Here, I'll get you my bathrobe," he said, and stopped on his way to the closet. "The melancholy Dane has come, the saddest of the year." He smiled at her.

"What made you say that?"

"Damned if I know."

"What was it? 'The melancholy Dane has come, the saddest of the year.' Did that have any special meaning?"

"No, not a bit. I just thought of myself as melancholy, and you as melancholy, and melancholy made me think of the melancholy Dane, and then I got melancholy Dane mixed up. The melancholy Dane has come, the saddest of the year. It's nothing. I get rhythms and words mixed. The melancholy Dane has come, the saddest of the year. You used to come at nine o'clock but now you come at ten. I'll get you the bathrobe."

"And the towel. The towel's more important."

"No, it isn't. Not in my present state."

"Oh—do you really feel—"

"No, no. Not seriously."

She got out of bed and put on his bathrobe with her arms folded in front of her and her shoulders slightly hunched. She smiled at him and he smiled back. "I guess—I guess I never felt worse. Not sad. It isn't sadness the way I and you think of sadness and everybody else thinks of it. It's just this, that the one thing we have—nope. I won't say it."

"Oh, you've got to finish it now."

"Must I? Yes, I guess I must. Well, it's awful when you think that you've stayed with so many men and made such a mess of your life, and then someone you really want to stay with because you love him, that person is the one person you mustn't stay with because if you do he immediately becomes like the rest, and you don't want him to become like the rest. The thing he has that the rest haven't is that you haven't stayed with him."

"No, that's wrong. I don't want you to think that. It isn't true. Maybe it is, but I don't think so."

"No, I guess not, but—I don't know. The hell with it. You go on out for a walk. Ten minutes, and when you get back I'll be dressed."

"I'll buy a coffee ring."

She stood at the bathroom door, watching him put on his coat. "I'm a real bitch, Eddie. Do you know why?"

"Why?"

"Because I know what's right, but I'm so strongly tempted. You've never seen me without any clothes on, have you?"

"I'll get the coffee ring."

"That's right," she said.

When he did not return in fifteen minutes she began to worry, but he did return in ten minutes more, and they had more breakfast. He brought also a container of orange juice for her and a morning paper. "Mm. Legs Diamond's arrested," she said. "I met him once."

"Who didn't?" said Eddie. "What did they arrest him for? Parking near a fire plug, I'll bet."

"No. The Sullivan Law. That's uh, buzz buzz buzz buzz. Weapons. Deadly weapons in his possession. By Joel Sayre. This is an interesting article. Yes, I met Legs Diamond. What did you say? Who didn't? Lots of people didn't. I met him and the boy I was with didn't know him, even by reputation, and he kept making cracks. Governor Roosevelt's mother is sick and he's going to Paris where she is. She's in the hospital. Did you know that he has infantile paralysis? I never knew that till about a month or two ago. It never shows in his pictures, but he's always holding on to a state policeman's arm. Mm. As an aftermath of the. It says here as an aftermath of the airplane crash in which Knute Rockne lost his life the Fokker 29's are being given the air by the Department of Commerce. I can use Fokker in a sentence."

"I can use identification in a sentence. I'm not going away this summer because identification till October."

"Mine was dirty. Oh, the Pulitzer Prize. 'Alison's House'? Now for God's sake. 'Alison's House.' And *The Collected Poems of Robert Frost*. Well, I suppose that's all right. Edmund Duffy. Have you read *The Glass Key?*"

"No."

"It's by the same man who wrote *Maltese Falcon*, but it's not nearly as good. Oh, here's one for you. Listen to this. This is old Coolidge. 'Collins H. Gere, buzz buzz buzz buzz belongs to a generation of strong character and high purposes. Their passing marks the end of an era.' Whose passing? Does he mean strong character and high purposes' passing? Maybe he does. Maybe he's right. Do you know anybody with strong character and high purposes?"

"You."

"No, that's insulting. Think of someone. It has to be our generation, not older people, because Coolidge says their passing marks the end of an era, I guess he means the era that had strong character and high purposes. You, now. Let me see. Have you a strong character, darling?"

"No character."

"I'd say yes. About the high purposes, I'm not so sure. How are you on high purposes?"

"Low."

"No character and low purposes."

"Not low purposes," he said. "I just said I was low on *high* purposes. It isn't exactly the same thing."

"No, you're right. Well, I can't think of anyone I like that has strong character and high purposes. The Giants beat Brooklyn, if you're interested. Six to three was the score. Terry tripled, scoring when the Giants worked their squeeze play, Vergez laid down a perfect bunt. That shouldn't sound dirty, but when you have a mind like mine. I must look at Bethlehem Steel. My uncle has some of that. Closed at 44⅝. That's enough of that. Oh, here *is* sad news. Clayton, Jackson and Durante are splitting up. Schnozzle is going to Hollywood and they're breaking up. Oh, that's sad. That's the world's worst. Why did you have to show me this paper? No more wood number? No more hats? No more telegrams like the one he sent: 'Opening at Les Ambassadeurs as soon as I learn how to pronounce it.' Ah. That makes me sad, really sad. I hope he divides his salary with the others. Do you like this hat? On the right hand page. . . . On me."

"No. It hides the eyes."

"All right. I must go home to the bosom of my family. A flat chest if I ever saw one. Shall I call you tomorrow?"

"Yes. Oh, how about that fur coat?"

"I don't know. I'll call you tomorrow."

"Well, aren't you going to give it back to this fellow?"

"Well, I can't just take the coat to him, can I?"

"I don't see why not," said Eddie. "If you want to return the coat, you can. The way you do it is up to you."

"All right, I will then, if it'll make you feel any better. I'll call him up right now." She telephoned Liggett. "He's out of town, his office said."

"Well, phone him tomorrow."

She went home and there was a telegram there from Liggett, asking her to meet him at their favorite speakeasy at four. They had told her at his office that he was out of town, but her life was full of inconsistencies like that.

She was there before four, and took a small table by herself and watched the world come in. That afternoon the speakeasy was visited by a fairly representative crowd. On their lips soon would be her name, with varying opinions as to her character. Most of these people were famous in a way, although in most cases their fame did not extend more than twenty blocks to the north, forty blocks to the south, seven blocks to the east and four blocks to the west. There were others who were not famous, but were prominent in Harrisburg, Denver, Albany, Nashville, St. Paul-Minneapolis, Atlanta, Houston, Portland, Me., Dayton and Hartford. Among these was Mrs. Dunbar Vicks, of Cleveland, in town on one of her three or four visits a year to see a friend's private collection of dirty movies and to go to bed with a young man who formerly worked for Finchley. Mrs. Vicks was standing at the bar, with her back to Walter R. Loskind, the Hollywood supervisor, who was talking to Percy Luffberry, the director. Percy owed a great deal to Walter. When Percy was directing "War of Wars" he had small charges of explosive buried here and there in the ground, not enough to hurt anyone, but enough so that when the charge was set off the extras in German uniforms would be lifted off the ground. The extras had been warned about that and were being paid a bonus for this realism. It went all right until Percy decided he wanted to have one extra crawling along the ground instead of walking. When the charge was set off the extra lost both eyes, and if Walter hadn't stood by Percy, Percy would have been in a hell of a fix. Seated directly across the room was Mrs. Noel Lincoln, wife of the famous sportsman-financier, who had had four miscarriages before she found out (or before her doctor dared tell her) that a bit of bad luck on the part of her husband was responsible for these misfortunes. Mrs. Lincoln was sitting with pretty little Alicia Lincoln, her niece by marriage, who was the source of cocaine supply for a very intimate group of her friends in society, the theater, and the arts. Alicia was waiting for a boy named Gerald, whom she took to places where girls could not go unescorted. Bruce Wix, the artists' representative, came in and tried to get the eye of Walter R. Loskind, but Walter did not look. Bruce stood alone at the bar. Henry White, the writer, was told he was wanted on the telephone—the first move, although he did not know it, in the house technique of getting rid of a drunk. On the way out he bowed to Dr. (D.D.S.) Jack Fry, who was arriving with one of his beautiful companions. It was after-noon, so the companion was not wearing the Fry pearls, which Dr. Fry always loaned to show girls and actresses while they were out with him. Mr. and Mrs. Whitney Hofman, of Gibbsville, Pennsylvania, arrived at this time, wishing they had been better friends so they could find something to talk about without self-consciousness. They were joined by Whitney's cousin Scott Hofman, a cross-eyed fellow who at the age of thirty did not have to shave more than once a week. Mike Romanoff came in, looked around the room, and went out again. A party of six young people, Mr. and Mrs. Mortimer House, Mr. and Mrs. Jack Whitehall, and Miss Sylvia House and Mr. Irving Ruskin, were told at the door that they could not come in because they had not made reservations. They had to make way for a Latin-American diplo-mat whose appointment to Washington showed what his country thought of this. He had had malaria *before* he caught *siflis*, which is the wrong order for an automatic cure. Inside again, banging on his table for a waiter, sat Ludovici, the artist, who had several unretouched nude photographs of Gloria which she wished she had back. He was with June Blake, show girl and model, who after four days was still cheerful over winning nearly a thousand dollars on Twenty Grand. The bet had not been made through a bookmaker, and involved no cash outlay on her part. It was a slightly intricate arrangement between herself and Archie Jelliffe, the axle man, who told June he would place the bet for her if she would agree to bring to his country place a certain virgin he wanted to know better. Was it June's fault that the former virgin was at this minute in a private hospital? Robert Emerson, the magazine publisher, came in with his vice-president, Jerry Watlington. Emerson was trying to make life pleasanter for Watlington, who had just been blackballed at a good club which Emerson belonged to. Emerson sincerely regretted the blackball, now that he had put it in. Mad Horace H. Tuttle, who had been kicked out of two famous prep schools for incendiarism, was there with Mrs. Denis Johnstone Humphries (whose three names seldom were spelled right), of Sewickley Heights, near Pittsburgh. Mrs. Humphries was telling Horace how she had to drive around in a station wagon because strikers stoned her Rolls. The worst of it was she was riding in the Rolls at the time, personally holding her entry for the Flower Show, and when the stones began to beat against the car she had presence of mind enough to lie on the floor, but forgot about the roses and crushed them. Her story was not interrupted when Horace nodded to Billy Jones, the gentleman jockey, who walked quickly to the bar with two dollars in his hand, had a quick double whiskey-soda, and walked out, with the two dollars in his hand. The bartender simply entered it against Billy's account—Billy was supposed to be a little screwy from knocks on the head. Kitty Meredith, the movie actress, came in with her adopted son, four years old, and everybody said how cute he was, what poise, as he took a sip of her drink.

"I'm sorry I'm late," said Liggett.

Gloria looked up. "It's all right," she said. "In five more minutes I'd have gone, or at least I wouldn't have been alone."

"Who? That one that's looking at you now?"

"I won't tell you," she said.

"Uh, what are you drinking?"

"Ale."

"One ale, and a brandy and soda."

"Well, what's it all about?" said Gloria. "I went home and your telegram was there. I phoned you at your office, but they said you'd gone away."

"Where were you last night?"

"Oh, no. Not in that tone. Who do you think you are?"

"All right, I'm sorry." He went through the business of getting a cigarette lit, then he remembered and offered her one. That doubled the delay before he said: "If what I want to ask you makes you very angry will you try not to hold it against me? First of all—please let me talk—first of all, I think you know I'm crazy about you. You know that, don't you?"

No answer.

He repeated: "You know that, don't you?"

"You said not to interrupt."

"Well, you do know that, don't you?"

"I'm not so sure. Crazy about me doesn't mean anything."

"Well, I am. In the worst way. Don't make a joke about it. I am crazy about you. I can't think of anything but you. I can't make sense for thinking about how long it's going to be before I see you again. When I don't know where you are, like last night. I was here and all over, trying to find you." He saw she was not paying much attention.

"You're right," he went on. "That's not what I want to talk about. At least not now. Or I mean I want to talk about it, now, but there is another matter."

"That's what I thought."

"That's what you thought. Well—Jesus, I wish we were some place else. Drink your drink and we'll get out of here. What I want to say I don't want to say in this madhouse, all these people yelling their heads off."

She gulped some beer and left some in the glass. "That's all I want."

He left two dollar bills and a quarter on the table and they went out. He refused the taxi at the door, but walked down the block towards Fifth Avenue and took a taxi that was moving. "Fortieth Street and Seventh Avenue," he told the driver.

"Where are we going?"

"That place you took me to the other night. The newspaper place." He took off his hat and held it on his knee. "You know, Gloria, I'm in a bad way about you. The thing that's happened to me usually happens to men I know who have been good husbands. I don't mean that I've been an especially bad husband. I've been good to my wife in most ways. I've always kept things from her that would hurt her—"

"You're the kind of man that would have a mistress and insult her in front of your wife because you thought that would mislead her."

"You're wrong. No, you're right. The only time I had a mistress that my wife knew I did say disparaging things about her, the mistress. How do you know these things? You're not more than I'd say twenty-two. How do you know these things?"

"How do I know them? What else has there been in my life but finding out things like that? But go on, tell me about what happens to men of your age."

"What happens to men of my age. What happens to men of my age is this, if they've been good husbands. They go along being good husbands, working hard and having a good time, playing golf, making a little money, going to parties with the same crowd, and then sometimes it's a woman they've known all their lives, and sometimes it's a filing clerk in the office, and sometimes it's a singer in a night club. I know of one case where it was a man and his sister. Not that they ever did anything about it, except that the man committed suicide, that's all. He'd been happily married—oh, what the hell am I talking about, happily married. Is anybody happily married? I often wonder whether anybody is." He stopped talking.

"What made you stop all of a sudden? You were going great."

"Was I?"

"I'll say."

"I just discovered something, or almost did. Wondering whether anyone was happily married. I wondered if I was, and then I wondered if I wasn't. God, I'm in a worse spot than anyone. I don't even know if I'm unhappily married. I don't know anything about myself. I must be happy, because whenever I've looked back and remembered times when I was happy, I always find that I didn't know I was happy when I was. Well, if I'm happy now it's because of you. Let me rave. I'm thinking out loud."

"A little too loud for the taxi driver, or else maybe not loud enough."

"Well, that's all he's going to hear. This is the end of the line."

This time they were not greeted by the voluble bartender, but by a tall sad man who looked as though he ought to be a Texas Ranger. They went to the small room off the bar where there were booths, and when the bartender brought their drinks Liggett began: "I didn't feel like talking about this in the taxi. Now I have to talk and get it over with. Gloria, did you take a fur coat out of my apartment Sunday?"

Silence.

"Did you? Are you not answering because you're angry, or what?"

"What do you think?"

"I'm asking you."

"Yes, I took it."

"Well,—will you give it back? It's my wife's coat, and I've had a hard time keeping her from telling the police."

"Why don't you let her tell the police?"

"Do you really want the coat that much?"

"I could have it, couldn't I?"

"Yes. You could, but not very easily. Uh, naturally it would break up my home. The first thing the detectives would do would be to question the employees of the apartment house, and the elevator operator would remember your leaving with the coat on Sunday. Then they'd tell my wife there was a girl in the apartment Saturday night, and while my wife might possibly forgive my being unfaithful, for the sake of the children, I don't think she'd forgive my bringing anyone into her home. It's her home, you know, even more than it is mine, or as much. Well, so that would break up the home, but that wouldn't be all. When the police are notified in a thing like that they like to make an arrest, so they'd probably find out who you were."

"From you?"

"No. Not from me. They could arrest me, I suppose, but I wouldn't tell them who it was. But from—did you take a taxi? You must have. Well, they'd find out where you went, and so on. They have ways of finding out, without any help from me. So you wouldn't have the coat long. And what if my wife told the insurance people? That would fix me in a business way. Not that there's much left to be fixed, but at least I have a good job. Well, if my wife became vindictive and told the insurance people to, uh, proceed just as though I were a stranger, they would arrest me for compounding a felony or accessory before the fact or something like that, and the tabloids would get hold of it. No, you can't win."

"Crime does not pay, eh?"

"I don't know whether it does or not, but I do know this, you won't gain anything by keeping the coat."

"Except the coat."

"Not even the coat. They'll take it away from you. Oh, come on, don't be unreasonable. I'll buy you a coat just like it."

"It's an expensive coat."

"It's insured for I think four thousand dollars. That's quite an item for an insurance company to have to make good on. What are you doing, having fun?"

"A little. You have fun with me Saturday night. Big stuff, tearing my dress and all that old cave-man act."

"I'm sorry about that. I've told you before I was sorry."

"It didn't sound very convincing before, but now that you're in a jam—"

"Listen, God damn it—"

"Don't swear at me. I'm going."

"Oh, no, you're not."

"Oh, yes, I *am*, and don't you try to stop me, if you know what's good for you."

"Listen, you little bitch, I'll go to jail before I let you get away with this, and you will too. Sit down." He reached for her hand, but she ran out to the barroom.

"Let me out of here," she said to the bartender.

"Don't open that door," said Liggett.

"Out of the way, Mister," said the bartender.

"What is it, Joe?" said a man at the bar, who Liggett saw was in uniform. The man turned, and it was a patrolman's uniform. The cop put on his cap and came over.

"Don't hurt him. Just let me out," said Gloria.

"Is he molesting you, lady?" said the cop.

"I just want to get out," said Gloria.

"Listen, officer—"

"Out of the way, wise guy," said the cop, and in some manner which Liggett did not understand the cop put his hand inside Liggett's coat and held him by the vest high up. He could not move. They let Gloria out and the cop still held Liggett.

"Wuddle we do with him, Joe?" said the cop. "You know him?"

"I never seen him before. Who are you, anyway?"

"I can identify myself."

"Well, identify yourself," said the cop.

"If you let me, I will," said Liggett.

"Stand in back of him, Joe, just in case."

"Oh, I won't do anything."

"Huh, you're telling me. You picked the wrong spot to try anything, fellow, didn't he, Joe?"

"Just leave him try something, he'll find out."

"I happen to be a very good friend of Pat Casey, if you're interested," said Liggett.

"A friend of Pat Casey's," said the cop. "He says he's a friend of Pat Casey's, Joe."

"Wuddia know about that," said Joe.

Whereupon the cop slapped Liggett back and forth on the face with the palm and the back of his hand. "A friend . . . of Pat . . . Casey. Don't give me that, you son of a bitch. I don't care if you're a friend of the Pope of Rome, any . . . son . . . of a bitch . . . that tries to . . . skeer me . . . with who he knows. Now get outa here. Pat Casey!"

"Go on. Get out," said Joe.

Liggett could hardly see. There were tears in his eyes from the cop's slaps on his nose. "Like hell I will," he said, ready to fight. The cop reached out and pushed him hard and quick, and he went down on his back. Joe, who had been standing in back of him, had knelt down back of his legs and all the cop had to do was push and down he went. He fell outside the speakeasy on the stair landing, and the two men began kicking him and kicked him until he crawled away and went down the stairs.

He had no hat, he could hardly see, his clothes were a mess of dirt and phlegmy spit that he had picked up on the floor, he was badly shaken by hitting his coccyx when the cop pushed him, his nose was bleeding, his body was full of sharp pains where they had kicked him.

To be deprived of the right to fight back when you have nothing left to lose is awful, and that made Liggett feel weak. They had beaten him in a few minutes worse than he ever had been beaten before, and he knew he could have gone on fighting now till they killed him, but they would not give him the chance, the bastards. Outside the world was disinterested or perhaps even friendly, but there was no fighting outside. It was inside, upstairs, where there was fighting, and he wanted to go back and fight those two; no rules, but kick and punch and swing and butt and bite. The only thing was, he was facing the street now, and it was too damn much trouble to turn around, and inside of him he knew he did not have the strength to climb the stairs. If he could be transported up the stairs and inside he could fight, but the stairs were too much. He heard the door upstairs being opened, then closing as his hat landed at his feet. He reached down painfully and picked it up and put it on his aching head, and walked out to the street. He stumbled along into a taxi. The driver didn't want him to get in, but was afraid to take a chance on crossing him. Then as the driver said: "Where to?" Gloria opened the door of the cab.

"It's all right, I know him," she said.

"Okay, Miss Wandrous," said the driver.

"Out. Get out. Get outa my tax'cab," said Liggett.

"Go to 274 Horatio Street," Gloria told the driver.

"Okay," said the driver, and reached back to close the door, which had clicked only once.

Liggett got up and opened the door, mumbling: "I'm not going anywhere with you." She tried to stop him but not very hard. It wasn't much use trying and the streets were full of people, little people coming up from the fur center to pile into the southernmost entrance to the Times Square subway station. She saw Liggett get into another cab.

"Will I folly him?" said her driver.

"Yes, will you please?" she said.

Her taxi followed his to within a block of his home. She stopped and watched him get out, saw the doorman at his apartment pay the cab driver. "Go to the Horatio Street number," she said.

Eddie did not answer his bell, though she rang for five minutes. She left a note for him and went home.

6

You COULD still read a newspaper in the street when Nancy and Paul Farley arrived at the Liggetts'. Nancy was wearing a printed chiffon frock, Farley was wearing a dinner jacket with shawl collar, a soft shirt, a cummerbund instead of a waistcoat, and pumps. The pumps were old and a little cracked, and in his hand he had a gray felt hat that certainly did not look new. Emily wondered where she had got the idea Farley would be dressed like something out of the theater programs. Where? From Weston, of course. Where, where was Weston? What had happened in Philadelphia?

"Good evening, Mrs. Farley, Mr. Farley. Let's go in here, I think it's cooler."

"It is cool, isn't it?" said Nancy.

"Bobbie did this building," said Paul.

"A friend of ours," Nancy explained. "Robert Scott? The architect? Do you know him, by any chance?"

"No, I don't believe I do," said Emily. "All right, Mary. The cocktail things. Mr. Farley, do you mind if I pass that job on to you? My husband hasn't arrived! He went to Philadelphia this morning and I expected him home at four, but I could have been mistaken. Perhaps he meant the four o'clock train, which arrives at six I think. He may have stopped at the office on the way uptown. It must be important, because it isn't a bit like him not to phone."

"Well, one thing, it isn't his health," said Paul. "I mean lack of it. When I saw him on Sunday I said to Nancy how well he looked."

"Yes, I only got a fleeting glimpse of him but I noticed too how well he looked," said Nancy. "He always gives the impression of strength."

"Yes, not like most men that were athletes in college," said Paul. "They usually . . ." he made a gesture of big-belly.

"Oh, he *was* an athlete?" said Nancy.

"He was on the Yale crew," said Emily. "I think he keeps well. He played some court tennis this past winter."

"Oh, really?" said Paul. "That must be a swell game. I've never played it. I've gone back and forth from squash to squash rackets and this winter I played a little handball, but never court tennis."

"I never know one from the other," said Nancy.

"Neither do I," said Emily. "Mr. Farley, would you like to mix a cocktail? If you have anything in mind. There's gin and French and Italian vermouth, but we could just as easily have something else."

"I like a Martini and so does Nancy."

"I think a Martini," said Emily.

"Tell Mrs. Liggett what you told me about shaking Martinis," said Nancy.

"Oh, yes," said Farley. "You know, like everyone else, I suppose, I've been going for years on the theory that a Martini ought to be stirred and not shaken?"

"Yes, that's what I've always heard," said Emily.

"Well, in London last year I talked with an English bartender who told me that theory's all wrong. American, he said."

"Scornfully," said Nancy.

"Very scornfully," said Paul.

"I can imagine very scornfully," said Emily.

"Well, we've always been taught that if you shake a Martini you bruise the cocktail. I've always taken a holy delight in not bruising a poor little cocktail until this English barkeep explained the right way, or his way, and I must say it sounds plausible. He told me a Martini ought to be shaken very hard, briskly, a few vigorous shakes up and down, so that the gin and vermouth would be cracked into a proper *foamy* mixture. He said Americans, especially in these dark ages—I mean Prohibition, not the depression. We have a tendency to drink a cocktail in two gulps, for the effect, whereas if you shake the cocktail the various ingredients go into solution more completely, and the result is a foamy drink—not very noticeably foamy, but more foamy than not—and you have a cocktail that you can sip, almost like champagne."

"Oh, I never heard that," said Emily. "It does sound like a plausible theory, as you say."

"You see, our cocktails, stirred, are syrupy and very strong. Two Martinis out of a stirred batch have much more effect than two shaken ones. Stirred cocktails are little more than straight gin and vermouth. So we've followed his advice and I must say I think he's right."

"Let's do it that way, then. I'll get the other shaker. This one has only the stirring kind of top."

"Oh, no, not if it means—"

"Not at all," said Emily. "I want to try your way." She went to the dining-room and came back with a shaker.

"I noticed you have new cocktail shakers too," said Nancy. "You know, we have newer cocktail shakers and things like that than a cousin of Paul's. She was married five years ago, and by actual count she was given twenty-two cocktail shakers for wedding presents. All sorts. And those she kept look positively obsolete compared with ours. Ours are all new, within the last two years."

"When Weston and I were married no one would have thought of giving a cocktail shaker."

"We didn't get a single one," said Nancy.

"There," said Paul. "I hope you like this after all my build-up, Mrs. Liggett."

She tasted her cocktail. "Oh, yes, by all means. Oh, even I can see the difference right away."

"Isn't it a lot better?" said Nancy.

"Yes. Weston will like it too, I know. His favorite drink is whiskey and soda. He'd almost rather not drink cocktails for that reason, that they're too syrupy. This ought to be the solution of the cocktail problem for him. Speaking of Weston, I think we'll wait five more minutes and if he hasn't arrived we'll begin without him. He's usually so punctual about meals, and I know he was especially anxious to be on time for the Farleys. I hate being late for the theater, so we'll give him five more minutes. I'm so glad you hadn't seen 'Tomorrow and Tomorrow.' Herbert Marshall has *such* charm, don't you think so, Mrs. Farley?"

"Just about the most charming man I know. Not that I know him. I did meet him."

"I don't see how he gets around with that leg of his," said Paul.

"I can't even tell which one it is, and I watch every time," said Nancy.

"He lost it in the war, didn't he?" said Emily.

"I believe so," said Nancy.

"Yes, he did. He was in the British Army," said Paul.

"*Not* in the Austrian Army, dear?" said Nancy.

Everyone laughed politely. "As a matter of fact he was in the Austrian Army," said Paul. "He was a spy."

"No, no. That's not getting out of it," said Nancy. "Besides, that's not original. Who was it said that first? You read it in the *New Yorker*."

"What was that?" asked Emily.

"Oh, you must have seen it. I think it was in the Talk of the Town column. George S. Kaufman, you know, he wrote 'Once In a Lifetime' and a hundred other plays."

"Yes," said Emily.

"Well, he and some of the Algonquin literati were together one night and there was a stranger in their midst who kept bragging about his ancestry, and finally Kaufman, who is a Jew, spoke up and said: 'I had an ancestor a Crusader.' The stranger looked askance and Kaufman went on: 'Yes, his name was Sir Reginald Kaufman. He was a spy.'"

"All right, except that it was Sir Roderick Kaufman," said Nancy.

Emily laughed. In one more minute she would have taken her guests in to dinner, but before the minute was up the doorbell rang and then the door was opened and Liggett came in, supported by the elevator operator and the doorman, who Emily noticed first was trying to take off his cap.

"Oh, God," said Emily.

"Good Lord," said Paul.

Nancy sucked in her breath.

"What in God's name happened, darling?" said Emily, going to him.

"I'll take this arm," said Paul to the doorman.

"Please let me walk by myself," said Liggett, and shook off his helpers. "I'm terribly sorry, Mrs. Farley, but you'll have to excuse me tonight."

"Oh, well, of course," said Nancy.

"Can't I give you a hand, old man?" said Paul.

"No, thanks," said Liggett. "Emily—will you—I think Mrs. Farley, Mr. Farley."

"Let me help you to your room," said Farley. "I think I ought to do this, Mrs. Liggett."

"I'd rather you didn't, Farley. Thanks just the same, but I'd really rather you didn't," said Liggett. "Apologize to you, Emily, before the Farleys."

"Oh, they understand I'm sure," said Emily. "Mrs. Farley, Mr. Farley, you will excuse us I know?"

"Of course," said Farley. "If you want me to do anything?"

"No, thank you. I'll manage. I'm sorry."

"Come on, darling," said Nancy. "Anything at all, Mrs. Liggett. Please call us."

"Thank you both," said Emily.

The Farleys left. Nancy could hardly wait till they got inside a taxi where only Paul could see her crying. "Oh, what a terrible thing. What an awful sight." She put her arms around Paul and wept. "That poor unhappy woman. To have that happen to her. Ugh. Disgusting beast. No wonder, no wonder she has such sad eyes."

"Yes, and the son of a bitch was no more in Philadelphia than I was. I saw him getting tanked up at the Yale Club at lunch time. He didn't see me, but I saw him." He waited. "But it's nothing for you to be upset about, darling. They aren't even close friends of ours."

"I'll stop," said Nancy.

"We'll go to Longchamps."

"No, let's go where we can drink," said Nancy.

When Gloria came home in time for dinner her uncle told her he would like to have a talk with her before dinner, or after dinner, if there wasn't time before dinner. She said they might as well talk now, before dinner.

"Well," he began, "I don't think you've been looking at all well lately. I think you ought to get out of New York for a month or two. I really do, Gloria."

Yes, she had been thinking that too, but she wondered how often he had had a chance to see her to decide she wasn't looking well. "I haven't saved anything out of my allowance," she said, "and as for work—well, you know."

"This would be a birthday present. It's a little early for a birthday present, but does it make any difference what time of the year it is when you get your present? I'll send you a penny postcard when your birthday comes, and remind you that you've had your present. That is, providing you want to take a trip."

"But can you afford it?"

"Yes, I can afford it. We don't live on our income any more, Baby"—he often called her that—"we've been selling bonds and preferred stocks, your mother and I."

"Oh. On account of me? Do I cost that much?"

He laughed. "No-ho-ho. You don't seem to realize. Don't you know what's been going on in this country, Baby? We're in the midst of a *depression*. The worst depression in history. You know something about the stock market situation, don't you?"

"I looked up your Bethlehem Steel this morning or yesterday. I forget when it was."

"Oh, that's all gone, long since, my Steel. And it was U. S. Steel, not Bethlehem."

"Oh, then I was wrong."

"I'm glad you took an interest. No, what I've been doing, I've been getting rid of everything I can and do you know what I've been doing? Buying gold."

"Gold? You mean real gold, the what do they call it—bullion?"

"The real article. Coins, when I can get them, and gold bars, and a few gold certificates, but I haven't much faith in *them*. You know, I don't like to frighten you, but it's going to be a lot worse before it's any better, as the fellow says."

"How do you mean?"

"Well, I'll tell you. A man I know slightly, he was one of the smartest traders in Wall Street. You wouldn't know his name, because I don't think I ever had occasion to mention it except perhaps to your mother and it wouldn't have interested you. He was a *real* plunger, that fellow. The stories they told downtown about this man, they were sensational. A Jew, naturally. Why, say, that fellow *couldn't* lose. *And*, he was shrewd, the way all Jews are. Well, as I say, he's always been a pretty smart trader. They say he was the only one that called the turn in 1929. He got out of the market in August 1929, at the peak. Everybody told him, why, you're crazy, they all said. Passing up millions. Millions, they told him. Sure, he said. Well, I'm willing to pass them up and keep what I have, he told them, and of course they all laughed when he told them he was going to retire and sit back and watch the ticker from a café in Paris. Retire and only thirty-eight years of age? Huh. They never heard such talk, the wisenheimers downtown. Him retire? No. It was in his blood, they said. He'd be back. He'd go to France and make a little whoopee, but he'd be back and in the market just as deeply as ever. But he fooled them. He went to France, all right, and I suppose he made whoopee because I happen to know he has quite a reputation that way. And they were right saying he'd be back, but not the way they thought. He came back first week in November, two years ago, right after the crash. Know what he did? He bought a Rolls-Royce Phantom that originally cost over eighteen thousand dollars, he bought that for a thousand-dollar bill. He bought a big place out on Long Island. I don't know exactly what he paid for it, but one fellow told me he got it for not a cent more than the owner paid for one of those big indoor tennis courts they have out there. For that he got the whole estate, the land, the house proper, stables, garages, everything. Yacht landing. Oh, almost forgot. A hundred and eighty-foot yacht for eighteen thousand dollars. That figure I do know because I remember hearing he said a hundred dollars a foot was enough for any yacht. And mind you, the estate was with all the furniture. And all because he got out in time and had the cash. Everything he had was cash. Wouldn't lend a cent. Not one red cent, for any kind of interest. Not even a hundred per cent interest. Just wasn't interested, he said. Buy, yes. He bought cars, houses, big estates, yachts, paintings worth their weight in radium, practically. But lend money? no. He said it was his way of getting even with the wisenheimers that laughed at him the summer before when he said he was going to retire."

"Uncle, did you say you *knew* this man?" said Gloria.

"Oh, yes. Used to see him around. I knew him to say *hello* to."

"Where is he now? I mean whatever became of him?"

"Ah, that's what I was going to tell you," said Vandamm. "I was inquiring about him, whatever became of him, about a month or two ago, and fellow I see every once in a while, a professional bridge player now. I mean makes his living that way, but he used to be a customer's man. I ran into him a short time ago at the New York A. C. and we had a glass of beer together, just friendly because he knows I don't go in for playing bridge for high stakes. We got to talking and in the course of the conversation Jack Wiston's name—that was his name, Jack Wiston, if you want to know his name. His name came up and I asked this friend of mine whatever became of Jack? 'Didn't you hear?' my friend said. Very surprised. He thought everybody knew about Wiston. Seems Wiston had the yacht reconditioned and started out on a trip around the world. I understand he had a couple of Follies girls with him and one or two friends. When they got to one of the South Sea Islands, Wiston said that was as far as he was going, and sent everybody on home in the yacht. Bought himself a big copra plantation—"

"I've always wanted to ask that, what's a copra plantation?"

"Uh, copra? It's what they get cocoanut oil from. So—"

"I've often wondered when I read stories in the *Cosmopolitan*—"

"Well, that's what Wiston must have done too, because it was one of those Dutch islands. The story that got back was that Wiston didn't believe in big nations any more. Large countries, doomed to failure, he said. The trend was the other way. There wasn't a single major power in the world that wasn't in sorry straits, but take any little country like Holland or Belgium and Denmark, they were weathering the depression better than *any* large country, irregardless of which one it was. The way I heard, he said he was thirty-eight, thirty-nine then, years of age, he had his good health and a reasonable expectation of at least twenty more years of an active life, and he didn't want to be beaten to death or shot next year, 1932."

"What?"

"That's his theory. Next year, according to Wiston, is a presidential year, and we're going to have a revolution."

"Oh, hooey."

"Well, I don't know. A lot of fellows are taking that seriously. A lot of people think there's going to be a change. Looks like Al Smith might get in or Owen D. Young. Some Democrat. But will things be any better? I doubt it. Hoover must have something up his sleeve or things would be a lot worse than they are right now."

"But you said a revolution. What kind of a revolution? You mean radicals? I know they talk all the time, but I'd rather have Hoover— well, not Hoover, but I wouldn't want to be governed by some of those people. I've met some of them on parties and they're awful."

"Yes, but what about the farmers? They're dissatisfied. What about in Pittsburgh, all those big factories closed down? I don't know where it's all going to end up. All I can do is do the best I can for you and your mother, so every chance I get I'm turning everything into gold."

"You're not a chemist. You're an alchemist," said Gloria.

"Ah ha ha ha ha. Very good. Quite a sense of humor, Baby."

"Dinner, you two," said Gloria's mother.

"I'm ready," said Vandamm. He whispered to Gloria: "I'll talk to you later about the vacation."

Liggett's story to Emily that night was that he and his friend Casey had gone the rounds of Hell's Kitchen speakeasies, trying to do their own detective work. An old enemy of Casey's turned up, Liggett said, and there was a free for all.

The next day he told her the truth, keeping back only the name of the girl.

He awoke that day stiff with pain and with an early realization that there was something ahead that he had to face. It was totally unlike the feeling he had in the war, when he would know each night that the next morning there would be a bombardment and the danger of an attack; it was less unlike the nervous fear in the days when he first began to row in college; the race day would be long until the race started in the late afternoon, and full of things to worry about, but then the boring alumni and muscle-feelers and door-openers would start coming around noon and by starting time the race was almost a pleasant escape. No, this was more like the time he had gonorrhea and had to force himself to the doctor's office, horribly in ignorance of what the treatment was going to be. He had known men with it, of course, but he was sure his was a special case and he could not talk to anyone about it. This morning was like that and like a time when he stayed away from the dentist for two and a half years. It was the knowledge that the unpleasant thing ahead was something that he himself had to force himself to do, that it was in his own hands, no one else could make him do it.

He thought he was awake very early and long before Emily, but when he groaned a little in a way that was like a sigh, she was standing at his bed before his eyes were fully open. She had been sleeping in a chaise-longue which she had moved into his room. His first angry thought was that she had done that to try to catch what he might say in his sleep, but her manner and her words changed this: "What is it, darling?"

He looked up at her, taking a good look at her for a change.

"Go on back to sleep, darling. It's ten minutes of six. Or shall I get you something? A bedpan?"

"No. I don't want anything."

"Does it hurt? Is it painful where they hit you?"

"*Who* hit me?"

"The men, the friends of Casey's that beat you up. Oh, you poor dear. You haven't tried to move. You don't know yet that you're hurt. Well, don't try to move. You've been badly beaten up, darling. Do you want me to get in bed with you? I'll keep you warm and I won't bump you. You don't want me to close the window, do you? Get some more sleep if you can."

"I think I will," he said. Then: "What about you?"

"Oh, don't worry about me. It's almost my regular time to be up anyway. The girls will be awake in another half or three quarters of an hour."

"I don't want to see them."

"I know. I won't let them come in. You go on back to sleep. I'll connect the buzzer." She referred to the line which ran from the button beside his bed to the kitchen, a line which had not been used since it was installed.

She had made the offer to get in bed with him and followed it up quickly with more talk because it meant something to her, and he had not taken up the offer immediately. She would not ask him again. Whatever he wanted she would do, and he did not want her to lie beside him.

She went to her own room. It was too early for the mail, too early for the *Times* and the *Tribune*. There was something wrong about reading a book so early in the day, like ice cream for breakfast. She thought she might have a bath, but it was too early for that too; that is, there was so much power behind the wide-mouthed faucet in her tub that it would be inconsiderate of the girls' sleep to run a tub now. It had been a source of unexpressed complaint; Emily meant to have something done about it, but it was one of those things that made her accuse herself of being a far from perfect housewife; one of the things she did not do because it was good enough, in satisfactory working condition, and only once in a while she would be reminded that there was room for improvement. Thinking of the girls she went to their room.

Barbara was actively at sleep, lying on her right side with her left arm almost straight up on the pillow. Compared with Ruth she was lying in a twisted position. Ruth was lying on her back with her mouth open just a little and her arms stretched out, at first reminding Emily of the Crucifixion, but then almost immediately of a Red Cross poster. Ruth was the daughter she would watch and be proud of; Barbara would be the one she would guard and protect and make sacrifices for if they became necessary. But it was Ruth who interested her now, because Ruth was closer to Weston, and it was Weston who was all on Emily's mind at present.

She might be dead, might Ruth, lying there so still, so quietly asleep with one leg bent a little but not enough to take away from the illusion of death which—knowing it to be an illusion—Emily created for the moment.

Ruth opened her eyes without moving any other part of her body, without moving so much as a muscle. She had that close but superior look of one who comes awake completely and effortlessly. "Mummy," she said.

"Shh."

"Is it time for school?"

"No." Emily whispered.

"Good." Ruth smiled and closed her eyes again, then opened them again to say: "Why are you up so early?"

"I don't want you to make any noise. Daddy isn't feeling well and we mustn't make any noise."

"What's the matter with Daddy?"

"He was beaten up in a fight last night." Emily did not know what she was saying until she had said it. It had not occurred to her to lie to this child of hers. The words were out, and Emily looked for a reason for the frankness. She could find none.

"Oh." Ruth said it and said it again: "Oh."

Emily could see what was going on in her mind, could tell it from the two ohs. The first was pain and the quick sympathy that you would expect from Ruth. The second was wanting to ask how, where, when, by whom, how badly—and a firm control of her tongue.

"He wasn't *badly* hurt," said Emily, "but they hurt him. When Barbara wakes up don't say anything about it to her, dear."

"She'll be noisy, though. You know how she always is."

"Tell her Daddy has a headache and not to make any noise."

"Is there anything I can do? I don't want to go back to sleep now."

"The best thing is to keep quiet, not to make a sound that will disturb Daddy."

"How did they hurt him?"

"In the ribs mostly, and punched him in the face. Don't worry about him, Ruthie. Try to sleep again."

She smoothed her daughter's hair, as though Ruth had a fever, and ended with a few little pats on the forehead. She went to the kitchen and started the coffee percolator. She sat down and waited, staring straight ahead and thinking about Ruth with her lovely intelligent innocent eyes, and her sing-song voice when she said: "What's the matter with Daddy?" All the innocent things about her eyes and her face and her ruffled hair and her voice—then she thought of the form outlined under the bed-clothes. At this minute, probably in New Haven or in Cambridge, some young man who would one day . . . No, it would be all right. It would be love with Ruth, one love. Barbara was the one to worry about, with one love after another, and many pains and the need for watching. Emily thought she knew for the first time why she thought oftener of Ruth. The reason was that Ruth and she understood each other; Ruth understood about Barbara, and she understood about herself. That was good—but it was too neat. No; if Ruth understood so much then she must be unhappy about something else. What? She went back to the thoughts of Ruth's little-woman's body. It was all there, ready to move in on life; the breasts were small, but they were there; the hips were not large, but they were there; and part of the intelligence, or part of the information behind the intelligent look of the eyes was the knowledge Emily had imparted to Ruth nearly two years ago. Ruth knew the mechanics of the female, as much as could be told in words. No, no. The look of those eyes, it wasn't an intelligent look; it was just that they were intelligent eyes. There was a difference. But Emily made up her mind that she would watch Ruth with boys, *because of* love.

She poured the coffee and took a cup in to Weston's room. "I brought you some coffee," she said.

What she did not know was that he had meanwhile manufactured the antagonism that was necessary before he could tell her the truth. Also he wanted to tell her because he felt that if he told her the truth as it was up to this minute, he would not be so much to blame if something else was going to happen—and he was not by any means sure that nothing else was going to happen. He had to see Gloria again, he knew that, and he knew that even though he didn't want Gloria now, the next thing he would want would be Gloria.

"Will you get me a cigarette out of my coat pocket, please?" he said. "Thanks. Emily, I want to tell you something. That's probably the last favor I'll ask you to do for me, and when I tell you what I'm going to tell you you won't want to do any more."

"Do you have to tell me now?"

"Right now. I won't go through the day wanting to tell you. I'll go crazy if I do."

"Well, in that case."

"You sound almost as though you knew what it was I want to tell you."

"I can guess. It's about a woman."

"Yes."

"Well, then I don't want to hear it now. I know you've been unfaithful. You've stayed with another woman. I don't want to hear the rest of it at this hour of the morning."

"Well, you'll have to hear it. If you don't mind, please, I want to tell you now."

"Why?"

"Emily, for Christ's sake."

"All right."

"I want to tell you the truth about this because it's a very special thing. Can you look at it this way? Can you, uh, think of me as someone you know that has nothing to do with you, not married to you, but someone you know? Please try to. Well, this man, me, last Saturday night . . ."

From the time he reached the point where he told about bringing Gloria to this apartment Emily did not try to follow his words. He told the story in chronological order up to that point, and she got a kind of excitement out of listening and wondering how he would reach what was for her the climax of the story; the awful climax, but the climax. She knew what was coming, but she never expected to hear the words: "So I brought her here." The words were not separate; they were part of a sentence: ". . . got in a taxi and I didn't have any baggage so I brought her here and we had a few drinks and . . ." But the last words that she paid attention to were: "So I brought her here." After that he went on and on. She knew his throat was dry because his voice broke a little but she did not offer to get him a glass of water. Every once in a while he would ask if she was listening and she would nod and he would say she didn't seem to be, and then continue. She had been sitting on the bed when he began. Once she changed her position so that she sat in a chair beside the head of the bed and she would not have to look at him. "Go on," she would say. Let him talk himself out. She didn't care how long he talked. She was back from Reno, back in Boston, it was 1932, the girls were at Winsor School, she was avoiding her father and his well-meaning solicitousness. Mrs. Winchester Liggett. Mrs. Emily W. Liggett.

What did people generally do with furniture? What did they do for immediate cash? Wasn't it a good thing that it was so near the close of the school year? Wasn't it a good thing New York meant living in an apartment? How awful if it had been in a house, a real home? Ah, but if it had been anywhere else he wouldn't have brought that girl here, to an apartment. No, it wasn't so good that New York meant living in an apartment. That was only a consoling thought and not a matter for congratulation. Let him talk.

". . . tried to swing at him, the policeman, but . . ."

Who cared? Now he was describing the fight. Why hadn't he been killed? He looked so foolish and unrelated to her, with his bandages and bruises. She knew he wasn't asking for sympathy, but she couldn't help denying it to him. What he had asked in the beginning and what she thought would be so hard—to think of him as someone she knew who had nothing to do with her, not married to her, but someone she knew—that was what she felt. Telling the end of the story, or the second half of it, or the latter two thirds, or whatever it was that remained after "So I brought her here," he was like someone who had nothing to do with her, someone not married to her, someone she knew and did not even like, did not even hate. Here was a man whom she could not escape, who was telling a long and pretty dull story about an amour and how he came to be beaten up. Come to think of it, she once knew a man like that, a man who got you in a corner and told you long dull stories about his love life, what a boy he was with the ladies, and how he got into fights. The man's name was Weston Liggett.

"Oh, no," she said.

"What?" he said.

The fool thought she was protesting at something he had said, when she only meant to pull herself together. "Oh, no. I mustn't think hysterically," was what she meant to say, but the Oh-no part had come out in spoken words.

"Well, and that's all," he said. "I wanted to tell you because I didn't —I couldn't stand lying here and letting you wait on me—what are you, what on earth are you laughing at?"

"You can't stand lying here. I just thought it was obvious that you can't stand and lie down at the same time."

"Oh, it's funny."

"No, not funny," she said, "but I don't know what you expect me to do. I won't congratulate you."

"Well, at least I've been honest with you. Now you can do as you please."

"What do you suppose I please?"

"How should I know. I'll give you a divorce. I mean, if you want a divorce in New York I'll give you grounds."

"You have. But I don't want to talk about that now."

"You haven't one word of understanding. Not a single instinct of understanding."

"Oh, now really."

"Yes, now really. You didn't even try to understand. The only thing that interested you was that I was unfaithful. You didn't care about anything else."

"I'm not going to quarrel with you. I'm not going to let you turn this into a little spat. I don't want to talk about it."

"You've got to talk about it. You've got to tell me what you're going to do. I was honest with you, I told you the truth when I didn't have to. You believed the story I made up."

"I beg your pardon, but I didn't believe the story you made up. I did at first, but not when I thought it over. I knew there was more to it than that. And don't tell me I've *got* to tell you what I'm going to do, or that I *have* to talk about it. There aren't any more have-to's as far as you and I are concerned."

"We'll see."

"All right, we'll see."

"Emily," he said.

She walked out.

He dressed and had breakfast after the girls had gone to school. He knocked on Emily's door and she called: "Yes?"

"May I see you a minute, please?"

"What about?"

"I'm leaving."

She opened the door.

"You can stay."

"Thanks, but I'm not going to. I just want to tell you, first of all, I'm going to a hotel. I'll let you know which one when I've decided. Probably the Biltmore. In the second place, I'll deposit some money for you some time today, five hundred now, and as much more than that as I can, later in the week. I'm going because I don't want you to take the girls out to the country at least for the time being."

"Why not?"

"Because they're looking for that Two-Gun Crowley, the fellow that murdered a policeman. He's somewhere on Long Island and there's a big reward out for him. Long Island will be full of crazy people with guns and policemen wanting to shoot this Crowley and it won't be safe. Now please take my advice on this. Stay here till they've captured him or at least till the excitement blows over."

"What else?"

"That's all, I guess. If you want a lawyer, Harry Draper's good. He isn't a divorce lawyer, but if you were planning to go to Reno, for instance, you won't need a divorce lawyer here. The New York lawyer will have a correspondent in Reno. That's the way they always do it, unless the divorce is contested, then sometimes they—"

"If you don't mind I'd rather not go into details now." She shut the door quickly, because she suddenly knew by his face that he wanted

her, and much as she loathed him, this would be one of the times when
he could have her. That was disgusting.

He knew some of that, too.

7

THAT SAME DAY, Wednesday, a coincidence occurred: Gloria decided
she didn't want to see Eddie for a couple of days, and Eddie decided
he didn't want to see Gloria for a couple of days.

Gloria went shopping with her mother, purchasing a beach hat with
a flowered linen band, for $8.50; a suit of beach pajamas with hori-
zontal striped top to the trousers, which cost her mother $29.50. She
bought a surf suit that tied at both shoulders for $10.95. A one-piece
bouclette frock cost $29.50 and a stitched wool hat with a feather cost
$3.95. Also a linen suit, navy jacket and white skirt, for the in-
credible price of $7.95, a woolen sports coat for $29.50, a tricot turban
with a halo twist was $12.50, and two pique tennis dresses (with cro-
cheted belt) for $10.75 apiece. Her uncle had given her mother $150 to
spend and the purchases were practically on the dot of that sum. Gloria
made the purchases with practically no interference from her mother
and she felt good and went home for the express purpose of sending
Norma Day's suit to the dry cleaners'.

She was wrapping the suit in newspaper but she could not resist
reading the paper. It was Monday's *Mirror*, and she was surprised to
discover that she had missed reading Walter Winchell's column. She
skimmed through it for a possible mention of her name (you never
could tell) and then she read more carefullly, learning that Barbara
Hutton was being sent to Europe to forget Phil Plant, that the Connie
Bennett-Marquis de la Falaise thing was finished, "Joel McRae being
the new heart." She read a few lines from that day's installment
of "Grand Hotel," which was running in the *Mirror*, and then she
turned to "What Your Stars Foretell": "Today in particular," it said,
"should bring encouragement to correspondents, typists, writers and ad-
vertisers. Tuesday may be a nervous and upsetting day in many ways,
but Tuesday evening as well as Wednesday evening are very satisfactory
for pleasure and dealings with the other sex on a friendship basis. Do
not expect too much of Wednesday. It is not a good day for anything
outside of the regular routine, and Thursday will be a discouraging day
for those with tempers. Beware of disagreements and quarrels in busi-

ness and with your sweetheart. Saturday should be a very encouraging day from almost any angle; you may act with confidence in either social or business matters. This week is favorable for those born Jan. 29 to Feb. 10, Mar. 3–11, April 1–10, May 5–12, June 2–9, July 7–12, Aug. 1–8, Nov. 15–20, Nov. 29–Dec. 5, Dec. 7–11, Dec. 24–28." Well, her birthday was December 5, so taking it altogether, by and large, if she would be careful today and keep her temper tomorrow—not that she had a really bad temper, but sometimes she did fly off the handle—she ought to have a good week, because Saturday was going to be a very encouraging day from almost any angle, the stars foretold. It might be a good time to plan a trip, and immediately she thought of Liggett. All these clothes, they were for the summer and the trip her uncle was going to give her, but if the weather was nice—but what was she thinking about? Had she gone completely screwy that she was planning anything with Liggett, when for all she knew he had a fractured skull? What if he had a fractured skull? It would be a nice mess and it wouldn't take the police long to get her mixed up in it. Why, there was a policeman right there in the speakeasy when she ran out. All he had to do was ask the bartender her name, and she'd be mixed up in it. She was frightened and she read over again what it said about Tuesday: ". . . may be a nervous and upsetting day in many ways." It certainly had been. It said Tuesday evening was satisfactory for pleasure and dealings with the other sex on a friendship basis, but her relations with Liggett had not been on a friendship basis, not by a whole hell of a lot, as Eddie would say. No, this stuff was right; ordinarily she didn't put much stock in it, but it was like superstitions; maybe there was something to them so it didn't do any harm to be careful. Besides, it was right enough about Tuesday being nervous and upsetting, and when you considered daylight saving time, then all that mess in the speakeasy was part of Tuesday the day, and not the evening. Do not expect too much of Wednesday . . . routine. Well, she would have Eddie's girl Miss Day's suit cleaned, and return the fur coat, those ought to be routine things. Tomorrow was Thursday, the day to be careful about disagreements and quarrels in business (that ought to cover the coat, so she would forestall any trouble tomorrow by returning the coat today), and she would guard against a quarrel with her sweetheart by returning the coat. How to do it would have to be figured out later. But she did not ignore the ease with which she was thinking of Liggett as her sweetheart. Whatever he was, she loved him. *"Don't* I?" she asked.

When he was alone in his apartment Eddie smoked a pipe. It was one of the few gifts his father had given him that was not cash outright. It had a "2S9" in silver on the front of the bowl, which was the way his father had ordered it, but it happened to be a good pipe and Eddie liked it in spite of the adornment. It was cheaper than cigarettes, and when he had money Eddie usually bought a half-pound or a pound tin of tobacco and laid in a supply of cigarette papers. Thus he almost always had something to smoke.

It was a furnished apartment, and probably had a history, but the only part of its history that interested Eddie was that it had come down in price from $65 to $50 a month. Something undoubtedly had taken place in the apartment to account for the lowering of the rental. As Eddie well knew, the depression did not result in decreases in rents of apartments that took in $100 a month or less. One-room and two-room apartments cost just as much as they always had, and renting agents could even be a little choosy, for people who formerly had paid $200 and more now were leasing the cheaper apartments, and paying their rent. So there must have been a reason why this apartment could be held for fairly regular payments of $50 a month. It must not be inferred that Eddie never had any interest at all in the processes that brought about the reduction. At first he wondered about it a little; the furniture was not the kind that is bought for a furnished apartment and the hell with it. No, this was hand-picked stuff, obviously left there by a previous tenant. Eddie thought it possible that the previous tenant had been slain, perhaps decapitated with a razor. He resolved some day to suggest as a magazine article the idea of going around to various apartments in New York where famous crimes had occurred. The apartment where Elwell, the bridge player, was killed; the Dot King apartment; the room in the Park Central where Arnold Rothstein was killed. Find out who lived in the apartment now, whether the present occupant knew Elwell, for instance, had lived there; what kind of person would live in an apartment where there had been a murder; how it affected the present tenant's sleep; whether any concession was made in the rent; whether the real estate people told the prospective tenant that the apartment had a past. It was one of the ideas that Eddie had and rejected for himself because he did not know how to write, but would have passed on to a writer friend if he had had any.

It was hard to tell whether this apartment had been a man's or a woman's. The distinguishing small things had been taken away. There was a bed that could be disguised in the daytime with a large solid red cover; a cheap (it was all cheap) modern armchair; a small fireplace that did not look too practical; a folding bridge table; three modern lamps; a straight-back chair like a "5" with the horizontal bar cut off. Over the fireplace was a colored map of New York with cute legends, and there was a map of Paris, apparently executed by the same cartographer, on the inside of the bathroom door. The pictures that remained were an amateur's replica of a Georgia O'Keeffe orchid, and a Modigliani print. There were a few ash trays from Brass Town via Woolworth.

Whenever he shaved Eddie would hum "I Got Rhythm." The reason for this was that he once had used the words in a sentence: "I had crabs but I got rhythm." He had first thought it up in the bathroom, while shaving, and he would always recall it, at least until something else took its place. Eddie never told anyone he could use the title in a sentence; it was not his kind of humor. Some day he would hear someone else say it and then he would stop thinking of it. That, exactly that, often happened to Eddie. He would make up puns, keep them to himself, and then he would hear them from someone else and they would cease to be his property. It made him wonder; he thought it was indicative of a great lack in himself; not that he cared about the puns, but it was just as true of his own work, his drawing. Once he had an idea that he turned into something; the drawings he did in college. But he also had thought and worked out a technique that was very much like that of James Thurber. In his case he knew it to be reminiscent of the technique employed in a 1917 book called *Dere Mabel,* by Ed Streeter, drawings by Bill Breck, but still he had done nothing with his idea, and then along came Thurber with his idea, and look what he did: everybody knew who Thurber was—and the people who knew who Brunner was were making a pretty good job of forgetting it.

All these things ran through Eddie's mind, which was like blood running through Siamese twins; there was a whole other half of his mind.

Then he began to consider the other half of his mind, and gave himself up a little to the pleasure of the day, the first pleasure of its kind since he had come to New York. For this day, not two hours before he had come here to this apartment and lit this pipe and looked at this furniture and wondered about this lack in himself—two hours ago he had been promised work, and given a half promise of a job. "I won't say yes and I won't say no," the man had said. "All I'll tell you positively now is we can use your drawings."

The work was for a movie company, in the advertising department, the art room of the advertising department. Eddie had gone there for a

job several times two years ago, because he knew there was a Stanford
man, a couple of classes ahead of him, working in the department. But
the Stanford man at that time had been terrified at the idea of being
responsible for increasing the company's payroll by another salary. He
knew that the officials of the company were worried about their own
nepotism and the cousins of cousins were being laid off. And so Eddie
had said well, he would leave a few drawings just in case, and never
heard any more.

Then this morning he had gone to that office for the first time in
nearly two years. He had asked for his old friend and had been told
that the friend was in Hollywood. Then could he see someone in the
department? Yes, he could see the man in charge of the art room. The
man in charge of the art room listened with a mystifying respect to
Eddie's account of his experience of two years ago. The man said:
"Oh, I see. You were a personal friend of Mr. De Paolo's?"

"Yes, I knew him in college. That's what I was saying."

"Have you heard from him lately?"

"Well, no, not lately. I understand he's in Hollywood," said Eddie.

"Yes, but we expect him back in a day or two. Thursday or Friday."

"Well, then I'll come in and see him then. Will you tell him Eddie
Brunner was in? Tell him I have some ideas for him."

"For Benny the Beetle?" the man said.

"No."

"He needs some for Benny."

"No, these are just some of my own drawings I thought he could use."

"Oh, do you draw?"

"Yes."

"Mm," said the man, and put on his thinking look. "Just a minute,
Mr. Brunner." The man left the office and was gone five minutes. He
came back with a batch of rough advertising lay-outs. "Could you do
something with these?"

"Jesus, yes. That's just my stuff," said Eddie. The lay-outs were for a
campaign advertising a college picture. "Do you want me to try?"

"Sure do. I think these are lousy, and the boys in the department just
don't seem to get the right angle. No yoomer. They can draw tits till
I want to chew the paper, but these girls are not supposed to have that
kind of tits, you know what I mean. What I want is more on the order
of John Held Jr. You know. Comedy girls. I want them female, but I
don't want to stress the sex angle." He smiled and shook his head. "We
did a campaign, God damn, boy, we had everything but the old thing
in every paper in town. The picture was a terrible turkey, 'Strange Vir-

gin,' but they almost held it over the second week it did such business, and every other company in town was bellyaching to the Hays office about our ads, so we got the credit for whatever business the picture did. Maybe you saw the campaign?"

"I sure did."

"The one where she's lying with her legs out like this, and the guy! I did that one my*self*. We even had squawks from Andre Jacinto on that. He happened to be in town making personal appearances when the ads came out and oh, he called up and he blew the house down, he was that sore. 'Listen,' he said, 'maybe I am like that and maybe I'm not, but you got no God damn license to put something in the ads that ain't in the picture.' That gave me a laugh, because when you take into consideration what that ad looked like he was doing, it'll take a long time before they put that in any picture they make in Hollywood. Maybe over West Forty-six Street, that kind of a picture. But for the time being. Well, anyway, that was some campaign. The other companies squawked to the Hays office, but I don't mind telling you I got myself two very nice offers from the companies that squawked the loudest. But with such a college picture we require an altogether different technique. You know? Dames, but cute, and comedy. Stress the comedy angle. I tell you what I'll do, Mr. Brunner. I'll take the responsibility on my own head. You go on in and sit down and just give me all you got on a couple roughs like what I have in mind, and if I like them I'll give you twenty-fy dollars top price for all we use, then if I like them maybe we can come to some kind of an arrangement about more work in the future."

Eddie did some drawings and the man said they were sensational. He'd take one anyway. Mr. De Paolo would be proud, he said. He made out a voucher for $25 and told Eddie to come back next Friday. "Oh, of course if you were going to see Mr. De Paolo maybe I'll see you before that." There was just a chance that there might possibly be a regular job there for Eddie.

Before he left the place Eddie of course had found out that his old friend De Paolo had struck it rich; he was in charge of the work on Benny the Beetle, the company's own plagiarism of Mickey Mouse. . . .

On twenty-five a week Eddie figured he could even go to a movie now and then and get a load of Benny the Beetle. It was too much to hope for a steady job in an art department, where they certainly would pay more than twenty-five a week, but if the friendship with De Paolo had got him this far, no telling how far he would get when Polly—De Paolo—came to town, always providing Polly hadn't gone high-hat and wouldn't pass him up. But he didn't think Polly would go high-hat. High-powered, maybe, but not high-hat.

And so Eddie breathed in streams of tobacco smoke, tobacco that he had dug out of the luxurious bottom of the can, where it was still faintly moist and had a flavor. He had $23 and some change, he didn't know how much, in his kick right now. Five dollars for canned goods would leave $18 plus, and would assure him of food for at least a week. Take Norma to a show, tickets at Joe Leblang's. Explain the situation to Norma, whom he had permitted to pay his rent on a loan basis, in return for which he put up her kid brother, a junior at the University of Pennsylvania, who came to town every other week-end to see a girl friend of Norma's. Norma had her own money, left her by a grandmother, and she also had a job as secretary to an assistant professor at N. Y. U. She and her brother were orphans and her brother had his own money too, but in trust until he was twenty-one years old.

What about Norma, anyway? Eddie now asked himself. He had the feeling that his troubles were over, temporarily, and he wondered if it wouldn't be a good idea to marry Norma. He thought back over the years, and it might as well have been Norma all along. His succession of girls always had been about the same general type; smallish, usually with breasts rather large for the girl's height; sometimes the girl would be chunky. They had to have a feeling for jazz that was as good as you can expect in a girl. They had to be cute rather than blasé, a little on the slangy side, and come to think of it, all of them including Norma had to go to bed for one day out of every twenty-eight. They were all fundamentally the same, and probably they were all fundamentally Norma.

About love Eddie was not so sure. The thing that he supposed existed, that kept together a man and woman all their lives and made them bring up children and have a home and that kept them faithful to each other unquestioningly and apparently without temptation—he had not seen that in his own home and so he was not personally acquainted with it. He was not sure that he ever had seen it, either. He knew, for instance, that he saw the parents of his friends in a way that was totally unlike the way his friends saw them. All through his adolescence he practically took for granted that Mr. Latham and Mr. O'Neill and Mr. Dominick and Mr. Girardot, fathers of his closest friends of that period, were unfaithful to Mrs. Latham and Mrs. O'Neill and Mrs. Dominick and Mrs. Girardot. He never spoke of it, because his friends never did, but if they had he was sure he would have come right out and said what he thought. He had it thought out beyond that: he believed that those fathers were human, and subject to desire, a thing which did not have to be forgiven except in the case of his own father. His own father had inadvertently taught him to accept infidelity in all other fathers but himself. On the other hand Eddie liked absolute faithfulness in a wife, not so much because his own mother practiced it, but because as a result of her practicing it she became finally a much better person in his eyes than his father. The years of being constant were a lot like years of careful saving, compared with years of being a spendthrift. It was just that it was easier to be a spendthrift than to save. Of course sometimes you saved for nothing better than a bank crash, but even though you lost everything that was in the bank, you still had something around the eyes, something in the chin, that showed you had been a saver. Sometimes he would say to himself: "Yes, but your mother was pretty stupid." All right, what if she was? She had kept her promise, which was more than his father had done. Eddie had no liking for the fellows in college who thought it would be swell to have a father who was more like an older brother. If his father had been an older brother Eddie would have been likely to give him a punch in the nose. Not that he idealized any other father he knew, but because he never met a father whom he regarded as the ideal did not mean that none such existed. Psychology and the lines of thought it indicated mildly fascinated Eddie, and he approved some of it; but he was not willing to ascribe, say, fidelity to a weakness or a dishonesty. Maybe it all did come down to the value of a promise. You gave your word that you would pay back some money, you gave your word that you would not sleep with another woman; in either case it was a promise, and if you couldn't depend on a promise then nothing was any good.

He was always telling himself that when he got older and knew more he would take up the subject of promises. But he hoped the day never would come when he did not believe a promise—just a promise, and not all the surrounding stuff about Gentleman and Honor—was a good and civilized thing.

He was lying on his bed, thinking these things, and he suddenly felt disgust with himself. For only yesterday he had come within inches of laying Gloria, and months ago he had promised Norma that he would not stay with anyone else. All his self-satisfied introspection went away and he could not find anything anywhere in his thoughts that would justify what he had all but done. It was not his fault that it had not been done. There it was, the first time his promise to Norma had been put to a test, and right away, without even thinking about it, he was ready for Gloria, very God damn ready; and it was worse because he had come so close without thinking about it. It was possible that if he had thought it out he would have found a reason, if no other reason than that he would stay with Gloria and stop staying with Norma. Then next he was thinking the thing he always thought when he was getting out of one romance and beginning another: the self-reproach that he was no better than his father; that he was his father's son. Maybe the psychoanalysts would tell him that that helped to explain how he would be faithful to a girl for months, then get another girl and be faithful to her until he was unfaithful. That's the way it had been, and almost the way it was this minute, with Norma and Gloria. But he had not stayed with Gloria; for that break he thanked his luck. If he had he would have had to tell Norma. But he hadn't. That seemed to him an important thing, one of the most important things in his life, and at that moment he decided he had found the girl he wanted to marry. A laundry called him on the telephone, and that prevented his having an affair with Gloria. Good. Something beyond his understanding had intervened, he was sure of that; maybe it was only his luck. Well, he wasn't going to fool with his luck. When he saw Norma tonight he would ask her to marry him. No money, no job, no nothing. But he knew she was the one he wanted to marry. He laughed a little. He was pretty proud of Norma, and he loved her very much. He was already loyal to her, too; in the sense that in his mind he could defend her against the kind of thing Gloria might say about her: he could hear Gloria calling Norma a mouse-like little creature (although Norma was the same size girl as Gloria, and, speaking of mice, it was not hard to imagine someone saying Norma had a mind like a steel trap). Eddie let his loyalty go to Norma and did not try to deny to himself that this probably was at the expense of his loyalty to Gloria.

It was strange about Gloria, how he always had had this feeling of loyalty to her. Offhand he could not recall a time when there had been any need for it; yet he knew that with the life Gloria led there probably were dozens of people who said things about her that, if he heard them, would evoke a loyal response and some kind of protective action on his part. He had been ready to defend Gloria at any time when he might meet someone who said things about her or did things to her. By God it was an instinctive thing: that first night he saw her he lent her money when money was life to him. It saddened him to think of the things implicit in his decision to marry Norma. One of these things was the giving up part. Maybe he was wrong (he admitted) but always it seemed to him as though he and Gloria were many many times on the verge of a great romance, one for the ages, or at least a match for the love and anguish of Amory and Rosalind in "This Side of Paradise" and Frederick and Catherine in "A Farewell to Arms." He nodded to an undefined thought: that yes, to marry Norma was a sensible thing and if out of the hundred pounds of the relationship between himself and Norma there was one ounce sensible thing, that one ounce was an imperfect, unromantic thing. All right; what of it? There never had been much romance in his past romances, and he distrusted romance for his own self; in a sort of Elks-tooth way his father had been a romantic guy, and he was not going to have any of that. He was in no danger of it, either, he was sure; his mother had not been like Norma. Disconnectedly he found himself off on a tangent, realizing how awful parturition must have been for his mother, all that stuff about getting up on a table and having a doctor look her over, and her realization that "the little one" she talked about and thought about and felt, also was a hideous little thing called a foetus. (He was able to think of this without any identification of the foetus as himself. You may say, "That was me," but you cannot imagine yourself as being no bigger than the present size of your foot.) No, it wasn't so disconnected as he called it; Norma never would speak of "the little one." If she were pregnant she would know beforehand what was going on inside her, and she would know about the placenta and all that. He hoped Norma would not have much pain. But what stuff this was! this thinking about Norma deliberately having a baby when he had not yet seriously asked her to marry him. She might fool him and say no; there was that chance. "A celluloid cat's in hell," he assured himself, but a chance.

He was already as married as though he were half of Mr. and Mrs. Eddie Brunner. Did babies sometimes come out upside down because that was the position of their parents when the baby was conceived? Could parents tell which lay had made the baby? How long did the husband and wife have to stop sleeping together when the wife was pregnant? (He had heard the story about an artist who tried to stay with his wife when she was being wheeled into the delivery room.) What if Norma had a dwarf: would the doctors let it live? What if they had a baby and it turned out to be an hermaphrodite? Would Norma's beautiful breasts get so painfully sensitive that he would not be able to touch them while she was pregnant? Did they always lose their firmness after pregnancy? What was this stuff about tearing? Did

it mean *literally* tearing? ripping open when she did not stretch enough?
Could doctors keep the size of the baby down so it would not endanger
the mother's life? How much did a baby cost?

Well, it cost more than he would be able to pay for a long time,
so he might as well stop thinking about it. He ought to be glad he
had enough money to take Norma to a show tonight, that's what he
ought to be.

8

WEDNESDAY PASSED for all those living in the world at that time, and
it was Thursday. It was for instance payday for James Malloy, who had
been living since Monday on borrowed dollars. For Gloria Wandrous
it was all of a sudden the day on which she would give up Liggett.
She had had a good night's sleep. Wednesday evening she had spent
in the bosom of her family, after trying without success to talk to Eddie
on the telephone. She had a good dinner at home, of things she liked:
her mother's cream of tomato soup with just a touch of sherry in it;
roast beef, scalloped potatoes, succotash, lettuce and mayonnaise (home-
made), ice cream with strawberries, coffee and a lick of Curaçao. Her
uncle had to go uptown after dinner and Gloria was left with her
mother. Her mother had not been so bad. They talked about the clothes
she had bought that day, and Mrs. Wandrous, who knew something
about women's clothes, reaffirmed her trust in Gloria's taste. She said
Gloria had clothes sense. "That's one thing about you I never had to
teach you even as a little girl. You always had good sense about clothes.
Oh, so few girls have it these days. Sunday before last, you know when
I went for a drive with Mrs. Lackland, we drove past Vassar College.
Now you'd think those girls would know how to dress, at least have
sense enough to put on something decent on Sunday. But no. Sweater
and skirt, sweater and skirt, all the way up and down the street from
Poughkeepsie proper to the college. And the same sweater, and the same
skirt. I said to Mrs. Lackland, if those girls were told they *had* to wear
a uniform the way girls have to in preparatory school, why, they'd yell
and scream and have school strikes and everything. But there they were,
just the same, wearing a uniform. And it isn't as though they dressed
any better when they came to New York. But I suppose they have no
style. *You have.* You have style. I noticed those things you bought
today. I was afraid for a minute when you asked to try on that one

dress at Altman's. I knew it was wrong for you but I didn't want to say anything till after you tried it on."

"Oh, I wouldn't have bought it."

"I know."

"I just wanted to try it on. They're handy."

"Well, I don't think so, Gloria. When I'm tempted to buy a dress because I think it's going to be handy, I think twice about it. Those handy dresses, so-called, I should say a woman won't get as much out of one of those as she will out of a really frivolous dress. I mean in actual number of hours that they're worn. Take your black satin . . ."

Clothes, and cooking, and curiously enough the way to handle men, were matters in which Gloria had respect for her mother's opinions. Packing, housecleaning, how to handle servants, what to do for blotches in the complexion, kitchen chemistry, the peculiarities of various fabrics—Mrs. Wandrous knew a lot about such matters. It occurred to Gloria that her mother was a perfect wife. The fact that her husband was dead did nothing to change that. In fact that was part of it. And any time anybody had any doubt about how well her mother could manage a house, all they had to do was count up the number of times Gloria's uncle had had to complain. No, her mother was a fine house-keeper, and she knew how to handle men. Gloria often would hear her mother say that if So-and-So did such and such she'd be happier with her husband. What Gloria meant was that her mother, dealing with her kind of man in her kind of life, was just as capable as she was with baking soda in the kitchen. Mrs. Wandrous knew what baking soda could be made to do, and she knew what the kind of man she would be likely to have dealings with (who bored Gloria to death) would do. It was almost a good life, Gloria decided. Without regret she recognized the impossibility of it for her; but a pretty good life for someone like her mother.

That Wednesday night after she went to bed she lay there trying, not very hard, to read, and thinking about her mother. Now there was a woman who had known (Gloria was sure) only one man in her entire life. Known meaning slept with. And that had not lasted very long. Yet after twenty years her mother was able to recall every detail of sleeping with a man, almost as though it had happened last night. She had not discussed it at any length with her mother, but now and then a thing would be said that showed how well her mother remembered. Think of living that way! Going to bed these nights, so many nights through so many years; some nights dropping off to sleep, but surely some nights lying there and saddened by the waste of shapely breasts and the excitement in oneself with a man, and the excitement of a man's excitement. And then nothing to do about it but lie there, almost afraid to touch one's breasts, probably, or anything else; and remembering one man long ago. There was only one possible explanation for being able to live in memory like that, and Gloria felt tears in her eyes at the thought of her father's and mother's love.

It showed, too. It showed in her mother's face. It worried Gloria a little to come around again to a theory she sometimes had that a woman ought to have one man and quit. It made for a complete life no matter how short a time it lasted. Gloria resolved to be a better girl, and after a long but not unpleasant time she fell asleep, preferring her own face but thinking well of her mother's.

She had breakfast in her room. It was too warm a day for breakfast in bed. To have breakfast in bed ought to be a luxury and not a nuisance, and it was a nuisance when covering over the legs was a nuisance, as it was this day. She drank the double orange juice and wanted more, but Elsie, the maid, had gone back to the kitchen out of call. Gloria drank her coffee and ate her toast and poured another cup of coffee. Then a cigarette. While having breakfast she was busy with her hands. With no one to look at her she swung her butter knife like a bandmaster's baton, not humming or singing, but occasionally letting her throat release a note. She felt good.

What, if anything, she had decided the night before had not been changed by the morning and the good night's sleep, principally because she had not fixed upon a new mode of life. The good night's sleep she knew had a lot to do with the absence of her usual morning despair, but it wasn't that she was happy, exactly. It came close to the feeling that she was ready for anything today, whereas if she had come to a solemn decision the night before to be an angel thenceforward, she would now be having a special kind of gayety—not removed from the despair—that was cap-over-the-windmill stuff. No; today she felt good. The big problem of Liggett would be settled somehow, not without an awful scene and maybe not right away, but it would probably be all right—and that concession was a step in the right direction, she thought. She felt good, and she felt strong.

She looked at the advertisements in the paper while smoking her second cigarette. She had a patronizing, superior feeling toward the advertisements: she had bought practically all the clothes she wanted and certainly all she would need. She had her usual quick visit to the bathroom, and then she had a lukewarm bath and she was dressing when her mother called to her that Ann Paul was on the phone and wanted to speak to her, and should she take the message? Yes, take the message, Gloria told her mother. The message was that Ann wanted to have lunch with her. Gloria said she would come to the phone. She didn't want to have lunch with Ann, but she had known Ann in school and did want to see her, so she asked Ann to come downtown if she could, and Ann said she could.

Ann lived in Greenwich where she lived an athletic life; sailing her own Star, hunting and showing at the minor league horse shows and in such ways using up the energy which no man had seemed able to get to for his personal use. In school Ann, who was very tall for a girl, was suspect because of a couple of crushes which now, a few years later, her former schoolmates were too free about calling Lesbian, but Gloria did not think so, and Ann must have known that Gloria did not think so. She called Gloria every time she came to New York, which was about twice a month, and the last two times Gloria had not been home for the calls.

Ann came downtown, parked her Ford across the street from Gloria's house, and went right upstairs to Gloria's room. Ann was in the Social Register, which fact impressed Gloria's mother as much as Gloria's indifference to it. Ann was always made to feel at home in Gloria's house.

"I had to see you," said Ann. "I have big news."

"Ah-hah."

"What?"

"Go ahead."

"Why did you say ah-hah as if you knew it? Does it show?"

"No. I knew there was something. You've never looked better."

"Look," said Ann, and extended her left hand.

"Oh, you *girl!* Ann! Who is it? When? I mean do I know him or anything?"

"Tell you everything. His name is Bill Henderson and you don't know him and he's at P. and S. and gets out next year and he went to Dartmouth before that and he's even taller than I am, and I haven't the faintest idea when we're going to be married."

"How long have you known him? What's he *like?*"

"Since Christmas. He's from Seattle and he spent Christmas with friends of mine in Greenwich which is how I happened to meet him. I sat next to him at dinner the night after Christmas, and he was the quiet type, I thought. He looked to be the quiet type. So I found out what he did and I began talking about gastroenterostomies and stuff and he just sat there and I thought, What is this man? He just sat there and nodded all the time I was talking. You know, when I was going to be a nurse year before last. Finally I said something to him. I asked him if by any chance he was listening to what I was saying, or bored, or what? 'No, not bored,' he said. 'Just cockeyed.' And he was. Cockeyed. It seems so long ago and so hard to believe we were ever strangers like that, but that's how I met him, or my first conversation with him. Actually he's very good. His family have loads of money from the lumber business and I've never seen anything like the way he spends money. But only when it doesn't interfere with his work at P. and S. He has a Packard that he keeps in Greenwich and hardly ever uses except when he comes to see me. He was a marvelous basket-ball player at Dartmouth and two weeks ago when he came up to our house he hadn't had a golf stick in his hands since last summer and he went out and shot an eighty-seven. He's very homely, but he has this dry sense of humor that at first you don't quite know whether he's even listening to you, but the things he says. Sometimes I think—oh, not really, but a stranger overhearing him might suggest sending him to an alienist."

"He sounds wonderful! Oh, I'm so glad, darling. When did he go for the ring and all?"

"Well—New Year's Eve he asked me to marry him. If you could call it that. Sometimes even now I can't always tell when he's tight. New Year's Eve he was dancing with me and he stopped right in the middle of the floor, stopped dancing and stood away from me and said: 'Remind me to marry you this summer.'"

"I like that. This summer."

"No, I guess not this summer. But I don't know. Oh, all I care about is I guess this is it, I hope."

"It sounds like it to me. The real McCoy, whatever that is. So what are you going to do this summer? Where is—what's his name? Bill?"

"Bill Henderson. Well, he wants to go home for a little while just to see his family and then come back. I—I'm sort of embarrassed, Gloria. I don't really know. When he gets ready to tell me something, he tells me, and I never ask him. But what I wanted to see you about, can you come up for the week-end tomorrow? Bill's coming, and I forget whether he's just getting ready for examinations or just finishing them. See? I don't know anything. I just sit and wait."

"That's good preparation for a doctor's wife."

"So everyone tells me. But what about it, can you come?"

"I'd love to," said Gloria. Then, thinking of Liggett: "I have a half date for the week-end, but I think I can get out of it. Anyway, can I take a rain check if I can't make it this week?"

"Of course. Do try to get out of the other thing. Is this other thing— would you like me to invite someone for you? I mean is there someone that—I could ask your other date."

"No. It was a big party, a lot of people, not anyone in particular."

"Then I won't ask anyone for you till I hear from you. Will you call me? Call me tomorrow at home, or else call this afternoon and leave word. Just say you're coming. And of course if you think you can't come and then change your mind at the last minute and decide you can, that's all right too."

"All right. I'll most likely call you tonight." Gloria noticed that Ann seemed to have something else to say. "What, Ann? What are you thinking?"

"I can tell *you*, Gloria," said Ann. "Darling, I've had an affair. Bill and I. We've had an affair. Almost from the very beginning. Do you think any the less of me?"

"Oh, certainly not, darling. *Me?*"

"I never knew about you. I've always thought you had, but I could never be sure. It's only in the last six months I found out why you can't be sure. It doesn't show on you. You know? You think the next day you're going to be a marked woman and everybody on the street will know. But they don't. And men. Men are so funny. Mothers tell us all our lives that boys lose respect for girls that they go all the way with. But they must have changed a lot since my mother was our age. At first I was so frightened, and then I saw that Bill was the one that really was frightened, not I. I don't mean about children only. But they're so helpless. When we're with people I'm quiet as a mouse and sit there listening to the great man, or when we're dancing I think how marvelously witty he is, with his sense of humor. But when we're really alone it all changes. He's entirely different. At first I used to think he was so gentle, terribly gentle, and it almost killed me. But then I realized something—and this isn't taking anything away from him. He *is* gentle, but the things about him that I used to think were gentle, they aren't gentle. The really gentle things he does aren't the same things I thought were. What I mistook for being gentle was his own helplessness, or practically helplessness. Yes, helplessness. He *knows* everything, being a medical student, and I don't suppose I'm the first for him, but—Lord! I don't know how to explain it. Do you see what I mean at all?"

"I think so. I think something else, too. I think you two ought to

get married, right away. Don't lose any of the fun. Right away, Ann.
He has his own money, and you have some I know. There's no reason
why you should miss anything. Get married."

"I want to, and he's crazy to, but I'm afraid of interfering with his
studies."

"It won't interfere with his studies. He might have to neglect *you*
a little, but he'll be able to study much better with you than he would
being in New York and wishing you were here or he was in Greenwich.
No, by all means get married. Just look at all the young marriages
there are today. People getting married as soon as the boy gets out of
college. The hell with the depression. Not that that's a factor in your
getting married, but look at all the young couples, read the society
pages and see, and there must be a lot of them that are really poor
and without jobs. If you got married now and he goes back to P. and S.
next year you'd have the fun of living together and all that, and then
he'll probably want to go abroad to Vienna or some place to continue
his studies, and that will be like a honeymoon. Your family aren't
going to insist on a big wedding, are they?"

"Well, Father thinks it's a good thing to keep up appearances. Mother
doesn't like the idea as much as she used to. She'd rather use the money
for charity, but Father says he's giving more to charity than ever before
and with less money to do it on. He's very serious about it. You see he
knows Mr. Coolidge, and I think he thinks if we invited Mr. Coolidge
to the wedding he'd come, and that would do a lot toward sort of
taking people's minds off the depression."

"I don't agree with your father."

"Neither do I. Of course I wouldn't dare say so, but I think Coolidge
got us into this depression and he ought to keep out of the papers."

"That's what I think, too."

"Well, you've given me something to think about. Not that I hadn't
thought of it myself, but whenever I broach the subject people say oh,
there's plenty of time. But you're the only one that knows we're practically married right now."

"Oh, no, you're not," said Gloria. "Where do you go?"

"Usually to an apartment of a friend of Bill's."

"Well, then you've—have you ever spent the whole night?"

"Once."

"That's not enough. *You're* not practically married."

"How do *you* know so much? Gloria, don't tell me you're married?"

"No, but I know how it is to wake up with a man you love and have
breakfast and all that. It takes time before you get accustomed to each

other. Who's going to use the bathroom first, and things like that. Intimacies. Ann, I can tell you a lot."

"I wish you would."

"I will. God! I know everything!"

"Why, Gloria."

"Yes, everything. I know how good it can be and how awful, and you're lucky. You marry Bill right away and hold on to him."

"I've never seen you like this. Why does it mean so much to you? Is the man you love married?"

"You've guessed it."

"And his wife won't give him a divorce?"

"Yes," said Gloria. "That's it."

"But couldn't you both go to her and tell her you love each other? Is she a nice woman? How old is she?"

"Oh, we've had it out. Not she and I, but Jack and I."

"Jack. Do I know him?"

"No." She was on the verge of confessing that his name was not Jack, but she did not want to tell Ann too much. "Look, darling, I'll call you tonight for sure and if you're not there I'll leave word that I'm coming or not."

"All right, my pet," said Ann, getting up. She kissed Gloria's cheek. "Good luck, and I'll see you, if not this week, perhaps a week from tomorrow."

"Mm-hmm. And thanks loads."

"Oh, I'm the one to thank you," said Ann, and left.

Gloria thought a long time about how uncontagious love was. According to the book she ought to be wanting to telephone Liggett, and she did want to telephone Liggett in a way, but talking to Ann, virginal Ann with her one man and her happiness and innocence and her awkward love affair (she was sure Bill Henderson wore glasses and had to take them off and put them in a metal case before necking Ann)—it all made her angry with love, which struck in the strangest places. It didn't seem to be any part of her own experience with love, and it depressed her. What possible problems could they have, Ann and Bill? A man from the Pacific Coast, comes all the way from the Pacific Coast and finds right here in the East the perfect girl for him. What possible problems could they have? What made them hesitate about getting married? She felt like pushing them, and pushing them roughly and impatiently. They would get married and after a couple of years Bill would have an affair with a nurse or somebody, and for him the excitement would die down. But by that time Ann would have had children, beautiful children with brown bodies in skimpy bathing suits. Ann would sit on the beach with them, looking up now and then from her magazine and calling them by name and answering their foolish questions and teaching them to swim. She would have enormous breasts but she would not get very fat. Her arms would fill out and look fine and brown in evening dress. And, Gloria knew, Ann would slowly get to disliking her. No; that wouldn't be like Ann. But Gloria would be the only person like herself whom Ann could tolerate. Every Ann probably has one Gloria to whom she is loyal. And the girls they had gone to school with, who had made the cracks about Ann's being Lesbian—they would turn out to be her friends, and she would ride with them and play bridge and go to the club dances. They would meet sometimes in the afternoons, parked in their station wagons, waiting for their husbands, and their husbands would get off the train, all wearing blue or gray flannel suits and club or fraternity hatbands on their stiff straw hats, with their newspapers folded the same way all of them. And she, Gloria, would visit Ann and Bill once each summer for the first few summers, and the men with the hatbands would make dates for New York. Oh, she knew it all.

She tried to laugh it off when she thought of the motion picture she had thought up for Ann's future, but laughing it off was not easy. It was unsuccessful. Laughing it off was unsuccessful because the picture was accurate, and she knew it. Well, every Gloria, she reminded herself, also had an Ann whom she tolerated and to whom she was loyal. Ann's was not her way of living, but it was all right for Ann. The only possible way for Ann, or rather the only good way. Hell, here she was in a bad humor, and for no apparent reason. You couldn't call Ann's happiness a reason.

In the rear of the second floor of the house in which Gloria lived there was a room which Mrs. Wandrous and the rest of the household called Mrs. Wandrous' sewing-room. It was small and none of the furniture made you want to stay in it very long. Mrs. Wandrous kept needles and spools of thread and darning paraphernalia and sewing baskets in the room, but she did her sewing elsewhere. Occasionally Gloria went to that room to look out the window, and for no other reason.

The sewing-room looked out on the yard of Gloria's house, and across the yard and across the contiguous yard was the rear of an old house which had been cut up into furnished apartments. It was nothing to look at. A woman in that house had a grand piano with a good tone, but her musical taste was precisely that of Roxy, the theater fellow. In fact Gloria had a theory that this woman closely followed the Roxy program, except when the program called for Ravel's "Bolero" and the César Franck and one or two others that Gloria and Roxy liked. The woman also sang. She was terrible. And this woman was the only human being Gloria identified with the house. On warm days she had seen that much of the woman that was between the shoulders and the knees. The woman did not close the window all the way down on hot days. She never had seen the woman's face, but only her torso. She had seen it in and out of clothes, and it was nothing to go out of your way to see. And that woman was the only human neighbor that Gloria knew anything about.

But a couple of yards away there was a garden; two yards with no fence between. Grass grew, there was a tree, there were some rose bushes, there were four iron chairs and a table to match with an umbrella standard in the center of the table. In that garden there was a police bitch and, just now, four puppies.

The last time Gloria had looked out the sewing-room windows the puppies were hardly more than little pieces of meat, not easy to count and completely helpless.

Now they must have been six weeks old, and as Gloria stood and watched them she forgot all about the woman who was playing the piano, for in a very few minutes she discovered something about the family of police dogs: the bitch had a favorite.

The bitch's teats had lost their fullness and had gone back into her body, but that did not make the puppies forget that they had got milk there not so long ago. The mother would run away from their persistent attempts to gnaw at her, but one tan little fellow was more persistent than the others, and when the mother and the tan had got far enough away, the mother would stand and let him nibble at her. Then she would swat him good and hard, but, Gloria noticed, not hard enough for him to misunderstand and take offense and get angry with his mother. The mother would open her surprisingly big mouth and lift him up and swing him away from her, then she would take a mighty leap and fly about the garden, chasing sparrows. Meanwhile the other puppies would be waiting for her and when she met them they would try again to take milk from her. Or maybe they were like men, Gloria thought; maybe they knew there was no milk there. And Gloria had a strong suspicion that the mother really liked their making passes at her. She guessed Nature provided the mother with the instinct to swat the puppies away from her. They were old enough to eat solid food now and as a good mother it was her duty to make them look out for themselves.

The mother was a marvelous person. Gloria found herself thinking this and since she was alone and not thinking out loud she went on thinking it. The mother was a marvelous person. Such good qualities as there must be in her, the way she held up her head and her ears stood straight up, and the way she would play with her puppies but at the same time not let them get too fresh or have their own way. Then the way she would lie down with her face on her paws, her eyes looking deceptively sleepy as she watched the puppies trying to eat grass or find something edible in the grass. It was really marvelous. There was one black fellow who wanted to play with himself, and every time he did the mother would get up and let him have it with her paw or else pick him up in her mouth and pretend to chastise him. She would put him down after a few moments and by that time his mind would be off sex. But all this time the tan was her favorite, and then Gloria saw something she did not believe. She saw it with her own eyes. She did not know anything about dogs, and maybe this was common practice among dogs, but she made up her mind to ask the next vet if dogs did this all the time. What she saw that she did not believe was a matter between the mother and the tan.

The mother was lying on the grass watching her children (about the way Ann would on the beach when she had hers). The tan was getting ready to squat for Number One. Instantly the mother got up and grabbed him in her mouth and took him to a bush. She put him down and grabbed his hind leg and lifted it. It was all new to him and he struggled, trying to get into a squatting position again, and he leaked a little, but the mother held on and shook him until he stopped leaking. That was all. It must have been one of the first times the mother had done this, but it was wonderful to see. It made Gloria wonder where the father was.

The father. That son of a bitch probably was out on Long Island or Connecticut or Westchester, where it was fashionable and cool, and here was the mother teaching her pup to stand up like a man and not sit down like a pansy. But the mother didn't seem to miss the father. She was self-sufficient, and that was a good thing about women. All that stuff about women must weep or wait or whichever it was. Give a woman her child or her children, and the hell with the men. It was incredible that before her very eyes Gloria had seen all the stuff about motherhood, which she thought was pretty much the bunk, being demonstrated by a police bitch and her litter. But it made her feel good again. It put Bill Henderson in his place as the mere father of Ann's children, and let him put his nurse up on the operating table or do whatever he liked. He wasn't important once he did his part toward making Ann's babies. If you loved a man, so much the better, but you didn't have to love him, you didn't even have to know him. They brought the stuff all the way from France and England and made mares have colts in this country, and they had done it successfully with people in New York, where the father was sterile and both parents wanted a child. Liggett. He had children. Gloria wondered about herself. Three abortions and all the things she had done not to have children probably had a very bad effect. For the first time she wanted a child, and she—

"Gloria! Eddie Brunner wants to speak to you," called her mother.

"I'll be there in a minute," she said.

Eddie might do it. But she didn't want Eddie. She wanted Liggett. Still, Eddie *would* do it. Only too glad.

"Hello."

"Hello, pal. This is Eddie."

"I know."

"I have good news for you, baby. I got a job."

"A job! Eddie, that's wonderful. Where? What doing?"

"Well, it isn't much, only twenty-five bucks a week, but it's something. Drawing for movie ads."

"Oh, swell. When do you start?"

"Right away. I work at home. They'll furnish the Bristol board and all that, but I can work at home. They called up this morning. Yesterday I was pretty sure I had it but I wasn't sure. I did some sketches for them and they seemed pretty sure I could do the kind of stuff they wanted, but this morning they called up and said it was definite. In fact it's going to be more than twenty-five bucks a week. That's what it was going to be originally, on a basis of part-time work, but now they said they could use some of my drawings on every picture. What they'll do is make mats and sell them. Do you know what mats are? Doesn't make any difference. I'll tell you at lunch. Will you have lunch with me?"

"Sure. But I don't want you to spend your money on me. We'll go Dutch Treat."

"Nuts. I buy this lunch. I'll be over for you how soon?"

"You can start right away. I've been up for over an hour. Come right over."

"I'll be over before you can say Jefferson Machamer."

"Jefferson Machamer," she said.

"That's not the way to say it," said Eddie, and hung up.

Eddie was full of plans, few of them making sense when his income was considered. All Gloria had to do was listen. "A small car, an Austin or one of those little Jordans. You know those little Jordans? They don't make them any more, but they were some cars. Or I keep seeing an ad in the paper for a baby Peugeot. I just want a small car."

"Naturally."

"Why naturally?"

"So you won't have to take anyone else for a ride. You want a car to think in, don't you, Baby?"

"That's right," he said. "A car I can think in."

"And Norma and I, we'll just sit around and sew on Sunday afternoons when it's hot. You go out to the country—the North Shore is nice and cool. You go out and you think and Norma and I will sit and wait for you, and then you come home and tell us what you've been thinking. Understand, if you don't *want* to tell us, or you're too tired, it'll keep. What else are you going to do with your money?"

"Well—" they were at the corner of Fifth Avenue and Eighth Street, halted by traffic. "You see those figures on top of the traffic lights?" At that time the traffic light standards were adorned on top with gilt statuettes of semi-nude men in trench helmets.

"Uh-huh."

"Well, I'm going to do something about them. I'm not sure what, but something."

"Somebody ought to."

"I may only buy them, all the way from here to a Hundred and Tenth Street, if they go that far, and send them to a silly old uncle of mine who loves to play with soldiers."

"No."

"No. You're right. I have a better idea, but I don't know you well enough to tell you."

"Certainly not."

"The idea is, how to control female jaywalkers. I would have instead of a light, when it is time for the red light to go on, all the little soldiers would uh, come to attention as it were."

"As it were."

"And all the women would stop, see? They would watch this phenomenon and meanwhile traffic would be rolling by. There's only one difficulty. When the women get tired of watching it we'll have jaywalking again."

"Ho-ho. Women—"

"I know. Women won't ever get tired of watching that phenomenon. This is a *nice* conversation."

"What about men jaywalkers?" said Gloria.

"We have a jaywalker for a mayor," said Eddie.

"Oh, stop it. That isn't even original."

"Yes, it's at least original. It may be lousy, but it's original. Anyway I never heard anyone else say it. That's always my trouble when I make puns."

"What else with your money?"

"Buy you lunch. Buy you a present. Buy Norma a present—"

"And get a haircut."

Eddie was gay all through luncheon, long after Gloria grew tired of his fun. She could see that it was more than the prospect of the job that made him feel good. The other thing was without a doubt Norma Day. Always before this when he was gay it did not last so long without encouragement from Gloria; this time he went on, and in a way that in anyone else she would have called stupid. Not stupid in Eddie. Eddie did not do stupid things. And God knows he was entitled to some fun. But twice in one day was too much for this: first it was Ann Paul with her Mr. Fletcher—Mr. Henderson, rather. Ann was all packed and everything and moving right out of Gloria's life. And now Eddie. She could easily have said the hell with Ann. She didn't like women anyway. Women had no spine. Gloria thought they were more intelligent than men, but they didn't get as much out of it as men did. Unless trouble was getting something out of it. Now that Ann was safe and happy Gloria admitted to herself that what their schoolmates had suspected might easily have been true. It was nothing special against Ann. Gloria had a theory that there was a little of that in practically all women; just get them drunk enough in the right surroundings. And a lot of them didn't have to get drunk. She had had passes made at her by dressmakers' fitters, show girls, women doctors, and—and then she pulled herself out of this. For every woman who had made a pass at her there were ten, fifteen, a hundred, a thousand, who had not, and who probably had not the slightest inclination in that direction. But admitting that she was factually wrong did not get her out of the general mood. She came back to wishing Ann well, and found herself wanting to be away from Eddie. She was tired of being with him. The only person she wanted to be with was Liggett. She wanted to be home or with Liggett. One or the other. Away from the whole thing, all that was her usual life; Eddie, her friends, the smart places or the gay places, the language she and they spoke, and all about that life. But if she had to have any of it, she wanted all of it. Here, with the bright sun on Fifth Avenue, she was thinking that the only thing she wanted was to be with Liggett, lying in bed or on the floor or anywhere with him, drunk as hell, taking dope, doing anything he wanted, not caring about the time of day or the day of the week and not thinking whether it was going to end. And if not Liggett, then no one. Then she wanted to be home where she could be within sound of her mother's voice, surrounded by the furniture that she would not bump even in the dark. She wanted to be moral. She would stop smoking. She would wear plain clothes and no makeup. She would wear a proper brassière, no nail polish. She would get a job and keep regular hours. And she knew she could do these things, because she knew Liggett would be back. Maybe.

Eddie asked her to have more coffee but she said she had to go home and wait for a call. Like that Eddie understood. His gayety disappeared, he was considerate, he remembered that she had not been participating in his fun. "You go on home," he said. "I'm going uptown, and I'll take a bus from here."

"I'm sorry, Eddie."

"You're sorry? I'm the one to be sorry."

"It just happens today—"

"I know. Go ahead. Kiss me good-by."

"No," she said.

"All right, don't," he said. But she did, and at least made the waiter glad.

She went home, feeling like crying part of the way, and then halfway changing to pleased with herself because she was on her way home, which was a path to righteousness or something.

Three o'clock was striking when she let herself in. Elsie, the maid, was dusting the staircase and could easily have opened the door, but not Elsie. Sometimes Gloria suspected that Elsie, who was colored, knew something of Gloria's Harlem benders. It may have been that, and it may only have been the contrast between the respectful, almost slave-like obedience Elsie accorded Mrs. Wandrous, and the casual, silent manner Elsie showed Gloria.

"Packages come from the stores," said Elsie.

"For me?" said Gloria.

"Yes," said Elsie. She spoke it on a high note, as much as to say, "Why, sure. Who else would be getting packages in this house?"

"Then why don't you say so? . . . Oh, don't answer me." This was a swell way to start the new life, but this nigger irritated her. "What's your husband doing now? Is he working?"

"Why?" said Elsie.

"Don't ask why. Answer my question."

"He's gettin' along. Now and then he gets sumpn. Now may I ask why?"

"You may not." Gloria was on the verge of mentioning Lubby Joe, a Negro big shot the mention of whose name was enough to command respect among most Negroes. But it would be hard to explain how she knew Lubby Joe, and it was a thing that could not be left unexplained. This made her angry too, to start something she could not finish, especially something that would have given her so much pleasure as throwing a scare into Elsie. "Where'd you put the packages?"

"Uh cared them all the way up to your room," said Elsie.

"Yeah man!" said Gloria, in spite of herself.

She was upstairs, trying on the new clothes, when Elsie came in, dust-cloth in hand. "Some man called you on the phone. He lef' this here number."

"God damn you, you black bitch! Why didn't you give me this message when I came in?"

"Uh didn't think."

"Get out of here!"

She called the number, which was a private branch exchange, and the extension number which had been given Elsie. The extension did not answer. The number was the Biltmore. It could have been a *lot* of people, but it *couldn't* have been anyone but Liggett. She sat there half dressed, too furious to curse Elsie, hating the Negro race, hating herself and her luck. In five minutes she called the number again. It was always possible he was in the bathroom the first time. This time she left word that she had called. "Just say that Gloria phoned. The party will know." She only hoped it was Liggett. She was sitting there and she heard the front door close in the careful but not noiseless way her mother closed it. Gloria called to her to come upstairs.

"Certainly is getting warmer. When did you get back? Is Eddie really working?"

"Mother, this is the last straw. I want you to fire Elsie. Today."

"Why, what's she done?"

"I just had a very important message and she forgot to give it to me till just this minute, and of course when I called the party had left."

"Well, you know Elsie has a lot to do. She's got this whole house—"

"You can get any number of niggers that will do twice the work and won't forget a simple little thing like that. I'm sick of her. She's lazy—"

"Oh, no. No, she isn't lazy. Elsie's a good worker. I admit she has her shortcomings, but she isn't lazy, Gloria."

"She is! She's terrible, and I want you to fire her. I insist!"

"Oh, now don't fly off the handle this way over a simple little telephone message. If it's that important the person will call again, whoever it was. Who was it, and why is it so important?"

"It'd take too long to tell you now. I want you to fire Elsie, that's what I want you to do. If you don't I'll tell Uncle Bill. I won't stay here."

"Now look here, just because Elsie does something bad isn't any reason why you should be rude to me. You have your own way quite a lot it seems to me. Too much for your own good. You go around doing as you please, staying away at night and doing dear knows what, and we permit it because—well, I sometimes wonder why we do permit it. But you can't come home and disrupt the whole household because one little thing goes wrong. If you can't appreciate all the things we do, all for you—"

"I'm not going to listen to you." She went to the bathroom and locked the door. In the bathroom was a dressing table with triplicate mirrors and many lights. Even the front of the drawer had a mirror, and whenever she noticed this she thought about the unknown person who designed the table, what he or she must have had in mind: what earthly use could there be for a mirror on a drawer, just that height? What *other* earthly use, that is? It reflected your body right where your legs begin. Did other women really look at themselves as much as she did or what? Yes, she guessed they did, and it was not an altogether unwelcome thought. She wanted to be like other women, now, for the time being. She didn't want to be the only one of her type in the world. She didn't want to be a marked girl, who couldn't get along with the rest of the world. It had started out a good day, and then came Ann, and her joy for Ann didn't hold over an hour; she was bored with Eddie, really her best friend; she fought an undignified fight with Elsie, and she had a quarrel with her mother. Why did days have to start right if they were going to turn out like this? Was it to give you a false sense of security, an angry God, a cruel God, making you feel this was going to be a lovely day, about as swell a little day as you could hope to find, and then—smacko! Four times she had gone smacko! So what about this stuff of starting the day feeling it was going to be a good one? Or maybe it was a merciful God who did it. He gave you a good night's sleep, thereby making you feel good at the beginning of the

day, because He knew you were going to have a tough one and you'd
need all the optimism you could command. What about God, for that
matter? She hadn't thought about God for a long time. Monday she
would begin again, because she noticed one thing about people who
believed in God: they were warmer people than those who didn't. They
had a worse time, but they had a better time too. Catholics. Catholics
had more fun on parties than anyone else. The Broadway people were
mostly all Catholics or Jews, and they seemed to have a good time. At
least the Catholics did. As to the Jews, they never seemed to have a
really good time. They were too busy showing off when they were
supposed to be having a good time. Like Italians. Gloria at this point
changed her classification from Catholic to Irish. The people that
seemed to have the best time, at least so far as she had observed, were
the Irish Catholics who didn't go to Church. Some of them would confess once a year and then they could start all over again. That didn't
seem right to Gloria, if you were going to have a real religion, but it
certainly made those Catholics feel good. She decided she wanted to go
to a Catholic Church and confess. What a story that would be if she
ever told the father all she could tell. The party she went to thinking
it was being given by a movie actress and it turned out to be a gangster
party, where they had all the girls from a show and the gangsters tied
sheets to one girl's wrists and hung her stark naked out the twenty-
first-floor window, and when they pulled her in they thought she was
dead. All the girls getting stinking as fast as they could because they
were afraid to stay sober and afraid to suggest leaving. The two virgins.
The dwarf. The very young and toughest of the mob, who never even
smiled unless he was hurting somebody. She remembered how frightened she was, because that young man kept staring at her, but the
lawyer with whom she had gone to the party told the big shot that she
was Park Avenue, and the big shot got enough kick out of thinking his
party was shocking her. And it was. She had seen wild parties, but
this was beyond wild: the cruelty was what made it stick in her memory. She looked around the bathroom and it made her think of Rome.
Rome never saw parties like that. Rome didn't have electric light and
champagne and the telephone, thirty-story apartment houses and the
view of New York at night, saxophones and pianos. Here she was, just
a girl on the town, but about the only thing she had missed was lions
and Christians, and she supposed if she hung around long enough she'd
have to see that. With an effort she made herself quit this line of
thought. It was so real to her that she was sure her mother could hear

her thinking. She opened the bathroom door. Her mother had left the bedroom.

She decided to go away. Alone. Think things out. She opened her desk drawer where she kept her money, and she counted more than thirty dollars. Where to on thirty dollars, without asking anyone for more? This place, that place, no, no, no. Then yes: at five-thirty she could take a boat to Massachusetts. The *City of Essex* was leaving at five-thirty. She had enough to go there and back, pay all her meals, tips, magazines. She would take a small overnight bag.

"Miss Glaw-ria, telephone." Elsie from downstairs.

9

THE *City of Essex* was built in the late 1870's, and though to this day she is a fairly sturdy craft, her designers were working to catch the custom of a public that was different from today's. Different in quite a few ways, the citizens of the Republic in the Rutherford Birchard Hayes administration were especially different from the Hoover citizens in regard to the sun. When the *City of Essex* was built, the American people, traveling on ocean-going and coastal steamers, liked to be in the shade, or at least did not feel like climbing from one deck to another just to get sunburned. Thus the *City of Essex* had a top deck that was little more than a roof for the dining-room. It had a sort of cat-walk around this roof, abaft the wheelhouse.

If they were putting that much money into a boat today they would have a place on the top deck where people could lie and sit in the sun when the weather was fine. They would of necessity have proper handrailing along the edge of the deck. The handrailing would be high enough and strong enough to withstand the usual wear and tear on handrailing.

The *City of Essex*, however, was built in the late 1870's, and no matter how amusing passengers might find the elaborate decorations and furnishings of the dining-room, they could not say much for the handrailing along the top deck of this old side-wheeler. That handrailing was too low; it was dangerous.

But one of the last things Weston Liggett was worrying about, two decks below the top deck, was the handrailing two decks above him. The big worry was whether Gloria was on board the *City of Essex*, and there were other lesser worries. He was a man who a week ago had a home and now had only a hotel room. He was insanely infatuated with a girl young enough to be his daughter (he would not call it love: he was too angry with her for that). He had reason to believe that the girl was aboard this old tub, but he was not absolutely sure. He was not positive. What was more, he did not want to take any step toward finding out. He did not want to do any of the things by which he could find out. He did not want to ask the purser (he did not want to have anything to do with the purser, who was a round-shouldered man with a neatly trimmed mustache; thin, and with a way of holding his cigarette between the knuckles of his first two fingers that made you think right away of a man fast drying up who at one time had been a great guy with the women—a man who would be nastily suspicious of any inquiry about a young woman, rather tall, well dressed, about twenty-two). He did not want to ask a steward or anyone else if such a young woman had come on board. Probably in the back of Liggett's mind all this and the preceding day had been a strong doubt that his marriage had busted up. The habit of married thinking does not break so soon, not if the marriage has had time to mean anything good or bad, and hence the precautions he had been taking: when he telephoned Gloria he did not leave his name, because he was not registered at the hotel under his real name but under the name of Walter Little. He had made the reservation on the *City of Essex* under the name of Walter Little (the initials were the same as his own). When he tried to reach Gloria he had not left the phony name because he was afraid she would not call back any Walter Little. He had not left his own name because he was almost certain she would not call any Weston Liggett. And so, all the precautions before getting on the boat, and after boarding it. Aboard the *City of Essex* he did not, as he thought of it, wish to show his hand.

So far as anyone could be sure, he was sure that Gloria had no suspicion that he was aboard. She did not know where he was. He had been in his room when she phoned, but he had deliberately not answered. He had not called anyone else from the hotel, and it was therefore reasonable to suppose that any call would be from Gloria. He did not at first know why he had not answered, but the moment the phone stopped ringing he congratulated himself on a master stroke. Gloria's phoning meant that she was home. It just possibly meant only that she had phoned her home to find out if there had been any messages for her, but that was unlikely. It was more likely that she was home when she phoned his room at the hotel. Acting on his hunches and as part of the master stroke he took a cab to within a block of her house. He dismissed the cab. He was going to be patient. He had his mind made up that if Gloria was in that house he would wait ten hours if necessary until she came out. He bought a couple of afternoon papers at the newsstand at the end of Gloria's block, and looking at his watch very big, so that anyone who saw him would think he had an appointment, he stood with his papers, one open, one folded and tucked under his arm. He did not have long to wait. Less than ten minutes after he—as he thought of it—took up his vigil, Gloria appeared, carrying a bag. He got out of her sight until she got into a taxi. Liggett got into a taxi across the street. He pretended to be undecided about where to go (as he certainly was until Gloria's cab got under way). Then noticing that her cab was turning into a one-way street he told his driver to go through that street until he made up his mind. His mind was made up for him. From one one-way street Gloria's cab went to another one-way street, westbound as was the first. He followed her cab and watched her get out at the Massachusetts and Rhode Island Steamship Company pier. He kept his cab a few blocks longer, got out and took another cab to the M. & R. I. pier, having given Gloria time to get aboard. He knew enough about the M. & R. I. ships, because he had taken them many times when Emily would be spending summers with her family at Hyannisport. He knew that they never left on the dot of 5:30, and he could take the *City of Essex* at the last minute if he so chose. He did so choose, because at next to the last minute a thought came that almost made him give up today's chase: What if Gloria was going on a trip with some other man? Some cheap fellow, to be going on a trip of this kind. It was common and cheap. Worse than Atlantic City. He almost didn't go, but then he thought what the hell? If she wanted to do that, now would be the time to find it out, and if she didn't, it would be a swell opportunity to talk to her and get her to listen to reason about the coat and all the other things he wanted to discuss with her. He felt weak and impotent when he thought how much of his life depended on her consent. Just her consent. A whim, perhaps. She might say no now to something that next week she would say yes to. So much depended on her consent, and her consent depended so much on his approach. If he went at her threateningly she might tell him to go —— himself, but if he went at it in the right way he might easily get her to agree to everything. And one of the things he was beginning to want very much to have her agree to was that she should sleep with him tonight. So when he came aboard the *City of Essex* his plan was to lie low and after dinner he would talk to her and then see what happened. He hoped she wasn't the kind that gets seasick on Long Island Sound.

On the *City of Essex* there is a narrow space of deck belting all the outside cabins except four on each side of the ship. On the starboard and on the port side are two sets of four cabins each which the reader must remember never to take when traveling in the *City of Essex*. These uncomfortable cabins are just forward of the housing that covers the side-wheels which propel the ship. Liggett had one of these cabins.

There was nothing to do but sit and look out the cabin window. The cabin was very narrow, and Liggett parked his ass on a little stool and put his forearms on the window sill and smoked cigarettes. He took off his coat and was more comfortable, and really it wasn't bad when you looked out the window. The *City of Essex* goes at a pretty good clip down the North River and up the East, under the bridges, past the (Liggett was on the port side) wasted municipal piers of the East River, the unheard-of tramp steamers docked north of the Brooklyn Bridge, and on up into the section from Mitchel Place north, occupied by Beekman and Sutton Place buildings which Liggett knew, inhabited by people he knew. He knew by the sound when he was near and under the Queensborough Bridge. There was so much hysterical noise of thousands of straphangers and motorists hurrying home to their hutches in Queens and Nassau counties. All the way up the river, and especially in the vicinity of Hell Gate Liggett kept thinking what a big job it is to be mayor of New York. All the dock employees, the cop on Exterior Street, the hospital people, the cops of the Marine Division, the people who worked on Welfare Island (which Liggett of course could not see), the hospital people on one island and the rat-fighters on another, the woman who had to live on a city-owned island because she spread typhoid fever, the men running the ferry-boats, the fellows making repairs under one of the bridges—there were enough of them to make up a good-sized (and probably very horrible-looking) city. And the only name they all knew was James J. Walker. Liggett wondered if Walker ever thought of that—and if he did was it a good thing for him to think of? Maybe he thought of it too often. It was too much of a job for one man. Liggett decided that the next time he saw Walker he would tell him he ought to have a rest (although Walker had just got back from one). Still daylight, and too early by his watch for Liggett to hunt out Gloria.

Blueprints. Did the average person know how many blueprints had to be kept on file for, say, a coal hoist like the one he was passing? There were prints of all the elevations of the building itself, and floor plans and so on; but the prints that a plan engineer had to use, for instance. The average man would look at a switchboard and not know

that there was a blueprint for the board itself, then prints for the wiring
and insulation, prints for a dynamo, a separate print for various parts
like a bearing. Good Lord! what if you could invent a blueprint material that would be a lot better than any now in existence, and marketa-
ble at a profit but selling a little lower than any other today? You'd
make a fortune that would be like gold. For all the blueprints Liggett
had looked at he knew nothing about how the paper was made. Oh,
well. That wasn't his line, but all the same it was a fascinating thing to
think about. All those thousands of blueprints. Why, in one plant
alone, like the Edison plant . . .

A commuting boat, owned by a fellow Liggett knew, and supported
by five acquaintances of Liggett's, caught up with and passed the *City
of Essex* like a bat out of hell. The commuting boat, a two-step hydro-
plane with Wright Typhoons, was up out of the water and going like
a bat out of hell. Why did people take such chances in the East River,
when a floating cigar box hitting the hull when the commuting boat
was going that fast, would smash through the hull and raise hell, probably kill all the passengers and the small crew. "Jesus, but some guys
are God damn fools," said Liggett. If that was their idea of a thrill, all
right; but as a way to get home it was lousy. Granted that the Long
Island was not the ideal railroad, it would still be better than getting
killed in a boat like that. It would be safer and quicker to take a plane,
because you could land a plane near the yacht club which was this
boat's home port. It wouldn't be more expensive to use a plane, either.
What God damn fools some fellows were! Every single one of them a
married man with at least one kid, and at least one of the fellows really was not in a position to pay his share of the tremendous cost of this
boat. Why did they do things that way, or anyway why go so fast?

But Liggett was only thinking from momentum after reminding himself that those fellows were married. He wasn't thinking much at all;
because the sight of a boat speeding husbands homeward did not make
him feel good. The next time he went home there would be strain even
between the girls and himself. Emily, naturally you would expect it of
her. But it would have communicated itself to the girls—if indeed Emily
had not actually told them that their father would not be living at
home any more. Ruth. The thing that made him kiss her hand in the
station wagon. The way she had taken charge at the family luncheon.
Oh, the things he wanted to do for her, the things he wanted to do with
her. He realized that for a couple of years now he had been having the
beginning of anticipation of the day when he would be able to take
her out to dinner and the theater and a night club, to boat races and

football games. Probably there wouldn't be many times like that; she was a beautiful kid. "Jesus, sometimes she takes your breath away," he thought. Not beautiful in a conventional way. It was more in the eyes, the set of her chin when she was sitting quietly on a porch or in a corner, not knowing she was being watched. He guessed there were no new things that a father could feel about his daughter. But he guessed no father felt so deeply, little though he might show it. You couldn't show it much with Ruth. Kissing her hand like that on Sunday—it had just come over him and he had done it, and he knew she liked it. That was good. Her liking it. She liked him better than she did Emily. No, but in a different way. And he liked her so much better than when she was a little kid. She got bigger, and your love got bigger. She was more completely a girl, a person, and your love was more complete. He wanted to be with her all the time she was pregnant, when she was having her first baby by the swell young guy she would marry. Not some older guy who had gone around and laid a lot of girls and was out of college five or ten years, but someone her own age. Like those two people in one of the Galsworthy novels, only they were cousins, weren't they? And they had to be careful not to have children. Ruth. Lovely, dear Ruth, that a father could love.

The tears were in his eyes and one or two out over the lower lid, and he became aware that he had not noticed it at first because dusk had come and darkness was coming. The light was gone. You were conscious of the curtains in the windows of the small yachts that the *City of Essex* passed. He was hungry. The clean feeling he had from loving Ruth did not last long. He remembered what he was to do on this boat.

Gloria was hungry too. One more discomfort. The other was that ever since she had come aboard the *City of Essex* she had wanted to go to the bathroom, and she was afraid to go. She had used toilets in speakeasies where to breathe the air seemed pretty risky. But there was something intimate about a speakeasy in the family. No one who went to the same speakeasy as you did would be so mean as to give you something. That was almost the way she felt about speakeasy toilets; but she always took elaborate precautions anyway. But on this old boat everything was so *old*. The women's toilet (as distinguished from the ladies' room in a speakeasy, the johnny at school, the little girls' room at a party in an apartment, and the wash-my-hands on a train) was clean enough, and an elderly Negress was there to sell you safety pins. Gloria took one look, went into one of the toilets, and then came right out.

The old Negress probably thought she was crazy, but this was not Gloria's day for caring what old or young Negresses thought. Finally, after failing altogether to win out by "not thinking about it," she gave in, went to the bathroom, came back and was ready for a fight or a frolic and a small steak.

She was working on the steak when a woman spoke to her. Gloria was alone at a table for two, the woman was alone at a table for four. "Always a nice breeze on Long Island Sound, isn't there?" said the woman.

"Yes, isn't there?" said Gloria.

"It's my first ride on one of these boats, although ha ha I've been to Europe several times. But I wanted to take this ride to see what it was like."

"Yes. Mm-hmm," said Gloria.

"Just about what I expected. I wonder where we're off of right now do you suppose? Think we passed New Haven? Because I have friends live there. I'm from— I'll bet you didn't come as far as I did for this trip. You're a New Yorker, I can tell that, aren't you?"

"You can tell it to anyone you please," was what Gloria wanted to say. "Yes, New York," was what she said.

"Want to come over and sit at my table? There isn't anyone else sitting here, and we're the only ladies traveling by ourselves I notice."

"Well—do you mind if I finish my steak? It'd be so much trouble to move now. But thank you. I'll have dessert with you if I may." She wished she had what some girls had: the ability to get rid of bores, instead of talking nervously and not thinking what she was saying. She didn't want to have dessert with this school-teacher or whatever she was.

"Then I'll come over to your table. I'm all finished eating, but I'd like to have a cigarette, only I hate to light one here when I'm sitting by myself. It looks funny. Yih know? When yih see a woman eating by herself smoking in a public restrunt. Where are you from? Oh, you did tell me, New York. Tsih. I want to go to New York for a real stay some time. I'm always going some place when I go to New York, on my way to Europe or else home after being to Europe. Oh, did I burn you?" Hot sulphur from the woman's match was scratched loose and stung Gloria's wrist. "Here, let me have a look. . . . No, it's all right. It may burn a little. I'd put something on it if I were you. Awful the way they make these matches. I suppose that Ivan what's his name made these. The match king, from Denmark. No, Sweden. Do you see that man over

there with the cigar? That's the reason why I wanted to sit with somebody. He's drunk."

"He *looks* sober," said Gloria.

"Not, though. Drunk as a coot. Tight as a tick."

"Tight as a tick. Did you make that up? Just now?" said Gloria.

"Oh, no. Why, we say that all the time at home. Tight as a tick?
Didn't you ever say that?"

"Never heard it before in my life. What does it mean? What is a
tick?"

"Well, I've always wondered that too, but I guess it must be something tight. It couldn't mean the tick of a watch, because I don't see
anything tight about the tick of a watch. What do they say in your
crowd when someone is three sheets to the wind?"

"I have no crowd."

"Well—I mean, your friends. What do they say when someone is under the weather?"

"Oh," said Gloria. "Well, I don't think you'd like what they say."

"Really? Why? Is it risqué?"

"Yes, a little."

"Tell me. What is it? I won't be shocked."

"Well," said Gloria. "Most of my friends, my *men* friends, they say,
'I was stewed to the balls last night.' My girl friends—"

"Really. I took you for a lady but I see I was wrong. Excuse *me*," said
the woman, and stood up and left the room.

"I didn't have to do that, but I guess I had to," Gloria told herself.
"Now I'd like a drink, and isn't it nice? I won't be able to get one." She
smoked a cigarette, hoping the strange woman would come back and
think she looked funny. She went out on deck, and on the radio on deck
the Connecticut Yankees were plugging Mr. Vallée's recording of "The
Wind in the Willows." The air was pretty good. There was no moon.

This was one of Gloria's nights for not looking at men. At a party or
at a ball, in a railroad station or a public speakeasy, on the street, at a
football game, Gloria always did one of two things about the matter
of looking at men. She either did one or the other: she either got the
eye of a stranger and stared him down, giving him a complete and unmistakable going over the way few American men have the nerve to do
with American women; or else she all but did what they call in the
movies "fig bar." Fig bar is a term which covers the whole attitude of
the very bashful child; the toes turned in, eyes lowered, and especially
the finger in the mouth. Gloria could be bashful when she wanted to,
and she frequently wanted to. She never got over her real terror of a

strange crowd. She could not recall a time when this was not true. It was true of her as a child, and on one occasion it had made her do something she never got over regretting. It was at a party, and it was that she had stayed with a man with four other people looking on; two men, two women. The other women wanted to do it, and did, but Gloria was the first. It was one of the few times in her life that she did something that made her repeatedly ask why she had done it. When she discovered that the reason probably was that she was showing off more intensely than ever before, and that the reason for wanting to show off was this unconquerable shyness—it didn't make the whole thing any better. She was glad when one of the women who had seen it, a second-string movie actress, died. That made one less person who had seen it. She wished the others would die, too. But she did not wish it very strongly, because she knew that the other woman, not the actress, probably wished Gloria dead too. And it did nothing to cure her shyness. It only made it worse. Sometimes just as she was about to enter a bar she would remember the time—and she could hardly force herself to enter the bar. Other times she would be passing a row of tables and she would hate her evening gown for the very things that had influenced her selection of it: its décolletage, the way it fit over the hips. Full well she knew the movement of her own hips as she walked, as though each hip were a fist, clenching and unclenching, and the rhythm locked forever, reminding her of a metronome. She knew, because she had watched other girls. A girl walks across a room, her hips going *tick-tock tick-tock*. The girl becomes self-conscious and stops at a table, interrupting the rhythm with the hip resting on *tick*; but when she resumes her walk, *tock* goes the other hip, and *tick-tock*.

It was dark on deck and on Long Island Sound. The thin bars of light on Long Island and Connecticut shore were better light than the cheap lamps on deck. Gloria told the steward to put a chair in the middle of the deck for her. She did not notice anyone.

Thus she did not see Liggett, who was leaning against the rail on the starboard side, looking at Long Island and being honest with himself in that he was guessing, and guessing only, the position of the *City of Essex*. When he heard Gloria's heels on deck he tightened up. He knew the sound for the sound of a girl's shoes. He turned and saw that she did not look in his direction. He watched a steward put a chair down for her. He left and went to the dining-room.

The Negro waiter was none too pleasant about giving him something to eat, as it was past the dinner hour, but Liggett was not in a mood for humoring waiters. When the Negro brought the soup Liggett said: "Take that back. It's cold." He knew the Negro was making a face at him and when he began to mumble Liggett looked up and said: "What?" so quickly that you could hardly hear the *t*. All aspirate. Then the white headwaiter came over and asked if there was anything wrong, and Liggett said no, thank you. The Negro picked up the plate and the headwaiter followed, obviously asking him what the hell was going on. The Negro answering the man said the soup was cold, the head-waiter telling him well, then for Christ's sake bring *hot* soup and be quick about it, and the Negro whining that cole soop want his faul, chef to blame for cole soop and anyway looka what time tis. Liggett was pretty well pleased with the way he had handled the situation, not snitching to the headwaiter.

Abruptly, he stood up. The headwaiter rushed over to him. "Anything wrong, sir?"

"I don't feel well. I think I'd better have some air." He didn't feel sick but he certainly didn't want to eat his dinner. "Never mind the dinner."

"I'm sorry, sir," said the headwaiter.

" 'T's all right," said Liggett.

He went up on deck again and Gloria was not in her chair. She was standing at the rail on the port side. It was noticeably colder and the only other people on deck were an Italian-American and his wife and two children, the Italian trying to get his money's worth of sea air, and the sleepy wife and children looking up to him for the signal to go to bed.

"Hello," said Liggett.

Gloria turned to give him cold stare Number 25, but said: "Good God!"

"I'm quite a stranger," said Liggett. "I'll say it for you."

"I wasn't going to say that. What—how did you happen to be on this boat?"

"You don't think I just happened to be on board, do you?"

"No, but how did you know I was going to be on this boat?"

"I followed you."

"Ooh. What a cheap trick. Followed me."

"Well, I had to see you."

"You didn't have to follow me. You could have called me again."

"Then I'd have missed you. You left your house a short time after you got my message."

"It was your message. I thought it was."

"Yes, it was my message. Do you want to sit down?"

"Not particularly."

"I do."

"I'd rather stand. Aren't you afraid people will know you?"

"Who, for instance? Those Italians? They look like friends of mine?"

"You never can tell."

"Anyway, there they go," said Liggett. "Now listen to me for five minutes, will you please?"

"I'll sit down now. I'm weak."

"Why?"

"Well, the way you suddenly appear."

"Been on the boat since five-thirty."

"You kill me."

"Here. Do you want to sit here?" he said. "Now look here—"

"Oh, no, thanks. I don't want any of those now look here discussions."

"I'm sorry. How shall I begin?"

"Are you all right? I mean after the fight? I thought you'd be hurt pretty badly."

"I may have a rib kicked loose."

"Well, don't fool around with that, then. I knew a boy had a rib kicked loose in football and finally it punctured his lung."

"You wouldn't want that to happen to me, would you?"

"No. Whether you believe it or not, I wouldn't."

"Why not? Simple humanitarian instincts or what?"

"No. Better than that. Or worse."

"What?"

"I love you."

"Aw-haw. That's a laugh."

"I know."

"What makes you think you love me?"

"I don't know. Nothing makes me think I love you. It's closer than that. It isn't as far away from me as something making me think I love you. It's knowing that I do love you. I don't expect you to believe it, but it's true."

"I beg your pardon. Have a cigarette."

"Oh, how nice. American cigarettes. There's a big fine if you're caught smuggling them into Massachusetts."

"Don't kid."

"All right."

He reached for her hand, but she would not let him hold it. "No. You wanted to talk. Talk, then."

"All right," he said. "Well, in the first place, I've left my wife. Or rather—I don't know how to put it. Technically I *have* left my wife—"

"Permanently?"

"Permanently? Why, yes. Of course permanently."

"Of course permanently," she repeated. "As a matter of fact you don't know whether it's permanently or not. I can tell by your tone, you haven't even thought about that phase of it."

"No, I guess I haven't figured it out by months and days and years. Are you cold?"

"Yes. But we'll stay here."

"You don't have to be nasty about it. I merely asked."

"I'm sorry."

"Well, to get back to the subject. My wife and I have split up. Permanently. I told her about you—"

"Why did you do that?"

"I didn't mention your name."

"That isn't what I meant. Why did you tell her before you told me?"

"I didn't have much chance to tell you, remember."

"Even so you should have told me. You should have waited. What did you do that for? I'm not a home-wrecker. You have children. It's the worst kind of luck to break up a home. You should have told me first."

"I don't see what difference that would have made. It had nothing to do with the facts."

"What facts? You mean my sleeping with you? Did you tell her I slept with you in your apartment? Did you?"

"Yes."

"Oh, you fool. You awful fool. Oh. Oh. Oh, Liggett. Why did you do that? You poor man. Ah, kiss me."

He kissed her. She put her hand on the back of his neck. "What else did you do? What else did you tell her?" she said.

"I told her everything except your name."

"What did she say?"

"Well, I didn't give her much chance to say anything. I told her I loved you."

"Yes. And didn't she ask you my name? No, she wouldn't want to know that. She'll find out soon enough, I suppose."

"I didn't want to tell her your name. I wouldn't have if she'd asked me."

"She wouldn't be in any hurry to know that now. What are her plans?"

"I'm not sure. I told her I'd give her a divorce in New York if she wanted it. I'd give her grounds."

Gloria laughed. "You already have."

"That's exactly what she said."

"Is she going to accept your kind offer?"

"I think she plans to go to Reno."

"Why go to all that expense? Get her to get one in New York. I'll be the unidentified woman in the lacy negligee."

"No. Reno's better."

"It's expensive. It costs a lot of money to go to Reno, so I'm told."

"But I think she wants to go to Reno, so whatever she wants to do is all right with me, except we'll have to have some arrangement about my seeing the children."

"How old are they?"

"Ruth, the older one, she's going on sixteen, or maybe she is sixteen, and the younger one, Barbara, she's two years younger."

"Yes, I remember now. You did tell me. But that's not so good. Isn't the older one going to have a coming-out party?"

"I doubt it like hell. Those things cost. Two years ago, yes. But not this year, or next year."

"Next year we're going to have a revolution."

"Where do you get that kind of talk? Revolution. In this country? We might have a Democrat president, but—or is that what you mean by revolution."

"I mean bloody revolution. Heads on staffs or staves or whatever you call them. Pikes. Your head, for instance. All the rich. Your head and a straw hat with a Racquet Club band on it. That's the way they're going to tell which heads to cut off. Dekes, Psi U's, Racquet Club, Squadron A."

"Will you marry me?" he said.

"I was trying to get your mind off that. You don't have to feel you're bound to ask me that."

"It's pretty obvious that I'm not doing this because I have to. It's because I want to. Do you *want* to get married?"

"To you, yes, but—"

"There are no buts. If you want to, we will. There isn't any other consideration."

"On the contrary, there are thousands of other considerations, but they don't matter."

"That's what I meant."

"No, it isn't. But we won't argue the point. Yes, I'll marry you. You get the divorce fixed up and all that and I'll marry you and I'll be a good wife, too."

"I know you will."

"Oh, not for the reason you think. You think because I've been around like a man and I'm ready to settle down. That's not the real reason why I'll be a good wife."

"Isn't it?"

"Absolutely not. Do you want to know the real reason? Because it's born in me. My mother. I was thinking today what a wonderful wife she was to my father, and still is after all these years. In a way of course you're right. Living the kind of life I've led then finding out that there's only one life for a woman. I know you'd rather not have me mention the kind of life I've led, but I can't just pretend it never existed."

"Where's your stateroom?"

"It's on my key. Where's yours? I'd rather go to yours."

He told her how to get to his. "I'll go down now," he said.

"I'll be down in five minutes," she said.

In his stateroom he thought what an awful place it was to bring her to. Then when she knocked on his door he was embarrassed some more. He sat on the lower berth and she faced him and he put his arms around her at the hips. Here she was, just under her clothes, standing with her hands holding the upper berth and ready for anything he wanted.

"No!" she said.

"What?"

"I don't want you to," she said.

"You will," he said. "Sit down."

"No, darling." She sat down on the berth beside him.

"What's the matter?" he said.

"I don't know."

"Yes, you do. What is it?"

She looked half way around the tiny stateroom and then brought her head back to looking straight ahead.

"Oh," he said. "But it won't always be like this."

"But I don't want it ever to be like this, ever again. Not even now."

"Then we can go to your room," he said.

"No. It isn't much better. It's bigger, but not better. It's still a dirty little stateroom on the *City of Essex*."

"Only for tonight," he said. "I want you so much. I love you, Gloria."

"Yes, and I love you even more. Ah, no. Look. Look at that bed. Those sheets. They weigh a ton. Damp. Cold. And we can't both stand up at the same time in this room. Oh, the whole thing. Like a traveling salesman and his chippy."

"You're no chippy, and I'm not a traveling salesman. We're as good as married now. Signing a lot of papers won't make us more so."

"Yes, it will. Not signing the papers, but what the papers imply will. I'm going up to get some air and then to my room. Do you want to come along?"

"To your room?"

"No. On deck. I won't stay with you tonight, on this boat. If you don't want to come with me, all right, darling. I'll see you in the morning. When we get off the boat we can go to a hotel and I'll go right to bed with you. But not here."

"Mm."

"It isn't scruples. You know that. It's just so God-damned—"

"Cheap and vulgar, I suppose. You're a fine one to talk."

"I know. That's just it. Good night. If you don't want to see me in the morning, all right. Good night."

He did not answer, and she left. He sat there, hating her for a moment, for the truth was he wanted her in this room almost as much as he wanted her at all. The very smallness of the room would make it good, like being in a box. It would be new.

And then he began to see what she meant. He was sorry for what he had said (but knew he could make it up). What he wanted to do was to see her before she went to bed, tell her he was sorry, and tell her she was right about the room. She was no common tart, and she had a right to object to lying on this bed. He put on his vest and coat and left the room.

The sounds that the boat made muffled the heavy thump of his feet on the deck. That was the only way he knew how noisy the boat was. Ordinarily he made a lot of noise walking, but the big pistons that turned the side wheels, and the wheels themselves, and the nose of the *City of Essex* pushing into the water, and the rather stiff offshore breeze —it wasn't sail. "Jeep," he said, when he meant to say Gee. The breeze filled his mouth and made him gulp.

One deck, two decks, and no Gloria. He saw a sign hanging from a cord, Passengers Not Allowed on Top Deck After 8 P.M. That's where she would be.

He climbed over the cord and the sign and walked slowly up the stairs. There was no need to proceed quietly. Apparently every passenger had gone to bed and it was Liggett's guess that no deckhand would be at work on the *City of Essex* at this hour.

At the top of the steps he could see only the outline of the wheel-house, and the *City of Essex's* single stack and some ventilators. There was one short string of light on the shore, and it was all dark otherwise. Then he saw Gloria, he guessed it was Gloria, sitting on the dining-saloon roof. She turned at that moment and saw him, her eyes having become better accustomed to the darkness. She got up and ran forward. Then she stopped and looked around.

"Oh, all right," he called, and turned and started down the stairway. Half way down he heard a scream, or thought he heard a scream. He ran down the few remaining steps, and this time he knew he heard a scream. He looked down at the water just in time to see Gloria getting sucked in by the side wheel. Then the boat stopped.

"There was nothing I could do," said Liggett to nobody.

10

THERE IS not much room between the blades of the side wheels and the housing that covers each wheel. It was half an hour before they got what was left of Gloria out from between the blade and the housing, and nobody wanted to do it then. If she had fallen overboard abaft the housing she would have been shot away from the *City of Essex* by the force of the wheel, but where she fell was just forward of the housing, and there is a tremendous suck there. The *City of Essex* is always pulling in floating timber and dead dogs and orange peel, and sometimes when the wheel makes its turn the stuff is kicked out again. Sometimes not. The men in the wheelhouse heard the second scream and signaled to stop. By that time Gloria was caught by the blades and was pulled up into the housing, counterclockwise, in one long crush. She probably was killed the first time a blade batted her on the skull, by the same blade that pulled her up into the housing. There was no place in her body where there was a length of bone unbroken more than five inches. One A. B. fainted when he saw what he was going to have to do. The captain of the *City of Essex*, Anthony W. Parker, had only seen one thing like it before in his life, and that was a man in the black gang of the old *Erma* when the *Erma's* boiler burst off Nantucket in 1911. Captain Parker directed the removal of the woman's body from the wheel. He and two A. B.'s entered the housing from inside the boat. The A. B.'s carried an ordinary army blanket. One of the A. B.'s accepted a slug of brandy from the captain's flask; the other man was going to take one, but he decided he could work better without it.

They put the blanket over the body first, then gently rolled the body over and into the blanket. Captain Parker helped them carry the body inside the hull. "Go on back and see if you can find the other hand," said Captain Parker. "She may have been wearing a ring. Have to find out who she is." The search for the other hand was unsuccessful.

"Keep that covered up," said Captain Parker, when the blanket fell open. "Go on back with you," he said, to the engine room crew who had collected.

The chief steward was called and he sent for one of the stewardesses, a middle-aged Negress. She screamed and was hard to manage, and it took five minutes for them to persuade her to examine just the girl's clothing, which they showed her by lifting a corner of the blanket. It took ten more minutes to get some answer out of her, and then she said yes, she recognized the dress, and gave the number of Gloria's stateroom. The captain sent someone there, and the someone returned, saying it must be her, her bed hadn't been slept in and the room didn't look occupied.

"She only come aboard to do the Dutch act," said Captain Parker. It was a hell of a thing. A young girl. Probably in the family way. The thought never crossed his mind that it was anything but suicide. A young girl, maybe eighteen, maybe twenty-one, according to the stewardess, who came on board alone, ate alone, according to the chief steward (who remembered her come to think of it, after hearing the stewardess describe her; and was corroborated by the purser), and was not seen talking to anyone. Captain Parker had to make a complete report for the owners and for the port authorities in New York and Massachusetts. Some assistant district attorney that wanted to get his name in the paper probably would be down snooping around and trying to make something of it. But here was one case of premeditated suicide and no two ways about it. It was too bad she didn't jump off the stern, but if you wanted to die that much it probably didn't make much difference which way you did it. Captain Parker hoped for her sake she got one on the skull when she was drawn in, otherwise it was a terrible death, judging from the looks of her. A terrible death. Well, girls got themselves in the family way these days irregardless of all the ways they had now that they didn't use to have to keep from getting that way. Captain Parker wondered whether he ought to say the Lord's Prayer over the body, but he looked around at his officers and men, and no, no Lord's Prayer in front of them. Fanchette, one of the A. B.'s, from Pawtucket, had crossed himself when he saw the body. That was enough. If the girl's family wanted to, they could have a service and all the prayers they wanted.

The *City of Essex* resumed her trip, and the next morning in port the passengers were asked to give their names and addresses before leaving the ship. Otherwise to most of the passengers the trip was as usual, and many left the boat unaware of what had occurred. Liggett had one awful moment when he almost forgot to write Walter Little instead of his real name. He took a taxi from the pier to the railroad station and from there took the first train to New York.

11

THE TRIP to New York was old, old scenery for Liggett—the years in prep school and college and at Harvard and on leave during the war and visiting Emily at Hyannisport. But he never took his eyes off the scenery, old or not. There comes one time in a man's life, if he is unlucky and leads a full life, when he has a secret so dirty that he knows he never will get rid of it. (Shakespeare knew this and tried to say it, but he said it just as badly as anyone ever said it. "All the perfumes of Arabia" makes you think of all the perfumes of Arabia and nothing more. It is the trouble with all metaphors where human behavior is concerned. People are not ships, chess men, flowers, race horses, oil paintings, bottles of champagne, excrement, musical instruments, or anything else but people. Metaphors are all right to give you an idea.)

Liggett thought he knew what had happened, and he called himself a murderer. Then he stopped calling himself a murderer, because he began to like it, and this was no time to like what you were calling yourself. A murderer is a man in an opera box with a black cape and a dirk; a man with a .38 automatic and an unfaithful wife; a man in leather chaparejos with many conchos, and a Marlin rifle. It is a hard thing to get away from the thinking you do as a boy, when you learn that a murderer is a noble criminal. You have to unlearn it. Liggett had seen one murder in his life. In France. He had seen many men killed, and some in hand-to-hand fighting, but only one murder. One of his men was fighting a German and getting the best of the German, with the German beginning to bend over backward against the trench. The American could easily have taken care of the German, but one of Liggett's sergeants, taking his time about it, came up and fired his pistol twice into the German's ear. That was murder. And in his way the sergeant was a murderer. He belonged to the long line of murderers and not of warriors. Gang killings were murder.

It was a reprehensible thing, but murderers bore some relation to history. What he had done bore no relation to history, and never would. He hoped it never would. He didn't want it to. He hated having this secret but he wanted no one else to have it—and knew that he was leaning forward in his seat so that the train would hurry and he could spill it all to Emily.

Now there was Emily. Always before there had been Emily and always would be. He thought away from that, the way on a train you think away from things. A good thought comes and is the big thing in your mind, but it sticks there and the click of the car wheels over the joints, especially on lines that use 90-pound and other light rail, lulls you to sleep with your eyes open, the thought sticking in your mind, then forgotten, supplanted by another thought.

Thus the thought of Emily, giving way to the thought of what had happened last night. He could see it all, including what he had missed. When Gloria ran and he called to her, he believed she could hear his voice, the angry tone, but not the words; and so she ran again when he called, "Oh, all right." She was headed for the stairway on the port side, behind the wheelhouse but pretty far forward, hoping to get away from him by running down the stairs. But in the darkness and on account of the motion of the ship she ran smack into the rail, which is extremely low on the top deck of the *City of Essex.* She most likely hit the rail just below or just about at her knees. The forward throw of the upper part of her body—and she fell into the water. The scream, and then the second scream, and he knew he could not save her, knew it the fraction of a second after he comprehended what was happening. Well, he could have died with her.

He would tell it all to Emily. Yes, he knew he was afraid not to tell her. If she told him to go to the police and tell what happened, he would do it. But he would not tell them without being told to do it. Yes, he knew he hoped she would tell him not to go to the police.

At Grand Central he went through the passage and up the steps to the Biltmore, got his key, went to his room, came down and paid his bill. Back to the Grand Central, he gave the bag to a Red Cap (he did not want anyone to see him carrying it). He told the Red Cap to check the bag and bring him the check. He bought the afternoon papers. The story was on the front pages of the *Journal* and the *Telegram*—the *World-Telegram,* they were calling it now, and it looked like something they got out during a printer's strike. There was nothing in the

Evening Post, the paper Emily read. The *Journal* had a headline: MYSTERY DEATH N. Y. GIRL IN L. I. SOUND. The story was to the effect that mystery surrounded the death of Gloria Wandrous, 18, brunette, pretty, and her leap to death from the *City of Essex.* She was identified by *her clothing!*

Liggett read no more. What about Emily's coat? Where in God's name was that coat? If Gloria had kept it at home it would be easy to identify it. The police never had any trouble identifying a thing like that, an expensive mink coat. They would go right to Emily. It was all right for her, but where was her husband that night? What was her coat doing in Miss Wandrous's apartment or house? Did she know Miss Wandrous? Did she know of her husband's relations with Miss Wandrous? Was she shielding her husband? Where was her husband that night? Then that cop in the speakeasy. He would make a report. The bartender would see it in the papers and he would comment on it to the cop, and the cop would report that the girl had had trouble with a man's attentions the Tuesday before she killed herself—*if* she killed herself. Then the people in the speakeasy the night he introduced himself to Gloria. They were the kind of people who reveled in anything like inside information when there was a scandal. "Did you read about poor Gloria? Gloria Wandrous? Yes. Why, yes. Why, we were with her and what's his name, Weston Liggett, at Duilio's the other night. Isn't it awful? The poor kid. I thought Liggett had taken quite a shine to her." Then there was that kid, Brunner. Just a friend, Gloria had said, but a friend would be worse now than a lover. All her lovers were checking their alibis for last night, and they would be only too glad to keep out of the whole thing, but not a friend. Liggett went home.

He still had his key and he let himself in. The maid answered his questions: No, there had been no callers or telephone messages; yes, Mrs. Liggett was out and would be back around three o'clock. She was shopping, the maid said.

Liggett chain-smoked cigarettes and poured himself a drink but could not drink anything but water. Then he sat down and wrote Emily a note. "Emily," he wrote. "Please meet me at '21' at four o'clock. This is terribly important and I beg of you to come. W." Then he called Lockheed, next in charge at the office, and told Lockheed he had been ill—"confidentially I've been on my semi-annual bender"—and Lockheed said everything was under control, no messages of any importance, he would send up bids on the Brooklyn job for Liggett's approval, but it didn't look like they would get the contract as old John McCooey was sore about something. . . .

Liggett had had an idea. He would go to Brunner and ask him quite frankly whether he knew anything about the fur coat. He was sure Brunner did know about the coat. It was the kind of thing Gloria would regret doing, and she would discuss it with a friend. And Liggett believed it possible for Gloria to have a friend. He believed Brunner was her friend. He had had a girl the other night. Not bad, either; and a man who was having an affair with Gloria wouldn't be likely to bring along an attractive girl. Anyway, Liggett's plan was to tell Brunner he had read about Gloria, how sorry he was, how much he loved Gloria. He might even go so far as to say he and Gloria planned to get married, but he would have to be careful how he did that. He would have to be ready to say that now that she was dead, there was no use having a lot of trouble—two young girls—the coat. If he knew how to get the coat or where it was, he was sure that was what Gloria would want done.

Liggett found the address in the telephone book, and went there by subway and on foot. Brunner, thank God, was in. He recognized Liggett, which encouraged Liggett but also put some worry in reserve.

"Mr. Brunner, I don't know whether you remember me," said Liggett.

"Yes. Mr. Liggett. What can I do for you?"

"Well—no, thanks. I've been smoking too much all day. I guess you know why I came."

"I imagine something about Gloria. You knew she—"

"I just saw it in the afternoon papers," said Liggett. "I don't know how to start. You were her best friend, she told me."

"Guess so."

"Did she tell you about us, about our plans?"

"Well, I knew you were having an affair," said Eddie. Eddie stood up. "Listen, did you come here about that God damn coat? Because if you did, there it is. Take it and stick it. I don't want you coming here with a long face and all you're worried about is are you going to get mixed up in a public scandal. You want the coat, so take it. I'm sure I don't want it. She didn't want it either. The only reason she took the God damn thing was because you tore the clothes off her. Guys like you put her where she is today. I wouldn't be surprised if you were the real—" The doorbell rang.

"Who's that?"

"Probably a friend of mine." Eddie pushed the release button and then poked his head out and looked down the hall. "Who is it?"

"Mr. Brunner? My name is Malloy and I would like to talk to you spare a minute of your time I'd like to ask you a few spare if you—"

"Talk sense, what do you want? Oh, it's *you*."

"I think I'll run along," said Liggett.

"All right," said Eddie. "I'll send you those drawings. Where do you want them? Home or your office?"

"Uh—home, if it isn't too much trouble," said Liggett.

"Just as much trouble to send it home as to your office," said Eddie. "Good day, sir."

"May I come in?" said Malloy.

"Not if you're going to get tough you can't."

"Oh-h, I remember you."

"Yeah, you oughta," said Eddie. "Well, what do you want? Are you looking for a piano player?"

"No, this is business. I'm a reporter. From the *Herald Tribune*."

"Oh."

"Well, it's a living. Or was till today. I think this may be my last assignment, so help me out, will you? I got drunk yesterday on the Crowley story. Jesus, did they shoot up that place! You know the story?"

"I haven't been out to get a paper."

"Two-Gun Crowley? They got him yesterday. They had the whole Police Department up there, Ninetieth Street, West Side. Crowley and another guy and Crowley's girl."

"Oh, did they kill him?"

"No, not him. But he'll burn. Whenever you kill a cop you burn. When two lines intersect the vertical angles are equal, and when somebody kills a cop they burn, and when I get excited on a story I usually get stewed. I told them I got some tear gas, but I didn't get away with it."

"Tell me some more about yourself, Mister."

"No, not now. Some other time. Maybe tomorrow. I came here to ask you about this Gloria Wandrous. You were a pretty good friend of hers, weren't you? You were, weren't you?"

"Not the way you mean."

"Well, that's what I want to know. Who was? I want to get a line on her friends. I'm not writing the story. I'm just what they call digging up facts. Me digging up facts, for Christ's sake. I *write*. I'm not a digger."

"You're an artist."

"In my way. So are you. You probably think you're a good painter.

Another George Luks or uh, Picasso, to name two. The only two I can think of."

"Listen, Bud, if it's all the same to you."

"Well, when did you last see Miss Wandrous?"

"About a week ago. No, I saw her Sunday night."

"Mm. That's very funny. Then it couldn't have been you having lunch with her only yesterday at the Brevoort. She left first and you took a bus uptown. But of course if you say so."

"Are you going to put this in the paper?"

"That's what I'm supposed to be, a reporter."

"Well, then you'd better get it straight."

"I won't get it straight if you hold out on me or lie. Listen, is this the first time you were ever interviewed by the working press? If it is, let me tell you something. The rest of the boys will be here in a little while. The *Trib* isn't a scandal sheet so you'll get a better break telling me the truth than telling me a lie. If you tell me the truth I'll know what to print. But if you start telling those boys from the tabs lies they'll have you tied in knots. They're real reporters. I'm not. I'm the kind of reporter that wants to be a dramatic critic, but those babies will tear this place upside down—"

"And where will the police be while all this is going on?"

"Probably outside to see that you don't get away. There's one guy on this story that was born in this neighborhood, and he knows all the angles. Now you come across with some straight talk and then I'll give you a lift uptown. Was she depressed when you saw her yesterday?"

"Yes."

"Why?"

"She didn't tell me. I thought she had spring fever."

"She didn't give you any hint of why she was depressed?"

"Nope."

"Was she pregnant?"

"Liss-senn."

"Who was she that way about? Quite a few, I gather, but which one in particular?"

"Nobody that I know of."

"Was she married?"

"No. I'm pretty sure of that."

"Now here's one you won't like. Is it true she took dope?"

"No, not since I knew her."

"How long is that?"

"Two years."

"Well, she didn't tell you everything. She took dope all right. What about her relations with her mother and uncle? What about that uncle, by the way?"

"They seemed to get along all right. The uncle gave her a lot of money, or as much as they could afford. She had a good allowance and she always wore good clothes. That's all."

"One more question. Did she ever speak of suicide to you?"

"Sure. The way everybody does. I speak of it. Even you I imagine."

"But specifically, jumping off the *City of Essex*. Did she say anything about that yesterday at lunch? Or any other time? What I'm trying to get at is, was suicide on her mind?"

"No, I wouldn't say it was."

"That's what I think. There's something screwy about this whole thing. I've read enough detective stories to know that a young girl, pretty and all that, she doesn't pack her bag the way Gloria did just to knock herself off. That was a love trip, if you don't mind my saying so. One more question, Mr. Brunner."

"You said that a minute ago."

"This is important. I just want to show you I'm not a complete dope. Have you been in communication with the family since yesterday?"

"No. I tried to get them by phone but they wouldn't answer. I guess the phone—"

"Has been disconnected. I thought you'd say that. And so has yours been disconnected. And you weren't out to get a paper today. So how do you know about this?"

"Say, you're not trying to—"

"Just giving you a sample of what you'll get from the boys and girls on the tabloids. Multiplied by fifty and you have an idea."

"Well, my phone isn't disconnected, so you're wrong."

"Yes, and you're lying. Oh, don't worry. I don't think you did it. Come on, I'll take you away from the wolves."

"Will they really break open the apartment?"

"Oh, probably not. I'm just taking you uptown as a friendly act. They aren't interested in you as much as in some elderly guy. That's all I know about him, and that's all they know. He was part of her past. A very big part, I should say. Coming?"

"All right."

"I'll buy you a drink. Jesus, guy, you don't think I like this, do you? Have you heard any of the new Louis Armstrong records?"

"No new ones. What ever happened to the little dame you had that played the piano?"

"Married. That's what we all ought to do. You too."

"I'm going to."

"I have a novel almost finished. As soon as I finish it and get the dough and stay on the wagon three months. You better lock your windows just in case."

12

"I'm PREPARING a paper on New York newspapers," said Joab Ellery Reddington. "Will you reserve a copy of all the papers for me every day?"

"Yes, sir. We don't get them all, but I can order them for you if you tell me how long you'll want them."

"A month. Shall I pay you every day?"

"That'll be all right," said the newsdealer.

And so every afternoon Dr. Reddington would go from his office in the high school building, down to the railroad station, and back to his office. He would open each paper so that the financial page was on the outside, and he would sit and read every word about the Wandrous case. With fear and trembling he watched the beginning, the growth, and the decline in references to an older man, a middle-aged man, an elderly man. Dr. Reddington still had in cash the money he was going to pay Gloria for her promise never to mention his name, and he carried this money with him all the time. He never knew when he was going to have to use it. He did not know where he would go, but he would go somewhere. Then one, then two, then all the papers described the man. A Major in the Ordnance Department during the War, whose name police refused to divulge. The police were good and sick of the case and only kept it open because one of the tabloids would not let it die down. The police said they only wanted the Major for questioning.

Then one day the police announced that the Major had died in 1925 of a heart attack on a train between St. Louis and Chicago. The body had been cremated and the urn reposed in a Chicago funeral home. After that Dr. Reddington continued to read the New York papers, but there were no more references to an elderly man, and in late August the doctor stopped the papers and joined his family, who were vacationing in New Hampshire. The Reddingtons always went to a hotel where the women guests were not permitted to smoke.

Hope of Heaven

1

MAYBE I am not the man to tell this story, but if I don't tell it no one else will, so here goes.

I was sitting in my office in the Studio one warm day last September. My feet were up on the desk, and I was admiring my new $35 shoes, and my $7.50 socks, and thinking how nice it would be to go out and get in my $2200 car and go for a ride. But that was out of the question. I was too far behind in my work, and they were beginning to turn on the heat. So I had to stay there and read the *Hollywood Reporter* and *Variety* and try to get my mind off the sound of the dynamo or the generator or whatever it was that made that sound. That sound never let up, and if you let yourself listen to it it had the effect of the dentist's drill, or the bastinado. That sound is in every studio that I've ever worked in, and I never have been able to determine just what it is. Some say it's a dynamo; some say it's the ventilating system; others say it's just water in the pipe-lines. Whatever it is, it's always near the writers' offices.

The door between my office and my secretary's was open, and I heard the phone ring. I looked up. My secretary.

"A Mr. Miller wants to speak to you," she said.

"What Mr. Miller?"

"A Mr. Don Miller—"

"What Mr. Don Miller? I know five Don Millers."

"If you'll give me a chance I'll tell you," she said.

"Are you still sore at me?"

"He says he's from Gibbsville. He says he's a friend of your brother's."

"Don Miller," I said. "He didn't say which brother he's a friend of?"

"No. I didn't ask him. He just said to tell you he was a friend of your brother's, and he came from your home town. That's Gibbsville, isn't it?"

"Right. Okay, put him on." I picked up the phone. "Hello."

"Mr. Malloy?"

"That's right."

"My name is Don Miller. I'm a friend of Pat, your brother?" There certainly was a question in his voice.

"Yes, I have one."

"Well, I wasn't sure. I mean, I wanted to be sure I had the right Malloy."

"Very common name," I said. "How *is* Pat?"

"Oh, he was fine the last I saw him. Uh—I don't exactly come from Gibbsville, Mr. Malloy."

"Oh, no?"

"No. I'm from Swedish Haven—"

"Well—four miles."

"That's right. Three and a half since they put the new road in. I guess you weren't home since they put the new road in."

"Nope. Two years since I've been home. How're things?"

"Oh, I guess all right. Uh—are you busy all day, Mr. Malloy?"

"Well, sort of," I said. Aw-haw, I thought; a touch.

"Well, how about tomorrow then? Are you busy tomorrow? I wanted to talk to you. I'm really a friend of Pat's, and I don't want to borrow any money, but I don't know anybody out here and I wanted some advice on something. I knew you were out here working, but I didn't know what studio till yesterday. I saw in the paper where you were working on some picture so I decided to call you."

"Well, I tell you," I said, "why don't you come around to the Studio around four o'clock. Do you know where it is?"

"Oh, sure."

"Okay. I'll leave word at the gate so they'll let you in, and if you have any trouble just have the cop phone me. Is that all right with you?"

"Oh, that'll be fine. Thank you very much. I'll be there promptly."

"See you then," I said, and hung up. "Miss *Wendell!*"

She appeared. "Yes?"

"Come here, dear?"

"Definitely no. Is that all you wanted?"

"It seems like quite a lot," I said.

"Well then, I'm going to lunch, *eef* you don't mind."

"Will you phone the gateman and tell him I'm expecting a Mr. Don Miller at four o'clock, and he's to let him in."

When I came back from lunch I busied myself for a while with Miss Wendell—Rose. It was no cigar; she was in one of her moods. I had kept her waiting an hour and a half in the Vine Street Derby the night before. She hated the Vine Street Derby because she said it was always full of Warner Brothers gangster types, and she had to wait alone. So I told her I was sorry, and then the story editor sent for me and when I finally got back to my office it was six-thirty and she had gone home. On my way out I remembered Miller and I asked the gateman if there had been a Mr. Don Miller to see me, and he said no; no one had asked for me since three o'clock, which was when this gateman went on duty. During the next few days I wondered about Miller, but I had other things on my mind. For one thing, the Studio let me go. They had decided to shelve the story I was working on, as they were unable to borrow Jean Arthur. So a month or so passed and I thought very little about Miller.

Then one night I was having dinner at a South Sea Island kind of restaurant, off Hollywood Boulevard. The girl with me was Peggy Henderson. Although she was only twenty-one or -two, Peggy and I were old friends. Sometimes I was in love with her, and sometimes she was in love with me; but never at the same time, as the saying goes. At this point neither of us was in love with the other. As a matter of fact she apparently was in love with a boy her own age, named Herbert, about whom she was very mysterious. For a long time she wouldn't introduce me to him or tell me anything about him, except that he was not in pictures and he was not a Californian. He was Jewish, she said.

"Well, that's hardly a novelty in your life," I said. "All your best friends are Jews. Except me."

"You're more Jewish than any Jew I know," she said.

I made her try to explain that, and she was explaining it when someone said: "Mr. Malloy?"

I looked up. "Yes."

"I'm Don Miller," he said.

"Oh, are you?" I said. I do not like strangers who introduce themselves when I am having dinner with a girl.

"Well, you don't have to get high-hat about it," he said.

"Oh, I'm not so sure," I said. "What do you want?"

"I only wanted to apologize for not keeping that engagement, but if you're gunna get high-hat, skip it."

"Oh, sit down," I said. "Miss Henderson, this is Mr. Miller. Will you have a drink?"

"No, thanks," he said. He bowed to Peggy. Nodded is a better word, although he kept looking at her. She looked at him the way she always looked at anyone new. She was always friendly, and she always studied new people.

"Have a drink, for Christ's sake. Don't sulk."

He smiled. "All right, thanks. I'll have a rye and soda."

"Mr. Miller is from my home town," I said.

"Gibbsville!" said Peggy.

"You're wonderful," I said. "He's a friend of my brother's. One of them. By the way, how did you know me? Don't tell me I look like Pat. Or don't tell Pat."

"No, nothing like that. Although I do see a family resemblance. No, I was sitting at the bar when you came in, and I heard the bartender call you Mr. Malloy, so I asked him if you were James Malloy. He didn't know, but the proprietor said yes, you were James Malloy."

"Mm. Well, what happened the other day?" I said.

"The other day? You mean a month ago? I called you since then but they said you weren't there any more."

"Well, that still doesn't answer my question," I said.

"Aw, I just couldn't get there that day."

"But why?"

"Why be so insistent, Jim? If he doesn't want to tell you," said Peggy.

"I'd rather tell you some other time," he said.

"All right," I said. "I suppose you don't need that advice any more?"

"Huh." He got a vague look in his eyes.

"Skip it," I said. "Drink up. Peggy?"

"I'm not ready for another one," she said.

"Waiter. A Tahitian Punch for Miss Henderson. A rye and soda for the gentleman, and I'll have a Scotch and soda."

Miller sat with us and got a little tight and insisted on buying some drinks. Presently Peggy excused herself and when she left the table Miller said: "Where can I get in touch with you?"

I was staying at an apartment hotel.

"Can I call you there tomorrow?" he said.

"Sure. But not before noon."

"Did you tell Pat you heard from me?"

"No," I said, "I never write home. Hardly ever. Why? Don't you want me to?"

"No. I wanta ask you a favor. Don't tell anybody you saw me."

Peggy came back to the table during the silence that followed his request, but I guess he understood that I would not tell anyone I had seen him, because right away he said: "Are you in the movies, Miss Henderson?"

"Oh, no. I work in a bookstore."

"Oh, you do? Where?"

"On Wilshire Boulevard."

"What's the name of it?"

"He's moving right in," I said.

Peggy laughed. "The Avon Bookshop. It's in Beverly Hills. Why, are you a great reader, Mr. Miller?"

"Me? I haven't read a book since Christ knows when," he said. From then on he relaxed and we had a good evening.

2

THE MORNING after we saw Don Miller I drove Peggy to the bookstore. Peggy did not have a car. Her kid brother, who went to the University of California at Los Angeles, had an old jalopy; a Durant Six roadster. She seldom drove it, although she paid most of the bills for it. How she managed so well I never will know. Her mother was dead, and she had not seen her father in years. Once in a great while she would hear from him, from Mexico, Texas, Montana, South America, Chicago. Never from New York or Europe or the Orient. Looking at Peggy and Keith, her brother, and having known their mother, and knowing as much and as little as I did about her father's life, I had my own picture of what Mr. Henderson was like. From him I imagine Keith got his height and leanness and casual, contemptuous good looks. Peggy looked so much like pictures of her mother as a girl that there couldn't have been very much of her father in Peggy's appearance. About the only thing Peggy got from him, as far as I could make out, was her independence, of which she had a complete set. Once in a great while Peggy would get a letter, forwarded, addressed to a house in which she had not lived for four years. The letter would be from Mexico City, Houston, Missoula, Quito, Clark Street, and it would be written on hotel stationery or on the stationery of some club, and in it would be a money order for as little as fifty dollars or as much as five hundred. "Dear Kids—" it always began. I remember one time Peggy showed me a letter from New Orleans and she asked me what I thought he was doing. Well, it was hard to say. Chicago and Missoula spoiled my theory that he was in the oil business. The money order from New Orleans was for five hundred, which led me to suspect that Henderson might be mixed up in gun-running, because in that racket they pay off good, and in gold, but I did not say so at the time.

There was a peculiar reason why I did not say so. Aside from not wanting to take away any of her pleasure at the mere fact of getting five hundred dollars all at once, there was a reason that would have been more important. Peggy was politically almost as far left as she could go, and she might have been afraid her father was running guns for the wrong revolutionaries. There was nothing transitory about her beliefs, and nothing new. Her conviction began in high school; the things she learned in the intervening years were really only additional information that made for stronger conviction, until now she had become a symbol to me. Whenever I read silly stuff about Reds I would think of Peggy, and not of Mike Gold. Just as, whenever I read silly stuff about Catholics I would think of my mother and not of Cardinal O'Connell. Feeling that way, it was a wonder Peggy and I did not get married, but it might as well be understood this early that she had something to say about that. We can get that over with now, so that it won't complicate things later.

On mornings like this, tooling my beautiful Buick out to the bookstore, with the car working fine and Peggy looking sweet and a good big breakfast inside us and the morning air and a cigarette and the pretty jail-bait on their way to high school and the sun and money in the bank and no hangover—I would reach over with my right hand and pull Peggy to me. (That was another good thing about her: there was none of that "Somebody'll *see* us.") "Do you love me?" I would say.

"No."

"Well, then, why don't you marry me?"

"I don't like you."

"Well, why don't you marry me? God damn it, we oughta get married. I think you do love me."

"What if I do! Suppose I did? I'd never marry you or anyone like you."

"We're friends, aren't we?"

"Yes, and that's all. Just because I *sleep* with you? Listen, we've had that out before—"

"Mm."

"Oh, now you're going to spoil it with your lousy puns and I'll be disagreeable at the shop. Why do you have to—why can't you just accept our relationship—and don't look hurt, and sulk. You know damn well, James Malloy, damn well you know it, if I said I would marry you you'd want to get out of it. If I said all right, you and I'll meet at two o'clock this afternoon and file intention to get married, I'll bet you'd be at the Vendome, drunk. Trying to get out of it."

"That's a lie, and you know it."

"It's the truth and *you* know it."

I always stopped the car about a block away from the bookstore. "All right. You're right. You're omniscient. You're Havelock Ellis. You're Dorothy Parker. You're Dorothy Thompson. You're Dorothy Dix. You're—whoever knows all about men and women and class-angling, and ideology, and human relations. Oh, you're so God damn smart. Why don't *you* face a fact or two? For instance, why don't you admit you're in love with this Herbert guy?"

"Because—why should I let you put words in my mouth? You object to my uh—omniscience. Well, I object to yours."

"All right, all right, all *right!*" I said.

"Major Bowes."

"That's corny," I said. "Well, then, listen, how about this? Suppose you don't love me. Suppose you don't even love this Herbert—"

"Why do you keep calling him this Herbert? Just call him Herbert. I'll get the idea. I'll know who you mean."

"Okay. Herbert. Suppose you don't love either one of us, this me, or that Herbert. All right. Now, I don't know what goes on between you two, but I think I can guess."

"No, you can't."

"Yes, I can. And I'll surprise you. My guess is, you're not having an affair with Herbert. Right?"

"Well, yes. You're right. As far as you go you're right. But only as far as you go. Listen to me, Jim. For a so-called intelligent man you don't seem to realize one important thing about me. I don't say you give the matter much thought. I have a strong suspicion that when I'm not with you you don't give *me* much thought. But anyway, what you don't realize is, even if I'm not sleeping with Herbert, he's much closer to me than you are. Except when you are actually sleeping with me. Why *can't* you realize that? I like you. I do like you. And, I like to sleep with you. But you've made me so mad this morning I'm going to tell you something. I'd rather marry Herbert, and not sleep with anybody, than marry you."

"Mm," I said. "Well, that about finishes that." I looked straight ahead. I was hurt, because she never had said anything as strong as this. We had had substantially the same kind of discussion many times before, usually under approximately the same circumstances, but this was the first time she had been blunt. And I guess honest. I punched the steering wheel with both fists. It was a "safety" steering wheel that yielded a little to the punches, as it was supposed to yield to your body if you were in a collision. For a second I forgot her in my misery, and then I felt her looking at me. She reached over and put her hand on my knee.

"Hello," she said.

"Hello," I said.

"I'm sorry."

"No, you're not. You're sorry you made me feel this way, but you're not sorry you said what you did."

She did not deny this.

"Peggy. I have a feeling this isn't the time to bring this up, but I have one more proposition. You're the most realistic person I know. I don't mean that in any way but honestly. It isn't flattering, and it isn't un-flattering. But you are. You're like Coolidge or somebody. I mean materialistic. Face facts. Good business head. That kind of thing. Well now, how about this? I would like to live with you. I have fun with you. I sort of love you. You have fun with me. You sort of love me. And even though we don't think the same way, or at least you think your way to things, for instance your leftist stuff, and I feel my way. But we arrive about the same place. Isn't that true?"

"More less."

"It is true. I haven't got a good thinking brain, but I have sound emotions. You can give me the party line on the Scottsboro boys or the Mooney case as though some God damn Jesuit worked it out for you. On the other hand, I know almost right away, without thinking, without using words like activize and ideology and dialectical material-ism and all that crap, I am on the right side. That is, the leftist side. Isn't that true?"

"Yes, that's true."

"Well, what difference does it make how we get there as long as we get to the same place?"

"Oh, a lot of difference. Emotions aren't trustworthy."

"Did you ever hear of the false syllogism?"

"I don't depend on syllogisms."

I lit a cigarette. I put the lighter back into the socket on the dash. "Well, anyway. We've got so damn far away from my proposition. You concede most of what I say. You're realistic. I'm emotional. You like me. I like you. Now then. You concede these things?"

"Sure. Go on, or you'll get lost again."

"Well, why don't you marry me on this basis. I make a lot of money out here. You make twenty-two-fifty a week at the shop. You get an occasional pourboire from your old man, which you can't depend on. Keith keeps you broke, and probably when he gets out of college he'll get a job as filling-station attendant. Your grandfather—"

"Oh, we don't count on him."

"Well, you see what I mean. Marry me for my money. Marry me for economic independence. To do the things you want to do. As far as I'm concerned, it's a damn good bargain, so you don't have to worry about that angle." I turned and faced her. "Well, what do you think?"

"James. Dear James. I'll be late for work. I *am* late."

"Well, for Christ's sake, give me some kind of an answer, or at least comment. Don't be so God damn patronizing and superior. Dear James. Dear James my ass."

She put out her finger and drew imaginary circles counter-clockwise on the crystal of the dash clock. "Uh, in the first place, you hate working for pictures, so as a realist I have to take that into consideration. How do I know you'll stick it out another year? Even one more year? I don't and you don't. So therefore I'd be taking that risk. In the second place, you said something about Keith. I'm not worried about Keith. He doesn't take much money. He practically earns his way through school. In fact, I'd say he does earn his way through. You know, he's a good athlete, and that's a great help. And then you mentioned something about my salary. Well, we don't live on my salary. We have some money from my mother's insurance. Enough to pay the rent and electricity and little debts, and the money I get from my father may not seem like much to you, but honestly, it does always come just when we seem to need it. I don't know why, but it just does. The little bluebird, or God, or something. And, one other thing besides. More or less covering the whole financial aspect. You talk about financial independence."

"Economic independence."

"Well—"

"No, not well. *Economic* sounds more like the kind of thing *you'd* say."

"Okay. But I wanted to tell you my theory. My theory is this. I haven't got the party line on it, Smartie, but it's this way. The only way to secure economic independence, is to be independent of—is to be economically independent. In other words, I'll put it this way. It's a curious thing, but the more money you have, the less independent you are, is my theory. In other words, the very rich are the least independent of money, that is to say, independent of economic or financial problems. The very rich are just not economically or financially independent."

"Well, now, I don't know about that," I said. "As far as it goes it sounds all right, but I imagine it's specious or Utopian. I don't mean Utopian Sinclair Utopian."

"Ooh!" she said. "And you talk about corny."

"Right off the elbow. But we gotta have money. We gotta have wampum, or scrip. Kale. Mazuma. Spinach. Cabbage. Gelt. Uh—or amperes or volts or bushels. You know why paper money is? Or credit? Because it's too damn much trouble to be lugging gold all over the place—"

"Yes, I know, dear, and besides, there isn't that much gold. Yes, I know all that. Probably better than you do."

"That's right. Do you love me?"

"Yes, now I do. And I'll tell you something else that ought to make you feel better, or at least restore your masculine pride. Herbert has offered me almost the same proposition, and I've turned it down. Except that with Herbert there wouldn't be any sex. Herbert—now don't you ever repeat this—Herbert has T.B. A spot. He just loves me. And without working he has more money than I'll ever need. Does that make you feel better?"

"In a way, yes, in a way, no. Doesn't make any difference. You know what I'd like to do?"

"I think so. You want to go back to the hotel, or to my house. Is that it?"

"Yes. You take the day off. We'll go to the beach, or the hotel, or your place, or San Luis Obispo, or the desert or anywhere. Let's go on a trip?"

"I'd like to. Honestly I would. But I'm not going to marry you or

Herbert or anybody, so I need my job. Now I have to go. I'm a worker."

"Arise, ye prisoners of starva-tion!"

"The first woman that comes in and wants to buy 'Gone with the Wind' I'm going to sell her 'The Coming Struggle for Power'—"

"Show her Strachey's picture."

"All right. I will."

"What if it's a man?"

"Men don't buy books in the morning," she said.

"Mm. And women don't buy enough of them."

"Right," she said. "Well, I have to go now. Oh, my."

"If you change your mind."

"I can't, Jim. I wish I could. What are you doing tonight, around ten o'clock?"

"No plans. Why?"

"I'm going to an anti-Fascist meeting. It ought to be over about nine-thirty. Do you want to meet me somewhere?"

We made the date and I sat in the car with my right arm stretched across the top of the seat. She was carrying her hat and she was wearing a sharkskin suit, not new, but one I liked. She always walked as though she were going some place. I liked her walk. I had nothing to do. When she turned the corner I got out of the car and went to a shop and bought some over-priced ties and then I went down Wilshire to Vine Street and Hollywood and bothered my agent, who had all the New York papers. I phoned the hotel and they said a Mr. Don Miller had called and left a number. I called him. He wanted to see me, so I said I'd take him to lunch, twelve-thirty.

3

IT WAS a boring meal, up to the moment when Miller said he never drank coffee except in the morning.

He was there first, sitting on a tube-and-leather chair in the front of the restaurant, which was one of those modern eating places, all tin foil and black cloth and marble. He stood up. He was wearing an inexpensive Glen plaid jacket, cheap gray flannel slacks, imitation suède shoes, a dark brown polo shirt, and the conventional Hollywood neckerchief. His hair was cut short, but not "crew cut," and he was taller than he had seemed before. Everything about him seemed newer than his sunburn, and he was a very handsome young man.

It was a very boring meal, because his attitude seemed to say: "All right, get it up. Say something. Start the conversation. What have you got to say for yourself?"—which was not quite the case. After all, he had called me, not I him. Several times, during silences, I wanted to say the hell with it and get up and leave. There were at least two hundred other people in Hollywood I'd rather have lunched with.

He was a good six feet tall, with the kind of athletic build that is athletic, but one look at his face and you knew that this was no athlete. Probably he could do hand-stands on a beach. Possibly he could dive well. Maybe he had played high school basketball or had picked up some golf or tennis. He undoubtedly was strong, but in a way that I was not afraid of. He had long fingers, with long wide nails that had been buffed to a nice shine. I bet myself that he played the piano, a sort of fraternity-house piano; competent, unimaginative piano; improvising-sounding, but someone else's improvisation. I could all but hear him, playing something like "Easy To Love," which at that time was brand new. Slow, not in any steady tempo, and all chords. That's what those hands were for—at least that was one of the reasons and explanations for them. I also could easily imagine them going to work on a girl. It is not often that I notice a man's hands, but I had to notice his, because by the time his steak arrived I had taken a thorough dislike to him, and that was the reason why I sized him up so carefully. It is often a good thing to look a man over carefully when you start out with such an active dislike of him, and all during the meal I had a far-off notion that a casual word, or a spilt glass of water might have us swinging at each other. Well, I kept telling myself, this was one decision I was pretty sure I could get.

We talked about what we were going to eat, and then what we were eating, and about a couple of dolls who sat across the room and the doll situation in Hollywood. There was no specific talk; it was all general, even when we talked about the food. I mean he didn't say his steak was good or bad; he said it was funny how in California the highest praise you could bestow on a steak was to say that it was "New York Cut." "Yeah, that is funny," I said. After a while the conversation settled down to a tempo: three or four mouthfuls of food, and some remark about movie extras and how some of them were easy to sleep with and some of them were difficult. Neither of us took dessert. One large coffee for me.

He didn't like my Luckies. He had Camels, which he took out of his shirt pocket. He reached in, surrounded the pack with his hand, slapped two fingers of his left hand on the top of the pack (noisily, and much harder than was necessary) until two cigarettes popped up.

He extracted one and put it in his mouth. He scratched a match and held it to the cigarette and cocked his head far over to one side and took a deep inhale. Enough smoke to fill a bicycle tire came out of his mouth and he blew out the match. Whenever you see a man go through all this you are looking at a man who has had plenty of time on his hands.

I could hardly look at him. I decided to shock him.

"What's on your mind, Miller?"

Some of his cockiness went away and he took another quick drag on his cigarette. He looked down at the cigarette, which he was rubbing against the ash tray. "Plenty," he said. "But I don't know—I'll be frank with you. I don't know if I want to talk about it."

"You mean to me or just to anybody?"

"Anybody, I guess. Yes, anybody. I might as well tell you this. No, God damn it, I don't know what the hell. Jesus, I don't know anything. God damn it."

I waited. I watched him crush the cigarette.

"You don't like me, do you?" he said.

"I don't know," I said. "Why? What makes you think that?"

"You gave me that impression. I guess you think I'm a fresh guy. Well, I am. I always was, I guess."

I waited again.

"You know, I used to know you," he said.

"Did you? When?"

"Remember when you used to come down to Swedish Haven and write up the football games? You were working on the *Leader*."

"I remember, yes."

"You wrote me up in a game and you spelt my name wrong. The only time you ever wrote me up."

"Miller? For Christ's sake, how could I spell that wrong?"

"It's not my name."

"Oh," I said. "Oh-h-h." Three notes. "What is your name?"

"That's the God damn trouble."

"You mean you don't want to tell me?"

"I don't want to tell anybody. Do you know anything about me? I mean, did you hear anything from Pat, today? This morning?"

"Nope. I'm not even sure Pat can write."

"Pat's all right. He used to be a good friend of mine. He's a good guy. We used to go out and get cockeyed together."

"You know, if you don't like Pat you don't have to say you do. I don't like him, so don't let that worry you. What's the matter? Are the cops looking for you, or what?"

"Mr. Malloy, I'll lay my cards on the table. Do you remember the Reverend Schumacher?"

"Sure. Pastor of the uh, Lutheran Church?"

"Reformed. That's the one. That's my father. He's dead, but that's the one you mean."

"A bald-headed man, a little heavy, about medium height. He was a Phi Beta Kappa."

"That's the one."

"Sure, I knew him. I liked him. I didn't know him very well, but I remember he wasn't a Kluxer. I think he was a patient of my father's at one time." I could see he wasn't listening much to this. Another silence.

"Some fresh coffee, sir?"

"Yes, I'll have some. Do you want a drink? One of your rye and sodas?" I said.

"No. No, thanks."

"Just some more coffee," I said. I lit a cigarette. "Well, listen, Schumacher—by the way, how did I spell your name?"

"S, h, u, m, a, c, h, e, r."

"That was a typographical error. I knew how to spell your old man's name, so I'd know how to spell yours. Anyway, you're in some kind of a jam, and you have some idea I can help you. That's right so far, isn't it?"

"Yes. I'm in a jam. I don't know why I phoned you in the first place. I had to talk to somebody, then when the time came, like the time I was to come to your office over in the Studio, I couldn't make myself go over. It's the same way now. I phoned you today because I wanted to talk about it."

"What kind of a jam is it? Money? A dame?"

"Well—money. Oh, what the hell, I might as well tell you."

"Whenever you're ready. I don't have to tell you I won't repeat it."

"Oh, that don't worry me." He smiled. "You know something? I remember one time Pokey Armbruster, when he was coaching S. H. High, he was worried the night before the Gibbsville High game because he remembered how you knew all our plays, and your brother Pat was playing on Gibbsville High. Remember that one play from a place kick formation where the guy holding the ball—"

"Sure. It was an old Lafayette play."

"Well, that was the one we beat Gibbsville on. So from then on, when Pokey realized how you didn't tell them the play, we all trusted you. Not that I ever had anything to trust you with, but all the same."

I let him talk on, because some of my antagonism was disappearing. He was letting himself go and was becoming a frightened kid who had to talk to somebody.

"It seems funny, sitting here in Hollywood, talking about S. H. High and all that stuff." He lit another cigarette, but not with all the motions he had gone through with the other. He took a sip of water, and a quick look at me. He watched the waiter pour my coffee, and when the waiter had gone he began: "When my old man died, for a while I lived with my aunt in Swedish Haven. She was my mother's sister and she was a strict old maid, so when I'd come in late at night she'd bawl me out the next morning, also because I didn't have a job. The only money I had was from my old man's lodge insurance, about enough to pay for the funeral and a little over. I had a Ford coupe and I used to go around with the fellas and sometimes lend the car out for a couple dollars, and when we'd go out on a double date I'd supply the car and the other fella'd buy the gas and I had a girl, she was stenographer for old Mossbacher, at the shirt factory, and he kept her. Old Mossbacher, he must be sixty-some years old, but I don't know. She'd never tell me much about him, but she was always good for ten bucks a week and a couple times we took trips. She used to get sore when I razzed her about Mossie. I used to say to her, 'Don't tell me old Mossie gives you the works.' And she'd get sore.

"Well, so anyway I was just about breaking even. I played a pretty good game of pool and I put up a good appearance because I had these clothes I bought when I was at State. I went to State for a year and a half after I got out of High, but I flunked out. I don't know. I got so I didn't give a God damn. So I used to pick up a couple bucks shilling at Jimmy's poolroom. That's new since you were there. But after a while the whole thing got on my nerves. I used to look at these muggs that used to come in the poolroom and I used to think, 'What the hell am I doing wasting my time with them?' Their idea of something hot was to be a brakeman on the railroad and have a regular run. They used to drive me nuts. And this dame got on my nerves. I felt sorry for her in a way, but I wasn't responsible. Mossie'd keep her at the office after everybody went home and after he went home she'd call me up at my aunt's place and my aunt knew who she was and she'd raise hell. Those old maids, you know they always know when there's something funny going on. I had a friend of mine had a dose and my aunt, I swear she knew he had it before I did, even if I did see him every day. And this kid I was traveling around with, my aunt used to raise hell about her, and the kid, she'd call me up after Mossie'd leave. She'd have to see me right away. So I'd go over and pick her up and she'd make me drive right out the Valley, without any supper, and I'd give her a jump in the car. Well, that part of it was all right, but I began to get worried. You know, I used to kid her about Mossie, about these times when he'd been at her. I remember in Psychology reading about some of these old guys and I thought it was a lot of crap. Oh, I'm no kid. But this stuff I used to read, I used to think those old English colonels and Chinks— but not Americans. Not old Mossie. You know, guys with whips or pushing pigeon's eyes out. This kid used to be nuts, absolutely screwy after he got through with her. She earned her pay, all right. Anyway, I got worried, because she'd cry and she was the hottest little babe I ever knew and I had some premonition I was getting into something. You know. Maybe she'd commit suicide, or Mossie'd do something to her and she'd die. And Mossie knew about her laying me. I'd see him on the street and he'd look at me with this dirty look in his eye and say, 'Good *eve*-ning, Harold, good *eve*-ning,' and give me a sort of, you know. Look. So I thought it was about time I got the hell out of there.

"There were no jobs, of course. It was all right with my aunt if I loafed around the poolroom all day and wasted my time, but take a WPA job or something like that? Oh, no. We were too good for that. I had to get out of town, so I went to a fella that knew Asa Merritt, the Congressman, and I got a letter to Merritt and I went to Washington. I sold my car and my aunt gave me fifty bucks and I went to Washington. I knew a guy there, he was a Beta, which I was and he flunked out the same time I did. I stayed with him. His parents were over in Europe.

"Well, it took me a couple days to get to see Merritt and he stalled me but he said he knew my old man and since I was in Washington anyway, I should stick around and maybe he could find something for me.

"Well, one afternoon I was walking along F Street and I kicked this thing, I thought it was a wallet. It looked like a wallet, and I picked it up and then I thought it was a checkbook. But do you know what it was? It was a book of these traveler's checks. A whole book of them, not one of them torn out. Brand new. I stuck the damn thing in my pocket, thinking sort of in the back of my head that I'd turn it in at some bank and probly get a reward for it. You know why? Because it was for five thousand dollars. Five G's. There were ten checks, each made out for five hundred dollars. A lot of money, you know.

"So the next day I had to go see Merritt, and this time the son of a bitch finally got around to telling me the truth. He said, 'Harold, I'm very sorry to tell you, but I can't seem to be able to find anything for you.' He was polite and all like that, because he probly was afraid he was losing a vote, and you know, like what if I went back home and said Congressman Merritt was high-hat? It might hurt him politically. But irregardless he didn't have any job for me.

"That was one thing. Then when I went home that day, late in the afternoon, back to this guy's apartment that I was staying at, Joe said to me, he told me his mother and father were coming back from Europe the following Monday and he had to go to New York to meet them and I'd have to get out of the apartment. We had to get a colored fella to clean the place up after the way we left it. Joe said why not go to New York with him, maybe I could find a job there. Fat chance, I thought, and anyway I didn't have more than about ten bucks and being stuck in New York on ten bucks.

"Swell luck I was having all of a sudden. Then I got this idea. I remembered about this book of traveler's checks. I didn't say anything to Joe about it, but I told him I'd let him know the next day in regard to New York.

"I went to my room and I got out this book of checks and I looked at it and looked at it. I never saw one before, so I studied it carefully and the idea came to me, when I was a kid I used to be able to sign my old man's name to excuses when I bagged school. I was pretty good at it. Right now I could sign the old man's name and if you knew his signature you'd think it was all right. So I sat down at a desk and I began writing out, Donald R. Miller, Donald R. Miller, copying it over and over again, oh, a couple hundred times. This checkbook was in the name of Donald R. Miller, and there was his signature right there in the book, ten times, so I studied it, the different ways he wrote it himself, and by the time I went to bed that night I could write Donald R. Miller better than my own name.

"Well, to make a long story short, I went to New York with Joe, my friend, only I went to a different hotel, a better one, and I told Joe I was registering under the name of Donald R. Miller. I gave him some phony reason like I was afraid I'd run into somebody or something. I put up a good front. I had these clothes and a couple good suitcases and I looked the part. I even went out and called up the hotel and left messages for myself. Please call Mr. Gump at the University Club. Call So and So at the Bankers Trust Company. Mrs. J. Archibald Smith would like you to come to dinner Thursday. Every day I'd have a lot of messages. Maybe the clerks didn't read them, but maybe they did. And I was there about three days and I got dressed up every night and when I'd go out I'd say to the clerk, if there were any messages for me I'd be at such and such a number, and then I'd go right out and call myself up. I had those guys thinking I was the most important guy in New York. They probly thought I was some rich man's son from Washington, D.C. I registered from Washington.

"Well, the third day, or rather night, I got all duked up and went out and ate a sandwich at some joint over on Third Avenue and went to a movie till around ha' past eleven and then I came back and I asked the clerk, I said I wanted to cash a traveler's check. I said it was pretty big and he didn't have to give me all the money all at once. I only wanted fifty bucks, I told him. So that made it look all right and he gave me a hundred. I signed that thing, boy, every minute I expected to have some cop thump me on the shoulder, but I guess they probly compared my signature with the one on the register and it looked the same. They had three signatures. The one when I registered, the one on the check, and the one I signed right then when I cashed the check.

"They gave me the rest of the dough the next day and I stayed there the rest of the week. I even gave a party right there in the hotel when Joe's mother and father came back. We got two nice babes, respectable, and the party set me back around seventy dollars. Joe sort of wondered, but I let him guess. Jesus, Malloy, I'm giving you all the chance in the world to get me thrown in the clink."

"Sure you are," I said.

"Well, I'm taking that chance."

"You certainly are."

"I guess if I tried to move in on your girl you wouldn't let me get very far."

"Well, then, don't try," I said. "But go on with your story. Didn't they ever catch up with you?"

"Never did. It was a funny thing. To get money I had to spend money. I went out and bought a new outfit, new bags, packed up, took a taxi to the Penn Station, checked the bags, came back a while later and got them, and registered at another hotel. I stayed at two hotels at the same time. I used the cash I got from one hotel to set me up at the second one, and then I cashed another check at the second hotel. In about two weeks' time I had over a thousand bucks cash, so I decided it was time to blow. All this time I was expecting some flatfoot to be waiting for me, but I got so I didn't care. I was living the way I always wanted to. There was a little dame at the place where they sold tickets to the shows, in the hotel. I'd go there and buy two tickets to a show and only use one. She got to know me, so I took her out and laid her, and through her I got to know some others. She was all right, too, this ticket girl. Oh, I did another little thing, just to make it all look on the up and up. I'd call Joe in Washington every couple days, just in case they checked up on the bill, I'd have these Washington calls. I was wishing I could have stayed there till I spent the whole five grand, but I had other plans. I wanted to get the cash and blow, which I did. When I was sure of having a thousand bucks all clear, and my bills paid, I checked out of the two hotels and I came out here.

"I been out here ever since. This place reminds me of those Western stories I used to read, where they don't ask you your name or where you came from or anything. I'm as much Donald Miller as I am anybody. I have a car and a license in the name of Miller, and for a laugh, I even told them at this place where I'm living, I said I was trying to get in the movies under the name of Don Mills, but my real name was Miller, but if any calls came for Don Mills, that was me. Oh, I've had a lot of laughs."

"But still you're worried. Why?"

"Wouldn't you be? What if they begin catching up with me? I can't understand why they haven't. This Miller guy, he must of been a crook or something, or else why doesn't he report losing five thousand bucks? That's the only answer I can think of. He must of been a crook." He took out a cigarette but did not light it. He held it in his thumbs and forefingers, fingering it as though he were rolling a cigarette. "Anyhow, it'd make a good story for you, wouldn't it?"

"I'd like to know the ending of it," I said.

"*You* would? What about *me*?"

"Uh, to get back to why you're telling me all this, you said you were in a jam. What kind of a jam? I mean, is it anything new besides your, uh, criminal record? You know, these banks and insurance companies are tough. If they ever do catch up with you they'll put you in that jail-house and throw the key away. My advice is, if you care anything about it, my advice is to be satisfied with what dough you have and try to get a legitimate job, under your real name. You could buy in on a hot dog stand or something like that."

"Me run a hot dog stand after the way I've lived! Say, that's the God damn trouble. Supposing I did buy a hot dog stand and went honest? Supposing I made enough dough to pay them back? That's just when they would catch up with me. Just when I was going honest. No, the hell with that. I considered going under my real name, but this hot dog stand idea stinks."

"Anyway, you're not in any immediate jam, other than what you've been in the past six months or so?"

"No."

"Then what are your plans? What's it all about? Why did you tell me all this?"

"Well, I had to tell you. I had to tell somebody. It may sound as if I was bragging, and I guess maybe I was, but I been thinking, I got away with this so far, why not use my brains to get into something honest, but where there was a lot of dough."

"Oh, I guess that's where I come in. Do you want to be a writer?"

"Don't kid me. Me write? Listen, when I write Donald R. Miller on a check or anything else."

"You're certainly one of the highest-paid writers I know."

"No, that writing, that's not for me. I haven't a big enough of a vocabulary, and I'm a lousy speller. No, what I want is some job that pays a good salary and I don't have to work too hard or get dirty. And I don't want to start from the bottom."

"It's too bad you're not a writer," I said. "Well, I'm sure I don't know what the hell I can do for you. Right now I'm not working myself. You have no ideas about what you want to do? No special training or anything like that?"

"Huh. If you call playing a good game of pool, or I can drive a car better than most guys. I'm a good dancer and I have plenty of clothes."

"You'd make a good dress extra. You know what that is?"

"One of those guys that has a full dress, long tails? Sure, I know about them. There's a couple of them living where I live. You can have that. No, I want a real job. I bet I could sell. Real estate, or cars. Cars I'd be good at. Good cars, like say a Packard or Duesenberg."

"How old are you?"

"You want to know the truth?"

"Mm."

"I'm twenty-two. I look older. I could pass for twenty-seven." He made a fist and punched the palm of his left hand. "Oh, Christ, Malloy, I don't know what I am, or anything. Here I started out to tell you about myself, and you listened, and I didn't tell you the truth. Not all of it. I left out some, and put in some. I'm gettin' so I don't know what's the truth and what isn't. I wasn't cut out for this stuff I'm doing. I'm no crook. I should of been a rich guy instead of a minister's son without any dough. I can fool people into thinking I'm rich, and all I need is a few bucks and clothes. I just sit around and look wise. When I'm doing it I get a great laugh out of it at the time, like with those checks, but when I'm alone, God, I don't want to go to jail. All I want is a good job and then I'd even pay back the money, providing I was sure I wouldn't get caught. When I used to make a living playing pool I was always honest. Oh, I used to lose a couple games on purpose and then make the bets bigger, but that's business."

"That's what they call a loss-leader."

"Sure. But anyway, I am honest. I'd like to sell a car that I wouldn't have to be ashamed of, maybe get the better of a guy on a trade, but that's business." He took a deep breath.

"It's after three," I said. "Give me your phone number and if I hear of anything I'll give you a buzz. Where do you live?" He gave me the address and phone number, and I paid the bill. He stood up, and by that act alone he changed. He was cocky again.

"Well, thanks for the lunch, old man. Gimme a buzz." He almost looked around to see if anyone was admiring him.

"Oke," I said, and he left me.

4

THE HENDERSONS lived in a little one-story house in the general direction of the Observatory. It took at least half a dozen visits before you knew the way, because of the winding roads and the names of the roads. They would take a name, say, Orchard, and there would be Orchard Road, Orchard Lane, Orchard Place, Orchard Drive, all together, intersecting and merging. It took a lot out of you to get there, too, because they have changed the ratios of steering-gears so you have to whirl your wheel continually all the way up to the Hendersons'.

I had the privilege of walking in without ringing the doorbell, and anyway I wore leather soles, which could be heard on the short cement walk and the wooden porch.

"Anybody home? Oh, hello, Keith."

"Hello, Jim."

"Don't get up," I said. "Sit still."

"Peggy isn't home yet." He was stretched out on a davenport. He rested his book, a fat textbook, on his belly. "What's new?"

"Nothing much."

He sucked his teeth, a habit of his. "Want a piece of pie? Millie baked a darn good pie tonight. Sweet potato pie."

"No, thanks, I just had dinner and a couple of drinks."

"I can get you a drink. Scotch? I think we have some Scotch."

"No, thanks. How're things out at Westwood?"

"Oh, 'bout the same as usual."

"Gonna make Phi Bete?"

"Me? Not a chance. Well, maybe. Accidentally. I won't try for it. I'm not altogether convinced of the, uh, uh, value of Phi Bete. I'm not so sure about it. There was a fellow in my fraternity last year, now he should have been Phi Bete. He was one of the most brilliant fellows I ever knew, really brilliant. Some of the nitwits that did make it, cats! They couldn't carry his books, this fellow. They weren't in the same league with him. But, he had some trouble with I don't know, English prof, or French. French I think. And, he just didn't get Phi Bete. Cats! I dunno." He rubbed the back of his head, fast and like a groom curry-combing a horse. "Do you think it's worthwhile?"

"In a way. A negative way. If you make it, if you have a key, then you can throw it away in the bureau drawer and forget about it. If you haven't got it and you pan it, then people naturally think you're sour-grapes. I guess that's about all it's worth. Get it and forget about it."

"Guess you're right. You've got something there. Yep. But I'm not going to try for it. If I get it, okey-doke. If I don't, well. What are you working on? Haven't seen you around for a while."

"I'm working on my agent right now. Otherwise, nothing. They aren't doing that picture I was working on, so I'm looking for another job."

"I guess you won't starve. I don't know what's keeping Peggy. Did you have a date with her?"

"She's at a meeting. Yeah, I had a date, but you never know about those meetings."

"Do you think that's a good idea, those meetings? I'm against Fascism. My God. But what do you think of those meetings? I don't mean for Peggy now, but just generally speaking."

"Oh, they don't do any harm. It's better than nothing. At least it shows the Fascists that we know they're having *their* meetings, and then also if it weren't for the meetings a lot of people would just forget about the whole thing."

"That's true. Um-hm. True. I went to two of them with Peggy, but, cats! I don't know, Jim. Same kind of people get up and do the speech-making there as at school. I mean the same type. Cheerleaders. What if there hadn't been a depression. I wonder if Peggy'd be going to anti-Fascist meetings. Or if there'd be any meetings at all. I'm too young I guess. I don't know enough, and all I learn is what they teach me. I'll grow up, I guess."

"You'll be all right, Keith. You're all right now. You can't have all the answers at your age. You can't at any age, no matter how long you live, so don't let it worry you. That's the difference between you and me. One of them. When I was about your age I thought I knew all the answers, but *you* know you *don't*. I guess this is Peggy. I wonder who's with her."

"Hello. Hello, brother darling."

"Peggy. Hello, Herbert."

"Hello, Keith. Good evening, Mr. Malloy."

"Hello," I said. This spoiled my plans.

"James, I brought Herbert along because I knew you'd have your car and I, Herbert has to go downtown and he'd have to take a bus. We can all go together, except Keith. You study."

"I don't want to go," said Keith. "Or, maybe I do. I'll have to give the matter a little more mature consideration. Do I want to drive downtown, or don't I? What advantage is there to be gained? No novelty in it. I've been there. Charming company. True. But is it worth—"

"While he's giving the matter his mature consideration let's go. Let us know when we get back," said Peggy. "By the way, don't take that seriously, little man. I mean, don't wait up for us."

"Little man. Lit-tle—man, eh?" Keith was more than six feet tall, and built on the lines we have been led to believe Lincoln's were. He very deliberately placed his book upon the table and very deliberately rose.

"Don't you dare! Don't you touch me," said Peggy.

"Lit-tle man. Lit-tle man," he repeated. He suddenly changed his posture and manner. He bent forward and held out his arms like a bear or an ape, and let out a Tarzan yell. Peggy ran and we, Herbert and I, followed her.

The three of us sat in the front seat, Peggy in the middle. "Where to, Herbert?"

"The Los Angeles Biltmore," he said.

"See what's on the radio," said Peggy.

"There's something wrong with it," I said. I switched it on, but it was bad, mostly static. On the way we passed the house I had had the first time Peggy ever stayed with me. I looked down, and across my shoulder at her, but she was looking straight ahead. We were silent for blocks.

"Malloy, tell me, how much did you make out of your book. I mean, about how many copies did you sell?" said Herbert.

"Which one? There were two."

"The—the popular one. The one about the policeman in Central Park."

"Oh, thirty thousand copies, including the English sales. Figure about thirty cents a copy and you have the amount," I said. He annoyed me.

"Mm. Nine thousand dollars. Imagine, a book of that kind making nine thousand. How long'd it take you to write it?"

"You mean in work-hours, or over how long a period of time on the calendar? And why? Are you writing one?"

"Oh, I've written several. Unpublished. I can't publish while I'm living off my family."

"What kind of books do you write?"

"Well, one is an epic poem, something like 'Buddenbrooks,' by Thomas Mann. You know Thomas Mann."

"Not personally. Do you?"

"No. But I know his work very well. In German."

"Are you, uh, writing this, uh, epic poem in German? I thought 'Buddenbrooks' was prose."

"Oh, it is. Of course. No, you see mine is *like* 'Buddenbrooks,' a book about a family, you *know*?"

"Yes. Family. *I* know."

"But mine's American. Jewish-American."

"I see. The last time I talked to you you were doing something for two pianos."

"Herbert doesn't play any more," said Peggy.

"I've given up the piano, permanently. It takes too much out of me. I'm not good enough at it, and the effect of even good piano is too ephemeral. De Pachmann dies, where is his art? Lost. Lost until one of these radio geniuses can recapture sound floating through the ether. You've heard of that, how they're going to be able to tune in and get the Gettysburg Address and the Sermon on the Mount. What kind of a voice do you suppose Jesus Christ had, Peggy?"

"Beautiful, I'll bet."

"Anyway soothing," I said.

"Soothing? Soothing I'm sure is precisely the word. Soothing. Soft.

Not exactly musical. Mildly hypnotic. The kind that the Hindu fakirs have when they induce mass hypnotism."

"You sound a little as if you had something against him," I said.

"Oh, shut up," said Peggy.

"All right," I said.

"No, don't," said Herbert. "I want to find out about books, from an author. You see, Malloy, I'm writing a novel about Los Angeles, present-day Los Angeles. The Angelus Temple. This fellow that killed his wife with the box of rattlesnakes. The Neon signs. The health people. No movie stuff. I'm going to ignore the movies."

"Who's your principal character? The fellow with the rattle-snakes?"

"No. In fact I may not even use him at all, but this town is full of people like him. It's a fantastic place, you know, Malloy. Fantastic. You know why? Because it's so incredibly ordinary."

"Mm."

"Fantastic. It's in a semi-tropical climate. It has a Spanish name, with religious Roman Catholic connotations. A rather large Mexican population and Oriental. The architecture, that is, I mean by that the Monterey house and the Mission stuff, is Mexican and Spanish and a little Moorish. And yet, Malloy, consider this: the really fantastic thing about it is that it's the crystallization of the ordinary, cheap ordinary American. The people. The politics. The cults. These Iowa people that come here and really assert themselves. They do what they wanted to do in Iowa but couldn't, for various and sundry reasons. The crazy clothes they all wanted to wear back in Iowa. And of course it's no city, except in population. Fantastically ordinary, cheap, commonplace. And I'm going to put it in a book, which is the reason why I've been plying you with questions about your books. I want my book to be a success, and I want to know what constitutes a successful book. Not a succes d'estime, but a financial success."

"Any book that makes any money is a financial success. From the author's point of view, any book that makes more than the two-fifty or five-hundred advance royalty."

"Well, of course I want mine to do better than that. Thank you very much, Mr. Malloy. I'm going to buy a car next week, and I hope I can repay this. Peggy, au 'voir. I had a pleasant evening. Thank you for my dinner. Now I go to face one of my capitalistic uncles, the bastard. Goodnight."

"Your heart's not in it, but as long as your body is I guess I have no kick coming."

"It's a nice body, so I'm told," said Peggy.

"Who told you?"

"You did," she said. "Light one for me, will you, please?" She took the cigarette but put it out after a few puffs. She was not what you would call an ardent smoker. She dinched it in the ash tray and then she settled back, apparently getting herself comfortable for a lengthy contemplation of the ceiling; but in a little while she took her hands from in back of her neck and lay over on her side and put her left arm across my chest. "I may marry you after all," she said, into the corner of the pillow.

"Oh, no. Not me."

"Yes, you," she said.

"Although it's as good an offer as I've had today."

"What is that? That's the last line of a dirty joke, isn't it?" She raised her head a little, angrily.

"I think so. But I don't know the joke."

"I'm glad, because—oh, Jim. I'm depressed, depressed. Why don't I tell Herbert to go away or leave me alone? Why do I feel so awful about the Jews under Hitler? Do you think Keith is a virgin?"

"Very likely."

"I wonder what he thinks about you and me," she said.

"He probably knows exactly where we are this minute. He's no dope. I've known about two kids like him in my life. They have an intelligence that transcends sex, or at least it keeps them out of that kind of trouble. Then, when the time comes, they get a girl, and the girl seems to be very well satisfied in that department. At least the other two guys I knew have wives that *look* very well taken care of, and content, and wouldn't cheat for anything. What about Herbert. Have you stayed with him yet?"

"Nope. I told you he has T.B. Put your arms around me. What are you thinking?"

"Nothing. I guess I may be in the middle of a train of thought. I have a theory that you're always thinking, always, always, always thinking. Isn't it awful? Think of being thinking all the time. Your brain banging away on all lobes."

"Well, that's what it's there for." She took a deep breath and gave it voice as she exhaled. "Hello."

"Hello."

"What's this?"

"Search me. I just happened to notice it there myself. Some kind of a growth, I imagine."

"Maybe you ought to see a doctor about it."

"I've seen enough doctors about *that*," I said. She lay on her back, I lay on my back, and she held my hand and we looked at the now dark white ceiling, and I don't know about her, but I had the illusion of walking hand in hand.

"This is nice, but I've got to go home tonight," she said. "I think you're right about Keith. I think he does know you and I go to bed, but I have a theory about that. Keith's a funny boy. If I went to him and said, 'Keith, I'm having an affair with Jim Malloy,' he'd probably say he knew, and from then on everything would be easy. I mean, I could stay out all night any time I wanted to, and he wouldn't hold anything against you. But I don't want to do that. I don't want to come right out with it, because the kind of relationship you and I have, it may break off any minute. Any day. You might fall madly in love with someone, or I might, and right after I'd told Keith, and then I'd have to tell him the same thing about someone else. Then he'd think his little sister is a tart. Which she isn't."

"No. She isn't."

"And he's going through enough right now without any additional worries about me. He likes you."

"I like him."

"I must go now," she said.

"No."

"Yes."

"No. No, I said."

"Ah, Jim. Jimmy."

"That's right, my sweet."

5

THEN FOR a few weeks Peggy and I did not see each other, which meant that I did not see Keith or Herbert. Also I did not see Mr. Don Miller, but that did not seem like much of a loss. Don Miller was the kind of man that for the most part it is a fortunate thing not to have to make up your mind about. There are people whom you see and you react to in a certain way, a way unfavorable to them, from your own point of view. You see them, like at a party or a racetrack or on a train.

You know them and you are on a first-name basis. Maybe you sit down and have a couple of drinks, talking about—well, just talking. If you ask this kind of acquaintance about a mutual acquaintance it invariably is a friend of *yours* whom he knows, and not a friend of *his* that you know. I don't know why this is so, because there are reasons why it should not be so. Maybe it is because in mentioning *your* friend, who knows him, you are subconsciously standing beside your friend, in a two-against-one alliance. You just plain don't like this Don Miller kind of guy, but the chances are about five to one that there never is an open break. You even give him credit for some good qualities, unimportant ones. I could and did readily concede, for instance, that Don Miller was a handsome young man. By the time this story was ended and I had seen him more frequently than I had at this point, I would have conceded that he dressed more like an Easterner than a Californian. I saw right away, the first time I met him on the Coast, that Miller was a guy who very probably could give me some trouble if we were both after the same girl. He also had a kind of courage that made him become Don Miller and stick to it. Under the same circumstances I would have been satisfied with the reward; or I might even have merely dropped the book of traveler's checks in a mailbox and let it go at that. The kind of courage that it takes to be a certain kind of phony is something I envy. In its way it's wonderful, the self-confidence of these guys. It's easy enough to go around being a jerk if your father happens to be President of the United States. But to make up your mind to be something, even if it is something you're not, and to be it, and to be successful at being it—well, maybe Joan Crawford did want to hire a bross bond, but that's a long way from five shows a day at the Capitol, and she made it. I'll take Mike Romanoff, and you can have Brian Ahearn. (But the trouble with all this is that you can also take the Lunts, and I'll take George Burns and Gracie Allen.) So anyway—Don Miller.

As I say, for a few weeks I did not see Peggy and the others. I could have got seven-fifty at one studio, but my last job, my last four jobs, had been paying me a thousand. Not that seven-fifty is tin, but about this time they were getting ready to release an epic that I helped with, on which I was getting screen credit, and I knew the picture couldn't miss. That meant that as soon as the picture was released I would be getting a thousand again, somewhere. I was four or five thousand dollars ahead, and I hadn't been to New York for a year, so it was New York.

New York was wonderful. The wonderful dirty old Jersey meadows. The wonderful Pulaski Skyway. Beautiful Vesey Street and the dear sweet asafoetida warehouses. Bert Lahr doing his swing song in "The Show Is On." The shrunken-looking kids in tails, trying to show that Twenty-One was an old story to them—but walking directly to the kitchen when what they wanted was the men's room. Jack White and Pat Harrington, than whom, and Screwball and Jerry and Doctor R. E. Lee. Sherman Billingsley making his million and not losing anything by it. Charlie Lucas, a good man to have on your side. My charming pals among the Swing Street taxidrivers. My waiter friends, Vincent and Karl and Georgetti and Stone and Nick and Joe and Tony and Fritz . . . Some time I'm going to write a book about New York, but this isn't it. In a little more than two weeks, maybe a little more than three, I was back in California, having done no Christmas shopping. My agent met me at the airport, which meant that he was proud of the deal he had made for me: a three months' hitch at a thousand dollars a week. On the way in from the airport the thing that kept depressing me was that for three or four or five days I would not be able to see a New York paper that I had not already read in New York.

There were some ugly bills waiting for me at the hotel. There were some swatches from some tailors, reminding one that Palm Springs was in full swing and that the same tailors who had the pleasure of serving Mr. William Powell, Mr. Joel McCrea, Mr. Robert Taylor, and their agents, would be pleased to meet one's Palm Springs requirements. They would whip up a pair of whipcord jodhpurs for a hundred dollars, and they begged leave to call attention to the midnight blue evening tails, now the accepted thing. Some excellent vintage wines had been included in the latest shipment to arrive at Vendome Spirits. Something new in supper club entertainment was being offered at the Club Something on Sunset Boulevard. Something new in night club entertainment was being offered at another club on Melrose Avenue. On the other hand, one's perennial favorites wanted to take the liberty of reminding one that it was not too early to make one's New Year's reservations at the Chez Something. Signed: the perennial favorites. There were about a dozen untelegraphed telegrams, written by persons of originality and taste (de gustibus non disputandum), inviting one to cocktail parties at private houses, new artists' agencies, and an automobile salesroom. There was an embossed, stiff paper opportunity to have a party of four or six at a dinner in honor of some Catholic big shot (my name got me on a lot of Catholic sucker lists). All I had to do was get up twenty dollars a plate. Black Tie. There were about two dozen splendid opportunities to help The Cause, from Tehachape to Tallahassee. There was a letter from my mother, a reminder that my school endowment pledge was unpaid, a request to straighten out an illegibly signed check. There was a Dutch Kalendar from a swell girl in Surrey, who wanted to be in plenty of time for Boxing Day. There were a few telephone messages to be ignored. And there was a note from Peggy.

It read:

> James: It was nice of you to write me from New York, you . . . A card or a telegram would have done (Heaven knows you send enough of them for no good reason). But this is not the kind of note I started out to write. Whenever you get back (some time this week, according to the *Hollywood Reporter*) please phone me, unless you arrive at an unearthly hour in the morning. As you may imagine, this is serious. Love,
>
> Peggy
>
> P.S.: It is nothing to worry about from your point of view.
>
> P.

I read the note in my room. It was around lunch time, so I phoned Peggy at the shop. For the first time in our life I failed to recognize her voice. "May I speak to Miss Henderson?"

"This is she. Is this you, Jim?"

Yes, sorry not to have recognized, etc. "I just got in. Do you want to have lunch?"

"I always *do*. What kind of a New York expression is that: 'Do you want to have lunch'? Of course I want to have lunch."

"My but you're snippy. I think I'll go right out and paddle that little round—"

"Yes, Mr. Bronson. I'll be glad to order it for you."

"I think I'll go right out and paddle those little round cheeks of yours, Miss Bronson. Would you like me to come out and paddle those little round cheeks of yours? Please be a little more respectful—"

"Thank you. I'll call you back," she said, and hung up. In a few minutes she phoned me. "Listen, you fool, the boss came in the shop and he could listen in on the extension."

"I'm sorry, I didn't know you had an extension."

"Is that another dirty remark?" she said.

"My God! What a really filthy mind! And you talk about me. You ought to be reviewing pictures for the Legion of Decency. Do you want to have lunch, *with me?*"

"If I can keep from throwing up. You make me sick. I'll meet you at the Derby, the Beverly one. Twelve-thirty."

It was only a short walk from her shop to the Derby. The boy parked my car in the lot across the street, and Peggy arrived by the time I got a table. That Derby is always so full of jabbering Beverly wives, pathetically dolled up as though for the Colony or Voisin, that it is a good place to talk privately, so long as you don't get caught in a lull. But some very funny things come out of those lulls. One time a woman was telling her companions a story, with her voice at the regular volume, and she got caught in a lull just as she was saying, ". . . I took opium." That was too bad, because she will spend the rest of her days telling people she never took opium.

Peggy was so pretty and sweet. She came in, took a quick look around and spotted me. It is easy to spot a man at lunch at that Derby. John, the headwaiter, brought her to the table.

"New coat?" I said.

"Twenty-five dollars, on the Boulevard. Plus tax. Do you like it?"

"It's the best-looking coat I ever saw. Twenty-five dollars."

"Yes. That makes it easy for me to tell you what I have to tell you."

"What have you done? Married Herbert? Let's see your ring."

"No. Nothing like that," she said. "After I wrote that note I tried to remember exactly what I said. It was a foolish note. Ill-considered. Inchoate."

"Whee!"

"I was a little worried about the effect it might have on you. I couldn't remember whether it had a postscript or not. I intended to write one but I wasn't sure I had."

"You did."

"Did you—were you afraid I was pregnant when you read the note?"

"Not after I read the postscript. What do you want to eat or drink, or be merry?"

"I think I'll have a straight whiskey. Rye. And a chicken salad, Russian dressing. Coffee with the salad. Melba toast."

"Did you get that, Bobbie?" I asked the waitress.

"Yes, Mr. Malloy. And you'll have?"

"A *sour* whiskey sour, not one of those banana splits. Corn beef hash without the egg, or *with* the egg. You know. Glass of some light beer."

"Thank you," said Bobbie.

"Okay. Well, what about the coat? Who gave you the coat, or how did you get it, or what's your story? So you won't talk, eh?"

"I'll talk," she said, with a nice smile. She lit a cigarette, scorning my assistance, because she liked to fool with those pull-out matches. She seldom smoked. "I got the coat from my father."

"Oh. Another check? Where from? Where's he spending Christmas?"

"Right where he is now. Right here. Seventy-two-sixty-eight Orchard Terrace."

"No!" I said. "Your father's here?"

"He's here, all right. In the flesh. Not a moving picture. Not a pretty picture, either."

"Peggy, what *is* this? Start from the beginning." Somehow I always had thought of her father as about as real as a character in some of the more entertaining virility fiction in *The Saturday Evening Post*. Now and then there would be an Anton Otto Fischer illustration of a story that would make me think: that probably looks like Peggy's old man. Now my jealous first thought was: How does she know it's her father? It's so long since she's seen him. I was ashamed of that, but there it was.

"A week ago yesterday," she said, "Herbert brought me home from the shop. He has a new car, and not that this has anything to do with the story, but if T.B. doesn't get him first, his driving will. I'm frightened to death to drive with him, but he comes for me nearly every afternoon and it's impossible to tell him how frightened I am. Most likely you think he's insensitive and he is, to other people's feelings, but—I'm sorry.

"Herbert came up to the porch with me, and Millie heard us and she came out looking frightened and began whispering, 'Miss Peggy, there's a man here says he's your father. He's been here most of the afternoon,' she said, 'and,' she said, 'I couldn't phone you because I was afraid. He sat right beside the phone and I couldn't phone.' And she said she wouldn't give him my address, meaning the shop, and didn't know when I'd be back and so that was that. So I went in and this man stood up and took a long look at me and said, 'Peggy, I'm your father.' I knew he was, too, right away. He knew me, too. It's true, Jim. There were some vibrations, is the only way I can explain it.

"Well, it was very embarrassing. Herbert, for instance. He wouldn't have been much help, but he insisted on coming in with me in case there was some trouble, so I had to introduce him to this strange man. 'This is Herbert Stern, Father,' I said."

"I never can remember Herbert's name," I said. "I'm not even sure I ever knew it before."

"It was terribly embarrassing, but Herbert had sense enough to leave, and my father and I sat there for an hour or so. We had plenty to talk about, naturally, but we'd finish one topic and we'd both sit there trying to think of what would be the next topic. Really, Jim. Have you ever had your father that you haven't seen for I forget how many years, suddenly return?"

"No, and I hope he doesn't. At least not on a dark night. Mine's been dead ten years or more."

"So was mine, really. Just think of it. It's an idea for a shocking short story. What if I were on a train, and this man decided I was nice-looking and I thought he was, and I let him pick me up and—so on. And he *is* at*trac*tive." She never used the word casually, but always as though she had carefully chosen it. "Or at least was this day. He was, well, if you can imagine Keith as he will be in about fifteen or twenty years or longer than that, but looking much younger than his age."

"What's he been doing all this time?"

"I'll come to that. We didn't really get into that the first few days he was back. That night Keith didn't come home until late and of course it would be the one night when he didn't call up and say he wasn't coming home to dinner. As a rule he's very considerate about those things. Then when he finally did come home. Oh, first my father wanted to take me out to dinner, to the best place in California, but I told Millie, she's darling, that we'd have dinner, my father and I, and to save something for Keith. Then after we had our dinner he wanted to know all about me and Keith. Then came the problem of where my father was going to sleep. That was embarrassing, but finally I had sense enough to ask him if he had his bags here or where, and he was stopping at the Hollywood Plaza, I think, and I insisted on his going to the hotel and getting his bags, but he refused and then he made a concession. He said he knew we probably weren't prepared for another person in the house that night, but he'd move over with us the next day, provided we had room. We have an extra room, so that was all right, although I'm glad he didn't stay the first night.

"Then he said he guessed I went to bed early on week-day nights, and he was saying goodnight when Keith arrived home. That was the worst part of that first day, because I could see Keith didn't take to him, immediately. He was surprised, and looked at my father as though

he'd come from some other planet, and in very short time I could
see Keith didn't like him. Of course Keith didn't show it, but I knew.
I was glad to get my father out of the house.

"After he'd gone Keith didn't go to bed. I could see he expected to
have a discussion about my father. You know Keith can suddenly get
older and very mature. He started to smoke his pipe and look at me,
waiting for me to start, but when I didn't he said: 'Well, what about
him?' And I said *what* about him, and he said: 'What are we going to
do about him?' And I said I couldn't think of what we were going to
do about him, and then Keith wanted to know, just as though it
were taken for granted, he wanted to know how we were going to get
rid of him. Did we have to be polite? I said of course we'd be polite, but
maybe my father's coming this way would change things entirely.
Well, saying that was stirring up a hornet's nest. Keith was furious, as
mad as I've ever seen him. 'Change things! It certainly will change
things. He isn't going to stay in this house. He's never been our father,
except the biological fact. He's never had any responsibility about us.'
Meaning he'd never taken any. Keith said: 'We're not going to have
him settle down here now, just because of some whim of his, or because he's afraid he's getting old and now he wants a home. You and I
have a nice home of our own, and to hell with him. If he's planning
to make our home his home, then I'm getting out.' Well, I never expected anything like this from Keith. In the first place I never realized
that he thought anything about our home. It *has* been nice, but I
never realized he appreciated it. I don't mean about gratitude, but in
so far as being aware of what a nice home it was. I was touched, because we're a very undemonstrative brother and sister. I'm touched
now, when I think of it."

I pressed her hand. She went on.

"'Well,' I said, 'maybe we won't have any difficulty with him. Maybe
he'll just stay a few days and he won't *be* any problem to us. Just control your feelings till we see what his plans are.' Then he wanted to
know how I felt about my father. I keep calling him my father.
Notice?"

"Yes," I said. "What do you call him when you're with him?"

"I try to avoid calling him anything, but I've been calling him
Father. Anyway, when Keith asked me how I felt about my father I
had to admit I didn't know, principally because I hadn't had time to
form any conclusions, but when I began to think it over, to give Keith
some kind of answer, I realized I didn't feel one way or another about
him. Then. I do now." She stopped.

"And?" I said.

"I can't stand him. I wish he'd go away. If he doesn't go away soon and if your offer is still good, I'll marry you. Or I'll live with you without getting married. I've just got to get away."

"The offer's still good. If you want to be tentative, come and live with me until he goes away. Or, if you want money. Why not take some of that larcenous dough of mine? I have a new contract, three months at a grand a week. At Metro."

"I always said I wouldn't take any money from you, but this time I might. Thank you anyway, even if I don't, but I knew I could count on you, without your telling me. Not that that's what I wanted to see you about. Mainly I wanted to talk to somebody. I've talked a little to Karen, but she has her own troubles. Father lost his best advertising contract. Mother just out of the hospital. Kid sister raising hell in school."

"Well, here I am," I said. "Whatever I can do, and any time. I'm going to take a house in Beverly, and there'll be more than enough room. And if Keith wants to come with me, now or anytime, the house I'd like to have has a room in a sort of wing of its own, with a separate entrance and so forth. He could come and go as he pleased."

"I'll tell him," she said. "I guess I ought to get back to the shop, and I haven't even begun to tell you. Are you going to be busy about five-thirty? You could pick me up at the shop if you weren't. I want to tell you the rest of it, and I need some sex, too."

"Let's plan to have dinner. I'll get you a little tight and get you out of this. You're in bad shape, aren't you, my sweet?"

"Am I. Pay the check and walk with me to the shop."

6

IN SOME respects Philip Henderson was an older Don Miller. Another way of putting it would be to say that Philip Henderson was what Don Miller might easily turn out to be if he continued his career. There are so many men who live as Henderson had lived. Their stories can never completely be told, for the reasons that it would take a detective with an unlimited expense account to follow them through the years, and since nobody cares that much, no detective is likely to get such an assignment. It would take a resourceful agent to check back on the story as Henderson's kind would tell it. There are so many lies in his version. Lies that he comes to believe himself. There are gaps in time, too, that frequently can be explained by jail sentences. Henderson himself undoubtedly had a criminal dossier or two, because there were two gaps of a year or more in his story.

But this much we did come to know about him: he was born in the '90's, in Buffalo, New York. His father was a railroader, a divisional superintendent of maintenance of way, which is a good railroading job. The Hendersons were old New York State, dating back to pre-Revolutionary times. Henderson took pride in mentioning the fact to Peggy and Keith, and was unable to understand their apathy when this historical information was forthcoming, as it frequently was. Philip, an only son, was sent to Cornell after high school. His college career was brief, and he soon was fond of saying that he hoped Keith was getting more out of college than *he* had. He was fond of saying, too, that he had carved his name in Cornell history—on a table-top in a beer-drinking establishment in Ithaca. He said he just got sick of college one day, and said the hell with it and quit. I had heard the same thing said in about the same vague way by boys who I knew had been kicked out of school for petty thefts. It was rather hard to believe that he had been quite as gay in college as he said he had been. No man earning the salary of a superintendent of maintenance of way could have afforded such a son. He probably was gay enough, but not in the financial league that his stories put him.

After he quit college he came out to California to "grow up with the country." Through Masonic and railroading friends of his father's he got a railroad job in Los Angeles, which he used only to get started. After he got the lay of the land and made a few thousand friends he went into the real estate business. Everybody in California was in the real estate business in those days. He did well enough to convince a girl named Margaret Keith that she was getting a good thing in him. Besides, she loved him. So they were married.

When the United States entered the war Mr. and Mrs. Philip Henderson had a large bungalow several miles east of Hollywood. They also had a snappy car, a second-hand Mercer phaeton. Their friends were Angelenos and a few young married people in the Pasadena-Santa Barbara group, and now and then some of the Navy. The Hendersons quickly went into great debt, which was not lessened by the death of Mrs. Henderson's mother. They had presumed that when the sad day came, they would be at least out of debt, but it turned out that there was not much more left than it cost to put the old lady's remains under the ground. It was a disillusioning experience to young Philip Henderson. The least a woman can do is to do something for her only grandchild (for at that time Peggy was an infant).

The Navy first attracted Henderson when he decided to do his bit for Uncle Sam. The uniform, the cleanliness, the travel, the social life that his Navy acquaintances led, all were selling-points. But he had better luck getting into an Army officers' training camp and it was as a second lieutenant of infantry that he went to France. After being shunted around here and there, always with the unhappy prospect of being assigned to the A.E.F. in Siberia, he was sent to France with a draft division, and he returned to California without having been shot either by the Germans or by his own men. He knew, of course, that in his absence he had become the father of a son. Also he rightly guessed that a deliriously grateful people had done nothing about his debts. A "college man," a successful realtor, a first lieutenant, a husband and father, he nevertheless was unable to command, as he put it, the kind of job he considered commensurate with his qualifications. He did not starve; a job selling real estate on straight commission, $50-a-week drawing account, kept food in the house. But it was not the large bungalow that he had left in 1917. That, like the Mercer and a lot of other things, had gone. Indeed, it became a piece of property that in his new job he once was asked to handle, but for sentimental reasons he asked another salesman to take it over.

It must not be inferred, however, that Henderson was all sentiment. He was not mawkish. In his service days he had come to face facts, such as the biological one that a man has to have a woman every so often. With Henderson it was pretty often, especially among the volunteers, the Junior League types who were there to run errands and things like that for the officers. In every good-sized city there were lovely young things in Sam Browne belts and beautifully cut uniforms. It was entirely up to you how far they could be persuaded to make a lonely and handsome young officer comfortable in what might be his last days on earth. Then there were women in France, and on the way to demobilization there were women at home.

And Henderson found out that there had been changes in his own home. His wife had had her hands full with the children and with the family finances. The presence of the children prevented her taking a job. She could not have made out financially by hiring a nurse. A nurse who was good enough for the babies would have taken all the salary the young and inexperienced wife could have earned. And in 1918 when the day came when she broke her last five-dollar bill, she went through a kind of terror that she never forgot. The next day she went to one of her rich Pasadena friends and borrowed a thousand dollars from him. He said he was glad to let her have it, and he meant it. He was married, and he had two children of his own and a mother who single-handed kept him out of the Army, and he told Margaret that he felt it was the least he could do, etc. A few months later she had to go to him again, and again he gave her money; more than she had asked. Then the first thing they knew they were having an affair. She was grateful to him, and he got from her a sense of being needed. Twice, then, she had had to transfer her love away from her husband; once for her children, and the second time for her benefactor.

The first time Henderson asked her if she had remained faithful to him she told him about the man in Pasadena, without naming him. Henderson took it calmly, and without a cross-examination—she didn't care—he confessed that his own body had not been inviolate. Her confession did make it easier for him to get around as much as he liked, and then one day he did not come home. He wrote her from Chicago, saying he imagined that she guessed that there was nothing to her marriage, and he was good and God damn bored with the life of a husband. He said he imagined she would get along all right; the fellow in Pasadena now had a clear track. If she wanted to get a divorce, that was all right too. He had no great feeling about the children; he'd never known them, and to tell the truth he wasn't sure Keith was his child. . . .

The fellow in Pasadena was frightened when Margaret showed him the letter, but when she convinced him that there would be no fuss, that her husband did not know who he was, they resumed the affair; a pleasant relationship that continued for four years. It was convenient for him, and it was a financial life-saver for her. She was able to have a nurse for the children, which in turn enabled her to go to business college and take a job in a department store. She became secretary to the head buyer of ladies-ready-to-wear, and then she worked into selling in the Paris Shop, a department that sold more expensive clothes. Margaret Henderson was prematurely gray, just a little on the stout side, and she was pretty in a way that women liked. That is, she looked as though she belonged where she was, a perfect saleswoman whom you would almost but not quite invite on a trip to Del Monte or the desert. She never bothered to divorce Henderson.

Henderson went only as far as Chicago with the woman who took him away from Los Angeles. She was on her way to New York a few days ahead of her husband. Together she and her husband were going abroad, and it was fun for her and Henderson to have the week on the train and in Chicago. She *was* a bit surprised when he said he wasn't going back to Los Angeles, and she suspected him of a form of blackmail when he borrowed some money from her, but she had had a good time, and it was an even chance that this would pay Henderson off. It did.

Now comes one of the gaps. Henderson's story as I have put it down was pieced together from conversations we had, he and I, and from things he told Peggy and Keith and that Peggy knew from her mother. It may have been presumptuous of me, but when Henderson turned up in California I made a point of seeing a lot of Peggy. I was nearer her father's age and his kind of life than anyone Peggy knew, and I didn't want anything to happen to her, so I saw a lot of Henderson. But of that, more to come.

This first gap, which Henderson not only left entirely unexplained, but even ignored as though for two years he had lived on air, may be traced to the Cook County (Henderson called it Crook County) criminal records. I don't know. Maybe he was skipping the gutter at that time and had jobs that were so lowly that he had succeeded in forgetting them. Maybe he had been mixed up in one of the many mobs that ran various localities in Chicago. He never admitted that, but he did have a pretty good account of the death of one of the greatest trumpet players in jazz, a youngster who offended a mob guy and for punishment a couple of hoodlums rammed the neck of a beer bottle up his rectum. The pain drove this trumpet player crazy, his hair turned gray, and Henderson's story was that this fellow became a hophead, dying of an over-dose. Henderson told it almost as though he had been there all the time, and better than I'd ever heard it before.

He must have known some of the influential gangsters, because he once picked up the silverware in a Sunset Boulevard night club and told us to an odd penny how much it was worth. When we asked him how he knew, he said he had had a job selling silverware to restaurants, and he said something to me about I knew what kind of restaurants. He wouldn't come out and say speakeasy; he liked unnecessary intrigue as much as he liked the necessary kind that must have been a large part of his life.

I had been wrong about the gun-running in New Orleans. He explained that part of his odyssey: he had been associated with Huey Long. He said, "Huey had work for a man that didn't have a Southern accent." I imagined Huey had plenty of work for a man who didn't have a Southern accent, although it might have been awkward to use him, say, as a repeater at the polls. Henderson must have been there more than a few weeks, because he pronounced Pontchartrain and Louisiana and New Orleans the way they pronounce them down there. He also was a bore about oysters Rockefeller, and he knew somebody named Legendre. He admired Huey. He said Huey knew as well as anyone else that the every-man-a-king stuff was so much sheep-dip, but Henderson said he sincerely believed that if Huey had reached the White House he would have done a good job. He admired Huey in the same way a faithful employee admires a paymaster who has been shot in a futile attempt to protect the cash.

This story was given to us in short takes, as they say in the newspaper business. One part he always left out was the woman's angle. He would start a reminiscence about a wild party in Boston or Memphis or Dallas, and even when Peggy was not present he would tell it up to a certain point and we who were listening would have to supply the women. It never entered my head that there weren't always women in Henderson's life. I never failed to get (and never tried hard to avoid) the impression that Henderson always had a solvent woman to turn to when he was not in the money. Somehow you would picture Henderson arriving at Atlanta or St. Paul on a train that got in around ten p.m. He would take a taxi to the second-best hotel, walk up very pleased with himself to the clerk, register for a double room, and before unpacking he would be on the phone, fixing up a party for that night with a handsome brunette of thirty-six, whose alimony came regularly on the first or second of the month.

He had covered the country pretty thoroughly from Denver east, and twice he had done it legitimately; once as a sort of promotion and publicity man for a tire company that was sending a small fleet of gaudily painted cars on an advertising junket. Another time he was with the William Bradwell Smith Associates, which I knew of old. The William Bradwell Smith Associates put on drives, big and little. The biggest ones would be for the Community Chest of some of the largest cities. The smallest ones they handled were for hospitals and churches. The minimum "quota" for the minimum drive was $500,000, and the William Bradwell Smith Associates, practical philanthropists, would take care of the whole drive for a guaranteed 5% of the minimum, plus a bonus over the minimum for as much as the traffic would bear. The William Bradwell Smith Associates, up to 1929, could turn any town in the United States into a frenzy of giving. The mayor, the "civic leaders," the clergy (sometimes excepting the

Catholics), the press, the luncheon clubs—all would get into a lather. There would be a forty-foot "thermometer" in the Public Square; stickers on cars; consommé-veal-ice cream luncheons at a dollar a throw (in the Y.M.C.A. cafeteria or in the local branch of a hotel chain); prizes for the team captains (usually boarded cowhide luggage donated by an unregenerate harness dealer who was tired of looking at it); a daily Page One story headed M'NULTY LEADS CHEST DRIVE, and two days before the drive ended Captain or General or Doctor Somebody would announce that he would give an additional, an *additional* $5,000 if that amount were subscribed before the final dinner. And it would be subscribed, thereby putting Middletowne over the top and saving it from disgrace in the eyes of the William Bradwell Smith Associates. In the picture I had of Henderson and the alimonyed brunette the William Bradwell Smith Associates played an important part. As a William Bradwell Smith Associate, Henderson would have met many of those handsome small-city women who campaign because they have nothing else to do. And of course when the Associates were running a drive for some college he must have made contact with many a co-ed alumna.

I could see Henderson in this, one of the more legitimate of his admitted enterprises during the '20's and '30's. He would have learned the ropes under a veteran Associate, then he would be put on his own. I could see him, even as I sat with him in Hollywood, getting up at one of those luncheons. He was not a short man, but he was not so towering tall that he would annoy the inevitable big shot who was bantam in size. Henderson, like as not, would stand up at the speakers' table. He would pick up a spoon and beat a tattoo on two glasses of water—a tinkling sound that was much more friendly than the rap of a gavel. Ling-cling-a-ling-cling. Shuffling of chairs as team members and captains faced the speakers' table. A sharp short whistle as one eater signaled a waiter to get some more coffee. The crack of silver-plate on heavy china as another eater snapped his spoon through a block of Neapolitan ice cream. Quantities of phlegm being pulled from its resting place in a hundred throats. Then—attention. All eyes, except those of the man bolting his ice cream, on Henderson.

Blue serge suit, two-button, ready-made, the coat open to give an occasional hint of Henderson's Sigma Nu pin under the upper left vest pocket. Soft white shirt with the collar kept in place by invisible tabs. Two-dollar small-figured tie. In front of him, on the table, a small pile of papers, which he arranged neatly until silence came. Then the surprise technique, which he would have figured out for himself.

Instead of going immediately into his little talk he would call to the waiters in the back of the room. "Would you mind closing that door, please?" A volunteer would get up from a table and nod to a waiter and repeat Henderson's request, and then the volunteer would sit down, feeling as though he had rescued a family of five and their dog from a dangerous surf. He would be rewarded with a beautiful smile by Henderson, and a quiet but audible "Thank you." Then Henderson would cock his head and look at a far corner of the ceiling, causing the less alert ones to wonder what he thought he heard. The wise ones were sure he was considering how best to phrase today's good news. The man with the ice cream would put down his spoon and light a cigar.

Then suddenly: "This morning at the corner of Smithfield and Wood . . ." And Henderson was off.

7

IN THE few weeks between the return of Philip Henderson and the annual observance of the Birth of Christ, there were certain developments and adjustments chez Henderson. Among them:

More money in the Henderson household. Apparently Henderson had not come to Los Angeles broke. He first took Peggy on a shopping trip. He was paying cash, and she thought she might as well take what he offered. Outstanding household bills were paid, and Millie, the colored maid-of-all-work, was given a $3 raise to $18 a week.

Less seen of Keith at home. He moved to his fraternity house so that he could study later and still get enough sleep. That was his story. The truth was that he had not changed his opinion of his father. He urged Peggy to get everything out of Henderson that she could. The night Henderson said he had worked for Huey Long, Keith said: "Did you ever work for Zioncheck?" But Henderson refused to be insulted.

More seen of Herbert. Herbert had much the same protective impulse as mine. He was always around, it seemed. When Henderson would mention some "dirty Jew" in a story, and quickly apologize to Herbert, Herbert would say: "That's all right. I don't like all of them myself. You aren't compelled to like people just because of your being of the same blood." Henderson didn't get that.

No word of any kind from Don Miller. No word of any kind from Don Miller.

A lot of drinking. The first party was the Saturday night after Henderson began his visit. "Tonight's my night to howl," he announced at noon. Peggy usually worked Saturday afternoons, but her boss had given her the afternoon off to make up for the evenings she would have to work when the Christmas rush began, Beverly Hills being a good book customer at Christmas. I brought Peggy home after lunch that Saturday and Henderson made his announcement. Henderson gave Peggy fifty dollars. "Go out and buy yourself a slam-bang evening gown, and if that isn't enough, there's plenty more where that came from." Peggy said it was more than enough. "Well, just in case, here's ten more for a manicure and hairdresser. We're going places tonight. Oh, by the way, do you think you could scare up a girl for me?" Peggy was obviously shocked, and he said: "Doesn't have to be somebody my age. Get one of *your* friends." Later she said she was *afraid* that that was what he meant. She called her best friend, Karen Waner, who broke a date to come with us.

Henderson looked well in what he called a "Tuck." He had chubby cheeks, but no double chin, and his hair dried quickly and became very light brown, making him look not much older than I. His eyes were green. His teeth tight and even and all present from bicuspid to bicuspid. The missing teeth went unnoticed except when he laughed his heartiest.

When I arrived at the little house Henderson was shaking cocktails in a Coco-Malt shaker. It was a strange sight. In the many times I had gone to that house I never had seen three persons in evening dress all at once. Once in a great while Peggy and I would put on evening clothes, but on those nights there would be Peggy in an evening gown, waiting for me, and *only* Peggy and I. Now there were three: Peggy, her father, and Karen Waner. My coming made it four, and there were still more to come. Keith had found it simply impossible to go along. I forgot what excuse he offered; something unflattering and final, that had to do with college life. And so at the last minute Peggy had asked Herbert to come and bring a girl.

The Martinis were watery and had too much vermouth. No one noticed it. Henderson had the floor, and did not sit down at any time. He kept busy pouring cocktails and urging us to drink up. Karen had made a very good impression on him, which was not strange. Karen's father, a photographer, had a favorite subject, and it was Karen. If I had been a photographer she would have been mine, too. She was about two inches taller than Peggy and this night she had on a blue and white dress; blue, with large white flowers printed on it in just about the coloring of Wedgwood. In a way it was a bad dress, so far as the colors went. It was a pattern that did not show off her figure. But to make up for this lack it was cut low enough in front to offer at least circumstantial evidence proving that she had nothing on underneath. Her breasts were large, and then you noticed that her thighs were large, but she had good calves and ankles. She had one of the most exciting bodies I've ever seen, but even without that she would have been a knockout. She had a small head, heavily lidded brown eyes, small curling lips, and a short straight nose. She did not look older than Peggy. They didn't look as though their ages could be compared by the same standards. Peggy was definitely a young girl, about twenty years old. Karen was a young woman who happened to be the same age. She also made Henderson seem young, or at least inept.

Henderson was trying not to be too attentive to Karen, and wondering how much she knew about him and his return. But he was in a spot; Karen knew everything about him that Peggy could tell her, and always had. Karen loved Peggy, needed her, depended on her.

But Peggy was in a spot, too. Now that the party was a reality, she wanted it to go off well. She was pulling for everyone, and for the first time I saw her as a conventionally timid hostess. It certainly was a new side—Peggy, who could get up before a hundred persons and say what she was thinking about Tom Mooney or Harry Bridges, was being a conventional hostess.

"You a Californian, Miss Waner?" said Henderson.

"I was born here, but my mother and father are from back East."

"Whereabouts in the East?"

"Columbus, Ohio."

"Oh, yes. I've been there," he said. "Yes, Columbus. I have some good friends there. But I guess you wouldn't know them. Have you been there?"

"No, I never have."

"It's quite a place. Yes, I've been there several times. You ever been there, Mr. Malloy?"

"Just for a short time. I've driven through a couple of times. Stayed there overnight I think once."

"At the Deshler?" he said.

"Some name like that," I said.

"You know, you have some cousins living there, Peggy," said Henderson. "Your second cousins. I haven't seen them—well, before I came to California. I never looked them up." This, he realized, was a slight mistake. "Where you from, Malloy?"

"Gibbsville, Pennsylvania."

"Gibbsville. No, I don't think I've ever been there. Pittsburgh. Philadelphia, of course. Just where is that in Pennsylvania? Is it near Pittsburgh?"

"No. Nearer Philadelphia. In the hard coal regions."

"Oh, the *hard* coal regions. Miss Waner? Dividend?"

"Yes, please," said Karen.

"Say, I wonder if you're related to the ballplayers named Waner?"

"I don't imagine so. I never heard of them."

"You didn't? Play for Pittsburgh? I guess you're not a fan, then. In 1927, in the World Series. Peggy, how about you? Mr. Malloy?"

Herbert arrived along about this time. In tails, and with a very tall Jewish girl, taller than he. Instinctively I knew that Miss Harris—Joan was her first name—was going to be my problem. She had good conventional manners and probably was a distant cousin of Herbert's. She accepted a cocktail without a word and took a quick look around, which was all she needed, and then settled down. She gave her attention to anyone who was speaking, and in between she would stare at Karen. I was thinking up a plan to snub her when Karen stared back at her, and then Joan smiled and it was a nice smile. After that I liked her. But she didn't help much in conversation.

"Well," said Herbert, after he told Henderson he didn't drink, "how do you like California? Oh, I forgot you've been here before."

Henderson gave three chuckles. "Well, this *is* all pretty new to me. By George, they certainly have done some building in the last eighteen, twenty years. You live here, Miss Harris?"

"Just for the winter. My home is in New York."

"Oh, is that so?"

"Mr. Henderson, Joan and I have a friend," said Herbert. "He'd like to join us later. Would you mind telling me where we'll be around half past eleven, twelve?"

"Why didn't you bring him along? Call him up and tell him to join us now. Extra man. I hardly ever dance, the girls—"

"Thank you, but he has an engagement for the early part of the evening. Joan's going up to San Francisco tomorrow and he wanted to see her."

"Well, I don't know. Peggy, where do you think we'll be around that time?"

"Ho-ho. Don't ask *me*," said Peggy.

"Why, of course I'll ask you, Peggy. What's the best place, after dinner? The Trocadero's about the only place I know of."

"Well, in that case you better ask Jim to get us a table, Saturday night."

"Will you do that, Mr. Malloy?"

"Sure. Be glad to, but I don't think we'll have to. The headwaiter's a friend of mine."

"Well, whatever you say. Mr. Stern, you tell your friend it would be a pleasure if he'd join us at the Trocadero."

"Tell him to ask for my table, Herbert," I said.

"All right, but remember, Mr. Malloy, this is my party. I want that understood before we start. Huh?"

"Sure," I said.

"Don't you think we'd better get started, Father?" said Peggy. "Jim, we can all go in your car, can't we?"

"Sure," I said.

"I'll take Joan in mine," said Herbert. "Both of us have to be home early."

And so we went to Lamaze and had a good dinner and everybody got tight, everybody but Herbert. Some ate filet mignon and some ate squab. All had champagne. Everybody danced, including Herbert, who was grim and silent with Joan, and loquacious with Peggy. He didn't dance with Karen. Henderson danced with each girl in turn. It was quite a workout for me, and only less so for Henderson. An armful of Karen made me forget that platonic basis we were on, and after I danced with Joan I told myself that if I weren't being temporarily faithful to Peggy I would certainly investigate Miss Harris. She liked to dance that way. When people bumped us out of that position she would settle back into it. Watching her face whenever she danced with Henderson, I was reminded of an engineer and a locomotive; his head sticking out of the cab was Intelligence; but it was the locomotive that was doing the work.

You could say to Karen: "Well, what about it, Karen?"

And she would say: "Why ask, when you know the answer?"

"Well, you might change your mind."

"I know. Let's go to bed together and see what happens. *That* old stuff."

"I warn you. You're taking the wrong attitude. I'll never make you a big movie star when I get to be a producer."

"You'll never make me, period," she said. "Besides, I'm no good. They all tell me that. A man like you, with all your experience, you'd want somebody to be very good. So. By the way, I hear you're out of the unemployed class."

We often talked that way, and the thing was, that kind of talk was full of truth. I liked Karen, and the things I said I meant, but without any optimism. Peggy knew all about Karen, and what I knew about her Peggy had told me. Their good friendship had begun when they were together in high school. It had the little beginnings: Peggy thought Karen was the prettiest girl in school, and with her usual generosity, said so. Karen was a pretty but frightened freshman of a few days, and when she heard what Peggy said she remembered that she *was* pretty. With this renewal of confidence in herself she was able to go out of her way to make friends with Peggy, and in a month or so each knew what the other was doing every hour of the day. So it had continued. Peggy, in her way, needed Karen. Peggy was not a pretty freshman; whenever she wanted to she led her class, but she was a rather fat little thing. She had no beau. Then the boys began to see that if they were going to get to Karen, it had to be through Peggy, which was how Peggy became a non-virgin. It was hardly more than a technical knockout for the boy who accomplished Peggy's change of status. There were no ill effects; in fact, only a great curiosity and surprise that there were no effects at all. Peggy often said she waited for someone to notice the change in her, but no one ever did. Even the first boy didn't realize or believe that he was the first. She promptly told Karen, who more or less promptly determined to change her own status; but in Karen's case there were effects. The first time was bad, and there was a frightened, hated boy, and a frightened, miserable girl. Then for Peggy a good adolescent love with a good, slightly older boy, but for Karen the next time—a year or so later—was as bad as the first; she had to have an abortion.

They lived near each other, and after high school the friendship was even better than it had been. They didn't *have* to see each other every day, as was the case in school, but hardly ever did two consecutive days pass without their being together.

Henderson paid the bill and we moved down Sunset Boulevard to the Trocadero. John, the headwaiter, whom I had known in New York night clubs, gave us a table in the second row from ringside. More champagne, and more dancing. Henderson was duly impressed with the movie stars, and completely unimpressed with the directors, not one of whose names he recognized, so I gave up trying to point out local celebrities who were not actors. Fan magazine photographers, trade paper owners, agents, brothers and sisters of the stars, visiting musicians, producers, press agents, Los Angeles politicians, and a large and rather badly behaved group of Pasadena-Santa Barbara younger set meant nothing to him, and they were the people I spoke to. I didn't know any star there well enough to introduce Henderson. I said: "Sometimes the stars sit downstairs in the bar, if you'd like to meet some. I might know someone downstairs. I'll take a look."

"Oh, that's all right," he said. "I've met some of them. Not the present-day ones. Wally Reid. I used to know Wally. Norman Kerry. There was a well-built chap."

"Well, I'll take a look." I went downstairs to the bar, not to do Henderson any favor, but to take a look around for my agent, who I was fairly sure would be there. But on my way to the bar I saw good old Don Miller, sitting in a booth. I immediately recognized the girl with him, and so would have at least half the men in the room. She was one of the girls; a free-lance. Miller was paying his bill, and he saw me. "Malloy, old boy. How the hell are you?"

"All right," I said. "Hello, dear."

"Huh. I didn't think you'd remember me," said Dear.

"How could I forget you?" I said. She was all right, but sometimes a trouble-maker when she got drunk and remembered that she had been Miss Potter County Texas or something.

"Just paying my check," said Miller. "How about a quick one. You're all duked out. What's it, a party?"

"Mm-hmm. Upstairs." I sat down. "What's with you?"

"You mean Charlotte?"

"No, I don't mean Charlotte. I wouldn't refer to Charlotte that way, would I, dear?"

"I don't know how you'd refer to me and I'm sure it doesn't concern me in the least how you refer to me."

"Oh, it's that way," I said. "Okay."

"You shut up," said Miller to Charlotte. "This is my pal. My pal Malloy, huh, Malloy?"

"If you say so," I said. "Scotch and soda."

"St. James, Mr. Malloy?" said the waiter.

"Yes. Oh, hello, Franz. Well, kid, you must be doing all right."

"You mean Charlotte?" he asked.

"No, I don't mean Charlotte. That's twice I don't mean Charlotte. I mean the Troc and so forth. Where you living?"

"Same place."

"Where are *you* living, dear?"

"I'm living in Honolulu, where do you think I'm living? Are you trying to pretend you don't know where I live? I suppose I'm not good enough for you in the Trocadero. Hunh. You don't have to take that attitude, *Mis*-ter Malloy."

"I don't think she likes me," I said. "I think I'll have my drink at the bar. Give me a buzz, kid. I'll be at Metro from now on."

"She's a little drunkie," said Miller. "I'll be seeing you."

I picked up my highball and went to the bar, and Miller and Charlotte departed. I talked to the bartender while I drank my drink, forgot about my agent, and rejoined the party upstairs.

In my absence they had decided to go some place else, but agreed to wait ten more minutes for Herbert's friend. In those ten minutes I had a strange conversation with Henderson. It began when I explained to Peggy that I had met Miller downstairs: "*Don* Miller. You met him." She remembered him.

"Don Miller? What Don Miller?" said Henderson, who I thought was busy with Karen's garter.

"You wouldn't know him," I said. "He's a kid—I beg your pardon. A young fellow from back East."

"Where from? Washington, D.C.?" said Henderson. "I knew a Don Miller there. What business is this fellow in?"

I didn't know whether to make up a whole new story to protect Miller, or to give Henderson some truth, or to stall. I stalled. "I don't know just what business he *is* in."

"How old a fellow is he?"

"Oh, I don't know."

"About twenty-four," said Peggy. "Wouldn't you say?"

"Somewhere around there," I said.

"What kind of a looking fellow is he?" said Henderson.

"Handsome. Tall, dark, and handsome," said Peggy, giving a very bad imitation of Mae West.

"It couldn't be the fellow you know, Mr. Henderson," I said.

"I don't think so either," said Peggy. "This boy is from Jim's home town."

"Oh, from Pennsylvania," said Henderson.

"That's the name of the *state*," I said. "No, this couldn't be the same guy. Peggy, how about a jig?" We danced.

I was not satisfied that Henderson was satisfied. I realized that I must have seemed unnecessarily evasive. If Henderson knew the Donald Miller on whose traveler's checks my Don Miller, or Schumacher, was living, he might also know about the checks. It was too bad that I hadn't told Peggy the real story of Miller, but it seemed better now not to take a chance.

We waited about twenty minutes for Herbert's friend, and he did not show up, so Herbert took Joan home. She was in a bad temper on account of her dilatory friend. Karen and Peggy and Henderson and I went to a couple of other places, to see Jerry Bergen and Louis Prima, and then I took them to their homes.

When I got home I called Don Miller and after a long wait a sleepy voice said he didn't think Mr. Miller was home, because his key was in the box. I left a message, but I had no hope of its ever being delivered or even written down. Then I called Charlotte's number, but no answer. I reread parts of Zola's "Germinal," stopping every half hour or so to telephone Charlotte. About five-thirty she answered.

"Charlotte, this is Jim Malloy. Is Miller there?"

"Oh, it's you. What do you think this—"

"This is important. If Miller's with you, I have to speak to him."

"Go —— yourself," she said. "You can't high-hat—"

"Tell Miller it's about Washington," I said.

"What'd he do, cross the Delaware?" she said, and hung up.

I tried to get her back, but she left the phone off the cradle. Of course there were two or three things I might have done—but there were reasons why I couldn't send her a telegram or go to her house, because I didn't know her last name, and I didn't know her address. She often had come to my house, but I never had been to hers. All I knew was that it was a three- or four-dollar taxi ride from a house I'd had in Beverly Hills, which wasn't much help. The best I could do was to send Miller a telegram to his house, which I did.

8

THE NEXT day I awakened five or six times with an inexplicable hangover; inexplicable in that I had not been drunk the night before. No blank periods; I remembered everywhere I had been, everyone I had spoken to, everything I had done. It may have been that I drank too much without getting stewed. Whatever it was, I had a hangover, and I awakened five or six times, dozed off again, changed my position in bed in the hope of getting rid of the throbbing headache. It was no use.

It was the middle of the afternoon. I sent down for a big orange juice and scrambled eggs and coffee and oatmeal and the Sunday papers. The eggs were not done the way I like them, but I put away the rest of the food and presently, after the usual natural functions, I felt well enough to tackle Miller on the phone. He was home.

"Say, what was the idea of calling me at Charlotte's? I call that a pretty lousy—"

"Listen, you punk, I don't care what you call it. You listen to me. I think you're in a real jam. You better come on out here and I'll tell you about it."

I read Louella and her daughter and W. R.'s editorial, and studied my favorite study, Ginger Rogers in color, and second-guessed the eastern football scores, and got mad about the latest ex-Communist who was telling all, and won a bet with myself that my name would not be in a list at a party I'd gone to, and read the second-hand automobile classifieds (but no Alfa-Romeo for $450 cash), and saw a fairly good wisecrack I had made three years before attributed to a New York orchestra leader, and read the titles of the Sunday sermons, and tried to calculate how much I would make if I were a sports writer again and on the take. I thought, as I thought every day, of the Paramount writer who came home from the studio one day and saw his father reading the paper. "What's in the paper, Dad?" he said.

"Huh," snorted the old man. "L. A. dog chases L. A. cat over L. A. fence."

I thought of Ginger and wondered how many youths at Yale and Kenyon and Stanford and Texas Christian and St. Bonaventure's and Clemson and Magdalen and McGill and Bowlder and Yale-in-China were thinking of her at just that minute. And the next minute I was sending flowers to Peggy. I had the clerk say on the card: These are New York Cut. Then the phone rang and it was Miller. He came up.

"Sit down," I said. "Want some coffee? Get the glass out of the can."

He got the glass from the bathroom and I filled it with coffee. He drank some, put the glass on the desk and lit a cigarette. "What's the jam I'm in?" he said.

"I *think* you're in one," I said. "Let me think how to begin this.

"Well, suppose I begin this way. I'll give you the worst part first. The facts. Then you can help me figure out if you're in a jam. Last night when I saw you at the Troc, one of the guys upstairs on the party I was on, when I came upstairs I happened to mention I saw you. I was with the Henderson girl. You met her with me that night at the South Seas."

"Sure, I remember her. Nice little number."

"Sure. Well, I mentioned your name, and immediately this guy wanted to know *what* Don Miller. From Washington?"

"Jesus!" said Miller.

"So I started to say I didn't know where you were from, but Peggy, the Henderson girl, she said you were from Pennsylvania. Then this guy wanted to know what business you were in. I said I didn't know. I said I didn't know you very well."

"Who was the guy?"

"And I told him I didn't know how old you were, but she volunteered the information that you were around twenty-four or -five."

"Who was he?"

"Just let me tell you the story, will you? Then he wanted to know what you looked like, and we gave him a sort of stall, but maybe not enough of a one. Peggy said you were tall, dark, and handsome, like Cary Grant in that Mae West picture."

"Jesus." He put his face in his long fingers and sat like a kibitzer or a condemned man. "Well, who was this guy?"

"I don't know whether to tell you or not. I don't know whether it'll do any good to tell you."

"God damn it, sure it will, Malloy. Give me a break."

"I'm giving you a break. These L. A. cops are tough, you know. I could just as easily be held as accessory after the fact or something, just sitting here talking to you. In my room, don't forget. All right, I'll tell you who it was. It's Peggy Henderson's father. He suddenly blew into town the other day."

"Jesus!"

"They don't know much about him, she and her brother. He disappeared when the brother was a kid, about fifteen, twenty years ago, give or take a couple years. Since then he's been traveling around the country, practically every place but out here. Different jobs. Advertising. I sat in on one session with the guy, and he's told his kids a few things, but I don't think he's a cop. Still, he may be. Not a regular cop. Maybe some kind of a special dick. An investigator. One of those. Maybe he works for that American Express or American Bankers or whatever it is. The people that issued those checks of yours."

Miller took one hand from his face and made a fist and pounded the air. "Oh, God."

"What?" I said. "The heat's on?"

"I guess so."

"What are you going to do? What are your plans?"

"Screw out of here, that's the first thing," he said.

"It might be a very good idea, but where, and how? Have you any dough?"

"Uh-huh. A couple hundred bucks. I owe a little, not more than fifty bucks. I don't know where to go though. Get a job on a ship, maybe."

"How? You've never been to sea, you don't belong to any union, and I wouldn't advise you to do any scabbing out here. But how do you know this Henderson is after you? It might be just a false alarm, or maybe he does know this Don Miller, maybe he's an older guy. All you have to do is change your name again, quietly leave this part of the country and go back to Swedish Haven or wherever you please."

"No, I got a hunch on this. This is it, all right. See, Malloy, they have my description everywhere I cashed one of those checks, and another thing, my pal in Washington, they probly got a description from him, so they'll be looking for me at Swedish Haven. So I can't go there, and I can't be Schumacher again, either. And there's something else makes me think this is the right guy. I mean by that, makes me think he's a detective. God damn it!"

"What's that?"

"Well, you were pretty swell to me so I might as well let you in on it. I cashed another check."

"Oh, you damn fool. What'd you do that for?"

"That bim I was with last night. Charlotte."

"Why, you dope, you didn't have to—why, she's a—she isn't any two-buck whore, but you could have been on the free list."

"Better'n that. She wanted to keep me. But I picked her up one night and I gave her this line of crap. I told her my old man was a big-shot banker in New York and I was out here to learn the business end of the movies. So I started in spending dough on her. I *was* on the free list, that's true, but I would of done better just giving her ten or twenty bucks every time I laid her. I spent that much on her every time I went out with her."

"Why?"

"I do' know. I liked her. Maybe she is a whore, but. Well, you laid her. I had to have more dough, see? I put on this act, banker's son and all that. I bought a new Ford. Aah." At this point I thought he was going to cry. "I was only sore last night because I thought you were trying to get her to come out, or you come down to her place."

"Nope," I said. "Last night was the first time I saw her since, oh, last summer. Are you in love with her?"

"I don't know. I never exactly thought of it that way. That's something I never was, in love with any girl. But she's all right. She often says to me, 'We don't have to go out.' She says I probly get a small salary and hardly any allowance and I don't have to spend it on her. That's what she said after she saw the joint where I live."

"Can you tell her the truth? Is she in love with you?"

"She offered to give up hustling for me."

"Maybe she'd be glad of the chance if she thought you could keep her. What do you honestly think? Is she in love with you enough so that you could trust her?"

"Well, it's so hard to say. Sometimes I think she is, but then I don't know. The first night I was with her, I went crazy. I never had anything like it. I thought, this dame must be nuts for me. She tells me I'm the only guy she ever enjoyed it with. We'll be walking along the street together or in a movie, and all of a sudden she'll start in, only talking. The other night we went to the movies and we no sooner got inside than she started in, did I like it last night, did I want to do it that way with the dame in the picture. Till I couldn't see straight."

"I guess you must be all right in the hay," I said.

"No, it's her. And she's only from Texas, only a plain ordinary American. Pretty, but, you know."

"Sure. Well now, listen, anything to get off the subject of tail, or I'll be sending down for the operator or somebody. Here's what I suggest. You figure out whether you can trust this Charlotte or not. That's entirely up to you. If you have any doubt about it, the hell with her. Don't see her any more, because she can be trouble. I imagine the cops know her, otherwise she wouldn't be able to operate even if she didn't have a record. As far as I know she's honest, and has no record. But they might be able to trace you through her, if they're going to trace you. Now what you do, you get rid of that car. Get out of that place where you're living and move to some place way the hell away from here, like on the other side of Western Avenue, or else go to Long Beach or any place, but don't stay around Hollywood or Beverly or any of these places.

"Change your name, and get a job. Get some kind of job that isn't a white collar job. Car-washer. Take any kind of dough, just to get a job. You have enough to stake you for a while, and if you need dough later I'll lend you some. Only don't get the idea that I'm going to keep you. How're your eyes?"

"Good, I guess."

"Well, go to some cheap jewelry store where they examine eyes and they'll find something wrong with them. They always do. Nobody has perfect eyes out here, and if one of these oculists saw perfect eyes he'd think there was something wrong with them. Get yourself a pair of glasses with steel rims, not tortoise-shell. Tortoise-shell look phony sometimes."

"Were you ever on the lam?"

"That's none of your business," I said. "I write for the movies, and whether I was on the lam or not doesn't make any difference. Another thing. You have to cultivate a new personality. Dress differently. Get yourself a cheap suit that doesn't fit so well, a coat that doesn't cover your ass. Did you pay cash for your car?"

"Yes," he said. "Traded the old one and the rest cash."

"Sell it at a loss, to get rid of it quickly. Maybe you ought to get a motorcycle, second-hand. That would certainly be a new thing in your personality. While I think of it, don't ever call me here. It's safer to call me at the studio. Let me know where you are, but don't get in touch with me except when it's absolutely necessary. Will you remember all this?"

"Yes."

"Don't forget it. I want to tell you something. You know, this may be a false alarm. But even if it is it'll be a good thing for you to change your identity again. If it'll make you feel any better, I *was* on the lam once, in New York, and I threw off the people that were after me by pretending to leave New York, but all I did was move to another hotel a block away, by way of Grand Central. Well, I guess that's all I have to offer."

"Well Malloy, I sure appreciate your kindness. I—"

"Skip it. By the way, where did you cash this last check?"

"At some gambling joint. They knew Charlotte and she told them my old man was a banker. All—"

"What gambling joint? The Surf?"

"Yes," he said. "It's *some place.*"

"My boy," I said, "you want to get the hell out of this section as fast as you can. You're in the middle, between the law and the mob guys. Beat it, and good luck."

He left, and I sat there in comfort, thinking about him and how I came to know him. The town he came from was a few miles from my home town, but it might as well have been a few states away, for all the mixing the people of the two towns did. As a reporter it was my job to know people like his father and all the other ministers, undertakers, cops, justices of the peace, politicians, station agents and other news sources. But this kid himself was not important enough to know, even though I had once written his name, wrong. Probably the only way he would ever get to be known outside of his home town was the way another townsman of his had become notorious. This other fellow was a sort of bush-league public enemy, who held up a dozen banks and filling stations before he was accidentally killed by a West Virginia deputy sheriff. The deputy didn't sound like the kind of minion of the law who goes around routing out public enemies. Anyway, this public enemy turned out to have been born in Swedish Haven, although he hadn't lived there from the age of two on. It gave us a good one-day story, and it made Swedish Haven feel that the eyes of the world were upon it, the way such towns feel when the local Elks take the lead from all the cities of that size in new members gained during the month of October, and get written up in the *Elks Magazine*. Or when the high school relay team wins its event at the Penn Relays. Or when some obscure housewife wins a Plymouth sedan for the very best last line to a prepared advertising limerick, and her name and address are announced over the radio.

And yet to me this kid was a sort of celebrity, the way anyone is who is wanted by the law. Sitting there in my room he was a frightened kid, the same age as one of my brothers, and he was about as unexciting a figure as there was in Los Angeles County. But the moment he left the room he began to be different. Already I was *remembering* him, not seeing him, and what I remembered was a figure that had passed, like a celebrity who has been pointed out to you just as he passed, so that you don't see his face but only his back. Miller was a tall young man, whose rounded shoulders contributed to the picture of a hunted man. All hunted men have rounded shoulders, in your mental picture of them. Sometimes they are turning their heads over a shoulder. I hoped Miller would get out of his own jam without any help from me, but that he would I neither doubted nor believed.

I put on a new brown double-breasted suit and a blue shirt and brown foulard tie and an old pair of brown Scotch grain brogues. I left the coat hanging until I had called Peggy and told her I would take her for a ride. She told me to come right over.

She was alone. She said her father had gone out to have a demonstration of a second-hand LaSalle that he was thinking of buying. He had wanted her to come along, but she said she expected a call from me, which was nice of her, as I had not mentioned that I would call.

"Oh, I just used you as an excuse is all," she said. "I don't want you to think of me sitting all alone by the telephone."

"Waiting for a ring, a ting-a-ling. Well I'm glad you waited, and I'm glad I called."

"And I'm glad you sent me flowers. Why don't you do that oftener?"

"I don't know."

"New York Cut," she said. "Oh! I just got it! You meant the steaks. Of course, of course, how stupid of me."

"No," I said. "You're *used* to seeing it, and it's still new to me."

"Why don't you send them oftener? I *know* why, of course."

"Why?"

"Well," she said, "if you were in love with Karen I'll bet you'd send her flowers, all the time. Every day when Karen came home there'd be a little box of flowers with some witty note."

"Not a witty note every day. Flowers maybe, but—"

"Yes, you'd try anyway. But with me—I'm not a glamor girl like Karen. I'm not beautiful. I'm a mere, oh, I don't know. Slightly pretty. Slightly intelligent. Pushover for you."

"Now don't talk like that, Peggy."

She laughed her fat little laugh that began low and went high and came back to low. "All right. But I'm a woman. Remember that. And I like to receive flowers. I may not *like* flowers, but—"

"Oh. So you don't like flowers. That's what you're carping about." I pretended to ignore her, and the first thing I knew I was ignoring her. There was a car ahead of us—we were driving out Wilshire by this time, with Malibu vaguely in my mind—and it was a convertible sedan like mine, with a low top so that I couldn't see who was in it. But the radio was on rather loud and it was playing something that I liked. It might have been the Toccata and Fugue, or it might have been the Three Oranges march, or it might have been Stack o' Lee Blues. It was something I liked and did not expect to hear from a California car on a Sunday afternoon on Wilshire Boulevard. It was the kind of thing that I expected every Californian to turn off. I switched on my own radio and tried to find the station that the other car had.

"You hurt?" said Peggy.

"Shh!" I monkeyed with the radio. "Trying to get something."

"You'll get something. A sock on the head if you shush me."

"Peggy, I'm trying to get the station that those people have. The Chrysler. The car like mine."

"I thought this was a Buick."

"It is. Please." I couldn't find the station, and then I got a break in traffic and drew up alongside the Chrysler. In it were four people: two girls, two young men. "What station have you got?" I said.

"I beg your pardon?" said the girl who was driving.

"I wanted to get that tune. What station are you tuned in on?"

They told me. It was one of those stations that broadcast nothing but phonograph records. I tuned in and it was what I wanted. Then the light changed. I was enjoying myself, and after I changed gears I reached over and took Peggy's hand. She took it away. "Wasn't that rather obvious?"

"Can't I hold your hand?"

"You know what I mean. I've seen you practically sock somebody that just looked at me when I was with you, but you, you drive right up to a girl on Wilshire Boulevard. What nerve! If I'd been one of those men . . ."

"Oh, balls!" The anger came first. Later I would be pleased that she was jealous. Now it was so unreasonable and so petty feminine that I wanted to hit her. "You must be getting change of life or something. I wanted to hear that music, and I thought the kind of people that listened to that music wouldn't mind if I asked them. I thought—well, what the hell."

"Don't try to explain it. You simply saw a pretty girl and so you picked a fight with me and *drove* the car fifty miles an hour through traffic to catch up with her, and then you couldn't think of anything better to say than, 'I beg your pardon, but as one music-lover to another I know I can't pick you up now, but if I see you again at the Trocadero will you remember me because you're very pretty and we have this mutual love of good music. Isn't it wonderful? Two souls, brought together by our passion for Bach!'"

"Who writes your dialogue? And what an actress! Boy, when you want to turn on the histrionics. I'll bet you wowed Hollywood High in Paolo and Francesca, or Green Stockings."

She burst out laughing, and she couldn't stop. "Well?" I kept saying. "What was it? Come on, what did I say?" I soon was laughing myself.

When she stopped laughing, she said: "I was *in* Green Stockings." Then she put both hands on my shoulder and it was all right after that. I kissed her and we were quiet. We turned off Wilshire and drove slowly up Rodeo Drive and across Carmelita and up Roxbury to Sunset and then back to Rodeo and down and around and around, and I said: "Pick a house. Look for one around three-fifty or five hundred. I'm going to rent a house, the hell with this hotel life."

"I wish you did have a house. I don't like where you live now. I don't like anything about it. I'd rather live where I live. You could have a house like ours and two servants for what you pay now, and still save money. Too many people can see me going in and out of your place. But I thought you had one picked out."

"I did, but I want you to pick one *you* like."

"If you live out here—well, the capitalists have got you at last. If they didn't always have you."

"Oh, yeah?" I said. "I lived here before, remember." Then I drove her around and pointed out houses that were owned or rented by the leftists in the movie colony. She pointed out houses that were owed by the reactionaries. "Sure, sure," I said. "I concede all that. My only point was that if the nice guys can live in these houses and still be nice guys, why can't I? Couldn't you?"

"I'd always be thinking of how much I could save by living somewhere else, and sending the difference to the Loyalists or the Scottsboro boys."

"You better learn to like this part of town, because you're going to live out here."

That afternoon we didn't do much more driving. I called up a movie writer I knew who had a house in Beverly, and he was going away and I borrowed his house. Late that night I told Peggy my suspicions of her father, and Miller's story, and she promised to find out what she could.

9

THE NEXT day I started my new job at Metro and the second day I was there I acted on an impulse, the overwhelming kind that I always got when I started a new job: the impulse to spend money in a big way. I left the studio that afternoon and drove over to a real estate agent I knew, picked out a house in Beverly for five hundred a month, had the agent hire a Negro couple, and the next day I moved in. I called for Peggy at the shop that day and behaved with all the mysteriousness I could summon. We drove in, stopped the car in the driveway, and I got out and said: "Come on, get out."

"What's this all about?"

"Get out."

She got out and I picked her up and carried her to the door and rang the bell, and Jonas, the Negro, opened the door and I carried her in, to the amusement of Jonas, who then left. I kissed her hard before putting her down. "I love you," I said. The strange thing was that that was impulse too; I had had no intention of saying it. I put my arms around her and kissed her again, long.

"Oh, Jim," she said. "This is the way to do it. Here, hold me here. Let me hold you. I want you. Where do we go?"

On the way upstairs we stopped again. She was two steps higher than I and I held her with my arms around her thighs. "It's like a first time, only better, isn't it?" she said.

"It is a first time, darling," I said. "Say it."

"I love you. I always loved you. I'm so excited. Let's stand here and think of what we're going to do. Let's talk about it. Do you know what I'm going to do to you?" She whispered.

"Let's do it now," I said. I was getting superstitiously apprehensive. I was in a hurry to have the first time accomplished. She kissed my forehead and turned and began running up the remaining steps. She took things off as she ran; her jacket, her sweater. She turned around and looked at me only once. I never had been so excited in my life— and ten minutes before I had only intended to show her the house. There was something new in her eyes. She seemed younger, too, and with her hands she was discovering her own body while she watched me. "Is it true about Chinese women?" she said.

"No."

"How do you know?"

"Well, it isn't true about Japanese women. I do know that."

"Oh, you do, eh? What about colored women?"

"Don't know anything about them. What about you, is it true about you?"

"Stop talking and hurry up."

"Yes," I said. She was right; this was one time when we could do without the talking and joking that we always did. Later on, when she was finishing a cigarette, we did talk.

"How much does this place cost?"

"Five hundred."

"Goodness! How long'd you take it for?"

"Three months."

"Has it got a swimming pool?"

"No. What good would a swimming pool be this time of year? You must have been reading the ads, the Year Round Club ads."

"You'll have to get a double bed. I don't like twin beds."

"I think there is a double bed in one of the other bedrooms. In fact I know there is. But I like this room better than the one with the double bed."

"I guess most people don't need as much room as we do. Otherwise twin beds wouldn't be so popular. The furniture is nice. Whose house is it?"

"I have to think. It's a strange name. A long German name. They aren't picture people. The husband came out here for Ford or General Motors, and I think he's been transferred. The rest of the house is nice, too. There's a pool table."

"Is there a nursery? I may need one after this."

"Oh, Peggy, you must know by this time I'm sterile."

"You mustn't be. Don't you want children?"

"I do if you do. I have no great feeling about perpetuating the name. I have enough brothers to take care of that."

"I wonder how I'd be as a mother."

"Wonderful," I said. "I really mean that."

"Why? What makes you think so?"

"You're sweet and kind and intelligent, and passionate. I think you have to be to be a good mother. I don't know, your breasts are so good."

"I used to hate them. I had them when I was fourteen, almost the same size as they are now. They are nice, aren't they? What do you like best about a girl's figure?"

"Her breasts."

"Not here?"

"Sure, but breasts mostly. Are you psycho-analyzing me?"

"No, not specially. Do you like Karen's?"

"*Do* I!"

"Did you ever lay Karen?"

"You know damn well I didn't."

"Did you ever make a pass at her?"

"Often."

"Do you want to lay her?"

"Do you want an honest answer?"

"If I asked her to, as a favor to me, she would, I think."

"What would you say to her?"

"I'd say I had the curse or I was pregnant or whatever it happened to be, and I didn't want you to go around with other women and get a disease. Or I'd just *say* to her, Jim wants to sleep with you and I want him to have what he wants, and she'd do it. I think she would."

"I'm not so sure. Sometimes I think she doesn't like me."

"Yes, she does. I think she'd like to sleep with you. She asked me one time how you were in bed. She's very curious about it. She never had an orgasm with a man. Something always goes wrong."

"She's never been in love," I said. "She'd be all right if she'd fall for some guy and have a long affair with him. She's a perfectly normal girl, and with the right guy."

"That's the great difficulty. I think you might be the right guy."

"Don't put ideas in my head. Your father certainly thinks—"

"He's horrible. He was trying to put his hand up her skirt all last Saturday night. He wanted me to ask her to spend the night with us, and I almost did but something stopped me. I wish he'd go away and never come back. I wish he'd never come here in the first place. Still, I guess I always would have been curious about him. Wanting to know what he looked like, and whether he was alive. Well, I know now."

"By the way," I said.

"I didn't find out anything. He carries a pistol. I found that out."

"How?"

"I saw it in his back pocket when he was coming out of the bathroom."

"Did he know you saw it?"

"No, I don't think he did. He didn't try to hide it, though."

"Has he said how long he's going to stay?"

"No. I didn't know how to broach the subject. I know he'll be here till after Christmas."

"Well, that's not very long. What does he do in the daytime?"

"Well, of course I'm never there, so I don't really know. He's home for lunch usually, Millie tells me. He gets up after I've gone to the shop and goes out and comes back with the Chicago and New York papers. Oh, yes. He buys racing papers. I imagine he must play the horses quite a lot."

"Good God, you don't think he's going to be here for the whole Santa Anita meeting?"

"God forbid! But I wonder why he carries a pistol. Maybe he is a detective."

"Well, let's us be detectives. Does he get any phone calls at the house?"

"Not that I know of."

"Mail?"

"Well, yes, but not at the house. General Delivery, I think."

"Doesn't he ever try to explain what he's doing out here?" I said. "I should think he'd feel that he had to say something about his plans."

"No. He sometimes gives me the impression that he thinks this is his home. Our house. And he's the father, and we're the children. Goodness knows I never have any such feeling."

"I guess we'll just have to wait and see," I said. I turned over and we lightly kissed each other and felt our passion slowly coming on again. "Ah, this is nice. This is what we're here for, isn't it?"

"Mm-hmm. Want me to stay all night?"

"Sure. It's a long time since we've done that."

"After a while I'll call Millie and tell her I'm not coming home, and I'll fix it with Karen. I want to stay in your nice new house, but let's sleep in the room with the double bed. Not now, but when we go to bed tonight."

"Anything you say. I'd like to christen every room in the house."

"In one night? Not if I know you. Am I good for you, Jim?"

"Yes, you're good for me. Am I good for you?"

"Yes. Yes," she said. "Yes. Yes!"

10

I HAD a friend, not exactly a friend, but a fellow I had known slightly in New York, although I had known him well by reputation. He was a hard one to figure out. He did a little tap-dancing in the Guinan days, and he was what we call around-Broadway. He had been a press agent, hoofer, errand boy for gamblers, and more than once I had seen him getting a nod from big shot public enemies. I seriously doubt whether he ever was convicted of major crime, or even was accused of it. He was not hopheaded enough or ruthless enough to be a torpedo. In fact, I am not even sure that he would actually steal, although he often referred to himself as "a larceny guy like me." This probably was his euphemism for chiseller. He was a chiseller, all right, but I liked him. He had come to Hollywood around 1930 or '31, as a "technical advisor" on a gangster picture. He appeared in the picture, and in several subsequent ones. Then he was an artists' representative for a while, and after that he sold an original story, based on fact. "I made a little," he was always saying, to cover his business activities.

He wrote and acted under the name of Jerry Luck, but everybody called him Red; I don't know why. I telephoned him from the studio the day after Peggy and I housewarmed. I made a date for breakfast, or lunch. We met at the Beverly Derby. He had not gone Hollywood in his clothes. He had on a one-button suit of Eleanor Blue, black pointed shoes with Spanish heels to give him a little extra height, soft white shirt that had been starched too much, and a spotless, almost white hat. He was carrying one of those wrap-around camel's-hair coats. When I got there, he said, "Jim boy," without looking at me. "Don't turn round now, but ain't that that Loretta Young?"

"Mm—yes," I said.

"That's for me," he said. "Where do we sit?"

We got a table. He carefully folded his coat, carefully laid down his hat, and smoothing his suit coat over his hips, he sat down, taking in the whole room slowly. He picked up the menu and read it item by item, and then tossed it in front of him like a disgusted cardplayer. "Frig dat," he said. "Hey! Miss!" he called the waitress.

She said hello to me, and gave him her attention. "Yes, sir?"

"You wanna go in pictures?" he said.

"Sure," she said.

"All right then, get this order and I and Mr. Malloy may have a part for you in our next picture. I want—" and he held out his hands like a man holding a watermelon. "I want some of that brannis wit' the portis salad dressing on top wit' a little—Jim, what's the name of that sauce?"

"Escoffier?" I said.

"Escoffyer sauce. You know?"

"I'm sorry, sir, I didn't get it," she said.

"She didn't get it," he said. "All right, once again. Now look. I want some of this brancovy portis like wit' the cullaba on *top! On top!* Usely you don't put it on top here, but that's the way I want it—"

"I'm sorry, sir—"

"You're sorry! Jesus Christ, she's sorry. What am I, talkin' Greek or Saskatchewan or sumpn? Calla head waiter. Calla captain." The poor girl brought the captain.

"You the captain?"

"Yes, sir."

"I'm S. J. Sterncliff from Gaumont British. Y'ever hear Gaumont British?"

"Oh, yes, sir," said the captain.

"Well, that's who I am, the New York representative Gaumont British. Now this here is my first trip to Hollywood and I'm accustomed to the best, the best. I ask this young lady to bring me a brannis salad wit' the portis on top like wit' the Escoffyer. You know."

The captain looked at me and smiled sadly, and then at Red. "Is this the double talk, sir?"

"Oh, a wise guy. Okay. Gimme a bacon and tomato on whole wheat toasted. Coffee. Wudda *you* eatin', Jim boy?"

I ordered corn beef hash. The captain and the girl left us.

"To what do I owe this honor, Kiddy?" said Red.

"A favor, Red," I said. "Do you know any private dicks?"

"Do I! You mean them gumshoe artists, Jim? Those hawkshaws? Those flatfoots, Jim?"

"Yes."

"Indeed I do. They have shadowed and tailed me all over the length and breadth of this fair land. Are you leveling? Why do you ask?"

"I'm leveling. Did you ever know one by the name of Henderson?"

"Henderson. No, not by that name. Why?"

"How's your memory for faces?"

"The best, Jim. A second Al Smith. A *first* Al Smith. A veritable photographic memory, if you know what I mean, Jim."

"I have a guy I want you to take a gander at."

"You mean give him the double-O, Jim? The onceover? The up and down, Jim?"

"Yes."

"Done, sir, done. You have my hand on it, and when a Luckman gives his hand, you better go right to Doctor Wharton, one flight up, leave this place as you find it. Is it you, or somebody else?"

"It's somebody else. A couple of other people, in fact," I said.

"What can I do? You want me to look at this guy and see if I know him."

"Right."

"Where is he, Jim?"

"I'll find out right away, if I can." I had a phone brought to the table, and called Peggy. She happened to be at the bookstore, and I told her to call her home and see if her father was there. I had a plan. She called me back and said he was there.

"If you're not doing anything for the next half hour," I said.

"All afternoon, Jim. Anything you say. Jesus, that Loretta Young. Who's that with her?"

"Eddie Sutherland. You know him."

"Eddie Sutherland the director. No, I don't know him. He was at Paramount when I was there a couple times."

"He's *still* there," I said.

"All right, pallie, you don't have to put salt in the wound. Here she comes."

"Hello, Eddie," I said. "Hello, Gretch. Gretch, this is Mr. Luck, Miss Young. Mr. Sutherland." Red did a scramble like Benchley in How To Behave, and they passed on. Red grabbed my arm.

"Pardon the vise-like grip," he said, "but anything you want, Jim. Anything you want. Anything she wants, too. A ray of sunshine in a drab life. A merciful angel. A lady bountiful whose very smile."

"I didn't know you cared, Red."

"Cared! For the pal who introduced me to Loretta Young—anything! Where is this Henderson? I will bring together the mains and the semi-mains and we will put the son of a bitch on the spot, Jim. We will rub him out. His number is up. We will *see* him, Jim. You know the sinister meaning of see, don't you?"

"Yes, dear," I said.

"You sure you don't want me to stop for my chopper? My type-writer? My tommy-gun, Jim? We'll let him have it, the rat."

"Just the double-O is all I want, Red," I said. "And the check, honey. Bobbie. Naomi. Betty. Ella. Check, please?"

My plan was simple. We would go to Peggy's house and pretend I had a date to meet her there. We would stay long enough for Red to get a good look at Henderson, and then retire. This we did.

Henderson was home. Millie came to the door and I motioned to her to let us in. "Is Peggy home yet?" I said, pretty loud.

"No, Mist' Malloy, she ain't home yet. Won't *be* home before six I guess."

"Yes, she was coming home. I was to meet her here."

"Well, in that case I guess you better come in wait. Will you rest your hats?"

"Ah, Malloy," said Henderson. "This is quite a surprise."

"I was supposed to meet Peggy here around two-thirty. Didn't she phone or anything?"

"Only to tell Millie what to have for dinner. About I'd say a half an hour ago."

"This is Mr. Luck, Mr. Henderson."

"Glad to meet you."

"Glad to meet *you*."

"It's funny she didn't call. She's usually pretty uh punctilious," I said.

"Why don't you try calling her at the store?" said Henderson. "Sit down, Mr. Lock?"

"Luck."

"Luck. Anything in the name, eh?" said Henderson.

"Lots of it. All bad," said Red.

I telephoned, putting on my act for Henderson's benefit. "She says she forgot all about it," I said. "Well—"

We left. On the way down the hill in my car Red was biting his lower lip. "We can go to the Bamboo Room and refresh your memory."

"That won't do any good," he said. "Of course we can *go*. I'll buy a powder."

We sat down in the too-low chairs of the Bamboo Room.

"I'll tell you the God's honest truth," said Red. "I don't know."

"Well, it was only a chance," I said. "One in a million."

"No, it's better than that," he said. "When we first got there I was positive I never saw him before in my whole life but while you was at the phone I kept looking at that kisser and, I don't *know*. You don't know if he took on weight or something? He couldn't of taken on *much*, but maybe just enough."

"Were you ever in Chicago?"

"A million times."

"For any length of time?" I asked.

"A week, two weeks. Split weeks in the neighborhood houses. I was to open in a club there once. I'm sorry, Jim. I'd like to straighten you out on this, but I honestly can't. I can't swear I ever saw him before, and I can't swear I didn't."

"When you were around the clubs did you ever meet a guy that sold silverware, knives and forks?"

"No, I wouldn't of been around doorn that phase. Of course a guy like that would come back and spend a little if he sold the silverware to the club."

"That's what I was thinking."

"Yeah. But that's no clue. I just have to give up till I can go to work on the old memory."

"Red. A personal question, and you don't have to answer it. Did you ever do time?"

"Yes," he said. "But he didn't. I'd bet on that."

"Thanks, pal," I said. "You're pretty sure?"

"Well, you can always be wrong about that. You hear about these guys that take a powder from some chain gang and they go and live in Ohio or some place and veil up and live respectable lives for fifteen years and nobody the wiser. But most of the time it's like the clap. I can tell you in this room who had the clap. You did, didn't you?"

"Sure."

"That guinzo over there. He had it. I had it, and I can tell just by lookin' at a guy. Usely I can wit' guys that did time, and I would say this Henderson never did. Jim, I'd like to be able to say I made that guy the minute I laid eyes on him, but I can't say that. If I did I'd be telling you a lie. But one thing I will say."

"What's that?"

"This much I will say. If I ever saw a wronggo, that Henderson is it."

"I'll go with you on that," I said.

So we sat and had a few powders and I got my load on and had to have Jonas come down in a taxi and take me home, as I never drive when I am a little stiff.

11

CHRISTMAS STANK. Maybe it is because I am a sucker for Christmas, and this was my first in Hollywood. Always before I had gone East, or happened to be East. It doesn't have to be White for me to like it, but it ought to be reasonably cold, and there never ought to be palm trees. Well, maybe palm trees. I could easily have made a better day of it in the Gauguin country, me in torn shorts and the girls in sarongs or better, and all of us drinking out of coconuts. As it was I took the day off on Christmas Eve and went around buying presents. I bought Keith a $25 shockproof wristwatch. I bought Karen a metal vanity case that looked like a radio set and weighed about two pounds, and cost $80. I bought Red a pigskin cigarette case for $15. I sent Millie a telegraph money order for $10 because I was sure she'd never had one before. I gave Jonas and his wife two weeks' pay, and I bought toys for the children of people who have no part in this story. I was glad to get a tie from Don Miller, sent to the studio. And I put down $400 on a star sapphire ring for Peggy. I had everything sent, except the ring, and then I went to a party at the studio and then a cocktail party at somebody's house and then had Jonas drive me to the bookstore to pick up Peggy. She would have kept me waiting, but that was all right, because I went to the bar at the Beverly-Wilshire and plied myself with Scotch and soda, humming the praises of good King Wenceslaus with a dash of Lord Jeffrey Amherst and I'm Only a Mercersburg Boy, which was to make me homesick. I got very drunk and they asked me to leave. I went across the street to the Brown Derby and distributed largesse of five dollars to each waitress except my favorite, to whom I gave $4.49. I told her if she was a good girl for the rest of the year I would give her the rest. I felt very good, but that was Christmas Eve.

Peggy was sitting in the car. I got in and took her hand and kissed it. "I have whiskey on my breath," I said.

"On your *breath!*"

"I've tried Sen-Sens and cloves, but no good. Now this little hand, which I now kiss, kiss, indicating kiss on hand, have you got a kiss on hand, Miss? I'll take—anyway. This little hand which I now kiss, I now decorate like gilding the lily." Then I put the ring on her thumb. "It doesn't mean anything unless you want it to, so put it whatever finger your heart's desire."

She took it off and looked at it and at me, and put it on the third finger of her left hand. "I don't care," she said. "Even if you are drunk." She put her arms around my neck and kissed me, and I started to cry because I loved her.

"I gotta cut this out," I said. "You like my house I bought for you?"

"You didn't buy it," she said.

"All right, I didn't buy it. All right. Very well. I didn't buy the God damn thing. I guess I didn't buy it, eh? Jonas!"

"Yes, sir."

"Have you got the deed of our house in your pocket? Do you happen to have it?"

"No, sir."

"Hmm. Well, maybe you're right, then. I didn't buy it. But I will. If you like it, that is. Contingent on your liking it only. Otherwise—the hell with it. We'll go set fire to the God damn thing. Let's do it anyway. Only fooling. Firemen are all drunk on Christmas Eve, drunk and home with their wives and little children."

"Will you take me home now?"

"Don't you want to go to our little home?"

"I want to go to my own little home. Next Christmas we'll go to our little home, and we'll have little children like the firemen."

"I can't have little children. Only big little children. We'll go to the Shelter and adopt two big little children and get a lot of publicity, like the movie stars. Wonderful, kind movie stars, adopting poor little waifs. Waives? Waifs. We get our picture in the paper. Mr. and Mrs. James Malloy with the poor little kiddies they adopted out of the kindness of their hearts because Mr. and Mrs. Malloy are so big-hearted. Especially Mrs. Malloy. Darling, I hope you don't mind being Mrs. Malloy? There's another one around somewhere."

"I know."

"Do you mind?"

"Sure I mind, but what can I do about it?"

"Maybe she'll marry somebody and then she won't be Mrs. Malloy. Maybe she'll marry the Duke of Windsor. At long last I'm gonna say a few God damn words of my own, you sons of bitches. Maybe she'll marry Oswald Mosley."

"Who? Mrs. Simpson?"

"Mrs. Malloy. I'm a great lover of music, Peggy."

"I know."

"Adeste fideles, laeti triumphantes. Venite, venite in Beth-le-hem. I used to be a boy tenor. At SS. Peter and Paul."

"SS. Peter and Paul sounds more like a ship."

"That reminds me. Jonas, you know where Miss Henderson lives? Well, start tacking, Jonas. That's where we're going. Everybody's tackin'. They hadda have something new. Tacking. I love all music, Peggy. You know that, don't you?"

"Yes."

"You know I love you, too, don't you, Peggy?"

"Yes."

"Do you know that?"

"Yes, I guess so."

"That's right. At least I love you as much as I can love anybody that isn't James Malloy. I hate him."

"I'm James Malloy, too."

"What?"

"I said I'm James Malloy, too."

"God knows I hope you mean what I think you do."

"I do."

"Kiss me."

"All right." She kissed me. "I think I'd like to get a little tight, too."

"I don't blame you. I always get nervous when I'm sober and someone's tight and I'm with them. But you gotta go some, my sweet."

We stopped at the Trocadero and there was hardly anyone there. We had Lanson 1926. "Drink up, sweet. You gotta go some. How I love music. Frère Jacques, Cuernavaca, ach du lieber August. All languages. A walking Berlitz. Berlitz sounds like you with that champagne, my sweet, or how you're gonna sound." We drank a quart of champagne and Peggy began to get a little tight.

"Waiter!" I called. The waiter came.

"There's a drunken man," I said.

"Where, sir?" he said.

"Here. Me," I said.

"Yes, sir."

"Oh, yeah? You wanna make sumpn of it? Where's Billy Wilkerson?"

"He isn't here, sir."

"If this place is good enough for me it's good enough for him. Let's get outa here, Peggy."

"All right. I'm willing. Woo-woo!" We left, both saying woo-woo quietly.

Jonas had the car parked on Sunset instead of on the parking lot, which was a good thing. We got in, and Peggy leaned forward. "Jonas," she said.

"Yes, Miss Henderson."

"The stockings were hung by the chimney with care. Finish it."

"In hopes that St. Nicholas soon would be there," said Jonas.

"Woo-woo," said Peggy.

"None of your lip," I said. "Yes. Some of your lip."

"Merry Christmas, cried the warden, and the prisoners shouted balls."

"Woo-woo. I drank that fast too champagne," said Peggy. "Woo-woo."

"Whose little home shall we go to?" I said. "Let's go to the Bide-a-Wee Home. The Ellin Speyer Home."

"Let's go to the Wee Kirk o' the Heather. Who is Ellin Speyer?"

"Ellin Prince Speyer? You don't know her? You must be drunk. I'll take you home and put you to bed."

"Aw, now you're hinting," said Peggy. She tried to whistle.

"How're you ever gonna wet your whistle, when the whole darn world goes dry? You're too young for that. Sahara, we sympathize with you, Sahara, we'll soon be dry like you. You're too young for that, too. How dark and still tonight, by the old distillery. I'm a different generation, Peggy. I'm too God damn old for you."

"Woo-woo."

"I am."

"Woo-woo."

"All you can think of is woo-woo."

"Woo-woo."

"Home, Jonas," I said.

"Woo-woo. No. My home."

"Stop at the Seven Seas, Jonas." We drove to the Seven Seas, and we were the only people there. We had more champagne. The waiters stood around trying to smile, now and then slapping imaginary dust off the table-cloths. "Are you my baby?"

"Yes."

"Bore a hole, bore a hole—"

"Stop it! I've changed. I'm dignified now."

"I like to think of old Bethlehem, tonight. Yes, I like to think of old Bethlehem. And old Allentown, and old Easton. And Catasauqua."

"I don't." Then suddenly: "I've got to go home. Come on."

Jonas drove us to her house. We sang on the way, and necked while we sang. She hummed Some Day I'll Find You, and I simply repeated, neeah-neeah, neeah-neeah. Outside her house she said: "How do you like my new ring that some man gave me for Christmas?"

"Well—ostentatious. I hope he does right by you. Who is the guy? A girl doesn't get a ring like that for nothing."

"He is my betrothed. I want you to be the first to know," she said. "Are you sure you want me to have it?"

"Well, temporarily. In about twenty years we'll wake up some day and realize it was only sex."

"Come in for a minute," she said.

We went in and Henderson was reading the paper. "Oh, there you are. Malloy. Say, are you drunk? Peggy?"

"Not very. Just a little."

"Now look here, Malloy. She's a young girl."

"She's twenty-one," I said.

"Twenty-one? That's young. How old are you? You must be thirty-five."

"Oh, for Christ sake."

"Did you wait supper?" said Peggy.

"I had mine. Keith just got home, too," said Henderson.

"I'll go tell Millie I'm home."

She staggered just a little and Henderson watched her. "You wait," she said to me.

Henderson stood there with the paper in his hand. "Malloy, I want to have a talk with you."

"Oh, for Christ sake."

"Yes, for Christ sake. We might as well have this out now, unless you're too drunk."

"I'm not too drunk but there's nothing to have out. You might as well get that straight."

"Oh, no? Where was Peggy last night?"

"At Karen's. Why?"

"That's a lie. I happen to know she wasn't at Karen's."

"Well, I happen to know she was. I took her there."

"Yeah? What time?"

"After work. Why? Are you implying she was with me?"

"Implying nothing. This is the second time she said she was at Karen's, and the other time I *know* she was with you."

"Listen, Henderson, it's a little late in the day for you to be coming around acting the stern parent."

"That goes for me, too," said Keith, in the doorway. He had a towel in his hand and was drying the inside of his ear.

"You. What kind of a brother *are* you? I guess you've known about this all along."

"Thanks for the watch, Jim. Cats, it was swell. I didn't get you anything but I just couldn't."

"Your money isn't wanted here, Malloy. I have enough to take care of my family."

"Aw, why don't you shut up?" said Keith.

"Now you listen here—" said Henderson, taking a step towards Keith.

"I wouldn't if I were you," I said. "He'll knock your block off."

"And you'd help him, I suppose."

"Gladly. But he wouldn't need my help. Listen, Henderson, why don't you get wise to yourself? These kids have got along without you for a long time. If you want to be a father you have to be it in a different way."

"I don't need any advice from you. I guess that's where they get their radical ideas from."

Peggy came in, apparently having gone from the kitchen to the bathroom which she shared with Keith. "I doused my face in cold water," she said. "Keith, look." She held out the ring finger.

"Cats! What is that?"

"Star sapphire. See it, Father?"

Henderson looked down and frowned, then looked at her and at me. Peggy came to me and pulled my head down and kissed me.

"Jim! Congratulations," said Keith, squeezing my hand. He kissed Peggy, and Henderson shook hands with me. "I'm sorry," he said, and then he held out his hand and kissed Peggy's forehead. I think it was the first time he had kissed her. Anyway, Peggy looked around at everybody, sat down on the sofa, and then quietly passed out. We all laughed and Keith went to the kitchen and got Millie to put her to bed. We had a few drinks and then I left as soon as I could and went to a Christmas-tree-trimming party out in Beverly, and Jonas got me home somehow.

I DID not go back to the studio until the Tuesday morning after Christmas, and when I did my stenographer said someone had been calling me almost every hour in my absence. That Tuesday afternoon she said I was wanted on the phone, and she said she was sure it was the same person who had been calling. Wouldn't give his name. I told her to put him on.

"Malloy?"

"Yes."

"This is that friend of Pat's. Don't mention my name if you recognize my voice."

"Yes. I know who it is."

"Will you do me another favor? This is a big one."

"What is it?"

"You know that place where I used to live?"

"Yes. I think so."

"That's all right, if you don't remember. I sent you a telegram with just the address."

"Yeah."

"Well, this is the favor. Will you go there and there's a fairy there that runs the switchboard. Blond-haired. About my age. You go to him and ask him if there was anybody there looking for me. Then I'll phone you tomorrow and you tell me. I can't call there myself because they may have the wires tapped."

"That sounds pretty melodramatic," I said.

"Well, will you do it? I'm going nuts," said Miller. "If there was anybody looking for me find out what he looks like."

"All right. I'll go this afternoon, late," I said. "By the way, thanks for the tie."

"Don't say that," he said. "Throw it away or they may trace it."

"Jesus," I said. "You've got it bad."

That was all the conversation we had. In a few minutes the telegram came, and late that afternoon I went to the address he gave, a sort of hotel on Gower Street. They called it a bachelors' club. You went up three steps and to the left as you went in there was a door and a window on one side of the hall. That was the office. The switchboard was behind the window.

"May I help you?"

I looked down and there was this fairy with a sunlamp tan and al-

most platinum blond, wavy hair. He was sitting on a low chair behind
the switchboard and he had to hold his head back, chin up, to see me.
With just a little narrower face I swear he would have made a swell
ad for Tangee lipstick.

"I'm a friend of Mr. Miller's."

"Oh, Donnie's? How is he? You're the second person asked for him
today."

"Well, that's what I came about. Could you tell me who else was
looking for him?"

"The party didn't leave his name. Very mysterious. He wanted to
know all about Donnie. Of course I couldn't tell him much."

"Oh, I'll bet you could."

"I *beg* your pardon?"

"Skip it. What about this guy. What'd he look like?"

"Well—he was about, ah, a man of forty, perhaps? Not quite your
height? With a nice head of hair for his age? That is, not bald. Nice
teeth?"

"How was he dressed?"

"Oh, very conservatively. Nothing flashy. The business man type, you
know?"

"Yes. What did he say?"

"Oh, just how long since I saw Donnie, and what did he look like.
Oh, yes. He asked me if I ever cashed any checks for Donnie. Me
cashing checks! Oh, I know who you must be. I've been wracking my
brains. Are you Mr. Malloy?"

"Yes."

"I *thought* I recognized you from your picture. I loved your book. It
was so true to life even if it was a fantasy. I mean I believed it all the
time. I really did. I wish I had a copy here, I'd ask you to autograph it,
but my friend went away and took it with him."

"Why the dirty thing," I said. "I'll send you one. What's your name?"

"Noel Sherman. Not Lowell Sherman. *Noel* Sherman."

"As in Noel Coward?"

"Yes, but it really is my name. My middle name," he said. "Will you
really send me an autographed copy?"

"Of course I will. Noel Sherman. It's a pretty name. Well, thanks
very much."

"Oh, notta tall, Mr. Malloy. Glad to oblige." He stood up and I left.

The next day Miller phoned and I told him Henderson was getting
warm. That was the last I ever heard from Don Miller.

For the next week I was as industrious as I could be under the circumstances, they being an average of two parties a day at my friends' houses. It just seemed as though all my married friends decided that the Christmas-New Year's period was the time to give parties, and I wanted them all to meet Peggy. Not many of them knew her, because they mostly patronized a bookstore in Hollywood, not the Beverly one where Peggy worked. The women were nice to Peggy, and of course the men were too. They all wanted to know when we were going to get married, to which Peggy's answer was that we hadn't made up our minds, but soon, she said. I went around glowing, because it was a new thing to me. I was proud of Peggy and glad people liked her. I felt much older than Peggy, which of course I was; but I felt younger myself than I had in years. Maybe ever. My other marriage had not been very good, and there had been no engagement. My first wife was rich and older than I and divorced, and her friends used to make me feel like a God damn Marchbanks, although I think I really loved her at the time. So it was all new to me, and it was fun, and I guess it was kind of fun for my friends, practically all of whom had settled down at their homes and work and children and some extra-marital dabbling. They were mostly newspaper men I had known in New York, and their first or second wives, and all the men wrote or produced pictures. There were only two movie actresses in the lot, and they knew their place and were always trying to improve themselves, like reading books and going to concerts and buying Picassos and publicly smuggling contributions to the I. L. D. I guess they were all right. Anyway the week passed, and there was a lot of talk about giving parties for Peggy. The parties never came off, because in the second week of the new year Peggy's father killed Keith.

13

On the second Wednesday morning after New Year's Peggy had gone to the shop early as it was her turn to open it. Every other day she opened up, her boss doing it on the alternate days. When she was leaving the house she called to Keith to snap out of it and get to school, and he called back to her that he was taking a couple of cuts to go down to Vermont Avenue to the dentist. Her father was not up yet when she left. (She had given notice at the shop. I wanted to get married right away. She told her boss, who always had been nice to her, that she would look around for a good girl to take her place. Now I wish she had quit right away.)

At about eleven-thirty that morning Millie telephoned her and told her to come, that something terrible had happened. Millie did not make much sense, and it took all of Peggy's pleading to get Millie to tell her what kind of terrible thing, and then Millie told her that her father had shot her brother.

I am trying to give the straight facts on this first.

Peggy told her boss what little she knew, and he closed the shop and they got into his car and at the corner of Santa Monica and Rodeo they saw a motorcycle cop he knew, and the cop gave them an escort out of Beverly, then they got another somewhere along Sunset and were at Peggy's house in less than fifteen minutes.

There were two police cars outside the house, and a small group of people. Peggy and her boss went in, and her father was sitting in the living-room with his head in his hands, with two cops leaning against a bookcase, their caps on the back of their heads, and smoking. Henderson had no coat or vest on and his shirt was open.

Keith was not there. They had taken him to a hospital.

Henderson looked up just once and said: "Don't ask me anything, Peggy. All I can say, it was an accident."

Peggy's boss picked out a nice cop and he went with them to the hospital. When they got there Keith was in the operating room, and Peggy had to wait. While she was waiting Karen's mother arrived at the hospital, and she waited with Peggy, and then before they brought Keith out of the operating room Karen arrived too.

The doctor in charge said it would be "some time" before Keith came out of the ether. He lied, and said Keith had about an even chance to live. He had lost a lot of blood, and there were internal hemorrhages besides. Then Peggy told Karen to phone me, but I was not in my office. I had gone to a projection room to watch a picture being run off, and after that I had gone to kill some time before lunch with Don McGinnis, a writer, whose office was nowhere near mine. I went off the lot for lunch, and did not get Karen's message until around three o'clock. I went straight to the hospital, but I did not see Peggy until around six-fifteen, five minutes after Keith died.

He recovered consciousness a little sooner than they expected. He opened his eyes, and when he did he was as conscious as you or I. A detective was there, and a doctor and two nurses and Peggy and Mrs. Waner. He said hello, faintly, and then the detective began to ask him questions, like, "Who fired the shot?" and "How'd it happen?" The poor kid knew he had to save breath, so he told the detective only two things: "It was an accident," and "It was my fault," and then he said to

Peggy: "Right hand up, Peggy. My fault." Then he said hello to Karen and she started to cry, and a sort of bored look came into his eyes and he made that noise in his throat and died. Peggy looked at him for a minute and then she heard the doctor say to the detective: "Remarkable. Seven hours. Why do you know, that bullet—" That was when she came out.

She came right to me as though she had known exactly where I would be, and she took my arm. I thank God I had sense enough not to try to say anything. Then I saw a cop coming out of the room and I asked him if it would be all right for me to take Miss Henderson home, and he asked the detective, who said he saw no reason why not. Peggy's boss came up to her and said: "Miss Henderson, anything I can do. If you want money, or anything. I'd consider it a privilege."

"Thank you, Mr. Milton," she said. "I'll let you know." Then she pressed my arm and we walked to the elevator and went out and got in my car.

I offered her a cigarette, and she took it, and the lighter wouldn't work. I reached for matches, but she said she didn't really want to smoke. She looked at me a couple of times. She wanted to tell from the expression on my face how she was taking it, or how I thought she was taking it. A cop came up and told me he'd have to give me a ticket if we didn't move on, and I showed him an honorary detective's badge that I had borrowed from Don McGinnis. "Well, don't stay too long," he said. "They blame me if this place ain't clear."

"Let's drive up to the top of the mountain," Peggy said.

We drove up, high above the broken Hollywoodland sign, and she took off her hat and rested the back of her head on the leather seat. Her hands were in her lap. Her pretty legs were stretched out straight under the dash. I sat and looked at her, and I wanted to kiss her, but I didn't. It was so quiet that I could hear the tiny sound as she moistened her dry lips.

"How does it feel to be a Catholic?" she said.

"Sometimes good, sometimes bad."

"Do Catholics believe that when you die your soul goes up in the sky? To heaven, if they go to heaven?"

"The poor people do. The educated ones believe that heaven is a state, a sort of metaphysical state. At least I think that's right."

"The soul doesn't rise, up in the air?"

"No."

She waited. "That was one of the reasons why I wanted to come up here. If *you* believe that, about their going up in the air, you'd be close to him. I don't believe it, but if you did I wanted to be with you while you believed it. Now I can never be a Catholic. The only thing I ever wanted from the Catholic Church I can't have. One little thing. But I guess he'll be just as alive down there, home. Oh, God! Oh, Jesus! He will be, Jim!" Then she broke, and so did I.

She stopped crying before I did, and this time she lit a cigarette and told me all she knew, starting by saying: "I have to be practical now. He said my father didn't do it on purpose, and I believe him. I wouldn't believe him, but now I remember how my father looked when I got home. I wouldn't have believed him, because he would have lied. That's the way he was. Look how soon it's the past tense. He was." She puffed on her cigarette. "What will they do?"

"They'll hold him, your father. Probably for manslaughter. I think probably involuntary manslaughter, if he has anything like an explanation. A lot depends on you, maybe a little on me, and a lot on Millie. If they knew Keith didn't like your father, he'd have a tough time. What do you want to do?"

"I want him to go away so I'll never see him again."

"Well, then I guess—I wish we knew what Millie told the cops. We can take a chance on repudiating what Millie might say. Hysterical colored woman saying anything in a crisis." I thought a minute. "I know one thing you can do."

"What's that?"

"You can say you're going to get a lawyer for your father. I'll give you the money. Then when they ask around they'll find out how much you loved Keith, so they won't think—I have to be blunt, Peggy."

"I know."

"Well, they won't think you were, oh, relieved by Keith's death. See what I mean? You're the loving sister, but you're also the loving daughter, convinced that it was accidental. I know a hell of a good lawyer in Pasadena. He doesn't try criminal cases, but he'll know the best one to get. I'll call him right away as soon as we leave here. By that time they'll have taken your father downtown and booked him. They won't let him out on bail. At least for a while. Depends on what they decide to do. This is a good time of year, you know."

"Why?"

"Well, no election going on or coming up. When there's an election coming up the D. A. tries to get as many convictions as he can to make him look good. If your father has a good defense, they're likely to figure on saving the expense of a trial. I'll do all I can."

"I know you will," she said. "All I want is to get him away from here and never come back."

I took my arm away from her and put my hands on the wheel. "What about us? You're alone, now. Let's get married as soon as we can."

"There's no hurry, is there?" she said. "Either way."

"What do you mean, either way?"

"Well, I don't know. There's no hurry."

14

WE DID it as we planned, and it came out as we wanted it to. I telephoned my Pasadena friend, and he made a good suggestion: not to get the local Leibowitz, but to get a less conspicuous but able lawyer for Henderson. The idea being that the Fallons and the Rogerses often get a case tried by the newspaper reporters before the suspect is indicted. People think the suspect is guilty because he hires the top lawyer.

They booked Henderson on suspicion of murder, but that was as far as it got. The detectives had to make a report that favored Henderson, and the Coroner's jury report that followed gave a verdict of accidental death, and so the complaint deputy in the D. A.'s office refused to issue a complaint. The only worry, Millie, was out of the picture, because she was not in the house when the shooting occurred. She was five blocks away, at a market. Peggy, acting the loving daughter, was convincing. They asked me a few questions, but they didn't pay much attention to anything I said.

It was a one-day story in the papers, and not a very good one. The father was a private detective for a surety company, and had a permit for the .38 detective special, not in California, it was true, but in New York, where the Sullivan Law is tough about carrying revolvers. This information must have interested Don Miller, because there was a picture of Henderson on an inside page of the *Herald-Express,* and one enterprising reporter wrote that Henderson was in California in connection with some stolen traveler's checks. This information cost Henderson his job.

He was released in less than a week after Keith was killed, and he aroused no suspicion by making preparations to leave. I never knew whether he made the decision unaided, or if Peggy told him to go away.

The day before he left he came out to see me at the studio.

I did not get up when the stenographer led him in. She knew who he was, and she could hardly take her eyes off him. For her benefit I was cordial to him, and then I got up and closed the door.

"Cigarette?" he said.

"I have some," I said.

"I guess you know I lost my job," he said.

"Peggy told me."

"I'm going away," he said.

"I know. When?"

"Tomorrow. I'm going up to San Francisco. I figure it's better not to leave the state. I used to know a couple fellows in the Army. I might be able to get something up there."

"Probably."

"Malloy," he said, "you're making it tough for me. I guess I know what you think. You're thinking, here's a man that killed his own son, the brother of the girl I'm going to marry. I guess you wish I'd get the hell out of here, the way Peggy can't stand the sight of me. Can anybody hear me?"

"Not if you don't talk too loud."

"Malloy, I'm a young man, comparatively. Or I was. Now I'm an old man. I'm not looking for any sympathy. Most of my life I've been a louse, a bastard. Some of the time I had a good time, sometimes not. I was kicked out of college for something I didn't do. I have a letter somewhere to prove it. My own fraternity brothers thought I stole a gold watch and chain, and they asked me to hand in my pin. I did, and I was so surprised I didn't make any stink about it, so they believed I was guilty and I was kicked out. Then five or six months later they caught the guy that did it red-handed, and they wrote me a letter and sent me my pin. Here it is. But by that time I didn't give a God damn. I was one of those fellows, give a dog a bad name, and by that time I was living off a whore in Binghamton, New York.

"Well, I've been a lot of things in my time. I was indicted twice, money matters, but they could never make it stick, so I never did time. Then I've been in legitimate business several times and twice in my life I've had a credit rating of over a hundred thousand dollars. But I don't know, I knew a dame one time that was pretty good at fortune-telling. Palmistry. She looked at my hand and she said she wouldn't tell me what she saw. I'll bet she'd feel pleased with herself right now.

"Anyway, one thing, I've always been pretty good at sizing up people, and I became a private detective, because I can get to know people easily, and I never forget a face. And, I'm a good liar. Convincing. But you know I'm telling you the truth. For instance, I was within a week of catching up with your friend Schumacher, alias Donald R. Miller. Now I have no job, which is a break for him. Probably for you, too, but that's not what I came to tell you about. You know what I came here for?"

"Money?"

"No. I'll take some if you give it to me, but I don't give a f—— if you offer it to me or not. I came here, Malloy, because you're going to marry my daughter. As bad a father as I've been, she's my own flesh and blood and I'm proud of her. Maybe she wouldn't have been as good as she is if she'd had the kind of breaks she deserves. Her mother was—well, her mother was all right, too.

"What I came here for. The whole world knows I killed my own son, but I'm the only one in the world knows how it happened. I'm going to tell you so you can tell Peggy some time, whether you like it or not. And it's the truth.

"The morning he was killed he came in my room and I was getting dressed. I had my gun on the bureau and I was tying my tie when he came in my room. He stood there and looked at me a minute, and I said, 'What is it, son?' And he called me a son of a bitch or bastard or something, and I asked him what was the matter? Then he yelled at me 'God damn you,' he said, 'if you ever put a finger on Karen Waner again, I'll kill you.'

"Well, I pretended I didn't know what he was talking about, but I knew. The night before I had a date with this Waner kid. I met her down there at Third and Rossmore. She came down there in a taxi and she got in the car I had and we drove to Long Beach. We had a lot of drinks. On the way back I lost my way, and it wasn't any gag. I was lost. We ended up near the oil wells. Well, I made a pass at her and I thought she liked it. Hell's bells, she was willing to go out with me without letting anyone know it, and I figured what I figured. What anybody'd figure under the circumstances. I was her friend's father and she looked like the most beautiful piece of tail—well, anyway, the first thing I knew she was fighting me off. I thought that was put on, but she kept it up so I started the car and we came back to Hollywood. I guess I tore her dress.

"The next morning she must have been afraid Peggy'd find out or something like that, because she called up and Keith took the call, and what she told him I'll never know, but he must have sat there a while, burning, and I guess he liked her more than he ever let on. Be that as it may, he came in and the way I told you, called me a bastard and I told him to calm down, and then he got up. Well, at that very minute I happened to have my gun in my hand, putting it in my hip pocket. It was a detective special, which is a very dangerous thing to fool with. The next thing to hair trigger, this was, and a .38. Short barrel. You probably know what they're like."

"Sure."

"I had it in my hand, and I was looking at myself in the mirror, when he grabbed my arm. The gun went off, and got him right here. I don't see how it didn't kill him right away. Instantly. I'm glad it didn't, though, because he knows what I said to him when he fell on the floor. That's between him and me, but I think the kid knew it was an accident. I sound like a heel to say it, but it was his own fault. He said so on his deathbed. I think for the first time he knew that no matter how much of a louse I was, I wanted to change. But with a guy like me, the life I led, these changes don't come all of a sudden." He stopped. "Or *maybe* they do, Malloy. Maybe they do. In the last week I've changed. I don't know.

"Well, there it is, there's the story. You be good to Peggy, and sometime the time may come when you can tell her what I just told you. I'll never bother you or her. I'm disgusted."

I waited for him to say something more, but he didn't. He started to get up. He reached for his hat.

"Would five hundred bucks help you?" I said.

"One hundred bucks would help me."

"I'll let you have five," I said.

"You'll never get it back," he said.

"I know," I said. I started to write the check. "Henderson, I think I believe you."

"I don't *give* a damn any more. I've told you the truth."

"I'll give you the address of my agent. If you get in a bad jam, I mean you're badly on the nut or something like that, you write me care of this guy, and I'll let you have some more. On one condition."

"That I never bother Peggy. Don't worry. And thanks for the offer, but I'll never bother you, either. I don't think I will. If I do, don't send me any money. It'll only go for booze. That's what this is going for."

He had half a load on now, but was carrying it well.

"Here's your five. The bank in Beverly will cash it right away. They may call me, but that'll only take a minute."

"Thanks," he said. "Well, good luck." He looked at me and half smiled. He picked up the check, which I had laid on the desk in front of him. "You wouldn't even hand it to me, would you?"

"Nope."

"Well, take care of Peggy," he said. "Good-by, Mr. Malloy." And he left.

15

PEGGY STAYED in the little house for about a month after her father left, and during that time I saw her nearly every night. We went to the movies a few times, but one night on the way from the theater to the car she said she couldn't help thinking that the way a shot sounded in the picture must have been the way the shot sounded when Keith was killed. After that we stayed away from the movies. Instead we would go for long rides, long conversationless rides to Pomona and Santa Barbara, or nearer places when we had less time. Then we formed another habit, that of going to a late spot that I knew of, where the fellows from the dance orchestras would meet after work and have jam sessions. Nobody knew Peggy. Nobody wanted to. The life of the place was the jam session, and non-musicians went there under sufferance. I kept my own liquor there, and it was a good place for us, because Peggy had been developing a fondness for brandy.

During that month or so I expected, and observed, changes in Peggy, just as anyone would have. Her drinking, for instance. It had become a serious matter with her, almost a job. She always had been one to take a drink, but she had given it a holiday spirit. Now she had become a drinker. Well, she was a healthy girl, and she could take it; never got mean or noisy. I drink too fast myself, but now she was taking drink for drink with me. I didn't like it, but I never said anything, because she would have tried to explain what needed no explaining.

Herbert often phoned her, but I don't think she saw him, unless he came to the shop (she wisely went back to work almost immediately). Otherwise she saw only Karen and me. One night as that first month was ending I suggested dinner at my house, and she said all right. It was the first time she had been there since Keith was killed. Jonas and his wife turned out a good dinner, and after dinner we sat in the library, a small room with sets of books and tennis trophies that had been left behind by the owner of the house. There was a Capehart in the room, and I put on some records and we sat and drank Courvoisier until about ten-thirty or so.

"Turn that thing down," she said. "Or turn it off altogether." I turned it off.

When I came back to the sofa, she said: "Jim, I know what you're going to say in a little while."

"Do you?"

"Yes. I'm sorry, Jim," she said, and held out her hand and I saw the star sapphire was in it.

"Oh," I said. I stood up and walked to the other side of the room and sat on an uncomfortable straight chair. "I don't suppose you'd have any reasons."

"You know the reasons," she said.

"Do I?" I said. "Well, anyway, keep the ring."

"No, you take it."

"No. When I gave it to you I put it up to you where you wanted to wear it. It was a Christmas present. So you keep it."

"All right. Thanks. You can always have it back. Do you want to take me home now?"

"Not unless you want to go."

"I don't, but I thought you might want me to."

"No," I said. We had a lot more to drink, and then we had a messy scene that I am ashamed of, and she made me take her home. I telephoned her the following night, but she told me she had a date with Herbert. After that I called her twice, late at night, when I was drunk and afraid, but she would not see me, and the next time I felt like that I remembered Charlotte, whom I had not seen since the night she was with Miller. Charlotte is all right.

Then my contract was expiring at Metro and there was some talk of a play of mine being produced in New York, and I was getting ready to leave, so I went to the shop to say good-by to Peggy. She was glad to see me. She started to smile when she saw me, and she kept smiling as she came up from the rear of the shop. "I hear good news about you," she said.

"About me?"

"The play. Congratulations. Is it the one I read last summer? Haven't they changed the title?"

"The title, and almost everything else," I said.

"Not the main idea, I hope. Remember I said I thought there were too many characters. When are you leaving?"

"Tuesday or Wednesday."

"Will you write to me?"

"What about, Peggy?"

"New York. The play. What you're doing."

"That's the kind of letter I'd write to Karen or somebody like that."

"You think I'm a heel, don't you?"

"No," I said.

"If I wrote to you, will you—no. You write to me and tell me where you're staying. I wanted to talk to you, but I think a letter would be better."

"Peggy, why don't you marry me and come with me? Are you in love?"

"I'd better write to you."

"Will you kiss me good-by?"

"Yes," she said. "Come to the back of the shop." We went to the back of the shop and I knew from the way she kissed me that she was not in love with someone else. I had a feeling at the time that she probably had not even kissed anyone else. "You must go now," she said. "Go on, Jim." I knew from the way she said it that she meant it and could not be made to change her mind.

The next I heard from her was when she wrote to me in New York. Here is the letter:

DEAR JIM:

I know now I never could have said what I have to say in a talk with you. The reason that I know it is that it is so hard to get started in a letter, without your distracting presence and equally distracting hands. With them I never could get started—if I ever do. (This makes the fifth attempt tonight.)

I love you, but as you have guessed and despite Francis Brett Young, love is not enough. It isn't even enough to know that not only do I love you, but that you also love me. I have known that since Christmas, but I did not entirely believe it until the day Keith died, when we went to the mountain. Since then, those first weeks, when you were kind and considerate and sensitive, I have wanted to do or say something to thank you, but when the time came at your house the same thing that kept me from telling you would not let me stay with you. The unreasonable aspect of that was that I wanted to stay with you, but here I am faced with the same suspicion, namely, that it wasn't only you I wanted to stay with. Almost anyone would have done. (Does this make any sense whatsoever?) Let me try again. Now don't go into a rage when I tell you this, but please read on and let me finish and then try to understand.

The whole trouble has been that you reminded me too much of my father, and at the same time you reminded me of Keith.

I could not live with or sleep with that combination. All I wanted from you was the thing that you were giving me: peace, or silence in which to think. To return to your reminding me of my father, I do not mean physically (although your head is shaped like his). I refer to the way you *are*, the kind of life you have led, which in curious ways remind me of my father. You are not his generation, but you are not mine, either. You both have the same attitude toward life, which in a phrase is "To hell with it." At a time when I needed stability in someone, you gave me stability, and for that I was and am grateful, but, dear Jim, that could not last forever. I am not blaming you, but I think I was right in not seeing you because your dutiful stability was apt to exhaust itself while I still needed it. In one sense, it did. The night we had dinner at your house, the stability was beginning to crack, too soon. One more week might have made the difference, but I will not swear to that.

As to your reminding me of Keith, that is true too, but for an altogether different reason. When you are gay, you seem as young as Keith (and sometimes when you are not gay). If we were married, or if we had been married these past two months, the resemblance or things you have in common with Keith would have been unbearable. What I really want to say is that I have known so few men intimately that when one of the three men I have known intimately in the past six months, kills the man I loved best in the world, the third man is unfortunately identified with the other two. I grew to know my father and to think he had a certain charm. Then he killed Keith, and that left you, and somehow I resented you. I begin to realize that I have been resenting all men. If Herbert were not a sort of "cripple" as he calls himself, I could not stand him; but because of his poor health he is not a normal man, and another good thing about Herbert is that he will talk to anyone who will listen, which makes it very easy for me. He sits with me while I get tight, talking away, and never letting my glass become empty.

I have been sitting here since I finished the last paragraph, and I have come to the conclusion that it was a good thing to write this letter, despite the fact that it is not a good letter and does not say half of what I wanted to say. But it is making me think, and it is about time I did some straight thinking. I think if you were with me this minute we would be closer than at any time since Keith died, but I also think it is better that you are in New

York. When you come back I will still be at the shop. My salary has been increased, and the boss is talking about taking a trip to Europe, leaving me in charge. Perhaps I will turn into an old-maid bookshop owner, an old maid with her memories. (But knowing myself, and knowing that inevitably you will return to Hollywood, I doubt that.) Be nice to the New York girls, but not too nice. I want you to be unattached when you come back here. Karen sends love and so do I, and I don't know which kind she means or which kind I mean. And write to me.

PEGGY.

16

MY PLAY was an inconspicuous success, and I stayed around New York half the summer, and then they sold the play to the movies for $60,000 and I went back to Hollywood for Universal. All I could think of on the plane was that I was going to see Peggy, and how rich I was. I did not tell her exactly when I would arrive. I had written her "news" letters, and had had two news letters from her. I arrived at the airport on a Sunday, just before noon, and I telephoned her at home, at her new apartment, but there was no answer. That night I saw her at the Troc, and she was with my friend Don McGinnis and two other people, all very tight. That next night I had a date with her, and she stayed with me, but never after that. She has not made up her mind about me, or probably anything else. She goes to the Trocadero often, but hardly ever more than two or three times with the same man. I guess we are all washed up. Karen thinks so.